READER'S DIGEST

CONDENSED BOOKS

THE READER'S DIGEST ASSOCIATION LIMITED
25 Berkeley Square, London W1X 6AB

THE READER'S DIGEST ASSOCIATION
SOUTH AFRICA (PTY) LTD
Reader's Digest House, 130 Strand Street, Cape Town

Printed in Great Britain by Petty & Sons Ltd, Leeds
Members of the BPCC Group

Original cover design by Jeffery Matthews FSIAD

READER'S DIGEST
CONDENSED BOOKS

CARTER'S CASTLE
by Wilbur Wright

Donald Carter is a pilot whose nerve has gone, and who feels he has little left to live for. But when he and three others miraculously survive a plane crash in the Cambodian jungle he finds his old flying skills may be vital in saving their lives. Before they can think of escape, there are mysteries in plenty to occupy Carter, the beautiful airhostess Liane, and teenagers Debby and Colin. Why was the landing strip abandoned, and what is the secret of the skeletons they find? And can the ancient aeroplane in the hangar be made to fly again?

A romantic and exciting adventure story in the tradition of *Lost Horizon* and *Raiders of the Lost Ark*.

Page 9

THE GREAT HUSKY RACE
by José Giovanni

The Iditarod, the great annual dog sled race across Alaska from Anchorage to Nome, is one of the most challenging contests in the world. Those brave enough to take part must survive deathly cold, icebound wastes, incredibly tough competition and every imaginable hazard that Arctic nature can throw at them.

Dan Murphy, the fictional hero of this amazing story, is just out of prison and desperately needs to redeem himself. With his courageous team of dogs led by the faithful husky, Eccluke, whom he has reclaimed from his great racing rival, Dan fights through. But there are a host of disasters on the way and a cliffhanging finish to the race.

Page 135

THE RED FOX
by Anthony Hyde

It all started with the discovery that May Brightman had been adopted. She was the girl Robert Thorne once loved and hoped to marry, and now there seems to be a dangerous mystery connecting her birth with the surprising suicide of her father and with the discovery of a man's savagely mutilated body. Anxious to help May and to solve the mystery, Thorne finds himself on a terrifying voyage of discovery which takes him halfway round the world, to encounters with men who will stop at nothing in their search for the truth, and then, amazingly, back to a dark secret in his own past.

This is a dazzling new thriller which is destined to be a bestseller.

Page 235

THE FLAME TREES OF THIKA
by Elspeth Huxley

Elspeth Huxley spent a rich and rewarding childhood in Kenya, and in this book she distils her memories and experiences in a loving recreation of that beautiful and wild country, her pioneering parents and their friends, and above all those who were most special to her as a little girl: the native Kikuyu and Masai tribesmen, and her collection of pet animals. Here is portrayed in vivid detail a way of life that no longer exists and which suffered its greatest blow with the outbreak of the Great War.

The popular television series, starring Hayley Mills, was based on this delightful book.

Page 403

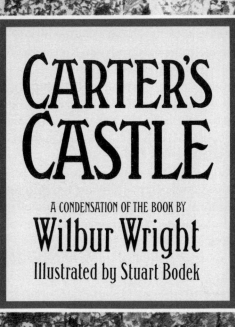

CARTER'S CASTLE

A CONDENSATION OF THE BOOK BY

Wilbur Wright

Illustrated by Stuart Bodek

To Donald Carter it is a miracle that he and three others have come down alive in the shattered tail section of the Boeing 707. Stranded in a remote Cambodian valley, surrounded by steep cliffs and impenetrable jungle, there seems no way they can get back to civilization. But then, on an abandoned US airbase where they have taken shelter, they discover an old, rusty Dakota with a valuable cargo. And the valley has more mysteries to reveal: what is the significance of the ancient and precious jewel found in the river pool? Why does the wild elephant respond only to Liane, the Cambodian airhostess? What is hidden in the cave behind the waterfall?

As Carter, Liane and their two teenage companions begin to find answers to these questions, great danger comes to the valley, and they must escape without delay. But can Carter, an ex-pilot racked by terrible fears, find the courage to fly the old Dakota and get them out in time?

Prologue

There is a fourteenth-century legend concerning the last of Cambodia's Khmer kings which tells how their royal city of Angkor was invaded by a vast horde of Siamese warriors. Like the waves of the Eastern Sea the warriors came, pouring across the plains to attack the walled city. But the city was already betrayed: its gates had been opened to the lethal horde by renegade Buddhist priests who cared nothing for the fall of Angkor, but only for the rise of the Lord Buddha.

Deep in an inner chamber of the royal palace, the Princess Indibaraja was awakened with news of the invasion, and urged by her father, King Jayavarman, to flee to safety. The king's last words to his daughter were these: "Guard with your own life those things which shall identify you on the day you return. This, my elephant ring, and this, the statue of our god, Siva. Take with you also all the treasure of our city, and find a place where it may be hidden until it is needed once more to bring justice back to the land of Angkor. And if any should then still dispute your claim to the Khmer throne, there is yet one more proof. The mark of the War Elephant which you bear upon your body, as do all females of the royal blood . . ."

So the princess departed with her husband, Prince Yasovarman, and upon an elephant they led a tiny procession of three bullock

9

carts across land and sea, searching for a safe resting place for the treasure.

They reached one morning a hidden valley surrounded by towering rock walls. There, following an underground tunnel, they came upon the place at last—a vast, dry cavern, shielded on the far side by a green curtain of falling water which tumbled into a frothing pool many hundreds of feet below. Yasovarman caught the princess's hand and smiled exultantly. Together they carefully laid the boxes of treasure in the hidden place. Just as they were completing their task, the skies above the cave opened to the violence of a monsoon storm, and a great flood of water surged through the underground tunnel, causing part of the roof to collapse and blocking the way by which they had come. Their only means of escape was destroyed.

Realizing that their fate was sealed, Yasovarman and his princess made love for the last time, surrounded by the wealth of the great kingdom of Angkor. Then Yasovarman lifted up Indibaraja, naked save for the great elephant ring, and approached the curtain of falling water. They kissed once more, and then together took a single step into eternity. . . .

The passing years left their mark upon the valley, and the sandalwood boxes containing the treasure decayed into dust, as did the fading garments left behind by Yasovarman and his princess. But the cave, the waterfall and the pool endured through the centuries, silently guarding their secret. It was as if they were waiting, waiting. . . .

Chapter One

At the time I became involved with the mysterious disappearance of Flight HK 108, I had lived and worked in Singapore for twelve years, and had recently retired. The minister for civil aviation, Mr. Lee Kuan Lok, was a close friend: we had flown Dakotas together in Malaya during 1944 and 1945, but it was twenty-odd years before I ran across him again, at a dreary party thrown by a senior British resident. He was as pleased and surprised to see me as I was to see him. I noticed he had a few extra inches around his black cummerbund now, and the lines on his face were deeper—but otherwise he had changed very little.

We met over an extended and most enjoyable lunch at Raffles some days later, and opened up some very old hangar doors in the process. Lee was interested in my accident investigation experience, gained during the years between our encounters, and told me that the government branch responsible at that time was both undermanned and inexperienced. My arrival must have seemed providential to him. He offered me a post as part-time but fully accredited consultant to his Investigation Department. Civil aviation and local airlines were booming. The salary offered was very attractive, but my decision to accept stemmed more from a real desire to re-enter the field in which I had spent so many years. And the additional income might even permit the purchase of a small light aircraft, such as a Piper Cub or a Comanche, to amuse me in my retirement.

In the years that followed, Lee—I am pleased to say—appeared more than satisfied. My salary was easily earned, for serious accidents were, luckily, rare at that time. One evening he came to see me in the small club hangar at Seletar, where I was working on the Cub engine for the Certificate of Airworthiness check, due next month. I took up a piece of rag, wiped my hands, and we walked slowly to the bar. The sun was low on the hills, and already the runway lighting glimmered softly in the dusk.

He told me, over a long cool drink, about Flight HK 108. It had disappeared over the South China Sea, en route to Hong Kong, after taking off that morning with a total of sixty-one passengers and crew. One becomes hardened over years of probing aircraft accidents, but I felt a sharp pang of sorrow when he told me that fifty-three of those lost had been children. We walked over to the Far East map on the wall of the clubroom.

"The last position report," Lee said gravely, "put Flight HK 108 some two hundred miles southeast of the Mekong Delta—well clear of Vietnamese airspace. They could have landed at Saigon—but communication is difficult with Vietnam at the moment."

That was an understatement. I stared at the map. "The weather?"

"Not good. A big depression over the Philippines, deepening rapidly—it's a full-blown typhoon now. Heading roughly north."

11

I set my glass upon the bar. "Local aeroplane?"

"The 707 operated by All-Orient."

I said slowly, "That one? Who was the pilot?"

"Eddie Wu Pak, their chief pilot."

"Well, he should know what he's doing. Been at it long enough. How long since they went overdue?"

"Three o'clock local time," the minister said shortly. "But the tower lost contact two hours before that time."

I put my forefinger on the map, in the middle of the South China Sea. A modern jet airliner could travel more than one thousand nautical miles in two hours. It could be almost anywhere. Lee agreed.

"I know, Alan. Look—we'd like you to take over the inquiry."

I stared at him. "Actually, I had planned to take the Cub down to Darwin in easy stages, after the C of A check."

He smiled blandly. "But you'll do it?"

I couldn't say no. The loss of the Boeing was the most serious incident in recent years. When such an aircraft goes missing over one of the world's most vicious oceans, there is little hope of finding it again. The only feasible landing places en route were the Paracel Islands and Vietnam itself. The former I could eliminate very quickly—but the latter was an unknown quantity. I managed to persuade myself that the inquiry would open and close very quickly indeed.

The hearing opened the next morning, Tuesday, and closed at noon on Friday. The final report was brief and inconclusive: there was no information from Vietnam (surprise, surprise) and no sighting of wreckage by shipping. That was in early May.

In the first week in October, I received a telephone call from Lee Kuan Lok.

"Alan," he said urgently, "you remember the inquiry on Flight HK 108? Back in the spring? You'll have to reopen it. A survivor has turned up at Khota Baru, on the northeast coast of Malaysia. We're flying him to Singapore today—you'd better go and see him in hospital tomorrow."

"All right. But how did he come to be at Khota Baru?"

"He crash-landed on the beach, with three other survivors. In a Dakota which has been missing for five years."

DONALD CARTER LOOKED UP at me from a newspaper. He was a spare man, in his fifties, and his hair was sun-bleached, fading to grey at the temples. He had been freshly shaven that day, his cheeks and body were two shades darker than his chin, and I judged that his hair and beard had grown long. He lay back against banked pillows, wearing green hospital-issue pyjamas, and looked remarkably fit and well, despite the lines of strain showing around his eyes and mouth.

I said, "Mr. Carter? My name's Napier. I'm attached to the Ministry of Aviation, Accident Investigation. We've reopened the inquiry into the loss of Flight HK 108—" He raised his eyebrows. "Your Boeing flight to Hong Kong," I went on. He nodded, laid down his newspaper and reached for the cigarettes on the bedside table.

I sat down. "Are you well enough to answer a few questions?" I asked.

He nodded. "I'm OK, Mr. Napier. But it's a long story—" He had a broad, engaging grin and penetrating blue eyes.

"When you're ready."

He stared down at the cigarette in his hand. "You'd better have the full story," he said slowly.

AFTER HIS WIFE DIED in 1975, Donald Carter's life had disintegrated inexorably, with quickening pace. He missed her, and he also missed the security and activity of service life. After twenty-five years in the RAF, he had found civilian life a depressing jungle. For years, he buried his nostalgia in a succession of underpaid, uninteresting jobs. Gavin, his son, was at boarding school, and Carter gradually lost touch even with the small group of fellow castoffs in the Ex-Apprentice Association.

He drifted listlessly from job to job. His wife Jean tried to help him—nagging, encouraging, even swearing at him at times, and always providing maximum support and comfort. And always Carter would come in and head for the sherry bottle. Then, suddenly, in 1975, Jean was gone. Cancer had consumed her with the speed of a forest fire.

Afterwards, Donald Carter aged visibly. He became careless about his surroundings and his person, drank a good deal too much.

13

Gavin, now a husband and father, and a qualified transport pilot, drove down from his Wiltshire base alone to make a final attempt to get him back on his feet.

He made Carter change before going to the pub and, once there, stared with distaste at his father. "Look at yourself, Dad! How long have you worn that suit? I know you miss Mum, but—"

"Let's leave her out of this, shall we?"

It wasn't just the clothes, Gavin thought. The old man was turning into—an old man? The once-dark hair was grey around the ears, a little thin on top; the strong hands that once had hoisted him overhead with ease trembled at times. He felt the dull ache of pity.

"Dad," he said, "I've got some news. You're going to have to look after yourself. I've been given a posting to Hong Kong. Hercules squadron. It's my first overseas tour. We all want to go—Shirley and Peter too. But Shirl's worried about you, Dad—she thinks you don't get enough to eat."

"Don't talk daft," Carter said equably. "Anyone would think I had one foot in the grave."

"Look, Dad, it's three years since Mum . . . I mean, she wouldn't want you to go on alone, you know. You're not past it—with a shave and a decent suit . . ."

"Thank you very much."

His son sighed, exasperated. "It's just that I'd feel better, knowing you were settled. Look, Dad—we'll be away two years, but I'll be commuting a bit—I'll drop in from time to time."

Carter said, "Gav, I can manage. I won't write every week, but I'll answer all your letters. A deal?"

"OK . . ."

Gavin, uncertain and worried, felt a poignant tide of emotion well up within him, as he remembered how his father used to be: tall, straight, uniform well-tailored and smart, the pilot brevet above the double row of ribbons; Mother beside him at some garden party, flowery dress flapping in the summer breeze.

He sighed, remembering. "I still think you should find yourself a rich widder-woman, Dad," he said, half serious.

Carter's eyes glinted. "You want a knuckle sandwich?"

His son grinned. "Reaction at last. Cheers."

14

GAVIN REPRESENTED the third generation of pilots in the Carter family. Charles Auckinlek Carter's Camel had collided with an Albatross in 1918. Donald Charles Carter was born in 1919, seven months after his father was killed—thus ensuring that he would be old enough to volunteer for the RAF in 1939. He crossed the Atlantic with the first wave bound for American training schools, and came home with 15,000 others in the *Queen Elizabeth*, early in 1942.

In learning to fly, he discovered a very strange thing. The moment he left the ground for the first time in the Tiger Moth, he was terrified; yet the sheer surging acceleration, the initial rocketing climb, overwhelmed his fears. And it was just as well. Surrounded by forty jubilant ex-schoolboys, he would rather have died than ask to be relieved of flying duties.

He began to learn to use the aeroplanes he had been taught to fly. Just as the involvement and complexity of flying training left no room for fear, neither did the operational training and the two tours of air fighting which followed.

His instructors recognized his terror, but they knew from experience that highly-strung young men under pressure tended to fight extremely well. They recommended him for fighters. Carter, despite his own misgivings, was neither a fool nor a coward. Cowards recognize their fears, succumb, run away. He recognized them, came to terms with them and lived with them—which is as close as one can come to describing a brave man. With his move to a Spitfire squadron, a flood of external distractions was released—most of them sporting black crosses—and for a long time he was unafraid.

He stayed on after the war, but with increased leisure and minimal activity, the old fears returned in strength. Lines from a poem about an imaginary castle—the terrible obstacle that fear conjures up, and that vanishes into thin air when approached with a stout heart—came to haunt his days:

> *Such castles rise to strike us dumb*
> *But—weak in every part—*
> *They melt before the strong man's eyes*
> *And fly the true of heart . . .*

He applied, with a friend, for a helicopter posting to Malaya, and came second in a short list of two. Three weeks later, his friend died when a helicopter main rotor snapped, near Kuala Lumpur. On an instructor's course a year later, he brought down a Vampire fighter, reporting it as "flying like a rotten crate"; a staff instructor took it up on test, and the machine broke up in midair, killing the pilot.

Carter began to imagine that some vengeful fate pursued him. How could all this be simple coincidence? In 1950, he was flying a Mosquito trainer from the south coast to Yorkshire on a day of frightening turbulence. An undercarriage doorlock failed: the door whipped open and the Mosquito headed groundwards in a violent near-vertical sideslip. Carter, fighting to bale out, found his head jerked back again and again towards the seat he had vacated. His radio microphone plug had jammed in the seat-frame. He saw the ground coming up very fast, and prepared to die.

The increasing speed ripped away the open door: the Mosquito lurched into a straight dive from which he barely recovered in time, swooping so low that the tail-wheel ploughed through soft soil and cabbages and was torn away.

Afterwards Carter suffered a nervous twitch, as if he were dragging his head against some unseen hindrance which bound him to a doomed aircraft. When the time came he left the service, threw away his medals, burned three fat logbooks. If he never saw an aeroplane again, it would be much too soon. . . .

Alone now, Carter settled down into something resembling normality. He washed, shaved most days, found a new job as traffic manager for an oil distribution company, and began to refurbish his small house on the outskirts of Southampton. More important, he worked on reducing his drinking, because he knew he was halfway to being an alcoholic.

This frightened him considerably. The letters to and from Hong Kong helped him a great deal, and a month after the family left for the Far East, Gavin began to hope that his father was truly a changed man. But inevitably, after exhausting every possible means of preoccupying mind and body, the old fears returned, and Carter began to drink again. The intervals between letters stretched beyond reason, and on the far side of the world Gavin gnawed at his fingernails.

16

"Three weeks, Shirl, and not a word. He could be dead."

His wife Shirley looked up from her book. "There must be something we can do. He hasn't been the same since your mother died."

"I know. I wanted to ask you something, Shirl."

"Like: should we bring him out here for a holiday?"

Gavin swung round, astonished and pleased. "You must be a mind reader! He could come out with the school holiday flight next month, stay about eight weeks. Maybe we can get him straightened out."

Shirley nodded, watching the light fade into glorious pink over Kowloon. She thought it would be very good, not only for Donald Carter, but for Gavin; he worried too much about his father. "Do it, darling," she said softly. "Do it soon. Life's too short to spend it apart from the people we love. . . ."

DONALD CARTER LIT UP with indecent haste the instant the NO SMOKING light went out, and settled back in the seat of the 707, staring out at the opaque greyness of the clouds through which they were climbing.

Fifteen-year-old Debby Worthington reached up and opened the overhead vent, and the cold current sliced through Carter's smokecloud; he turned, said, "Sorry," and put out the cigarette.

Debby smiled, nodded. The man in the seat next to her was human after all. His lined face was like the antique dresser at home, she thought—it had taken a few knocks in its time, but stayed in reasonable shape. He seemed—careworn? No, not exactly. She glanced curiously at him, wondering why he was on the flight: the only other adults were escorts, and two new teachers bound for the colony schools.

She turned her head away, looked at Colin. They had travelled together several times. At first, he had taken the lead to which his two years' seniority entitled him, infuriatingly superior. She was grown-up now, wore make-up by choice and a bra of necessity. But he persisted in treating her like a younger sister. He was totally engrossed in his paperback, the cover of which depicted a three-decker of Nelson's navy. Debby turned again to Carter.

"I'm Debby Worthington. This is Colin Todd."

"Hi, Debby. Donald Carter. Colin—pleased to meet you."

They shook hands self-consciously. "Col and I are going to Hong Kong for the holidays—eight whole weeks. Are you going to stay?"

"Only for a while," Carter said equably. "To see my son and his family. He flies transport aeroplanes."

"Colin's airforce, too," Debby confided. "My dad's a major in the army." She groped in her bag for sweets, offered one to Carter, watching surreptitiously as he fumbled to remove the wrapping. His fingers were long, brown, and trembled periodically. His hair was a little grey, his eyes distant and surrounded by tiny wrinkles which shifted attractively when he smiled, yet he wasn't really old. He was tall—as tall as Daddy, even—and a bit podgy round the middle, but his voice was nice, deep and vibrant. She decided she liked Mr. Carter.

Debby recognized intuitively that he was afraid. As the veteran of a dozen holiday flights, she found this vastly mysterious, intriguing; she stared down the length of the Boeing, taking in the subdued lighting, spotless russet carpet, gleaming décor, all pleasing and reassuring.

Debby watched the movement within the cabin. Four of the staff were recognizably Chinese—small, lithe creatures in flat-heeled shoes. Another was a gaunt Sino-American blonde with a grating voice and nicotine-stained fingers, who seemed to be in charge; the sixth was a slim, black-haired girl of startling beauty. Not Chinese, but Debby couldn't yet distinguish between the half dozen races she had encountered in the East. The girl could be Vietnamese, Laotian, Thai—perhaps even a Philippino; her face was an integrated medley of parabolic curves, encompassing cheeks, eyes, chin and small, sculpted nose. Debby thought herself ugly, and was constantly searching for the ideal on which she could plan her own metamorphosis; the tall stewardess came very close to it. She watched the way the Asian girl moved within the blue uniform, and sighed.

Colin nudged her in the ribs. "I fancy her!"

"She's old enough to be your mother," Debby said contemptuously.

"Rubbish—she's only about twenty."

"And the rest, fatty. You can't tell, with these Eastern women."

Colin grinned wickedly. "You know what they say about them?"

"It's probably rude, and I don't want to know," she said tartly. Then she turned back to Carter. "Do you like flying?"

He was silent for a moment. "I've done a lot of it, at one time and another. It's not a thing I liked or disliked—just a job."

The schoolgirl, mature beyond her years, sensed he was hedging, but hesitated to probe further. "I used to be scared stiff," she said presently, "but I'm all right now."

Carter nodded. "Everyone is, to start with. It takes some people longer than others to get used to it."

She thought about that, caught his eye and smiled, and the innocence and candour of her youth caught at his heart. Old age was ten per cent self-pity and ninety per cent envy, he thought. He had lived most of his life to the full, enjoyed it; yet he begrudged these children the future he would never see. What wonders would they see, in the century to come? Sixty or seventy years, he thought drowsily: such a short time. The design, he thought, was incomplete, flawed. Mankind deserved a hundred years at peak . . . and memory should be inheritable . . . if one could be born with the knowledge and experience of one's parents, learning from their mistakes, steeped in the depths of their love . . . He fell asleep, a faint smile around his relaxed mouth.

WITHIN THE PORT WING of the Boeing, close to the root end attachment points, a double row of titanium bolts passed through spacer tubes to secure a massive steel member, nestling in alloy channels. Around several of the bolt holes, tiny cracks radiated outwards, concealed beneath the large plate washers of the bolt assemblies, and by the thick anti-corrosive coating on the metal.

Between one pair of bolts, upper and lower, two cracks wandered randomly but inexorably towards each other. As the mainplane flexed in flight, and upon landing, the cracks extended almost imperceptibly, a millimetre of movement requiring hundreds of flying hours, and the metal absorbed infinitely small quanta of energy from the imposed stresses. The energy was stored within the nuclear lattice of the metal itself, which would eventually become crystalline in structure, brittle, with almost none of the strength and elasticity of the original metal, of which it would become an isotope. This was metal fatigue, well known to the Boeing engineers in Seattle, who had produced, years previously, a system of inspections involving the removal of the bolts and the use of X-ray spectroscopy to identify any change in the metallic structure.

But the old Boeing had changed both owners and identity a number of times. Her new Chinese engineers believed, from the aircraft logs supplied by the previous owners, that these and other inspections had been carried out properly. Indeed, they had—but on a 707 which was now a disintegrating wreck in the Arizona desert. From that wreck, spare parts and a new logbook had been cannibalized to give 10026 a new lease of life.

On the previous flight the cracking process had accelerated enormously, and an hour after takeoff the spar metal underwent an abrupt and significant change in structure, and the cracks raced towards their final rendezvous. With each successive positive and negative deceleration, the wing structure began to groan, the noise remaining inaudible above the slipstream and jet roar. One of the bolts, now resting in an ever-widening channel, began to rotate, and at intervals it blurred visibly, in violent reaction to the subsonic vibrations within the wing.

Thirty-eight thousand feet below the Boeing, the sea rolled and tossed, reacting to the pressure wave of the storm-front eight hundred miles to the north, across the China Sea.

Chapter Two

Eddie Wu Pak was uneasy. All pilots have a sixth sense for danger, an innate awareness defying description, that warns them when something may be amiss. Maybe it was the weather, he thought numbly. . . . Climbing out of Singapore, he tried to justify his decision to go ahead with this flight in the light of the forecast weather, and found it hard. That damned typhoon up near Manila could move any which way, and alternative landing sites were hard to find around Hong Kong. He made another slow, methodical scan of the instruments; they were climbing in cloud on autopilot, passing 20,000 feet. The altostratus contained scattered "cobble-stones"—regions of heavy turbulence which made the plastic beaker on his console vibrate jerkily towards the edge. Wu Pak turned to the flight engineer.

"Any problems, Charlie?"

"Board all green, skipper." They spoke in English, the *lingua franca* of the airways.

Eddie shrugged and lit a cigarette. Very soon they broke through cloud-top, still tail-down in the climbing configuration. The sun overhead gave a strange luminosity to the cloud tops; at 30,000 feet, they formed a roughly level plateau, horizon to horizon. Scattered along the northern skyline, mountainous cumulonimbus clouds were bursting like nuclear explosions. The upper air was unstable; the thunderheads reached 40,000 feet within minutes.

He turned to the copilot. "Nasty, Chang."

"Yes, captain. With luck, we'll clear the tops. If not . . ."

"Then we'll work round them. The vertical winds in those things are unbelievable. But we're not at full load. We can make forty-two thousand feet if we have to."

The copilot frowned. He had flown with Eddie Wu Pak long enough to realize that the captain was worried.

Eddie stood up, spoke briefly to the flight engineer, then went aft on his customary walkabout. He found Dolly Feng in the aft galley, talking to the new girl. Eddie looked at the small waist and long legs, and liked what he saw.

"Captain, our new girl—Liane Dang Ko."

The girl put a hand out nervously: he noted the long, slim fingers, translucent nails—fingers which seemed boneless and capable of bending far back towards the wrist. She flushed, and her pale lemon skin seemed to take on the glow of fresh honey. Eddie retained the hand, complimenting her.

"I was trained as a ceremonial dancer, captain. The finger exercises were painful, but we learned. My parents died when I was small, and I lived at the dancing school."

The pilot blinked. "You must dance for me some time, Liane."

"I have not danced for years, captain. It is necessary to keep up with the exercises and movements." Her English was grammatically correct, but stilted and spoken with a lilting accent.

Eddie nodded. Plenty of time, little bird. "Tonight in Kowloon, we will all eat together—all the crew."

21

Dolly Feng shot a glance at the young girl: the lashes were long and dark on smooth cheeks. This one isn't for you, Eddie Wu—stick to your bar girls in downtown Hong Kong. She looked at the captain.

"The weather is not good?"

"We can fly over most of it. The landing forecast is good."

Dolly Feng's lips tightened dubiously. Dolly was strong, experienced, full of guts, yet she had a frail, pinched look about her. Nerves? Strain? Eddie wondered. He allowed his old confident smile to break out, but later, back in his seat, he anxiously watched the storm clouds marching towards the scudding Boeing.

DONALD CARTER DOZED lightly on the fringe of wakefulness, aware of the noise in the background as a hypnotic resonance. When had he last flown? Fourteen, fifteen years ago? It didn't seem as long as that. He sank a little deeper into sleep, groaning quietly at long intervals, and his hands, palms upward in his lap, twitched spasmodically. Sometimes his head jerked sharply to the right and the escape hatch would not open . . . he could see each individual cabbage in the field, swelling in the windscreen, and pieces falling off the aeroplane, until he sat in sickening horror in a glass capsule, fitted with controls connected to nothing, and fell down the endless vault of the sky.

MOST FLIGHT EMERGENCIES originate in some minor occurrence, in itself only a temporary inconvenience; but when it is the first in a series of associated events, the aeroplane eventually reaches a point at which the situation becomes irretrievable.

The Boeing was doomed because a flight mechanic should have replaced eighteen inches of old iron locking wire on the cabin-condensation drain plug—but that would have involved a half-mile walk in the heat of the day. Instead, he used the old wire again. Too often twisted and strained, it broke at the locking lug, allowing the plug to rotate slowly. Then the cabin pressure exceeded the resistance of the few remaining threads and the plug blew out with catastrophic violence.

At 38,000 feet, cabin pressure was maintained at an equivalent 8,000 feet altitude by pumping in air. When the plug blew out, this was instantaneously raised through 30,000 feet to very low air pressure and intense cold, with insufficient oxygen. The effect on the passengers, and particularly upon the children, was devastating. Eddie Wu Pak slammed the plane into a 45-degree bank, and forced the 707 into a steep dive, heading for thicker and warmer air. In the cabin, adults and children were flung screaming against seats and roof.

Veteran of a hundred emergencies, Eddie slowed all engines, lowered some landing flap, got the wings level, dropped the main gear. The forward speed slowed, the vertical rate of descent built up and they entered cloud at 30,000 feet, flight deck and cabin already thick with the grey fog of condensation. On instruments, the pilot left Chang to concentrate on the internal problems; the compass was swinging wildly, and he made a rough mental calculation of position: southeast of Saigon, over the sea, outside Vietnamese airspace.

The headlong descent slowed, stopped, and the Boeing levelled out at 14,000 feet, within ten degrees of its original course—an outstanding feat of airmanship by any standards. Eddie sent the flight engineer down into the hold to investigate.

"We have a hole you could put your foot through, skipper. Looks like the condensation drain valve blew out."

Eddie Wu Pak winced. "Can we make a temporary repair?"

"Let's hope so. That sea's too rough for swimming. I'll check back with you." The engineer went below again.

The captain checked with Dolly Feng. "What's the score, Doll?"

"Some of the kids are hysterical, captain. One woman has a broken leg. Two kids with nosebleeds. What happened?"

"Explosive decompression. If we can seal the hole, we can work up cabin pressure, get back to altitude. I—"

He never completed the sentence. The Boeing, ploughing through turbulent stratus cloud, had no chance of avoiding the thunderhead buried within. There was a brief sensation of sinking, followed by a raging climb that pinned the crew to their seats. The aeroplane vibrated, surged, twisted, fighting the vortex of air currents, the almost solid rain, in a hideous globe of thunder and blue light.

The lightning bolt hit the forward radio antenna. Carter heard it

23

as a dull explosion, jerking him into a paralysis of fear. Millions of volts flooded the aircraft systems, jumping circuit breakers, starting a dozen small fires.

The cabin lights failed instantly, yet the long fuselage was lit almost continuously by searing blue-white fire from the lightning, which flickered all around through the churning storm clouds. There was a reek of ozone and burning rubber.

Beside him, Debby wailed and buried her head in his shoulder. Shaken and disorientated, Carter held her tight, pressing her oxygen mask close to her face. He had been fully aware of the enormity of the emergency from the moment it began; he had fought to secure oxygen masks for himself and the children, and held them in their seats by brute force until he got their belts fastened round them.

Now he sat frozen in a cocoon of terror. His eyes recorded the sequence of light and shadow, but his brain ceased to transmit signals in terms of duration or meaning.

THE CREW FOUGHT the electrical fires until the last flickered and died; the compartment was filled with the fumes of burning rubber and seared molten plastic.

Eddie Wu Pak sat coughing harshly, watching the few remaining instruments. Everything electrical was shot; only the Turn and Slip, altimeter and airspeed indicator, remained to assess aircraft altitude.

The flight engineer had completed his temporary repair, and the altitude was creeping slowly back up through 18,000 feet. They had breached the worst of the storm, but lightning still flickered eerily in the grey depths, and the turbulence persisted, jarring and hammering at the aeroplane. They had no accurate indication of heading: the gyrocompass rotated madly, out of control, and the small E2 emergency compass was little better.

"Charlie—status?"

The flight engineer came forward, leaning over the centre console. "Not good. All electrics out. Engine instruments shot, but we seem to be getting full power—no problems there. All fires out—and we are also out of extinguishers."

"Any systems left? Radios? Radio compass?" Eddie asked dully.

"Not a thing, skipper. That flash really cleaned us out. Hydraulics seem OK, but we've no instrumentation."

He turned to the copilot. "Chang—any idea of position? Did we get a mayday out?"

"Negative, captain. No time. We were about two hundred miles off the Mekong Delta when that flash hit, say thirty minutes ago."

Wu Pak nodded slowly. "Check. We were close to course at the bottom of the hill—between 020 and 030 degrees. We could be anywhere between Borneo, Manila and Hainan Island by now."

"What are you steering now?" asked the copilot tightly.

"God only knows, Chang. That emergency compass is going round like a roulette wheel, and I don't feel lucky. I'm working her round to a westerly heading; we'll never make Hong Kong at this altitude, and if we climb, maybe that patch over the hole will blow again. I figure our best bet is Saigon. If we hold this heading for an hour, we should be over land. I'll let down slowly in about thirty minutes. With luck, we'll come out over the sea near the Mekong Delta."

Chang nodded. "Better call it Ho Chi Minh City, Eddie. There'll be no red carpet for us there."

Suddenly the storm burst around them in renewed fury. The depression had worked itself up into a king-sized typhoon. If only they had got a mayday out, thought Eddie. He would have to let down soon, he told himself, but he shied away from the thought. Even kamikaze pilots wouldn't let down through cloud when they got lost. Hold course for another twenty minutes, maybe. It wasn't good, but in this situation he had the tiger by the tail and couldn't let go. Whoever heard of an aeroplane with so much trouble and still flying?

CARTER STOOD IN THE GALLEY, a stinking shambles of spilled food and other debris swirling to and fro round his feet. He felt jaded, battle-weary. He had left Debby and Colin to help the cabin staff, while he and the Asian girl Liane had worked like demons, pacifying children and getting them into their seats. Carter helped the stewardess lift the woman passenger with a broken leg into her seat, watched her remove one of the woman's stockings and use it to lash a fire-axe splint to the leg. Liane made the woman drink four brandy miniatures. Maybe it was against all medical practice, but it had the desired effect: soon she fell into an uneasy sleep, and they left her.

Back aft in the cabin, Carter had time to look at the Asian girl closely. Her nose had bled copiously and her right temple was swollen and a deep purple colour. The long dark hair was disarranged: she put up a tired hand to straighten it, abandoned the attempt.

"You OK now?"

"Yes—thank you, Mr. Carter."

"Donald."

She smiled wearily: the wide generous lips, rose pink, parted to reveal even white teeth.

"You'd better let me fix that bruise," Carter said. "It doesn't look good to me. Head aching?"

"Only a little."

"Double vision?"

"No. Go back to your seat, Mr. Car—Donald. I'll be fine. Please." She smiled tremulously.

"Just checking you had no concussion. But you should rest here for a while—that was a bad knock."

The girl shook her head. "I have to go. The children . . ."

". . . are all right. Panic's over. Take it easy—I'll be back in a moment." He went forward, located the senior stewardess. "Miss Feng? Donald Carter. Look, your Asian girl took a bad knock on the head, but she'll be fine after a rest. Do you need her right now?"

Dolly Feng wiped her hands on a paper towel. "You mean Liane? No. Things are more or less under control here. How bad is she?"

"No concussion, but badly shaken."

Dolly nodded. "She's lucky, Mr. Carter. We all are."

Carter said, "That's right. The pilot did well. I was in the game for years myself. Would he mind if I spoke to him?"

Dolly waved tiredly at the flight-deck door. "Be my guest."

He went through, closing the door behind him. In the cramped dark cabin, flash-photographed on his vision every few seconds by bolts of lightning, the pilots sat motionless.

"Name's Carter. I was a pilot myself. Anything I can do?"

"Mr. Carter. Thanks—no. We lost cabin pressure, but my engineer made a temporary repair. He's down below checking it out now. How are things back there?"

"Don't even ask," Carter grunted. "We'll be late in Hong Kong?"

"We can't make Hong Kong. Don't have the altitude. We can make Saigon OK—plenty of fuel. Only . . ." The pilot hesitated. "Only . . . we have no radio."

Carter stared at him. "But we got a mayday out, surely?"

"Negative. Happened too fast. We're shot on all bands."

Donald Carter was silent for a long moment, digesting an unpalatable fact. "Weather?"

"Lousy. We've no aids to get down at Saigon, no landing forecast. We can let down soon, lose altitude out to sea, come back in under cloud. We'll hit the coast somewhere . . ."

Carter bit his lip. "Lucky we were out at sea when we took the dive. There's some very solid green clouds on the mainland."

"Damned right. It was real rough for a while." They stared at each other in unspoken understanding.

"Tell me," the old pilot said stiffly, "what are our chances?"

The captain turned back to his controls, shrugged his shoulders; there was no need of amplification—Carter read him loud and clear. Dazed and uneasy, he stumbled back to the galley, made sure Liane was resting and made her drink a little coffee, lukewarm from the rapidly cooling urn. At intervals the cabin staff came in for supplies, smiling tiredly, making tense little jokes at which no one laughed. They were all doggedly summoning up every last ounce of stamina and courage.

It made a difference, keeping busy. How well he knew it. He looked at Liane, who stood swaying loosely as the plane hit more turbulence, both hands cupped round the coffee beaker. He could see the lines of strain round the wide, mobile mouth. He tried to draw her mind away from their problems.

"Been flying long, Liane?"

"About three years, Mr.—I mean, Donald."

"With this crew?"

"No. This is first time with them. Before, I was with Captain Charles on the Viscount. He's an American." Her voice was low, musical, with an odd lilting accent.

"Your family in Singapore?"

"No. I lost my parents when I was a little girl. My uncle took me in. He was a teacher at the dancing school in Battembang."

"Battem-which?" he said, puzzled.

She laughed. "In Cambodia—Kampuchea now."

He smiled. "I get it. What happened to your parents?"

"They . . . were killed, when I was six."

"I'm sorry," he said softly.

The girl began clearing up the galley, and as he helped her, he saw that her skin was unusually smooth, a pale, delicate shade of lemon; her lashes lay long and luxuriant upon her cheeks, natural and untouched. He had little experience of Asian women; he was only vaguely aware of the TV version—short, flat-footed, snub-nosed, with oddly shaped eyes. This girl—woman, rather, for she must be in her late twenties—had a beauty which made him catch his breath.

She was almost as tall as he was, yet her small-boned body was lithe and balanced. His eyes returned again and again to the sensitive oval face, the large, luminous eyes: they had the slightest hint of angularity, characteristic of her race. In London she could have taken the fashion world by storm, yet here she was, working as a servant on some nondescript Third World airline. She was beauty in an alien mould, and he felt disturbed by her presence.

Carter, he told himself ruefully, you're too old to understand women of this age—any age, maybe. He left her there, and groped his way back to his seat. The lightning still flickered in the cloudy depths, and the turbulence seemed to be increasing.

Debby turned to him. "Mr. Carter? Are we going to die?"

He looked at the face of the girl, compassion gripping his heart; it was a time for prevarication, false optimism. Besides, much could happen in the hours to come. . . . He checked his watch. They had been airborne for four hours.

"I think we'll be OK, Debby. The captain thinks he'll get us down, probably at Saigon. He's very experienced. But keep strapped in—it's still very rough. Hang on to me, if you like."

Debby smiled uncertainly, gripping his hand. Colin sat rigid and terrified, with clenched teeth. Carter thought the boy did not look too good, but there was nothing he could do about it. Seat belt tight,

Carter sat back, bracing himself against the storm, watching the play of St. Elmo's Fire around the wingtip, listening dully to the pounding of his heart.

Chapter Three

Some ten minutes after Carter resumed his seat, the Boeing began to resonate in waves of a periodicity of about one minute, like a railway carriage bumping over rails. They flew into very heavy rain, and the clouds took on an eerie glow, a luminescence born of the incessant lightning. Numbly Carter gazed out at the hellish panorama. Then abruptly he sat up, wiped the window clear of condensation.

No—he had not been mistaken. In the instant between two lightning flashes, the appearance of the wing had definitely changed in some way. He waited for the next flare, and was sure.

Along the joint of wing and fuselage, rivets were popping. With each flash, a few more black holes replaced flush countersunk rivets—sometimes singly, at other times in a group. Even as he watched, stunned, a row of four neat holes appeared. He stared fearfully along the length of the wing. In addition to flexing, it was also twisting—not much, perhaps only a few degrees at the tip—but enough.

Donald Carter sat back, feeling curiously calm. Would he die when the aircraft broke up, mangled in tearing metal wreckage? Or would he survive long enough to experience the long nightmare fall through miles of cloud to the sea below? His fear had gone, replaced by a consuming ghoulish curiosity. How long? He shot an appraising glance at the wing joint. It could go in thirty seconds, or it could last thirty minutes.

HIS MIND DRIFTED back over the years to a bright March day in 1945, somewhere south of Bremen in Germany. At 25,000 feet, his Tempest squadron was operating sixteen aircraft out of Volkel airfield in Holland, against German fighters launched to attack the incoming stream of American B17Gs and B24 Liberators heading towards Bremen.

More than thirty years later, the scene remained sharp in his memory: the day was glass-clear; a single block of sky, a five-mile cube, was virtually filled with bombers, flak, fighters, parachutes, bombs, debris, burning aircraft, flares.

A B17, both port engines on fire, broke away from its group, sideslipping to keep the flames at bay; Carter saw three, four parachutes open like white fungi behind it. Suddenly a black Me210 slid shark-like through the little knot of survivors, hammering cannon shells into the stricken bomber.

The port wing of the B17 folded back, almost gently; it began to break up. The entire tail section, aft of the gun blisters, separated from the rest and glided away in some grotesque parody of a real aeroplane. It assumed a weirdly stable attitude, descending in shallow, wide orbits towards the ground so far below that Carter thought wryly that the tail gunner would be the only survivor, if he could just fly the thing to earth.

Fly it?

Carter's eyes opened wide. It would never work . . . and yet . . . and yet . . . he had nothing to lose. Worth trying? Damned right, he thought, if only because it gave him something to do, instead of just sitting there, waiting for the worst. He got out of his seat awkwardly, went aft to the galley where Liane was alone.

Carter said urgently, "How do I get into the tail section?"

"The . . . tail?" she said, uncomprehending.

"Show me!" he said violently. "Where does this door lead?"

She hesitated. "It's—I'm not sure. A cargo space, I think, but it's empty—all the baggage is in the hold. Why?"

"Look, Liane, you mustn't panic. I've been a pilot all my life—I know about aeroplanes. This one is just about finished—the wing joints are cracking up. Do you understand?"

Her eyes opened very wide. "We are going to die?"

"Maybe not. People have survived things like this, usually when they're sitting near the tail. How do we get in?"

"There is a key, I think—here." She opened a bulkhead panel, took out a small square-section T-key. It fitted the two holes in the door. Carter twisted, pulled, and it came open. It was dark inside, and Liane found an emergency torch in the galley and together they went in.

The space was twelve feet long, tapering from ten feet wide at the door to less than four feet at the aft end. The compartment was filled with cable looms, control rods and electrical and hydraulic pipelines; the metal floor was fitted with recessed eyebolts for lashing down cargo, and hanks of inch-wide canvas webbing were neatly stowed on the bulkhead. Across the far end of the compartment stretched a massive shelf: the centre section of the huge tailplane.

Donald Carter took a last look round, and followed Liane back to the galley. "Time's short. Just do as I ask, and no questions. Go and get the boy and girl sitting next to me—quietly, no fuss. Get them in here. Find all the blankets, food and torches you can. We'll strap ourselves down back here and pray the tail end holds together. Hurry, now—"

He walked without haste up to the flight deck. "Captain?"

"Mr. Carter—what now?" Eddie Wu Pak's face was lined with strain.

"Bad news," Carter told him. "You've got serious problems at the port wing root. Rivets popping everywhere—and the wing's twisting badly. Any chance of finding smoother air?"

"Such as where?" Wu Pak yelled above the tumult. "Thanks a lot—it's just one more problem on top of all the others. We have no electrics, we're lost, unable to climb. I'm starting a let-down soon. Best get back there and hold on!"

"But the wing—"

"We'll just have to take a chance on that. But thanks for the warning. In case we don't make it—God go with you."

Carter stared. The captain grinned tiredly. "I'm Chinese, but I went to a Christian school. Much good it did me."

Leaning against the door for support, Carter smiled. "You're all right, captain. If anyone can get us down, you will."

He turned, left the flight deck, and went back through the cabin to reassure the harassed women and frightened kids. There was nothing he could do to help really—he wasn't even sure why he thought the four of them might survive. But he did what he could, with a smile and a brief word here and there. It was odd: he was no longer scared.

The others were already in the tiny compartment, and Debby's and Colin's eyes were asking questions he could not answer. He took a last look down the length of the main cabin, then closed the door. The torchlight showed white, strained faces.

"We've very little time left. This thing is going to break up very soon. We have one slim chance—back here. Often, in cases like this, the tail comes down in one piece. If we lash ourselves down very tightly on the floor, heads towards the door, we may just come down with it. OK. Quickly, now."

They folded blankets, made four rough palliasses; Carter secured each of the others to the deck with webbing straps until they could not move a finger, and placed a roll of blanket under their heads. Liane was last. As he pulled the loop of material tight around her, he muttered a brief apology. She smiled wanly in the torchlight.

In one corner, he tied down the small bundle of stores Liane had collected, before taking his position beside her. He worked frantically, getting the webbing tight across legs, thighs, chest; finally, with one arm free, he found the torch, switched it off and jammed it under his knee.

There was nothing to do now but pray, and that had never been Carter's style. With mouth dry, heart pounding, body soaked with sweat, he lay there, waiting . . . waiting. . . .

DESCENDING SLOWLY, the aeroplane reached 15,000 feet, ran into a sheer plane of vertical winds, and fell like a stone for a thousand feet, before slamming into an updraught moving at close to 180 miles per hour. They might as well have collided with a brick wall: the accelerometer needle wound round to 7-G and jammed; the port wing bent slowly upwards through 45 degrees, twisting half a turn before fracturing at the root end.

The doomed plane yawed violently to starboard, and then equally hard to port. This reversal of stress snapped the fuselage at the aft end, just forward of the tailplane. Still in cloud, the aeroplane began to break up, rolling very fast and shedding the remaining wing and engines.

In the tail, Carter and the others tumbled in a three-dimensional whirlpool, their heads whipped cruelly back and forth with the sharply reversing forces, bodies compressed agonizingly under webbing straps which became steel bars. They could hear a background pandemonium of thunder, whistling winds and the clatter of hail upon the metal surfaces of their coffin. There were times, in that endless fall, when they seemed to slow and stall, hanging suspended while the airflow appeared to stop. Carter abandoned all attempt to distinguish between up and down. At times he winced in pain as his ears ached from pressure imbalance. He opened his mouth to scream, joining the others in a united wail of terror.

Later, he realized that they had lost altitude in the manner of a falling leaf, descending obliquely in a shallow dive, until a shift had occurred in the balance of lift and drag upon the tailplane. This shift had been followed by a gentle climb, a semi-stall, a sideslip in the reverse direction, and another shallow glide.

The shattered tail section dipped below cloud, skimming diagonally across the valley and into the upswing as it approached the steep, jungle-clad slope. At two hundred feet above the rocky ridge, it slowed, rotated gently, started the glide back, following the curvature of the slope. The speed was low—perhaps only sixty miles per hour—when it ploughed through the slender treetops and bamboo thickets, sliding ever more slowly, remaining upright but swinging violently on impact with the trees of the forest along its track.

Carter's straps slipped a little, then gave way. He slid clumsily down the metal floor, ramming his head against the bulkhead. He was aware, fleetingly, of intense pain, before he dived headlong into a whirling silence.

IT WAS DARK, and the rain smashed in endless fury against the metal roof. Carter lay still, totally confused, wrapped in blankets. He felt as if his head had been split down the middle. He fumbled for he knew not what, and touched a warm face.

"Mr. Carter? It's Colin. Are you all right?"

That, Carter told himself sourly, was a moot question. He could hear Liane and Debby somewhere in the darkness. Groping, he found the torch and switched it on.

As he sat up in the dim light, the shadows whirled sickeningly around him, but soon things began to steady themselves. Turning his head with difficulty, he found himself staring at Liane, high above him, her eyes wide and shining. Painfully, he clambered up, fumbled at her straps.

"Liane—are you hurt?"

"No, only my neck. It hurts when I move . . ."

"Mine too. How's Debby? She all right?"

Debby answered him. "I think so. Can you get me loose?"

"Just a minute, girl. . . ."

He freed Liane from her straps, made her hold the torch and then released the others.

"Easy now, don't wriggle around, Debby, or you'll slide down. Hang on to this loop."

Soon they were stretched out on the tilted metal floor, staring at each other in the stark light, unable to comprehend that they were all alive. The door key was lost somewhere, down at the bottom; Carter crawled down, groped—and there it was. Opening the door was not so easy: Colin helped heave it over the point of balance. It crashed out of sight and the blessed rain sleeted in, warm and somehow reassuring in its discomfort.

Hurriedly, they stacked the blankets in a sheltered corner before they crawled out into the downpour, slipping on the thick mat of vegetation underfoot. The slope was precarious, the clouds low overhead, and they stood mutely in the grey half-light of the rain forest, drenched to the skin, faces raised to the sky whence they had fallen. Thunder rolled and crashed. They were lost—they did not even know in which country they had landed. They stood close together, constantly touching to seek reassurance, shaking with delayed reaction. They had survived. Against all the odds, they were alive.

TOWARDS DUSK, the rain stopped and a light, watery sun peered through the clearing overcast. They saw that they were surrounded by thick, green, rain-soaked jungle, from which came the deep, orchestrated humming of a hundred different species of insect. They heard unidentifiable animal sounds; birds of many colours and small monkeys moved through the trees, and from nearby there came the sound of running water. They sweated in the high humidity. A gamut of smells drifted on the wind: rich rotting undergrowth, brief traces of perfume from exotic flowers. They saw orchids, azaleas, a red and orange flame tree etched vividly against the dark background.

Carter stood alone, debating priorities, while the others talked in muted whispers of impersonal things—the forest, the rain, the heat—shying away from emotions and anything to do with aeroplanes and falling. They were not quite ready even to think about their escape, let alone talk about it.

The tail section was their only shelter: they would have to move it to a more level position. Fighting the lethargy which threatened to envelop them, they levered away with bamboo poles, and by the time darkness came they were able to retreat into their lair like jungle animals. Their only torch was failing now. Carter made them drink their fill from the flask of cold coffee Liane had brought along, and they wrapped the damp blankets round themselves. Colin and Debby huddled up together for comfort, while Liane sat in a corner against the slope of the floor. The door stood open a few inches, and Carter could see her face in the dim light. She caught his eye, smiled wearily. Her dark hair was limp on her shoulders, and the white uniform shirt clung damply to her body.

"Get some sleep, Liane. Tomorrow . . . tomorrow, we'll see."

She turned her head towards the sleeping boy and girl.

"They'll be fine," he said tiredly. "They're young. It's a great adventure for them."

"But I think of all the others—" Her voice was husky, uneven.

"Don't," he told her bluntly. "We couldn't have saved them."

For a long time she looked out at the darkness beyond the door. In the end, she lay down and drifted into a restless sleep.

Donald Carter remained awake for some time, his memory replaying terrifying images of the breakup, the descent. His thoughts explored labyrinths of speculation. Where were they? Could he keep them all alive until they were rescued? Could they walk out of here? What dangers faced them in the jungle? Uneasily, he listened to the enigmatic noises of the night, until sleep finally drowned him.

HE AWOKE, cold and stiff, staring at a sunbeam on the curved metal wall opposite. He stretched and winced: every bone ached. Liane lay beneath her blanket, a still, shapeless bundle; the boy and girl lay stretched out, blankets thrown aside. His watch had stopped at some point during that nightmare yesterday. To all intents and purposes they were dead, to those who waited in Hong Kong: the kids' parents . . . Gavin and Shirley . . . Liane's—what? Was there a husband waiting for her somewhere?

He began to think back. According to the captain, no distress call had been made. The flight had been entirely over sea, so a search of this area was unlikely. The pilot had said they were heading for Saigon. Maybe they were on the Asian mainland, or perhaps an island? One thing was for sure: if they ever got out of this place, it would be by their own efforts.

Sitting still, waiting, the recommended practice after crashing, was a non-starter: they must move, explore, advance or retreat. Jungle survival . . . his thoughts went back to training days, and he began stacking up the problems: heat, humidity, lack of salt; food shortage; impure drinking water; bugs; snakes; prickly heat, malaria, dysentery—all the old nasties of the tropics.

Speculation was a waste of time at this stage; he fumbled in his jacket, found cigarettes: the packet was damp, unusable. He got up carefully, laid out the cigarettes in a line on the warm, sunlit floor to dry. He sat with legs crossed, thinking. One thing stood out: no more flying. Ever! He had pushed his luck too far already.

"Donald?" Liane was sitting up now, the blanket round slim shoulders, her knees drawn up close to her chest. "Your head—it hurts still?"

"Only when I larf."

"Please?"

"Never mind. Did we bring any food with us?"

She nodded, reached behind her into the corner. The plastic carrier, freed from its straps, held an assortment of goodies: cigarettes, biscuits, potato crisps. A few liqueur miniatures, some chocolate.

Carter grinned, pleased. "Could be worse. Anything else?"

"Some coffee left in the thermos. But it is cold."

"We can warm it up. And make hot chocolate, if we can get a fire going. Come on, you kids, show a leg!"

They sat up, bleary-eyed, hair tousled, flushed with sleep. Colin yawned. "What time is it?"

"My watch stopped," Carter said. "Any offers?"

Debby sniffed. "I make it half past three."

"You're worse than me," Carter said cheerfully. "We'll have to have a guess at it. Let's say seven thirty. Come on, we'll have a look round."

The wrecked tail section lay in a small clearing, partly of its own making; a steamy haze lay close to the ground, and the metal skin glistened with condensation. It had come to rest on a steep, jungle-clad slope, upon which they stood with difficulty.

Wet thickets of fern, bamboo and coiled vines surrounded them; lush undergrowth, agleam with water droplets—a profusion of yellow-green, blue-green, red-green foliage, under canopied banana trees, laden with hard green fruit. Vines as thick as Carter's arm were strangling palms, club moss infested the skeletons of once-proud banyan, neem and jacaranda trees, and there was a rank, overpowering stench of rotting vegetation.

They stood transfixed: Colin had shed his jacket in the steamy air and was now wearing a blue shortsleeved shirt and charcoal-grey trousers, already stained and torn. Debby's green shirt was ripped at one shoulder, a fragment hanging down over her short black skirt.

Carter turned slowly, scanning the vista of mountains and forests. Behind them, the steep slope terminated at the base of a high, rocky escarpment, stark grey walls of granite laced along the ridge with trees and brush. The wall curved away into the distance to encircle the valley below, an almost circular depression with a flat floor a thousand feet below them. It was some five miles across, he judged, seven in length. At the foot of the escarpment, the jungle slopes fell away steeply in verdant growth to the valley floor. Across the flat, overgrown plain, a river snaked a devious course, sections of it glinting in iridescent ribbons where they caught the sun; far away to the right the stream disappeared, it seemed to Carter, into the rocky face of the escarpment, near a huge "V" in the forested slopes. In many places around the valley, thin feathers of waterfalls showed creamy-white in the clear, warm air.

On the flatland below, beyond the river, there stretched a long strip of vegetation in a lighter shade, in stark contrast to the multi-hued undergrowth around it. For one blinding moment, Carter thought it was an airfield, but he changed his mind a millisecond later. It couldn't be: too overgrown. It might have been an airstrip once, a single, cleared rectangle, hacked from the forest. Shading his eyes again, he took another look.

God's teeth . . . it was true. On the left of the strip, roofs of buildings—two, three, four, in mottled camouflage, almost invisible, betrayed only by the angularity of outline. And beyond . . . his eyes narrowed, searching. Beyond, an old-fashioned hangar, a low, sweeping arc, ground to ground, festooned with brush and grass.

He turned—a tall, spare figure in crumpled cavalry twill trousers, checked shirt, suede shoes now black with moisture.

"Look! That was an airstrip once. But it's been deserted for years. Derelict—that brush on the strip is as high as a man. But it seems the best place to go. First we'll build a fire, heat up coffee and chocolate. Then . . . we'll see."

An hour later, with the sun higher and hotter, they stumbled downhill, blankets rolled and tied with webbing straps to form backpacks. Carter led, with the girls behind and Colin as rearguard. Carter was worried more about Liane than either of the others: she coped, but sluggishly, with an air of puzzled detachment that was a very bad sign. They were all suffering from delayed shock, and the natural palliatives of rest and sweet, strong tea were in short supply. Liane would have to take her chance until they found shelter of sorts—and if this was the rainy season, which seemed likely, judging by yesterday's cloudburst, they had only a short time to find it.

The slope was too steep for direct descent, and they were forced to traverse to and fro, avoiding dense thickets of brush and bamboo. In the process, they had to ford half a dozen streams again and again. The few game trails they came across were enmeshed with sodden tangles of undergrowth. Twice, small deer scrambled across the path in terror; swarms of flies attacked every bare inch of skin. Within an hour they were near exhaustion, wilting in the heat and humidity. In the end Debby sat down and burst into tears. She was near collapse. They rested for ten minutes, then set off again, more slowly.

After another hour Carter began to feel a steel band of pressure tighten across his forehead. Fighting for breath, drenched in sweat, he found a clear spot beneath a banyan tree and ordered another

halt. The girls fell asleep instantly; Colin, perhaps the fittest of them all, with head bowed between his knees, sucked in air like a drowning man. Carter stared at his team despondently. Then he lay back, breathing hard. He slept restlessly, waking very much the worse for it.

By noon, the ground levelled out. They stopped by a ledge where a stream broke free from its runnel, tumbling into a deep pool. Without a word they plunged in, washing away the sweat and dirt, revelling in the cool, fast-flowing water. Afterwards, they lay on the flat granite slabs, clothes steaming dry in minutes, ate a little fruit and watched Colin trying to catch a fish in the pool.

Carter caught Liane's eye, smiled. "You know this sort of country?"

"I think so. The rain forest is the same in Kampuchea, Laos, Vietnam. I can show you the fruits to eat, the berries my people use for sickness."

"That's something, at least. Animals?"

"Not so many. Deer we have seen. Elephant—they work in the teak forests. Many small monkeys—and snakes. Bad snakes."

"Poisonous?"

"Yes. Cobras—not so many in the mountains. The long black snakes—very bad."

He nodded seriously. "We'll have to be careful. We have nothing for treating snakebite. What about tigers?"

"Not many here now. More dangerous, the spiders."

Carter looked gloomy. "I'd better warn the kids. Time we were moving. Those clouds are building up."

Progress became painfully slow. By Carter's reckoning it was ten minutes short of three in the afternoon when he finally lurched round a bamboo thicket and saw the river, some yards ahead. It was fifty feet wide, and the burble of the water against rocks was music in their ears: the current slowed at level spots, before tumbling into deeper pools full of green shadows and flat sandstone boulders. Wading in, thigh-deep in the shallows, they crossed in pairs—Carter and Debby, Liane and the boy.

Soaked, dog-weary but exultant, they stood on the far bank, sobbing for breath—and the heavens opened.

"We'll have to keep going!" Carter bellowed above the tumult of

40

rain and thunder. "Take your packs off—use the straps to keep together. If you get lost, stand still, don't go rushing about."

Doggedly they thrashed their way through trackless brush, endless mazes of whipping bamboo, stinging thorn, clinging creeper, sodden fern and bracken. Beyond speech, past caring about anything except the next step, Carter agonized over direction. Visibility was less than a yard, and his only guess was the oblique slant of the rainflood, from right to left: he staggered, reached for the next tree ahead—and suddenly there were none. He lifted his eyes: ahead, a sea of young brush and elephant grass, chest high, a marked delineation extending away on both sides. The airstrip.

"This is the runway," he yelled hoarsely. "Buildings that way— not far—stay close."

They nodded mutely. Carter plunged away along the airstrip's boundary, breaking a trail through heavy underbrush, feet sinking into thick, gooey clay.

The hut loomed up through the water curtain like an apparition. Carter squelched his way across what was once a path, climbed stiffly and carefully up rotted timber steps onto a debris-filled veranda. Water cascaded from holes in the roof. Resisting a crazy urge to knock, he pushed open the door, the others close behind him, staggered inside out of the relentless downpour.

They stood open-mouthed, the rain beating a devil's tattoo on the roof overhead, unable to believe what they saw before them.

Chapter Four

The room—office—was almost dry. A brace of rotting reed mats lay upon the plain wood floor, and in a corner a warped bamboo pole supported the remnants of a United States flag; there were two cane chairs and a glass-topped coffee table, stacked with mildewed magazines—Carter recognized a *Saturday Evening Post*, long out of print. Two wallcharts hung from twisted wooden frames.

On the right stood a long desk, flanked by two corroded filing cabinets. Behind the desk, the remains of a man sat through eternity in a metal armchair. Only the bones remained, flaked with grisly fragments of skin and muscle; much of it, including the skull, had fallen to the floor. The torso was still contained within an open flying jacket of brown leather, adhering to the rib cage. The olive drab shirt hung in tattered strips, and skeletal arms met on the desk top in a huddle of finger- and wrist-bones. A dull, corroded automatic pistol, a Colt .45, lay inches from the hands. Carter moved slowly round the desk, peering at the skull on the floor. There was a hole an inch in diameter above the left eye, and another, much bigger, in the back of the skull.

On the floor near the desk lay the dried, shrunken skin of a black snake, some six feet in length; the head was missing, the hide shredded and stringy at the neck.

Carter absorbed the picture in seconds, but calming Debby down took a great deal longer: she screamed, dropped her blanket roll and bolted out into the storm, Carter and Colin in pursuit. She fought like a wild thing, hysterical, in the pounding rain. They dragged her back into the shelter of the veranda, but she refused to go a step further. In the end Carter left the boy with her and went back inside.

"Liane?"

She waited patiently, face pale but composed. "I am here, Donald. Do not be afraid. Dead men harm no one."

He filed that for future reference, nodded. "Give me a blanket. No—I'll do it. Tomorrow, we'll bury this poor sod properly— meanwhile, he has to be moved."

As he gathered up the pitiful debris, his mind was calm and unruffled, the storm a muted background to the scene. He knew he must not unloose the hysteria that was yammering away at his mind.

"I can see it all now, Liane. He must have been left behind. Then the snake . . . maybe he couldn't face the agony alone, waiting for the poison to . . . he killed the snake, but it did him no good, poor bastard."

Picking up the tiny bundle, he collected the snake by the tail, went out of the back door onto the veranda and hurled it into the distance. He stopped for a moment, looking round: each of the four huts was connected to the other by a bamboo bridge, four feet above ground; he went down, pushed the bundle under the hut, wiped his hands with a shudder and went back.

Liane had been busy: the floor was clear, and the wastepaper basket in the corner had been filled. The rain was a decibel less noisy on the roof, and he brought the children inside and closed the door. It was no time for propriety: they all stripped and he built a fire in the small stone hearth.

Debby huddled in a blanket, averted her eyes from the desk as she watched Colin drying and folding other blankets to make her a bed; she refused food, but managed a drink of water before lying down. She slept instantly, her face fixed in a frown, lips working, and Carter thought grimly that it was going to be a long time before she got straightened out.

He fed the fire again, using the old cane chairs, and hung their clothes up to dry; Colin sat against the wall beside Debby, utterly drained, a blanket round his shoulders, his eyes closed.

Carter, in bare feet and shorts, got up from the fire, and glanced at Liane in her bra and panties. He grinned tiredly. "If my son could see me now!"

Liane found some string, rigged up another line and hung her skirt before the crackling fire.

"Your son—he is married?"

"Sure. Seven years now. He's a pilot, too—in Hong Kong."

Liane was silent, staring into the flames. "You—your wife?"

Carter said briefly, "She died three years ago."

"I'm sorry, Donald," Liane apologized.

"It's strange," he said ruefully. "First you miss them, yet remember what they looked like. Then you get over missing them, and the memories come flooding back. We had a long time together."

She nodded. "I know. I will never forget my own father and mother. I was only six, but my uncle often told me about them. My father was in the government. I do not know what he did."

"What happened?" he said gently.

"He disappeared one day, along with many others in his department. They say he disliked what the government was doing and spoke out. Some, they never found. My uncle searched for my father a long time, and when he came out of the forest, he found my mother dead in the garden. I went to live with him in the dancing school."

Carter gazed for a long time at the glowing tip of his cigarette. Then: "Your . . . husband?"

"I am not married. There have been . . . men. Rich men. With promises of dresses and big houses. But none brought the gift I wanted."

Carter looked up, questioningly.

"Love," the girl said simply, and flushed.

Carter grinned again. "Makes the world go round, I suppose. But don't miss out—find someone. Have a family . . ."

"Like yours?"

"Sure! Take Gavin—I brought him up, sent him to school, and what does he do? Joins the airforce, gets married, and moves to Hong Kong. I came out to see him—and hey presto! Here we are." He smiled. "Here—your shirt's dry. Put it on and I'll fix up a bed for you."

She turned her head, shirt half on. "Please, Donald—you will sleep close? I am not afraid, but I will be happy, I think."

"OK," he said softly. "We can keep each other warm, like those two." And he nodded at the recumbent pair in the corner.

Liane came to him trustingly, and they stretched out upon the folded blankets near the fire, another blanket covering them, her head resting in the crook of his arm. The sun was down, the rain had stopped, and all around the forest was stirring. He lay quietly for a while, watching the fireglow fade, listening to the soft breathing of the girl beside him and wishing he was thirty years younger.

UNACCUSTOMED TO SLEEPING on floors, he felt sore when he awoke, but at the same time rested. The hut was cool, silent, an odd mixture of makeshift and modern: the metal windows were rusty, the timber structure was lined with unpainted weatherboard, and the trusses and purlins of the roof were exposed. An electric bulb hung from the end of a white cable.

A Far East map on oiled paper was stuck on the far wall and, beside it, a large-scale map of the Vietnam-Laos-Cambodia area. Carter nodded, pleased: at least that narrowed it down a little. He padded across the floor in bare feet, and stood, hands on hips, studying the map. With his forefinger, he traced a dotted line from Saigon, northwest towards the Dangrek Mountains near the Thai

44

border. The line ran up through the Vietnam-Cambodia border country, to an area with very few towns and villages, hachured to indicate high ground. It stopped in the middle of that area, and many lines radiated out to unnamed locations in Thailand, Cambodia and Laos.

So that's where we've ended up! He shook his head in disbelief. They were hundreds of miles from anywhere, deep in the high rain forest, surrounded by rolling virgin ranges covered with thick jungle, uncharted rivers. . . .

He bit his lip sharply and went out onto the veranda. The morning was cloudless, perfect, the air cool and fresh, and he stood there, breathing deeply. Liane came to stand beside him, securing the stained but dry skirt at her waist.

"Hi," he said evenly. "Sleep well?"

She grimaced. "The floors are very hard here."

"We'll sort out something better for tonight."

Her eyes followed the valley rim, above the trees. "Where is this place?"

He took her inside, showed her the map. "I think it was an American airstrip in the war. They must have moved out very quickly at the end—was it April, 1975?"

"May, I think."

"May. OK. God knows how that poor sod got left behind, not that it matters. We are here"—he jabbed a finger at the map—"way up in the border country. We may even be in Cambodia."

"Kampuchea now." Liane frowned. "Will there be people looking for us?"

"Not a chance." He told her about the mayday message that was never sent. "We must be hundreds of miles off track."

"Perhaps someone will see the aeroplane?"

"No way," Carter said firmly, a finger on the map. "Look—the wreckage must stretch over fifty miles of mountain. And besides, they don't even know we're on land."

"We can walk to Saigon? Such a little way on the map . . ."

He grinned. "Bloody sight further on the ground. Let's talk about it later. It's time we got those lazy kids out of bed."

Over the last of their chocolate, heated over a small fire, with water added, Carter put Colin and Debby in the picture.

45

"First, we go through this place—every inch of it. Anything we can use is a bonus. If that pistol works, I might be able to bag one of those small deer." He avoided Debby's eyes. "The first priority is survival. The second is getting out of here. Now listen: we have no doctors here, so we can't afford scratches, ulcers, sprains, colds or snakebites. We all stay fit and we all stay together. We go in pairs everywhere. Do you read me loud and clear?"

Three heads nodded.

"OK. Let's take a look round."

The adjoining hut proved to be partitioned, a dining area with a Formica-topped table and half a dozen chairs at one end, leading to a kitchen almost filled by a rusted gas stove, worktop, storage cabinets. Beyond, a storeroom—and Carter's eyes gleamed. Vast supplies of canned goods, sealed packages, crates of bottles; best of all, a dozen Tilley lamps with fuel.

"Colin—know how to light these lamps?"

"Yes. They have one in the boathouse at school."

"Fine. Get half a dozen or so working. Two in the sleeping hut, the rest in here. Then see if you can find anything to catch the rainwater; the river may be clean, but I'm taking no chances. There's coffee in those jars, and I can see breakfast coming up. Let's see what we have here. . . ."

Over the squeals as the girls discovered fresh delights, Colin stuck his head round the door and said, "Don, I've found a stack of gas bottles out at the back. If we can get that stove working, we could have a hot breakfast!"

Breakfast was indeed hot, and delicious. Porridge oats with hot canned milk, fried corned beef with scrambled dried eggs, and unlimited coffee. Carter sat back, lit two cigarettes, gave one to Liane and ignored a pleading look from Colin. "You're too young—wait another year."

Debby said, "Oh, Mr. Carter—Donald. We've smoked for years. Be a sport."

He grinned, pushed the packet towards them. That breakfast was too good to spoil with petty argument.

They were in much better shape this morning: Debby's face and hands were reasonably clean; Carter suspected Liane's influence there. Colin wore only trousers and shoes, and Liane had knotted

46

her shirt up under her breasts for coolness. The bruise on her temple was fading, and her hair was swept back into a ponytail. Looking at them all, Carter felt considerably more confident.

"Well, we won't starve. There's enough food here for months—but there's to be no waste, no raiding the pantry. Liane can show us what we can get from the forest, and I don't want you kids experimenting. We ought to keep the canned goods for emergency only."

"You talk," Colin said gravely, "as if we'll be here for years."

"We won't get out tomorrow," the older man said phlegmatically. "We'll be spotted eventually. We can build a signal fire, and if anyone sees or hears an aeroplane, light the fire." He paused, gathering his thoughts. "Liane, can you and Debby manage the catering?"

"I will enjoy it, Donald. Perhaps we can find some wild rice—I could make some of the dishes of my country."

"Sounds good. OK, Colin, we'll have a prowl round today and see what we can do about sleeping arrangements. That floor is hard. Debby, can you keep some kind of diary? I reckon today must be Thursday, somewhere around the twentieth of the month."

"I'll try. If I can find paper and pencil."

"Fine," Carter said comfortably. "Let's assume that we'll be here at least a month, maybe more. If we walk out, it'll have to be in the dry season. Of course, we may get lucky."

CARTER PUT HIS GLASS back on the bedside table and looked at me with those penetrating blue eyes.

"We didn't get all that lucky, Mr. Napier," he said slowly. "We were in that valley darn near six months. But I think it was the best time I ever had. It was a beautiful place—fantastic trees and flowers—and apart from the rains and the morning fogs, the weather was wonderful."

He stared at the wall opposite for a long time, and I thought I could see tears in the corners of his eyes. But that was stupid. After all, he had survived a major air crash. There was no reason for him to cry. None that I could see.

When I sat down with him next morning, Donald Carter seemed unwell—yet I could not put his condition down entirely to reaction following his ordeal. As he spoke, he shifted about frequently in his bed, seeking a more comfortable position, and I saw him wince at times.

It had been, he began, a time which none of them would forget. Survival was not difficult: supplies were adequate, and they had companionship, too, as they worked together to build up their odd little society. There were times, in fact, when they were very happy, he told me.

The way back started that very first day—and Donald Carter did not like the shape of it at all.

It came about in this way.

After breakfast, Carter and the boy explored the remaining huts, one of which proved to be a bunkhouse, with spring frames under rotting mattresses; the girls brought in huge bundles of rushes from the bank of the river, stitching up rough palliasses which proved to be excellent beds. The fourth hut was jammed with boxes, cartons, packages, but nothing of immediate interest.

The hangar was some hundred yards distant. They had to wade through the deep wet brush to reach it, and Carter saw that the arched roof had been overlaid with soil in which grass and brush grew luxuriantly. From the air, he suspected, the building would be all but invisible. The roof soared forty feet above ground level.

They stepped cautiously into the dim coolness. Instantly, a raucous horde of multicoloured birds took flight, streaming through the doorway into the sunlight, showering droppings as they went. Carter and the boy ducked, laughing, until the last screeching bird disappeared, then turned to survey the silent hangar. On the far wall sunlight streamed in through four plastic-covered apertures. Carter stopped dead in his tracks.

Colin gaped. "An aeroplane!"

For a moment, Carter saw salvation on three rubber wheels. Then he ran his fingers through damp hair and sighed.

"Once, maybe, Colin. It's a wreck now."

The old DC3 was painted olive drab and grey camouflage on the upper surfaces, the paint almost hidden by a thick layer of guano. Along the fuselage, in white block lettering, were the words AIR AMERICA.

Carter began to walk critically round the Dakota. The landing flaps were fully down; both main tyres were punctured, the main wheels resting upon cracked rubber hanging in strips. The side windows were cracked, the main cargo door missing; the port engine seemed to be intact, but the starboard one was minus propeller and cowlings, and surrounded by an aluminium servicing platform.

Carter climbed three or four steps up it until his head emerged above the metal floor; he saw tool kits, oily rags and an apparently new cylinder assembly, still wrapped in oiled paper. Climbing down stiffly, he went on round the aeroplane, Colin following hot on his heels, full of questions but loath to intrude. Carter rubbed a toe in congealed pools of hydraulic fluid on the concrete floor, pulled tentatively at the port propeller blades. The resistance was solid, without a trace of movement.

"Seized solid, Col. It's had it. It'll never fly again. It was probably scrapped. Look at it. Rust everywhere."

Colin looked doubtful. "It doesn't seem *too* bad, Don."

"Listen, it would take ten years and half the mechanics in the Douglas factory to get this heap off the ground. Come on. . . ."

A small box of an office occupied one corner of the hangar; an open-topped store made from wire mesh another. Carter pushed open the office door and went in. Piles of mildewed publications lay on a desk: service manuals, fragments of Form 1, the servicing log used to sign out an aeroplane as serviceable. There was a big metal toolbox against one wall: he slid out the butterfly trays of spanners, wrenches, screwdrivers and pliers. All were heavily greased and in good condition. Who had accumulated this kit? The dead man? He sensed some strange story here—tragic and hidden through the years in this quiet valley. At the height of the Vietnam war, six, seven years ago, this place must have buzzed. Overnight it had been deserted, and a dead aeroplane and a dying man had been left behind. Why? He shook his head, disturbed and uneasy.

Back in the hangar, he found the girls listening to Colin's explanations.

"It's all beginning to fit in," Carter told them. "Air America—that was the cover name for the CIA air transport organization. They ran it like a civil airline, mostly on secret missions from bases like this. Remember those routes on the map, from here up into Cambodia,

Thailand, Laos? I checked the date on one or two papers in the office. Nothing later than April 1975—nearly five years ago."

Liane nodded eagerly. "Donald, I remember reading in *Time* magazine that they flew in agents, supplies."

"Right," Carter said. "Well, you can't get any more secret than this place. As far as I can see, the only way in or out is by air."

Liane said hesitantly, "The aeroplane—it will not fly?"

Carter repeated his verdict. The girls looked disappointed, as indeed he was himself. Or was he? He took a long, slow look into his own soul and recoiled from what he saw there; the truth was that he was glad the old beast was beyond repair. Better spend the rest of his life here than kill himself trying to coax that heap of junk into the air.

The Asian girl said softly, "I wonder how long he lived, after they left him here."

"The guy in the office? Maybe he was the anchor man, detailed to clear up after the rest. Perhaps the plane they sent for him never made it. The last few weeks of the war were pretty chaotic. Maybe he'd just made a start on that engine when he got bitten by the snake."

"Poor, poor man," Liane said sadly.

"I may be able to get the radio working," Carter went on. "Colin—how about tracing the electrical supply from the office? They must have had power from somewhere. You girls have a look round the hangar and see what you can find."

He climbed stiffly into the plane's open cargo hatch. Clearly the DC3 had been loaded and ready to go, crates and boxes lashed down. He grimaced, nauseated: suddenly he detected a rank, squalid stench, permeating every corner of the old aeroplane. Unable to make any sense of the stencils on the crates, he moved forward into the cockpit.

He recoiled, sickened and afraid.

The cockpit was festooned with cobwebs, all alive and jerking with the passage of unseen, scuttling creatures in dark crevices; in the port seat was the macabre caricature of a man, wearing a peaked cap green with mould upon a naked skull, leaning on the seat back. One skeletal hand rested upon the centre control console, the bones of the forearm showing through the decomposed fibres of a flying overall; a wristwatch hung gruesomely loose on a corroded metal strap.

The webs, sparkling with water droplets, gleamed in the reflected sunlight from the hangar doors. By the same light, Carter saw that a snake as thick as his wrist was coiled round the starboard control column, its head aimed directly at him. The long black tongue slithered out, waving sinuously, then disappeared.

Carter gulped, retreated slowly and with infinite care, and closed the door behind him. Reaching the alloy steps to the ground, he got his feet onto solid concrete and tried breathing.

"Donald?"

He said sharply, "No one goes near this aeroplane until I say so. There's a snake in there—and another dead man."

They nodded, shaken. After a pause, Liane spoke. "There is some sort of machine behind the hangar. Debby thinks it is a . . ."

"Generator," the younger girl said firmly. "Can't be anything else, Don. Lots of cables going in and out."

"That sounds like it, Debby," he agreed. He stopped, looked at her sternly. "What's wrong? Spit it out."

"The aeroplane . . . if it was fixed, would you be able to fly us out of here?"

He sighed irritably. "Debby, my love, it's out of the question. That plane's been standing here rotting to pieces for more than five years. Besides, I've never flown a Dakota before. And the airstrip is overgrown. It would take months to clear it. I don't think we should waste time even thinking about it."

Liane said abruptly, "I think if you wanted to fix it, Donald, you could do it."

"Now, let's get one thing straight!" Carter said furiously. "I'm not going anywhere near that damned wreck—it's nothing but scrap! I don't want to hear any more about it!" He stalked out of the hangar, leaving them standing in stunned silence.

Liane stared discontentedly at the section of valley framed in the hangar doors. "I do not think he wants to leave this place, Debby. He has no wife . . . his son is married and does not need him. What has he to go back to?"

The boy and girl looked at her with ill-concealed dismay.

"Look," Colin said carefully, "it's early days yet. He's done so much . . . getting us down from that aeroplane . . . organizing things here. Let's leave him alone for a day or two—let him settle down. Agreed?"

The girls nodded reluctantly.

"OK. I'll go and see if he wants help with the generator. And remember—no talk about the Dakota. Not just yet."

CARTER WAS ON HIS KNEES, checking the machinery. He looked up at Colin. "I might be able to get this thing working, and there's plenty of fuel in these drums. Let's find some tools."

They took off the cylinder head, heated some engine oil over a Tilley lamp and poured a mixture of oil and petrol into the cylinder bore. Carter levered away at the turning handle and the crankshaft turned a few degrees. Fifteen minutes later, he primed the cylinder, gave the handle a swing and the little motor bellowed triumphantly, bringing the girls running and sending every bird within earshot squawking into the air. In the hangar half a dozen lights glowed, dispelling the shadows. Carter stood up, beaming.

"Now for that radio shack."

The set was old, damaged beyond repair by water and corrosion; there was a hole in the roof of the shack and the rain had poured through. Carter turned away at last, admitting defeat. "It's completely kaput. Short circuits all over the place; some of the tubes are shot. It's so old it doesn't even use transistors."

Debby, her voice breaking, seemed to lose control.

"The way you talk, you don't want to get home! You keep saying this is no good, that's broken, this won't work . . ."

Gently, Carter laid a hand on her shoulder. "Debby, why on earth should I want to stay here? I want to see my family again, the same as you. But I won't go raising false hopes. You have to trust me. It'll take time, but I'll get you home, you'll see."

She stared at him, tears welling. "I don't believe you! You're useless. . . . A stupid, useless old man, and I hate you!" Her face was twisted, ugly with emotion as she whirled round and stumbled away towards the line of huts.

Liane ran after her, calling to her to wait; Colin walked away, face set and angry.

Was she right? Carter asked himself. After all these sterile years, he had a chance to prove himself; yet there was something about this place, something that drugged the mind, blotted out memory. It was a little Eden, his own kingdom. Be honest, Carter: if that thing in the hangar was ready to fly, would you try it?

He sat down heavily on the edge of the generator housing and pondered. What was the big deal in getting back to civilization? A lonely house? Empty, futile jobs? He was happy here. Suppose they had to stay—would that be so bad? He was fifty-seven, old by some standards, but he was fit; a few weeks here would shift the spare tyre round his waist. There would be problems, yes: those two kids, for instance. And then there was Liane. She could waste her best years in a place like this.

Thoughtfully he got up and walked back slowly towards the huts; crossing the strip, he looked at it again, with the eyes of a pilot. It would take a bulldozer to shift that little lot. No use brooding: no one was going anywhere. Not for a long time.

Chapter Five

Evenings, invariably, were spent around the mess table, under the naked electric light, the generator thudding comfortably in the distance. Debby found a pack of cards in the storeroom and they rotated the games often, to avoid boredom. But, despite Carter's efforts, the talk always centred on their predicament, their chances of rescue, until he angrily tried to put an end to the speculation.

"Listen," he growled, "all this talk about rescue—forget it. You're only making things worse. Take my word for it—that plane's finished. And forget about walking out. You know what it was like the day we came down from the mountain; it took us all day, and that was downhill! Besides, we've no compass, no suitable maps, no travelling rations. We'd need a truck to carry what we'd need for three months—and that's how long it would take us to walk to Saigon."

He sat in seething silence for a long time. "Two other possibilities. We may be spotted by a passing aeroplane, or we may be found by people who've been alerted by a plane that's seen our fires or lights at night. And that's it—nothing else."

Colin wasn't so sure. "I think we should check out the rest of the valley, Don—especially where the river goes."

Carter nodded. "OK, we'll go take a look-see tomorrow. And when we get back, we're all going for a long short walk."

He grinned at their expressions. "I just remembered, talking about being spotted from the air. Way back, in the RAF, we were taught how to survive in winter. Part of the drill was treading out a big 'SOS' in the snow. Well—we'll do the same on the strip."

Debby held a hand to her head. "A long short walk?"

"Sure. One man can make a path by walking the same route five hundred times. Or a hundred men five times, five hundred men in one go. We mark out our 'SOS' and spend an hour a day at it—letters a hundred feet across that an aircraft can see miles away."

Debby clapped her hands in delight. "Oh yes! Smashing!"

Carter smiled with pleasure. "And one more thing—"

They waited expectantly.

"There'll be no walking out—and I mean it. When the rains end, I'll walk out myself. No"—he held up a hand—"I mean it. I can get along better alone. I've had training in escape exercises, years ago. I'll have that gun, and as soon as I make contact with any kind of civilization, there'll be a helicopter on the way for you. I can't do it in the monsoon, so if we're still here in September, October, I'll go. And no arguments."

CARTER AND COLIN left camp early in the morning; there was a trace of ground fog along the strip, but the air was filled with the rich smell of flowers, the sky a pale china-blue bowl overhead.

They had heard odd animal noises during the night, coming from far down the valley, and Carter took along the rusty .45 just in case. It was old, but it worked.

The river was broad and clear; fish were plentiful, as were the wading birds that fed upon them. Towards the end of the valley the river descended in a series of natural pools, flanked with red sandstone slabs, before wandering around a stand of dwarf pines and entering a region of heavy undergrowth. From here onwards, progress became a dogged business, until finally, towards noon, they glimpsed the towering grey wall of the escarpment above the trees, and began to encounter boulders of all sizes, clearly the results of past landslides; the stream twisted through mazes of small canyons between rock walls, and the going became dangerous.

Carter was never absolutely certain how it happened. One moment, he was edging carefully along a sandstone ledge ten feet above the frothy green torrent, Colin a few yards behind; the next instant, he was deep in cold, surging water and being swept along at enormous speed for some twenty yards, into a wide pool dotted with rocky outcrops. It was all he could do to keep his head above water, until suddenly his body drove hard into a rock slab. The massive force of the river pinned him to the rock, bent forward as if in obeisance, his mind stunned by the welter of water breaking over him. He knew that if he was to go on living, he had to get out very quickly; he had never imagined that water could be so cold in the tropics. Once the feeling left his limbs, he would be as good as dead.

One arm was under the surface, jammed into a crevice by sheer weight of water; the other was half free. Cautiously, he explored the surface of the rock until he found a narrow crack which accommodated four fingers, full length. Gripping hard, he began pulling up on his right arm, seeking to slide it round the rock, rather than lift it free. Inch by inch the arm came round and up, until his hand crawled out of the water just before his eyes, and he stopped, sobbing for breath.

He jerked at his trapped right leg again and again: it was caught fast. The left seemed better; he dragged it upwards, inching it up until he found an outcrop on which he could get leverage. Painfully he fought his way upwards, until he lay with his upper body flat on the sandstone slab, the torrent ranging about him in frustrated violence.

TO COLIN, IT WAS as if Carter had vanished off the face of the earth: for an instant he had taken his eyes off the man in front to check his footing, and in that instant Carter was gone. The boy let out a great cry of anguish, rushed forward, saw the broken section of rock on the ledge; he plunged forward recklessly, following the stream until it debouched into a rocky side pool, and he turned pale. At the bottom of the pool, fifty yards away, the river entered a stark "V" of rock which ended almost instantly, the black water flowing under a shelf and disappearing entirely. Colin's tears flowed freely; he visualized Carter already a mile away in some underground drain, his drowned body battering against the rocks.

Then, quite suddenly, he saw Carter drag himself from the turmoil like some wounded animal, to lie exhausted across the sandstone slab. Colin worked his way downstream to stand on the shore where he could yell to Carter, twenty feet away from him across a boiling maelstrom. Carter made no move. For a desperate moment, Colin thought he was dead. Then a hand flexed, moving crab-like upon the rock, and he sobbed thankfully, before haring away upstream to the bamboo grove they had passed—was it only minutes ago?

Sweat streaming, he manhandled a heavy four-inch-thick fallen bamboo trunk downriver, dragging one end waist-high, inching it around the sharp bends of the ledge, until he reached Carter once more. This time the head turned, and the slim brown hand on the rock lifted an inch or two in salute, then fell back exhausted.

The boy saw that if he simply allowed the twenty-five-foot bamboo trunk to fall across the stream, it would be swept away. Worse, it would be smashed down onto Carter's unprotected body in the flood.

He turned and ran back, searching frantically; the vine he selected was a tough, twisted growth some thirty feet in length. He coiled it over one shoulder, hurried back to the pool and tied one end to the thinner end of the bamboo, eyeing closely a second rock which protruded from the torrent six feet upstream from Carter, and another four feet out into the pool. Moving with care, he jammed the thick end of the bamboo into a recess between two rocks on the shore, grasped the vine, and pushed the top end of the pole out into the flood, taking the strain on the vine. Foot by foot, he paid out the rope, fighting to prevent the river from snatching the pole away from him.

As the bamboo caught more and more of the pressure as it extended, the boy had to dig in his heels and battle for every inch. With the pole a bare three feet upstream of the target rock, Colin allowed it to surge free and jam in position; he now had a bridge of sorts to the furthest rock.

Next, Colin took up a second length of vine, fashioned a rough

loop round the bamboo pole and entered the water, pole against his chest, facing downstream. Gingerly, holding on tightly, he edged outwards, pushing the vine loop before him and fighting for breath with each step. Inch by inch he made his way towards the centre of the span until he reached a position directly upstream of Carter. Playing out the vine gently, he brought it against Carter's body; Carter, half drowned, searched with his left hand and pulled the vine tight. With painful sluggishness he found the loop in the end of the vine and got his head and arms through. Then the boy moved further out towards the anchor rock against which the pole rested, taking the end of the vine with him: he knew the bamboo would never stand their combined weight. He straddled the rock, then jerked the vine slightly, beckoning Carter to move; then he set his feet hard against the rock and began hauling.

It seemed an eternity to Colin before Carter reached up a trembling hand to grasp his wrists; the boy heaved him almost clear of the water and they lay together, fighting to draw breath and still their pounding hearts.

Presently they worked their way back across the bamboo span: Carter first, secured to the long vine which Colin paid out slowly as he went, then the boy himself, until at last they staggered onto the small beach and collapsed, feeling the warmth of the sun on their backs.

"That," Carter said thickly, "was a bit too close for comfort."

Colin nodded weakly. To him, it was the understatement of the year. But the sand and gravel were warm and comforting under his shaking hands, and a great wave of exhaustion swept over him, carrying him into sleep. Yards away, a long-legged wading bird lifted its head, regarded the two recumbent bodies with incurious eyes, and began searching again for tiny freshwater shrimps.

When they started back in the early afternoon, the rain clouds were already stacking up in the northwest. Four miles of ceaseless trudging later, with only a half mile to go before they reached base, the monsoon suddenly swamped them, washing out the game trail they were following. By sheer luck, Colin recognized a clearing where he and Debby had gathered fruit the previous day, and they stumbled into camp at dusk, barely capable of movement or speech.

The girls ushered them into the hut, white-faced and concerned. Colin collapsed onto his bed, and Carter, stripping quickly, snapped out instructions. "Get those wet clothes off him, Liane; wrap him in a blanket and rub him down hard. Debby—hot coffee, as fast as you can. Where are those brandy miniatures?"

The fiery liquor revived the boy considerably. He sat up on the edge of his bed, watching Liane dry his legs.

"Debby," said Carter, "that boy saved my life."

"Donald!" cried Liane, her face stricken. "What happened?"

"Let's just say I fell in the river, and Colin hauled me out. If he wants to tell you any more, that's up to him. But I'll tell you this—when we get out of this place, Colin will never pay for a drink in any pub I visit."

Colin grinned. "I'll hold you to that, Don."

Later, as Liane stood by the fire, watching the sleeping boy cocooned in blankets, there was a strange look of tenderness on her face. "He looks so young," she said gently, staring down at the flushed face, tousled hair.

"He did a man's work today, Liane."

Carter sighed. There was a deep pain within him, reinforced by the events of the afternoon. Pain and sadness that she and the others should be trapped here, with almost no chance of rescue.

For him, it was simple: another ten, twelve years and he'd be out of it. But Liane and the rest? It didn't bear thinking about.

"Look Liane, I've covered most of the valley, and there's no way anyone can get in here, short of flying."

She sat down on Carter's bed, hands clasped in her lap, looking up at him apathetically. There was little comfort he could offer: it was best that she should know the truth and accept it.

After a while, she went away. Carter stretched out on his bed, trying to find some ache-free part of his anatomy to lie down on. The last light was fading along the rim of the escarpment, a black, brooding wall. The valley was large, beautiful, a pleasant place in which to live. But a prison, nonetheless.

DR. SINGH MET me in reception the next morning at the hospital. He smiled briefly and asked me to go with him into his consulting room.

"Mr. Napier," he said quietly, "I would be grateful if you are not seeing Mr. Carter today."

I raised my eyebrows. "What's the matter? Has he taken a turn for the worse?"

He said, "We are wanting to do some tests on Mr. Carter's back today. You know, when he was flown down from Khota Baru, he could not walk?"

I stared at him. "No, I didn't know that. He's been in bed each time I've seen him. Is it serious?"

He tightened his lips. "We are finding severe bruising of the lower back muscles, Mr. Napier. Also, a slight misalignment of the spinal column."

"Caused when he crashed?"

The doctor shook his head. "We do not believe so. We are asking Mr. Carter and he is not telling us anything about that at all. But I think he has carried something heavy on his back. Something very heavy indeed."

I could not quite see where this was leading—and it seemed to me to be none of my concern: I had already established to my own satisfaction what happened to All-Orient Flight HK 108. But I wouldn't have been human if I hadn't been fascinated by Carter's story. I said, "Have you asked the others? The stewardess and the children?"

He leaned back and steepled his fingers. "I am hoping that you would do that, Mr. Napier."

I sat in silence for a moment, thinking uncomfortably that it was rather going behind Carter's back—but on the other hand, it was for his own good.

"All right, doctor. What do you suggest?"

"The girl, Liane Dang Ko, is very well now. We are letting her get up this morning, and in a day or two we are discharging her."

"You think I should talk to her?"

"Yes, please. But I would not be rushing things too much, Mr. Napier. She has been through much strain. Just talk with her—and do not be letting her think she is being made to give evidence. Do you see?"

I nodded. "I understand. Don't worry, doctor—I won't upset your patient."

60

LIANE'S ROOM was a pleasant one, looking out onto the hospital grounds, with the harbour in the distance; there were flowers, tastefully arranged, and the windows were open, carrying the scent of the blooms through the room. Carter had told me she was beautiful, but that, I thought, was an understatement. Her long black hair, secured by a wisp of blue ribbon, hung unobtrusively over one shoulder, and she was playing absently with the loose end with one hand while turning the pages of a magazine with the other.

She stood up when I came into the room, slim, composed. I held out my hand.

"Good morning, Miss Dang Ko. My name's Napier—from the Ministry of Aviation. I'm handling the inquiry into the loss of your Boeing—All-Orient Flight HK 108. Do you feel up to talking about it?"

The girl smiled. The facial transformation was startling—there are few people who can inject genuine pleasure into a simple smile of welcome.

"Of course, Mr. Napier. Will you sit, please?"

"Thank you. I have talked to Mr. Carter," I began, "and he has told me much of what happened to Flight HK 108. It seems to me that you were very lucky to escape, Miss Dang Ko. I have found that most survivors have been seated in or near the tail of a crashed aeroplane. But the odds against striking the mountainside at exactly the right angle . . . I've only heard of one comparable case."

She leaned forward, her eyes intent. "Please tell."

"A man who jumped from a burning bomber in the war, over Germany. He landed on a hillside covered with snow and little trees."

She nodded, keenly interested. I went on, "Tell me . . . what sort of a man was Carter? Out there in the mountains?"

IT WAS CURIOUS, she said, how her feelings towards Carter changed during their time in the valley. In the beginning, he was more of a father figure—the kind of person she dreamed her own dead father might have been. He organized them, protected them, told them what to do with a quiet firmness. During that early period, Carter cushioned her against reality and relieved her of the need to rely upon her own strength. It wasn't long before she began to depend upon the tall, spare Englishman, falling in with his every wish, anticipating his every need.

As the weeks drifted by, she found the group was welding itself together in close companionship, and her dependency upon Carter began to diminish. She threw herself into the business of finding food, briefing the others on edible fruits and plants, building fish traps, collecting the wild rice which grew along the river. They even selected a flat, muddy patch, built a dam, and diverted water into their own paddy field. None of them really believed that they would still be there in three or four months, when their first crop was ready. It was a game, something to pass the time.

But the Dakota haunted Liane. In those early days, when Carter had demolished with sheer logic all their hopes of flying home in the old aeroplane, she had accepted it without question. Her acceptance lasted less than two weeks.

Most aircrew eventually pick up a smattering of aircraft technology, and Liane was no exception. There was nothing very magical, she reasoned, about aeroplanes; she had once heard them described as "large collections of spare parts all going in the same direction at the same time." Breakdowns were a part of life. It seemed to her that the stores available in the valley were more than enough to meet the Dakota's needs.

She began making secret visits to the hangar when Carter and the boy were in the valley, and she looked at the aeroplane critically. She figured that if the larger faults could be rectified, the smaller ones wouldn't matter too much. She checked the replacement tyres, stripping off part of the protective plastic covering, and found them as new. She stood precariously upon the servicing platform, staring at the partly dismantled cylinder, ready and waiting. She climbed down, examined the engine cowlings: they seemed complete, undamaged.

Four days passed before she found the courage to approach Carter, but when she did, she recoiled from the stark, bleak anger in his blue eyes. They were alone in the hangar, out of the blazing afternoon sun; the multihued birds were back, and she had asked Carter if he would find some eggs for her.

Then she asked him, falteringly, about the Dakota. He rounded upon her viciously. "For heaven's sake, Liane! I told you before! There's not a hope in hell of repairing this junkheap! Stop needling me about it! Enough is enough!" And he walked away, stiff-legged, hands bunching into fists, leaving the girl in tears.

She almost believed him. Almost. Until he began finding other reasons for staying in the valley. The mountains were too high . . . the cliffs too steep . . . the forest too dangerous . . . not enough food . . . bad drinking water . . . no maps for walking . . .

What was there for him to go back to? Liane wondered. Life alone, back in England; no wife; family away in Hong Kong for two years. She knew about his job troubles, the drinking, the way he had let himself go. They had sat for long hours talking on the veranda in the evening sunshine. She had looked at him then with critical and unbiased eyes. He was probably fitter than he had been for years; the hint of a paunch had disappeared, the tall, lean body was tanned a deep brown after five weeks in the valley, and he went about habitually in his only pair of trousers, cut short at mid-thigh for coolness.

In retrospect, she realized that they had been in the valley almost five weeks before she saw the light: Carter wanted to stay!

SITTING IN THE COOL hospital ward, she turned to me again.

"You see, Mr. Napier, it was deadlock. I couldn't get through to Donald."

I leaned forward in my seat. "But you came out all right, Liane. What happened to change Carter's mind?"

She smiled brilliantly. "Why, something happened . . . something quite strange, I think. . . ."

THEY MOVED SLOWLY downstream, Colin stalking fish in the shallows with a length of bamboo tipped with a knife blade. Sooner or later, Debby thought resignedly, he would catch one—and become even more unbearable. She perched on a smoothly rounded boulder, savouring the warmth through her tattered skirt, watching Liane on the far bank, picking fruit. Time had improved Colin in looks, at least, she mused: his body was now deeply tanned, and he was wearing cut-down trousers like Carter, his hair bleached near-white by the sun. He had matured, broadened out, and since that episode with Carter and the river he'd lost that juvenile sense of humour she had always loathed so much. She realized that a stranger might take him for a man, not a boy. She sighed. If only he wasn't such a beastly bore.

"Debby?"

She started from her reverie. Colin was twenty yards further downstream, on the brink of a little sandy beach.

"Take a look! Here!"

Debby waded down through the shallows, eyes narrowing against the sun's glare. The boy knelt on the coarse sand. There were imprints—large, flat, round depressions, and, nearby, a massive heap of droppings.

"It's an elephant, Deb! Liane—what do you think?"

The Asian girl waded knee-deep through the water towards them, holding her fruit before her in the fold of her skirt.

"It is an elephant, Liane, isn't it? Do you see what it means? If an elephant can get in, we can get out!"

Liane smiled at his excitement. "Maybe. Let me see . . ." She knelt carefully, still holding the fruit before her. "It is a big one. There are many elephants in my country—they work in the teak forests. This one, I think, is wild. We must be careful."

"I don't think we should go anywhere near it," Debby said anxiously. "Maybe we should fetch Donald?"

"Oh, forget Donald!" Colin exploded. "This is the best thing we've found so far. We won't go looking for it, but we'll keep our eyes open. I just want to take another look at the big pool by the waterfall. Come on, you two."

They began to move upstream, leaping from rock to grassy bank and down into rippling shallows, driving clouds of brilliant birds into the air.

Soon the brush became more dense, a green wall along the water's edge. The stream narrowed, and they waded thigh-deep through the dark, shady tunnel, out into the sunshine and the soaring rainbows of the waterfall. Hard under the base of the cliff, the air was filled with fine spray, the two-hundred-foot cascade feathering out randomly with the air currents. The water fell into a great semicircle of froth upon the surface of the pool as a constant shower of fine rain.

Colin walked slowly along the brink, examining the sandy areas where animals came to drink: there were tracks aplenty, but none of elephant. He stood at last on a little promontory, shading his eyes, staring at the falling water and the cliff beyond.

"If this was an adventure story," he said wistfully, "there'd be something behind that water—maybe a cave. I think I'll swim over for a look-see."

Debby raised her voice above the thunder of the fall. "Be careful!"

He grinned, revelling in the superiority of two extra years in age and six inches in stature. "Tarzan wouldn't think twice about it, Deb."

"You're not Tarzan!"

"You not Jane, either. Go get some bananas for lunch." And with that he was gone, ploughing across fifty yards of water in an untidy, thrashing overarm crawl. He slowed, approaching the edge of the water curtain, and went on cautiously, disappearing in the welter of foam and water vapour.

"He'll be all right," Liane said cheerfully. "He is a very strong boy, I think. Come, Debby—we swim too."

They stripped quickly, and Liane slid into the water with hardly a ripple, down into the green world of silence, where the noise of the fall subsided into distant drumming. The water was glass-clear, and small bubbles escaped from her mouth as she glided down the smooth, sandy slope into deeper water. She was about to thrust for the surface when a small, glowing light on the floor of the pool caught her eye. She pushed downwards, grabbed a handful of sand and shot up into the sunlight, uncertain if she had managed to grasp the tiny glittering object.

The air was cool and sharp in her lungs: she trod water, gasping, laughing, fighting to draw breath. Debby was nearing the shore with her slow, hesitant breaststroke, and Liane thrashed in behind her. Together, they hauled themselves out onto the flat sandstone ledge and lay back, feeling the burning sun on their bodies.

Liane opened her palm, allowing the wet sand to filter out. She bent forward, staring at what remained, drawing a quick gasp of astonishment.

"Liane? What is it?"

"I . . . do not know, Debby. I do not understand. Look."

The ring was a heavy loop of solid gold, adorned with a garland of small rubies. The setting formed a flat mounting almost an inch square, in which rested a single enormous emerald. Inlaid into the glowing stone was the image of a war elephant in black obsidian; on its back was the outline of a fighting turret in delicate silver filigree, and round its legs, spiked anklets; its tusks were picked out in white ivory, topped with bronze points.

"Liane! It's marvellous. Did you find it in the pool?"

"Yes. But I do not understand, Debby. I am afraid."

"Silly—what is there to be afraid of?"

Liane was silent for a moment. Then she stood up, tall and slender in the sunshine, turned her back on Debby and pointing, looking down over her shoulder, asked, "What do you see?"

Debby stared. At the base of the long, smooth back, just above the swelling curve of the buttocks, she saw a mark. Surely it must be a birthmark? It was raised slightly above the skin, in dark, almost black pigmentation: an outline, without detail. But it was staggering in its implications. Perhaps two inches long and an inch high, it was an image of a war elephant, and identical to that displayed on the ring.

It was quite impossible. Debby's mind spun in disbelief.

Liane sat quietly, gazing out across the pool, turning the ring over and over in her long, slender fingers.

The younger girl came to sit beside her, silent and thoughtful. At last she spoke.

"Liane, what does it mean?"

"I do not know. I am much afraid, Debby. I have never been here before—and yet I know this place so well from my dreams. It is beautiful, and yet it holds much sorrow for me. I want to run, yet I know I must stay. I look around and it is all different, yet nothing has changed. Only I . . . only I have changed."

Debby shivered involuntarily as the girls slipped on their shirts. Despite the warmth of the sun, it was as if some cold hand had been laid briefly upon the young girl's heart.

Liane turned to look at her. "Do not be afraid, Debby. There is no danger here for us. That much I know. There is much to be told, much that remains hidden. If the Lord Buddha so wills, we may be told the meaning of this thing."

66

BEYOND THE THUNDER of falling water, in the calm backwater under the cataract, the air was humid and cold. Colin hauled himself up onto the rocks, shaking violently in the sudden chill. He stared upwards. The rock face wasn't quite vertical, leaning back slightly from the shoreline, and the fall issued from an aperture in the rock some twenty feet across and about two hundred and fifty feet above the pool, plunging in a long, sweeping parabola to meet the surface close to the shoreline.

The boy scanned the cliff face systematically. He reckoned that it might just be possible to climb the rock face as far as the top of the fall itself.

Halfway through a horizontal scan his head jerked suddenly upwards. Was it possible? No—no, it couldn't be. The shadow was indistinct in the spray-heavy air, some fifty feet below the fall's exit point, but the more he looked at it, the more convinced he became that it might be a cave of sorts. But it would be no help to them—no way of escape.

But the fall, now—what about the fall? Would it be possible to follow the flow back to the high lands from which it came? He stared again, shrugged. Then he came thrashing back across the pool, to drag himself out with a great porpoising and blowing.

"Nothing. Not a damn thing. Except there might be a . . . what's up with you two?"

They looked at him wide-eyed. Debby was unusually pale. He leaned forward, touched her arm. "You OK?"

Liane held out the ring in the palm of her hand.

"That's nice. Where did you find it?"

Debby answered. "In the pool, Col. But it's the strangest thing. We don't understand it at all. It's scary. . . ."

"For God's sake, Deb—*what's* scary?"

"Show him, Liane."

The tall Asian girl stood up, turned her back and remained motionless for a long moment before sitting down once more. Colin stared.

"Good grief. That's fantastic. Liane—that thing on your back: have you always had it?"

"Yes, Colin. I did not know until I was five or six and started the learning of the dance. I could not see my back, you see. But the

67

exercises and movements—they had a mirror in the dancing school."

The boy considered that briefly. Then: "You don't know if your mother had the same mark?"

"No. And I have never seen it again until today. I see many pictures of elephants, but no elephant like this. Do you see? It is a fighting elephant—the tusks made to sharp points with bronze, the spiked war anklets, the war tower filled with soldiers."

Colin looked up sharply. "How do you know, Liane?"

"Please?"

"About the tusks being tipped with bronze. Have you ever seen a war elephant?"

She smiled. "No war elephants now. How could I see one? Perhaps in a museum—I do not know. But it is not important. We have talked too much. Now we go home." And she stood up.

Debby opened her mouth, avid with curiosity, caught the look on Colin's face and remained silent.

Colin gave the ring back to Liane. "All right—let's see if we can find *our* elephant on the way back. Did you find any decent bananas, Deb?"

They moved towards the pool outlet where the river began. The heat was oppressive and they kept in the shade, stopping to rest and eat on the tiny beach where Colin had discovered the elephant spoor. For a while he wandered around idly. Debby turned to Liane.

"This is your country, Liane. It's beautiful. But we don't want to stay here always, Colin and I. Do you think we'll ever find a way to get out?"

"Perhaps. Much depends on Donald. I do not think it is good for him to walk to Saigon by himself, even if he could climb the cliffs. And he cannot go the other way, not now. There is great hunger in my land—many die. When Pol Pot drove the people from the cities onto the land and into the forests, none knew how to grow the food they needed. And when other countries send money and rice, the government takes it for itself. No white man is welcome in Kampuchea now."

Colin, joining them, heard Liane's last words.

"She's right, Deb. Besides, Saigon and the delta are nearest, and

68

even they're hundreds of miles through that forest. He'd be mad to try it."

He stood on the bank of the little river, staring along the game path used by the elephant.

"Look," he said persuasively, "it won't do any harm to explore a little way in. What do you think, Liane?"

"I think we should go back," the girl said uneasily. "The elephants of the forest are dangerous."

Grumbling, he gave up the battle, turned to the river. Just as he was about to move, he stopped, one foot raised.

"What was that. . . ? Listen!"

From somewhere close by there came the sound of branches being shaken and snapped; an odd muffled groaning. They stood transfixed. "Well," said Colin, "we seem to have found our elephant."

Chapter Six

Thirty yards across the little glade, a wrinkled grey back, large floppy ears and a prehensile trunk were visible above the lush grass and fern. They watched the beast stripping fresh young leaves from a branch.

Colin whispered, "Smell him? We're downwind, he can't smell us. Careful, now. Let's get a little closer. . . ."

Debby shrank back. "Colin—"

"Oh, come on. It'll be all right so long as we're careful."

They moved forward into the shelter of a small jacaranda. The beast stood quietly, munching stolidly, trunk now sweeping the ground, now lifted in alert sensitivity. It was a male with small tusks, some ten feet at the shoulder, wiry black hair sprouting around ears, and busy, mobile mouth. It moved ponderously to the right and Colin stiffened with excitement.

"Debby! Liane! See that? On the hind foot?"

They could see, but the boy's sibilant whisper had alerted the animal. The huge head turned, trunk lifted in interrogation of the afternoon breeze, sampling the odours of the air. The leathery ears twitched spasmodically, turning to detect the slightest sound. Then the elephant lifted a hind leg, and they could see the chain and iron anklet clearly, dragging as the beast moved.

"It's a tame one, Liane—a runaway! Do you suppose . . . ?"

"Stay away from it, Colin. When these elephants return to the forest, they become wild again very soon."

"Well, it certainly looks gentle enough. I want it to see me. If it charges, run like hell back to the river. OK?"

"Colin—*no!*"

"Hang onto Debby, Liane. Here goes!"

The boy stepped out into the sunlight, moving very slowly. He stood quite still; the great bull raised its trunk higher, rumbling angrily in its belly, rocking from side to side. Colin could see the small bright eyes, faintly pink, and tried to recall if the rocking was a good sign or bad.

For a tense moment elephant and boy watched each other across the width of the clearing. Then the beast blew a great angry breath and trumpeted in clear warning, the sound echoing round the valley.

"Colin! *Please* . . ."

"It's all right. Calm down," the boy hissed irritably. "Liane—what do you think?"

He turned, receiving no response. The golden-skinned girl was silent, her face tense, and he saw that her eyes were suddenly glazed, almost as if she were asleep. She stood, tall and slender, twisting the great ring upon her finger, mouth set and determined.

The elephant exhaled again, a great menacing gust.

"*Colin!*"

"It's OK, Debby. I think he's going to . . . *Watch it!*"

The grey mountain moved with incredible speed, feet pounding the earth, charging half the width of the clearing, and Colin dodged into thick brush, his guts constricting in cold terror. The beast stopped, breathing hard, barely fifteen feet away, towering over him: its sides heaved, trunk questing, head weaving from side to side.

"Colin!" Debby's voice was a terrified whisper. "Come away!"

"For goodness sake," Colin muttered, "let him cool down a bit. Liane, what do you think?"

To Colin's astonishment the Cambodian girl walked slowly past him into the glade, raised an arm imperiously and called to the bull in some strange tongue, her voice full of authority. The elephant's head swung sharply round to face her. He trumpeted again, quietly, as if in plaintive question.

Liane said something softly to the beast, and the trunk descended slowly. She picked up a length of bamboo, strode forward and tapped the right foreleg; it lifted, forming a step, and the trunk came to form a looped handhold. The girl swung lithely up onto the broad, grey back and tucked her knees in behind the elephant's twitching ears.

The bull rumbled contentedly, and Liane rapped smartly with the bamboo, moving the animal forward to the very edge of the glade.

"It's all right now, Colin. He will not hurt us."

Debby and Colin emerged nervously, eyeing the beast with ill-concealed distrust. The Asian girl laughed. "Come on!" She spoke a word or two, and the elephant raised its knee; Colin helped Debby up, clambered aboard himself, grinning all over his face.

"Liane, that was amazing! I didn't know you could handle elephants!"

She turned to stare at him, uncertainly. "I . . . I cannot, Colin. I was never on an elephant before. It is strange . . . it seems that I remembered what to say, what to do. See!" And she kicked her heels gently, coaxing the bull with soft-spoken words; instantly the elephant responded and they moved off towards the river.

They made good speed, following the stream, and once accustomed to the rolling ship-at-sea motion and the sliding skin of the back, they even began to enjoy the ride. Colin leaned over, pointing to the dragging chain. "We'll have to get that thing off the old boy, Deb. But just think what Donald'll say when he sees us!"

The young girl turned to him, whispering, "What did you make of that? Talking to the thing like that?"

"Search me. What with the ring, and that birthmark—and now this. Something's going on. But I'm damned if I know what."

CARTER, DOZING in the afternoon sun on the veranda, heard them coming down the airstrip and held a hand to his brow, incredulous.

Liane tapped the elephant's great head with her cane and the beast stopped five yards from the hut. The three slid to the ground and came clamouring around the man.

"Isn't he fine, Donald? Liane can talk to him!"

"He's tame—a runaway!"

Carter walked slowly round the bull, and it followed him impassively with small wise eyes as he bent to look at the drag chain. The ankle ring was of rusted iron, two sections hinged together, ending in flanges through which a screwed bolt had been inserted tightly. "That's been on there a long time; it's rusty, and he's got an almighty callus under it. Have to cut it off. Colin—nip over to the hangar, will you? A hacksaw, some blades, a hammer— you know the score."

Half an hour and three hacksaw blades later, the restraint finally gave way. Colin hefted the heavy iron curiously. "There's something stamped on the ring, Don: 'KHAN 62.' Khan must be his name—I like that. '62'—could that be a registration number?"

"Could be 1962—maybe the year he was born. That would make him seventeen. Is that old for an elephant, Don?" asked Debby.

"Haven't a clue," said Carter. "But I think they go on to around ninety."

Liane stepped back and stared up at the sculpted head, silhouetted black against the afternoon sky. "Khan, Khan. Come!" The beast rumbled deep in its belly, tossed its head, raised its trunk and trumpeted exultantly, moving towards the girl. Liane had clearly established an instant authority over the bull.

Carter said, "Poor old lad. Must have been years since he heard his own name."

Colin frowned. "How did he get here, Don? I mean, if an elephant can get into the valley, surely we can get out?"

Carter's brow wrinkled. "That makes sense. But maybe the Americans brought him in by air, to clear the strip. Their C130s can land in open country if necessary. Then, when they all got out in a hurry at the end, they left him behind."

Debby said sadly, "How lonely it must have been for him."

"Maybe," Carter nodded. "He had plenty of food and no enemies, but he'd miss his own kind—elephants are gregarious by nature. No wonder he was so pleased to see you. How did you find him, anyway?"

"Colin saw his footprints. He was a bit scary with Colin at first, until Liane spoke to him."

"Until *what?*"

"Don," Colin broke in, "how about some coffee? We can tell you all about it."

CARTER PUSHED his empty mug away and lit another cigarette. "That's the strangest thing I ever heard. And this is the ring?"

He held it at an angle for a better view. "It's the sheer coincidence that gets me. This *and* the birthmark. There's just no logical explanation."

He paused, deep in thought. The ring itself was no mystery, although the odds against finding it must have been astronomical. Technology capable of producing such workmanship had existed throughout the world for centuries. Gold? That was common enough—and he knew that precious stones had been mined in Southeast Asia when Ancient Britons were still painting themselves blue. It was the link with Liane that baffled him completely.

Carter shook his head, uncertain and troubled in his mind. All his life, he had abhorred anything connected with the paranormal. Most unusual occurrences, in his view, could be explained as simple coincidences, the rest imagination. But how far could imagination be stretched? Where did coincidence end and the supernatural—if it existed—begin?

Then there was that damned business with Khan. Liane had firmly refused to talk about it, but the fact remained that she had somehow established an instant authority over a bull elephant which had spent years running wild. It made no sense at all.

"Donald?"

He jerked out of his daydream. "Yes, Debby?"

"It's a pity you can't fix that plane. I mean, with Khan to help us, we could clear the strip in no time, couldn't we, Liane?"

Liane's dark, shining eyes remained shadowed, withdrawn. "Donald says it cannot be mended, Debby."

The child stared mutinously at the pilot. "My dad would soon make it work. At least, he'd try!"

Carter took a long, deep breath, gritted his teeth and made for the door. They watched him walk away, stiff-necked, heading

73

towards the hangar. Women! Damned insolent kids! He ground his teeth in angry frustration, stalking through the long grass to the hangar door.

That filing cabinet in the office: time he got that open. Could be all sorts of things in there. And those crates in the Dakota, and the dead man. Time he sorted that lot out, too. He had left the door and all hatches open, weeks ago; with a bit of luck, the snake would be long gone.

There was no sign of a key for the filing cabinet. In the end, he jammed a long steel bar into the top drawer and levered until the lock broke. Bingo! Ten cartons of cigarettes just when stocks were running low! Eight bottles of bourbon—Carter hefted a bottle in his hand, debating whether to try a sample. He decided against it. The ease with which he made the decision pleased him: all at once, he knew he could take it or leave it. He left it, went on probing.

There was a crumbling set of aircraft documents, which he lifted out with care. Beneath, he found a large buff envelope marked STATE DEPARTMENT—TOP SECRET—BY HAND ONLY. He took it over to the desk, sat down under the single light bulb and opened it.

The first few documents were copies of operations orders dating from January 1975 onwards, detailing certain aircraft for flights to widely separated destinations. The targets included Phnom Penh, Da Nang, several others in Cambodia and Laos. There was an original of an order with two copies, scheduling a special night flight to a point in western Cambodia, in the mountains beyond Phnom Penh, with detailed instructions on landing-strip identification, the lighting to be provided by Task Force Baker Five, the recognition signals to be expected. Carter stared: the date was 30th April 1975—the time of the American Dunkirk from Saigon. Commander of Task Force Baker Five was given as Major Carl F. Macbain.

The receipt attached to the operation order completed the picture. He stared at the document. Now Carter knew, with absolute certainty, what was in those crates stacked in the silent Dakota. Face pale and drawn, he put the papers back and closed the drawer.

He checked his watch, listening to the thunder of the inevitable rain on the hangar roof. An hour before dusk: it would ease up soon.

74

He shrugged, turned back towards the old DC3. No use putting it off. Might as well do it now.

Carter lit a Tilley lamp, climbed aboard, moved up cautiously to the flight deck. He peered round apprehensively. No sign of that damned snake, thank God. He got out his knife and worked on the fabric webbing of the lashings; the wooden crates were intact, solidly made, unaffected by the moisture and decay which attacked most timberwork on the base. He began unstacking and checking the contents.

Three cases of M1 rifles, in mint condition. Two crates of Browning automatic rifles, two cases of grenades, still live, pins in position, made safe for transit with tape. He went on. Forty boxes of assorted ammunition followed the weapons out of the door. And there was an unexpected bonus—sixteen cartons of US army "K" rations: the standard field issue of canned meat stew, hard biscuits, sweets, coffee and powdered milk, cigarettes, gum. He grinned. No doubt Liane would be able to make something of that lot—especially if they had to walk out. His face darkened. On second thoughts, it seemed good sense to stash the "K" rations out of the way, under a heap of camouflage netting in the corner of the hangar.

Forward, near the flight-deck door, he found three strong timber boxes, painted black, metal-bound at the corners and spot-welded shut. He took the receipt copy from his pocket, checked the serial numbers on the crates and nodded with satisfaction.

Finally there was a single metal container, eighteen inches square, twelve deep, painted olive-green; the lid was stamped with the State Department seal, the lid welded shut, the whole lashed down very tightly. Carter cut the bindings, tried to lift the box; it was extraordinarily heavy. He nodded. There must be a lot of money in it. He lashed the crate down again and went aft, to sit in the cargo hatch, looking far out across the valley in the fading light, through the open hangar door. He smoked a cigarette, thinking very deeply, oblivious of the occasional bird returning to roost in the roof members.

In the end, he got up and set about the worst job of all. Carefully, he bundled up the remains of the man in the pilot's seat. The flying overall was as brittle as burned paper, decayed and rotten, but not enough to hide the two bullet holes in the back. Carter sucked in his breath sharply, leaned round to look at the back of the seat. The two holes in the metal were neat and round where the bullets had penetrated.

Sombrely, he carried the burden out into the underbrush, where he scraped a hole beneath a banyan tree.

On the way back to the hut, his face was set in a frown. What in God's name had happened here in those last few days of the evacuation? The contents of those boxes could have had a great deal to do with it. Major Macbain: was he the dead pilot or the man in the hut? It made no difference: Task Force Baker Five had blown their last mission when the Dakota had blown an engine.

Later, when he told the others about the rest of the Dakota cargo, it seemed to mean little or nothing to them, faced with the greater realities of their survival. What was the use of money here, in Lost Valley?

TEN DAYS PASSED in deceptive peace and quiet. Debby and Colin were working on a guitar, knocked up from plywood taken from spare crates. Colin carved the fingerboard from a single teak sapling, breaking four hacksaw blades and as many fingernails in the process. Debby made the strings from strands of control cable, pre-stretched to remove the kinks. Carter was surprised: the finished article was excellent, agleam with glossy aircraft-grade varnish. Colin turned out to be a passable player, and Debby's voice was young, immature but strong. They spent hours writing down what they could recall of pop song lyrics and country and western music.

The storeroom yielded a new stock of playing cards, and one evening Carter started a bridge training course, but the youngsters were impatient, unruly, unwilling to learn stupid conventions they might never have to use. He finally told them to forget it and suggested to Liane that she might like to amble down with him to switch on the generator.

The sun was a fire balloon rolling along the rim of the western cliffs; cloud remnants were breaking up. It promised to be a clear, warm night. The first few stars glowed. Together they trod the well-worn path. Carter felt a sense of exaltation, and he halted a moment, gazing up at the valley rim, listening to the insect chorus, the sighing of the wind through the bamboo thickets.

"It is beautiful, Donald."

"Mm . . . as if the rest of the world didn't exist. Reminds me of Shangri-La."

"Please?"

"A story in a book. About a valley lost in the mountains in Tibet, where people lived for ever and the sky was always blue. But it was only a story—not real, like this."

She turned her face towards him, her hair catching the fading gleam of the sun. "You would like to live here for ever, Donald?"

He was silent for a long moment. "I don't know. At home, there was always trouble, problems. Money. Houses. Bills, more bills. And it's not easy, unless you have someone with you."

Liane hesitated. "I . . . I think you loved your wife very much, Donald. I think, maybe, you still love her."

"Maybe I do. Strange—you love people even after they've gone, but in a different way. You get the feeling they're still alive somewhere, if you can keep them fresh in your memory. When you forget their faces, it's as if you've murdered them all over again."

Liane looked shocked, but Carter continued. "It's true," he said fiercely. "I killed her, sure as I stand here. For half a lifetime, she worked to care for me and Gavin. I could have helped; maybe got her a home help or an au pair. I could have found myself a decent job, given her a real home, so that she wouldn't have had to work so hard. And when that . . . thing . . . caught hold of her, began to eat her alive, I could do nothing . . . nothing to make it up to her. God, Liane, those were the worst days of my life."

"Donald . . ." There was a world of understanding and pity in her voice. Tears on her cheeks, she reached up and drew his head down to her, and the dam broke: he buried his face in her shoulder, his arms holding her with an intensity which took her breath away. Suddenly he felt her lips pressed close to his ear, whispering words in a tongue he could not understand, her voice lilting and musical, almost as if she was singing softly to him. He kissed her softly, without thought. Immediately he felt the fear and anger and uncertainty draining away. Her fingers ran lightly through the hair on his neck, and he caught her distinctive fragrance. Until suddenly he felt her writhe away from him desperately, avoiding his lips.

"Liane . . ."

She shook her head in the gloom. "Please, Donald . . . go. I will follow you soon."

He stumbled away, filled with remorse. No need to wonder why: he was nearly thirty years older than the girl. Yet, for an instant, he had been young again. Since Jean had died, he had consciously sublimated his emotions, drifting from job to job, drinking— anything to black out her memory. And now . . . He found his hands were shaking, and he had to force himself to concentrate on the task of priming the generator, swinging the handle, waiting until the lights came on in the huts.

Colin was alone when he returned. He looked up at Carter.

"What's wrong with Liane, Don?"

The pilot avoided the boy's eyes. "Got a bit upset. Nothing to worry about. Has she gone to bed?"

"She and Debby both. Was she on about that aeroplane again?"

"In a way," Carter said heavily. "Listen, I may have been quite wrong, Colin. It needs proving, one way or the other. We'll start work on the Dakota in the morning."

"And if we find it can be fixed?" Colin said breathlessly.

"If pigs could fly," the pilot said caustically. "All I'm going to do is prove it's impossible."

THE NEXT MORNING he went alone to the hangar, paper and pencil in hand, at a loss to know where to start. The main wheel tyres were shot completely, but there were spares available. Luckily, the brakes had been left off, so with luck the wheels would turn all right, provided he could get the thing jacked up. In the remote event that the plane ever moved again, he would have no brakes: the metal hydraulic lines were solid with congealed fluid, flexible pipes perished and decayed.

Main shock-absorber legs collapsed . . . which meant taxiing on solid legs. Suppose they used the elephant to tow the thing down to the end of the strip? Brakes wouldn't matter, and they'd have the full length of the strip before the wheels caved in from the pounding. Carter! What are you thinking about?

Start from scratch. Aim for an irreducible minimum of services for a one-way flight. Flaps? They could take off without, but they'd need them for landing—if ever they got that far. Undercarriage? "Up" system only: it would have to be a belly-landing. Electrics? The engines would hand-start on the inertia system, and they'd be going in daylight, so no instruments needed. The radio was shot anyway. So who needed electrics?

He looked at his list and grinned, despite himself. He wasn't about to put the old bird into airline service. The engines would run fine on magnetos, without a battery; all he needed was an altimeter and an airspeed indicator and a compass. Of course, the whole enterprise was mad, but he had to admit a quickening of the blood, a certain something long-dead coming to life within him.

He started jotting down notes. On the flight deck, he found the hydraulic reservoir and sight glass. Contents: nil. What else? He found a stick, went back and used it as a dipstick: it came out of the tank thick with a brown jelloid substance, all that was left of four gallons of hydraulic oil. He checked the controls from the cockpit: all were free, but accompanied by shocking grating and squeaking noises. Back near the tail, he found himself glowering at a collapsed tail-wheel assembly. Suddenly the ludicrous insanity of the whole business swamped him. He stepped back, looked again at the sagging wreck, laughter bubbling up within him.

Carter walked out into the sunshine, shading his eyes with the sheaf of notes. That strip, shoulder-high with brush—could it be cleared? Maybe they could bodge up some kind of harness for Khan so that he could drag a log behind him, or something. Or burn the stuff down first. It *could* be done, one way or another.

Supposing they got the thing running. He'd never flown a Dak before. He had no flight manual. Maps, yes. Once out of the valley, he'd know where to go. But that takeoff . . . he turned slowly, eyes searching the rim of the cliffs. He would have to make a screaming, climbing turn on takeoff, gain at least fifteen hundred feet before heading out over the mountains. He began sweating profusely, not from the heat.

If he lost an engine in that climbing turn, it'd be curtains. There was a minimum speed below which the rudder couldn't hold the plane straight against the pull of one engine. The critical speed . . .

Carter shivered. He walked back slowly to the hangar office and slumped down at the desk. His head ached and he felt confused. Liane . . . How stupid can you get, old man? Of course she wanted to run away from you. And that damned aeroplane: half of him wanted to set fire to it—anything rather than risk a nightmare flight ending with a last plunge into the ground, Liane and Colin and Debby all screaming, seconds away from death. And yet, at the same time, how he craved to be free of this place! Free of this desperate yearning for a girl half his age. The sooner they got away the better.

But then the pendulum swung again. Carter's castle was back, that terrible obstacle that fear conjures up. "Such castles rise to strike us dumb . . ." The old, hideous fear gripped him in a vice. He got up, seized by an impulse, opened the filing cabinet and took out a bottle. He placed the bourbon on the desk and sat back, looking at the rich, gold liquid behind the glass.

Carefully, he broke the seal, opened the bottle, sniffed gently. He tilted the bottle, let the smallest drop rest on his palate and held it there for a moment, savouring the smooth, rich taste, until the first big swallow came to rest in his belly. Suddenly, he coughed, guts on fire, eyes watering, and put the bottle down smartly. Talk about rocket fuel!

The next one, bourbon and water in equal parts, went down more easily. It was better than anaesthetic, this stuff. He poured himself another shot. If he ever got out of here with those boxes on the Dakota, he could afford a bottle like this every day, maybe two.

There was a faded map on the wall. He got up, drank deeply again, and wandered over to take a look. With those boxes aboard, Vietnam was a non-starter. There they would take the lot, probably shove the four of them into Ho Chi Minh pokey and throw away the key.

It had to be somewhere else, preferably with the shortest sea crossing, given the state of those engines. Hong Kong? No way. Four hundred miles of rain forest, six hundred miles of sea. More than seven hours' flying time—and in the monsoon. It was impossible. How about Malaysia? Five hundred miles, four of 'em over the sea. That northeast coast . . . Koora . . . Khota Baru . . . whatever. He took another stab at the bourbon. Say, four hours' flying an' the sea full of sharks? You gotta be jokin', Carter! Hey, no life-rafts either! Kids'd tried them for skylarking on the pool—damn things were rotten.

"Donald!"

"Huh?" He lurched round, mug in hand, grinning crookedly. "Liane, ole girl . . . wanna li'l drinky?"

She shook her head. "I think you have too much now, Carter. I came to see if I can help with the aeroplane."

Carter sniggered. "Call that an aeroplane? You're blind . . . blind an' daft. Should be inna museum. I should be inna museum, too."

Liane frowned. "But you said you would try to fix it."

"Try? 'Course I'll try. Lots work, though . . . lots spares we ain't got. Lots mechanics we don't have. . . ."

Carter was at the filing cabinet, trying to get the drawer open. Liane saw the bottles, whipped one away from his groping hand just in time. He bellowed with rage, clutching at her, staggered and went down like a felled oak, without a twitch of movement. His face was a sick, grey colour. She found water and a cloth and tenderly wiped the sweat from his face. Then she fetched an old engine cover and made a pillow for his head.

It was wrong of her to have rejected him. It was little enough to give in exchange for the lives he had saved. But over the long weeks she had come to feel for him as a father. And fathers did not do what Carter had tried to do. In the way of her race, Liane believed that she had lost face, yet she knew she would lose more face by apologizing to him. She would have to find some other way.

If he was at peace with himself, he would work well upon the aeroplane. She would find some way to bring him that peace. She would help him overcome the fear which gripped him.

THREE DAYS PASSED before I next saw Donald Carter. His back was responding slowly to treatment, X-rays having disclosed no fractured vertebrae.

"I talked with the stewardess, Miss Dang Ko, a few days ago," I said, as casually as I could. "She's leaving hospital soon. Has she spoken to you?"

He raised a hand in disclaimer. "No—and I don't think she will.

Things were . . . difficult when we left the valley." He stared at me. "What did she say?"

I smiled. "Nothing bad, Mr. Carter—quite the reverse. She seemed to think you performed miracles."

"That's a load of rubbish," he said sourly. "I had my own reasons for wanting to leave in the end. I don't care what Liane says, I *did* want to get out of that place."

I said carefully, "I think you did—in the end. But it must have been a wonderful place—peace, quiet, plenty of food. . . ."

He looked at me, eyes heavy. "It wasn't that, Mr. Napier. Not that at all. I'll tell you what it was: I was just plain bloody scared—frightened out of my wits."

He moved his head restlessly. "I was a fool, Mr. Napier. I should have left that booze alone. I was out for nearly eight hours the day I took a really close look at the old wreck for the first time. They worked on me, all three of them—got me over to the hut and into bed. They were marvellous; they needed me to get them home, depended on me, trusted me—and I'd blown it."

"It seems you owe Liane a great deal, Mr. Carter." I stood up. "I'll leave you now. If you decide you don't want to talk any more, I'll quite understand."

After a pause, he looked at me in an odd manner. "You still fly, Mr. Napier?"

I told him I still had a private licence for a small aircraft, the size of an Apache or an Islander, and he smiled.

"When I get out of here, I want you to fly me up to Khota Baru, in something capable of carrying a decent load—say, eleven or twelve hundred pounds. Could you do that?"

"I could—if I knew what the load involved."

He said slowly, "We brought something out of that valley, Mr. Napier. Something the Americans left there five years ago, something of great value. Why it was ever left there, I don't know; perhaps the pick-up plane never made it. The CIA used that strip for agents penetrating Thailand, Cambodia, Laos—agents who carried money for bribes, supplies, you name it. Money was their main weapon: given enough, they could and did buy governments, start revolutions."

"What are you trying to tell me?" I said curtly.

"I brought out two boxes of mixed currency—dollars, sterling, Swiss francs, local currencies from half the countries in the Far East. Plus a box of gold ingots weighing four ounces each—six hundred of them, weighing a hundred and' fifty pounds, near enough."

I looked at him very hard. "That's a remarkable story, Mr. Carter. Do you realize what you're saying? Two thousand four hundred ounces of gold . . . the current rate is around $400 an ounce, I think. That's nearly a million dollars!"

He smiled complacently. "You've heard nothing yet. There was nearly ten million in dollars, used bills, and perhaps another four in other currencies. If you said $15 million, you wouldn't be far off. And it's still all there, up on the beach at Khota Baru. Waiting to be picked up."

I took a deep breath. "I . . . I don't know what to say, Mr. Carter. And it won't be as easy as that, if what you say is true. The government here will have something to say."

Carter's voice was determined. "I have to go back for those boxes, Mr. Napier, because I need the money for something important— something I can't keep to myself any longer. But first I have to have your promise of absolute secrecy. Well?"

My thoughts were in turmoil but I agreed, and leaned forward in my seat expectantly.

"You'd better switch that recording machine of yours on again," he said, amused. "You won't want to miss any of this next bit."

Chapter Seven

Debby lay stretched out, drowsily staring up at the dark leaves of the trees silhouetted against a china-blue sky. Her eyes moved along the rim of the escarpment, climbing halfway to the sky. Suddenly she stiffened.

"*Colin!*"

Colin, who had been dozing on the grass beside her, rolled over, looked at her raised hand held to her mouth in sudden alarm. Then he too saw a group of tiny figures moving along a clear rim of the cliff to the left of the falls. They were too small to identify at such a

83

distance, but he sensed the sameness of clothing, the carefully measured distance between each tiny figure.

Soldiers!

Debby got to her feet, sobbing with excitement and fear. "Who can they be, Colin? What do you think?"

The boy spoke with a new authority, his voice calm. "I think we may be in trouble. They're soldiers—a patrol. They could be Vietnamese, Cambodian, anything."

"Can they see us?"

"Don't think so. We're under the trees, and Khan is back in the brush somewhere. Listen, we're ready for this. Donald's drilled us often enough, God knows. And the first thing we do is keep cool. I want you to get back to Donald just as fast as you can. And stay under the trees, keep out of open space, OK? I'm going to stay here and watch them."

"Will they come down?"

Colin considered. Strange, he thought, that now that it had finally happened, he felt quite undisturbed. "I think they've been up there for some time, Debby. They'll have seen the hangar, maybe our lights at night, or our 'SOS' message. There's only one place they can get down—right here. Don't worry. Just get to Don, he'll know what to do. He'd better bring some guns—but he'll know that."

"You mean we'll fight?"

"Damn right we will. You think Don and I will let them get their hands on you and Liane?" the boy said truculently.

She turned white as a sheet. "Oh, God . . ."

"Stop worrying. Get going as fast as you can. Take care."

COLIN LAY MOTIONLESS, his vantagepoint affording a view over the whole cliff face. They were up to something over there, messing about with sticks? . . . or trees? He scowled, shading his eyes against the glare. Of course! A tripod—they were building a tripod of sorts, sticking out over the cliff-edge. They were getting ready to come down!

The hot afternoon drifted past, until the sun was an hour above the western escarpment. Donald's voice in his ear was a welcome sound indeed. Colin turned, and saw Liane and Debby crouched behind him.

Carter said calmly, "So, we have company, eh? What are they doing up there?"

"Knocking up a tripod, I think, so they can let a rope down. I think there are seven or eight of them altogether."

The older man nodded. "That's how I'd tackle it, if I had enough rope. But how did they know they'd need rope?"

"Because they've been here before?"

"Perhaps. Or they may be a local unit who spotted us some time back and returned to their base for equipment."

Debby crawled forward for a better view. "It's awfully high—how will they get down?"

"Rappelling. They'll hang a rope from that contraption and come sliding down in no time at all."

Colin licked his lips nervously. "And then?"

The pilot frowned. "That's where it gets difficult. If they've come for that American money in the Dakota, they won't want to leave anyone alive to tell the tale. Also, there are the girls. . . ."

Colin said thickly, "I already thought of that."

"Right. Which doesn't leave us much choice. It's going to be rough, and I can't do it alone. You're going to have to do what many men go through life and never do."

"We're going to kill them." It was a statement, not a question.

"It's them or us. Now, we can do it two ways: either you take the girls away down the valley and go to ground . . ."

"*No!*"

Carter grinned. ". . . *or* we all work together to set up an ambush. We're a good three miles from the base, and with luck they'll think they can get down to ground level without being seen."

Colin looked up at the group of figures working away on the edge of the cliff, and shivered. Donald kept treating him like a man, and he wasn't. Yet ever since he had saved Carter from the rapids, he'd stopped feeling like a schoolboy. Besides, plenty of people his age had done braver things.

"What do you want me to do?"

Carter said, "I want you to do murder, Colin. Give those swine up there half a chance and they'd crush us like a steamroller. They're professionals. Our only chance is to hit them from cover with everything we've got. The girls and I brought along four M1s with

85

plenty of ammunition, and a box of grenades. You all know how to handle grenades. We'll get into position before dusk. When I give the word, we each throw four grenades as fast as we can; the girls will then get out, head back to camp and hide. You and I, Colin, will then open up with the M1s directly after the grenades, and keep firing until they're empty. Then we get out ourselves. Is that all perfectly clear?"

Three frightened faces nodded.

"None of us has experienced anything like this before," Carter said bleakly. "I was in the 1939 war, but not on the ground. It's not going to be easy, and we may get hurt. What we *do* have on our side is surprise. And we also know the valley from end to end. There's only one real danger: that one or more of them may get away. Now—I don't think they'll tackle that rope at night, and there are only a couple of hours before dark. They'll probably come down early in the morning, and start off down the valley. We'll wait until they're bunched together, ready to move, then open fire."

Colin swallowed hard. Killing? He glanced at Debby, who was now on her knees, peering up at the escarpment. His jaw clenched tight in determination. He'd do what had to be done. . . .

Keeping well under cover, Carter reconnoitred the area round the base of the cliff, at the side of the falls. The soldiers' ropes would bring them down the vertical face to the point where the cliff bellied out, level with the falls. From that more gentle slope, they would climb down, gaining ground level in a small natural clearing. Carter moved around cautiously, taking in the ground contours, possible arcs of fire.

Satisfied, he went back to the others.

"I think we've got a good chance. But I want you three to stay under cover here for the moment. They may send a couple of men down to check out the area. Also, they may keep some men up top, and even if we write off the main party, that spells trouble."

High on the rim, a coil of rope arced out, unwinding as it fell, reaching, with feet to spare, the slope of broken scree at the bottom of the rock face. It hung there, swaying gently, more than four hundred feet in length.

The pilot stared up. "Well, there's no turning back now. We'll have to play it by ear."

WITH PERHAPS HALF AN HOUR of daylight left, he sat wedged between two rocks not thirty yards from the danger zone, watching as two figures rappelled down, swinging out from the cliff and falling in short pitches until they reached the lower level. Once they left the rope and began descending the scree-covered slopes, he could see them clearly, and grunted in surprise.

One, the leader, was a white man, big, husky, dressed in tan trousers, lumber boots, a leather jacket swinging open to reveal a holster. The man who followed was a slim Asiatic, almost certainly Vietnamese. He wore dark green coveralls, jungle boots, peaked cap, and an automatic weapon was slung over one shoulder.

The men worked their way down through the boulders and scree until they gained level ground. Carter froze in sudden fear: no more than ten feet away, in the little clearing, they stopped and stripped off the strong gloves they had worn for rope work.

"OK, Tran?" asked the bulky man with a wolfish grin. Carter studied the pale eyes, the square, underhung jaw, strong white teeth: it was a face of exceptional strength and viciousness. Carter shivered involuntarily.

"What now, Macbain?" the Asian said in a highpitched voice.

Macbain? thought Carter dazedly. *Macbain! Task Force Baker Five was back!*

"Now—nothing. We stick to the plan. There's not much daylight left. You can bring the team down at first light. We're OK down here tonight for rations and water. You left your glasses up top?"

"Yes . . ." Carter heard the prolonged, sibilant hiss of oriental English. "Sergeant Pak Trang Dok is a good man. If he sees anything, he will warn us. Those people—you said nothing of them in Saigon. The money—you think it is still here?"

The big man scowled. "I told you, the money's here, in the valley. I'll tell you where when I'm good and ready, and not before."

The Vietnamese said bitterly, "Still you do not trust us."

"You're damn right I don't," the big man snarled. "I didn't work my guts out for five years getting this thing together for a bunch of gooks to cut my throat. I spent fourteen months in this godforsaken hole with the CIA. I'd rather have done the time on Alcatraz."

"You said you were last man out of the valley. Why you not take money with you?"

"I took what I could. You wanna know what happened? We got four planes out of here after Saigon fell; I was with the last, waiting for the gooney-birds to bring in the field men and their war-chests. Then we got shot up by your Migs, and I missed the last plane out. There were three of us left here—Simmonds, the pilot; Garvey, the mechanic; and me. The plane was in the hangar with a blown cylinder head, or it would have got shot up too. Then the last chopper came in with room for one guy only. Simmonds wanted to argue—I hadda kill him, right there in the plane. Garvey was no use to me: he was no pilot, so I left him here to rot. I filled my pockets, got into the Huey and made tracks."

The Vietnamese said coldly, "Why you no tell me this in Saigon?"

"Because you'd have called in your secret police. It took me a long time to find a guy like you, Tran, but you came well recommended. I knew you'd prefer half a million bucks to working in a paddy field."

Tran said in the thickening gloom, "You were a brave man to come back to Vietnam. We do not like Amis very much."

"Which was why I came to you, instead of the government. And why I told you as little as possible. OK. Your guys know what to do?"

"Pak will send the six men down at first light, staying on top with the radio. You go first, with one man—we follow."

"Right. And tell those guys to keep their gook hands off the women. They're mine."

"I tell. You have American cigarette, yes?"

"All the way up-country you've smoked my cigarettes. Maybe once we get our pinkies on that dough you'll buy your own."

The Asiatic soldier laughed. "First, I think I buy an air ticket to South America, my friend. Then cigarettes."

"Yeah? You mean, you don't like your cosy little Commie state?"

Carter, listening, grinned broadly.

"Communism . . . capitalism . . . two names, same thing. I think. Already, we have boss class in Vietnam—people with power, with big cars, new houses, plenty food, money in foreign banks. What different from capitalist country, hey? You tell . . ."

Silence. Carter eased his stiff body a little. Then he heard a muffled snore. Macbain had nodded off. Well, thought Carter, sweet dreams. He began working his way back towards the river.

So, he thought grimly, that answered a whole lot of questions. It solved the mystery of those two poor sods back on the airstrip. Just possibly, guys, I might be able to square the account for you.

HALF AN HOUR before dawn.

Carter moved slowly, rubbing his numbed legs to stimulate circulation. There was a pink glow in the east, and the shadow of the escarpment, projected onto the far rock walls, left a brilliant band of sunlight along the western rim. He groped cautiously for the M1, checked the safety catch was off and hoped to God that Colin was awake. He was a hundred feet away, deep in a bamboo thicket with the girls.

Last night they had talked for an hour about the task that lay before them. It would have been easier, Carter reflected, if Macbain had opted to stay with the main group. The surprise attack he'd planned would alert the big American out there in the valley.

Carter had refused flatly to allow the girls up front. They could throw a grenade up to forty yards, and that was as close as they'd come.

"None of us," he had told them acidly, "has any experience of action—so no one plays the bloody hero. As soon as you girls hear the first bang, you throw your four grenades at the same place and get the hell out. Col will be on the right, me on the left, so you don't have to worry about hitting us. Get back to the tail unit on the hill and wait for us there. Colin, you know what you have to do?"

"Yes. I fire off the full magazine, shooting low, chuck the gun away and run like the clappers back here. We pick up the spare M1s and ammunition and go after Macbain."

"Very good. I think that's it, then."

Liane had said anxiously, "And you, Donald?"

"I'll be OK. From my spot, I can see the whole clearing. I'm counting on getting most of them first time round. But I'm not stopping to check—we *have* to get Macbain. With him out of the way, we can deal with stragglers. Colin?"

"Huh? I'm fine. Terrified, of course."

"You and me both, pal," Carter had admitted. "I'm too old and you're too young for this game, but what the hell. Like the man in the film said, 'You wanna live for ever?'"

"Yes, please . . ."

Carter had grinned in the darkness. "You'll be fine. Get some sleep. When we let rip, they won't even know what's hit them."

CARTER STOOD FROZEN, legs apart, listening to the echoes rebounding down the valley. He had lost count of the grenades in the continuous overlapping explosions. Now he stood still, lean and predatory in the early sunlight, gun at the ready.

Far away shocked birds were screeching anxiously, and down the valley Khan trumpeted stridently twice, three times. Carter walked forward stiffly, slipped a new magazine into position, set the gun on auto and moved into the clearing with almost painful care. He whirled. Something had stirred in the brush. Panicky now, he sent a long searing burst into the undergrowth. Then silence. He dropped to his knees and vomited helplessly, time and time again.

There had been seven men in the team, excluding Macbain. Carter walked round gingerly, counting heads, or what was left of them. He found six, in various states, including the lieutenant— which meant that Macbain had taken one man with him, dammit.

WORKING HIS WAY DOWNSTREAM, Carter kept in cover and shade. He had told Colin and the girls to retreat to the tail-section rendezvous after the clash. Colin, he knew, would not wait when he failed to show up—if the older man were dead, the girls would be his first and only concern. Carter gripped the spare M1 tightly, feeling the weight of the bandoliers on his shoulders.

Item: Macbain, inevitably, knew he had a problem.

Item: Macbain was going to be a very angry man, and a very, very careful one. He would understand that he, now, was the quarry. Undoubtedly, the American was a seasoned CIA killer who would use that .45 automatic to good effect.

Item: maybe it was Carter who was on the spot, Macbain who was lying in wait? So? So he had to out-think the man.

Supposing he was Macbain . . . for a start, he probably knew that only one man, two girls and a young boy opposed him. Ergo, he would concentrate on the man first. It made sense. Carter paused at the edge of a stretch of open ground, then began working his way round. About a mile to go to the base . . .

"*Don!*"

Carter hurled himself forward, hit the ground, rolled twice and finished up under a thorn bush, breathing hard. Who the hell?

"*Don!* It's me, Colin!"

Carter raised his head, saw the boy emerge upright from the bushes fifty feet away. He surged forward, covered ten yards at a dead run, weaving sharply, went in waist-high with a braced shoulder.

Suddenly the two of them were rolling deep in the brush, entangled with vines and with each other.

Carter sobbed for breath. "You could have got us both killed!"

Colin's face was ashen. "I—Don, I'm sorry . . ."

"Oh, belt up, Colin. Suppose Macbain had been waiting for us here? We'd both have been pork, for sure."

"Did you—? I mean, are they—?" asked Colin weakly.

"We did all right. We only have to worry about Macbain and one man he took with him. There's one more up on the cliff, but he shouldn't worry us. Did the girls get clear OK?"

"I—I think so."

"All right. We've been lucky, Col. But now Macbain'll be waiting for us, and he's a pro. So you do exactly as I tell you."

"Yes," replied Colin, a little shakily.

"If we run into trouble, keep your head down and leave the field clear. I don't want to risk hitting you. OK?"

The boy nodded, crouching on his heels in the thick scrub.

"One more thing, and it's important. When we move, I go first, twenty yards ahead; you watch our backs. Stop often to listen. If you see anything move, let fly. Now, if he's on the base, he'll expect us from this direction, so I'm going to make a big loop round and come in behind the hangar. If we get separated, don't shout: get back to the tail unit and sit tight. All clear?"

"All clear, Don."

"Right. Come on."

ALMOST THREE HOURS later the sun was high overhead, as Carter parted the fronds of fern in front of him with his gun barrel and stared at the rear of the hangar. Nothing.

He turned and waved Colin on. The boy crawled forward,

lay prone beside him. "Don? We've no choice, have we? We have to go in, look for them. Question is where?"

"The huts, maybe—that's what I'd go for. There's a back door with a clear view down the strip. Those huts are two or three feet clear of the ground. If I can make the last in the line, I can move down the rest and listen out for them. If you work round a bit so you can see the front walls and doors you may have a clear shot. Set your M1 on auto. And sight down fully—it's only fifty-yard range. If I hear them in the huts, I'll put a short burst up through the floor. That should start them moving out of the front door, giving you a clear shot. If you miss, they'll be under the hut, looking for me."

"My God, Don . . ."

"You said it. Pork. You think you can handle this?"

"I can handle it."

By God, Carter thought amazedly, I think he can, too. He moved off to the right, Colin to the left, crawling with the M1 across his forearms, the way he'd seen it done in many a movie. Under the first hut the air was cool and moist, away from the sun. Carter sat up, head bowed under the floor, listening.

Silence.

Maybe he'd guessed wrong . . . maybe Macbain was miles away. Try the next hut. . . . He got moving again, body sliding very slowly over the rotted vegetation, heading for the bright avenue of sunshine between the buildings. Carefully, he started across the gap. Behind him, he heard the faintest creak and found time to think about dying before the weight landed solidly on his back, flattening him across his rifle, ramming his face and mouth into the dirt. He tensed, then erupted in a volcanic surge of energy, smashing aside the reversed pistol swung by the soldier. He had a glimpse of green cloth and staring oblique eyes before a hurtling body hit the Vietnamese from one side and the weight came free, leaving Carter gasping.

Colin, later, confessed he had no real idea of what happened: when he saw the soldier jump Carter from the veranda, a red fog seemed to swim before his eyes. There were clouds of dust and a heaving body under him, and he had a forearm under the man's chin, a knee in the small of his back; his right hand found his left, forming a bar of immense strength. He pulled back savagely; heard

92

a crack, felt the man jerk spasmodically and dissolve into immobility.

He lay motionless on top of the green-clad body, chin resting on a still shoulder, great shudders passing down his body in waves; hands were pulling at his arms, a voice in his ear. "All right, boy . . . easy, now . . . you can let go. Colin—it's finished."

He turned his head. Carter knelt close by, pushing him clear of the body. Colin rolled onto his back, looking up at the clear blue of the sky, tears welling; he didn't know if he was crying for himself, or for what he had done.

Carter rolled the body of the soldier under the hut, reached up onto the veranda and brought down the Kalashnikov with the curved magazine and the exaggerated front sight. The boy needed time to adjust. Waiting, Carter squatted in the shadow, staring round at the panorama of waving grass, trees swaying in the wind along the strip, the noises of birds. It all looked so damned peaceful—and menacing.

Macbain had known they would come looking for him and had left a booby trap: a Vietnamese soldier, a deserter along for the easy money the American had promised. Colin sat up and stared with dazed eyes at the pair of dirty jungle boots sticking out into the sunshine. He looked away quickly, shuffled over to Carter, sat down, rubbing his right arm.

"It aches," he said wonderingly.

The pilot grinned. "I'm not surprised. Good work, Col. That's twice you've saved my bacon. I won't forget."

"What about Macbain?"

"That," Carter said grimly, "is a good question. He's likely not here, but we'll check the place out just in case."

Twenty minutes later they were in the mess hut, wondering what to do next. Both were uncomfortably aware that despite their search, Macbain could be nearby in the bush. While Carter made coffee, Colin was near the window on watch.

"Don! Macbain. He's out there. With Liane."

"*What?*" Carter came out of the galley like a prowling tiger, and crossed to the window.

The big man had his left arm round Liane, pulling her close to him. With his right hand, he jammed the barrel of the .45 up under her chin, forcing her head back at an acute angle. A white-toothed grin split the tanned face a hundred yards away.

"You hear me in there?"

Carter kept his eyes glued to Macbain. "I hear you."

"I wanna talk. Truce—unnerstand?" Macbain yelled.

The pilot set his teeth, picked up the M1, checked it, walked out onto the veranda where he and Liane had sat watching so many sunsets. Macbain urged the girl forward brutally.

"Listen, fella, you answer a few questions, or I'll kill the girl and take my chance. You read me?"

"You're doing the talking," Carter said harshly.

"That firing—my team?"

"—that was," the pilot said, with some satisfaction.

Macbain scowled. "And my man here?"

"Gone to join his friends."

The American nodded. "For an old guy and a kid, you've done OK. I guess you saw us come down yesterday?"

"We saw you, Macbain. Cut it short."

The big man started. "How come you know my name?"

"I was . . . handy, when you talked to Tran."

"Seems I underestimated the problem."

"Go easy on that girl!" Carter's voice was filled with venom.

Macbain caught the inflexion and scowled. "Listen, don't push it too hard, Limey. You want this broad back in one piece, right?"

"Yes, damn you!"

"OK. That DC3—any chance of fixing it?"

"I'm no engineer. How would I know?"

"On account of you've been spending most of your time in that hangar—we've been watching for a week while we looked for a way down. We all need to get out, right? And I've got the girl."

"Don't bank on it," Carter said heavily. "You have to sleep some time, and there's two of us."

Macbain said nastily, "I could soon set those odds right. Look, I'll do a trade: I let the girl go, and we work together to get out of here. And we split the money down the middle. Deal?"

Carter said bluntly, "No deal. Don't get any stupid ideas that that girl means anything to me—you want to kill Liane right now, you go ahead. But you'll go the same way ten seconds later. And try to move away, I'll kill you both myself. I don't have many years left, maybe you'll be doing me a favour, killing me. But you won't walk away from here. Because the boy's got a gun on you too, Macbain. Right, Colin?"

"I'm here, Don."

Macbain scowled. It all seemed totally unreal, Carter thought, standing here with a loaded gun in his hand, on a day when he had killed six or seven men already. Was it really only a few brief months ago that he was drinking himself to death in Hampshire pubs?

There was so much now that he wanted to do, *needed* to do. Liane's eyes were staring at him accusingly, and time seemed to slow down, stop with a shudder.

FEW PEOPLE REALIZE how fast a large elephant can travel in the charge. With no warning, Khan burst from the trees fifty yards away from Macbain, legs going like pistons, ears spread wide, tail ramrod-straight, trunk uplifted. And as he came he bellowed in fury, the trumpet call echoing round the valley.

The big American jerked his head round, stood transfixed. Dropping the girl, he used both hands to fire the .45, but it was like using a peashooter to stop an express train. Great jagged wounds appeared on Khan's head and trunk; the gun was empty now and Macbain hurled the weapon at the raging beast, then turned to run.

The elephant caught him in mid-stride, a single fat coil of trunk snaked round his waist, and he was lifted off his feet, legs kicking frantically, while Khan half skidded to a halt on the very edge of the runway strip. The bull trumpeted again, brought the man to earth, holding him down firmly. With almost ponderous ease and lack of haste, it bent at the front knees, and Macbain disappeared from view into the long grass. Carter heard a single, searing howl of agony, abruptly cut off; then he walked stiffly towards Liane, a frail figure down on one knee in the dust. . . .

THEY FOUND DEBBY stumbling through the river shallows on her way back to camp. In the late evening, when Carter's trembling had subsided and Colin had returned from his solitary communion with himself, the girl filled in the details. She had moved uphill, away from the tail section, to see what she could see in the valley; meanwhile Macbain had moved in quickly, caught Liane and hustled her away. Debby had heard her screams, but could do nothing to help.

Carter lit a cigarette. "We've been incredibly lucky," he said, "and that's not detracting from what everyone did. I think it may well be the end of it. Macbain left one man up on top, who pulled the rope up when the firing started; but none of his men were regular soldiers. Macbain had a deal of some sort with the other one, Tran. All in all, I doubt if anyone will be looking for them."

Debby said tiredly, "What about the one left up above?"

"He's alone, up in the mountains, with nowhere to go and all his friends gone. I shouldn't lose any sleep over him. How Macbain expected to get the money out undetected, I don't know—maybe he had a helicopter waiting somewhere. It doesn't matter."

They sat round the mess table, watching his face. "All the same," he went on, "we should move as fast as we can on the aeroplane and get out of here as soon as possible, just in case Macbain has friends who'll come looking for him.

"And one more thing. I'm not given to making speeches, but I want to tell you, Col, in front of the girls, that you did well today. Not many lads of your age would have managed to do what you did. But I don't want you to get hung up over the deaths of those men. You saw what they were like and you know what they would have done. We had no choice. End of speech."

Debby came round the table, eyes brimming. She slipped an arm round Carter's shoulder. "You're a very nice person, Donald. Thank you for saying that about this great lout here—we'll never hear the last of it, I'm sure. You'll have the best meal we can fix for you."

Carter got up, jerked his head at Colin. "Come on, lad. Let's leave them to it. We've got a different job to do."

Outside on the veranda, Colin stopped. "What job?" he asked.

"A little digging," the pilot said sombrely. "Let's get this place cleaned up."

LIANE SAID QUIETLY, "Debby, will you be all right if I leave you for a little time?"

"Why, yes. What is it?"

96

"I must go to Khan—he is hurt. He saved us all today, I think. Perhaps I can help him now."

"Liane, let me come with you."

"No. This I must do myself. It is strange . . . there is an understanding, a bond, between Khan and myself. . . ."

She shook her head, confused and disturbed, and walked slowly out of the hut.

Chapter Eight

September drifted into October on the makeshift calendar in the hangar office, and as the list of outstanding work on the Dakota dwindled, so too their memories of those fearful days when evil burst into their paradise, faded.

The ingenuity of the girls and Colin surprised Carter every day: when the replacement wheels had been assembled, they brought Khan into the hangar and positioned his broad back under the wing, edging him forward until the old wheels lifted clear of the ground and Carter could slide the screw jack into position. The beast's wounds, lovingly tended by Liane, were healing cleanly. Colin rigged up a spare gas burner under an empty forty-gallon drum to produce a supply of hot water, and the girls set about removing the layers of encrusted guano on the upper surfaces of the aeroplane. Slowly the original paintwork began to emerge, the freight cabin was cleaned out, scrubbed spotless the bullion and cash boxes replaced.

Carter had been surprised at how little impact his discovery of the American money had had on the others. Perhaps it was because of their total lack of news from the outside world: everything beyond the valley assumed an aura of unreality.

There were, on the other hand, serious problems which Carter concealed from them. One was food. Their supplies of canned goods were all but exhausted; the local deer and other animals were too wary of the M1 rifle to come within three miles of camp; the rice in their paddy field was finished, the natural supplies of fruit waning with the season; increasingly, Carter had to turn to the dwindling "K" rations. If the aeroplane failed them and they had to walk out (assuming they could find an exit) the rations wouldn't be sufficient for any long journey.

But they worked on steadily enough—until the day Carter's worst fears were realized.

IT BEGAN much like any other. It was noticeably cooler in the mornings now, and the monsoon was drawing to a close, the rains lighter and less frequent. Carter had found an engine service manual for the Pratt and Whitney, and he and Colin were working on the starboard engine; they were deeply involved in fitting a new cylinder, high on the front bank of cylinders.

The rocker gear and cylinder head were easily freed, but the piston itself was seized solid in the bore. They toiled for an hour or more, cleaning the bore with light oil and emery cloth. Suddenly Colin looked up, head turned towards the hangar door. "Wait a minute . . . it's Debby!" The boy was gone through the sliding doors, with Carter following ten yards behind. Out in the sunshine, far across the strip, Debby screamed wildly.

"Something bit Liane's leg . . . *There!*" Debby's voice cracked.

Carter knelt down, and Liane sagged against his shoulder, grey-faced, eyes half closed. There was a dark blue patch around two deep punctures on her right calf. Carter reached up and tore away the loop of cord Colin used to secure his trousers. He tied it round the soft thigh, ripping the remnants of the skirt out of the way. Then he poked a piece of wood through the loop and started tightening the tourniquet savagely.

"Knife, Col—quickly, dammit. Debby, get some hot water organized. And something for bandages. *Move.*" He bent forward, knife poised. "Hold tight, Liane . . . this'll hurt. . . ."

Gritting his teeth, Carter cut deeply across the bite mark, cut again at right angles, and placed his mouth over the wound. He sucked, spat, sucked again, to extract as much blood as possible. Liane screamed, thrashing about, until Colin threw his weight on her.

"Good lad . . . hold her, now. Almost finished."

The blood tasted salty, with a nauseating metallic rancidity that turned Carter's stomach. Debby returned with drinking water. *Thank God . . . rinse mouth, start again.*

At last he raised his head, sick and shaking. "Debby—down to the hangar. Whisky in the office filing cabinet . . ."

Liane's face was pale, with a deep greyish tint. She was still now, eyes closed tight. The heartbeat was a faint flutter.

Debby returned with a bottle and the first-aid kit from the aeroplane. Carter released the tourniquet, allowing the blood to flow again, poured whisky liberally over the wound. Liane groaned.

"We have to get her in now, Colin. Take her feet. Ready . . ."

When the hut was close by, he braced himself for a final effort. "All right, calm down, Debby. You're not going to help her by panicking. Get that door open. Fine."

They lifted her onto the bed and wrapped her in blankets, for despite the warmth of the evening, she had begun to shiver violently, making strange, small animal noises that gripped his heart in a vice. She was drenched with sweat, yet her skin was cold.

He straightened up, looked at the boy and girl; it seemed to him that they had aged perceptibly that day. They were ashen-faced.

"Debby," Carter asked, "what was it? Did you see?"

"No, there was something round her ankle. She kicked, and it flew off into the grass."

Carter bit his lip. "Colour?"

"Black, dark brown . . . I don't know!" Debby ended in a wail of terror. "She's going to die, Donald! She'll die. . . ."

Carter smiled. "Take it easy, now. The worst's over, with luck." He sat down heavily, while Colin ran a damp cloth over Liane's face. "I wish to God I knew more about snakebite. I know she mustn't have stimulants—her heart rate's high enough already. Deb, make her some diluted canned milk, plenty of sugar."

After Debby left them, Colin looked Carter squarely in the eye. "She's going to die, isn't she? We can't do much."

"Shut up," Carter said. "She's going to make it, you hear?" He knelt by the bed, rubbing the girl's cheeks, wrists, talking to her. Terrified to see how quickly she was losing body fluid, he forced her to take the diluted milk. If she became dehydrated . . . He made Debby and Colin bring in relays of soft-drink bottles filled with hot water, loaded the slender figure with blankets, made a fire in the stone hearth.

Colin bit his lip. "Don? What do you think?"

"I'm past thinking, but I want you and Debby to get some rest. I'll need a break later—someone will have to take over from me, so get going."

Alone, he reached for a cigarette, drank a cup of the coffee Debby had made for him and sat by the bed while the single Tilley lamp hissed and glowed on the table. At intervals, he removed Liane's bandages, washed the wound.

After midnight, her condition began to deteriorate. Her hands became restless, fluttering on the blanket, her head turning incessantly. Just after one o'clock she began to run a fever, her skin dry and scaly to the touch and with an unpleasant sheen. When he lifted an eyelid, he was shocked: the pupil was enormously dilated.

Exhausted, he worked on steadily, sponging down her body, checking the wound, dripping a little cool water between her lips. In those dark hours before dawn, her eyes were glazed and delirium possessed her; she spoke jerkily, frenziedly, for minutes at a time, in a language he couldn't understand.

It seemed to him that she was slipping away slowly, into a land and a time far remote from him. Her heart beat slowed down until Carter began to fear it would stop altogether. He knew that unless something was done, she would drift away into the long night. Agonizing that, in his ignorance, he was helping her to her death, he poured a dose of neat brandy down her throat and began rubbing her chilled frame with all his strength, using a dry, rough blanket. Ceaselessly he talked to her in a low voice, urging her to fight on, calling her back from the brink.

As the first, tentative glow of dawn stained the window, colour began stealing back into the pale, almost translucent skin, and her breathing became easier. Now Carter called in Colin and Debby, had them make a great pot of black, sweet coffee, and hot soup made from "K" ration canned meat. Liane opened her eyes.

"Donald . . ." He sat by the bed, holding her hand, swallowing hard. Too much damned pepper in that soup, he thought irritably; makes your eyes water. Debby too was shaking away the tears, smiling defiantly, and Colin was beaming as if he would never stop.

"Liane, how do you feel?"

"Tired . . . so tired, Donald. But it is so nice to be back . . ."

101

"Back?" said Carter, confused.

The girl on the bed lifted her hand, laid it on his own. "I have been on a journey, Donald—such a long journey! I remember cities on fire, great armies fighting, the elephants on the plain, and a tunnel . . ." Liane turned her head on the pillow. "I remember now: the ring . . . and the cave behind the fall. . . . Such unhappy dreams, Donald . . ." Her head sagged a little, and Debby cried out in alarm.

"It's all right," Carter said softly. "She's sleeping now. And when she wakes, she'll be much better." He stood up, swayed and put out a hand to Colin to steady himself.

"Easy, Don! You've been up all night, remember."

"Yes—yes, I have." The point seemed a little academic to Carter. A great weariness was breaking over him like a tidal wave. He stumbled towards the other bed, falling face down, asleep before he could even comprehend the fact.

Colin found a blanket, covered the lean, suntanned body, and stared down at the sleeping man with a feeling of deep compassion. Then, having made sure that both he and Liane were sleeping peacefully, Colin and Debby went out into the morning sunshine, down to the river to bathe and to prepare Khan for the day's work.

THREE WEEKS LATER, Carter was trying to come to grips with the knowledge that all his good intentions had evaporated, just like so many others before them. They were beginning to have trouble finding things to do on the Dakota; very soon, he'd be forced to move the old wreck outside and try to start the engines. But before things got to that stage, he promised himself he'd start planning his walkout. Once he got past that rock face at the fall, he reckoned he could make it in three or four weeks, but he needed supplies. He started squirrelling away candy bars, even whole "K" rations; spent time surreptitiously looking at maps.

In the beginning, he'd sworn no one would get him up in an aeroplane again, not after that 707. But now that Colin and Debby had almost cleared a usable strip by driving the elephant up and down towing a log, the proposition had become horribly feasible.

It hadn't helped, the way Liane had blossomed after getting over that snakebite. The kids had made sure she ate properly, took plenty of rest, but the trouble was in Liane herself: the way she kept looking at Carter with a troubled, almost puzzled air. When she came into the hut that evening, he was totally unprepared.

"Donald?"

"Liane, come on in. The kids back yet?" Colin and Debby had taken Khan up to the waterfall pool for their evening swim.

She shook her head, standing in the doorway, the orange disc of the sun behind her. Shading his eyes, he could see the clean, sharp outline of her body through the worn, patched skirt, as she stood with a slim hand on the door, the long strand of black hair tied at her neck, hanging free over her right breast. He thought achingly that he had never seen her look so lovely.

She said, "Not yet. They are swimming. You want to talk?"

"OK," he said lightly. "How's your leg?"

"It is good now. It hurts only a little when I walk."

He grinned. "That's fine. What's on your mind?"

"This." She opened her hand. Carter's stomach contracted; he thought he'd hidden those fuses where no one could ever find them.

"Why do you do these things, Donald? The aeroplane is nearly ready—otherwise you would not have done these bad things. Making the wheels to go flat; hiding little pieces like this . . . why do you wish to stay here until you grow old and die?"

He shook his head, aware that she would never understand.

Liane's eyes were hard. "The aeroplane is ready; we have found much money—enough to make us all rich; we have fixed the airstrip with Khan, there are few things left to do. There is only one reason we cannot go: Carter is afraid."

He stared at her, mutely, his mouth working. Then, "All right. Maybe so. You and the kids want to make it out of here alive. But I *know* we can't make it. Liane—if there was even one chance in a million we'd make it, I'd try it. You have to understand that."

Her mouth twisted. "You say this, Donald Carter. But I say you lie. It is because you are afraid to fly again."

Carter shook his head in frustration. "Will you listen to me, just for a moment? If we get the engines started, we've no brakes to keep the plane straight until it flies. So I have to use the rudder—when we're moving fast enough. But at the beginning, the tail will be down, so I won't be able to see the strip. You follow that?"

"Go on, please."

"Right. With a wide strip, it might be possible . . ."

Liane shrugged. "The strip can be widened, Donald."

"Never mind. There's worse to come." He took a deep breath. "If we get off the ground, we'll need at least five minutes to get enough height to leave the valley, but if an engine stops in that time, we crash. Understand?"

"I am listening."

He stared at her, disgruntled. "OK. And making a single-engined landing without brakes or flap on a narrow strip is suicide. Now— the nearest place to go is Khota Baru, in Malaysia. It's five hundred miles from here, most of it over water. If a motor stops then, we go into the sea, without life jackets or rafts, and the water's full of sharks."

"Is there much more?"

"Yes, damn it. I could list a dozen more: engine on fire, fuel leaks, controls giving way; burst tyres on takeoff; runaway propeller . . . Add it all up and you get only one answer: stay here, we live; try it your way and we die. Very unpleasantly. All of us. You want to load all that responsibility on me, girl?"

She leaned forward, laid a hand on his arm. "Donald," she said very softly, "I know all these things. You have said them before, many times. There are risks—but do you not see we would rather die that way than die of loneliness here? Colin and Debby miss their families. I know you hate me—"

"Hold it right there," Carter said quickly. "You've got that all wrong, you know. I could never hate you."

"I think so. For the way I sent you away that night. I know you wanted me . . . I wanted you, too, Donald. But my thoughts were wrong."

"I know why you changed your mind. I'm twice your age, Liane. I don't blame you at all." He was finding it difficult to speak clearly.

She smiled then, white teeth gleaming in the fading lights. "Such fools, men. Why cannot you understand? Since we met on the Boeing, since you saved us, cared for us, Col and Debby think of you as their father. It was the same with me. All my life, I had had only memories of my father, a photograph or two—until you came

104

to care for me as my father would. That night I was two people: part of me a woman, wanting you so much, and part a daughter."

At last Carter began to understand. He held her hand tightly, in silence. She was very close to tears, and he sat up on the bed, pulled her close to him. Time became unimportant, and he wiped away the salt tears, smoothed back the straying hair with a gentle hand, diffidently, as if he were almost afraid to touch.

He said hoarsely, "I don't want to be a father to you, Liane. I wanted you from the first moment. You were so kind—but I knew all you could feel for an old man like me was pity."

She sat up, amused. "Old? You are not old, Donald! Your mind is as bright as the sun; and since we came to this place, you have become strong and hard." Absently she drew a long forefinger down his chest, and his breath caught quickly in his throat.

"Listen, my love," she said very softly, "soon we must fly away. We may be killed, but I do not want to die until you have loved me."

"Liane—if you only knew. Why are you doing this? You must know I want you, but . . ." His voice died away, his uncertainty and disbelief yielding to the dawning realization that a miracle might happen.

Her eyes widened. "And you must know that I have loved you for many months, Donald. As I have never loved anyone in my life. Women of the East find love only once, did you not know?"

Carter laughed deeply. "I love to hear you talk this way, Liane. I always wanted you—but I was afraid . . ."

She laid a cool hand on his cheek. "You cannot be afraid now, Donald." Gazing into his blue eyes, she knew he was lost, afraid of being afraid, without confidence—but she knew she could help him. If she could but give this man back the desire to live, to be young again, what could they not achieve together?

AFTER SUPPER ONE EVENING some days later, the conversation, as always, turned to means of escape from the valley. They had been over every inch of it, looking for a way out, and they were all feeling claustrophobic, knowing there was still perhaps two or three weeks' work left to do on the aeroplane.

"I forgot to tell you something," Colin said importantly. "I think I saw a cave under the waterfall. That day Liane found her ring. I mean, if that stream comes down from the top of the plateau, there may be a way up to the top through the cave."

Quite suddenly Liane said in a small voice, "The way back is blocked."

Carter shot an uneasy glance at her. "What was that you said, Liane?"

She said diffidently, "There is a cave. But the way to the top of the mountain is closed."

Colin and Debby started speaking together, excitedly, but Carter held up a warning hand, frowning.

"Shut up, you two. Liane, what exactly do you mean?"

She smiled. "It is nothing . . . only a dream I had, after the snake . . ." Her voice tailed away, as if she lacked the confidence to go on.

Carter nodded. "I remember you were saying all sorts of things. None of it made much sense. What can you remember?"

"Only that there was a cavern filled with black water, and a second cavern beneath the first, with—oh, Donald, it sounds mad. . . ."

"Go on, please," he said intently.

"The second cave had a window in the end—a great window made of green glass. And there was someone . . . someone . . . I can't remember any more."

Carter looked at her very hard. "OK. Don't worry about it. Tomorrow morning we'll go and take a look."

THEY REACHED THE POOL early in the morning, before the sun began to roast the valley mercilessly. Carter and the boy carried large coils of white parachute cord, as strong as rope ten times its thickness, plus bolts, hammers—anything they thought might be of use in scaling a cliff. Carter proposed that he and Colin should swim under the fall and examine the cave Colin claimed to have seen. This suggestion, however, was immediately shouted down by Liane and Debby.

"All right," Carter said resignedly "I'm outvoted. We all swim out to the fall, right? Just stay close to me."

Ten minutes later, all four of them stood in a wet and shivering row at the base of the rock face, their backs to the cascade, craning their necks upwards.

"You could be right, Colin," Carter said critically. "The fall starts about three hundred feet up. The cave—if it is a cave—is fifty or sixty feet below it, slightly to the left. It doesn't look too bad a climb—not absolutely vertical, plenty of foot- and handholds. Suppose we tackle the drier section there, over to the left, then work our way across?"

"You're the boss," Colin yelled, above the thunderous roar of plunging water.

THE CLIMB WAS PHYSICALLY arduous, but straightforward. Colin went up thirty feet, belayed the rope around a rock snag and waited until Carter was beside him, red-faced and breathing hard, but otherwise in good shape. Then the boy went on again. At the end of the fifth pitch, they stopped on a broad ledge to rest, to wave down to the girls and survey the situation.

Carter stared up and across. "The cave must be behind that overhang. We can start angling in soon. I don't know how the hell people can do this sort of thing for a hobby."

Twenty minutes later, Colin climbed up onto the ledge, got three turns of the rope round another lump of rock and helped Carter over the last few feet. They waved frantically to the girls below, then turned to the cave opening. The ledge was smooth red sandstone, with a central trough which had once accommodated the stream which formed the cavern. The ledge was covered in places by a film of mud formed by spray, and it felt gritty underfoot. It was some twelve feet wide and seven high at the entrance, widening considerably inside. Slowly they moved forward and paused, allowing their eyes to adjust.

Against the left-hand wall what had once been a long row of sandalwood boxes had disintegrated with age. Protected from the winds, they had formed vague piles of grey dust through which countless stars seemed to beckon. The pilot walked forward slowly, went down on one knee.

"Oh my God . . ." he said, in a stunned voice. "Colin . . ."

Some of the boxes crumbled into dust at a touch; Carter brushed away the detritus carefully. Each contained a specific type of jewel.

He recognized the translucence of emeralds, the blood-red of rubies, the silver sheen of pearls—the sheer volume of the stones was mind-shattering. His fingers scrabbled in the encrusted debris of centuries and he saw that he was holding a marble-sized black pearl of such lustre that his eyes seemed to be drawn into its very depths. His mind reeled with the unimaginable wealth assembled here. He could hear Colin, alongside, gasp in astonishment, half mouthing words of disbelief.

In a fever of excitement, Carter moved on down the line of boxes and came to a double mountain of emeralds, flanked by a scattered hoard of great Burmese rubies—heavy, fat-bellied wonders, some of them exquisitely carved. The impact was overpowering. With but a fraction of the great store exposed, he rose to his feet, walked out onto the ledge near the green curtain of falling water that hissed past, filtering the sunlight like a stained glass window in a cathedral. *Glass? Window?* He remembered Liane and her dream, and shivered involuntarily. There was something about this place. . . .

Colin came out to join him, his face pale and disturbed. Neither of them would ever be the same again, thought Carter. He grasped the boy's arm.

"Colin, we should bring Liane and Debby up here—but I'm worried about Liane."

"About that dream of hers, you mean? I had already thought of that. You remember she said the way was closed? How about taking a look at the back of the cave? It's just possible that . . ." He left the words unfinished, hanging on the air.

The older man grinned, a strained expression on his face. "There's plenty of time for that. In any case, we'll need light of some kind—a Tilley lamp."

"OK, I'll go down for the girls. I'll lash up some hand ropes on the way down. You'll be OK?"

"Why shouldn't I be?"

Colin smiled. "Any idea what all that stuff is worth?"

"A hell of a lot. About a hundred times more than the Crown Jewels. Go on—get on with it."

Time passed as if in a dream for Carter. In the half-light of the cave he worked busily, moving the scattered heaps of jewels into neat piles on the smooth rock, clearing away rotted wood and

108

debris. In a corner he noticed something odd, blew the dust away carefully and uncovered the rotting remains of some garments and a curved bronze sword jammed into a jewelled scabbard.

When the girls finally gained the ledge, Carter was cleaning the encrusted dirt and filth from a magnificent statue of a god, twenty inches high. The multi-armed figure stood in awesome majesty, surrounded by an arc of lambent green flames—huge emeralds set in a filigree of gold wire like a halo.

Carter turned to see Liane staring at the statue with a face as pale as death. He rose, reached her just as she slumped to the floor of the cave in a dead faint.

"Debby, quickly—there's a gold bowl over there. Get some water from the fall."

With infinite care, he wiped the sweat and dust from Liane's face and poured a little of the fresh cold water into her mouth. Presently she opened her eyes and stared up at him, uncomprehending for a moment. Then she looked over his shoulder into the cave, and remembered.

"It's all right, Liane," Carter whispered, as he helped the Asian girl to her feet.

She stood immobile for a long time, staring at the cave and its contents. "It is the place from my dream, Donald. What is it that you have found? Colin talked about treasure. . . ."

"Come and see."

Liane went with him, kneeling to run slim fingers through the gleaming pyramids of riches. He brought the statue of the many-armed god to show her, and she nodded calmly.

"This I have seen in school, and in museums in my country, Donald. It is Siva—the old god, before Buddha came to save us. And these words around the base—they are in the old language of Cambodia."

"This is all from your country?"

"I think we are in Cambodia now," she said calmly. "In the high mountains the border is never marked or disputed. And I will tell you one more thing, Donald—it is no accident that we are here."

"That's crazy talk, Liane—how could that be? That damned dream . . . that snake . . ."

She smiled tiredly. "You in the West, Donald, you do not believe. You *cannot* believe, because it would make nonsense of everything you learned as a child. Your coming to Singapore so that you could save us from the Boeing . . . the way in which we came to the valley . . . my dream . . . all steps on the way."

He turned his head to look at Colin and Debby. They had drawn close for mutual comfort, disturbed by the presence of something quite beyond their experience.

He shook his head stubbornly. "I can't accept that, Liane, You're saying that the future is already fixed, unchangeable? That time itself . . . no, I don't believe it. I *won't* believe it."

Liane laid a hand on his arm. "Then do not believe, Donald. Just accept the proof that lies before you. This is a royal treasure, Donald, from the temples of old Angkor. Some day maybe we will know the truth about how it came to be here. But for now it is enough that we have found it." She looked past him, to the green curtain beyond the cave. "It grows dark. A storm, I think."

Carter pulled himself together. "You're right. We'd better get back as quick as we can. Another day we'll come and see if there's a way out. Let's take the statue along for now, and leave the rest here. After all, nobody's going to steal it while we're gone."

Hurriedly they began to prepare for the descent, the statue of the god wrapped in Carter's shirt and tied firmly to Colin's back. None of them would get much sleep tonight, that was for sure, thought Carter, as he worked his way down the rock face. He began to wonder about the centuries that must have elapsed since long-dead hands brought the treasure to this place. How long ago? Before Columbus sailed west? Before the Armada sailed?

He was still in a state of mild shock, combined with euphoria. It was impossible simply to say that they were rich: wealth of this magnitude required a whole new definition. But it was not only about wealth that he was thinking as he made the descent; it was also about responsibility.

Reaching the end of the scree, Carter gained the rocky shore of the pool and stopped, watching Colin help Debby over the last pitch. He had an uncomfortable feeling that someone, somewhere, was watching, would be watching, his every move. Easy, Carter, he told himself angrily, you'll be seeing ghosts next.

110

LOOKING BACK, CARTER couldn't recall ever having worked so hard in his life. Using Colin as a fitter's mate, he returned to the task of the cylinder replacement, and spent three nerve-racking days refitting the new cylinder over the rings of the piston—a nightmare, because they had no replacement rings, and to break even one would spell disaster. All day he toiled, drenched in sweat, with Liane constantly at his side, making him eat salt tablets and drink huge quantities of water to prevent dehydration. If it hadn't been for the rotting and mouldy manuals he found in the hangar office, the whole thing would have been quite impossible.

His salvation lay in a profound gift for improvisation. He coaxed the old cylinder off the piston with a mixture of oil, petrol and judicious swings of a hammer; he removed the spark plugs of both engines one at a time, cleaning and setting the gaps; he drained the oil from each engine, cleaned out the filters and replenished the oil.

The landing flaps were jammed down: it took him four days to dismantle the "up" system, clean out the coagulated oil from pipelines and valves, refuel the system and bleed it free of air.

Carter drove them all like slaves now, and himself hardest of all. There were times when Liane, taking a late cup of coffee down to the starkly lit hangar, would find him on his knees against a main landing-gear wheel fast asleep, a wrench still in his hand.

Slowly, the outstanding items on his list were being whittled down, yet still there were tasks that seemed never-ending: the patient tracing of control runs through the structure; checking, greasing, tightening, replacing, tensioning, testing.

The girls were a revelation to Carter: each time he left the hangar, the strip seemed a little longer, a few feet wider, and from his work on the aeroplane he could see them far off down the strip in the hot sun, urging on Khan and the massive log he towed, mowing down the short brush and stubble.

Through it all, they never lost faith. They talked, not of "if" they made it, but "when". In his darker moments, when Carter lay awake, too tired to sleep, he thought fearfully of the hundreds of miles of jungle and sea, the stark, precipitous hills, the thousand-and-one things that could—and probably would—go wrong. But he worked on, in a constant nausea of panic and foreboding, like a condemned man forced to dig his own grave.

111

Chapter Nine

Carter opened the side window, peered down at Colin, who was getting ready to throw his weight on the turning handle.

"Contact port, Col. Wind her up, boy!"

It hardly seemed right calling Colin a boy now. There was nothing of the schoolboy left in those hard hands, knotted muscles, that set jaw. Steadily the sound of the inertia starter wound up from a low groan to a highpitched whine, but Colin was tiring visibly; Carter yelled "*Contact!*" and pulled the "engage" toggle. The noise changed down in pitch, the propeller turning in brief kicks, smartly at first as Carter primed like mad; then, almost at the last moment, the motor fired, stopped, fired again and stopped for good.

"She's almost there, Col. One more time!" Carter yelled.

This time she fired almost at once; Carter primed furiously, catching it on the throttle. The motor caught, roaring, smoke pouring aft as the over-rich mixture settled down. "*Go, you great buzzard. . . . Go!*"

Below, Colin was turning cartwheels, laughing like a maniac, and Carter saw Liane come running across from the hut, summoned by the noise. The speed built up to 1000 revs, and Carter chopped it back a little to a steady tick-over. He leaned out of the window, stabbed a finger at the other engine.

Trouble. Four times they tried to start the port motor; four times they failed. Eventually Colin staggered off to one side, falling exhausted in a patch of long grass. The fifth time, it caught, fired, but ran very unevenly. Carter switched off the twin ignition switches one at a time to test the dual ignition system—and on the port magneto, the revs fell sharply, from 800 to 450. He groaned; spark plugs, almost certainly, or maybe magneto contact points. Trouble, whichever way you looked at it.

The hydraulic pressure built up satisfactorily, but there was no way of testing either flap or undercarriage systems, since he had isolated the return systems in each case. Everything had to work right first time. Still, it was an enormously encouraging start. Switching off the engines, he climbed down to ground level to be met by a babel of joy and enthusiasm.

112

"So far, so good. Still some work to do on that port engine. But they work—at least they work!"

Liane flung her arms round his neck. "Donald—we go home soon? Tomorrow?"

"Optimist," he mocked. "A week, maybe more. Besides, we've got to bring the treasure down from the cave first, and that'll be two or three days' work, at least. How much more to do on the strip, Debby?"

"One more full-length cut, Donald. You'll have your hundred-yard width by tomorrow night."

He stared round at the eager young faces. "OK. Now, let's not get too excited. There's a hell of a lot to do yet. We have to improve that towing gear. Khan will have to pull the Dak down to the end of the strip. There's a few more things to check, but we can start loading in a day or two. Put everything we load into that square I've marked on the floor, Colin; that should keep our centre of gravity within limits." He stood silently for a moment, looking at the Dakota. There was a ghost of a chance that they would make it.

THE PAIR OF MIGS flashed over the valley from end to end, soaring up into the cloudless sky in tight formation. At the top of the climb they slowed, went into line astern, rolled over the top gently and came down in a long, slow orbit, tracking along the escarpment.

Carter yelled frantically, "Under the aircraft, everybody!"

Flat on his belly between the wheels, he could see only the top of the waving elephant grass and a glimpse of Khan's back in the distance. Thank God! Liane had gone to ground. But his heart was like lead within him: those boys were no amateurs—they'd spot the aeroplane, the cleared strip, put two and two together . . .

Two passes . . . three . . . Carter was terrified that they would do a strafing run which would destroy the aircraft, and the three of them beneath it. But after the third pass, the Migs drifted eastwards in a steep climb towards the rim of the escarpment.

Long minutes passed . . .

Behind him, Liane said fearfully, "Is not good, Donald?"

"Is bloody awful. They were Vietnamese. That last man of Macbain's, the one left up on the rim—maybe he got through, spread the word."

Debby said tensely, "What'll happen now, Donald?"

"I don't know. Maybe a ground party trekking in, maybe helicopters. Most likely they'll drop paras on the strip."

"How long have we got, Don?" asked Colin.

"No time at all, I reckon. If they use paras, I'd guess tomorrow morning at the latest." He hesitated, terrified of what he was about to suggest. "We have to go—first light tomorrow morning. I'll have to work all night clearing that port engine, and you'll have to do what you can on the strip." Carter stared at the stricken faces around him. "Look," he said firmly, "we've been expecting this ever since we got here. What we didn't expect is that the people who found us wouldn't want us around to tell the tale. All they're after is what's in those boxes. We *have* to go now, whatever shape we're in."

Later, setting up the aluminium platform round the port engine, Carter turned to Colin. "This thing could really go bad on us if those Migs come back and catch us after takeoff. We won't stand a chance: they'll blow us away rather than risk us getting away with it. We have to have some sort of surprise ready for them."

"What had you in mind?" There was no apprehension in the boy's voice, only a plain recognition of the emergency.

"It'll take hours to fix this engine. But we do have those Browning automatic rifles. . . ."

"You mean we're going to fight them?"

"Don't panic, it's just an idea. Suppose we rigged up a timber frame, lashed half a dozen BARs into it, to fire straight out of the aft door. With a wire or something, to make them fire all at once. I wonder what those boys would do if they found us? Hack us down right away? Not on your life—they'd want us for propaganda value. Think of the headlines: Americans back in Vietnam . . ."

"That's all very well," Colin said nervously. "You think they're going to steam up alongside and take a look?"

"Why not? The old Dakota doesn't carry guns—they must know that. We may get lucky though—blow at least one of them out of the sky."

"All right, Don." Then suddenly Colin grabbed the pilot's arm savagely. "My God—what about the treasure!"

Carter stared. "I forgot all about that! Well, I'm sorry but there's no time to collect it now, Col. We can take the statue, some-weapons, the American money. Nothing else. Come on, we've a full night ahead of us. First light, remember—no later."

COLIN WOULD NEVER FORGET that last night in the valley. Carter drove them all on relentlessly, as if to atone for his earlier attitude, working them a straight twelve hours until midnight and ending up with a walking inspection carrying a Tilley lamp on a pole. At one in the morning he had Liane bring Khan round to the hangar, ready for towing. At three, he located the ignition problem, an intermittent short circuit in the lead from the switch to the magneto.

At the first thin streamers of light in the east, they hitched up Khan and began the Herculean task of dragging the aeroplane down to the end of the strip. The ground was soft, and they fought for half an hour before Carter finally released the elephant, started the engines and taxied down to the takeoff point, using fuel he could ill afford. Once there, Carter had Colin wedge a piece of wood under one wheel as a chock, belted the starboard engine and got the old aeroplane facing up the strip towards the west.

The girls began ferrying their meagre belongings to the Dakota, riding on Khan's broad back. They had little enough: a few keepsakes, the guitar. The boy handed the statue of Siva up to Carter, who was standing in the cargo hatch: it must have weighed forty-five pounds, and Carter was breathing hard by the time he got it stowed away behind a bulkhead on the flight deck.

"Anything else, Col?" he said anxiously.

"That's the lot—I just have to drag the BARs into position. I hope to God we don't have to use them."

Carter sat in the left-hand seat, settling down, fastening the lap strap. It was a fine, unclouded morning, the sun a half disc above the valley wall. He sat fighting to control his breathing and the pounding of his heart. It was sixteen years since he had flown an aeroplane. And he had no experience of Dakotas at all. Through the windscreen, the strip ahead looked like the back garden path of a suburban house—too short, too narrow, too rough, too everything.

The girls came forward and stood behind him, pale and dark-eyed from lack of sleep. Below, Colin stood legs apart, holding the engine turning handle and staring up at the cockpit.

Carter slid the window open. "All clear?"

"All clear."

"Stand by to start port engine. Priming now . . . turn her over!"

The inertia starter began the long, slow buildup from a bass moan to a highpitched whine. As the speed peaked, Carter yelled "*Contact!*" and yanked the "engage" toggle, priming like fury. The motor turned, fired, missed, backfired, then roared in triumph. Carter heard the girls scream ecstatically behind him, and turned a grimy face to them, smiling wearily.

Starboard now . . . the propeller turned, slowed, turned again. Soon, with both engines at fast tick-over, Colin obeyed Carter's signal, dragged away the chocks, waved frantically at the cockpit and ran for the cargo hatch. Seconds later he was in the cockpit.

"All right, Don?" he screamed above the engine noise.

"Fine. Get the girls set. Liane here beside me, Debby behind to carry messages, you down back. All right, Debby?"

Her eyes were shining, brimming with tears. She nodded, beyond speech. The pilot turned back to Colin, waiting for the engines to reach operating temperature.

"We've a few minutes yet. Got those BARs lined up?"

"Just have to drag them into the doorway."

"Remember what I told you. Pull the string, they all fire. Wedge them in tight, there's a hell of a recoil. Check all the safeties off, like I showed you. And don't fire unless you've got a clear shot—I'll send Debby down to tell you. OK?"

"I . . . I think so, Don."

Carter settled himself in the seat more firmly, glanced briefly at the sun swelling over the valley rim, and took a long, shuddering breath. The moment he had feared all these months was upon him. The great blunt nose of the Dakota obscured most of the strip ahead; he looked through the side window, at the roughly trimmed margin barely fifty yards away. It just couldn't be done. . . . *Couldn't be done*.

He wound on full forward trim to get the tail up as soon as possible, opened up both throttles before he had time to regret anything, and the old aeroplane surged forward, sluggishly at first, wheels ploughing through the debris of grass and brush. He kept his eyes glued to the strip edge, closing one throttle or the other fractionally to keep straight, stick hard forward. No time to look at the speed indicator. Correct direction again. Pedal hard on the rudder . . . no feeling yet. God—nearly overcorrected that time. Engines still running, miracle, thanks Lord, keep going. . . . Was that a hint of reaction in the rudder at last? The tail came up slowly and now he could see the strip—what was left of it. A few hundred yards, no more. He started winding back on the tail trim, keeping the nose straight. Rudder good now, and she felt lighter, bouncing along. Controls dreadfully stiff, but working.

Seventy knots . . . eighty . . . she *wanted* to go, with two hundred yards left. He hauled back viciously on the stick, and the Dakota lifted, bounced, lifted again and they were away and free, the gear coming up. They passed over the end of the strip, the escarpment dead ahead, and Carter rammed on left aileron and rudder, grinding her round in a steeply banked turn, wingtip scraping the treetops, until the river and strip came into view in the top left-hand corner of the windscreen. Now he began to straighten her out, climbing steadily at 120 knots. He yelled dementedly, banging both fists on the control column, grinning madly at Liane, strapped in the right-hand seat. She smiled stiffly as she glanced down to the valley below, her face alive with mixed emotions. Carter turned back to the side window, checking his position. The valley wall was looming up again: he coaxed the old plane round in a more gentle, climbing turn, keeping the engines running flat out. Then he opened the cooling gills a shade, coming out of the turn to parallel the strip once more.

He stared down at the peaceful valley: the tiny base, the stream where he had bathed so often, faithful Khan grazing in the elephant grass, the hut where he had found what he thought never to find again: happiness.

He felt a touch on his shoulder. It was Debby, laughing exuberantly. He winked, shouted above the roar of engines.

"All right, Deb?"

She nodded, beaming. "Yes—it's going to be all right!"

Well, Carter thought happily, it could be a great deal worse. Fifteen hundred feet . . . he pulled back the propeller levers, let the engine speed drop, the noise falling to bearable level. He reefed the Dakota round to a heading of 255 degrees on the emergency compass, set the old-fashioned gyro and rechecked his heading.

Now the rim of the escarpment was receding, becoming just another ridge in a long series stretching far away to the horizon. The forest-covered ridges were divided by steep valleys with sparkling streams. He levelled off at 2,500 feet, throttling back to cruise settings.

He had his head bent over the compass, setting the grid ring, when he heard the sudden thunder of the Migs flashing over the cockpit. They were terrifyingly close. He jerked upright, staring through the front screen, watching them pull ahead, turning to port in a tight pair, in echelon. Carter turned to Debby, his face working with rage and ill-concealed fear. "Get back to Colin—get ready; keep covers on guns and wait. Got it?"

The pilot held his course, shaking with helpless rage. After all that damned work! The dark, fish-like silhouettes drifted astern, turning in again, disappearing from sight behind the tail. Seconds later, they slid back into view on his port beam. Carter noticed that they had full flap down: the Dakota's cruising speed was very close to the stalling speed of the supersonic jets. They were painted silver grey but with no national markings, though they must be Vietnamese; the leader's aircraft had a large black "06" painted on the side. The fighter's clear plastic hood slid back, and a black-helmeted figure turned to stare at Carter through a dark green sun visor. A gloved hand came up, finger pointing downwards; it stabbed down, once, twice, and then waved in unmistakable command: "Follow me."

Carter gritted his teeth. *Like hell, buster. I'm not going to provide free propaganda.* He turned, yelled for Debby.

"Listen," he bellowed, "I'm going to try to get them to fall back. Colin has to wait until he can see both clearly. And don't forget the bloody safeties."

The girl's face was ashen with fear, but she nodded vigorously, then turned away.

COLIN TODD HAD NEVER felt so alone in all his life. He sat with his back to the vibrating side of the Dakota, facing the open cargo hatch, six feet square. In front of him was the makeshift frame he and Carter had devised—six loaded BARs lashed down into place,

muzzles pointing straight out of the hatch. All six triggers were tied with wire to the short length of wood in his hand. The faded green canvas sheet was lashed to the frame; from outside the aeroplane it resembled stowed cargo.

From the moment the two Migs appeared in their opening pass, he knew he was going to have to fight. He tried to stop thinking about what would happen if he managed to down only one of them: the furious survivor running in again and again, shells ripping through the fuselage . . . fire . . . explosions . . . he had read plenty of war books. He wiped cold, wet hands on his grimy trousers, reached under the canvas to release the safeties on the guns.

Debby came down the cabin between the stacks of boxes, lurching from handhold to handhold; she squatted down beside him, shying away from the open hatch and the terrifying chasm beyond it. She gave him Carter's message, and he nodded almost absently.

The Migs came round again, sliding up alongside like two monster fish. Colin could see the pilots clearly. He waited, stomach heaving as he watched the fighters rising and falling as if on some bumpy invisible road.

UNCERTAIN, AFRAID, Donald Carter glared at the Mig leader. He saw him look forward, and saw his oxygen mask moving as he transmitted a message; then he saw him turn back to look at the Dakota.

The Migs began sliding back, reducing speed, past the wingtip, almost out of sight. Carter held his breath in agonized silence for a moment, then screamed to Debby, "They're moving back! Tell Colin!"

The green canvas cover erupted into a roaring wall of flame. The Mig, staggering under the pounding of the automatic fire, slid sideways into the second aircraft, and in front of Colin's horrified eyes the sky flared into a nightmare of flame and disintegrating metal, swelling into a fireball of horrendous proportions before falling away astern.

Colin dropped the triggerstick, turned his head to stare at a horrified Debby, and buried his face in his hands. Then he slowly lifted his eyes to the girl's and stared at her defiantly.

120

"Well?" he said, above the wind noise. "Don't just bloody stand there—go and tell Don it's all right."

Then he went to the door, hanging on desperately, gazing down at the distant drifting smokecloud. "God," he whispered, "God . . ."

CARTER HEARD THE CRASHING ROAR of the BARs, which seemed to go on for a terribly long time: a sustained, shuddering broadside followed by something that sounded like a distant street accident. But he could see nothing from the side window. He hauled the DC3 round in a tight turn to port, peering out and aft, and there it was: miles away, curving groundwards, a long trail of grey-black smoke, flecked with debris. He sucked in his breath. No sign of any others. Was it possible? *Both* gone?

He continued the turn round to his southwest heading, straightened out, shouted to Liane, who throughout the action had sat immobile, hands clutching the armrests. He leaned across, touched her gently. "It's all right, my love. They're gone. Colin did it! That boy—*he did it!*"

THE HOURS DRIFTED PAST. The engines were still turning, the speed a steady 145 knots. Carter munched candy from a "K" ration, smoked the occasional cigarette, looking constantly from the map on his lap to the ground below. An hour after takeoff, they sighted the coast, the shimmering silver sea beyond, and screamed with delight. He started to climb, explaining to the others, grouped behind his seat, "We need all the height we can get, once we're over the sea—if we have any problems, it'll give us that much more time."

Later, Carter wondered about the decision. Was he psychic? Did he know all along, deep down, that they'd never make it? They climbed up past 6,000 feet, going for 7,000. He checked the fuel. There should be no problem there.

They were some fifty miles out from the coast, cruising in clear sunshine at 140 knots, when the starboard engine let go. It simply cut dead, propeller windmilling, and the Dakota yawed violently to starboard under the offset power of the live engine.

Carter trod hard on the rudder, reefing the tail round into a straight course, jammed his thumb on the feathering button. The propeller slowed, came to a stop with blades edge-on to the airflow.

"God," he said thickly, "that was close." He wound on some rudder trim to take the strain off his left foot, opened up the live engine to take the additional load. The revs went up to the takeoff setting, the single propeller roaring flat out. When he had everything straightened away, fuel cocks set, he sat back to take stock.

"We still have two hundred miles to go—almost as far if we turned back. And I'm damned if we're going to turn back. At this speed, it'll take the best part of two hours. *If* that port engine keeps going."

Colin leaned close. "What happened, Don?"

"Who knows? At least there was no fire. I figure it was probably a blocked fuel line. I'm not surprised, the amount of crap we found in the filters. We'd better look out for ships: I want something afloat nearby. Maybe we could thumb a lift."

It was a poor joke, but they grinned dutifully, found a window each and started looking down at the endless wastes of ocean below, furrowed by the wind.

That day the Gulf of Siam seemed as deserted as the sky itself, and visibility was barely two miles into the sun. Carter sat at the controls in an agony of anticipation, dreading with each passing second the explosion of the overworked engine, a sudden burst of flame. They had reduced altitude to 3,000 feet, losing precious height slowly to a level where the single engine could hold the Dakota in level flight.

At this reduced speed, their time over water lengthened interminably. Five hours had passed by now, and fuel was becoming a desperate problem: the single engine at full power was using more fuel than would both engines, throttled back to maintain a steady 100 knots.

At ten minutes before noon by his watch, with the sun almost overhead, Carter spotted a long, grey shadow on the horizon which could only be the land; ordering the others to strap themselves in tightly, he did all he could to prepare for a crash landing.

Now he could see the coast: they would intercept at an angle, the beach stretching from under their left wing, obliquely away into the distance to starboard. He began looking feverishly for a pinpoint of some sort: far away to starboard he could see the mouth of a river, with buildings on each side of the estuary—a small town, sitting in a clearing surrounded by a semicircle of forest, which thinned out on either side at the beach. The sand was white in the brilliant sunshine, and far inland the green hills rose and fell in ridges all the way to the horizon. Ten miles . . . five . . . we've damn well made it! he thought exultantly. *We've made it!*

At which point the port engine cut, backfired, caught again, then stopped for good. For a few frantic moments, he panicked, getting the trim off, feathering the windmilling propeller, getting the aeroplane into a stable glide. It was quiet now in the cockpit; he found, amazingly, that he could speak naturally to the others, who were watching him anxiously. He heard his own voice, sounding composed and full of a confidence he didn't feel.

"Sit tight, we're going to be OK. We're only a couple of miles off the coast, with plenty of height. I'm going to put her down on the beach. Get your heads down between your knees, you two—up against the bulkhead in the cabin. Liane, pull that lap strap tight. And hold on!"

Now, Carter, just for once in your life, do something right. . . . He checked the descent indicator: they were losing 500 feet a minute. Height: 1,500—that made it about three minutes to touchdown. And wind? Too far out to see. This was going to be a dead-stick landing with wheels up, but he couldn't have wished for better conditions: the beach was wide, perhaps a hundred yards, rising gently from the water's edge and with a long, harmless curve to the northwest.

No flap for landing . . . the thought came to him quite automatically. In fact, all the old habits and skills were flooding back, as if he had flown regularly for years. He'd have to come in fairly fast, a flat, shallow approach, keeping the beach in sight until the last moment. At five hundred feet, he began a descending turn to starboard, allowing the speed to build up to 90 knots for safety, keeping the white ribbon of sand high right in the windscreen. Straighten up a little. Still curving in gently, like a fighter attacking a target from beam to astern. Speed back to 80 . . . hold it there. He sat at the controls, relaxed, resisting a ludicrous impulse to whistle nonchalantly, head turning like clockwork: airspeed . . . beach . . . airspeed . . . beach . . .

123

It was time: the old Dakota was skimming in over the lines of white surf, a hundred feet, fifty, the waves breaking now under the right wing. He swung the controls firmly, bringing the wings level, trimming back hard, miles of beach ahead, shelving slightly from the left, black seaweed on the white sand. . . .

Hold her there! She's trying to go nose down. Trim back all the way . . . now, hard back on the pole, airspeed falling—*Wham!* Tailwheel digging in, he thought fleetingly. Hold her one last second, and—*Crunch!* The impact on the belly of the Dakota was solid, teethshaking, but she stayed down. With sand grinding underneath, she skidded slightly to port, towards the treeline. Finally, she stopped, twenty yards from the trees, nose pointing straight inland.

The old crate could burst into flames any moment. *"Everyone out!"* Carter yelled, and he dragged Liane down the cabin to the open hatch, shoving Colin and Debby ahead, astonished that he could step from plane to ground, a distance of eight or nine inches. Together, all four of them scrambled up the beach, collapsing on the sand well clear of the Dakota, laughing, crying, finding it impossible to believe that they were down, and safe.

Chapter Ten

There was no fire. The pilot sat with head bowed, physically exhausted, mentally stunned, the healing sunlight warm on his bare back. Carter knew, instinctively, that he was closer to collapse than at any time in his life; Liane sat beside him, an arm round his shoulders, and Colin brought water from the plane, made him drink. Debby knelt alone on the white sand, fifteen yards distant, face buried in her hands, shoulders shaking.

Carter looked at Liane wearily. "Go and take care of her, Liane. She's at the end of her tether."

Liane stared blankly, unfamiliar with the term. She looked at Carter with a strange, distant expression, then did as he asked.

"Don? You OK?" Colin said anxiously.

Carter grinned feebly, punched the boy's upper arm. "That guy must have had a shock when you opened up. Did they all fire?"

124

Colin nodded bleakly. "I think so. I didn't like doing it."

"Don't worry, lad—all be the same in a hundred years. Here . . . where are the guns?"

"Shoved them overboard when that engine stopped," Colin told him with some satisfaction. "I thought the less weight the better, and I didn't think we'd need them again."

Carter nodded absently. "Sure. Listen—we don't have much time. We're somewhere near Khota Baru. There's a town about three miles up the beach, that way. I want you to take the girls there—no, listen to me: I want to get our money stashed away safely, where we can collect it later. It's best I'm the only one who knows where it is. I'll explain later. The girls won't go without you, so get going. Tell them, no arguments."

The pilot waited until they were three remote specks far up the beach, plodding through the soft white sand, then he turned, went into the Dakota and began stripping away the covers and lashings from the cargo. Fifteen minutes later he was out on the beach, leaning on the money boxes, sucking air into aching lungs. No time . . . no time . . . tying a length of webbing to the first crate, he dragged it fifty yards along the beach to a particular tree, found a piece of sheet metal from the wreck and began digging.

Long before the first hole was finished, the sweat was pouring off his body, and a dull ache was spreading through his chest. The three black-painted boxes went down solidly, and he began shovelling sand over them. The gold box, he thought despairingly. It was too heavy to drag through the soft, yielding sand. He staggered up the beach, scooped out a second hole, large enough for the single crate. Back at the Dakota, he dragged the steel box to the cargo hatch, spent five minutes hollowing out a shallow trench in which to stand, hauled on the straps. Sobbing in sheer agony, he got the box onto his back and one shoulder; then, bent double, he moved jerkily and stiffly up the beach, before collapsing six feet from the hole. Four feet . . . two . . . at last the box slid into the hole, and he knelt, shovelling sand on top with his bare hands.

Totally spent, he swayed onto his feet and limped back towards the Dakota, smoothing out the flattened channels gouged out by the crates. He felt his knees buckle. Head on fire from the sunglare, he crawled like a wounded animal into the shade of a wing.

CARTER WAS SILENT for a long time. Finally he looked at me pleadingly and said quietly, "You said you'd respect my confidence, Mr. Napier—does that still go?"

"Of course."

"OK. What I have to tell you now has nothing to do with Malaysia, or Singapore for that matter. You know the situation in Cambodia—Kampuchea—now?"

"Broadly speaking," I admitted.

"After the war," he said calmly, "the Pol Pot regime took over. Revolutionaries, crackpots with unlimited powers, criminals who committed genocide in the name of Communism. They emptied the cities, drove everyone into the countryside and told them to work or starve. Well, they've gone now. But they left behind a famine which may kill more than twenty million people."

His voice faded away, and I waited patiently. I was beginning to have a great deal of respect for Mr. Carter.

"Some nations are trying to help—but it's too little, too late. And much of the aid is diverted—stolen—by corrupt government officials. Have you any idea how much money is needed to save that country, Mr. Napier?"

I shrugged. "Millions, I suppose."

"Far more than that," Carter said sombrely. "Unlimited cash, that's what they need. Spent on supplies delivered right to where they're needed. Food, clothing, portable buildings, farm machinery, fertilizer. And that's what I can give them, Mr. Napier—unlimited cash. Because what we left behind in that valley is worth maybe a thousand times more than what we brought out. It makes the gold looted from the Aztecs look like a piggybank."

Carter eased himself into a more comfortable position. "Can't even begin to describe what we found. People talk of Morgan's treasure in the Caribbean, the contents of Tutankhamun's tomb. I tell you, this thing is bigger still—big enough to buy Fort Knox and the Bank of England. Disposal is going to be a headache. I've lain awake at night here, trying to work out ways of dumping the stuff on the market without debasing the world's entire currency."

His voice died away, and I sat there for a long time, watching the play of emotions on his face. Some minutes later, he looked up at me again.

126

"I need that American money to go back to the valley, Mr. Napier. And I desperately need help to work out the best way to help the people of Kampuchea. After all the treasure is their property, no matter how long ago they lost it. You see, I'm not important—none of us is. What matters is the people of Cambodia—Kampuchea. Liane's people. You have to talk to your government, tell them I need help. Will you do that for me?"

A FEW MINUTES before four o'clock the next afternoon, Lee Kuan Lok came round from behind his desk, opened his liquor cabinet and poured out two glasses of brandy.

"Alan, I never drink as early as this normally," he said huskily. "But I have never heard such a story in all my life. If any other man but you had told me, I would never have believed it. If half of what you say is true, there's enough money in that cave to give every family in Kampuchea an income for life. Provided the aid can be delivered where it's needed, it can save a whole nation from starvation. Carter has a tremendous responsibility."

"Yes," I said thoughtfully, "and he's going to need some help, Lee. I told him I thought I could probably arrange some sort of deal on the American money—two thirds to the Singapore government, one third to Carter and the others. Of course, he's obsessed with the problem of getting the Angkor jewels out of that place."

Lee topped up his glass. "That US money is spoils of war, finders keepers—call it what you will. The Americans wrote it off at the end of the war. Now we don't want to go messing up their bookwork, do we? We'll take a share—officially—without releasing any details; in return, we'll help Carter retrieve the treasure. But that belongs to the people of Cambodia—Carter is quite right there, and I'm all for it. What we *can* do is offer him advice, help, a base of operations—anything he wants. None of us has any claims to the treasure. Alan, I know a great deal more than you about conditions inside Kampuchea now, and they need every penny the world can scrape up."

I stood up, satisfied. "Very good, Lee. Carter will be out of hospital in a day or two and I'll bring him along to see you. After that, you're on your own. You can have my report on Flight HK 108 within a week. By the way—"

"Yes?"

"I've an idea Carter may want to get married, quickly. He's not the sort of chap to hang about. I'd be grateful if you could oil the wheels a little."

He smiled. "Of course, Alan. Be glad to. Tell me—Liane. Is she really as, er, good-looking as you say?"

"Better," I said slowly. "If I were thirty years younger . . ."

"Go away and let me think," Lee ordered, grinning hugely. "You're a disturbing influence."

FOR ME, EVENTS SEEMED to move very quickly in the weeks that followed. Carter, it was plain, was beset with impatience and found the waiting intolerable. It was remarkable to see the change in him after he left the hospital. He and Liane were married quietly at a civil ceremony in Singapore, at which Lee and I were happily in attendance as witnesses. Carter's son, Gavin, flew down from Hong Kong, bringing with him the others—Colin Todd and Debby Worthington, and their parents, all of whom seemed quite prepared to insist that the sun rose and set on Donald Carter. Typically, Carter had told his son little or nothing of the events before his arrival at Khota Baru, and Gavin had to trap me at the reception, in a private room at Raffles, to learn the truth. Thereafter, he spent the evening walking round Carter in small circles, as if expecting him to vanish into thin air. It was obvious the boy was blissfully happy about his father's wedding—he and Liane developed an instant understanding and liking.

I have a small holiday home in a tiny fishing village a few miles outside the city. I packed off Carter and Liane in a hired car, with instructions to stay as long as they pleased. But he pestered me over the telephone every day about the Dakota cargo, and in the end I brought him back for the recovery operation.

This was a classic exercise in disguised intervention. The boat Lee procured for the job was a fifty-foot seagoing pleasure cruiser, with two massive diesels and a shallow draught. Carter landed on the beach one morning an hour before dawn from an inflatable dinghy, accompanied by two trusted men. The transfer of the three boxes and the steel crate took rather less than an hour, and before he left, Carter went back to the Dakota for one last time, to collect the Siva statue from behind the bulkhead. Luckily it hadn't been found by the local inhabitants, who had otherwise ransacked the plane and removed everything that hadn't been screwed down.

A plain closed van transferred the load to the Williams bank in Palembang Boulevard, where it was counted, checked and deposited in Carter's private account. Lee, through his connections, was able to dispose of the gold at very favourable rates, and two days later Carter sat in Lee's office with Liane, trying to thank him.

Lee nodded benevolently. "Mr. Carter . . . Mrs. Carter . . ." Liane smiled, a little self-consciously.

"I now have full authority to give all the assistance you need in recovering the Angkor treasure, short of involving Singapore forces on the Asian mainland. All our resources, other than that, are at your disposal. More important still, Singapore has agreed to grant you indefinite residence in this country for the purpose of administering your proposed Kampuchea Distress Relief Fund."

Carter flushed. "Minister, that's far more than we expected. Thank you."

"As for organizing and operating the relief operation in Kampuchea, Mr. Carter, have you any idea of the magnitude of the task you intend to take on?"

The pilot nodded. He said uncomfortably, "I have. And it scares me. I'm going to need all sorts of help. But the more people are involved, the greater the risk of supplies going astray. We're talking about millions of dollars of food, equipment, vehicles, clothing, housing. . . ." He paused, extremely disturbed. "I don't know how I'm going to cope, Minister, and that's the truth."

Liane spoke out in a quiet, firm voice. "Donald, there are many people in my country who would help us in this work. People who want to see our country whole again. We can find them if we try hard enough."

"What do you suggest, Li?"

"Let us first bring the treasure to a safe place. Then let us build a proper charity organization approved by the United Nations. And then, when the people of Kampuchea learn that the treasure of Angkor Vat will be used to rebuild their country, they will come forward and help us."

Carter said doubtfully, "They may take some convincing."

"I know," she said calmly. "That is why, when we go back to

129

Phnom Penh, we shall take to them the proof they need."

Carter shot her a questioning glance.

"The statue of Siva, from the temple of Angkor," she added in a quiet voice.

"Frankly," Lee Kuan interrupted, "I think you should consider handing over the money to the Kampuchean government, or the United Nations."

"No!" Liane's voice was emphatic in denial. She came to stand beside Carter, slipped her hand into his.

The minister frowned.

"Please—" Liane held up a slim hand, upon which flashed the great elephant ring. "The old Chinese knew, Minister, that our lives are planned by Buddha—perhaps by One even greater than He. We can make small changes, but all our lives we follow the path. Since I was born, I have followed my path—the path that led me to Donald, to the valley, to the treasure. Donald's own path, as was intended, met mine in Singapore, and from that time onwards, we travelled together. Now, the way is clear to see. There are many people in my country who would help us in this work. I think, Donald, that we shall see much sadness, but we shall also bring happiness to many people. It will mean a heavy load upon us, but together we can do it. Will you come, Donald?"

The tall, lean pilot turned his head to the woman at his side.

"Together, Liane . . . together."

In that moment, I found it hard to swallow. I turned to the window, staring out across the busy streets towards the harbour, but the view was blurred, indistinct. As I heard the door close behind the Carters, I somehow knew, with absolute certainty, that they would accomplish the huge task which had been set before them.

Wilbur Wright

"Any pilot called Wright in the RAF in those days used to get nicknamed Wilbur, and with me it just sort of stuck." It is particularly apt that Wilbur Wright, who was originally christened Evan in South Shields in 1919, should have come to share the same name as one of the famous Wright Brothers, for a large part of his life has been devoted to aeroplanes. He not only writes about them with the sure touch of someone who knows his subject inside out, but he has also spent most of his life flying.

He began a long and varied career in the RAF after leaving school at sixteen. He was trained first as an engineer and later, at the beginning of World War II, was sent to America to train as a pilot. He recalls volunteering, along with some of his fellows, to be posted to a flying school in Miami. "Marvellous, we thought, Florida: sundrenched beaches. You can imagine the shock we got when it turned out to be Miami, Oklahoma!"

After that minor disappointment, Wilbur Wright went on to fly fighter planes for the next fifteen years. As well as the exhilaration of flying, he well knows the fear that plagues Donald Carter in *Carter's Castle*. "When you think about it," he explains, "everyone who flies has got to be afraid. It's a dangerous job. Any pilot who's not at least a little scared must be an idiot." He adds, "If I'd been Donald Carter, in that valley surrounded by mountains, I wouldn't have wanted to fly out in an old Dakota."

Asked about his interest in the subject of reincarnation, one of the themes of *Carter's Castle*, he responds: "There is so much reliable documentation of the phenomenon now that it would be a brave man who denied at least the possibility of its existence."

Wilbur Wright lives with his wife in Southampton, and they have one son and one granddaughter. He describes himself, nostalgically, as "a bit long in the tooth for flying now", and says he is currently busy restoring a Lagonda Tourer and turning the nine acres of woodland which surround his home into a bird sanctuary. His seventh novel, written under the pseudonym of David Graham, is due out shortly, and will be entitled *Seven Years to Sunset*.

THE
GREAT
HUSKY
RACE

A CONDENSATION OF *LE MUSHER* BY
JOSÉ GIOVANNI

ILLUSTRATED BY NEVILLE DEAR

A world of snow,
solitude and intense cold: this is
the part of Alaska, with its sparse human
settlements, in which Dan Murphy lives. He
treasures the wildlife of the North, and his anger
at unscrupulous hunters has already led him to
extreme violence and a prison sentence.

Now Dan is free, and to exorcise the past he
decides to take part in one of the most difficult
and dangerous races in the world—the Iditarod,
the great dog sled race across Alaska, between
Anchorage and Nome. Almost everything
depends on the courage and strength of his dog
team, led by the faithful Eccluke and by Dan's
new dog—and Eccluke's rival—the fiercely
proud Bull. As the miles roll by, dogs and man
face the toughest challenge of their lives, and
Dan must prove himself again in his own and
others' eyes.

CHAPTER ONE

The train had just left Anchorage and, as it rattled north towards Fairbanks, Dan Murphy watched the onset of winter. The snow beside the railway line was still very fine. But the brown and grey plumage of the ptarmigan was already turning white, foretelling the coming snow and frosts of the Alaskan tundra.

For the last five years Dan had spent his life in inactivity, either sitting or lying down, and all he wanted was to stay on his feet—to walk, and to get accustomed to wide open spaces again.

He wandered down the corridor of the train. A native of Quebec, born of a phlegmatic Englishman and a Frenchwoman who was something of a rebel, Dan Murphy, as he approached the age of forty, was a man of measured actions. His stride, a bit on the slow side, tended to disguise his slight limp, legacy of a childhood attack of polio. On some days the stiffness in his left leg was more severe than on others, but he knew that all real improvement had stopped a long time ago and he would carry the limp to his grave.

The train was practically empty. Dan paused to listen to an Eskimo from the Seward Peninsula and another from the Kuskokwim Delta amiably arguing over the merits of their different dialects. Each was making fun of the other's accent. Eventually the older one asked Dan to judge.

"Which is the best one, the most musical?" In his own dialect, the old man had continued, "The one that comes closest to the wind that heralds the thaw?"

135

Not wanting to upset either of them, Dan replied in a more generalized Eskimo language that the main thing was to continue to speak your own native tongue and not that of the foreign profiteers who came to exploit the country and its people.

Dan settled in the next compartment. Through its windows he looked only ahead: never behind. He knew that if he looked back, he would be able to see Cook Inlet, and the enormous petroleum platforms throwing their ghostly, fantastic light on the glacial waters. And those were what he was leaving behind.

He could have called ahead to Bob Leeve, the only friend he had in this country, at his home in Fairbanks. But he preferred to drop in on him unexpectedly. He needed far more to shake hands with someone than a chat on the telephone.

The train braked now and then, slowing so that local farmers could throw on their mail. It also stopped to unload groceries and supplies that the isolated inhabitants had ordered from Anchorage.

Dan was in no hurry. It was October now and he had until February to carry out his plan. He took a sandwich out of his pocket and ate it absent-mindedly. The train had been climbing ever since Talkeetna. Dan was familiar with these vast slopes at the foot of Mount McKinley, with their wolves, their grizzlies and their herds of caribou. He had once nursed an injured ram in these parts. It was a cousin to the wild sheep of the Rocky Mountains, and each of the dark grooves on its horns corresponded to a year of its age.

Dan looked at the reflected image of himself in the dirty glass of the compartment. Did each one of the wrinkles on his face correspond to a year of his life? He ran his fingers over his cheek, wondering what all these years had been good for—except for the day of the "accident", his confrontation with the vile Dr. William Bettniger.

At Nenana, the train crossed the Tanana River. At Nenana, with one dollar you could win a hundred and twenty-five thousand dollars. All you had to do was buy a lottery ticket and write down the day, the hour and the minute of the thaw. A tripod on the frozen Tanana was connected by a wire to a clock on land. As soon as the ice cracked and began to move, the wire snapped and the clock stopped.

Dan needed money, but he hated gambling. He preferred to forget this questionable hundred and twenty-five thousand and settle instead for the more modest fifty thousand his plan would bring in—a plan that depended not on chance, but on genuine effort.

In Fairbanks, as he left the station, Dan was gripped by the bitter cold of the October night. He must find new boots and a heavier fur jacket—but first he had to sell his car, always assuming the garage man in Nome hadn't already got rid of it. He turned his head away when he passed people, to avoid being recognized. Downtown the old log houses of the pioneers were still standing among more modern buildings; the frontier's past was still alive. Some of the inhabitants still caulked the cracks of their log cabins by boiling water so that the steam would seep into the fissures and freeze, sealing them for the winter.

Bob Leeve's house was at the end of a street on the outskirts of the town. From there he could see the landing strip. Bob would have lived in his plane if he hadn't been married. Dan hesitated. The house was a different colour, and it seemed to him that the veranda was new. Light filtered out through the curtains, along with lively rock music. He approached the door and knocked loudly.

Bob's wife opened the door. Eleanor Leeve was thirty-five years old and looked exactly her age. She was no cheat. Seeing him in the doorway, she didn't seem at all surprised. She held out her hand to him in a straightforward manner and called over her shoulder, "Hey, everybody, it's Dan Murphy!"

Inside, the living room was still just the way he had always loved it, its white-painted wooden latticework reminding him of the Quebec of his youth. At the table eight people were sitting round a cake that had just been sliced.

Bob had hardly changed, except for a touch of grey about the temples. He stepped forward, his arms wide, and embraced Dan.

"This is Charles, and that's Gregory—they're both pilots," Bob began. "And Geraldine and Eva, their wives. These two rascals are at the university."

One of the young men had carroty hair; the other was dark. Dan extended his hand to no one, not wanting to run the risk of seeing it refused.

"What do they get taught there?" he asked, smiling. "The positive effects of petroleum on Arctic fauna?"

The young men looked at each other awkwardly, and the two

pilot's wives peered curiously across the room at Dan. But they all squeezed more closely together so that Dan could sit down between Bob and Eleanor.

"We've heard about you from our professors," blurted out the red-haired boy.

"Bad things, I hope," Dan replied.

"Yeah," volunteered the other. "But we think what you've done in this country is pretty classy."

Bob cleared his throat and leaned towards Dan. "You know I've got a new plane?" he said.

"Will it be able to take me to Nome?"

"Are you kidding? It's a Piper 750 with an inverted propeller. I can land almost like a helicopter."

"Trouble is, I don't have anything to pay you with."

"It'll cost you ten per cent more by the time you *can* pay," said Eleanor cheerfully. "That Piper cost a fortune," she added as she filled his glass.

Dan grinned. "On the same basis, can I sleep here?" he asked her.

"Next door, though it's not well heated."

The two boys started laughing. "I guess you're probably used to that," said one.

"And why would he be used to it?" Bob cut in dryly.

Uneasiness rippled round the table.

"Jeeze, I dunno. . . . They say he used to be tougher than a wolf."

Now it was Bob's turn to burst out laughing. "*Used* to be, did you hear that? He *used* to be!"

"Well, it's not so bad to be a 'used-to-have-been'," Dan concluded peacefully.

Later that evening, when his guests were gone, Bob seemed worried. "You're sure you really want to go to Nome?"

By then Dan was stretched out on a narrow bed in the older, unheated part of the house. To warm himself, Bob was taking little sips of grain alcohol from a flask.

"I've got to get back my things."

"I can go for you, you know."

"I've things there I could sell. I've just got to have a little money to hold me over until the end of March."

"Speaking of money," said Bob, "there are some new openings

around. There's work over on the Skagway Harbour. Silver, lead and zinc are all coming in from the Yukon. The harbour's going to be enormous!"

"I don't really want to work," said Dan. He folded his arms and rested his head upon them.

"But you'll never last here. They'll be keeping an eye on you the whole time."

"Come March, I'm going to make fifty thousand dollars."

Bob recorked his flask. "Some lottery, I suppose?"

"No. And I'm not telling you, either. You're going to have to guess."

He pulled the covers up over himself. He had taken off just his boots. Bob left him the flask, placing it near the head of the bed, but Dan was already asleep. The only evidence that he was alive was a small drop of moisture that appeared at the end of his nose with every breath.

People said of him that he could make up for twenty hours on the go by catching fifteen minutes of sleep.

THE PIPER WAS BLUE with white stripes. Bob, who had worked in the Alps as a glacier pilot, claimed it could go through storms like a needle through a ball of wool. This morning, however, the air was calm. Bob flew low so that Dan could reacquaint himself with the terrain, its isolated villages and snowbound farms.

They moved in over Nome's airfield, and Bob touched down. The bar was open, so they went in and had a cup of coffee. The owner, who took pains to pretend he had not recognized Dan, lent Bob his jalopy.

Nome was waking up gently. A sweeper was working on the wooden sidewalk on Front Street.

"Really, are you sure you don't want me to go for you?" Bob asked again.

Dan declined the offer. They were silent then until they reached the house belonging to Virginia Finsson. Bob knew it well. Virginia was the daughter of a man who exported bulldozers. She had lived with Dan for two years, during which time he had never made up his mind about marrying her.

The man who had replaced Dan in her life was Greg Harway,

assistant director of the Petroleum Company. Virginia's father had once called him "solid stuff"—in comparison with Dan, an idealist who would have liked, single-handed, to hold back the commercial development of Alaska.

Virginia's house was elegant but simply built. Dan noticed that his whaleskin lantern, which he had liked so much, was no longer hanging over the porch. It occurred to him that this could be a bad omen for the rest of his belongings.

Bob stayed in the car. A woman Dan didn't know opened the door. "What do you want?" she asked aggressively.

"I'm a friend of Miss Finnson," replied Dan.

The woman disappeared and moments later Virginia emerged, wearing a dressing gown. When she saw Dan, her mouth dropped open and then closed again. Her green eyes crinkled slightly, and she cast a quick glance over her shoulder.

"I came early to be sure I'd find someone in," Dan began.

"There's always the telephone," she suggested.

"And there's also the mail. But nobody answered my letters. I've come to get my clothes, and a couple of other things."

A door opened behind her, then closed again. Greg Harway came forward and planted himself directly in front of Dan. He was wearing a sweater over trousers that fitted tightly round his ankles, showing off his boxing shoes. He was smaller than Dan but had broader shoulders. His gaze was humourless.

"What other things?" he said.

Dan pointed to a glass cabinet. At issue was the carved ivory comb inside it, an ancient Eskimo artifact. He also wanted the little statue of a mother clasping a child to her breast.

"That dates back to 2400 BC, and I didn't give it to anyone," he said firmly.

Greg consulted Virginia with a glance. She nodded, then fetched the Eskimo objects and handed them to Dan.

"The best thing you can do now is never to turn up here again," said Greg.

"Or else?" Dan asked politely.

Greg clenched his fists. At that point Virginia stepped in. "What with the scandal and everything," she said gently. "I think you should just leave here. Go back to Quebec. Or somewhere else."

140

Dan was studying Greg intently. "They did give me your name, Mr. Harway, but I'm only just now making the connection."

"That's right; you've got it—you beat me in the Kenai dog-team race," he growled. "But didn't they tell you in that bloody place you've just come from that I won the Iditarod that same year? You know—the one when almost all of your dogs croaked on the trail. But of course, that one's no race for a cripple!"

Dan nodded peaceably. A childhood spent going to school on crutches every day had been an experience that built character.

"Speaking of dogs," he said, "I happen to know you've been keeping Eccluke here. She was my lead dog. I heard her yapping a little while ago."

Greg rocked back and forth on his short legs. "She's a total has-been.... More than ten years old. I was just about to have her destroyed!"

"I'd rather take her with me."

When Greg hesitated, Dan put the Eskimo sculptures down on a chair, leaving his hands free. It was the same old story. For an animal he was ready to sacrifice everything. He was thinking that a couple of swift jabs in the belly would do Greg Harway a world of good.

Greg turned to Virginia. "Let him have his asthmatic old bitch, and give him his stinking clothes from out in the garage."

"That's real friendly of you," Dan told him.

Eccluke was alone in one of the cubicles of the kennel. As leader of the pack, she couldn't be put with any of the other dogs. As soon as she recognized Dan she began jumping wildly and yelping. But she soon calmed down when he clasped her in his arms.

Virginia was watching them. Briefly Dan smiled up at her. She stood quite still—suddenly everything had become too difficult for her. She didn't know what she would do if Dan should put his hand on her arm, or his arm round her shoulders.

But Dan was taken up now with the dogs in the other cubicles. He counted about eighteen huskies, two to five years of age, unusually fine-boned animals. Perhaps they had been crossbred with grey-hounds to increase their speed.

There were two sleds made of light wood hanging from the wall. "The sport does Greg good," said Virginia. "It distracts him from worrying about his oil wells."

141

Dan ignored the remark. He would gladly have thrown Greg and all his kind to the bottom of their wells.

Stashed in one of the garage cupboards were the boots and clothes Dan used to wear out on the ice field. Virginia stuffed them into a large bag. Eccluke got a scent of the clothes and lifted her great, Siberian husky's muzzle towards Dan.

He took a lead down off the wall and fitted it to her collar.

"What are you going to do with yourself now?" asked Virginia. She seemed to him suddenly vulnerable, despite her rich father and her grand house. The scandal must have shaken her deeply. A tenderness crept into her gaze and Dan felt flattered, more alive.

"Be a *musher*," he answered simply.

Together they took a few steps towards the door. His hands were burdened by the bag, the two Eskimo relics and Eccluke's leash.

"That's not much of a profession," Virginia reproached him.

"I've had a good deal of time to think about it," he said, as they stood in the garden by the wicket gate.

From the car, Bob watched Dan hand something to the young woman. It was the chiselled ivory comb. "I remember you liked it a lot," Dan said.

Her fingers trembled slightly as she took it. She seemed to sense the weight of the centuries behind the ivory.

She turned away and stood there by the gate until the car had disappeared.

Eccluke sat in the front, between Dan's legs.

"Now where?" asked Bob.

"North Garage." It was where Dan had left his car, a four-wheel-drive vehicle that was capable of handling ice, snow, and mud up to its axles.

The garage owner recognized Dan with no great joy. "Do you realize what it's cost to store your car here for five years?"

"People have seen you doing road repairs with it. That much use of it should pay you for the storage."

"Look, I don't want to deal with people like you."

Dan grabbed him and pushed him up against a workbench.

"I've come to sell you the car." He brought his face close to the other man's. "Don't force me to do anything else."

"Oh, so you w-want to sell it?" the fellow stuttered.

142

"Yes. Three thousand five hundred dollars. Cash. You know you'll easily get five thousand for it."

The guy knew that. Hastily he counted out the money while Dan wrote a receipt.

Eccluke was waiting outside. "Can you take me to Kotzebue?" Dan asked Bob. Kotzebue, at the tip of the Baldwin Peninsula, was one hundred and seventy-four miles away. "I can pay you now," Dan said.

In the Piper, Eccluke didn't move a muscle, her head resting flat down between her front paws. It seemed to Dan that she was a bit on the skinny side, especially for going any great distance.

The Piper touched down in Kotzebue at almost the same moment that a Douglas was landing. Dan wanted to buy one or two *malamutes*, North American sled dogs, from an Indian he knew, one of the best mushers in the region. In spite of a growing influx of tourists, the town still retained its rough frontier character. The Indian's name was Mayapuk, and he bred malamutes for their pulling power: they were slower than huskies, maybe, but stronger. Mayapuk also took tourists around on his sled.

Dan asked a few people where to find him. A mechanic gestured towards the Douglas, now rolling into its hangar.

"Those guys get around a lot in this area. They're bound to have seen him."

Two men jumped down from the plane. Bob and Dan moved closer and saw them dragging the carcass of a grizzly from the cockpit. The grizzly's head had been chopped off. Separate, head and body would provide a double trophy: a cover for the bed and a head to hang on the wall.

Mart Mieldost, the pilot, must have recognized Dan and Bob from a good way off. When he turned to them he had a carbine automatic in his hand.

"Hold it right there, Murphy!" he shouted.

"Come on, Mart, you're crazy!" said Bob.

"You! I don't know you any more!" roared Mart. "I don't want to know anyone who associates with that bastard Murphy!"

Mart's companion was dressed in style. His leather boots looked custom-made. Obviously this was one of the fancy clients Mart guided around on bear hunts.

"Mart, I wonder how bigmouthed you'd be without that gun in your hand," said Dan.

"I swear to you, Murphy, one of these days, if you don't leave this country, I'll get you!"

"That'll be a bit harder than killing a mother bear with little ones in her belly must have been." Dan turned to the client. "Are you also a murder expert?"

"Leave the gentleman alone!" Mart bellowed.

Bob took Dan by the arm and tried to drag him away. But Dan pulled free. He stared coldly into Mart's eyes.

"Yeah, take a good look at me," Mart blustered. He turned to his client. "These days we're only allowed six animals. But before this son-of-a-bitch started interfering, the sky was the limit."

With one crisp, unexpected motion, Dan kicked a hole in the plane's rudder. "There. Now you won't kill anything for a few days," he said.

There was the sound of the carbine being cocked. Bob positioned himself in front of Dan.

Mart's client was studying the damaged part. "Sir!" roared Mart, "I ask you to witness what that man's done!"

Already, however, Dan was moving off at his unhurried pace. From a distance his slight limp was noticeable. As Bob ran to join him, the blast caused the pilot to spin round, but Dan didn't even check his stride. Mart, his gun slightly raised, had evidently fired over their heads.

"One of those hunters is going to have your skin some day," Bob said to his friend. "You don't have the administration behind you any more."

Dan walked on towards the Piper in silence. Bob was beginning to feel exasperated. "Try to understand, for God's sake! You're no longer Professor Dan Murphy. The Institute of Arctic Biology doesn't want to know you. Even the Boone and Crockett Club have crossed you off their list. And yet once upon a time those guys fought just like you against aeroplane hunts!"

They were nearing the Piper now.

"Not really," replied Dan. "They made compromises; they weren't ruthless enough."

"Well, who can be? You tried, and you've seen what came of that."

144

"I'll tell you what I've seen," Dan said. "I've seen nothing as beautiful as a polar bear." He climbed into the plane. "I can tell you also that an ice field without polar bears is not really an ice field."

Bob sat down at the controls beside him. "I could take you back to Quebec, if you wanted."

"Look. Suppose you do. In that case we'll be flying for at least an hour over that area down by the shore; there's a good chance we could find Mayapuk there."

Grumbling, Bob repeated that even if they did find him, the best thing Dan could do would still be to leave the country.

On the Arctic coast in early winter the winds from Siberia bring squalls of snow and ice. Bob had to wait for a "hole in the wind" to avoid making the plane pancake on takeoff.

Finally, though, the Piper set off again over the snowbound landscape, sombre under a grey sky. Everything below them was trapped in ice, everything except the sea, which heaved lazily. Inland, the streams that in summer still attracted stubborn gold prospectors were now frozen and deserted. Abandoned dredging machines had left rust stains on the snow.

The plane was flying at an altitude of forty feet. As it rose above one of the dredgers, a sled came into view with a team of eighteen or twenty dogs. The sled was long, and four Europeans were sitting on it in single file, their legs muffled up under blankets. An Indian stood at the back directing the dogs. Dan recognized him as Mayapuk.

Bob retracted his wheels, preparing to land on his runners. The snow was hard, and the Piper skidded a hundred or so yards.

Dan jumped out first, in the path of the approaching sled. A driver cannot stop a sled by himself if the dogs want to go on pulling it, so Dan seized the lead dog by its harness. The four passengers seemed to be a single family: father, mother and two children. Surprised, the father looked back at Mayapuk, who had recognized Dan and returned his greeting.

"It's good to see you again." Mayapuk spoke in his own dialect.

Dan thanked him. They talked together and Dan asked if he could spare two malamutes, three to five years old, to put at the tail of a team.

"One mile or so from the northern outskirts of Kotzebue you will see my house," said Mayapuk. "There are sleds and other dogs around it. Come this evening."

He let out a raucous cry, and the dogs hurled themselves forward again. The four tourists craned their necks to stare at this white man who had dropped from the sky and who spoke Indian.

MAYAPUK, who had originally come from the village of Minto, lived in the old way, in a single large room with a fireplace. In one corner there were two camping cots, arranged bunk-style one on top of the other. Mayapuk made a living and fed his dogs by taking tourists for rides on his sled, and he also hunted fur animals. But he killed only in order to stay alive, not to hang trophies on his wall. His friendship with Dan went a long way back, and had to do with Dan's efforts to put a stop to the wholesale slaughter of polar bears.

Dan and Bob arrived around six o'clock. In the course of their evening together a Land-Rover drove up and braked sharply in front of the house. The Indian lifted the edge of a shabby curtain to look out, and said laconically, "Police."

There were four of them: three policemen and one plain-clothes man, a dry, narrow little guy. "I'm the Chief Inspector, Bureau of Aliens," he announced. "Are you Dan Murphy?"

"Your lieutenant knows me well," said Dan, pointing to one of the uniformed officers.

"Well, I don't. You have a visa?"

The chief inspector held out his hand. Dan sat down calmly, elbows on the table. "I've lived in Alaska for fifteen years."

"Last place of residence?"

"Anchorage."

"The address?"

"Everyone knows it. Why all the questions?"

The lieutenant gazed down at his boots.

"I can vouch for Dan Murphy!" Bob burst out, kicking violently at a stool. "He owes you nothing. That whole business of the accident is over and done with, and if you've come here to strut around on Mart Mieldost's behalf, let me tell you I'm not impressed!"

"Don't get excited, Bob," the lieutenant said.

"A murder, you call that an accident?" the inspector asked. He pointed at Dan. "You killed an honourable citizen—"

146

Mayapuk interrupted him, spitting on the floor. The policeman repeated his words, carefully separating the syllables.

"An *hon-our-able cit-iz-en!* Just a few miles from this town! And you're not going to go on staying here! Get it?"

Dan began to laugh gently. "You're really marvellous, inspector," he said. "You've actually guessed my intentions."

"Oh, sure! No sooner did they let you off at Anchorage than you turned up here again!"

"To visit a friend," Mayapuk cut in.

The inspector rocked back and forth on his skinny legs. "Want to know what I think?" he snapped. "I think we'd be doing you a favour if we had you expelled from Alaska, period." He surveyed Bob, the Indian, Dan, and the three policemen in uniform.

"Does anyone want to disagree with me?"

There was silence. Satisfied, the chief inspector signalled his men towards the door. He followed them out, calling over his shoulder, "That's all. For today!"

The door clicked tightly shut behind him. With temperatures of forty below outside, cracks weren't taken lightly.

The Indian spread a skin in front of the fire and lay down on it, leaving the bunks to his guests. Since the Piper couldn't take off over unlit ground they were going to stay the night.

"I think that cop's right," Bob acknowledged.

"Could be," said Dan.

In a single swift movement he hoisted himself onto the upper bunk and stretched out contentedly. Down below him Bob had decided just to sit, elbows on his knees, head in his hands.

The fire hissed softly, its burning wood still damp. Dan realized that the poor old bitch Eccluke must be pretty bored in the Piper by now. But he was asleep before he could do anything about it.

CHAPTER TWO

Next morning, aloft in the Piper, Dan ran a strap round Eccluke's black muzzle to help her to resist the temptation to butcher the two malamutes that the Indian had sold him, for a ridiculously cheap price.

The Piper bounced along in the wind. The squalls would either pick up its nose or cause it to dive, tail in the air like a frisky horse. The three dogs were howling as Bob headed for Fairbanks, and the blizzard continued to blow.

Bob had thought Dan was planning to return to Fairbanks with him; however, as they flew over the Tanana River, Dan gestured towards the wooden houses of the Indian village of Minto, scattered between the river and a forest that was not yet completely white. There was room enough to land.

The Piper bumped across dangerously rough ground. This was not the first time, however, that Bob had landed in this benighted place, usually to deliver vitally needed supplies. Kids ran up, their eyes large in round faces over which the skin was stretched tightly. Dan held the three dogs with a firm hand as he pulled one of the sacks full of his possessions from the plane. Bob hefted the other one down just next to it. There was also a 30–.30 carbine automatic.

Several men were standing at a distance, while the kids were patting the malamutes. The big furry dogs looked like huge stuffed toys.

"A guy of your abilities, living in this lost outpost," snorted Bob.

"My abilities? What abilities?"

"With all your studies and everything—why, you've even written books! You're just going to stagnate here!"

"I'm going to take advantage of the fact that it still exists."

Dan gave the malamutes' leash to the children and released the muzzle of his bitch from its strap. From one of his sacks he pulled out the ancient Eskimo statuette, and gave it to Bob.

"You can sell it to one of the professors from the university, or to a museum. With the money, I'd appreciate it if you'd buy me some dogs. I'll tell you where."

Bob asked what price the little carving might fetch.

"At twenty thousand dollars, it's a steal. I found it near a pipeline construction site. She's got forty centuries behind her."

As Bob walked with him over to the houses, about fifty Indians had gathered round. A good-looking fellow with tufts of white hair escaping from under his fur cap introduced himself as the chief. His name was Kougar. He reminded Dan that the two of them had gone fishing together on the river one summer about ten years back.

Dan pointed out the house where he had lived in those days, and the Indians began to laugh. Yes, that was certainly the one. He had sure done a bunch of funny things, with a pile of odd gadgets, and the house had remained empty ever since.

The white paint job round the door and windows, which Dan had had such a good time doing, had held up pretty well against the weather. Inside, however, a large dark spot in the centre of the floor showed up the unreliability of the roof. There was a stove, and a mattress of dry straw on a wooden frame.

Bob looked round, shaking his head in dismay. An Indian lit the fire and soon a heavy, whitish smoke was finding its way out of the stove by various routes.

"This is a rat hole!" Bob said in disgust.

Dan attached his bitch to one of the posts that held up the roof and left the two more sociable malamutes to run freely. He unpacked a few things and set them on the table.

"In the past," he declared, "at the Institute, I used to try to understand why it was that the seal's flippers, the caribou's nose, the beaver's tail and the wolf's paws can all function at temperatures far too low to support the nervous system of ordinary warm-blooded animals." He fixed an intense gaze on Bob. "In fact, the cold flesh of their bare extremities serves as insulation and prevents their vital centres from getting cold too rapidly."

He stopped abruptly, then took up the thread again. "Bob, do you think it's really essential to know why nerves continue to function in the coldest temperatures?"

Bob cleared his throat, his eyes watering from the smoke. Dan rose and opened both the windows.

"Well, you know that better than I do," Bob answered.

"Before the accident," Dan continued, "I had already come to believe we were wasting our time and the state's money. From my own humble point of view, it seemed to me that the only real usefulness would lie in opposing the disappearance of any and all species. It struck me that the slaughter of the polar bears injured the whole of creation."

Now Dan had his carbine in his hand and was looking for a place to hang it up. He smiled.

"Listen, you're going to go to Huslia, on the Koyukuk River. It's the village with the best mushers. They've got huskies. Ask for the slowest animals they have and buy four of them, to start with."

"Good God! What are you planning?"

"Above all, don't say that they're for me."

They went out of the hut and walked together back towards the plane, escorted by a gaggle of kids.

"Let's see: four, and the three you already have, will bring it to seven," Bob calculated. "You wouldn't be thinking, by any chance, of taking on the Iditarod?"

"Yes. Just a little fantasy."

"You all but died in one a few years ago," Bob reminded him.

"I've got to make up for that. I don't want to leave too many failures behind me." He patted his weaker leg with his hand. "It's really on account of this. He's extremely demanding, you know. Way back, from the beginning, he never could accept being different."

Before climbing into the plane, Bob shook Dan's hand. "It's no use arguing with you," he said.

"It never was," said Dan.

They were almost laughing. Then Bob started the engine, and the Piper tore away, nosed up a bit, and took to the air. Dan turned and walked back towards the village.

He moved among the houses, stopping in front of the enclosure that served as a communal kennel. The Indians of Minto tended to let their dogs live and fight as they pleased, believing that natural selection preserved the fittest. In fact there were now thirty or so pitiful-looking dogs in the place, their ears hanging or torn, their fur glued down in bloody patches. Kougar came over and explained to him that they were no longer happy with their dogs, because of coyote crossbreeding. As a result of it some dogs no longer ran, but trotted like coyotes, instead.

What a place, Dan thought, to have ended up, hoping to form a winning team! But he merely asked if they could sell him a sled and some harnesses.

They offered him a basket sled six feet long and one and a half feet wide, with a nice curve to its side members. A few of the stays mounted at right angles to the runners were broken, however. Also, when dogs get bored at a standstill they gnaw at their harnesses and pulling ropes; to prevent the harnesses' destruction, one must dip them into oil or carbonyl, and the harnesses sold to Dan had not yet been properly treated.

Dan got to work in the very long house, which was used by the community both as a boathouse and a workshop. First he tackled the sled. The physical labour did him good. He was managing to rehabilitate himself at the same time that he reconstructed the sled.

The first two weeks passed like a single day. Almost every family invited Dan to share a meal. Not by one word, not by one glance, did they suggest that anyone knew the slightest thing about the "accident", or where he had been for the last five years.

The two hundred or so Indians who clung to this dying village had a sense of respect for the next man, for his physical and moral freedom, that was totally lacking in large cities. When old people die in the houses where they were born, their grandchildren by their side, there must be a wholeness in their hearts. Neither nursing homes nor social security will ever replace that wholeness.

The snow on the ground was still thin, but there was enough for the sled. Dan harnessed his three dogs in a triangle, the two malamutes parallel to each other and Eccluke at the front. His aim was to form a team that would only trot. No walking, no running. Just trotting.

The Iditarod team race would be held in March, four months away, on a course of 1,050 miles. Replacing dogs during the race was forbidden. Mushers could leave sick or exhausted animals at certain organized locations, but on no account could they harness new ones. Dan had worked out a theory proving that a team would make better overall time by trotting steadily throughout, at an even pace. He would not profit from points along the course where it was possible to pick up speed, but neither would his team ever slacken its pace to a walk. He intended to cross the starting line with about twenty dogs.

Eccluke, a speed husky, thought only of running. She would do so until she collapsed from exhaustion, which would happen well before the end of a long race. She would run until her courageous heart burst.

At the beginning of training the two malamutes, who preferred to trot, let themselves be carried away by Eccluke's galloping frenzy. Dan tied some old tyres to a rope and let it drag behind her. This seemed to quieten her down a bit. Then, the moment she began to run again, he would crack his whip in front of her.

Dan tested a few of the village's half-coyote dogs. To determine if a dog is in good condition, you put your hand on his hindquarters just in front of his tail, fingers pointed towards the head, your palm resting on top of the pelvic bones, then grip. If he's firm and round, yet you can still feel the bones of his pelvis, he's in good shape. If you cannot feel the bones, he's too fat. If his spine protrudes and his flanks are flat, then he's too thin. Beneath his hand Dan felt the hard ridges of the crossbreed's backbones. He decided to feed up four of them for a few days before trying them in harness.

And that was about where things stood with him when one quiet afternoon Bob Leeve touched down in his Piper. Surrounded by children as usual, Dan walked over to the plane. Bob had brought him four huskies, selected for their slowness. They had good, foxlike heads and their tails turned up. Their fur was heavy and soft, the colour of a wolf's, with shades of grey running through it. Their shoulders were powerful-looking. While Dan inspected them closely, silently, lifting their paws and staring into their pale, white-blue eyes, Bob began to show signs of irritation.

"Aren't you going to ask me for some news from the civilized world?"

"I prefer the dogs," replied Dan.

He had improved the inside of his house. It was now warm. The roof no longer leaked, and the stove no longer smoked. Bob even found the kitchen arrangements acceptable. Dan had been living on rice mixed with fish and also on the fresh meat of caribou killed by village hunters.

Bob had sold the ancient sculpture for a little more than twenty thousand dollars. He laid what remained of the money on the table, along with a list of expenses: dog purchase, clean laundry, books, ammunition—in short, everything Bob's wife had thought it necessary to procure for Alaska's newest hermit. Dan put the money on a shelf and stuffed the list into the stove.

"There's something I wanted to talk to you about," Bob began, seeming slightly embarrassed.

He stopped. Pouring him a glass of the French wine Eleanor had sent as a present, Dan encouraged him to go on.

"Actually, it was Eleanor's idea: that you should have a radio transmitter. You could keep in touch with us. She says you could have an accident or get sick, and no one would ever know it. She says that would be just plain stupid."

"For a man of my abilities," Dan remarked ironically.

"I've got the equipment in the plane."

Dan sat for a moment, deep in thought. Finally he gave his consent. He didn't want to be bound to society again, but he also didn't want to disappoint Bob and Eleanor, whose friendship clearly knew no limits.

"You'll have to mount the antenna on the roof," Bob explained, putting the radio set down on the table.

"That'll ruin the landscape."

"No more than the tacky corrugated iron of this little shanty already does!"

"I gather you're not too fond of the place." Dan smiled. He took the rest of the twenty thousand dollars and stuffed the bills into Bob's pocket. "Come back in a month, and bring me four malamutes and two more huskies."

They strolled over to Bob's plane. Dan stuck his head inside, rummaging around, and pulled out Bob's old chest-expander, left there from his body-building days.

"Planning to make a slingshot?" teased Bob, as he climbed back into the Piper.

"It's for a kid I know."

Bob took off and disappeared among the clouds.

But the chest-expander wasn't going to be a toy. Irik was twelve years old and had a withered right arm. The movement in his shoulder joint had been severely impeded, and the kid had gradually acquired a habit of not using his arm any more.

Dan made a wooden handle which he fastened to one end of the chest-expander. He attached the other end to a wall. Then he taught Irik a number of pulling movements designed to force him to exercise his weak arm. Dan told him that with patience he could become like everyone else. And Dan saw himself as a child again, rehabilitating his leg after the polio attack. Living in this village, Irik had at least not been teased by the other children. Back in the city, Dan, with his crutches, had been frequently subjected to cruel taunts and thoughtless practical jokes.

At first, Irik could stretch the chest-expander only three or four centimetres. Dan made marks on the ground to record his progress. And to reward the kid, he began taking him along on the sled during training sessions with the dogs.

The system of using the whip and of making the dogs drag old tyres was a success. In less than two weeks they forgot they had ever known how to run. Tails turned up, they trotted along indefatigably, pulling a load whose weight Dan kept increasing. Meanwhile the four crossbreeds picked out in the village had fattened up a bit. But if their breeding helped when it came to training them to trot, it hardly served to promote harmony.

The huskies had clearly been biding their time, just waiting for a chance. The coyote crossbreeds were always harnessed in front of them. But on the day Dan chose to begin practising sharp bends, the huskies suddenly threw themselves on the crossbreeds, and in a split second's time there was nothing but a seething mass of fur, a confusion of fangs, of slaver and blood, of snarls and yelping.

With furious blows of the whip's handle, Dan and Irik drummed away at the heaving mass of dogs. With his free hand Dan pulled the tail of the dog closest to him to tear him away from the fight. But as soon as he released it to pull out another dog, the first one jumped back in again.

Dan took his hunting knife and severed the central tether. With Irik still helping, he pulled on the section linking the four huskies together. One of them had his fangs clenched in a coyote mongrel, dragging him along. Dan had to hammer the husky's muzzle with his fists to make him let go.

They hitched the huskies to a tree and the dogs calmed down, licking their wounds. One coyote crossbreed lay dead on the snow. They left him at the edge of the forest, where his flesh and bones would no doubt enable some scavenger to prolong its own life for a few days. The three surviving coyote crossbreeds were still hitched to the sled. Dan unfastened the one that seemed in the worst condition. His ears, three quarters torn off, hung down pathetically beside his head. Dan placed the dog on the sled.

"We might have to harness the huskies in front," Irik suggested.

They went back to fetch the huskies, untangled them, and Dan retied the central tether. The whip cracked over the heads of the newly harnessed dogs and they started back to the village, each with an ample share of bloody bites.

At the house Dan muzzled the injured dog and shackled him, intending to sew his ears back together. It began to dawn on him that one day he would have to consider getting a second lead dog. For a fight to the finish like the Iditarod, this would not be a luxury. He thought about it, knowing already that Eccluke wouldn't stand for the idea.

That evening Dan felt like giving up the whole venture. He told himself that his leg was demanding too much of him—once in a while it would just have to put up with a failure.

A bit later Bob and Eleanor called. Grateful to the apparatus that

155

connected them, he found himself telling them that the dog team was entirely satisfactory. Would he like to come and spend two days in Fairbanks with them? No, thanks all the same; he did not feel like cutting himself off from his life here in the village.

He hung up and stretched out, thinking. Could it be he was growing less sure of himself? Or was it that he felt he had to subject himself to some kind of iron discipline? Born in a city, surrounded by people, he had started out earning a living by teaching. Talking all day to students—and listening as well. Then came the aeroplanes, the hotels, the international conferences, the world. Was there not some consistent thread that ran through all of this and that should not be cut? Not even by an accidental bullet from a thirty-thirty?

IN THE FOREST there was not a murmur to be heard. The frost had reduced even the river to silence. And this peace, so magnificent and so potentially deadly, was barely disrupted when Dan passed through on his sled. The squeaking of runners on hard snow and the panting of dogs were part of this country's heritage.

Dan kept his weak leg propped on the rear of the sled; to help the dogs when they climbed the slopes he would shove with his other leg. Other mushers ran behind their sleds. Dan couldn't run. But pushing steadily, he had the regularity of a piston and the endurance of a wolf. To integrate Eccluke into the team, he took her out two hours a day with the other dogs one at a time, and soon enough they all came to acknowledge her as lead dog.

Young Irik's family dropped off a stream of presents at Dan's door. They left embroidered moccasins to wear around the house, and fine sharkskin gloves to put on underneath his mittens so that he could safely take his hands out of his mittens when necessary without exposing his fingers. In strong blizzards, people had been known to have the ends of their fingers frozen in seconds.

One morning Dan decided the time had come to yoke together the four huskies, the two malamutes and the five crossbreeds that he was now training. At the kennel, things went pretty well. Dan let Irik have the honour of harnessing Eccluke at the lead. There were eleven dogs bound to the central tether. The day of the race there would be almost twice that number, and they would have to act and obey as one: not get tangled up, not fight, not run, not get sick. Just obey, and trot to the last.

Now Dan tore out the anchor that held the sled. The anchor was a harpoon with curved spikes attached to a long rope. When a driver threw the harpoon on the run, it would hook itself onto a tree or a post and the taut rope would stop the team.

Freed from restraint, the dogs set off together in perfect harmony, but running. Dan had started them out on a rise that soon put a damper on their zeal. He trailed tyres behind him to slow them down further. When they had climbed a bit, he asked Irik to let himself be dragged along too, holding on to the back of the sled with his arms. A few of the dogs looked back, curious as to why the load had suddenly become so heavy. It must have dawned on Eccluke that the situation was hardly normal. She stopped, bringing the rest of the team to a halt.

Irik had had a great time being dragged along, and Dan was just thinking about unharnessing Eccluke to see if he could bring her down to the rhythm of a trot on her own, when the unpleasant noise of a snowmobile motor broke into the silence. The vehicle was

157

cutting its way across the frosted hill in the direction of the village. From a distance they could make out two men.

Dan reached for his binoculars. He saw silver badges pinned to the bulky fur jackets the men were wearing.

"It's the police," he said.

"Why?" asked Irik.

Dan hoped that their visit did not concern him. But why else would they be coming to this desolate spot? He grabbed his carbine from the sled, leaving Eccluke at the head of the team, and they headed off back towards the village.

The arrival of the two policemen there had aroused a certain cautious curiosity. The Indians had often had run-ins with these uniforms. On their own turf though, in this village, they felt within their rights. Kougar, the chief, explained politely which house Dan lived in and that he was not in.

Where was he, then?

When an Indian gestures vaguely towards the Infinite, it often gives the policeman the impression that he's being laughed at. The policemen, resentful now, became very interested in Dan's radio transmitter. To communicate with whom?

Another vague gesture.

But when the two men entered Dan's house with the obvious intention of confiscating his radio, Irik's father and two brothers took up places in front of the door to stop them getting out.

The larger policeman—a Texan, who seemed unhappy in this cold—put down the earphones he was holding, and clenched both fists. But the first punch he let loose at Irik's older brother had no effect. The Indian's body didn't budge. Blackish blood ran down his chin, but his lips remained closed over his broken teeth. Then Yosepi, Irik's younger brother, struck at the policeman's wrist with a club, a sort of truncheon used by local fishermen to strike fish when pulling them out of the water.

The Texan's hand dangled limply, his wrist broken. With his other hand he took out a revolver, shouting that he was going to wipe out all Indian scum, and started firing shots into the air.

As Dan jumped from his sled, he saw frightened villagers backing out of his cabin. He took up his carbine and moved forward. Inside his house the two guns faced each other. Dan looked past the Texan at Irik's wounded older brother and at the second policeman, who was holding the radio transmitter.

"That set is mine," he said calmly.

The policeman decided to put it down.

"We came to see what you might be doing in this village of savages," said the first one.

"There aren't any savages in this village. The savages are out there shooting polar bears on the ice field, for fun," said Dan, moving further into the cabin. He put the radio back in its place and then looked up at the bullet holes in the ceiling. Water would seep in through them.

"Who's going to repair that?" he asked.

The policeman put aside the revolver and, to save face, grabbed hold of Yosepi.

"We're taking him with us. He smashed my wrist."

Dan beckoned the older brother to come forward.

"And this kid, did he bash in his own jaw?"

The two policemen exchanged glances. "We're on duty," said one.

"I'll testify to that," said Dan. "And also to the fact that you were about to steal my radio. That's abuse of power."

The two men burst out laughing. "If I were you," the big one said, "I'd shut up. Half of Alaska is spitting on you, and the other half is just living for the day when you're kicked out."

Outside, the Indians stood in a watchful group. The two policemen eyed Dan's sled and dogs suspiciously. And they held on firmly to Irik's brother.

"Listen," said Dan, "you can't charge me with a thing! And you shouldn't take out your frustrations on this young fellow."

"He's going to pay for what he's done!" The Texan lifted his dangling hand. "As for you, we know where you are now—and that's all we need for the time being."

They forced the Indian up onto their snowmobile. Dan seized Irik's older brother, who was about to throw himself at them.

"Hold on. That'll only make things worse," Dan said, speaking Indian. "He'll come back safely. I promise, I'll take care of it."

Irik hurled an old cooking pot that clanged against the sheet-metal side of the snowmobile, and the policemen took up their weapons again. It occurred to Dan that if a blizzard came up and the

159

snowmobile's motor died, there was no one here the two men could count on for help.

Two men had come here: three had left. Dan could sense the Indians' anger. He asked Irik to gather his family together, and they grouped themselves round the radio while he tried to reach Bob Leeve. He got Eleanor. Bob would not be back until the next day—he was ferrying some experts along the pipeline.

Dan told her the story. It turned out that Eleanor was a good friend of a judge's wife in Fairbanks. Dan told her that if necessary he would use every penny he had left to pay for Yosepi's bail. He felt responsible for bringing this evil on the village.

That very evening, Eleanor called back and told him she had seen the judge's wife, who was planning to wait for the right moment before speaking to her husband about the matter.

Leave it to a man's wife, Dan thought, to know how to choose that "right moment". Even so, he didn't want to hold out false hopes to the villagers, so he said nothing. He wandered about that week amid glances which had the decency not to question him openly. He tinkered with his sled and harnesses, but Eccluke yelped in vain to remind him that the date of the race was approaching; he still did not take the sled out.

One day he took a sheet of paper and wrote down the names of all the people he knew well. Then, one by one, he crossed off the names of those he knew he could not ask to help Yosepi. Eventually only one name remained—Virginia. The woman with green eyes whose life he had once shared.

If she did not say she was doing it for Dan, she might possibly be able to influence Greg Harway on the matter. For a petroleum boss in Alaska, getting a wretched Indian out of prison would present no great problem. Still, how to go about approaching Virginia? He framed her name with his pencil. The next day he ran a second square around the first one. The day after that, he added further embellishments: doodles, trees, sketches of dogs' heads.

And then, unexpectedly, Bob Leeve circled over the village. Before landing he dipped a wing in greeting. Eager for news, the Indians ran to the plane as it landed.

Yosepi himself jumped out and the villagers' astonishment soon gave way to joyful hysteria, a mingling of shouts, tears, laughter.

160

Everyone wanted to touch him, to be sure that he was real. Yosepi disappeared within the heaving, disorganized mass of arms and legs and bodies. Dan had hung back. Now he went over to Bob. "Many thanks, on their behalf," he said.

"It was the judge's wife—and your dollars," replied Bob.

There was something else in the plane. Something lying curled in a semicircle, head between its paws. It was reddish, with white spots on its muzzle: a greenlander. The dog stood up, and Dan figured he must be about five years old. Under his throat the dog had deep scars, evidence of a terrible fight. He had one brown eye and one clear, grey one.

"His name is Bull, and he's a lead dog," explained Bob. He added that this had been an idea of Yosepi's, who considered Eccluke a bit old to take on the longest race in the world.

Bob held out a dollar bill from his pocket. "This is all you've got left."

Dan took the dollar and the dog. They walked to the house, and Dan tacked the dollar up on the wall to the right of the door.

"No one knows you supplied the bail. The people over at Justice would never have accepted it."

Justice. Dan repeated the word with various inflections. However he said it, the word seemed to lack meaning.

Kougar came to invite them formally to a celebration of Yosepi's return. First, they had to do a grand tour of the village. The grain alcohol was strong enough to clean out a sewage pipe. Fortunately, as they reached the third house Bob remembered that he had a plane to fly home. The warmth of the alcohol seemed to lift him up into the Piper, and soon his wheels were grazing the tops of the trees.

Dan didn't even hear the takeoff. By the time he arrived at the sixth house, pushed and pulled by the embarrassingly grateful Yosepi, he had forgotten his birthplace and his own mother's name. They fed him salty fish, and the beat of Indian music kept time with the throbbing he felt behind his temples.

Rocked by the growing din, Dan didn't hear anything any more. When the group moved on to another house, Dan tried to stay outdoors, revived a little by the glacial air. But the crowd propelled him along and shoved him into yet another house—Kougar's. There was meat here, as well as even stronger alcohol. Dan made half-

161

hearted attempts to coordinate his tongue with his brain. Kougar was saying that happiness was to be found in this village and nowhere else. Dan tried to answer that that was absolutely true, but the words came out sounding like slush.

He saw Kougar burst out laughing. Dan drew himself up, offended. But he didn't have the bearing of an Indian chief, nor of any Indian for that matter. He reeled over to a bench instead, and slid down onto it. Dan Murphy, brilliant university scholar, was drifting serenely into the primitive. Poor but free, he was slowly learning that tomorrow's fears need not always take precedence over today's happiness.

CHAPTER THREE

Dan was finally returning home. And, as there were no street lamps or pavements, he was not obliged to walk straight.

When he saw Virginia at the corner of his house, he hesitated, narrowed his eyes, ran a hand over his forehead. He recognized her woollen cap. Had she dropped from the sky, or was the grain alcohol causing him hallucinations? He came close enough to touch her, to see the hint of irony in her green eyes.

"It's really me," she said. "I flew in on one of Greg's company planes."

The fire was still going in the house. Dan invited Virginia in and the warmer temperature cleared his head. She took off her cap, her hair falling free, and looked around. Her glance seemed to be saying, "So this is how he lives!" She tapped the dollar tacked up on the wooden wall-board inquisitively.

He shrugged. "A fetish," he said.

He felt more at ease now. She stopped in front of the sheet of paper that was covered with scratched-out names—she had noticed her own, framed twice and decorated with sketches.

"Is this a marriage proposal?" she asked.

Her tone was friendly. Dan realized he had been right not to cross her name out.

"Could be." He smiled.

The only chairs in the place were hard. Virginia preferred to

162

remain standing. "Maybe you won't listen to me," she began, "but I'm going to tell you all the same. Because I really believe it." She suddenly stood up very straight. "It's pure madness for you to take on the Iditarod. Why are you doing it, honestly? Because Greg's going on it?"

Dan weighed the question honestly.

"I didn't even know he was planning to when I made my decision. I'm doing it for myself."

"Except that the whole country sees it as a gesture of defiance, of pure bravado."

"The race is open to anyone."

"You're not just anyone. You killed the eminent Dr. William Bettniger, to protect a polar bear."

"People shouldn't go around assassinating pregnant bears, simply to make pretty bedside rugs. Besides, the court decided it was an accident."

"Try to understand, Dan! They all figure you're going to start interfering again. Mart Mieldost's been all over the place telling people you've deliberately settled here so as to wipe out more hunters. That's why the police are watching you." She came closer and looked him straight in the eye. "They say that the race is an alibi—that you're really staying in these parts just to meet up with another Dr. Bettniger."

Dan looked out of the window. He saw Irik over by the kennel and Eccluke standing up on her hind legs.

"I'm a long way from being able to win," he said. "My team is not trained, it's not even complete." He turned back towards her. His hand touched her shoulder, the nape of her neck. "But it's rough, you know, going from one failure to another. I hope that this time I'll win—and the hope keeps me going."

"And afterwards?"

His response was a vague gesture, like that of an Indian.

"But this race can't possibly help you. And what if you lose? The whole way, the whole thousand miles, you're going to run up against hostility and traps. Then it will be just one more failure for you—a disaster."

Her hands gripped one of Dan's muscular arms.

"For the sake of the past," she said, "for the sake of what was once between us, I'm begging you, Dan. Get out of this country. Go back to Quebec."

He looked at her for a long moment.

"Does my being here really complicate your life that much?" he asked softly.

She let go of his arm and took a few steps towards the stove. "I'm also thinking of you." She cocked her head slightly. "When I think of what you used to be, and what you've become!"

She looked around at the shabbiness of everything. Instinctively Dan passed his hand over his unshaven cheek. "But I'm happy," he said at last.

"You were also happy as a lecturer. The university in Quebec would take you back."

"No doubt," he muttered. He was thinking: life goes on, and you can't always be happy with the same old things.

She came and sat down next to him. "You're not going to remake the world. You're not going to change people, either. When they band together it's in order to be 'right'. And you're all alone—which means you're 'wrong'."

He loved the tenderness that drifted warmly back and forth between them.

She sighed. "And you don't care one bit. Well, anyway. Tell me what I can do to help you."

He wrote a few lines on a piece of paper and handed it to her. "Find out what's going on, and try to get the whole business taken care of. It has to do with an Indian who lives in this village."

She promised, leaned over abruptly and kissed him on the cheek. Then she stood up.

Irik had been waiting patiently outside on the doorstep. Dan called him over and the boy came awkwardly into the room without once taking his eyes off Virginia. To do something, he tugged at the chest-expander fixed to the wall. Virginia noticed his withered arm, and when she looked from him to Dan she felt that perhaps she understood the simple stuff from which happiness was made in a place like this.

She preferred to return to the waiting plane alone. Walking out towards it, she looked back just once, furtively, as if afraid she might be intruding on something.

Dan listened to the noise of the plane's engine growing fainter. Watching Irik, now pulling conscientiously on the chest-expander, he reproached himself for not having asked Virginia how she was these days.

HIS DRINKING BOUT had left Dan feeling weak at the knees. He went out for a walk with his new dog, Bull. According to Yosepi, Bull had been outstanding as a lead dog in the south of Greenland, and had come to Alaska with a timber merchant who no longer competed in races. The fellow realized that the dog was miserable at not being asked to pull sleds any more, and he hadn't tried to make a huge profit when Yosepi had proposed putting him at the head of a team about to take part in the greatest race in the world.

Whenever Bull passed Eccluke's kennel, she would foam with hatred, and tear with her teeth at the wooden floorboards. Bull might *look* placid enough, but Dan felt him quite capable of slaughtering the older dog if given a chance.

He was still at least five dogs short and had just one dollar left. The only solution would be to try out the rest of the coyote crossbreeds from the village. With no great hopes, Dan picked out five of them to train. The breed was a mystery: one moment they gave the impression they could cover at least five thousand miles, and the next they seemed ready to collapse by the end of the next mile.

During the first week he spent with them, Dan increased their mileage daily—from twenty-five to thirty, then thirty-five. The dogs had no problem when it came to trotting. This pace was instinctive, a result of their crossbreeding. Dan was becoming fairly happy with his own form, also. His scooting pace was steady; his weaker leg, pressing down on the sled's runner, did not tend to get numb. Now and then he would push with it for a while, just to keep it supple.

The day he was to do forty-five miles, he decided to harness Bull in the lead, with the five half-trained dogs behind him. Irik had just finished hitching them when Dan strode over with the greenlander on a leash. He had tried Bull out at the rear of the team, but the greenlander only attempted to savage the dog in front of him. Without even receiving a fang in his side this coyote crossbreed flattened himself on the ground, acknowledging Bull as his leader.

165

Dan tried him out in another position, but it was clear that Bull would stand for, and deserved, nothing less than the lead.

Irik stationed himself at Bull's side, continually pulling him back to keep him from running. Bull reacted by inching along like a crab; then by turning his muzzle anxiously up at Dan. A dog harnessed at the lead believes he owes it to himself to run as fast as possible, and Bull did not understand.

Dan was unnerved at the thought of all he still had to do to get Bull and the rest of his final team to trot without endless arguments and fights. He gave Bull a few lashes of the whip every time the dog started running, and now, as soon as he trotted again, Irik would lean over to offer him a piece of meat.

At the end of the forty-five miles the dogs were fine. Dan's shoulders ached, however—not a sharp pain, just discomfort, but it worried him. That evening he examined the sled. He preferred to think that his mushing position was faulty, that he had maybe been holding his wrists too high, rather than believe that he was succumbing to fatigue. For he knew that when the race was on, he would have to clear a daily average of sixty miles.

He dedicated the next day to lowering the height of the handles on his sled. Eccluke spent that Friday watching Bull's every movement. The mere sight of the greenlander transformed her into a wild thing. Dan avoided the thought that one day, ideally, Eccluke and Bull would have to pull the sled together, with mutual understanding and goodwill, over the infernal Iditarod course.

Saturday dawned, and for the next distance of some fifty miles Dan harnessed the two malamutes at the rear, then the five coyote crossbreeds, with Bull in the lead again. The heavy sky, sallow grey, appeared to blend with the frost on the ground. Irik was sitting on the sled, his head slightly lowered against the gusting wind. They skirted a forest of motionless birch trees, the dogs causing no trouble. With his hands held lower down, Dan too was feeling better.

Rather than take the next hill straight on, he made the team cut obliquely across the slope, and walked ahead of the sled to prevent it from skidding sideways. Walking complicated matters, but he knew that the Iditarod course would include a number of very steep ridges. Along these ridges, the pressure on his weaker leg made the going even more difficult.

A light wind came up. With the slightest breeze, the temperature dropped several degrees. By the thirtieth mile, Dan had just started looking around for a spot that might afford some shelter, when one of the coyote crossbreeds decided to stop and urinate.

Bull spun round, lunging violently at the dog, and blood spurted. Only Dan's swift intervention kept Bull from even more deadly corrective measures. But hardly had Dan returned to the rear of the sled than Bull hurled himself on another of the crossbreeds.

Dan rushed up to the front again and struck a volley of blows on Bull's muzzle. Bull gave up, but these comings and goings carried out at a fast run, and their struggles to separate the dogs, must have cost them at least fifteen miles in terms of sheer physical energy.

As long as Dan stayed near him, Bull kept calm. Dan and Irik had a bite to eat. The wind was rising now, and the two coyote crossbreeds were licking their wounds. Sitting up very straight, Bull eyed them imperiously. He avoided looking directly at Dan.

Before setting out again, Dan ran a rough hand over Bull's back, hoping the dog would realize that while his master appreciated the idea of him coaching the others, he disapproved of the method. And he put him back at the lead, with Irik running beside him. One way or another, the sled made its way back to the village.

Then, while being unharnessed, and despite Irik's efforts, Bull again threw himself on one of the coyote crossbreeds. His nerves ragged, Dan passed the thong of the whip round Bull's neck and pulled him backwards. He would gladly have strangled the beast had Bull not released the wretched crossbreed into which he had sunk his teeth.

With a few swift kicks, Dan drove Bull into his kennel. He let Irik do the rest and, returning home, stretched out on his bed. He could hear Eccluke growling; she was undoubtedly foaming with jealous rage, her eyes streaked with red. He got up suddenly and plugged in the radio, to talk to Bob and Eleanor, to tell them they could come and get him: he was throwing in the towel. But no one answered: apparently his friends were out. He set the receiver back down and put water to boil on the stove and set about a few of life's other domestic chores.

All that night the wind howled, but by morning it had calmed a bit, and Dan was longing once more to be back behind his team. He took the dogs Bull had already bitten and placed them directly behind the greenlander. Bull acted as if he was a reformed character.

Ideally they would cover fifty-five miles that day. As they started off, the wind blew directly into Dan's face. For the dogs, heads bent sidewards, struggling forward made them forget their petty quarrels. Dan too was trying to catch his breath as the wind spat bits of hard snow at him.

To win the Iditarod, the first thing to do was develop a resistance to this wind. Today's blast, relatively speaking, was a mere caress, and anyway, this evening they would all be back in the village. But when the race was on, they would have to withstand whole days and nights of it. Today, also, Irik was on the sled, his back to the dogs, and occasionally Dan caught a glimpse of the smile that split his face into a moon-shaped crescent. It occurred to Dan that during the race he would not see that smile. He would be alone.

A few miles from Livengood, Dan saw a Land-Rover broken down on the road, its windows covered with a layer of frost. Curious, the dogs slowed down. Dan took advantage of this to stop the team.

He walked round the car. There was no one at the wheel, but next to it he could just make out two people clinging to one another. They were women, as far as he could tell from their bundled-up clothes.

He knocked on the window and opened the door. "Need anything?" he asked.

They looked at each other, apparently taken aback by his wild appearance. The older one was still young. The other must have been her daughter.

"We've broken down. We tried getting back to Livengood on foot—my husband is district attorney there—but six miles in this wind ..."

Dan had been around enough Americans from New York to recognize the accent. More petroleum people, he said to himself.

"Out of gas?" he asked.

"No. And the car's brand new. But the engine just stopped. No warning—it just stopped."

"All I have is a dogsled," Dan told her.

The idea of going home by sled struck them as "real cute". Dan took a folded rug from the Land-Rover's back seat, Irik got off the

168

sled so that Dan could settle them there, and he wrapped the tarpaulin round them. The young girl chatted on about how she had once been on a sled belonging to a school chum of hers, but he had only had *three* dogs.

Dan started Bull off, and the others followed. Their round trip would be much longer because of all this, but Dan looked forward to seeing the district attorney's face when he found out who had rescued his wife and daughter.

Eventually they spotted the first houses and several parked cars, and two snowploughs opening up the approaches to the little town. The few passersby in sight were hurrying. The coyote crossbreeds were turning their heads in every direction. They had never seen so many houses.

The woman directed Dan to a small dead-end street. Her house, faded grey, was bordered by neat flowerbeds. She suggested that Dan and Irik come in for a hot drink, and they followed her in after securing the sled to the railings outside.

The house smelled of furniture polish. There was a good deal of bric-a-brac, and lace, and silver gleamed in several glass cabinets. Irik was made nervous by all this bourgeois comfort. Despite the heat, he had kept his cloak clasped tightly about him, the fur hanging raggedly in places.

A mirror made Dan suddenly conscious of his own attire: the elbow of his parka was patched, and one of his cuffs was frayed. He took his teacup with the other hand to stop loose threads trailing in the tea. The mother and daughter did their best to keep the conversation going, but they were increasingly distracted by the boots of their guests: the ice on them was now thawing. Pretty soon there would be four very definite puddles on the carpet.

The Indian woman who had brought in biscuits fixed scornful eyes upon Irik. The way he ate embarrassed her, the way he scattered crumbs and licked his fingers.

Dan stood up, preparing to go. He was afraid nightfall would sneak up on him.

"My husband, Attorney General Spencer, will certainly want to thank you in person, Mr. . . . ?"

She waited for Dan to introduce himself.

"Murphy," he said. "Dan Murphy."

She nodded politely, and he couldn't be certain if the name meant anything to her or not.

"Thank you again, Mr. Murphy. If it weren't for you, we'd have died from the cold."

He was about to reply when a howling and yelping of dogs interrupted him. He and Irik rushed to the door. The sled was still hitched tightly to the railings, but the central tether linking the eight dogs together had been left slack enough for them to be able to close in around a plump little boxer.

Dan forged his way at once into the thick of the scuffle, in an effort to rescue it, while Irik stayed back along the fringes, trying as best he could to separate the dogs. But the poor boxer, its shrieking master still clutching its leash, had already been reduced to a bloody pulp.

Disapproving townspeople were gathering. Dan heard talk about destroying the dogs, about barbaric behaviour in a supposedly civilized age. The dead boxer's master still tugged on its leash, wailing.

Dan planted himself between the people and his dogs. If he had to choose, he would be on the dogs' side, just as he had been on the bear's side against the respectable Dr. Bettniger. After all, he himself was no longer the respectable Professor Murphy. To all outward appearances he was just a savage, dressed like an Indian, rejecting everything respectable society stood for.

He ran his eyes over the scowling faces. Each one seemed to judge him. But they would not get to him that easily.

By now Irik had untied the sled from the railing. Not quite knowing how, Dan took a grip on the handles once more. With the dogs trotting forward he pushed through the crowd, and their angry voices receded behind him. He didn't look back. If people wanted an explanation they could ask the wife of the district attorney. If society wanted to destroy the dogs which had rescued her and her daughter, Dan could almost wish he had just left the two women to fend for themselves in their broken-down Land-Rover.

Dan headed back towards the Indian village, the wind now behind him. The sun was setting fast, but with the radar all lead dogs seem to possess, Bull knew without hesitation which direction to take. All the dogs trotted briskly along, doing what they loved most in the world: pulling a sled.

170

Night fell, and in the darkness Irik's teeth were bright in his crescent-shaped smile. Standing on the runners, shoulders broad and square in his parka, with the wind swirling up inside it as if it were a sail, Dan gripped hold of his very existence, stripping from it all that was superfluous. Purging it of the trivia that make civilizations grow old too soon.

CHAPTER FOUR

With the race eight weeks away, Dan could no longer put off his moment of truth: he had to harness all the eighteen dogs together.

He rose before daylight to go out and offer encouragement to Eccluke. He talked to her while he carefully checked her physical condition. None of her joints seemed to cause her any pain, not even her hindquarters, where age has a way of showing up first. But he could hardly tell her that, considering her age, she was superb. Females do not forgive that sort of compliment. Still less could he tell her that this race was too long, that Bull was going to relieve her and spend a good part of the race at the lead, and that he was taking her along mainly for old times' sake.

So how was he going to ask her to forget the hatred she felt for the younger dog?

He inspected her paws between the pads. Hoping to prove she was his favourite, he attached to each paw protective leather bootees he had sewn himself. For the race he would have to provide all the dogs with these bootees. Along one part of the course erosion had left veritable needles of ice projecting from its surface.

When he led Eccluke over to the team, now harnessed in place, she was clearly quite proud of her bootees. Also, when her eyes searched for Bull, she was immensely satisfied to see him back by the side of the sled, harnessed there alone.

Eccluke installed herself in the lead. Behind her, in order, came the ten coyote crossbreeds, the four Siberian huskies, and finally the two malamutes. The team was a good twenty metres in length. Bull, enraged, tugged furiously at his leash, but it was short enough to keep him from throwing himself on the dogs nearest him.

With this dynamite in reserve, Dan started off. He had loaded the

171

sled with about two hundred pounds of ballast, of which Irik accounted for about half. The dogs were harnessed in pairs to either side of the central tether. Using this system, it was theoretically possible to head up the team with two lead dogs pulling side by side. But this time Eccluke was alone up front, and after the first hour Bull could no longer bear his humiliation.

First he left off trotting and merely walked; Dan nudged him a bit with his foot. Then he stopped altogether and let himself be dragged along; Dan bent his whip and struck him a couple of times. Bull didn't even look up. The harness pulling him backwards was mangling his ears. He lay like a dog at death's door, and the others went on dragging him along.

Dan now had to bring his emergency brake into action: a wooden lever tipped with iron. During training this was sometimes enough to bring a sled to a halt. Eccluke turned her head and fortunately stopped. Eyes closed, Bull remained stretched out on the ground. Dan unhitched him, wrapping the short leash round his wrist. The dog stood up again and wriggled as Dan led him to the front of the team.

Dan now placed himself between Eccluke and Bull as he harnessed the greenlander alongside his bitch. He then sat down facing the two leaders as their lips curled up over their fangs and the fur on their backs bristled with mutual hatred. Irik came over and sat down next to Bull. Dan waited for the growling to subside and for the fur to lie down flat again. Then he got up slowly, feigning a total lack of interest in either dog. But when they lunged at each other, both standing erect on their hind legs, he just had time to stick his leg in between the two fighting bodies.

Pulling on the collars of their harnesses, Dan and Irik managed to separate them. Quickly Dan unfastened the snap-hook that connected Eccluke to the central tether; he lifted her and carried her to the sled. He dropped her roughly onto it, then attached her to a very short leash to prevent her from jumping off.

With a lash of the whip, the team set off once more. Irik had positioned himself at the front of the sled. Bull was happy and tugging conscientiously. Eccluke, however, raised an outraged muzzle towards her master. She wriggled, trying to jump from her perch, and promptly received a blow from the whip handle. Dan now

172

realized that if he wanted to take both lead dogs along on the Iditarod, he would have to put one on the sled when he or she was not pulling. Eccluke weighed fifty-two pounds, and Bull weighed eighty. Dan wondered if having two strong lead dogs working in shifts could compensate for the extra load. Should he not leave Eccluke behind?

Worrying about this question, he was surprised by a sharp right turn as they emerged from the forest. The dogs on the left tried to turn between the ones on the right, crossing the central tether and causing total confusion by tangling all the separate pulling ropes.

Bull alone, by virtue of his position as leader, had managed to stay clear of the muddle. Behind him everything crisscrossed and jammed, and a fierce tug on his chest harness brought him to an abrupt halt. He turned, heading back towards the sled, and went round the other side of a tree. At that point the whole mess became inextricable. Dan and Irik began working on it from all angles. Some of the dogs were being strangled by others who were trying to get free. In a fury Dan grabbed his hunting knife and was about to sever every single leash when he heard the raucous call of an approaching musher.

A sizable team was coming into view, its dogs running smoothly. The musher was legging it behind his sled for several metres at a time, then putting his feet back on the runners. The man's breath had formed frost on his chest. This was an Indian whom Dan had met during other races. He was undoubtedly training for the Iditarod.

The man passed by with a cheerful wave of the hand. He had twelve dogs, all Siberian huskies. The track was narrow, and the Indian carefully manoeuvred his sled to avoid colliding with Dan's, which was wedged between the raised verge and the forest.

Watching the man take a sharp bend without a hitch, without even slowing down, Dan stood dismayed in the midst of his own bogged-down team. Behind him Irik began to unfasten the leashes, untangling them one at a time with the patience so typical of his people. Once released, all the dogs were carefully tied to trees, for if polar dogs are allowed to escape and happen to catch the scent of game, they can take off for days at a time.

If this sort of mishap had occurred in a blizzard, the knots would have been frozen solid and Dan would indeed have had to cut all the pulling ropes to extricate the dogs. Afterwards they would simply have abandoned the sled and tried their luck on foot, Dan and Irik together with the dogs roaming loose.

As it was, they still had to put in two long hours reorganizing everything from top to bottom. And although the rest of the day went by without incident, the dogs' trot now seemed to Dan impossibly slow, and as he went into his house he realized that his weak leg was pulling on his hip more than usual. The eighteen dogs had been seen to, Irik had gone home, and Bull still snarled at Eccluke from the opposite side of some wire netting.

Once again, Dan asked himself if the challenge this race held out to him was really worth it. His chances of winning were so slim that it seemed ridiculous.

He was mixing up some fish and rice when Bob Leeve called. Things were fine in Fairbanks. Bob wanted to talk to Dan about what was still needed for the race. Above all, he wanted to talk about the re-supplying points. Mushers couldn't possibly transport twenty days' worth of provisions for their dogs and themselves. It was common practice to have supplies dropped off at specific locations.

"But I only have one dollar left," said Dan.

Eleanor's voice cut in. "I lend money at ten per cent. I've figured out that you need a thousand dollars."

"What if I don't win?"

"There are second, third and fourth prizes."

"It's possible I might not make any money at all," Dan pointed out.

There was silence at the other end of the wire.

"Well then, why get involved in the first place?" Bob demanded.

"I'm unemployed," Dan replied, "so why not?"

"People are too kind to the unemployed," scoffed Bob. "They let them go on dogsled races!"

Dan heard Eleanor's laugh. "OK, then? So I'm lending you a thousand dollars, and you'll pay me back a thousand, plus a hundred. Agreed?"

"Agreed."

"Give us your list."

"But I don't know the prices of things any more."

The very words, as he spoke them, explained to him his longing to live in the wild. A gulf existed between himself and civilization, and he would be wasting his energy trying to bridge it.

174

"Maybe you're just a frustrated poet," joked Bob's wife.

"And a poet always needs sordid people like us, who know the prices of things," added Bob.

Dan didn't argue. He thanked them and then, as he had noticed a burning smell from his simple meal, he hung up. But he knew his morale had been boosted all the same.

Dan now worked at improving his starts. Leaving the faithful Irik behind in the village broke his heart, but he had to get used to the solitude that would be his during the race. Irik spent his time waiting, and invariably Dan found the young boy watching out for him a mile or two from the village. He would then let Irik guide the sled the short distance back. Bull and Eccluke spelled each other in the lead, and took it in turns doing punishment time on the sled.

And then one day Bob arrived, landing his Piper on the rough ground for the last time before the race.

"I've got all your things," he announced. "And I've put some food in storage at Fairbanks."

He climbed out of the plane carrying an oblong sack that was almost as tall as he was.

Irik helped them lug it over to the house and spread its contents out on the floor. There was a change of clothes, a pile of heavy socks and a spare pair of tall boots. A musher must certainly expect to get wet, and then the polar cold could turn his clothing into a rigid vice capable of paralysing him. So Dan would need several changes of clothes.

He also had an isothermic, moisture-proof tent, a double-layered down-filled sleeping bag, and medication for the dogs and himself, enabling him to give injections, immobilize fractures, sew up wounds. He had a tarpaulin to cover the dogs in case the weather got too bad to go on. He had maps and a compass, extra harnesses, and duplicates of every leash. There was a small, very sturdy folding shovel and an alarm clock to wake him when he couldn't afford to sleep more than an hour or two on the trail.

His one-piece underclothes were very fine wool, and Eleanor had included a silk hood for his head; he could wear this underneath his fur caps, and it would prevent chafing. He had a special grease to smear on the exposed parts of his face. Also he had one thing that none of the other competitors would have: a gammy leg.

They cleared some space to lay out the maps. The race was from Anchorage to Nome, a distance of 1,050 miles.

"To have any hope at all, I'll have to do it in eighteen to twenty days," Dan said.

Bob thought for a moment. "That means you'll have to do at least fifty miles a day."

Dan estimated that he could survive on his own for five days at a time as long as he had food for the dogs.

"Then I should plan to intercept you three times," said Bob. Leaning over the map, he pencilled small circles round three points spaced out equally over the total distance.

"As far as my own food is concerned," said Dan, "I can get along on my own till I reach Ruby."

Ruby was well past halfway. "That's a long way to go," said Bob.

"A few supply points will be set up by the race committee."

Bob conveyed his doubts with a wave of his hand. "Don't count on anyone but yourself," he said.

He was referring, Dan knew, to the hostility people had shown towards him, but he didn't want to think about that. Instead, he began to discuss with Irik the weight of the supplies he should carry from one stopping point to the next. Finally, they arrived at a figure of three hundred and ninety pounds, including the camping gear and his personal belongings. Bob thought it was a lot.

Dan was careful not to mention the additional weight caused by the dissension between Bull and Eccluke—the fact that each of them would be loaded onto the sled in turn.

Bob mentioned the inevitability of a blizzard, and how it might become impossible for him to drop off supplies.

"We'll cross that bridge when we come to it," replied Dan.

The answer didn't please Bob, but he had a hard time improving on it. They decided that Dan would immediately go as far as Fairbanks with the sled and dogs so that he could test the equipment. From Fairbanks, Bob would transport everything to Anchorage by plane. It was February 18. The race would begin on March 3.

Bob drained his cup of coffee. Proudly Irik pulled on the chest-expander with his crippled arm, showing him the progress he had made. Dan's eyes, recently clouded with gloom, lit up. To all three of them life suddenly seemed inexpressibly good.

DAN HAD FINISHED stowing the baggage on the sled; he placed the carbine within reach of his hand and put the boxes of cartridges in a dry place. Irik helped him harness the dogs. Bull was at the head of the team and Eccluke remained behind her wire netting, not making a sound. Dan had finally made up his mind, with enormous regret, not to take her along.

Kougar, the chief, came forward, the villagers grouped behind him.

"When you come back, the ice will have cracked," Kougar said.

He added that there would be a big celebration on his return. Touched by his simple words, Dan patted him on the shoulder as a gesture of farewell. Kougar then patted Dan back—the Indians started laughing and it seemed that the pantomime might go on and on. . . . Dan broke off to grab hold of Irik and swing him into the air.

"When I come back I want to see you do this." He stretched his arm backwards, far over his shoulder. "Swear it?"

Irik spat on the ground to seal the vow. "I'll take good care of Eccluke," he said.

Dan raised his hand to start the dogs, and the sled took off like a shot. It was then that Eccluke's howl of agony rose into the leaden sky.

Dan's heart turned over in his breast. Instinctively, he flung his anchor round the guardrail post in front of a house he was passing and the team jerked to a stop.

Eccluke was still howling, her muzzle raised towards the sky. She was announcing her death from abandonment. Already, however, Dan was opening the kennel. She jumped into his arms, making herself so small and light that he could not possibly leave her behind. He unhooked her harness, and then she knew for certain she was going on the journey.

He placed her on the sled; there was no need to tie her. She stood erect, facing him, paws resting on the rear springs. Her back was turned to the entire team: the better to show her scorn for the dogs, the better to show her love for the musher.

Companions in adversity from way back, Dan and Eccluke stood facing each other, Dan's body swaying slightly as he pushed with his one good leg.

DAN REACHED FAIRBANKS in two short stages. He had camped fairly comfortably in his tent. He wasn't eager to venture into Fairbanks with his sled and dogs, so he bedded down in the corner of an aircraft hangar on the landing strip.

The start of the race was now just six days off. Bob had bought some pemmican, concentrated meat in tablet form. During prolonged effort the dogs should eat six and a half pounds of this a day. With eighteen dogs, that would come to a hundred and nineteen pounds.

Dan and Bob revised their calculations. Dan couldn't carry more than three days' worth of provisions for the dogs, so he would try to buy fresh meat in villages along the way.

Eleanor wished Dan loads of luck—claiming that all she wanted was to see her thousand dollars back, plus interest.

It took the Piper two trips to transport Dan and his whole circus to Anchorage. There, too, Dan decided he would stay in a hangar at the airfield. He had no desire to show up in town or to leave the dogs. With the race only forty-eight hours off, the excitement was growing, with bets of up to a hundred thousand dollars being taken, and he was afraid someone might poison them.

Before leaving him for good, Bob stuck his head out through the open window of his Piper. "Eleanor's betting on your winning or coming in second," he called out. Dan didn't bother to answer that she was crazy. This country, having once known gold fever, had kept its taste for gambling.

He made his dogs trot, saw to their needs and slept next to them on the same ground. Eccluke always managed to get closest to him. Then, on the final silvery dawn of March 3, he loaded the sled and harnessed the team. Bull was on the sled, Eccluke at the lead. With three days' worth of food the sled held its heaviest possible weight, but tomorrow morning the dogs would have lightened it by a hundred and nineteen pounds.

He didn't hurry. He was properly registered, and he wanted to arrive at the start just before the number cards were distributed. He was not anxious to satisfy anyone's curiosity.

On the outskirts of town, other teams were gliding in ahead of him. A fine layer of snow covered the road. The sleds ran alongside parked cars, and a few traffic lights blinked on and off in the empty streets.

Low houses lined the main avenue. Shop signs were lit up, as were the street lamps.

Number cards were being drawn in front of a pub in the centre of town. Dan saw the mass of people, and various officials up on a platform. Beyond the people, dogs jumped up and down in special cages set up for them in removal vans. Sleds were being taken down from the roofs. Harnesses were being put on. A banner flew overhead, blocking off the street and indicating the starting line.

The moment a team arrived, it was surrounded and eagerly scrutinized. Gamblers assessed the chances of the man and his dogs. Jokes flew to and fro in the cold. But the faces of the mushers all reflected the same degree of gravity, the same apprehension at the prospect of the journey ahead and the risk of dying somewhere on the trail.

All the teams were being helped to get ready. Someone must have uttered Dan's name, for all at once silence seized hold of the gathering, and every eye turned towards him. He attached his sled to a lamppost well out of reach of other dogs and stared impassively back.

A few smart alecks approached him nevertheless, offering caustic comments about his gear—his old-fashioned sled basket was patched with leather and pieces of tin; the coyote crossbreeds, with their heads lowered, tails between their legs, did not seem inviting prospects to bet on. A voice called out that they wouldn't even have the strength to get past the town boundary.

Dan counted thirty-four competing teams. The most popular was Greg Harway's. He was the favourite; he had won the previous year. Virginia, by his side, smiled now and then. Her gaze met Dan's, but he restrained himself and gave no sign of greeting.

Among the mushers, Dan had recognized Rocky Bent, Aklosik and George Smith. Except for theirs and Greg's, the other faces were new to him. Dan preferred it that way. Shared memories were often a handicap; at times they were a source of suffering. Even so, Dan was secretly pained that an old friend like Rocky had not come over to shake his hand. In a way he understood: few men liked to owe another anything and, in fact, Rocky owed him a great deal. One of life's little accidents, during which his emotional debt to Dan had become enormous.

179

Dan had drawn number seven. A magic number. The seven days of the week; the seven layers of the skin; the seven deadly sins; the seven wonders of the world; the seven colours of the rainbow. Greg Harway was wearing number three.

An official was briefly going over the regulations. The runners travelled and camped at their own pace. They were asked to stop at all the checkpoints, set up every fifty miles or so, along the way, where dogs that were incapable of going on would be dropped off. Such dogs would be cared for, and later returned to their owners, by the committee. No runner should drop off a dog at a location that wasn't a checkpoint.

The police had cordoned off traffic on the main road for the start of the race. Runners were starting out every two minutes, each team

aided by friends who held the sled steady at the starting line.

The dogs, unnerved by all the waiting about, were tugging furiously at their central tethers. Each dog's pull was around five hundred and fifty pounds. The teams had a minimum of sixteen dogs, the longest one numbering twenty-five. Thus, on average, each sled was being dragged by a force of eleven thousand pounds.

Dan had no one helping him hold back his sled. As Number 6 went forward to the starting line, Dan turned his team round. No one moved to make room for him. He gripped Eccluke, the leader, by the harness, and forced her into a sharper turn. In the process he found himself passing close to Virginia, and it seemed to him that she had placed her hand lightly on his shoulder as he went by.

He attached his sled to another lamppost and again gripped Eccluke's harness. Seated on the sled behind the baggage, Bull looked around defiantly at Eccluke and the other sixteen dogs in the team.

Number 6 had just taken off. Dan had his seventeen dogs at the ready near the starting line. But because of the angle of his sled Eccluke was a few yards short of the line. Laughter broke out. Someone said snidely, "The race isn't long enough for the famous Dan Murphy!"

The countdown was under way. The dogs pulled anxiously, tightening the strap that anchored the sled to the lamppost. Dan moved back to calm them down, and with starting time ten seconds away, they were still.

Dan waited for the signal, then unhitched the sled, and when his dogs started off at a peaceful trot, scorn rippled through the crowd. It was to the accompaniment of this that Dan took off on the Iditarod. The sun had failed to break through the clouds, so there would be an hour at the most of pale daylight, that day.

181

CHAPTER FIVE

March 3. Anchorage to Knik. In the course of the first twelve miles Dan overtook five mushers who had left before he had. One more remained: Greg Harway.

Dan's dogs kept up the trot that had so amused the bystanders at the starting line—after a few miles the teams that had taken off like rockets had begun to walk, and Dan soon made up for his slow start. Bull clearly wanted to take up his place at the lead and was squirming fiendishly on the sled, but eventually he settled down. Now, near the Eagle River, he spotted Greg at the top of a slight rise, running behind his sled.

Dan pushed down with his good leg, maintaining a slow rhythm that meshed well with the dogs' trot. But Greg, turning round and seeing Dan, feverishly began to increase his speed. It made no sense, with the finishing line still some twenty hard days off.

Passion, Dan knew, was a dangerous counsellor. He spoke calmly to his dogs. Eccluke turned her head up to him. He told them the journey would be long and very difficult, but that they would make it in the end, no doubt about that.

Once they had passed through Eagle River, Dan saw Greg suddenly fork off. It seemed to him that Greg was making a mistake, so he kept pulling straight ahead. The trouble was that there were no more trail pointers. The army was supposed to have put up markers, but they had no posts, so that whenever there were no trees to fix the markers to, they simply tossed them out on the snow, where they were soon covered over.

In time Dan found himself altering his own course. Instinct guided him, and he tried to follow the least difficult route. His main concern was to save wear and tear on the dogs' paws. Although there were hard areas of melted and refrozen snow here, he saved their leather boots for later, reminding himself that much further north the needles of ice were waiting for him.

During this stage, in fact, Dan covered around twenty miles more than he had to. Aklosik, who had begun as Number 13, overtook him. But then, two hours later, having changed direction a few times, Dan met up with him again near the Knik River.

Three or four miles beyond the Knik, Dan had to drop off an exhausted coyote crossbreed at a checkpoint. He took advantage of the stop to inspect all of the others meticulously. There were three men at the checkpoint, an isolated shack that had served as a stopping point along the old overland postal route.

One of the men there was very old, a man who had trailed a great many of these races. He watched Dan's every movement. "Seems to me you've got five more dogs there who are goners," he said, speaking painfully through cracked lips.

He had not bothered to examine the team closely, but Dan knew he was right. His observation had simply pinpointed what Dan himself had realized without really wanting to admit it.

Dan ventured to ask how the other mushers were doing, but no one answered him. He noticed, however, that the old man was shaking his head at him. What did that mean? That no one else had yet passed through this checkpoint? Or, on the contrary, that he was in fact the last to do so?

He gave small portions of food to the dogs. For his own part, he gulped down some vitamin tablets, and then switched Bull for Eccluke. When she began acting up on the sled he clipped her two or three times with his whip and she calmed down.

A bonus of a thousand dollars was waiting for the musher first across the finishing line at the town of Knik, the end of the first stage. Still not knowing whether he was first or last, Dan set off again at his trotting pace. The loss of the coyote crossbreed didn't seem to make any difference.

Then one of the four Siberian huskies began to limp. Dan kept an eye on it, hoping that the problem wouldn't get worse before nightfall, when they could all rest.

He first knew they were approaching Knik when he saw houses in the distance. Shortly afterwards, a sign announced the name of the next checkpoint, two miles from the town itself.

One of the army scouts overtook Dan on his snowmobile, making a terrible racket. It occurred to Dan too late that this fellow would have known the exact standings and was now taking them to the gamblers assembled at Knik. People were allowed to change their initial bets during any part of the race. Even near the very end they could make new bets, though the odds then would obviously be less interesting.

Even so, all kinds of reversals were possible right up to within a mile of the finish line.

The limping husky's condition was pitiful now, but Dan couldn't stop. There was no more room on the sled, and he couldn't harness Eccluke in his place without setting off a battle royal. But at least the ground was flat, not too bad; still, the husky let out its first moans. They grew more and more distinct until they came with every movement of his hindquarters.

Dan finally abandoned the dog at the next checkpoint. This meant two gone out of eighteen. Two dogs disabled in a single day.

As Dan was reorganizing his team, Greg Harway arrived behind him at the checkpoint. His team was complete, but his dogs' tongues were practically touching the ground and he had obviously forced them in order to catch up with Dan. He asked the man in charge of the post which teams were in front. Greg got an answer: no one had passed through ahead of them.

Dan was the first to set out again. There were still two miles to go before the day's finishing line and that bonus of a thousand dollars. When Greg overtook him, Dan asked himself if the prize was really worth straining his dogs' hearts—maybe losing the eventual fifty thousand by trying to get hold of a mere thousand. Besides, he had based everything on his trotting theory, and he must not yield to any temptations. So he let Greg go by and curbed his impulse to fight shoulder to shoulder.

Another team caught up with him: Number 6. But scarcely had it overtaken him when its dogs fell back from a sprint to a walk, the difference so dramatic that it seemed to Dan the other sled had virtually stopped. He passed it easily and realized he was again catching up with Greg, whose dogs by now were walking also.

With the thousand dollars two hundred yards off, Greg tried to speed up his dogs. But he had to make do with a poor trot, and Dan cruised past him.

Greg was furious. He didn't need the bonus, and he probably didn't give a damn which of the other contestants won it, as long as it wasn't Dan Murphy. He didn't want to be on hand for the presentation, so he went back alone to the area encircled by huts that was reserved for the men and their teams. And he fed his dogs without even unharnessing them.

184

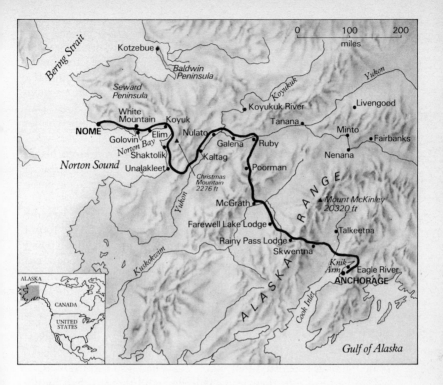

When Dan arrived at the encampment, he realized that Greg was planning to continue the race by night in order to regain the lead. As for himself, he tended his dogs and made himself a bed on the floor of one of the huts.

Darkness fell: it was the blackest of nights. Using a lamp on his forehead to leave his hands free, Dan examined the paws of all his dogs. Two more huskies were slightly lame. If he took off with them again tomorrow, and if they collapsed before he reached an official checkpoint, he would have to abandon the race. On the other hand, if he left them here and it turned out that they could have recuperated en route, he would be needlessly depriving himself of two good dogs. Crouching down near his team, he weighed the risks. And in the profound darkness that enveloped the camp, he identified several teams heading out. Greg was the first. Then Rocky Bent, and Aklosik, and George Smith.

185

Finally he made up his mind. He put the two huskies on a leash and walked them to a large stone house about a hundred yards away. A cafe-pub-restaurant, the haze inside it gave the impression that a steam locomotive had just passed through. Hanging lamps gave barely enough light to penetrate the smoke. With his dogs, Dan stayed near the entrance, waiting until he had got accustomed to the atmosphere.

A rowdy character was shouting odds in front of a large black-board, on which was listed the names of the mushers, with a row of figures in front of each. Dan noticed that opposite his own name there were only two, fairly insignificant, numbers.

He finally spotted one of the race officials and asked where he could leave any dogs not able to go on. The man asked Dan to put them in a cubicle out the back, behind the building. He gulped down the beer he had bought, then dug a couple of pieces of cardboard out of his pocket, which he fastened round the dogs' necks, with the number seven marked on them, along with the name of the town where the dogs would be returned to after the race.

Dan left without anyone else paying him the slightest attention. The two huskies were only too happy to lie down in their cubicles. When Dan scanned the place in the light of his torch, the presence of some ten dogs suggested that other teams had also had troubles.

Dan had lost four dogs in a single day, and the race had hardly started. He smiled, thinking that at this rate he might well end up by pulling the sled himself.

He got back to the mushers' sleeping huts at the same time as Greg Harway staggered angrily through the door. Greg had lost his way. He had gone round in a circle in the darkness, ending up back in Knik, and he was swearing like a trooper.

He paused to deal a few savage kicks to those of his dogs who weren't wise enough to get out of his way. But he still didn't unharness them. Dan knew he was stubborn enough to try setting out again. Seeing him, Greg declared emphatically that he was "perfectly capable of going faster than a filthy murdering cripple."

"Not this evening, you weren't," said Dan, as he walked away. He lingered by his window for a while, and before long had the satisfaction of seeing Greg starting out again, spurred on by his vicious temper.

Dan stretched out on the floor. He was unable to doze off, but that didn't bother him. He would sleep well enough once he was wholly caught up in this race, far out northwards towards Bering, and on the ice field. He loved the purity of the crystalline ice, and participating in a natural contest untainted by the slightest compromise of conscience. And, best of all, the kingdom of the polar bear.

His memories kept him awake late enough to hear Greg returning. The darkness had thrown him back on Knik the way the tide spews back shipwrecks.

March 4. Knik to Skwentna. Dan started off again at around five o'clock. He had heard a team leave a short while before him, but he didn't know which one. And as he left the hut area he heard another team being hastily prepared.

The track was better than it had been the previous night. The sled was gliding well and the dogs' trot was lively. Suddenly Dan was confident and felt that the old man's prediction about the number of dogs he might lose had been unnecessarily gloomy.

In the night Rocky Bent had managed only five miles beyond Knik. He was barely awake when Dan arrived at his camp. He had gained absolutely nothing by going on beyond the Anchorage–Knik checkpoint. He watched Dan approach and then, kneeling up, slowly raised an arm in greeting. They were alone now, free from the judgments of other people. Dan gazed impassively at him, the man who had once said to Dan, "As long as I live, I will always owe you something."

Had Dan stopped to speak, he would probably have been welcomed warmly. But Dan simply waved back and went by without stopping.

Fresh sled tracks stretched ahead of him. He hoped they weren't from Greg's sled. He caught up with the team in the hollow of a small valley. It was Number 9, however, and Dan didn't know the musher. This man's dogs were trotting, too, but only because they were tired, and their trot was less efficient than Dan's.

Dan overtook Number 9 and soon, still barely twenty miles beyond Knik, he came within sight of a camp with two mushers heating coffee over a bright fire close to some woods. Dan recognized Aklosik and George Smith.

They greeted Dan as soon as they recognized him. Aklosik raised his tin mug, inviting him to join them for coffee, and George Smith stopped the greenlander, Bull, by grabbing hold of his harness. Dan attached the sled to a tree, then shook hands with both men. He remembered that they worked in the timber business. He had met them once before in a race during the fur-market fair at Anchorage.

That had been almost ten years ago. And now, in the freedom of the wilderness, they felt no embarrassment about Dan's past. Their friendship warmed Dan far more than the coffee did. They chatted, forgetting about the race for a short while. Smith was of the opinion that, this far away from everything, a few hours one way or the other made no difference.

Number 9 passed them. Aklosik knew him. His name was Leavey, and he was a gunsmith from Fairbanks.

"He competes every year and always finishes up two days late."

Also, according to Smith and Aklosik, Number 9 was the only team ahead of them. So Greg was still behind.

When Rocky Bent came into view, Aklosik and Smith glanced questioningly at Dan. He nodded his consent, and the other two invited Rocky to stop and finish up the coffee. He halted his team, and Dan sensed from the strength of his handshake that he genuinely wanted to make up for his pettiness at the starting line. His son owed his life to Dan Murphy, whose unfailing presence of mind saved the boy, after the newly sharpened runners of a snowmobile had severed his femoral artery.

"The kid is just fine," he announced.

"Great," said Dan.

There was an awkwardness which was every bit as obvious as the rising wind.

"Right now he's working in Italy. They're doing excavations in the south, He's never forgotten you, you know."

"Me neither," said Dan.

He stared into his mug. Rocky was clearly trying to rid himself of an enormous burden.

"If he'd been around during that stupid business of yours, he'd have come to see you in ..." He left the sentence dangling.

"Prison." Dan supplied the word.

"Yeah, right! That's it, prison." Rocky was almost shouting.

Dan was charitable enough not to ask Rocky why he, the father, had not come to see him in prison either.

Aklosik and Smith exchanged a few jokes, and laughing did the four men good. But Dan was restless, looking at the landscape around him. The coffee was already frozen in the bottom of his mug, and the wind was buffeting his tall frame.

"I should have come myself!" Rocky said at last, his voice hoarse.

Dan put a hand on his shoulder. "It's OK," he said simply. He thanked them all for the coffee and went over to his sled.

"If you ever need anything, don't hesitate," added Rocky.

Dan unhitched the sled. "On this race, we'll all find ourselves needing something sooner or later," he said, stepping onto the runner of the sled as it started forward.

Rocky clenched his hands together and shook them above his head. Clearly he was not about to forget that Dan had saved his kid's life.

Dan knew that the race had already brought him a thousand dollars, plus the happiness of finding himself once more among men. He had been right, so far at least, to entertain such high hopes. And his team was carrying on tirelessly at its fast trot. All in all, the prospects were quite reassuring.

As he neared Skwentna, another of the huskies began to limp. Again Dan thought about the old fellow at the checkpoint and his prediction. "Five more dogs who are goners," he had said. This one would make it already four goners. But the surface was good. Admittedly the wind hadn't let up, but it hadn't grown any stronger either. It blew across the surface, erasing the tracks as usual. Even so, the route presented no problems. The army had put up markers galore. In places it looked like a village fair. And yet the husky's limping was getting worse.

At the checkpoint on the outskirts of Skwentna, Dan left off the husky, with one of the now familiar tags round its neck. Nevertheless, each time he'd fed his team that day he'd lightened his load, and the loss of so many dogs seemed to have no effect. After all, even if he had not yet caught up with Number 9, no one else had either.

He had covered eighty-three miles since Knik, and he decided to bypass Skwentna, pitching his camp a few miles beyond the town, alone, and in peace. Daylight was growing faint. He stopped just before seven o'clock, seven miles past Skwentna. He unharnessed the dogs. Bull and Eccluke had each led for half the distance between them, and both were in splendid form.

He decided to warm the dogs' food tonight, and to cut down some branches for their bedding. A polar dog can eat frozen food and sleep on the ice; however, if his food is warm and his body insulated from the ice he will have more endurance.

Dan worked swiftly, cutting litter for the thirteen dogs. Then he made a fire and was melting snow in his cooking pot when three teams appeared in the gloom. The light from his camp stopped them. The unrelenting climate and the vast open spaces were an encouragement to see the tiniest glimmer as a refuge, perhaps as a friend.

Hearing the newcomers speak, Dan at once recognized Greg Harway's voice. He was talking the loudest, deciding for the others that they would stop here for the night. Torches flicked over Dan's camp, and one of the fellows called out, "Hey—it's Number 7!"

Dan had a feeling these guys were up to no good. He remained seated and began mixing dogfood into the warm water. He heard branches cracking as the other fellows broke them up to make their litters.

"Hey! I just found a pile all ready to use," said one of them.

"Those are mine," Dan called out.

He had barely moved. He got up only when he saw them beginning to carry his branches away. Greg loomed in front of him, a short carbine in his hand.

"We're not going to argue with a guy like you," Greg warned.

A torch shone into Dan's face. He sensed one man behind him, another to the side.

"We could do to you what you once did to another guy," said one.

"I never stole anything belonging to a fellow competitor."

"We're not your fellows, though," sneered the other.

Dan thought of George Smith and Aklosik, camping safely in Skwentna. And here he was, all alone, facing these three vicious men. He turned away without answering and began to feed his dogs. He forced himself to eat a few bites also, listening as the men, who were suspiciously close to his pile of branches, came and went around him.

He crisply loaded his 30–.30 carbine, and the others suddenly

190

grew quieter. A sullen silence fell over the mushers, and Dan slid into his sleeping bag. He didn't want to tire himself further, and he knew he would have to keep alert, ready to protect his dogs. Dan had placed his carbine at a slight angle, its barrel to hand so that he could grab it quickly. He was ready to kill to protect his dogs.

He dozed off, without really sleeping. More than once he sat up to see if there was any movement in the camp, but after some swaggering remarks about the outcome of the race, the others had apparently fallen into a deep sleep.

Dan knew that the click of his carbine had made them think twice. An armed truce had its merits.

March 5. Skwentna to Rainy Pass Lodge. At two thirty in the morning Dan figured that he would be ready to leave again in about an hour and a half, at four o'clock. In future he would always start out at night, and thus be able to stop earlier in the afternoon. He could then set up his new camps by day, in more comfortable conditions.

And so he extricated himself from his sleeping bag, fed and harnessed the dogs in almost total silence, and treated himself to coffee, biscuits and a few thin slices of bacon.

He vanished into the night, leaving Greg and the other two still sleeping heavily. Two miles further on he passed Number 9, who had put tent canvas in front of his sled to protect himself from the wind. He, too, was still asleep.

Dan hadn't seen anyone overtake him during the night so he knew that he was moving into the lead. Bull was on the sled and Eccluke was guiding the team. Her days went better when she was able to pull at the start.

Before daybreak Dan cleared a series of fairly steep hills, and as soon as the darkness faded into grey light, the poor condition of the trail became apparent. Some areas were naked rubble. Army scouts were already busy trying to re-route the course.

After a while one of the coyote crossbreeds began to limp. At first he limped only every ten yards or so, but then almost constantly. "Seems to me you've got five more dogs who are goners." The old fellow's remark was turning out to be more precise than a Swiss watch.

The next checkpoint was still a long way off when the course started zigzagging through the forest. To slalom between the trees, Dan slowed the team to a walk. On steep slopes the sled tilted dangerously, and Dan had to use all his strength just to keep it straight. He also had to push to help the dogs, the zigzags cut down on their momentum. He kept looking up at the sky—some time that day Bob was supposed to drop off new supplies, but in this dense forest his friend wouldn't see him. They would have to meet later, maybe at Houston Pass.

Dan inhaled deeply as he left the forest. Visibility was improving, but Bob's Piper was still nowhere to be seen. The coyote crossbreed was suffering more and more. The dog wasn't complaining, but his pulling rope stayed slack. He no longer kept his proper station and this cramped the dog trotting just behind him, which bit him cruelly. Bravely the injured dog tried to take up his place again. For the space of a few yards his rope was taut; then it slackened again, and again the other dog bit him.

Dan took advantage of a new slope to halt the team. The checkpoint was still twenty miles away. The crossbreed couldn't make it that far.

Dan got Bull off the sled and put the injured dog in his place. The pads of the crossbreed's right front paw had opened up like an over-ripe fruit. Dan then harnessed Bull in front of Eccluke, who immediately threw herself forward to attack him, restrained only by her short pulling rope.

Dan started the team up again and at once realized he would no longer be able to keep them at a trot. Spurred on by Eccluke's rage, Bull was galloping, while Eccluke was pulling flat out on her own rope to catch up with him.

The other dogs were being swept along at a sprint. The slope did not help to slow them down: Eccluke's blind fury was too strong. On level ground, the pace accelerated even more. Standing on the runners of the sled, Dan could do nothing. He knew, though, that pushed to extremes like this, a dog could drop dead as if struck by lightning.

The pace slowed gradually as the miles streamed by. Dan wasn't happy with the lead he had taken; he feared that he would pay for it later. The dogs were now running at a slower pace, but they hadn't yet slackened to a trot.

The checkpoint was in sight, at the edge of the next village. Dan pressed on his brake, plunging its steel teeth into the hard ground. But Eccluke hardly seemed to notice. Foaming, she still hoped to catch up with Bull and rip him to pieces.

A hundred or so yards short of the checkpoint Dan noticed the wooden post of an old telephone line, and threw his anchor, hooking onto the post and stopping the team abruptly. With his injured dog he went forward on foot.

At the village Dan was welcomed by two men and a young woman, who marked down his arrival time at the checkpoint and gathered up the dog. Dan asked them if they had seen an aeroplane, a blue Piper, but they hadn't. The young woman walked with him back to his sled. She was well dressed, wearing such elaborately worked furs that Dan thought she was probably waiting to cheer on one of the competitors.

"Who are you waiting for?" he asked, as he tried to calm Eccluke and put her back on the sled.

Surprised, the woman told him, "I'm waiting for Jacques Loff, Number 8."

"I've never seen him," said Dan.

"Well, he's the one who's going to win this race," she said confidently.

"Good for him."

She peered at him closely with clear grey eyes. "You're Dan Murphy, aren't you?"

He nodded, then released the sled, with Bull now alone in the lead.

"Good luck anyway!" she called after him.

The dogs had resumed their regular trot, and the sled was smoothly on its way towards Houston Pass. Dan helped it along at intervals, giving it a shove with his good leg.

Suddenly, the faint droning of an aeroplane engine broke into the solitude. Dan practically got a crick in his neck as he anxiously looked up, trying to spot the plane. But although the noise grew louder, the low clouds, greyish-white like dirty cotton wool, still hid the plane. When Dan finally saw it, Bob's Piper was very low and already greeting him, dipping first one wing and then the other. The plane set down gently.

"Everybody's saying you're in first place!" Bob exclaimed.

"The finishing line's still a long way off," Dan answered soberly.

Bob unloaded food for the dogs. "I see you're missing some," he said, looking over the team.

Dan smiled. "You might say that."

At least, now that he had fewer dogs, he needed to load less onto the sled. Bob waited, jingling a pair of eight-pointed crampons from his fingers.

"Present from Eleanor. She says there's not enough snow this year, and there'll be slopes of sheer ice."

"What's it like to have a wife who's always right?" asked Dan.

gratefully accepting the crampons. Bob conceded that it took some getting used to.

They soon ran out of conversation. Dan, totally wrapped up in the race, was no longer in Bob's world. They agreed that their next meeting would be on March 8, in McGrath. Bob flew the Piper companionably over the sled for a few minutes before leaving them to their struggle: to the relentless wear and tear on man and dogs, as the miles eroded their resistance.

Dan stopped around three in the afternoon, six miles from Rainy Pass Lodge. He left the trail and went into the woods to set up camp out of sight of the other mushers. He gave the dogs more food than usual, for he'd noticed they were losing weight. He made good litters for them and for himself with some dry wood he could use for fuel at breakfast time. And he hoped that while he slept, no one would overtake him.

March 6. Rainy Pass Lodge to Rohn Roadhouse. The alarm rang at two thirty in the morning. Dan opened his eyes to merciless cold. But at least there was no wind. When he moved, Eccluke also stirred. He greased her and the other dogs' paws; they were all in very good shape. He also increased their regular morning rations. By the time he struck camp he had already been up for an hour and a half.

When he arrived at Rainy Pass Lodge, people were just beginning to stir. Clearly a great early-morning occupation for those who didn't have garages was to run out of their warm houses and check whether their car engines would start or not.

A tall fellow, who had just removed a bundle of old blankets from inside the bonnet of his small truck, waved to Dan and invited him in for a meal. In this country, a bit of warm nourishment was not to be refused. Dan tied up his sled and went into the house.

The man shouted to someone that there was a guest, and then went out again to start up his engine. In the kitchen, a woman invited Dan to sit down. Opposite him a teenager was huddled, still half asleep. His father was in the transportation business, and always dropped his son off at school. School was far away. Everything was far away in this country.

"So, is the race going well?" asked the woman.

She must have seen his sled through the window. The young boy sprang awake at the mention of the race, wanting to talk about his dogs. Dan saw a list of the competitors fastened to the inside of the kitchen door.

The father came in and sat down. There were pancakes for breakfast, served on white plates with yellow daisies on them. The man broke the news to Dan that one Jacques Loff, Number 8, had passed through the village at one o'clock in the morning. This fellow Loff was a local—he came from Galena, right on the Yukon—and he could navigate with a handkerchief tied over his eyes.

"He will still have to stop to let the dogs rest," said the boy.

His mother added that a man can't keep going all day and night, either. This Loff, she said, was a doctor, a general practitioner, and in the winter he had found no more reliable means for visiting isolated patients than a sled and dogs.

"Still, this is the first time he's been in this race," said the father. "He told me it was his wife's idea."

"Wives sometimes get those kinds of ideas," said Dan, remembering the young woman with grey eyes, back at the last checkpoint.

He stood up, thanking them for their hospitality. From the doorway they watched him leave.

So now Dan was second—but he had lost six dogs in three days. Some caribou cut across his path as he crossed Ptarmigan Pass and emerged onto Rohn River. The sun formed a crown of light on a round-shaped stand of trees. In places the rays mapped out zones of shadows as slender and tapering as swords. He thanked fate for having safely brought him so far.

About twenty miles past Rohn River, Dan ran into melting ice and gravel. The slush came well up the sides of his boots.

He didn't know which path to take, since there was no route marked out. Theoretically there should be scouts preceding the first musher, but Dan had caught up with them the day before. They had been having trouble with their snowmobile and were probably still a long way back.

Dan knew there should be a cottage somewhere nearby, and he began looking for it. When he found the place, it was inhabited by a young couple who told him that a team had just passed through and that the man was having problems with a dog who had suddenly gone as weak as a kitten. It was Number 8.

Dan cut short his stop there and caught up with Jacques Loff three miles further on. Loff had come to a full stop and was leaning over a dog stretched out on the sled. Dan asked if he needed anything. Loff had an open and pleasant face, with grey eyes like those of the young woman who had taken it for granted he would win. He said he would be all right, that he was just waiting quietly for his dog to die. Some people might have helped the animal along with a bullet, but Loff preferred to stroke him and talk to him like a friend.

Dan went on. He had travelled faster than usual, and got all the way to Rohn Roadhouse, which he reached towards seven. That evening only the army scouts on their snowmobile caught up with him.

Dan bought fresh meat and allowed the dogs to eat as much as they wanted, for a treat.

The scouts had had to take a sick musher all the way back to Knik. Three teams had given up, disgusted by the condition of the trail. There were now only thirty-one sleds competing on the remaining eight hundred and seventy miles to Nome.

March 7. Rohn Roadhouse to Farewell. Although he got up a bit later next morning, Dan still left before the army scouts. But they caught up with him five or six miles further on, along the river. All around was nothing but melting ice, sand and gravel, and deep, water-filled potholes. It was impossible to distinguish the water from the ice.

Farewell Lake Lodge was still forty miles off. The wind grew stronger by the minute, and once or twice it completely overturned Dan's sled. The dogs had to work hard to keep to their trot.

The scouts also were having problems. Water holes are a curse to snowmobiles. At times the scouts were ahead of Dan; at other times he was ahead of them. At one point he crossed the river, thinking he could find a shorter and more sheltered path through the forest, but he had had to go back, for there was simply no way through.

Late in the morning he arrived at Farewell Lake Lodge. He ate with the scouts and bought some food for the dogs. The scouts left to mark the trail as far as McGrath, and Dan himself covered another twenty or twenty-five miles, pushing on until four in the afternoon.

Before setting up his camp, he noticed a plane flying in circles above him, hovering in the wind like a kite. This was a group of reporters from the United States, but Dan didn't know that until he spoke to the pilot in McGrath the next day. Apparently they had landed on a lake a few miles ahead and waited for him in the hope of getting some pictures.

But Dan had not shown up. As usual he had camouflaged his camp. Because of the strong winds he had had trouble tipping over his sled and pitching his tent. He wanted to be sure of getting a good night's sleep, and the dogs felt the same way; they grouped themselves in a straight line behind him for a little protection against the gusting wind.

At Farewell, he had been told that the other competitors were pretty far behind him. Still, Dan preferred being alone and going at his own pace, doing exactly what he wanted. As he went to sleep that night he tried his best to think of the Iditarod not as a race but just as a long journey.

March 8. Farewell to McGrath. The sound of the wind must have lulled Dan to sleep, because once it stopped he found himself awake again. It was only one in the morning, but he decided to get ready anyway. Later in the morning the snow might have melted, and all signs of the trail might be wiped out. But his pace, and every movement he made that day, even when he stopped for a while to feed the dogs, was like an automaton's.

In the afternoon he scanned the cloud cover, hoping to see Bob's Piper break through. Then he tired of that and thought only of getting to McGrath. He noticed that Bull's gait was stiffening; the greenlander's paws were frozen, and Dan quickly switched him with Eccluke.

They arrived at McGrath at nine in the evening. The dogs were exhausted. He found a hangar where they could shelter and then, stopping off at a store on his way to a modest restaurant to eat a hot meal, he ran into some of the excitement stirred up locally by the race.

A man listening to his radio was keeping track of the general situation and bringing people up to date. The news was that Dan Murphy had taken the lead, with six dogs gone, and a friend was supplying him by plane; Jacques Loff was second by a few hours, and was carrying a dead dog with him; Greg Harway, in third place, had broken one of his sled's side members but was coming back strongly, with all his dogs in perfect condition; Rocky Bent, Aklosik and George Smith were travelling together a day behind; and anybody who had placed bets on the others badly needed to light a candle to Saint Musher.

Dan went back to his hangar and his dogs. Bull was lying on his side. His paws were now numb, and Dan realized he should have dried them off when he switched him with Eccluke. There had been a lot of water on the trail and, immobilized as he was on the sled, Bull's extremities must have been literally freezing.

Dan got up several times in the night to check on Bull. He was so preoccupied with his dog that he didn't even remember that Bob Leeve had failed to show up for their McGrath rendezvous.

NEXT MORNING, when Dan examined Bull's paws, the circulation in them was still not good. The other dogs, still exhausted, hardly moved an ear. Fatigue had drawn a cloak of inertia over the team. Dan bought fresh food for them and decided to stay where he was, telling himself that Bob would surely find him.

On a bulletin board, regularly updated for the gambling men, he was still listed as in the lead, but with a note beside his name: "Team tired out."

Rumour had it that Jacques Loff had carried his dead dog all the way to a checkpoint and then lost a ridiculous amount of time trying to dig a grave for the animal in the frozen ground. Greg Harway had passed him.

Dan had taken six days to get to McGrath. Yesterday, when he arrived, the army's trail ahead had still been good. Had he set out again that morning, the signs would still have been there to guide him. But by the time Greg Harway entered the little town, around noon, a full blizzard was blowing.

Some hours before, Dan had noticed two men in a van parked on the outskirts of town. Now Greg stopped his team just abreast of these men. He still had all his dogs, but they weren't in good shape. For two miles as they came into town they had had to weather a driving wind blasting straight at them.

As Greg walked swiftly towards a restaurant next to a group of

199

houses, the two fellows from the van began loading his sled with provisions.

A moment later Dan saw Greg coming out again, running. Someone must have told him that Dan Murphy had not yet taken off, and he launched his sled again in a frenzy. Sheltered there by the houses, he wouldn't appreciate the ferocity of the blizzard. But once past the village there was the open trail to confront.

Dan watched Greg disappearing, now at the front of the race. He went closer to take a look at the men with the van. The bigger one had an odd upturned nose sticking out of his balaclava helmet. They drove off, and Dan went back to look after his dogs.

The wind beat against the hangar. Dan tried to telephone Bob. He was worried, thinking there might have been an accident. When a snowstorm comes up around McGrath it can last three or four days, and aeroplanes can neither take off nor land.

No one answered Dan's call. Returning to the hangar, he found Jacques Loff there, his dogs looking like balls of ice. It was now three o'clock in the afternoon and Loff had decided to stop for the day.

Before night fell, nine more teams had shown up in McGrath, making eleven in all. Rocky Bent, Aklosik and George Smith were among them. They all got together at the restaurant, and during dinner the man in charge of the bulletin board noted down that back at Farewell Lake Lodge twelve other teams were shut in by the storm.

Then, just before dark, he announced that a scout had found Greg Harway five miles from McGrath, practically at death's door. He had helped Greg and his team back into town; luckily the wind had been at their backs, assisting them along. It was then that various caustic comments made it clear to Dan that Greg Harway, last year's winner, was not well liked. Undoubtedly he was too rich, and his position as assistant director of a large company didn't fit well with his being a musher. After all, many of the mushers earned their living by breeding polar dogs, or as craftsmen who made sleds, and they relied on the prizes they won in races.

Since society at large—except for Bent, Aklosik and Smith, who were now rallying around him—was also against Dan, he began thinking how mighty hard society was to please. Even if you tried to conform to it totally, it often rejected you. But what was the true face of society? Did it really have one?

March 10 and 11. McGrath to Bear Creek. Dan was the first to wake up. It was still snowing, ·but as the wind was now gentle and the dogs seemed eager to leave, he harnessed them. Greg Harway had stayed over at a friend's place, no doubt in a comfortable bed, Dan hoped.

On the way out of town the fresh snow slowed down the runners of the sled, and the dogs alternated between a trot and a walk. But Bull's circulation was fine again, and he tugged along conscientiously at the lead.

Even so, Jacques Loff caught up with them within a few hours. They stopped together to feed their dogs. Dan had brought only enough fresh food for this and the following day.

Loff drank deeply from his thermos. He explained to Dan that, for the kidneys, you could never drink enough during sustained exertion. There was snow on the beard that ran along the edge of his jaw. He was tall, his muscles well defined, and he inspired confidence.

That day the dogs were constantly in snow up to their chests, and Dan and Loff covered only sixty miles despite valiant efforts to go further.

The two mushers slept over in a hunting cabin belonging to a man named Arny Post who worked in McGrath. A fire burned in the hearth, and there were turkey pancakes and bacon and eggs to eat. Arny was there for the weekend, but his wife would be staying on through the following week, offering hospitality to other mushers. It occurred to Dan that society did have a better nature after all, and that Arny Post and his wife were a proof of it.

DAN LEFT THE POSTS' CABIN a good half hour before Loff, setting out on what would prove to be a trying day. Almost immediately he ran into scouts retracing their tracks. They confessed to Dan that they had lost their way, but they thought they knew where to pick up the route again. Dan turned his team round to follow them. The scouts stopped frequently and finally lost the trail altogether. In this region of vast, virtually treeless plains everything looked the same: white on white.

While the scouts were deliberating about which route to take, Loff, Aklosik and Smith caught up with Dan. They told him that Rocky Bent's dogs had been fighting. He had one with its throat torn open and another dying, and he had had to go back twenty miles to a checkpoint to leave the two dogs.

Dan and the three others were seven miles from Bear Creek when they unexpectedly reached a forest where the scout's trail markers hung from the trees as clearly as lanterns. But when they crossed the forest all was chaos. The slopes turned out to be so steep that Dan had to get off the sled and really push—using both legs, the good one and the bad. Only Jacques Loff stayed on his sled, since his dogs seemed to be in better condition.

Dan had only a day's worth of food left. Bear Creek was the simplest of stopping posts, but since it did have a radio telephone, Dan called McGrath to send for some food. The supplier claimed he would do everything he could, but he doubted if the delivery would be possible for several days.

Tex Gates, the fellow in charge of Bear Creek, lodged the mushers in a cabin and fed them that night. Dan chalked him up as another of society's positive aspects.

March 12, 13 and 14. Bear Creek to Poorman. Dan was again the first to set out the next morning, with Eccluke at the lead. The weary dogs could only manage a trot that was much slower than their pace at the beginning. In the end no one had shown up with food from McGrath, but Dan decided he could not afford to wait for a delivery. He had no more provisions for them, and very little for himself. He could only hope that he would see Bob's Piper appear in the course of the day.

Greg Harway had arrived at Bear Creek so late the previous night, after badly losing his way during the day, that he had found it impossible to get up with the others.

At that difficult moment between darkness and daylight when one doesn't know if it's dawn or still night, Dan was crossing a wide snowy expanse when he saw a landing strip ahead, with an aeroplane on it. It turned out not to be Bob's, and it flew off before Dan could reach it. He found a large heap of dried fish that had been tossed onto the ground nearby. He couldn't decipher the name written on the makeshift sign stuck in the middle of the pile, and he assumed the fish had been dropped off for some other musher, so he didn't take any. He learned later, to his great annoyance, that the delivery had in fact been left there for him, but the supplier working out of McGrath had misunderstood his name.

The trail was bad again today. Going round in circles, Dan kept crossing his own tracks. He was only five miles from Bear Creek, but he had already travelled ten miles. Far off in the valley he could see the army scouts, who seemed to have lost the trail also. Aklosik and Smith caught up with him. It struck Aklosik as pretty funny that here they all were, after two whole hours, virtually back where they had started.

One thing was not so funny: the sickness that had swept over Jacques Loff's team, probably from their eating bad food. When he woke up, Loff had found four of his dogs as limp as newborn puppies, and was unable to set off with the others.

Smith also reported that Greg Harway had taken another route. "He says the scouts are imbeciles, we're all too far northeast."

The three men had lost their bearings. They didn't even know how many miles they had gone, having drifted around so much during the day. They set up their camp and the dogs lay down quietly, not eating, not demanding a thing. They seemed to sense that the supplies had been used up. Dan and his buddies had sugared tea and a few thawed biscuits, a meal rather less spectacular than turkey pancakes and bacon and eggs.

In the morning they got up and set off together again. Without the faintest idea where they were and with scarcely any provisions, none of them wanted to split off from the others. Dan had maps, but had completely lost track of his position. The commotion created by two scouts whirling up on motorsleds, also lost, only made the situation seem worse.

Jacques Loff would have been able to get them out of this: he came from these parts. But was it worth waiting for him? With his dogs sick, he had probably given up. Dan finally decided on the direction they should take to reach the little settlement of Poorman, and the scouts opened up a passage.

A bit further on, unsure of what to do at the junction of two valleys, Aklosik suggested that they leave their teams; they could search for the trail more easily on foot. They wandered for two or three miles, until Smith declared they could not possibly be in the right area.

Returning to the dogs, they found that one of Dan's malamutes had been badly tied and was gorging himself on the few remaining provisions the mushers had had.

Just then Greg Harway appeared, seemingly out of nowhere. He was flailing his arms, like someone talking to himself. He announced that he had seen animal tracks and proposed that the best thing to do would be to organize a hunting party, all four of them, to go out and bring back fresh meat. He began to brandish his automatic rifle.

"But the hunting season hasn't opened yet," observed Dan.

"So what!" yelled Greg. "I'm hungry. We're all hungry, the dogs are hungry, and we're not about to listen to one of your damned lectures on the survival of game in Alaska." He turned back towards the others. "Hey, c'mon! I saw really big tracks a couple of miles south of here!"

Aklosik and Smith glanced over at Dan. Greg went on, "Let's leave this saint of a man to starve to death if he wants to."

To get Aklosik and Smith off the hook, Dan unhitched his team and ordered his dogs to start out again. He didn't even look back. He knew Greg and the others would go hunting. And he had to admit that he might do the same himself a bit later on, if the situation deteriorated.

Then the sound of a plane made him shout with joy. It was coming from behind him, and he swung round—only to see a plane he didn't recognize diving straight down towards him, almost grazing the ground. Dan had to drop down behind his sled as the plane's wheels passed above it, only a few feet away from his terrified dogs.

He was just hoping that this was no more than someone's pretty cruel joke, when the plane veered back from the opposite direction. It was flying even lower. The wind from it brushed the dogs' fur. Flat on his stomach, Dan thought he saw one of the wheels touch the greenlander's ears.

Dan swore. He now recognized that the plane belonged to Mart Mieldost, the bear-hunting guide whose client he had killed one day long ago on the ice field.

The plane had vanished, but Dan had a deal of trouble prodding his dogs into action again. They seemed determined to hide in the snow. And as soon as they heard the engine of the plane again, they stopped pulling the sled. Eccluke was the first to come to a halt. She scratched furiously at the ground trying to bury herself in the snow.

The plane was hurtling towards them, again forcing them to flatten themselves.

After an hour of this, the already famished team was more exhausted than it would have been after twenty hours on the trail. Mart Mieldost was getting his revenge. Much more of this and Dan would be forced to give up. He lay down beside the sled and waited. He simply refused to watch his whole venture go down the drain—he preferred to load his rifle.

The plane came up again, from behind. In shooting position, his gun propped on the front of the sled, Dan waited for it to pass overhead. He then fired all his magazine into its tailplane. The dogs' hunting instinct was roused by the shots and suddenly they were alert again, no longer scratching at the ground. That was at least a positive step.

The plane now zigzagged, climbed a bit, then dived. It veered to the left as if trying to land, then disappeared behind some woods, but from the sounds he heard Dan knew that it had landed safely.

He managed to coax the dogs into setting out again. He started off in a wide semicircle to go over and have a look at those woods. Through the trees he saw the grounded plane. He attached the sled to a tree, took up his rifle, reloaded it and moved forward into the narrow strip of forest.

On the other side Mart Mieldost was examining his plane and trying to assess his chances of taking off again. He, too, had a carbine in his hand. Dan watched him for a long moment. Oblivious to everything around him, Mieldost put down his gun and got out his toolkit. When he turned round he found himself facing the barrel of Dan's gun.

It was an ideal place for killing someone. The wolves would clean up everything, down to the bullet lodged in Mieldost's heart. There was fear in the hunting guide's eyes, along with that refusal of man to believe in his own death, even when it is very close.

"So you're the one who chose to come," said Dan.

Mieldost's numbed features moved slightly.

"Not on purpose. I happened to be in the area," he muttered.

He could not keep himself from glancing over at his rifle which was propped against the plane. Dan picked up the gun and threw it a long way away.

"So you were just passing through? And you decided to attack me and my dogs as some kind of joke?"

The guide didn't dare say yes.

"Did Greg Harway pay you to do this?"

Mieldost denied this emphatically. When it came to Dan, no payment was necessary. Mart Mieldost's own hatred was reason enough.

"You could be helping him to hunt, you know, instead of using me for flying practice," Dan said lightly. "He's off hunting just a few miles from here. It's been two days since we ran out of food."

Mieldost straightened his shoulders. He knew what it was to be isolated without supplies in these parts, knew that one day he might find himself in the same spot. "I've got some food," he said, waving a hand towards his plane. "Not much, but I can go and get more for you."

Dan wasn't prepared to accept the offer. "Something must have happened to Bob Leeve," he said.

"Didn't you know? He crashed his Piper in a windstorm, taking off from Fairbanks."

The blood drained from Dan's face. "And Bob—how is he?"

"A bit cut up around the forehead. But he's OK."

As Dan was no longer openly threatening him, Mieldost slipped open the door of the plane and pulled out a sack, which he dropped on the ground.

"Some cans of beef and some wholemeal bread. There's a good day's rations there for you and the dogs."

And then, in tacit understanding, they helped each other repair the plane's elevator cable. A wolf howled nearby. Perhaps Mieldost regretted having come here with the idea of putting Dan out of the race, of making life more difficult on a trail that was hellish enough as it was. But of course he would never say so.

They turned the plane so that the wind would be coming from the right direction for takeoff.

"Do you want me to drop off food for you somewhere?" suggested Mieldost.

Although Dan was happy to see this change of heart, he declined the offer. He retrieved Mieldost's rifle and gave it back to him. "I'll manage. Make sure Bob knows everything's OK."

He picked up the sack of provisions and moved away as the plane took off. He opened the cans, and he and the dogs stoked up. They would eat again tonight. And then ...

DAN'S TEAM WAS ALONE again on the plain. He ran into a scout on a snowmobile who told him that all the other snowmobiles were completely bogged down in deep snow. Dan's dogs had recovered some of their energy, but the deep snow made the going painfully slow. And he didn't need to consult his thermometer to know that the temperature was around forty degrees below zero.

The scout camped with him. They had no news from any of the other competitors. Dan thought he might be the front runner again, but then some sensible calculations made him realize he could hardly have travelled more than a mile or so all day.

With the aid of the dogs he finished off the rest of the beef and bread and got to sleep very late. On top of everything else he had a nightmare. Undoubtedly it stemmed from the shots that had been fired, the whole hunting business, and the presence of Mieldost. In his dream he relived the past, seeing himself once again on the ice field, capturing a polar bear with a tranquillizing dart gun. He was going to land him in a net, brand him and then weigh him. A helicopter lifted up the net, which was hooked onto the scales he was using. Dan was reading the weight of the bear as it hung suspended about a yard above the ground. And the helicopter then put the bear back down gently on the ice field. When it woke up it would stagger a bit, get its wits back, and then forget about the whole incident. And with the animal marked, Dan could keep track of its movements. In this way, he was gradually making a census of the bear population.

But these images blended gradually into an argument with the hunter Dr. Bettniger, who was just loading his rifle with explosive bullets, ready to slaughter a pregnant female. In his dream Dan saw Dr. Bettniger very distinctly. Bettniger fired and missed the bear and Dan began running towards him. He managed to push away the man's rifle barrel before he could fire again, but then Mieldost appeared and kicked him brutally to one side.

At that point, Dan had loaded his own rifle.

"If you shoot, I'll kill you."

Those had been the exact words Dan had spoken. Now they came back to him, along with the gunshot and Bettniger toppling backwards in a grimacing somersault, his arms thrashing wildly.

Dan woke up. Sitting in the cold of the night, surrounded by these round balls of fur that were his dogs, he found relief in the solitude of this frozen plain.

Eccluke, who breathed when he breathed, raised her bright eyes to him. Shining in the night, they lit up her Asiatic mask like the crowning jewels of a pride that even her love for Dan would not bring her to surrender.

Reassured, Dan let himself fall back again, and slept.

ON THE MORNING of March 14, after the scout had left for Poorman, Dan covered only ten miles. The sled was sinking into the snow; the dogs were weak. Bull seemed to be the most resilient, thanks perhaps to his heavier fur.

When Dan was still some miles from Poorman, Aklosik caught up with him and told him about their hunt. Greg's dogs had bolted so much caribou meat that they could no longer run. Aklosik gave a bit of the meat to Dan's team, who hadn't eaten anything since the previous evening.

According to Aklosik, they were in the lead, with Greg and George Smith not far behind. No news of Jacques Loff, and it was likely that the majority of the other runners were a long way back.

Towards six in the evening they arrived at Poorman, a hamlet with a few army units camped in tents. Dan set off in search of food for the following day, while Aklosik went to get news from a younger brother, a sergeant supposed to be taking part in manoeuvres on this part of the trail.

Greg Harway and George Smith arrived later. Greg sardonically offered some fresh meat to Dan, who declined it.

Around nine in the evening three men from Ruby, the next stop along, drove in on snowmobiles. One of them, named Beckman, was from Galena. They had heard that some of the mushers were lost, and Beckman was worried about Jacques Loff, who was married to his sister. Dan told him that Loff was fine, that he had met the young woman at a checkpoint, and that she was gallantly spreading the word that her husband was winning.

Greg Harway remarked that family matters had no place here,

that the race was not supposed to be a boring little village party, and that if Loff wanted to be the first to arrive in Nome he would do well to finish off his sick dogs and take a plane.

March 15–18. Poorman to Galena. Dan had only been able to find a commercial dogfood, not really nutritious enough for racing dogs. He took off again next morning just behind Greg, but found himself gradually outdistanced.

It was sixty miles to Ruby, and by the end of twenty Dan already had two exhausted crossbreeds on the sled. With Bull and Eccluke taking their turns, of the original eighteen Dan had only ten able-bodied dogs left, and only nine were pulling the sled.

As he neared Ruby, one of the largest centres on the Yukon, Dan began meeting volunteer helpers along the route. Often they handed him things to eat and provided coffee for his thermos. He stopped only rarely. He was determined to get to Ruby and take care of the two coyote crossbreeds, for he didn't want to abandon them at the next checkpoint. He would soon be tackling the last third of the race, the most gruelling trek of all, and he wanted to keep as many dogs as possible.

Rocky Bent had finally caught up with the group again, and he slipped past Dan in the company of Aklosik and George Smith. A few others whom Dan didn't know also passed him in the middle of the afternoon. Dan pushed as hard as he could on his good leg, trying to help his team along. But he arrived in Ruby in eighth or ninth place. Once there, he rushed to the vet. The man took his time, checking the dogs out in every detail.

"They've got flu," he said, finally.

"All of them?"

Dan's every hope depended on the answer. The vet put Eccluke to the side, then did the same with Bull. . . .

Dan watched him, not wanting to believe his eyes. These were the ones he had thought were in the best condition!

Next, the two malamutes; then the two huskies. The vet hesitated, feeling the four others. "Those six are still OK," he decided, pointing to Eccluke's group.

Dan breathed a sigh of relief, grateful for small mercies. The vet began preparing medication.

209

"These are antibiotics you can give the others. You don't have to, but they'll get well sooner if you do."

Leaving the place, Dan dropped off the six ailing dogs at the checkpoint, emphasizing that they would be infectious for a few days. He arranged with the committee to have someone send them on to Fairbanks for him.

That same evening the word spread that Dan Murphy had only six dogs left.

ON MARCH 16 Dan took the precaution of leaving even sooner than usual. His next stop, Galena, was fifty miles off. All he had to do was follow the Yukon River. He was carrying only about twelve pounds of provisions and his camping equipment. Of course, in addition there was the weight of either Bull or Eccluke.

During the past few days he had tried setting Bull free while Eccluke was pulling at the lead. He had thought that Bull would be delighted and would follow the team. But all Bull did was try to bite Eccluke. The same thing happened, Dan found, when he let Eccluke go free while Bull was pulling. She wanted her position back as leader.

Eight teams passed Dan that day and he was very discouraged when he arrived in Galena, still some eight long days from the finishing line. He found a house where he could shelter his dogs, so he decided to stay over for a day and let them rest. He fed them meat and rice every six hours, made sure they stayed warm, and also gave them vitamin injections.

It was thanks to the kindness of a Mrs. Ganel that he was so comfortably set up here. Her husband worked for an insurance company, and joked with Dan about his life insurance, and her two children spent the greater part of their day with the dogs. They amused themselves by slipping the little leather boots on the malamutes, who held up their paws good-naturedly.

Mrs. Ganel knew the wife of Dr. Loff very well, and Mrs. Loff came by to visit Dan. He got the impression, though, that her real reason for coming had been to check out the condition of his dogs. She announced that her husband had cured the illness that had attacked his team, and he would soon rejoin the race. And naturally he was going to win it.

"Your confidence will certainly help him on his way," Dan told her.

He felt uneasy staying here, knowing that the other mushers were gaining ground. But his dogs needed the rest. To cheer himself up he bought all kinds of wax for the runners of his sled.

Many of the folk who lived in Galena had bet on Jacques Loff, their beloved "doc of the ice". And their faces were now gloomy: Greg Harway was the front runner. He now had a good day's lead on Dan; and sixteen other teams had leads of several hours on him. Dan was glad to learn that Rocky Bent, Aklosik and George Smith weren't far behind Greg.

Mrs. Ganel had noticed how jealous Eccluke was. She told Dan that the dog might accept the idea of sharing with Bull if Dan made their shares truly exact ones. Dan listened to her advice. That evening he lay with Eccluke on one side and Bull on the other, one hand on each back, his fingers gently—and equally—stroking them.

March 19–21. Galena to Shaktolik. Dan left Galena at last. Eccluke was pulling at the lead, and Dan, in the spirit recommended by Mrs. Ganel, had placed two light saddlepacks on Bull's back. Given this new feeling of responsibility, Bull ran freely alongside the team and no longer tried to rob Eccluke of her place.

The sled was therefore lighter. The dogs, now well rested, lengthened their stride, and in two hours Dan passed a team that had left during the night. He gazed happily at his dogs' broad backs and decided not to force them to do too long a stretch. He cleared fifty miles, to stop at Nulato, having passed another two competitors on the way. From now on towns were more frequent and he would undoubtedly be able to take along a single day's worth of food at a time. He would go faster as a result.

The people of Nulato were wonderful. They helped care for the dogs, and a family took Dan in for the night. They spent all evening talking about the progress of the other teams and the fitness of their dogs. In these long-distance races, nothing was certain until the very end.

THE NEW SYSTEM of sharing was working: Bull and Eccluke took turns running alongside the sled. Dan quickly reached the Kaltag checkpoint, and passed two teams as he left town. From here the trail turned away from the Yukon River, down to the bay of Norton Sound. The army snowmobiles had left winding tracks on the snow, which made the sled sway awkwardly from side to side. To be safe, Dan had fitted all the dogs with their protective boots—as there were only six dogs of the initial eighteen, they would have three sets each.

Fifty miles out of Kaltag, Dan caught up with another competitor. He figured there could be only eleven teams in front of him now—and then Greg Harway's, much further ahead.

By dusk that evening he had done ninety miles, so he stopped at an old cabin he'd spotted on the map. He started to make himself some tea, but the dogs, although they had been driven hard, still seemed eager, ready to head out again. And Dan found himself thinking the cabin didn't make all that great a camp, so he might as well get back on the trail again.

It was totally dark by the time he arrived at Old Woman. He had covered more than a hundred miles that day. No lights shone anywhere in the place. Moving down the one street in the place, Dan came to a checkpoint with two teams halted in front of it. So he continued on a bit further, crossing two more contestants off his list. Ahead of him now there were nine teams, plus Greg's. He quickly set up his camp, determined to take it down again even more quickly, well before daybreak.

HE CLIMBED OUT of his sleeping bag at two in the morning and set off again at three, travelling light, with only a few pounds of provisions left, for noon and the middle of the afternoon. The sled glided swiftly through the night. Despite his weak leg Dan ran at times, to make it easier on the dogs. At other times he would ride, pushing vigorously with his strong leg.

At daybreak he unhitched Bull and put Eccluke at the lead. He did it on impulse, for no clear reason. Neither of the dogs seemed tired, nor was either of them trying to take the other one's place. But he did it anyway.

In this area Dan had to cross a wide hard-frozen stream. But ice has its mysteries, and suddenly it gave way beneath his foot as he pushed down to urge the sled forward.

Everything happened very quickly: Dan's boot caught under the rim of the hole it had just made; surprise, along with shock from the

212

stumble, made him loosen his grip; the sled went on its way, the ice broke up around him, and he found himself in the icy water, held up only by his outstretched arms. He tried pushing down with the flat of his hands to pull his body clear, but he heard the ice crack the minute he put pressure on it. His clothes were becoming weighted down with water. It seeped into his boots, pulling him towards the depths.

The sled was almost out of sight. Dan called the dogs, but they weren't trained to return on command like German shepherds. The cold tightened around him, gripping him to the bone. His body seemed to weigh a ton. With his mittens full of water, he could no longer feel any solid surface at all. His head was level with the ice.

Suddenly, it seemed to him that the sled was turning round. He watched, scarcely believing, as it came back towards him. Eccluke, in the lead, was approaching his left side. She had instinctively chosen the thickest ice.

The dogs went past him, Eccluke stopping them when the sled was behind his back. Dan cursed—the hole was lined with jagged ice, very hard to turn round in, and he was afraid that if it enlarged he would disappear into it once and for all. He exhaled, then inhaled as deeply as he could; he flung one arm backwards in the direction of the sled and managed to catch hold of it. Then he wrenched himself completely round. He shouted to Eccluke, who started up again very gently, her head turned back towards him. His hands holding onto the sled's lowest side member, Dan let himself be pulled along. Slowly his waterlogged figure emerged from the hole and slid along the ice. After a short distance Eccluke stopped and Dan got painfully to his feet. Each time he took a step water spurted from his boots, and he knew that the cold would soon transform his wet clothes into a shroud of ice.

As quickly as possible he made his way towards a dark line of forest where at least he would be able to light a fire. He had worn through his other pair of boots on the gravel-filled track before McGrath. He was wondering how long his clothes would take to dry out when, miraculously, he caught a glimpse of a cabin among the trees.

At least here he could change his clothes out of the wind. Inside it, however, he was startled to find a man and a woman, two indomitable old Eskimos who presumably fished the bay in the

summertime and hunted fur animals—surely with little success—in the winter.

On the bare earth in the middle of the room a faint fire was smouldering. But Dan's attention had been attracted by the man's sturdy walrus-skin boots. He showed the couple his own frozen boots and ventured a few words in their language, proposing an exchange.

They shook their heads.

Dan returned to his sled and came back with a few dollar bills in his hand. The old woman's expression grew interested. She drew closer, speaking privately to Dan between the five or six teeth she still possessed.

Dan nodded. She hung onto the dollars and while Dan held the old fellow firmly round the waist, she quickly dispossessed him of his boots. The Eskimo flung himself about in a rage until the old woman wrapped his feet in a blanket.

Dan then took off his own sodden boots and changed his clothes in the cabin. The woman put his boots to dry and while they waited he rolled his wet clothes into a ball and stuffed them under the tarpaulin on the sled. The old man's boots felt tight, but they were very warm.

Eccluke had saved Dan's life, and the entire team seemed delighted. They set out again, their trot lively, and at noon they arrived in Unalakleet, on the coast. It was a dismal scene, the shore merging with sky and sea in the same shade of dirty white.

To feed the dogs, Dan sought shelter from the wind behind the first house he found. Some people came along and reported that a team had just passed through, and that another one had been held over in the village. It seemed its musher had acute stomach pains.

Wondering if the man might be Greg Harway, Dan went across. But it was poor Rocky Bent, who clung to the bedposts as his body twisted and convulsed in spasms, his face sweating, a light froth at the corners of his mouth. His stomach was hard to the touch, and his pain made Dan suspect an attack of peritonitis. He gazed at Dan with eyes that cried out for help.

Dan put his hand gently on Rocky's forehead, and then left. His powerlessness to help drove him away. All Dan could do was to hope that the wind would drop long enough for a plane to land in the village, collect the patient, and fly him to the nearest hospital.

Dan raised his eyes to the northern sky, which was turning to radiant silver as the day drew to a close, and thought he might cover forty miles before stopping at Shaktolik, on a hilly part of the trail along the coast. And even though the sea salt mixed with the frost prevented his sled from gliding easily, the dogs hardly lowered their heads against the force of the wind, and Dan managed to keep them trotting. For himself, the trail had taken so much weight off him he was practically swimming around in his clothes. But at least his feet had become accustomed to the Eskimo's boots.

About three miles from Shaktolik he passed a team, and then, coming into the village, he caught up with Aklosik and George Smith again. There were only five competitors ahead of him now, apart from Greg Harway.

The people of Shaktolik were sheltering the mushers in the National Guard armoury, and when the dogs had been taken care of Dan and the other two went over to talk with some scouts who were sorting out the problems of two broken snowmobiles. No one spoke of Rocky Bent. George Smith was suffering badly from arthritis. His knees were swollen like balloons, and Dan wondered how he had even managed to get this far. From the betting crowd they learned that Greg was just six hours away.

Then, between beers, a late piece of news reached Dan, Smith and Aklosik: the five teams up ahead had been immobilized by a blizzard just before reaching Christmas Mountain, which they had to cross before threading their way down to Koyuk, on Norton Bay.

Later, there came another piece of news, which caused a shout of joy to go up from the gathering. They had just found out that Jacques Loff had rejoined the race, and everyone there loved the guy. Dan liked him a lot, too, and he liked the grey eyes of Loff's wife.

He stood up, telling his friends he was planning to go and buy some provisions for the next day's journey.

"What next day's journey?" Smith asked him.

Only then did Dan realize that the other two were going to wait there until the weather got better.

March 22. Shaktolik to Koyuk. Dan got up alone in the dark and readied his gear while waiting for daybreak. The wind was just as violent as it had been the evening before. In only a few minutes outside the cold had numbed his whole face. He went back into the armoury, and an old truck driver from the area who had travelled every one of these trails, advised him against leaving.

"The dogs could freeze, and you'll freeze, too," he said. He told Dan a sledding story about a musher and his dogs who had been turned into statues by the cold.

As Dan hesitated, Eccluke and Bull sniffed each other, then Eccluke gave the greenlander's muzzle a furtive lick, and the big redhaired dog put his head down to rest on the neck of the bitch. Dan was no longer listening to the old fellow talking about death. The affection springing up between these two dogs on the final lap of this odyssey had given him new courage.

He reorganized the team: the two malamutes side by side, then the two huskies, and finally Bull and Eccluke, the two leaders. He outfitted all the dogs in their leather boots.

Drawn on by the momentum of the two loyal and tireless leaders, the team leaped forward into the wind. Dan realized he now had a real chance of catching up with the front runners. He was in no mood to think about his weak leg, which was growing increasingly numb. He pushed on with the other leg, and summoned every ounce of strength he had left to keep the sled on course despite the eighty-mile-an-hour blasts of wind coming from the sea.

After three hours of grim struggling he saw two teams coming towards him. They crossed his path at a run and yelled to him that they were turning back, that their only hope of surviving lay in stopping over at Shaktolik. From the look of things they would be there soon, for the wind was behind them, helping them on. With only three runners ahead of him now, Dan felt still more encouraged. His dogs showed no signs of faltering. They kept on going, and their physical condition seemed, if anything, better than it had been on the very first day. Dan began to bless the long hours of rest he had given them in Galena.

He crested a long hill and came upon a team that wasn't moving. The dogs had huddled up against each other. Instinctively they were conserving the little energy they had left, feeling confident enough within the insulation of their fur.

A few yards beyond them was a man, Number 20, sheltering from the blizzard beneath his tarpaulin. Dan could not stop. In this cold, to stop would be to die. For that reason, too, he considered it useless to turn back.

On uneven stretches the wind scattered the tops of the snowdrifts and blurred all visibility along the trail, as if it were still snowing. At other times a whirlwind would tear away the curtain of white for a few seconds.

During one of these brief breaks Dan saw an animal dart past, followed by another. They looked like wolves, yet his team showed no signs of anxiety.

Further on he saw a third, closer up. It was a husky, with its harness still on. Dan counted eight dogs crossing through the storm. He did not recognize them as Greg Harway's, so they must have belonged to the runner who had been in second place.

Once again Dan prodded his dogs into a trot. Their breath had completely frozen to their chests. Dan's rough wool balaclava helmet was now a mass of ice around his mouth. His fingers were cold inside his mittens, but so long as he could still feel the cold, it would be all right. In dangerous frosts, blood can stop circulating to the extremities and one's hands become virtual blocks of stone dangling from one's arms. His feet, too, were all right. The Eskimo's traditional boots were better than any sophisticated trekking gear. Dan now realized that, ironically, he might even have been lucky to have fallen through the ice on the river. It was hard to judge how things would turn out when one was right in the midst of them.

The wind wasn't letting up. Dan had to wonder just where it got its strength. Visibility was very poor, but he seemed to be approaching the wooded foothills of Christmas Mountain. He could see his two malamutes well enough; he could just make out his two huskies; but he could no longer see Bull and Eccluke at all.

Suddenly the two leaders switched direction, veering to their right. Dan assumed Bull and Eccluke must have come upon some obstacle that he couldn't see in this haze of snow. The dogs slowed from a trot to a walk. Then, just as he was trying to figure out what had happened, the dogs lurched to a halt, and he found himself in one of those large wooden sheds that isolated foresters build to store their equipment. In the half-light of this windowless place Dan could make out another team, with its musher still muffled up in fur, and a big fellow dressed in a long military parka like the ones worn by forest rangers.

Watching the man unhitching Bull's harness, Dan suddenly understood: this fellow was not a competitor—he had simply intercepted his team on the trail. No doubt he had intercepted the other team, too. And since the other musher was not Greg Harway— he was wearing Number 12—Greg must still be somewhere up ahead. Dead or alive.

"It would be madness to go on," said the man in the parka. He explained that the storm had brought all activity in the area to a standstill. The weather report predicted only the very worst.

"Have you seen Greg Harway pass through?" asked Dan.

The man thought for a moment, then shook his head. He added that no human being, musher or otherwise, could cross the ravines of

Christmas Mountain in a blizzard. Dan changed mittens and balaclava and fed his dogs. Then he removed some of the icicles hanging from their chests.

The other musher, Number 12, was dozing off despite the cold. His head drooped. He seemed annihilated by his ordeal, his mind sunk into a stupor.

Dan glanced over at their good Samaritan. He felt sure he had seen the guy somewhere before. He set his memory to work—yes, that rather odd, slightly upturned nose was familiar. The man was one of Greg Harway's suppliers. There had been two of them waiting with a van back in McGrath, and Dan had watched this character loading provisions onto Greg's sled.

"This Greg Harway—do you know him?" Dan asked.

Again the man shook his head. Something didn't fit. Dan turned his dogs and the sled round.

The fellow planted himself in front of the door. "No one's leaving. I'm in charge of this sector, and I don't want to have to go out searching for you on the mountain."

"Especially since you've been paid by Greg Harway to make sure no one goes up there. I don't doubt you're also in cahoots with the bookmakers. Come on! Open up that door!"

The other man picked up several boards and placed them in front of the door to bar the passage. Dan ripped off one of his mittens and aimed his rifle at the man.

"Are you going to open the door or not?"

"This is my place," the fellow replied.

Dan's first bullet pierced a board barely a yard away from the man's shoulder. He didn't wait for the second but quickly threw open the door. The storm blew in, and the dogs shrank back. Dan lowered his head, since the wind coming at him impeded his breathing, and urged them on. The other man didn't interfere.

After a few yards Dan picked up the trail again. In tandem, Bull and Eccluke brought an impressive continuity to the pulling. Their mutual understanding, perhaps even affection, had entered Dan's life at a crucial moment.

In places the wind had scraped the ground down to bare ice, and in order to negotiate two very steep descents, Dan had to wrap chains round his runners. One climb of scarcely a mile took them three hours. His boots kept slipping backwards as he tried to push the sled. He did not have the strength to pull the team uphill, either, and on ice the dogs' paws in their protective leather boots had little traction. Yet it would have been out of the question to have them run bare-pawed again in this cold and across these sharp ridges of ice. Dan took advantage of a narrow valley, shielded from the wind, to stop and put on his crampons. They'd been Eleanor's idea and at this particular moment, as far as Dan was concerned, they were the best idea any woman had ever had.

He was careful not to tighten the straps around the tops of his boots and block his circulation. Climbing on out of the valley, he tackled a series of slopes that seemed to lead up to a plateau. Visibility was better here, yet his vision narrowed until his boots and the ice beneath them were all he saw.

The wool of his balaclava helmet was again as hard as an iron band round his mouth. The dogs climbed the steep incline, their muzzles touching the ground. On his crampons Dan pushed the sled with all his strength. To his right was a cliff that dropped off dizzyingly into a ravine strewn with boulders. The more he climbed, the more precipitous the chasm became. At times the runners of his sled would lurch dangerously close to the edge, and Dan would desperately lean back to his left to keep the sled safe from disaster.

He did not let himself glance up towards the plateau. He focused all his attention on his boots and the sheer cliff edge. He counted up to fifty paces, then set his mental calculator back to zero and started again. He hoped he would wear away the plateau's defences almost unnoticed, just counting from one fifty to the next.

And then the sled jerked to a halt. Dan felt the impact of its full weight, straightened his body, and looked ahead. Two unfamiliar dogs were blocking the trail, and two others were trying to regain a foothold, their front paws still on the path but their hindquarters hanging over the icy precipice. And on a ledge part way down, Dan could make out the rest of the team and its sled—and, at the back of the sled, Greg was hanging by his arms, his body pressed close against the cliff.

The two dogs who were trying to climb back up onto the trail were sliding desperately on the ice. The bottom of the ravine lay in wait for them, the whole way down covered with treacherous spikes of rock, as sharp as sharks' teeth. They were wearing out their paws, scratching furiously, and had thus far managed only to avoid being sucked down into the void. Certainly they were making no headway towards the top.

Dan shuffled past his own team, seized the harness of these two dogs and, braced on his crampons, tried to pull them back up onto the trail. But with their weight plus Greg's six other dogs and the sled, and Greg himself, the task was beyond his strength.

His breath harsh from his straining, hindered by the cold and the gusting wind, Dan looked ahead to see if he had room to pass with his own sled. It would be possible, if he thrust past the two huskies clinging to the trail. But if he did that, they would swing into the void, taking with them the rest of the team, and Greg.

He went back to his sled for a spare length of towing rope and his first-aid kit. He drove a stake deep into the ice and attached his sled to it. He was about to do what few men would have done in his place: to save the life of the man who had taken Virginia away from him, who had slandered him, and put him through so much hell.

Was he going down out of pride? Out of fear that people might otherwise accuse him of having killed his enemy? Dan did not consider such questions.

He started down the cliff, moving cautiously, his crampons crunching each time he pulled them out of the ice and drove them in again. With his knees bent and his weight resting on his thighs, he kept his body perpendicular to the slope.

Suddenly, Greg raised his head and saw him. He shouted something incomprehensible. Dan saw him let go, first with one hand and then two seconds later with the other, and begin to slide down the ice, still shouting.

Dan's crampons dug into the cliff, and he reached the back of Greg's sled. He started to push it up the cliff; above him two dogs regained a foothold, and then two more of them. The weight shifted, and the sled was suddenly up on the trail again, facing Dan's.

Dan went down again. He found Greg beside a large boulder, lying on his back, his clothing torn by rocks, his face lacerated by the ice. The fresh blood on it was already freezing, but under his frosted lashes the eyes still moved and saw.

There was no wind at all at the bottom of this chasm, there was only an unnatural silence. Greg put his arm round Dan's neck: he wanted to speak but could manage only feeble movements in his throat. What was left of the man he had been? A body freezing up beneath a face torn to shreds; a bundle of fur. At all events, fate was bringing him help from the man he had hated the most, a man he had wanted to see dead.

Dan tried getting up, pulling his burden with him. He made it onto his feet, but after only two steps Greg's legs folded beneath him. Dan laid him back down. His life was fading fast and with his little emergency kit Dan couldn't hope to save him, but still he tried a shot of camphor. His numb fingers had trouble holding the syringe, and it broke. The whole episode was turning into a cruel farce.

And still life had its incalculable resources. Greg lifted his face up, and Dan could feel the lips move against the balaclava close to his ear. Greg wanted so much to speak. But all he had now was the will; the strength to do so had ebbed and departed.

Dan tied his rope round Greg and began to pull him up the treacherous slope; but in fact, after some thirty steps, he saw that he was pulling a corpse. He abandoned the body halfway up. Here, at least, the wolves would have a hard time climbing down to devour it.

And so it was over. Greg Harway, leading the race, had fallen into the abyss, and now was dead. Dan did not see his team on the trail when he reached it. As there wasn't a single track up ahead, he supposed that the dogs had passed his own sled and gone back the way they'd come.

As soon as he signalled his own dogs to leave, Dan realized that they were half frozen. He himself had been in constant motion on that slope; they had stayed at a standstill, exposed, cruelly chilled by the wind after all their recent exertion.

Things didn't go well. Even when they reached the plateau the dogs weren't moving with their usual smoothness. And Dan was in trouble too: heaving at Greg's body, he had been so hot that he was soaking wet, but now the first layer of wool next to his skin was freezing as it absorbed his sweat.

He would gladly have gone many miles out of his way to get out of the wind and set up a survival camp. But there was nothing but flat ground to be seen. No signs of the descent that should lead him back down to the coast. With no tree in sight, he couldn't build a fire. His clothing was tightening round his chest. That, and the ceaseless wind, made it hard to breathe. He stopped helping the sled along, and the dogs slowed to a walk. The change in pace was enough to make him feel he was hardly moving.

Between the two malamutes and the leaders, the two huskies were weakening. Eccluke turned round, sensing that the team was at odds behind her. Big Bull walked on placidly, but even he was unable to muster a trot again. And Dan wasn't pushing any more. Indeed, he was close to turning back. Anything, just so long as the wind was behind him.

When at last the sled bogged down in a drift of finely blown snow, the impact flung Dan against the sled, and he stayed there for a while, doubled over, his dogs at a halt. Then he moved, instinctively, mechanically. He could go no further. He unhitched the dogs so that they could take their chances; he pulled off, for better or worse, the tarpaulin that had been tied over his belongings, and eased himself under it.

An ominous drowsiness—that feeling called the white death—moved in with him beneath the tarpaulin. He had tucked it between his body and the sled, but part of it still flailed in the wind, slapping about more noisily than a whip. This was his flag, it kept him awake, but it was hardly a flag of victory.

Finally he began to doze off, so that he no longer heard the wind, no longer cared whether it was day or night, cold or hot. But before losing consciousness completely he found himself wondering how Irik was doing, and whether he was still working with the chest-expander to strengthen his arm.

And then something was tugging at his cover, and there was a weight on his chest and something breathing into his eyes. He struggled, still disorientated, and felt a body, fur. A wolf. He came alive, crying out hoarsely from beneath his frozen balaclava.

Eccluke was gazing down at him with her moon-coloured eyes. He sat up. She seemed to have a piece of white fur in her mouth. It was a mountain hare, and it was still warm.

Feverishly, sensing the life for himself that was in it, Dan cut open the hare's throat with his knife and drank its blood. All the numbness he had felt inside seemed to thaw. He gave the hare back to Eccluke; she took it delicately and carried it away.

Then, to restore his own confidence, to prove to himself that he was still there and still fairly strong, Dan rolled up his tarpaulin and stuffed it back onto the sled.

The dogs must have roamed about, but they weren't far away. He harnessed one malamute, and the second one appeared at a trot. Then came the others; Bull was yipping with pleasure. While Dan hitched Eccluke she put both her paws on his shoulders. He had returned from the dead. He felt giddy, a bit lightheaded.

When they had gone a hundred yards or so, he saw the remains of a lynx that had been slain by the dogs. All that was left of its carcass was the skin—and the dogs were trotting eagerly, obviously revived by their hunting expedition.

Dan didn't know exactly how many days, how many hours, he might be from the ribbon at the finishing line, but he wanted only to be done with it. Done with it, done with it, done with it: this was the chant repeated in his head with every thrust of his good leg.

When he saw the curve of Norton Bay, he realized that he had at last finished with the mountain. Koyuk was situated high up on the bay. Night had not yet fallen. This close to the Bering Strait, darkness descended suddenly, and was very black. Dan had been so dazed by so many interminable hours of wind that he could no longer judge its intensity. But looking at the dogs, who were trotting along now with their heads well up, he guessed that it had eased.

He arrived in Koyuk at about eleven o'clock. People were still awake: gamblers, obviously, and others who were anxious for news of survivors.

At the checkpoint they reassured Dan that he was indeed the front runner. He talked to them about Greg Harway's death, and about the others who had run into difficulties before reaching the mountain. He tried to mark the position of Greg's body on an ordnance survey map.

He was offered a garage for the dogs and a room for himself. He preferred to stay with the dogs. Instinct told him not to leave them any more—they had become companions in peril.

March 23. Koyuk to White Mountain. Dan spent a bare three hours in Koyuk, stretched out on the bare concrete, not even bothering with his sleeping bag. The heated garage was a paradise and he suspected that if he started to sink into the comfort of a soft bed he might never leave.

For the first time he had not taken off the dogs' harnesses. They, too, seemed to share the tense determination of the musher, straining onwards towards his goal.

Koyuk was sleeping as the sled glided through, making a pleasant crunching sound. The wind was now a mere gentle puff of air. Dan had taken off his crampons and at last his body was dry inside dry clothes.

He pulled into Elim. He was one hundred and fifty miles from Nome, and from the finishing line. At Elim, people gave him food to eat. He was asleep on his feet, and one young couple was determined to make him stay over and rest. He was on the verge of giving in when the radio announced that another team was approaching Koyuk.

Dan left again. The radio was also announcing the deaths of Rocky Bent and Greg Harway. He told himself that if the sled just behind him stopped, he would stop too. The only thing keeping him awake was the thong of his whip, slapping at him. He looked back frequently, like an exhausted runner on his last lap. As far as he could see, he was alone.

He arrived in Golovin at six in the evening. He ate, and bought some fresh meat for the dogs. By now he was down to his last few dollars.

At nine he left Golovin. The news was that the musher behind him had only three dogs left. He had no number card; undoubtedly he had lost it. He had passed through Koyuk without stopping and he had been seen in the vicinity of Elim.

Dan figured that he couldn't have more than a three-hour lead over this fellow. It was dark, and he was heading towards White Mountain. The dogs were finding their own way along the trail.

They reached White Mountain around midnight. This close to Nome, the race had stirred up such a pitch of excitement that people were staying up all night to see the front runners pass by. Everywhere there were comments on the dogs' condition, the fatigue of the musher, his chances. Dazed, Dan no longer heard them. His own voice had become as slurred as a drunkard's.

He pulled in somewhere, again without bothering to unharness

225

the dogs. He simply sat down, leaning against the sled. He hadn't really slept in forty hours. He wondered how long the other musher, with his three dogs, would be able to go on without sleeping. He decided to allow himself a couple of hours' rest, and he asked some youngsters standing nearby to wake him. He told them to make absolutely certain to do so, otherwise he would lose the race. He added that his dogs didn't deserve to have that happen.

March 24. The last day. When they shook him, Dan jumped like a lunatic. Opening his eyes wide, he gazed round at the place, at his team, and—not knowing quite where he was—he searched for the other team, the one that had been chasing him.

The youngsters handed him some coffee. Dan gulped it down burning hot, making his eyes water. He saw that the dogs were eager to start out again and he marvelled at their endurance. As long as he himself could stay on his feet, they'd never let him down.

He had just finished feeding them when a young girl, her transistor radio slung across her shoulder, came up to report that the man with three dogs was less than an hour away. He hadn't stopped anywhere but had just kept on going, not eating or sleeping. Sixty miles from the finishing line, Dan had only a one hour lead. He called start-up orders to his dogs, launched the sled, and ran behind it for a good few yards, pushing. It didn't matter that he had never before limped so badly at a run.

He had started this race as a pariah, jeered at on all sides. And yet, throughout the long ordeal, he had always found helping hands. Even Mieldost's hatred had proved no match for the spirit of this race. And the experience had brought Dan back in touch with the world. How long would it last? Would it just be for the duration of this one race?

THE DOGS LENGTHENED their trotting stride. It was a beautiful dawn; gripped by ice, the shore sparkled brilliantly. People cheered Dan from their doorways. He left the houses behind, cut across a deserted plain, the last he would have to traverse before coming to roads, cars, and the densely built-up areas of the metropolis.

Half an hour later, at the far side of the plain, he looked back—and saw the black dot of a sled. It was clearly gaining ground. Dan took

226

advantage of a short descent to launch his dogs into a gallop. He still had a half-hour's lead. If the dogs could go on running, everything would be all right.

They, too, sensed the end approaching. They had easily broken out of their usual trot. Bull set the pace, straining with all his might. Despite her age, Eccluke threw herself into the effort. Again and again, Dan looked back. He could no longer see the other team because of the trail's twists and turns. He thought that he had at least succeeded in maintaining his lead.

When he reached a road, two Land-Rovers greeted him with toots of their horns. A bare two hours from now he would be at the finishing line.

He headed into a series of upward slopes, some of them several miles long. To rest his dogs he was running behind his sled, gasping for breath. They were managing to trot as they climbed, then to run flat out on the descents. The moment Bull and Eccluke had dealt with one slope, they would head straight into the next, trying to take it at a run, with the other dogs and the sled still halfway up the previous one.

And it was then that Eccluke collapsed. She hadn't even sensed the coming of death, such was her courage. Bull sniffed at her tentatively. Dan ran up, fell to his knees, lifted her, laid her down again: and he wept in the cold, which froze his tears, welding his eyelids together.

Eccluke was still soft, still warm from her efforts. But she would not see the flags at the finish. She was gone, and with her she took the joy of the man who had loved her so much.

He spread out the tarpaulin and laid her down on it, her head raised, her delicate paws folded beneath her as if ready to soar on into the journey she had just begun. Carefully, he folded the tarpaulin and carried it to the sled, Bull watching him. With his mind still elsewhere, he headed his team out again. And then the man with the three dogs came down on him.

It was Jacques Loff. His empty sled was swaying in the wind. He had nothing left. No more provisions, no camping gear. He had stripped himself of everything. Empty sled, empty stomach, empty brain; he just kept on going.

He appeared to Dan to be even taller and thinner than he really was: just a dark ghostly line behind his sled. His dogs, too, stretched out beneath their backbones, were just three living skeletons.

The speed and silence with which Jacques Loff's team passed Dan added to the impression of ghostliness. He wore neither a fur cap nor a balaclava. Only a headband for his ears. He was letting the cold bite into his cheeks and forehead.

Dan's dogs, spurred on by the competition, took off again close behind him. But still Dan had lost around twenty yards, which slowly became thirty, then fifty.

There were only five miles left. Lurching up one last slight incline, Dan threw off his provisions and all his gear at the side of the trail, and soon afterwards saw that Loff was no longer pulling away from him.

Lost in another world, the two mushers were not even aware of the people beginning to appear beside the trail. All they knew was the panting of their dogs. Dan picked up about ten yards more. If he could lighten the sled even further, he could again be in the lead. But all that remained on his sled was the body of Eccluke. Throw Eccluke onto the trail? Drop her off, like excess baggage, at the last checkpoint, a hundred yards from here?

He left the checkpoint behind. Only a mile to go before the line, and still Loff's lead was forty yards. Dan shouted encouragement to his dogs and for the first time since the start he cracked his whip.

Thirty yards. Fixing his eyes on Jacques Loff's back, he made out new details on his clothes. He figured he was coming closer—he might even beat him in the final five hundred yards.

One year the race had been won in the final sprint, by a fraction of a second. This time it was won with a twenty-five yard lead—twenty-five yards out of one million, eight hundred and forty-eight thousand.

Jacques Loff had won. People were running up to stop his team. Then Dan also crossed the line. The two teams converged in the midst of the crowd. Jacques Loff and Dan looked at each other; then they took off their mittens and shook hands awkwardly.

The woman with the grey eyes was there. She smiled at Dan but he had nothing to say. He was wondering what he was doing in the middle of this mad throng. He seemed to see everyone and yet no one. He felt himself being shoved along towards the speakers'

platform. He would rather have stayed with his dogs. The sea of people swept him on. Martial music burst forth.

He climbed the wooden steps, walking as though he were being dragged onto a scaffold. They hung a medal round his neck, and they gave the trophy to Jacques Loff. Fifty thousand dollars went to Loff, forty thousand to him. A difference of twenty-five yards.

It was only after all this that he found himself face to face with Virginia. She took his arm, and he read the questions in her eyes. Greg's death.

"He swerved off course," Dan said simply. "There was a cliff."

He did not add that he had done what he could for Greg. She would have guessed that. She stayed next to him, not caring what people might think. A loudspeaker was blasting the news that the third runner was a few hours away, and that those following him were a day behind, possibly two.

A voice shouted his name. It was Eleanor. She ran up, embraced him, reminded him about her bet that he would win or come in second. She told him Bob was recovering, and the insurance would pay for the damage to the plane. He must come to Fairbanks; they would celebrate. He promised he would.

He turned back towards his team. He would have to bury Eccluke. Virginia felt that the best place would be here in Nome, in her garden. Dan agreed, and he put together a coffin. The frozen ground gave him trouble, but he was content to labour a little more for this dog.

He drove a knife into the ground as a marker on the grave site. It was the one with which he had sliced open the hare's throat.

"When all the competitors have crossed the line," Virginia told him, "there's going to be a huge banquet."

Dan looked over her head, staring into some vague middle distance. "I don't think I'll go," he said.

He was too tired to rest. He didn't know what he wanted to do next. His heart was still in the race, on the trail.

It would all sort itself out. He limped visibly as he moved off, but as he did not want her to see the limp, he walked away as steadily as his weary legs would allow.

José Giovanni

It is not easy to arrange a meeting with the Corsican writer José Giovanni. The immense success which greets the publication of each one of his books in France has not turned the head of this novelist and scriptwriter, but it has taught him the necessity of protecting his private life. As a result, he has chosen to live quietly in the mountains of Switzerland with his wife, his children and his dogs.

His literary debut happened quite by chance, the day after the liberation of France at the end of World War II. He was waiting for a visa which would allow him to settle in Australia. In order to pass the time, he decided to jot down on paper what he could remember of his troubled teenage years when he had, not long before, had certain brushes with the law. Those jottings were to become *Le Trou*, his first novel, which was a great success. Film director Jacques Becker's interest was roused by the book, and he offered the young author a job as technical adviser on his next film. Two doors had just opened wide in Giovanni's life: one into the world of books, and one into the world of films. Over the next few years he wrote many novels, some of which, through his skill as a scriptwriter, were to become equally successful films.

José Giovanni introduced into his detective novels a new element of adventure. The heroes of his stories are inspired to act with almost superhuman courage, to be stretched to their very limits. The challenge made by the Iditarod to its contestants could not fail to attract Giovanni as the subject for a novel.

The course of the race—sometimes called The Last Great Race on Earth—began as a mail and supply route from the coastal towns of Alaska to the mining camps of the interior. Mail and supplies went in and gold came out, all via dog sled. Heroes were made, legends were born, and in 1925 part of the trail became a life-line for Nome when it was stricken by a diphtheria epidemic: the mushers and their sturdy huskies brought in vital supplies of serum to save the town.

Now this great race is run every year, and new legends and heroes are added to the old.

THE
RED FOX

A CONDENSATION OF THE BOOK BY
ANTHONY HYDE

Illustrated by John Heseltine

It is a
shock to Robert
Thorne when May
Brightman, the woman he
had loved and lost years before, comes back into his
life. There is a troubling mystery connecting May's
birth with the sudden disappearance of the father
who is so important to her, and now she implores
Robert to help her find him.
The discovery of Harry Brightman's body in his
car, apparently a suicide victim, is only the
beginning of an amazing quest which takes Thorne
from the forests of New England to a doctor's
surgery in Nova Scotia, and from a canal barge in
Paris to a remote Russian village. As Thorne pieces
together the Brightmans' story he also finds himself
penetrating the dark world of international
espionage, and the solution to the mystery reaches
even into Thorne's own past.
Thorne knows that powerful and dangerous men
are following the same trail as himself, men who
think nothing of killing and torturing to discover
the devastating truth about the Red Fox . . .

1

I was to learn that all the real secrets are buried and that only ghosts speak the truth. So it was fitting that all this began in a graveyard, among mysteries, memories, and lies.

That year October 28 was cold and threatened rain, and as I walked away from the little frame church with Father Delaney, our breath misted in front of us. The three tall oaks that screened off the graveyard were stripped bare as old bones and the summer's grass had died down. I came here only one day a year, but every step brought a rush of memory: the flick-flick of the old priest's heavy trousers as he walked beside me; the smell of wet leaves; a rusted iron cross glimpsed in the undergrowth: JENNIFER, AGE THREE WEEKS, 1907. Year after year, none of this changed, and when we finally stopped before my father's stone, all the old emotions welled up—the shock, the grief, the fundamental disbelief.

The old priest murmured a prayer in Latin. Half kneeling, I placed a bouquet of cornflowers against the smooth stone, then drew myself up and raised my eyes. My father's grave was right on the crest of the hill; you could see for miles across a spur of the Tuscarora Mountains, northwest of Harrisburg, Pennsylvania. Low grey clouds trailed tendrils of showers over the opposite ridge and the wind bit at my cheek.

My mother had died the previous winter; for the first time I was making the annual trek by myself. Every year she had come, out of love and loyalty—and the desire, above everything else, to disprove the doubt I'd seen in so many eyes. *A hunting accident. Leastwise, that's what they're calling it. . . .* But I knew that everything my mother had refused to believe was perfectly true. My father had killed himself. For me, the only mystery was why.

I glanced back towards the headstone. It occurred to me that its carved letters were growing into an obscure kind of hieroglyphics. My mother was gone; now I was the only one left to decipher them.

MITCHELL SVEN THORNE

FEB 17 1902—OCT 28 1956

London Paris Cape Town Mexico Rome

Father Delaney asked, "Those cities . . . I was trying to remember why they were there?"

"He worked for the State Department, Father. Those were the places he served."

"You were fourteen, weren't you, when your father died?"

"Yes. Almost fifteen."

He shook his head. "I still remember how you looked at the funeral, Robert, and then those first years when you came with your mother. You were always so stiff and silent. Sometimes I thought you must be terribly angry, and then I wondered if you weren't afraid, like someone who has a secret they're too frightened to tell."

I looked at him, startled. Had he guessed that I knew for certain what everyone else only suspected? I turned away quickly, and found myself looking straight into the past. *Sunday, October 28, 1956.* A cabin, not ten miles from where I stood now. My bedroom, cold and bare, the mattress stripped of its sheets. Myself, stretched out on the bed, staring up at the ceiling. Beside me, voices emerging from my transistor radio.

We're closing the cabin for the season and my mother has been cleaning in the other room, but now the screen door snaps shut as she steps outside. A moment later, I swing my legs over the edge of the bed and sit up. It is now that I see my father through the window. He is hurrying away from the cabin, and just as he enters the woods I see his shotgun. In that instant, the tension I've felt both in him and in my mother all the previous week suddenly crystallizes. *I know.* My heart pounds. *No one, under any circumstances, should take a gun into the woods without warning everyone else about what he's doing.* It's his own golden rule.

236

"Robert?"

Gently, Father Delaney gripped my arm and brought me back to myself. "If you don't mind, I'd like to ask something personal."

"Of course, Father."

He hesitated, then looked up at my face. "When your father died, you knew there were all kinds of rumours?"

"Yes."

He shook his head. "Those rumours weren't true, Robert. I never knew your father well, but I knew him well enough. Believe me— they weren't true."

For the briefest instant, we looked each other in the eye and finally, in gratitude to this old man, I managed the lie: "Thank you, Father. I know . . . I believe you."

FOR FIVE MINUTES, as Father Delaney made his way back to the church, I stared into the valley.

Advancing like a heavy mist, the curtain of rain drew closer, until I felt the first drops, cold and prickling, on my face. I looked down at the tombstone; as the rain grew heavier, it began to shine with a slick, velvety sheen and my mind again slid back to that day. Again, in horror, I watched my father disappear into the woods. Again, in terror, my heart began pounding. And again there was nothing to do but run, but never quite fast enough. Finally, at the edge of the woods, I slumped to the ground. My breath trembled in my chest. I tried to shout, but my strength—no doubt like my father's—was exhausted, and not even the birds were disturbed by my cry. And then, with the great roar of the shot, the question exploded within me: *Why? Why did you do it?*

More than twenty years later, as I wrenched myself back to the present, I knew it was still the only question to ask.

Then I told myself what I always did: Let it lie, forget it. But I could never forget, of course; not quite. And perhaps my mother's absence this year made it even more difficult. As I drove away through the autumn hills, I could sense her beside me and hear her voice, low and murmuring, as she remembered him.

My French mother had first met my father when he'd been posted to Paris in 1938. The bright young diplomat had helped a manufacturer with some permits, received a dinner invitation in return, and then walked off with his daughter. She and my father had been falling in love just as Europe staggered towards war and had hurriedly married as the Germans raced towards Paris. After that my father, fearing that his diplomatic status might not guarantee my mother's safety, had rushed her out of the city when the British embassy was evacuated in the first week of June.

I ARRIVED HOME shortly before noon.

For me, "home" is now Charlottesville, Virginia, a small town about a hundred miles southwest of Washington. I could never quite believe that I'd actually settled there. Its population is only thirty-five thousand, whereas I was brought up in a succession of world capitals and spent most of my journalistic career in Berlin, Warsaw and Moscow. Nonetheless, when I tired of the rat race Charlottesville won out for two reasons: it is the seat of the University of Virginia with its excellent research facilities, and it is near Washington, where I have most of my contacts. Now, after three years, I fitted right in.

I live in a white frame house decorated with Victorian gingerbread. I left my Volvo in the lane, let myself in through the front door, and went straight through to the kitchen. The house felt cold, so I laid a fire in the old woodstove, then made coffee and carried it into the living room.

Usually, the visit to my father's grave was just a day's excursion, but this time I'd worked it in as the last leg of a two-week trip to New York, so the room had a forlorn, abandoned air. I went around plumping cushions and opening curtains, then slumped down on the sofa. The coffee table was directly in front of me, a large pile of mail strewn across it. Perhaps it was the peculiar quality of this day, but I saw nothing unusual in this and, almost absently, began sorting through the envelopes. When I had finished my coffee, I carried the whole mess into my workroom.

Like most workrooms, I suppose mine gives a fair portrait of its owner. It's converted from an old screened porch running the full length of the house. Bookshelves cover the inside wall (two thousand volumes, mostly about the Soviet Union), and on the outside, under the windows, there's a maple counter that is my principal work-space. The tools of my trade were scattered there—

238

drafts, offprints from journals, illegible notes to myself, a couple of tape recorders, an old Underwood I'd been dragging around for years as a sort of lucky charm, and my latest toy, an IBM personal computer.

You should be able to guess from these bits and pieces that I love my work. In a sense, that's also connected to my father. Soon after he died, Sputnik was launched, and in the great panic that followed, my high school in Washington began offering courses in Russian. I needed something to lose myself in, and soon I was totally enthralled by the language, the country, the people. It's a fascination I've never lost, and for most of my adult life I've earned my living, in one way or another, as a "Russian expert": as a journalist in Eastern Europe and Moscow, and now as a freelance writer. Even on that afternoon I couldn't resist, and flipped on my new machine, but I was too tired to do anything useful, so I went back to the living room and went to sleep. When I awoke, it was after three and the phone was ringing.

When I answered it a girl said, "Western Union. We have a telegram for you, Mr. Thorne. The text reads: ROBERT, TRIED TO REACH YOU ALL WEEK. URGENT. PLEASE CALL 416 922-0250. LOVE MAY."

May. May Brightman . . . even after all these years, hearing her name was like a blow to the pit of my stomach. I cleared my throat. "Could you tell me where that was sent from, operator?"

"Yes, sir. The point of origin is Toronto, Canada." May was Canadian, though I'd never known her to live there.

"And could you read back that number again?"

She did so, and I hung up.

May Brightman. I stood there, my hand on the phone. It had been a long time since I'd heard from her. But she always did keep in touch—maybe a woman who rejects you can never quite leave you alone . . . . Except that sounds bitter, and that's not what I felt. Enough time had passed, God knows—I was over her now—so there wasn't that pain. But there still was a strange lack of completion. What had happened between us? Standing there, almost twenty years after the fact, I still didn't know. She'd loved me, she'd never denied it. But when I'd asked her to marry me (I was very young and sufficiently romantic to do the deed on a bench in Central Park), she'd said yes right away, only to change her mind the next week with no clue as to why. I thought how uncanny it was that she had called today, for there was another link to my father. I'd lived my life within the shadow cast by his death, and May had been my great attempt to step outside it.

What could she want?

I poured myself a whisky as I pondered the question. Working it out, I realized it had been five years since we'd last met. At the time I'd been fairly hard up and she'd offered me the use of her place near Sancerre, in France, while I finished my first book. This was typical of our contacts over the years. You couldn't say that we were now "just friends", for the original relationship had been too complicated and intense, and its ending too mysterious, to permit anything so neutral. She kept in touch, almost protectively—perhaps she felt a shade guilty. I wondered if that was all she wanted now, just a word to know how I was keeping.

Except the telegram had said "urgent" . . . not a word you'd normally associate with her. Her father had money, she'd never worked, and she'd always had the calm, cool confidence of the rich. In fact, the only time I'd seen her truly afraid was the night she'd tried to tell me why she'd decided not to go through with our engagement—but, almost twenty years later, that could hardly be the cause of her anxiety. What the hell, I put down the whisky and picked up the phone.

She answered on the first ring, obviously very upset.

"Robert . . . thank God it's you. I phoned every day last week. I sent another telegram on Wednesday—"

"I was in New York. What's the matter?"

She took a breath. "It's my father. He's disappeared."

I'd never met her father, but I knew he was important to her. I'd suspected that her refusing me had some connection with him, for her change of mind had taken place after she'd flown up to Toronto to see him.

"When did this happen?"

"Ten days ago."

"You've told the police?"

"Yes. They . . . they were worried he might have been kidnapped, but there hasn't been a ransom note and now they say he's just gone off on his own for a while, but he'd *never* go off

240

without telling me." The intensity of her voice was startling—but then she caught herself and added, "Robert, maybe I shouldn't have called—"

"No, no. Of course you should have. I'm just trying to think. What can I do?"

She hesitated. "I'm afraid—I'm afraid he's killed himself. I know all the reasons why you'll say he hasn't—but I'm still afraid . . ."

Suicide. On this day, of all days, it wasn't a possibility I could easily dismiss. "You have a reason for thinking that?"

"Yes. The police don't think it means anything. That's why I called you. I need someone who can find things out for me. You're a journalist, Robert. You can get things out of bureaucrats. But I'd rather not say what things till you get here."

"So you want me to come to Toronto?"

"Yes. I know you must be busy . . ."

She was right. I was anxious to get back to work. She said, "And of course I'll pay your way—you—"

"Don't be silly." I was certain I couldn't help her but I could at least hold her hand till her father showed up. "You're sure you can't tell me anything more?"

I heard her sigh. "You know I'm adopted?"

"Yes. I remember."

Remember: I could sense her falter as I said the word, but then she went on, "It has something to do with that. That's what I'd want you to find out about."

"All right. I can probably be there tomorrow."

A breath, all relief, fluttered down the line. "Thank you, Robert. Bless you." She told me where she lived, we said goodbye and hung up . . . and right away I knew that something was wrong.

It was an odd sensation. For a moment, I thought it was just the call itself—fears about the suicide of a father on precisely *this* day.

But the intense unease that now swept across me was a more particular sensation—as if I was being watched, as if someone else was with me in the house. . . . And then I knew what it was.

May had said she'd sent me *two* telegrams: the one I'd received today, but another last Wednesday when I'd been in New York. It hadn't been in my mail, I was certain, and now I checked again to be sure. It wasn't. Carefully, I played my arrival back through my mind. After I'd come in, I'd gone straight through to the kitchen. From there I'd carried my coffee into the living room. *And that's when I'd discovered my mail:* two weeks' worth, scattered all over the coffee table . . . instead of lying in the hall, under the letterbox, where it ought to have been.

2

Like most Americans, I don't know Canada at all—it's where the winter comes from—and I hadn't been there in years, so Toronto struck me as a great deal bigger, richer and noisier than I remembered when I arrived there the next day. May lived downtown, in an area the cabbie called Kensington Market. I had him drop me at the edge of it and walked a little, passing through crowded streets jammed with stalls selling everything from lobsters to African beads. This was obviously an old immigrant district but the immigrants, I suspected, were on their way out. On May's street, exotic plants dangled in windows, young matrons pushed wicker prams. This was a slum-in-transition; five years from now, it would be a chic address.

I went up to the door and rang the bell. No answer.

Setting down my bag, I walked around to the side of the house. There was a lane here, with an orange Volkswagen Beetle parked halfway up it—the only car May ever drove—and a board fence down one side. Peering over this, I could look into her narrow garden. A brick path ran down the middle of it and on either side grew shrub roses, grey thorny canes dabbed here and there with clusters of blood-red hips. I could see May halfway along the path, squatting with her back to me. Her long, reddish-blonde hair cascaded over a blue wool poncho which, in turn, was worn over an ankle-length burgundy dress.

I watched her in silence. May had always possessed a mysterious quality—and now I felt it touch me again. The garden, in the wan autumn light, was like a faded old photograph of girls in large bonnets whose eyes are lost in shadow as they squint into the sun. That was May's quality: she didn't quite belong to this time.

But now she stood up. Holding her dress in front of her, she walked down the path towards a compost heap where she spilled dead rose canes from her lap. When she turned round, she saw me and smiled. "Robert . . . Robert!" I stepped through the garden gate; then, with a sigh that was almost a groan, May fell against me and I held her. "Thank God you've come," she whispered.

She started to cry, and I squeezed her against me. "Don't worry," I whispered. "It'll come out all right."

Getting her breath, she eased away and tried to smile. "I think I brought you all the way up here just to be able to do that."

"A trip worth making, then."

She took my hand and led me inside, to a large, comfortable kitchen. Sitting on the edge of a table, I watched her make coffee—Braun grinder, Melitta filter—and was again struck by the sense of dislocation I'd felt in the garden. There, because the garden itself seemed out of time, she'd fitted right in; here, where everything was right up to date, she seemed out of place.

She started to talk, questions about my trip, Charlottesville, my writing. As best I could, I brought her up to date on my life. Her own hadn't much changed. She was still studying music; she had her house, loved the garden, saw just a few friends. As she went on, she became more composed, though nothing could hide her anxiety.

When we were sitting with second cups of coffee in front of us, I said, "Do you think you can tell me what happened?"

"There's not much to tell. On Saturday, around three in the morning, a police car drove past my father's place and saw that the door was open. One of the patrolmen rang the bell, but there was no answer and he went inside. No one was there, so they sent in a report and locked the door. They sent another car in the morning, but there was still no answer. A neighbour gave them my name."

"This was Saturday . . . the eighteenth?"

She nodded. "The police made their checks—they were serious to begin with because they knew he was wealthy. But he wasn't in hospital, he wasn't in the morgue, he . . ."

Her voice trailed away. She'd been in control of herself, but all at once she was right on the edge.

"Were there no signs that he'd gone on a trip?"

"He could have taken a couple of suitcases of clothes and I wouldn't know."

"Does he drive a car?"

She nodded. "It was in the garage." She closed her eyes for a second. "I've been all through this, Robert. There's just no sign of him at all."

I leaned back, wanting to put a little distance between us. "All right, I accept that he's missing. At the very least, he's been damned inconsiderate—but what I don't see is suicide."

She glanced down. "I told you I had a reason."

"Yes. Something to do with your being adopted."

She reached out for her cigarettes and, as she lit one, I watched her face. It was broad, girlishly freckled, with a slightly snub nose. In a way, she did look her age, but something was missing—she was like a young girl who'd suddenly woken up to find she was forty. As she brought the cigarette to her lips, I noticed her thin, delicate wrists, very long, like those of some wistful Pre-Raphaelite maiden. But the fingers themselves, practical and strong, belonged to a real country girl. Bloomsbury girl . . . hippie lady . . . princess . . . peasant . . . she was a little of each.

Now, guardedly, she said, "I was adopted when I was just a few months old. I only remember Harry . . . my father. I don't even remember his wife—my legal mother—because they separated just a year or so later. He's the only family I've ever had. Or wanted." She looked up at me. "I didn't even know I was adopted till I was fourteen."

"And what did you feel?"

"I was dizzy for a second, that's all." She hesitated, then continued. "I don't want you to miss the point in all this. It didn't make any difference. It never has. That day, he told me everything I know about my adoption—it happened in 1940, in Halifax. The subject hasn't been raised since. . . . That is, until a few weeks ago."

"Then what happened?"

"He started to talk about it. He began asking if I didn't want to know where I came from. . . . Then he started to press—didn't I want to know who my real father was . . . ?"

"And?"

"*He's* my real father. I don't want another one. But something about the whole subject was bothering him."

"He's an elderly man. He probably won't live much longer.

Perhaps he only wanted to give you one final chance. . . . And why does any of this make you think he's killed himself?"

She flinched at the words. "I'm not sure. What if my biological parents came back? Or . . ."

"Or what? If you were still a child—yes, I could see it. But now? You'd all go out to lunch, shake hands, and that would be it."

"Not necessarily. Say there'd been something illegal about the adoption . . ."

I waited, but she didn't say anything more. I said, "Did you tell the police all this?"

She nodded. "They're sure he wasn't being blackmailed, because of his bank records. They told me they'd look into it but I don't think they have."

"And you want me to?"

She looked me square in the eye. "Yes."

"So far as you know, this was the only strange element in your father's recent behaviour?"

"Yes. It's the only thing I can think of."

"All right, then, I'll do it. But even if I do find out something, it probably won't be connected to your father's disappearance."

She smiled. "Bless you, Robert. I knew you would."

I squeezed her hand. And then I sensed a certain embarrassment come over her, so I said, "I just thought of something. I left my bag on your front porch."

She laughed. "Don't worry, the neighbours are honest. Go and get it, then I'll show you to your room."

She led me up to a bedroom on the second floor, and after taking a shower, I stretched out on the bed and began to think . . . though more about May than her father. I had few worries about him: Harry Brightman, I was willing to bet, was pursuing an old man's folly, chasing a woman whose existence he'd been too embarrassed to admit. The police, I suspected, had also reached this conclusion, and in fact I could see only one point contradicting it—May's fear itself. Undoubtedly she was genuinely upset. And she wasn't the sort to cry wolf. On the contrary, self-sufficiency had always been one of her hallmarks, so that her call for help now was ample testimony to the devotion she felt towards her father.

I drifted off to sleep and when I awoke it was completely dark outside my window. I dressed and went downstairs to find May.

"I've woken up starving," I said. "Why don't we get something to eat? On the way over here I thought I saw a Jewish restaurant. If they make a good borscht . . ."

The restaurant was just around the corner, one of those old-fashioned Jewish restaurants with a counter where ancient men drink tea with lemon.

As I dunked a piece of potato into my soup, May said, "This is like Russian food, isn't it?"

"Some Jewish cooking is, but this is more Polish. Russians and Poles and even Germans are raised on good yiddisher food."

"I remember Harry once saying something like that. He's German you know. His parents died in the First World War and an uncle in Winnipeg adopted him. When the uncle died, he left his fur business to my father. Actually, you'd enjoy talking to Harry. He always says that he made his real money out of Russia, not Canada."

I swallowed cabbage roll. "I don't get it."

"As well as manufacturing furs—turning them into coats—he had an import-export business. In the thirties, he brought in fur from the Soviet Union."

Once, in Leningrad, I'd gone to one of the fur auctions. It was enormous, with buyers from all over the world. I said, "Did he ever go to Russia?"

"Oh yes, several times. I know he got to meet one of the important Bolsheviks . . . not Lenin but . . . Zinoviev?"

"Yes." It made sense. Zinoviev, a close friend of Lenin's and the first head of the Comintern—the organization the Russians use to control Communist parties outside the Soviet Union—had been relatively cosmopolitan and well-travelled, qualities that would have made him interested in a foreign businessman intrepid enough to visit post-Revolutionary Russia. Of course, those same qualities had made him the first of the major Bolsheviks whom Stalin had purged. That had been in 1934, so presumably Brightman had gone before then.

I said, "I take it that his business was really his life."

"No, it wasn't. He sold out about fifteen years ago and he's been happy since. He travels a lot. He loves art and collects it. And there's me. He's very devoted to me, he always has been."

246

After we'd finished eating, I suggested we walk. We headed up
Spadina—a broad, barren, windy street—then turned east along
Bloor. As we came up to a corner, May pointed down a side street.
"Harry lives just up there . . ."

"Can we look?"

"All right. It's not far."

Almost at once we were in a solid old residential neighbourhood
with large Edwardian houses reposing on generous lawns. May
stopped under a streetlight and pointed across the road. "That's the
house. Behind the fence."

The house was dark, almost lost behind an immense elm, but
plainly very large. May said, "It's too big for him but he can't bring
himself to move."

"Are you collecting his mail?"

"No . . . I suppose it still comes."

"Let me get it, then. Do you have a key?"

She didn't want me to, I could see that, but after a moment she
fished a key out of her purse and I crossed the road. The iron gate
opened with a squeak and I went up a stone walk to the door. This
was large, glossy, black, and bore a knocker appropriate to a fur
dealer—a brass snowshoe rapped a fox on the nose. I fitted the key
and pushed the door inwards, ploughing a heap of mail ahead of me.

I couldn't find a light switch, but after a moment my eyes
adjusted to the gloom and I picked up Brightman's mail and stepped
into a hall. The doors on my left were partly open, so I stuck my
head in, peering across a shadowy vista of furniture towards the dark
glitter of glass-fronted cabinets. I stepped back into the hall and felt
ahead to the stairs. There was a lamp on the newel post and I put it
on, then started up, the banister guiding my hand. The landing was
pitch black, but I groped ahead and almost immediately felt a
doorframe. The door was open. I stepped into the room and
punched on a light.

I had found my way to Brightman's library. It was very large,
with dark oak panelling. Despite its size, the room felt cramped, for
it was jammed with books, cabinets, display cases and heavy
furniture. The display cases were filled with stuffed animals, each
caught in a natural pose (a beaver was chewing a twig gripped in its
paws; a lynx padded furtively over a log), and this made the glassy

glitter of their eyes all the more gruesome—though I suppose such a collection was reasonable given Brightman's business. And yet this collection, I realized, was only an afterthought compared with the framed prints and engravings that occupied one whole side of the room. There were five rows of them; they were filed on that wall, not displayed, and didn't invite you to look at them so much as count them. All of them were modern, and many had that heavy, romantic quality you find in the propaganda art of the thirties. One, I saw, was by the Russian artist Vladimir Favorsky: Cossacks, workers, soldiers, Lenin and Trotsky, their figures all pulled and stretched into a map of Russia.

I ended my circuit of the room by Brightman's desk. On it was a photograph of him in a plain wooden frame. He was a big man, with a broad chest sloping into a heavy belly. His face was genial, his hair thick, though receding slightly from a high forehead. It struck me as a little peculiar, having a photograph of yourself on your desk, but when I picked it up, I saw its real value. Pencilled on the back were the words: *Harry Brightman, taken by May Brightman with her own Brownie, Georgian Bay, Aug. 1, 1949.*

I set the photograph back in its place. Harry Brightman, as May had seen him. But what sort of man had lived and breathed in this room? And why had he left it? For the first time, it occurred to me that the answer to this question might be more interesting than I'd assumed. But I wasn't going to answer it now. Taking a last glance over my shoulder, I turned off the light . . . and froze.

Before me, the hall was pitch black. But I knew I wasn't alone.

Steps, soft as breaths, were coming along the corridor. Towards me. Right past me. And then, for an instant, I saw a face—a glint of red hair—and with a wild glance that face looked right into my eyes: a face as thin as a weasel's and very pale.

And then it was gone.

My heart thumped—thumped so hard it was all I could hear. I strained to listen. The carpet on the stairs was very thick, but I made out quick, padding steps . . . and then only silence . . .

Cautiously, I edged into the hall. The stairway was black as a. well, but then I reached the landing and the newel-post light glimmered up from below.

Three steps from the bottom, I stopped and listened again.

Nothing. He must have gone . . . but if he hadn't, if he was waiting along the hall leading to the back of the house, I would be completely visible the moment I stepped off the staircase.

Gripping the banister, leaning forward, I switched off the light on the newel post.

Red spots danced in front of my eyes. I waited, letting them fade, then stepped silently down the last couple of stairs. Nothing moved. I felt my way along, towards the back. There was a little grey light here, and after a moment the kitchen loomed up in front of me. The fridge coming on nearly made me jump out of my skin, but there was no one here, and when I checked the back door it seemed firmly locked. Quickly, I made my way to the front of the house. He'd either gone out this way or through the basement. I opened the door and stepped into the night.

I DIDN'T TELL MAY. She was already frightened and there was no point in alarming her further.

Up to this point, I'd been a rather reluctant good Samaritan. And of course that still might be my position—Brightman, after all, was a rich man, he lived in a rich neighbourhood, and perhaps I'd only interrupted a burglar. On the other hand, if Brightman's disappearance had a darker side then conceivably his concern about May's adoption *might* be linked to it. The next morning, for the first time, I began taking the whole business seriously.

I worked fast. I began searching for information at the main branch of the Toronto Public Library, first with *The New York Times Index*, then in a microfilm reader. I read through a dozen stories about adoption, mainly concerned with the United States, but one compared American practices with those in other countries, including Canada. I discovered that in Canada adoption was under provincial jurisdiction, and that most of the provinces had established official bodies called children's aid societies to handle the whole business. And it appeared that the basis of their entire system was absolute secrecy. Someone trying to track down their parents would probably run right up against it.

If May had been adopted through a children's aid society there was only one way to find out who the birth mother was: a contact inside the society. There were, however, still private adoptions, arranged through lawyers and doctors, and if the case were one of these, the lawyer would be the key.

It was around three by the time I got back to May's house and told her the gist of what I'd found out.

"So it's going to be very hard," she said, "if I was adopted through one of these societies?"

"It would be a big help if you knew someone inside the system. It would be easier, though, if we knew whether or not you were adopted privately."

"All I know is what I told you.".

"But your father must have a lawyer?"

"Of course. His name is Stewart Cadogan."

"He'd probably know. Phone him and find out. If he says you *were* adopted privately, we'll go see him."

May glanced quickly at me. "If you need to see him, I'd rather you went by yourself. I don't like him. We never get along."

Her fear—I felt it flicker again. "May . . . you're sure you've told me everything you know?"

She reached up with both hands, combing her fingers back through her hair, but then she smiled. "You have to understand, I've lived all my life with one story and I'd prefer not to change it. Even if my adoption is connected to Harry's going away, I'd rather you take that connection to the police and let them find him. If it's possible to do it like that."

I nodded, though I wasn't exactly happy about it. "I'll try . . . but you know, this lawyer may not be prepared to see me alone. Your adoption is confidential—"

"Don't worry. I'll fix it."

I waited in the kitchen while May used the phone in the hall. In ten minutes, she was back. "Good news. My adoption was private."

"But he won't talk about it?"

"Well, he didn't want to, but I persuaded him. I have to write a letter giving him formal instructions."

Stewart Cadogan QC had agreed to see me that day at six thirty. I set off at dusk in May's Volkswagen for his office.

Old, rich law firms can be very impressive, and Cadogan's fell into that category. A black-suited porter ushered me through a door into an outer office, and an elderly secretary took me over and held the door as I stepped into Cadogan's sanctum. It was large and gloomy. Greeting me, Cadogan lifted himself out of a chair behind a desk. He was very tall, somewhat stooped, with a large, bald head. Accepting May's letter, he indicated a leather chair. I sat, and he began to read, frowning and suspicious. When he was finished, he laid the sheet of paper on his desk and pressed it flat with a huge bony hand. Then he glanced at me.

"You'll understand, Mr. Thorne, that your situation is somewhat equivocal?"

"Yes, I suppose I do."

A smile flickered. "Then you'll be aware that mine must be too."

I said nothing. He got to his feet. "It's after six. You'll take something to drink, Mr. Thorne?"

"Thank you, sir. That would be very pleasant."

He stepped to a lacquered cabinet and took out bottles and glasses. "You're a young man and will prefer whisky. I am old and must make do with sherry." This was a joke, so I smiled. I watched him pour, then he brought me my glass, and settled himself behind his desk. "As I understand it," he said, "you're trying to find Miss Brightman's father."

"Not quite that. May thinks her adoption might have some connection to her father's disappearance and has asked me to look into it."

His eyes didn't leave mine, but his hand edged over his desk to a file that was lying there. "Adoption. Intimate business. You realize, I suppose, that I offered to tell Miss Brightman everything I know about the matter, but she asked me to tell only you?"

"Yes."

"Without wishing to give offence, Mr. Thorne, I must tell you that I am under no obligation to tell you anything at all. May Brightman is my client, as well as her father, but these papers come from Harry Brightman's file, not hers. Only he, strictly speaking, can give you permission to read them."

"I'm sure that's true—strictly speaking." I hesitated, then I said, "Can I ask if *you* think there's some connection—that is, between Brightman's disappearance and his daughter's adoption?"

He frowned. "I don't say yes, Mr. Thorne . . . but I don't say no, either. In any case, I'll let you see these because I know that Harry

Brightman would wish me to do as his daughter has asked . . . and because, as you will see, they contain very few secrets." Abruptly, he shoved the file across his desk. "However, May Brightman's adoption has a peculiar interest because of a quirk in the law of the time. You'll understand as you read."

I opened the file. An old memo summarized the Nova Scotia Adoption Act. It concentrated on the "consents" that had to be obtained before an adoption decree would be granted. According to the memo, if a person whose consent was normally required couldn't be found, the court could advertise for that person and then declare, if he or she still hadn't come forward, that consent was taken as given. The memo concluded: "NO, the child's physical presence would not normally be required in court; and YES, our client would have to be married. *This is not stated as an explicit provision of the law but in practice is almost always required.*"

I looked up at Cadogan. "I assume this was drafted after a request by Brightman?"

"Yes. His request is not in the file. Probably he came into the office and spoke with my father personally."

The next items in the file were some letters and a clipping from *The Royal Gazette*. It was old and yellowed; in the middle of it was the heading: *Adoption Act; re Florence Esther Raines.* Beneath it was printed:

TO: Florence Esther Raines, whose present address is unknown and who is the mother of Elizabeth Ann Raines:

TAKE NOTICE that pursuant to the provisions of the Order, you are advised that a petition has been presented for the adoption of the child Elizabeth Ann Raines, and that said petition will be heard and considered at County Court Chambers at the Law Courts, Spring Garden Road, Halifax, Nova Scotia, on Friday, the 28th day of June, AD 1940, at the hour of ten o'clock in the forenoon.

I skipped down the page. The petition itself was the legally certified story of May Brightman's adoption.

I read that Harold Charles Brightman, and his wife, Ellen Sarah Brightman, were desirous of adopting a female child, Elizabeth Ann

Raines, the illegitimate child of Florence Esther Raines of Halifax.

The child had been born on the 12th day of June AD 1939 and abandoned into the care of Charles Grainger, MD, within a few weeks of her birth.

The last item in the file was the adoption order itself. I looked up at Cadogan. "So this means that May Brightman's adoption has always been public knowledge?"

"Yes. There have never been any secrets about her adoption and, as you see, it was all entirely legal."

"But not," I thought aloud, "entirely regular."

"How is that, Mr. Thorne?"

"I'm thinking of Brightman's marriage . . ." I flipped back through the file. "In this first memo, there's the clear implication that he wasn't married when the proceedings began. Your clerk stressed that he'd have to be. So it must have been a marriage of convenience."

Cadogan gave me a frosty smile. "Perhaps so," he conceded. "But I suspect that Harry Brightman wasn't the first man to desire a child without having to put up with a wife. And like many wealthy men, he simply arranged matters to suit him."

Brightman, a wealthy man, wants a child. But not any child—*this* child. So he travels all the way to Nova Scotia because . . . but then the thought slipped away.

"You don't entirely rule out a connection between Brightman's disappearance and the adoption?"

Now, for the first time, Cadogan seemed uneasy. His eyes dropped. "Mr. Thorne, when men say they wish to speak frankly, they usually intend to tell you a lie, but in fact I want you to know what's in my mind. On the last occasion I saw Harry Brightman, I sensed that something was troubling him. He mentioned a woman. It was clear that he meant a liaison in his past . . . but it was all very fleeting."

"Did he mention a name?"

"Anna. He said, 'When I look back, Anna is my deepest regret.' We'd been talking about the past, the war."

"And you didn't like to ask who this woman was?"

"It would have embarrassed us both."

"I see. . . . But there are no Annas involved in any of this."

He lifted his hand from his desk in a dismissive gesture. "A nickname, a pet name . . ."

And now, at last, I had it. I could hear May's voice: *He said he wanted to tell me who my real father was.* But surely the usual focus of interest was the mother's identity. . . . All of which must have showed on my face, for now Cadogan said, "I take it you've drawn the obvious conclusion, Mr. Thorne?"

"Yes, sir."

I had. In adopting May, Harry Brightman had been adopting his own illegitimate daughter. I said, "Did you just reach this conclusion then, during that conversation?"

"No, it was a suspicion I'd held for a good many years." The old man looked at his watch rather deliberately. "If you don't mind . . . I think I've told you all that I know."

"Yes, sir. And I thank you for doing so."

I rose. Cadogan didn't hold out his hand. I nodded goodbye, turned, and went out. The porter was waiting and I followed him down the stairs and through the big oak front doors to the street.

The pavement was dark and deserted; a drizzle was falling. Standing there, I let it prickle, cold and sharp, on my face. I took a deep breath. Would I tell May? I really had no idea what to do. And all at once—it must have been the rain—I was back in that graveyard where my father was buried and an uncanny sensation passed through me: a distressing feeling that I was not here by accident, that somehow Brightman's fate was intimately connected to my own. Should I keep back what I'd discovered? May's instructions had been clear enough: she didn't want to know unless it became absolutely necessary. Perhaps, given that, I had no right to tell her, for there was still no certainty that the adoption and Brightman's disappearance were connected. And why, given the facts, should he have fled?

As I walked along, a soft voice began whispering: Let it alone, let it alone. But even then, I knew I wouldn't. I'd found out something that no one had been intended to know, and there had to be more.

As I reached the car, I remembered what the White King had told Alice: "Begin at the beginning, and go on to the end."

For May Brightman, and perhaps for her father, the beginning lay in Halifax, Nova Scotia, during the spring of 1940.

254

3

I flew into Halifax the next morning, my aircraft descending blindly through a dense fog, and took a cab into the city. It was a Victorian garrison town mellowed by time: grey, narrow streets; weather-beaten clapboard houses; and that odour of salt, fish and diesel oil that is common to ports the world over.

My hotel room overlooked the harbour. Eating breakfast, I peered out the window while the mournful note of a foghorn shivered the glass. A warship nosed into view, sullen and menacing as a shark, and the sight of it brought my mind back to business. May Brightman had been adopted in June 1940, the same month that France had fallen. The United States was still eighteen months away from war, but in this harbour the first of the Atlantic convoys had been preparing to run the U-boats' gauntlet. I wondered if Harry Brightman had watched them. It was possible, though he must have had other things on his mind. The woman he'd made pregnant, for example, Florence Raines. Or Charles Grainger, the doctor who'd taken possession of the child. Or possibly the child herself, the little girl he'd called May. Forty years later, I began backtracking over his problem.

I began by trying to find Florence Raines, a search that took me to an old stone edifice that housed the registry of vital statistics. Within an hour, I established three facts. First, Florence Esther Raines had been born in Springhill, a small mining town in the northwestern section of the province. Second, she had married one James Luton Murdoch, in Halifax, on March 22, 1943. And third, she had died, also in Halifax, on June 12, 1971.

This final fact set me back on my heels. Florence had been the obvious person to relate the story of the adoption. But I told myself that her death wasn't the end of the world and went back to the hotel and checked the phone book for Murdoch, her husband. When I called, a female, youngish voice told me he wasn't at home.

"Could you tell me when he'll be back?"

"Not till the end of the month. He's in Montreal, with his sister."

"It's important that I get in touch with him. Could you give me this sister's address?"

She gave it to me, but for the moment I filed it under "last resort". I had one better hope: the doctor. He was listed in the telephone book and I dialled the number. A woman answered the phone.

"Oh, no, the doctor's not in, I'm afraid."

"Do you know when he'll return?"

"That's hard to say, sir. It's Friday, you see. His day at the clinic."

So he still practised. She gave me the clinic address and I went straight downstairs and hailed a cab. The city slipped by, grey, old-fashioned, oddly appealing. Gradually the streets grew scruffy. Shabby houses. Cheap shops. People scurried along the pavements with their heads down. White-bread faces; draught-beer faces; black faces. . . . I suddenly realized that there were quite a few black faces, which surprised me enough to mention it to the driver.

"You American?" he replied. I nodded. "Well, slaves used to come here to escape. The Underground Railway, they called it. This whole section of town was called Africville."

The clinic was located in a small frame house on one of the meaner streets. I went up the path through an open door and into a shabby hall. There was a scent of poverty, masked by carbolic. A bespectacled girl with lanky brown hair was sitting behind a desk talking into the phone. "I know . . . I know . . . exactly. . . . You just can't treat people like that . . . exactly. Just a sec." Resentfully, she looked up at me. "Yes?"

"I'd like to see Dr. Grainger."

"He's pretty busy right now."

"It isn't a medical problem. Could you say I want to talk to him about Harry Brightman?"

She looked dubious. "Well . . . you'll still have to wait. Go down the hall, to your right."

I followed her instructions and passed through an arch into a large, square room. Around the walls, perched on straight chairs, sat a variety of people, all poor. I took a chair beside a pregnant black lady and asked, "Do you know Dr. Grainger?"

She looked at me suspiciously. "Sure, I know him."

"I've never been before. You'd recommend him?"

Softening a little, she placed her hand on her belly. "Well, Dr. Charlie brought me into the world, he brought my mother into the world, so he might as well do the same for this one."

I smiled. "I guess he's been here a long time."

She nodded. "As long as I can remember. My mother was born in 1933, so as far back as that."

Dr. Charlie: doctor to the poor; medical man with a social conscience. A strange friend for Brightman? This was an interesting question, and I pondered it until at last the girl from the office appeared looked towards me. "Could you come with me, please?"

Along the hall, through a doorway, into the staff room: the girl held a door open at the back of the room. "This is his study. Could you just wait here?"

Oddly, the room I entered immediately reminded me of Brightman's, though it was almost exactly the opposite—small, dim and cramped. It was a retreat, in the same way as Brightman's room, and overstuffed in the same way—though with books rather than pictures. There were some medical texts and a sagging shelf of journals, but mostly there were thousands of old paperbacks. My eye caught a row of uniform red hardbacks and pulling one down, I saw they were all Left Book Club editions from the thirties: *The Coming Struggle for Power* by John Strachey. *Soviet Communism: A New Civilization* by Sidney and Beatrice Webb. Once upon a time, it seemed, Dr. Charlie's do-gooding had possessed an edge: he'd had at least an intellectual interest in the left.

But just then he came into the room.

It was hard to imagine this old gentleman as a rebel of any kind. Dr. Charlie was over seventy, very short, with a kindly, lined face and a shock of fine white hair. He eyed me. "Now then," he said, "you're not Harry Brightman."

"I'm sorry, doctor. The young lady misheard me. I want to talk with you about Harry Brightman but my name's Robert Thorne."

"Charlie Grainger." He stuck out his hand—small, firm, warm. Then he grinned. "To tell you the truth, I'm relieved. If you had been Brightman, I would have been seeing a real ghost from the past." He pointed. "Have a seat."

He sat down behind a desk in front of a pair of battered French windows. Folding his hands in front of him, he eyed me with a bright, questioning concern.

I said, "I assume you haven't seen Brightman lately?"

"I haven't heard his name in thirty years, Mr. Thorne."

"Well, he's missing. I'm a friend of his daughter's. She asked me to help look for him."

He shrugged. "That's too bad. I hope nothing's wrong. But you don't think he'd come here? You realize, I only knew him very briefly, and that was a long time ago."

"I understand. But part of the mystery around Brightman's disappearance is the motive. In the weeks before he vanished, the only thing troubling him was his daughter's adoption. He seemed to want to tell her about it."

For a moment he looked uncomfortable, but then, recovering himself, he smiled. "*Did* he tell her about it?"

"No. And I don't want to put you on the spot. But let's say that I've read the petition, talked to Harry Brightman's lawyer about it, and have drawn the obvious conclusion."

"Which is?"

"Brightman was adopting his own illegitimate daughter."

There was a moment's silence, but finally Grainger gave a little wave of his hand. "Let's proceed as though your conclusion were true. What difference does it make?"

I said, "I'm not sure . . . or that it makes any difference at all. His daughter doesn't know the true story, but I'm sure that it wouldn't disturb her. If anything, I think she'd be pleased . . ."

"Then why not tell her? Perhaps some people would feel a certain embarrassment about that sort of confession, but not enough to make them disappear." He leaned back. "It sounds to me, Mr. Thorne, as if you're barking up the wrong tree."

"Well, probably I am . . . but think about what you just said, doctor. Why not tell her? I'm sure that most adopted children are sometimes anxious about their relationship with their adoptive parents. Brightman could have allayed all those anxieties. Yet he never told her the truth, even though the true story would only bring them closer together. What's more, Brightman somehow communicated to May her idea that she'd be better off not knowing what the true story was. You see? It implies that the 'true' story either may not be true or is incomplete. There has to be more."

He shrugged. "If there is anything more, Mr. Thorne, I don't think I know it."

His gaze met mine and held it. It seemed pretty clear that he was telling the truth. Finally I said, "How did you first meet Brightman?"

"He imported and exported furs in the late twenties or early thirties. After Montreal harbour closed down for the winter, he'd ship them through here. One of those times he fell ill and consulted me. Did you know him at all?"

Did. . . . But that was natural; he hadn't seen him in years.

I shook my head. "We've never met."

"He was a fascinating fellow. He'd been to Russia early on and even claimed to know some of the big Russian leaders. In those days, I was a bit of a socialist, so that interested me. He played chess as well—one of my hobbies. When he came to town, we'd have a few games. Beat him, mostly."

"And what about the adoption itself? How did that come about?"

A moment's hesitation. "I suppose there's no harm telling you. He said he'd made a local girl pregnant. He didn't want to marry her, but he wanted to see that the child was looked after. The question was, would I see the woman through her pregnancy and then arrange for the adoption? I agreed."

"Wasn't this a little unusual?"

"Of course. Let's say, Mr. Thorne, that I talked to Brightman for a long time about it, then talked to the woman—also at length—and *then* agreed."

"I'm sorry. I didn't mean anything. But you did get to know the woman, Florence Raines?"

"Not really. She was a pretty blonde thing, I remember. Healthy. Once the agreement was reached, I saw her in the usual way, then took the child after it was born. Beyond the medical necessities, I didn't get to know her at all." He leaned forward. "You understand that, legally, it was all perfectly normal . . . the only difficulty I can remember was that this woman disappeared without signing some papers, so some extra legal steps were necessary."

"And you're sure that was the *only* difficulty?"

Grainger leaned back in his chair. "Let's not mince words, Mr. Thorne. Brightman was a wealthy man and I'm sure he made it worth her while. So why would Florence Raines have made difficulties?"

He was right. Besides, Florence Raines couldn't be making

trouble today, since she was dead. Yet, more than ever, I sensed that trouble—of some sort—existed. Why had Brightman never told May details of the adoption? And someone had been poking around in his house . . . even in mine—at the very moment May had been trying to reach me. Frustration must have shown on my face, for the old doctor said, "I'm sorry, Mr. Thorne. I wish I could be more helpful." Then with a smile he added, "Of course, when you're as old as me, you sometimes don't know how much you've got in your head, so if you want to keep asking questions . . ."

The hint was perfectly reasonable. "You've been very patient, doctor. I shouldn't take any more of your time."

He nodded, and then, as I began to get up, he asked, "How do you go on from here?"

I shrugged. "Florence Raines married. She's dead but apparently her husband is still alive. I can speak to him."

His eyebrows lifted. "Most wives have a few secrets to keep from their husbands. Why would Florence Raines tell anyone about what she had done? And you know—you might end up causing a great deal of pain for no reason."

I nodded; it was a valid point. "On the other hand," I said, "May Brightman is going through a great deal of pain. She's afraid her father might have killed himself. At least Florence Raines is dead. No one can hurt her any more."

"Perhaps. But why don't you think a bit, Mr. Thorne? I didn't know Brightman well, but clearly knew him better than you do. If Harry Brightman didn't tell his daughter about the adoption, he probably had good reasons. And if Harry Brightman has chosen to disappear for a time, I suspect he knows what he's doing. I wouldn't tell you to mind your own business, Mr. Thorne . . . but you might give Harry a chance to mind his."

A nice speech, nicely delivered. I extended my hand. "Thank you, doctor. I'll bear that in mind."

He came around his desk, and I followed him out through the staff room. We said goodbye in the hall.

Back in my hotel room, I thought about the meeting with Grainger. More than ever, I was convinced that something was very, very wrong. Grainger had given me a much clearer picture of Brightman; indeed, I could just imagine the young doctor—

bookish, full of ideals—and the young businessman—well-travelled, with artistic interests—getting together for their chess games. But this was a far different image of Brightman from the one I'd been carrying around in my head. I'd begun with the assumption that Brightman had fallen prey to some old man's folly. That assumption had been modified by my visit to his house, and now I discarded it altogether. *If Harry Brightman has chosen to disappear for a time, I suspect he knows what he's doing. I wouldn't tell you to mind your own business, but you might give Harry a chance to mind his.* But what was Brightman's business?

It was about two thirty now. Frustrated, feeling at a loose end, I went down to the restaurant for a coffee. Then I had an idea: something that would keep me busy until tomorrow. May had told me that as a little girl, she had been briefly curious about her mother; at least I could tell her where her mother was buried. I walked up to the main branch of the public library, where I obtained the Halifax *Chronicle-Herald* on microfilm, and discovered that Florence Murdoch was buried at the West Baptist United Church, Old Guysburough Road.

As I handed the microfilm back, it occurred to me that I might as well drive out to the cemetery. Back at the hotel, the desk clerk showed me Old Guysburough Road on a map; it was out in the country. This meant renting a car, and it was four o'clock, raining and almost dark when I set off. Tacking against the rush hour, I made my way across town. Suburbs flickered by, and then scrub farms, and then scrub bush. On Old Guysburough Road, the landscape grew even more desolate—rocks, brush and tar-paper shacks. Finally, coming over a rise, I spotted the church propped against the side of a shallow valley. Over the entrance drive, a rickety trellis proudly proclaimed: *West Baptist United Church*.

I parked on rough ground rutted by the parishioners' pick-ups. The rain was pelting down, but I had borrowed an umbrella from the hotel doorman; getting out, I popped it open, then slammed the door shut behind me. I stepped forward, my feet squelching in the mud. A path led around the side of the church, then cut through an open field. Beyond was a fence, with a gate; beyond this, the graveyard.

The graves were laid out haphazardly; bending forward a little—

the rain deftly trickling under my collar and down my neck—I passed among them. Florence Murdoch, née Raines, was at the back. Her stone was a piece of granite with a bevelled edge and simple lettering: FLORENCE ESTHER MURDOCH, 1919-1971, "Home at Last".

In the rain and gloom I stared down at it, just as I'd done in front of my father's grave only a few days before . . . .

But then I peered harder.

For my father's grave, year after year, was mute, ignoring the questions I put to it—while Florence's, to my surprise, eloquently answered them all.

On one side of the stone I saw an oval, silvery protrusion about six inches long, like a large locket. It had a hinged lid, and I bent forward to lift this up. Underneath was a smooth plastic oval, vaguely reminiscent of a brooch, and on this, transferred by some new miracle of mortuary science, was a colour photograph of the deceased.

I stared at it, and swore under my breath.

She was a pretty blonde thing, I remember . . . .

Well, not exactly.

Just possibly, Harry Brightman had been May's father—but Florence Raines, this very black woman, had never given birth to such a lily-white child.

I DREW MYSELF UP and stepped back from the grave.

Lifting my eyes, I watched the rain glitter against the gloom. Beyond the low, crouched shadows of the headstones lay a sagging wire fence and then a muddy field, jagged with the broken stalks of last summer's corn. The fence grated and squeaked in the wind.

For a moment I was stunned, but as the numbness began to wear off, what I felt was so strong that I shuddered. I felt fear—but not my own fear, someone else's. A long-buried odour was finding its way up from this grave: the smell of fear that springs from mortal danger. What I'd discovered today was proof that someone had once been terribly afraid.

Just then I turned around. A light had come on at the side of the church. The side door swung open, a figure emerged. And in the spill of light from the door, I could see he was black. Of course—this was a black Baptist church. Bent over and clutching a plastic raincoat closed at the neck, this figure pulled the door shut behind him, then turned. At which point he saw me. I shook my umbrella in acknowledgment and began walking towards him. He watched me approach him.

"Good evening," I said.

He nodded. "May I be of assistance? Were you looking for a particular stone? It's quite dark . . ." He was a rotund little man, and his expression, both solemn and welcoming, would have told me he was a pastor even if I hadn't caught the white flash of a collar inside his coat.

"Thank you, Reverend. I apologize. I'd intended to call, but there didn't seem to be a light."

"That's perfectly all right. You're entirely welcome."

"I'm interested in a woman who's buried here, I believe a former parishioner. Her name was Florence Murdoch."

"Yes. She did attend here. I only knew her in the last years of her life, but she was very devoted . . . to the church, to her family . . . I take it you were a friend?"

"No. I never met her."

"Then I'm afraid I don't understand."

"It's confidential, Reverend. I'd like to tell you, but I shouldn't."

He frowned. "Tell me," he said, "is it important—to this confidential matter—that Florence Murdoch be black?"

I hesitated. "And why should that be important, Reverend?"

"I've no idea—but it was important to that other man."

"What other man?"

"He came to see me, about a week ago. He asked me was Florence Murdoch black? He was . . . unpleasant about it."

The ceaseless drum, splash and drip of the rain filled the silence. Another man, asking after Florence Raines. Brightman? "Was this an older man? A big fellow, but—"

"No. This man was short, with red hair."

I shook my head. "Then I don't know him." Except I did . . . it was the red-haired ghost who'd flitted through Brightman's house while I was looking through his study.

"Well," the Reverend said, "let me tell you what I told him. Let her rest in peace. If she sinned, her sins were paid for long ago."

263

"Reverend—"

But now he smiled and held up his hand. "The church is closed, but if you wish . . . ? No . . . ? Then, I'll say goodnight." He turned, his plastic raincoat stiffly rustling, and headed down the path.

I slogged back to my car. It was full dark now; as I started the engine, the rain flashed in the beams. Turning onto the highway, I put my foot down, impelled now by a sense of urgency that seemed fully justified. I thought of May: *she'd* been afraid. Had she lied, like Grainger? And who was this other man burrowing into Florence Raines's past?

I decided to drive to Grainger's home, but when I got there, it was empty. I worked it out. Despite his skill, Grainger must have known that I'd find out he was lying—because I'd told him I intended speaking to Murdoch, and once I'd laid eyes on *him*, the truth would be obvious. But what could Grainger do? If he tried to hide he couldn't expect to get very far. I could go looking for him— but I could also just wait; eventually he'd have to come back. But I could still taste the odour of ancient fear. So, though I didn't have much hope, I put the car into gear and headed back to Grainger's clinic: it was the only other place I could check right away.

Almost by accident, I found the right street. In the dark, and under two inches of water, it looked no better than it had this afternoon. I pulled up in front of the clinic, then splashed up to the door. A sign was pinned to it: CLOSED TONITE *j. penny*. I knocked anyway and rattled the knob . . . nothing. I didn't like it. Places like this stayed open till all hours, and the sign's very presence indicated that such an early closing was out of the ordinary.

I stepped off the porch and walked around to the lane. Halfway along it, under a little peaked roof, was a side entrance with cement steps leading down to the basement. Feeling forward in the dark, I went down them, plunging from the last into ankle-deep water and groping ahead to the door. Which was locked. I waded back again. That's when I heard someone come down the lane.

I stood still.

Grainger? Sharp and grinding, the footsteps came on quicker. And though Grainger was a spry old party, such steps couldn't be his. I pressed against the wall. Whoever it was paused . . . and came forward again. And then stopped at the top of the steps. I held my

264

breath. A second later, I heard a little *snick* and a torch came on. A narrow beam darted down, found the door, then winked out. And then, as a yellow blotch pulsed in front of my eyes, the footsteps went away.

Cautiously, I edged up the steps. I looked back towards the street, but both the lane and the pavement were empty.

Moving towards the back of the house, I stared into the darkness. Shadow folded in upon shadow, and rain sounds filled my ears: the metallic drumming of the drops on the roof, a plopping drip from the eaves . . . . I stopped. I'd now reached the back of the house, where I'd sat this afternoon talking with Grainger. I waited and listened, then took a step forward. Now I could see the yard, overgrown with weeds and clearly visible in the oblong of yellowish light spilling out from the back of the house.

I took two more steps and now I could see the French windows at the back of Grainger's study. One of them was ajar, and a man in a tan raincoat was bending over the desk where Grainger had sat. . . . Then he turned and saw me. He hesitated; I didn't move and, quite calmly, he stepped through the doors. As he did so, the light fell on his face and I recognized him at once: it was the man I'd seen in Harry Brightman's hall, the other man who wanted to know if Florence Raines had been black. He had a thin face, his teeth were pushed forward in his mouth, and his crew-cut hair had a reddish tint. In Brightman's hall I'd seen him for no more than a second or two, but I had absolutely no doubt—it was the same man.

Did he know me?

I wasn't sure. He had a good look at me as he came through those doors, but nothing moved in his eyes. Perhaps, to him, it didn't make any difference, for he had a gun in his hand. I froze.

He had to come towards me, because I was between him and the lane. Slowly, his shoulder brushing the back wall of the house, he edged past me. Then stopped. He was at the corner of the house; to go up the lane, he'd have to turn his back to me or walk backwards along it. He chose the former, but as he began turning he slipped: with one foot in the muddy yard and the other on the asphalt, he did the splits between them.

He swore under his breath.

And I went for him then, taking him down so easily that my

momentum carried me right over him. On my back in the wet, I frantically clawed for his right hand, the one with the gun, desperately jerking it into the air before I realized the gun was long gone. Still hanging on to him, I scrambled up. He kicked . . . and then swung with his other hand, which now held a knife. Jerking his right arm, I whipped him away from me. He staggered, lunged, and with a ripping sound his raincoat came away in my hand. The sudden release of his weight sent me staggering backwards, the raincoat fluttering off in the dark. I fell to one knee—and when I looked up, I saw he still had the knife in his hand.

Slowly, I got to my feet. Took a step back.

Useless. Because he'd only trap me in the yard . . . .

But in fact he took a step sideways, to his right. Which I countered with an identical movement. Then another. Two more—we were circling each other. His eyes darted about and now, as he moved, I realized he was edging towards his raincoat, which was spread, like Sir Walter Raleigh's cloak, across a puddle. He was welcome to it—my only concern was to stay out of his way. So I took a step back . . . and my foot grated down on the gun.

At the sound he stopped dead in his tracks and for a frozen instant we stared at each other; but then I bent over, scooped the gun up, and levelled it at him.

Flee a knife, charge a gun . . . . It sounds good, but when the barrel's pointed at you, *discretion is the better part of valour* sounds better. He took one last look towards the raincoat, then jumped back into the darkness and ducked down the lane.

I lowered the gun. . . . Now it was over, my heart started pounding as if I'd just run a mile. I stepped into the lane, picked up the raincoat, and stared out towards the street. It was easy to imagine figures lying in ambush on either side of the lane, but after three soaking minutes I was sure it was safe. I eased the hammer back on the pistol, slipped it into my pocket and walked to my car.

Driving slowly up to the corner, I turned right, cut back and forth for the next dozen blocks but saw nothing. When I finally parked and lit a cigarette, my hand was still shaking.

Now, sitting in the dark, I took a look at the raincoat—apparently the prize we'd been struggling over.

It was ripped at the shoulder, but otherwise intact. An inside pocket contained a ballpoint pen and an empty Air Canada ticket folder. In the left side pocket I discovered some notes and coins and three keys, one with a Hertz tag. I found something a great deal more interesting in the right pocket: a brown manila envelope which had obviously been taken from Grainger's desk. Clipped to it was a note: JENNY. *You'll remember the man I spoke to in my study this afternoon, I expect he'll be back. Try to get rid of him, but if he starts making a fuss, give him this envelope. I'll be gone for a week, so cancel my appointments next Friday. Dr. Charlie.*

I'd been right, then. Grainger had realized I was going to discover the truth. When I tore the envelope open, I found half a dozen handwritten sheets, addressed to me. Making sure that the black, wet street was empty, I turned on the interior light and started to read:

"Mr. Thorne—

"If you have this in your hands I can assume that you've now discovered that what I told you this afternoon wasn't the truth. I told those lies to fulfil a solemn pledge made many years ago to Harry Brightman. You will know by now that our story is false, and your attempts to discover what I can easily tell you may only distress many innocent people.

"Having said this, however, what I'm going to tell you here is only the truth as I know it—and I'm certain I was told a good many lies.

"Harry Brightman told me those lies in 1939, just after the outbreak of the war. By then I'd known him for a number of years, and we were a good deal closer than I implied. I liked him, almost to the point of fascination, and I think he liked me. He was making his fortune out of the Soviet Union, and I was attempting the difficult feat of being a practising doctor and a practising socialist at the same time. I think my youthful idealism amused him, but I believe he also respected me for it. When I opened up my first clinic, he made—unasked—a large contribution.

"In any case, by the autumn of 1939 we were close friends, and I suppose the story he told me, even if it was false, was the sort of story you can only tell to a friend. It all began (he said) shortly before he'd first met me, at the time of his first visits to the Soviet Union in the mid to late twenties. He went there originally to purchase furs at the invitation of the state agency concerned with fur exports. The whole business was of great importance to the Soviet authorities: fur was one of their only exports to the West, and was therefore one of their few sources of hard currency. Consequently, Brightman and the other buyers were looked after in great style.

"In the course of this courtship Brightman met a man named Grigori Zinoviev, a major figure who had been a close friend of Lenin's and the first head of the Comintern. Brightman had often told me about his meetings with this man—but now he told me that he'd had an affair with a woman on Zinoviev's staff named Anna Kostina. It was clear that he loved her. Their affair, he claimed, had begun on his first trip and continued on subsequent ones. The last of these had been made in 1933 or '34, and on the eve of his departure Anna Kostina had told Brightman that he had made her pregnant and that she intended to bear his child.

"Brightman was telling me all this in 1939. If his story was true, Anna Kostina would have given birth five or six years before. But during that time the Great Purge had begun and Zinoviev had fallen. He was sentenced to death, and a number of his friends and associates fell with him, *including Anna Kostina.* Apparently she hadn't been executed, but had received a long sentence in what we'd now call the Gulag.

"Brightman claimed to have received word from inside the USSR that it might be possible to get his child out and he wanted me to provide him with the necessary papers. As it happened, I had two children of my own, one six years old, the other newborn. If I applied for a passport, submitting Brightman's photograph instead of my own, and had my two daughters included on it, Brightman could travel overseas as me and return with the child.

"I agreed to do this and shortly afterwards, having received 'my' passport, Brightman departed for Europe. A few months later— early in 1940—I had the unique experience of meeting 'myself' at the dockside. But I was now given quite a surprise. The child Brightman had brought back was an infant in arms, not a six-year-old. He had no difficulty bringing her into the country, for she merely took the part of my younger daughter rather than my older one. He claimed that it had proved impossible to bring his own child out, so instead he'd rescued the child of another Russian friend who was in some sort of political danger. He wished to adopt the child and asked for my help. I was reluctant to give it to him—I was now convinced I'd been lied to—but I was involved so deeply that it was hard to object.

"I looked around for a way to do what he wanted and we had a stroke of luck: Florence Raines, a young black woman, who had been my patient for several years, discovered she was pregnant. She had a job with the Board of Education which she would have lost on 'morals' grounds, so, desperate, she asked for an abortion and I agreed—until a further examination convinced me that it would have been dangerous, for medical reasons. I helped her though, as best I could, providing a letter to her supervisor requiring she take an extended medical leave. She went to stay with her mother outside the town, and there I brought her child, Elizabeth, into the world. Then, a few weeks after Brightman's return from Europe, Florence called me. Her child was very sick. A day later, despite my best efforts, it died, and I saw my opportunity at once.

"Normally, when someone dies, the doctor prepares a death certificate, which is submitted to the local authorities. But I explained to Florence that the normal burial of her child would probably lead to her own exposure, and that if she 'looked after' the burial on her own, I would ignore the requirement of the death certificate. Florence agreed immediately and so I acquired, as it were, a bona fide infant identity. Brightman was doubtful at first, and insisted that Florence be kept in the dark, thereby necessitating a 'public' adoption procedure. Even this was a help—it removed any mystery about his new daughter's identity. The only problem seemed to be the mother's colour. But race was not a part of a child's birth records in Nova Scotia, and so long as no one met Florence (a sheriff, say, serving a paper), we'd be all right. Now Brightman's money came into play. Both Florence Raines and her mother quietly disappeared (until you told me, I had no idea that either had come back to Halifax). And so the adoption went through. Once it was complete, my contacts with Brightman became infrequent, and I haven't seen him at all since 1945.

"I have no idea why he has now disappeared, and let me also say that I'll answer no more questions about this.

"As a last word, I might as well give you my theory as to who the child was. I assume that some of what Brightman told me was true. He did go to Russia, after all; I'm still certain he had an affair with Anna Kostina, and I'm sure he did get to know many men in the senior Communist leadership. So I suspect that Brightman's daughter was (is) the child of one of those men—someone who believed he would soon fall victim to Stalin's Terror. If this is true, you may agree that neither Brightman nor myself has cause to feel any shame.

Charles Grainger, MD"

I lifted my eyes from Grainger's letter, and I felt something like awe. Revolutionary Russia . . . Zinoviev, chief of the Comintern . . . a child snatched from the jaws of the Red Terror . . . even if it wasn't true, you couldn't ask for anything more melodramatic. Question: who was May Brightman? Answer: a fascinating political mystery.

I put the car into gear and made my way back to the hotel.

That evening the questions began piling up. How much had May known? If she'd known nothing at all, then the last few days had been a proof of woman's intuition, par excellence. And I wasn't sure I believed it. Perhaps she hadn't known what I'd find, but she'd known I'd find something. Then that incident with my mail was still working away at the back of my mind; I'd been involved, somehow, even before I'd known there was something to be involved *with*.

But why was I involved? Why had May turned to me in the first place? There was another coincidence—a big one: Russia. At first, Brightman's connection with the country had seemed peripheral, but now it was obviously central. *And Russia was central to my life as well.* I didn't need Grainger's little lectures about Zinoviev or the Purge Trials—those subjects were my bread and butter. Wasn't it passing strange that someone like myself should have stumbled into this peculiar eddy of Soviet history?

Sitting there, my feet up on the heater and whisky warming me inside, I played through that scene in the alley. When the red-haired man had taken his tumble, he'd uttered a curse—*moy tvoyou mat!* A curse I'd recognized at once, but only because I'm fluent in Russian. He was a Russian: a real, live Soviet Russian. . . .

What could he want? Why would he care about Florence Raines, or what Harry Brightman had been up to in 1940?

By eleven fifteen I hadn't found any answers to my questions.
Then the phone rang.
It was May, about to go into hysterics.
They'd found her father, dead, in Detroit.

4

He spoke deliberately, with the patient condescension of a professional coping with a layman.

"Mr. Thorne," he said, "have you ever seen someone who's killed himself with a shotgun?"

I am moving in a dream. Sweat burns on my skin, my eyes sting, and when I emerge from the forest onto a road, dust cakes against my lips. I start running again. He must have come here, I think, he must have come here. Finally I see a tumbled-down shack. That's where he is. He must be inside. And so I run faster. And then, glistening—

"Yes," I said. "I have."

Katadotis, a lieutenant in the Detroit police force, raised his eyebrows. "It was a hunting accident," I quickly added. "Not very pleasant. So I know what you're talking about, and I appreciate your concern for Miss Brightman. I just want you to understand that I never met Brightman and it's stretching things to describe me as a friend. Accepting that, I'd be happy to identify his body."

He hesitated, convenience and duty struggling together, and I glanced at my watch. It was now twenty past two. Early that morning, I'd flown from Halifax to Toronto, and then May and I had come on to Windsor, and across the border to Detroit. For two hours now, we'd been shuffled from office to office at the headquarters of the Detroit police, waiting, answering questions, filling in forms, waiting again. To begin with, May had stood up to it well, but finally she'd broken down. A policewoman had now taken her off to see a doctor.

Wearily, I watched Katadotis's face. He finally shrugged, making up his mind. "I don't think it makes much difference, Mr. Thorne. He took both barrels of a twelve-bore shotgun right in the face, so there's not much left to identify. I don't see that we need trouble

Miss Brightman. All I need is someone to go through the motions and sign my form."

"All right. I can do that."

"There's no doubt, you see. It's him . . . and it's suicide."

Yes. By this time even I was ready to set my doubts aside. The shotgun that had killed Harry Brightman had been purchased at a Grosse Pointe sporting-goods store with his Visa card. There was no doubt about his signature on the form, and no doubt too about the handwritten note he had left addressed to May. *You know how much I love you, but I can't go on. For me, this really is easier. Your loving father, Harry.* He had left this on the dashboard of the car, and must then have manoeuvred himself and the long gun into a practical posture of self-annihilation—the gun braced against the door on the driver's side, his body half reclining on the passenger seat. Death must have been instantaneous.

Taking a breath, I asked, "Will there be an inquest?"

"That'd be routine, Mr. Thorne."

"What about Miss Brightman? Would she have to attend?"

"I'd guess they'd want her to, but probably they'd be satisfied with a deposition." He cleared his throat. "There's the matter of Mr. Brightman's remains. Pending the inquest, we hang on to them, but once that's done we release them. She'll have to get them over the border on her own. You'll want to talk to Canadian customs."

I closed my eyes: I could just imagine the bureaucratic niceties involved in transporting a corpse across an international boundary. But I nodded. "I'll look after it, lieutenant."

Katadotis shuffled papers on his desk, his eyes screwing into a frown. He said, "That's about everything, except for the car. According to this, they're done with it. You could take it back with you now."

"Lieutenant, I sincerely doubt that Miss Brightman wants to return to Toronto in that particular vehicle."

"I guess not. I was just thinking that it'd save you a trip."

Brightman, it had turned out, had killed himself in the front seat of his Mark VII Jaguar saloon—a model that was about as large and conspicuous as the *Queen Mary*. How could May have forgotten about it? The police had found one car, a Buick, in the garage of Brightman's house, but May claimed Brightman never drove the

Jaguar and garaged it miles from his home so it had just slipped her mind. Now I cursed the thing under my breath. "Couldn't one of your men drive it back?"

"We wouldn't want to take that responsibility, Mr. Thorne." Then he brightened. "But supposing you did want to take it back, I'd probably be able to detail a policewoman to go with Miss Brightman."

I sighed. "Perhaps I should discuss it with her."

He drew the telephone towards him and made three calls: the last of these showed that May was sitting right outside his door. We rose. His office was merely a cubicle within a larger partition, its walls formed from varnished wood and frosted glass like the principal's office in an old-fashioned high school.

I crossed the room to where May was waiting on a wooden bench in a corner. Her face was terribly drawn. I took her hand and whispered, "How are you doing?"

She managed a smile. "Better. I'm sorry. All of a sudden . . ."

"Just take it easy. We're almost finished, but there are still one or two details. I'm going to have to identify your father's body."

She glanced at Katadotis, who was busy on the far side of the room. "You can't," she whispered. "You never met him."

"Don't worry, they understand. We've worked it all out." I hesitated. "But we have to decide what to do about the car."

She closed her eyes. "I feel sick about that. If only I'd told them . . ." I held her hand. If she'd remembered the car, the police might have found him. And if only I'd called out to my father—just once—he might have stopped. Yes. That was true. But if people want to kill themselves, they'll find a way.

Beside me, May whispered, "What about the car?"

"They'll release it now if we'll take it away. I could drive it back to your place and they'd send a policewoman with you on the plane."

She nodded. "All right . . . you drive the car, but I'll go over to Windsor and take the train alone. I'll have time to pull myself together." She touched my hand. "But you're sure you don't mind, Robert? You've done so much already, I feel badly . . ."

It was clear to me that I was going to end up dealing with the car one way or the other, and I preferred doing so now. I levered myself up and crossed the room to Katadotis. "I'll take the car," I told him, "but she wants to go back alone. Can we get a car to take her across the border?"

"No problem there."

He went into his office. I helped May on with her coat, and when Katadotis returned we all went outside. November was here; there was a wintry chill in the air and the sunshine was brittle as glass. May took my arm as we went down the steps. I said, "I'll probably be back tonight, but late. Are you sure you're going to be all right?"

She nodded. "I don't know what to say, Robert. If you hadn't been here I don't know how I would have got through this."

"Forget it. I'll see you tonight."

She gave me a quick kiss, then got into the police car. Katadotis and I watched it disappear, but as soon as it did I could feel his mood shift. Now, man to man, we could get down to business.

We walked to the morgue, which was across from the Water Board, behind Sam's Cut Rate Drugs. Katadotis signed me in and I followed him to a large, low basement room. Fluorescent lights gave off a wan blue haze and every sound seemed to echo in the chill air. Four steel tables were spaced through the room, with three men grouped around the one furthest away.

Katadotis marched off. I grew conscious of a wet, washed smell as I waited. After a moment Katadotis beckoned me to a wheeled stretcher in a corner. I stared down as Katadotis opened the body bag in which Brightman was encased.

A smaller man than I'd expected . . . .

Harry Brightman, taken by May Brightman with her own Brownie, Georgian Bay, Aug. 1, 1949.

I tried to summon up that photograph, but in thirty years Brightman had changed. The hair, though, was more or less right, still thick, an indeterminate brownish-grey colour. As for the rest of his face . . . there was scarcely anything there. For one ghastly instant, I was back looking down at my father.

Steadying my voice, I said, "He must have held the gun away from his face."

Katadotis, surprised at this professional observation, gave me a look. "They do it like that if they want to wipe themselves right off the face of the earth." He took up his clipboard and intoned, "Do you, Robert Thorne, to the best of your knowledge and belief, identify the human remains you now see before you as those of Harold Charles Brightman?"

"I do." My voice sounded ridiculously solemn, but Katadotis nodded and filled in his form.

"If you could just sign here, Mr. Thorne . . ." I scrawled. "Great. That's it." Eyes front, we made our way out. We travelled in the lift in silence, and when it jerked to a stop, made straight for the open air. Katadotis said, "You wait here a minute and I'll get a car. Then we'll head out to the pound."

Turning my back to the wind, I got a cigarette going. So that was the end of Harry Brightman. There was nothing anyone could do to him—or that I could do for him. And perhaps it was all for the best. I looked at my watch. Getting on towards three. I probably wouldn't get away until four, and I guessed that Toronto was a good three hours away. I'd have to spend the night at May's—but if she was feeling all right, I'd go home tomorrow. Yes. Get this out of my mind, get back to work . . . . But then I swore under my breath. The trouble was, I didn't want to get back to work, I wanted to find out what had happened to Harry Brightman.

Katadotis pulled up and I got in beside him. Turning down towards the river, we passed blocks of low, anonymous buildings: cheap furniture stores; liquor stores; abandoned warehouses.

We turned onto St. Jean Street. Thistles and weeds were invading it and the car lurched over ruts in the ruined road. On the left-hand side, a chain-link fence appeared, with the car pound beyond. I began to understand why they'd wanted to release the car today—in this neighbourhood, no one wanted responsibility for an antique Jaguar any longer than necessary.

Katadotis turned in at the gate and drew up beside a small shack. I waited while he went inside. A smell of exhaust and burned rubber tainted the air; a winch whined in the distance.

Katadotis reappeared, accompanied by a mechanic dressed in overalls. "This is Jerry, Mr. Thorne."

I nodded, and Jerry said, "That's some kind of car you got, Mr. Thorne, but I'll be glad when you take it."

Brightman's Jaguar was at the back of the yard. To its left was an enormous pile of old wheel rims; behind it, arranged in an arc, were a dozen black motorcycles.

276

I stared at the Jaguar. As a boy, I'd been crazy about cars, and I recognized it at once. A white Mark VII, circa 1955, its lines rounded and flowing—a rich man's horseless carriage from an era when liners still plied the Atlantic.

"It seems to be missing some hubcaps."

Jerry grinned. "Yeah. And one of the guys must have cut the Jaguar out of the bonnet."

Fishing keys from his pocket, he opened the door and slid behind the wheel. The engine caught first time, idling with true British discretion. Jerry got out and patted the car. "Runs like the lady she is. She was kept real nice."

Yet May had forgotten the car's very existence . . . you couldn't help thinking this. But she had no use for cars; all the time I'd known her, she'd only driven Volkswagen Beetles. This great boat just hadn't registered.

Katadotis stepped forward, holding a large manila envelope towards me. "The contents of the glove compartment, Mr. Thorne. You have to sign for them, and of course for the car itself." He handed me a form and I read it through, signed it, then stepped forward warily and slid onto the seat. I looked around inside. The carpet on the passenger side was stained, and you could see that someone had tried to towel off another stain on the roof.

Katadotis leaned through the window. "You OK, Mr. Thorne?"

"Yes. Thank you, lieutenant."

"Well, I'm sorry that we had to meet under these circumstances, but you've been a great help, believe me, Mr. Thorne."

We shook hands. Jerry shouted directions. I eased off the clutch . . . . As the transmission took hold, it was as if a great locomotive was delicately nosing me forward. I reached the gate, still in first gear, then daringly shifted to second as I started down St. Jean Street. How bizarre this all was. I was Churchill, touring the lines after D-day . . . . I put my foot down a little and changed up into third. The Jag moved as if in a dream, with no sense of effort or strain. I decided to count my blessings. Tomorrow, I'd be home. In a month, this would all be forgotten. All those unanswered questions were frustrating, but as a journalist, you learn that 90 per cent of your questions never get answered.

I hadn't eaten since early morning, on the plane, and I was more than a little hungry. Looming up on my left were the towers of the Renaissance Centre, a massive hotel and office complex that's supposed to "revitalize" downtown Detroit. I knew I'd find a restaurant there, and so I ponderously turned the great car and rolled sedately down an access ramp to a car park. Lighting a cigarette, I tore open the envelope Katadotis had given me, searching for some clue the police might have missed. But there was nothing: just maps of Ontario and the New England states, and a membership in the Canadian Automobile Association.

And then a face leaned down towards the window. "Mister?"

It was the young black attendant who'd let me in at the gate. "I got an urgent call for you, up in the booth."

"I don't understand. A telephone call?"

"Yessir. The man said, the man in the big white car."

"What's his name?"

The black kid looked impatient. "Your name's Brightman, isn't it? He just said to go fetch you."

"Hang on," I said, "I'll be there in a second."

"MR. BRIGHTMAN?"

"Yes, I'm Brightman."

"But I know it is you, Mr. Thorne. I only wished to get your attention." The voice was male, the accent Russian.

"Who are you?"

"Never mind, Mr. Thorne. We've never met—but now I think that we should."

"I'm not so sure. Perhaps we already have."

A pause. Then: "I assure you, Mr. Thorne, we've never so much as laid eyes on each other."

And I believed him—it wasn't the Russian from Halifax. But he must have been following me, whoever he was. I looked around. The booth had tinted-glass windows on all four sides. I knew he had to be close by, but there wasn't much I could see: the booth was on the downslope of a hill, so I could just make out the tops of the cars passing along the road while the far side was completely hidden from view.

"I can tell you everything, Mr. Thorne. How it was done. What has happened to Brightman. Everything."

"I'm listening."

"No. It is better to meet face to face."

"There might be other things besides Brightman to talk about," I said. "You're Russian. Maybe we should talk about that."

"If you like. We can talk about anything . . . . We can talk about the *byliny* or the *beguny*—anything. Just ask me and I'll point you where you want to go. It is four o'clock now. In one hour and a half come to 362 Grayson Street. It is just an old garage, but from there we can go somewhere else."

"All right. I'll be there."

"Very good. And of course no police. It has nothing to do with them. I will tell you about Brightman, but I will tell you something personal also. Something you wouldn't want a policeman to hear."

Silence . . . then the line went dead and I was standing there, the phone squeezed in my hand.

Something personal. Something you wouldn't want a policeman to hear . . . .

I put the phone down. My palms had started to sweat. From the beginning, I'd had the feeling that all this would double back on me. None of it was tied to me personally—there was nothing I wouldn't want a policeman to hear, yet my skin had gone clammy, and I'd begun to feel very queasy, as if . . . *as if, somewhere inside, I already knew*—

When I left the booth, the wind, gusting off the Detroit River, pressed my raincoat tight to my body, and grit, blown across the huge car park, stung my cheeks. I tried to calm myself down. Should I call Katadotis? But even as I thought this, I knew that I wouldn't. My mysterious caller would obviously be very cautious and at the first hint of the cops he'd take off. But if I kept our appointment, what would happen? One Russian yesterday, a second today—and the first had had a gun. Certain initials began blinking at the edge of my brain. But it was too incredible and it just didn't feel right. *Komitet Gosudarstvennoy Bezopasnosti* may be hard to pronounce, but after eight years in the USSR I could smell a KGB officer a mile away. This smell was different; not official at all.

I didn't have the faintest idea what it all meant, or could possibly mean. But I knew I'd go anyway. But not in Brightman's car, which had already been recognized.

I caught a taxi out front. The cabbie headed back downtown, and dropped me at a Hertz office where, after the usual routine, they put me into the driver's seat of a Pontiac and the clerk showed me Grayson Street on a map.

Heading north, I resolutely kept my mind on my driving: it was the easiest way of forgetting how nervous I felt. Five o'clock. A gloomy dusk hung over the city as the rush-hour crowds fled outwards. I let the traffic suck me down the Chrysler Freeway.

I fought clear of the expressway at the Plymouth Plant exit and began hunting for Grayson Street. Trapped between the expressway approaches and an old railway spur, it turned out to be almost impossible to get to; but I made it on my third pass, bumping across an abandoned siding.

It was getting dark now. I slowed down, trying to spot house numbers on shabby breezeblock bungalows. Just then the garage itself loomed up. It appeared abandoned.

I continued past it and turned down a side street, where I parked and looked at my watch. Ten minutes early. I stared down the street. Lights were on in the houses; a door banged somewhere and a woman's voice harshly called out a name.

I got out of the car and locked it, then walked back towards the corner. At Grayson Street I paused a moment, looking around. To the left, a block away, a few indistinct figures were grouped round a car. Somebody laughed. Kids, I thought, horsing around. On the far pavement, a man was walking towards me, hands thrust into the pockets of his windcheater; on this side, beyond the garage, two men were walking away from me. As they passed into the area of a streetlight, I saw that they had green rubbish bags over their shoulders: heading for the launderette before the crowds came after supper.

I started ahead. Each step made a precise, distinct sound. The man in the windcheater passed by me on the far side of the street; up ahead, the two men with the laundry bags disappeared in the dark. And then I could see the garage. Quiet. Recessive. Like some forlorn country crossroads petrol station on a lonely stretch of road.

I angled across the asphalt apron towards the two old-fashioned pumps. I stopped and looked around. The dark building, the black asphalt, merged with the gloom. And the street was now completely deserted. Stepping closer to the pumps, I realized that their hoses were cut and the glass over their gauges was broken.

I had a sense of being out in the open. . . . But he had to be able to see me. I began to fidget, tugging my gloves over my fingers, putting my hands in my pockets. A couple of minutes slipped by. I walked across to the office, thinking that he might be inside and still hadn't seen me. When I shaded my eyes and looked through the window, the old, dusty glass filled my nose with a dirty, coppery smell. Inside, there was rubbish everywhere—no one had been here in weeks. I tried the door and the knob turned easily. Inside, it was darker. Colder. I stood in the doorway and stared ahead. Feeling an urge to call out, I repressed it, then changed my mind. "Hello? Hello? Anyone there?"

Whistling in the dark . . . . Now the silence left me feeling more than a little foolish. There wasn't even an echo, just grit grinding under my heel as I shifted my weight. To the left was the grey patch of the doorway into the service bays. Slowly, I edged into the gloom. My toe nudged a can. Deciding that no one was there, I flicked on my lighter and looked at my watch. Five forty-six. Was I being stood up?

I began moving around, just to keep warm. My eyes were getting used to the dark. I realized that the place had been abandoned for years; half the floor had crumbled away; at some point vagrants had built a fire in the corner. I continued along the back wall . . . and that's when I heard a slight sound, a rustling . . . . It came again. I stepped further along till I reached another doorway, blocked on the outside by one of those big metal dumper trucks for picking up rubbish. I listened again, but didn't hear anything—it was probably nothing more than a rat.

Deciding to walk around to the front of the building, I began to edge sideways between the dumper and the back wall of the garage—and then the sound came again, from inside the dumper. A settling sound, a weight shifting. I reached up, grabbed the top edge of the dumper, and pulled myself up. I looked in. Dropped back. I wasn't sure what I'd seen. I took out my lighter, adjusted the flame as high as I could, then hoisted myself back up. With a grunt, I leaned my chest across the top rail, and stuck out my right arm.

The orange flame of the lighter hissed in the darkness. I looked down. There wasn't much to see at the bottom of the dumper: bits of piping, and a painter's plastic sheet that was wrapped around something. All twisted and folded, the clear sheet was shot through with wrinkles and fissures, like an ice cube. But the wrinkles were wet and red. And frozen at the centre was the body of a fat, hairy man with no head, hands, or feet.

I fell back, my knees banging the dumper. *Dear God!* Then I blundered away, charging back down the gap between the wall and the dumper. Weeds grabbed my legs. The wall grazed my cheek. Falling to one knee, I reached down and touched the cold ground and steadied myself. And then I remembered those men with the laundry bags and understood what they'd contained, and I was sick.

For a moment, I closed my eyes against the horror.

I opened them slowly.

It didn't happen to you. It's all right.

Catching my breath, I pulled myself upright. My ankle was throbbing, my knee ached, there was a stinging scrape along the side of my face. I peered around the corner of the garage. Night uncoiled down the street. Windows glowed like cats' eyes, but I couldn't see anyone, so I forced my legs to move. Across the asphalt apron of the garage. Then the pavement. Left. *Don't run.* The corner . . .

I made it to the car and got in, locking all the doors . . . . Five minutes, I thought, maybe less: I'd come that close to seeing a murder, maybe being murdered myself. My heart began to race and I felt faint. Who was he? Who had killed him? Why? Who, except you, knew he was going to be there? Are you in danger? And the answer was no, not now, not here. Whoever had killed him hadn't waited, which must mean that they hadn't known I'd be coming. Or maybe they didn't care.

I started the car. I only wanted to get away from this spot, but, like a careful drunk, I made myself do it slowly. I turned away from the kerb, lightly put my foot down . . . and maybe that's why I saw it. As I came up to the next corner, I stopped the car dead.

I twisted back in my seat.

Behind me, stretching along the kerb, were the half dozen cars that had been parked in front of me. They were all rusted, dented heaps—except for one, a late-model Pontiac as bright and shiny as the one I was driving. I reversed down the street, stopped, and walked back to the other car and peered in the driver's-side window. I didn't have to see the Hertz sticker to know it was rented. I tried the doors, but they were locked. It was obvious, though. He'd done just as I had: parked here, then approached the garage circumspectly . . . though not circumspectly enough.

For some reason, this little discovery steadied me. By the time I was back in my own car, I felt more under control, and I just drove around for a while. Bit by bit, my nerve came back and I realized I was hungry. I pulled into a shopping centre where I found a bar. I ordered a whisky and a steak sandwich, and by then my mind was more or less back on the rails. I tried to work out where I stood. Point one: there was no reason to panic. The man who had called me, assuming he was the man in the dumper, had known I was involved in all this, but whoever had killed him probably didn't; or didn't care if I was. Otherwise, they would have hung around and killed me as well. Point two: I didn't want to go to the police, at least for the moment. *Something personal, something you wouldn't want a policeman to hear* . . . . And I'd come this far on my own; I could go a bit further. Which is why, when I'd finished eating, I walked through the plaza until I found a hardware store that was still open and bought a five-pound sledgehammer.

It was after seven now. Back on the freeway, heading south, traffic was thin. In Grayson Street again, the garage was as dark and calm as I had left it. But there was no reason why it shouldn't be. They might not find that body for months—they might never find it.

I turned down a side street and parked about three cars ahead of the Pontiac.

Headlights off, motor running. When I eased open the door, a cold wind struck my eyes. I left the door open a crack, then walked back towards Grayson Street. The Pontiac was parked right in front of a house where the lights were on, but the place next door was dark. I drew back the sledgehammer and swung as hard as I could. The first blow starred the car window like a piece of old ice. I pushed bits and pieces away, then reached in and opened the glove compartment. And found what I wanted: the rental form. I pulled it out, and two minutes later I was back on the freeway.

I headed south and went right downtown before pulling off. Then

I parked and read through the form in the glow of the dashboard light. His name had been Michael Travin. He had a Maine driver's licence that gave a home address in Lewiston. The car had been rented from Hertz in the Renaissance Centre and the local address was room 909 in the Detroit Plaza Hotel—the hotel that's part of the complex. Hertz had imprinted his Visa card.

Decision time. I drove down to the Centre, parked in the same car park where I'd left Brightman's Jaguar and went in by the main entrance. I found the hotel desk right in front of me, but I walked around for a moment, getting my bearings. The main lobby was a brightly lit, five-storey atrium where trees breathed the man-made air and fountains splashed into artificial lakes.

Smile. "Hi. I'm Mr. Travin in 909. I can't find my key, so I must have left it with you. I hope." *Smile.*

"Just a—yes, Mr. Travin. Here you are."

"Thanks."

I strode firmly away from the desk and followed a bellhop into a lift, which then shot me up to the bedrooms. Emerging, I followed the hall around to room 909. I hesitated a moment then just inserted the key and went in.

I flipped on a light. I was in a little hall, the bathroom on my right. I stuck my head in. Neat. Tidy. The main part of the room was a standard first-class American hotel room.

And no sign of Michael Travin at all.

There were no clothes in the bureau or closet. The bed was made. Ashtrays were clean. The room was so neat you would have thought he'd checked out. But he hadn't—otherwise I wouldn't have been able to get the key in his name.

Now a creepy feeling came over me—a prickling at the back of my neck. I hadn't felt it in years, not since I'd lived in the USSR . . . and then I knew what it was and I spun right round and began searching for the signs of a search, a search that would have been made so carefully that even if you did find traces of it you wouldn't be sure. On my hands and knees, I felt along the edge of the carpet, and yes, it was loose. Had the contractor been sloppy or had somebody lifted it? Then I traced out the seams in the wallpaper, feeling along with my fingernail. Loose again. Natural wear, or had someone been using a razor? I checked the TV—and found three screws that might have been freshly scratched. They'd been looking for something small, I thought, some sort of paper or document. But, whatever they'd been looking for, I was now certain of one thing. There was only one source for the lingering scent I sniffed all through this room: KGB.

Which didn't especially excite me. I was more accustomed to the *Komitet* than I was to dead bodies. But I began to think fast. They, after all, must have moved *very* fast. At four o'clock Travin calls me in the car park and we set up our meeting for five thirty. So, some time between four and five, they'd picked him up and started following him. They probably would have had this room under surveillance, and then followed him to Grayson Street.

When you thought about it, all they'd really taken trouble about was his identity. They'd cut off his head, hands and feet, so that establishing the identity of the corpse would now be a forensic miracle. But then they'd been very sloppy, for they'd forgotten the car. Or maybe they'd just ignored it, and come here and searched the room instead. Which might mean they already knew that the Travin identity was false, and that by itself, it wouldn't help establish who the man actually was.

Using a Kleenex, I picked up the phone.

"This is room 909, operator. I'd like to speak to information in Lewiston, Maine."

"Yes, sir. Just one moment."

When the long-distance operator came on, I pulled out the Hertz form, spelled Travin's name, and gave his address. After a moment, she said, "We have no Travin listed there, sir."

I hung up . . . but then had another idea. I called the desk.

"I'd like to check out. Mr. Travin in 909. Could you have someone bring up the bill?"

"One moment, sir . . . . Yes, will that be on your Visa card?"

"Please. I think you already have it."

"Yes, Mr. Travin. Someone will bring it up to your room."

Ten minutes later, careful to hide my face, I stuck a dollar around the door and received Travin's bill in return. But it wasn't very informative: same address, same phone number, same Visa number as on the Hertz form. He'd been staying at the hotel for six days; unfortunately, he'd made no long-distance phone calls. So . . . the name Travin, his driver's licence, the credit card, his hotel bill, added up to a dead end.

I took a long breath, walked over to the window, and looked out at the night. *I can tell you everything, Mr. Thorne. How it was done. What has happened to Brightman. Everything.* Had Travin been killed because he knew? And was that why they hadn't worried about me—because as long as I didn't get to talk to him, I *wouldn't* know? I sensed that I'd reached a turning point.

There was a knock at the door.

I froze, then took a deep breath. "Yes?"

"Valet service, sir. They called up from the desk, sir, and said you were checking out. Don't want to be forgetting your suit."

"Just a minute." I was even more careful than I'd been with the bellhop and made absolutely certain that the woman didn't get a look at my face.

The suit was perfectly ordinary. But then I saw a little brown envelope twist-tied to the hanger. *We Found This in Your Pockets.* I tore it open, spilled it out on the bed.

One book of matches. Seventy-seven cents. And a claim check from a photo store. . . . I picked up this last item. It was a grey strip of envelope, overprinted with a number and the store's name and address: *Jack's Photo Supplies, Berlin, New Hampshire.*

And right then, I made up my mind. I wasn't entirely sure why. Russia, and all I felt about that country, was part of it; and so was May Brightman. But there was something else—that feeling, present from the very beginning, that all these events, however impossible it seemed, led back to me.

With Travin's suit bundled under my arm, I took the lift down to the lobby, and, after I had returned my Hertz car, I drove Brightman's enormous white boat back over the Canadian border.

5

Windsor to Toronto to pick up my bags at the airport, Toronto to Montreal, then south across the border again . . . . Twenty-four hours after leaving Detroit, I was sitting in a restaurant in Washington, DC, but on that trip you'd have to say I took the long way around. Most important of all, I drove through Berlin, New Hampshire, to pick up Travin's photographs.

As the miles rolled by, my mind hummed along with the tyres. But the further Detroit receded behind me, the more unbelievable my speculations seemed to become. Brightman had killed himself: I had no reason to contradict that conclusion. And I had no *certain* knowledge that anyone had searched the hotel room. But just as I grew convinced that I was making a fool of myself, my mind headed off in another direction. Someone had killed Travin. No: something very peculiar was happening . . . . I suppose, even before I picked up those photographs, that I was convinced of that.

Berlin, when I got there, turned out to be a pulp and paper town whose smokestacks trailed a livid, sulphurous haze across the New England hills. Pleasant; a little ramshackle; even pretty if you looked away from the smokestacks. Of course, I noticed this only in passing: my mind was entirely concentrated on the photo shop, where I laid down $65.48 and received two oversized grey envelopes in return.

I had no idea what to expect when I opened them, and for the past fifty miles had been bracing myself for something completely banal. Still, even as I took them from the woman in the store, I knew that I hadn't entirely wasted my time. The two envelopes were stapled together, and scrawled across the first was: *M. Travin, RFD 2, Berlin, tel. 236-6454*. This, I thought, was more likely to be his real address than the one on the driver's licence. But when I opened the first envelope, I hit the bonanza. Twenty-four five-by-seven enlargements spilled onto my lap. Each shot was different, but they all had one subject: May Brightman.

I began sorting through the photographs. All of them were "candid": May, clearly, had had no idea what was happening. Three had been shot as she came out her front door, another caught her in a crowd, and three frames showed her sitting on a bench in a park. Her expression was calm and composed and though you could see her age in the wrinkles around her eyes, there was something girlish about her—a patter of freckles high on her cheeks, the way her loose fair hair spread across her rough-knit sweater.

The next shot was a direct contrast to this: she was wearing a white business suit, her hair was pulled into a bun, and she

287

reminded me of a proper suburban matron—perhaps European. But then the next four shots reminded me that her special quality wasn't national at all, for Travin had crept down her lane, and photographed her working in the garden. All four of these shots caught precisely the quality I'd seen that first day: there was something other-worldly about her—she contained contradictions that removed her from this time and place. In Travin's photos, she was wearing a large straw hat and a long, high-necked dress worked with lace; draped over her shoulders was a long, tasselled shawl. The effect of all this was like watching a highborn Edwardian lady at play.

As I flipped back through the prints, it was obvious that Travin's principal interest had been her face, as if he'd wanted to compare this face, *her* face, with another. Travin had also been asking the question: who was May Brightman?

Naturally, I was hoping to find the answer inside the second envelope. And maybe it was there, if I'd only been able to see it.

This envelope held only three six-by-eight enlargements that were all identical except for slight differences in the developing. They showed fourteen men very informally posed in the backyard of a house, with a large wooden shed in the background. On the far right stood a picnic table covered with bottles and dishes; a few canvas deckchairs had been placed around the table, and two of the men were sitting in them. Two other men had been circled with white marking pencil and, in the same pencil, a single line had been written across the bottom of the photograph. *Halifax, 1940*, it read.

I stared hard at the smaller of the two circled figures. It was Brightman. It had been impossible to connect the bloody head in the Detroit morgue with the face in the photo May had taken "with her own Brownie", but there was no doubt about this. He was standing at the back, a big, barrel-chested man. Thick hair, receding a little and pulled straight back from his forehead . . . Harry Brightman, as he'd looked when he'd adopted his daughter.

Fascinated, I examined all the other figures but especially the second man who was circled. He was standing in the foreground, short but powerful, with a broad, fleshy face and heavy lips turned down in a sulky scowl. I hoped such a heavy, determined face might ring some bell; but it didn't. Nor did the others. And yet . . .

288

Russia.
Brightman.
Halifax, 1940.
Dr. Charlie. . . .

I felt that I was closer to some real answers than I'd been before. The men who'd searched Travin's room had been looking for these photographs; I was almost certain of that. In addition, the photographs brought Brightman's disappearance and May's adoption irrevocably together, for Travin had been interested in *both* father and daughter. May's adoption gave a particular focus to her father's past—a focus that had burned its way right into the present. Who was May Brightman? This question, the question Travin had been asking, now seemed only one aspect of another: who was Harry?

That afternoon, as I drove away from Berlin, I had some real clues to play with, and I began putting them together. May and Harry, together, made up the mystery, and Russia was the key to its solution. And I suspected that I knew more than I yet understood. I needed one final hint . . . I had the photograph but I still needed the caption.

I began looking for it in Washington—and found it three days later in New York.

As searches go, this one was not that hard, and indeed it was a pleasure for me: something like work, a return to civilization. Retrieving my own car, I ditched the Jaguar in a parking garage, and though I stayed at my mother's house in Georgetown, I kept away from my friends and haunts, and kept my head low. With May, I was vague. She'd returned to Toronto without mishap, but she was still upset—naturally enough—and tried to make me promise that I'd give up what I was doing. Once I was satisfied that she was all right, I told her a story about having trouble with the car and said I'd call her again in a couple of days.

A week, in fact, was the deadline I gave myself. I knew the sort of job I had to do, and experience told me that I'd either wrap it up quickly or not at all. Who were the people in the photograph? What had they been doing in Halifax in 1940? Above all, who was the other man Travin had circled?

I had three clues: Brightman, Halifax and 1940. The first I dispensed with quickly. My second clue, Halifax, was more productive—a huge explosion in 1917, innumerable royal visits, naval activity all through the war. And 1940 was a bonanza: all those war stories my mother had told me scrolled through the scratchy, glaring field of a microfilm lens. There were plenty of pictures: Molotov, Chamberlain, Churchill, Roosevelt, Lindbergh . . . My man, obviously, would be a minor figure, an assistant or aide. But I was sure he was a public man. If the photo had no wider reference, why search Travin's room trying to find it? Pushing on, I checked all the papers, the Library of Congress, then made copies of the photo and showed them around.

Finally I got lucky. In New York, in the Bettman Archive, which houses one of the largest collections of historical photographs in the world. My first break came under "War, Spanish Civil": a picture of a stocky man hoisted on the shoulders of some grinning members of the International Brigade—but I wasn't sure he was Travin's man. I quickly found three other shots, the best of them in the "Date File" for 1933. It showed a man in his mid-forties with dark, thick hair and dark eyes. His powerful shoulders bunched the cloth of his suit and, even in this casual portrait, the force of the man's personality was evident. The index card said:

> *Georgi Dimitrov (1882–1949), Bulgarian-born Communist leader, was accused by the Nazis of conspiring to set fire to the German Parliament buildings (the Reichstag) on Feb. 27, 1933. His trial at Leipzig made Dimitrov a hero of anti-Nazi groups around the world. Dimitrov brilliantly defended himself and was finally released. He subsequently became head of the Comintern and was later premier of Bulgaria.*

Setting the two photographs side by side, there was absolutely no doubt. The second man whom Travin had circled was Georgi Dimitrov, the man the Nazis had tried to frame for the Reichstag fire, last head of the Comintern.

As I leaned back in my chair, there were no fanfares, no ringing bells. Just that hush that surrounds any true secret. For that's what it was. From the middle thirties, Georgi Dimitrov had been one of the most important of all the Communist leaders. And Brightman had known him. What's more they'd both been together in the

290

spring of 1940—just after Brightman had returned from Europe with May and started Dr. Charlie along the devious course of the adoption.

What had the two men been doing? Who were the other men with them? That afternoon, as I boarded the shuttle back to Washington, I knew I had to pick someone's brains, and by the time I landed, I had decided on Leonard Forbes. When it comes to the Comintern no one knows more than he does.

At six thirty he was still in his office, but readily accepted my invitation to dinner. "I have an ulterior motive, so it's on me. How about Chez Odette's in half an hour?"

"Terrific."

When he arrived at the restaurant, Leonard was his usual self, his understated wit slyly poking away at the universe. We talked friends, doings at Georgetown University where he was a professor, politics. But when our coffee arrived, Leonard lit up a cigar, folded his hands on his paunch, and grunted, "So what's it all about?"

"Take a look at this," I said, and handed him the best of Travin's "Halifax, 1940" prints.

He peered at it for a moment then put it down and looked at me. "That picture wasn't taken in Halifax in 1940."

"Because," I said, "Georgi Dimitrov wasn't in Halifax then?"

"So you recognized him?"

I smiled. "Not in thirty seconds, I didn't. But eventually. Could you swear he *wasn't* in Halifax?"

"No, I suppose not. But it's unlikely. He didn't travel around incognito. He was one of the best-known Communist leaders in the world then. Besides, the Comintern, especially the foreign sections, had just been hit by the Purges. I expect he was spending a lot of his time on Gorki Street holding hands with the survivors."

Leonard, on his home ground, can be hard to keep up with, so you don't want him to get too far ahead. "Gorki Street . . . you mean the Hotel Lux in Moscow, where all the foreign Communists stayed?"

He nodded, then frowned. "Let me see that again." He stared at the photograph. "What the hell, that's *Browder!*" I leaned across the table to look. I saw it now: Earl Russell Browder, general secretary of the Communist Party of the USA. Still staring

291

down at the picture, Leonard murmured, "You know, I wouldn't swear to it, but this guy with his arms crossed—I think he was the head of the Canadian CP. . . . Tim Buck." He looked up at me. "If this is one of your stunts, I'll admit it's very ingenious. How did you do it?"

"It's not a stunt, I promise. So what this might show is a meeting, in Halifax, between the head of the Comintern and a bunch of top North American Communists?"

"If it's real."

"Don't worry, it is." I picked up the photograph and looked at it again . . . and now I recognized the yard the men were standing in: it was the yard behind Dr. Charlie's clinic in Halifax.

"Len, I don't understand most of this, but my way into it was the man at the back, the other one who's been circled. He's dead now, but he was a Canadian businessman. He made several trips to Russia in the twenties. Apparently he got to know Zinoviev pretty well, and even had an affair with a woman on his staff. Her name was Anna Kostina—I don't suppose you've heard of her?"

He pursed his lips around his cigar and shook his head. "No. I don't think so."

"What I'm driving at is this: could this businessman, through people like Zinoviev and this woman, have become close to Dimitrov?"

"I suppose it's not unreasonable. Zinoviev was the first head of the Comintern, and already in the twenties Dimitrov was head of the Comintern's Balkan section. So if this Canadian fellow knew Zinoviev well enough to have an affair with a woman on his staff, I guess he might have run into Dimitrov."

"But Dimitrov, back then, wasn't very important?"

"No. His break didn't come till 1933, when the Nazis tried to frame him for the Reichstag fire . . . his trial turned him into a celebrity. The next year—or the year after, I guess—he was elected head of the Comintern."

"But what was his position in 1940?"

"Well, he survived the Purges in 1937."

"Why?"

Leonard shrugged. "Why any particular *individual* died—or escaped—is almost impossible to say."

"But—again going back to 1940—Dimitrov might still have been *afraid* he was going to be purged?"

"Oh, I'm sure he was. It would have been an especially bad time. In August 1939 Stalin and Hitler signed the Molotov-Ribbentrop Pact—and the next week invaded Poland together. Overnight, the Nazis were the good guys, and Dimitrov was an embarrassment made flesh. Now I think of it, it's a miracle that he survived."

"But he *did* survive, and he remained head of the Comintern. And in that capacity—if you accept the photograph—he made a secret trip to North America in 1940. Why?"

Leonard shook his head in his most professorial manner. "No one could say, not on the basis of this."

"Guess."

He hesitated for another half minute—then took a sip of brandy and propped the photograph against his coffee cup. "I'd say that your best bet is to work back from the time and place of this thing as much as from the people in it. Nineteen forty was a very interesting year. By the spring, the Nazis have already invaded Poland and divided up Eastern Europe with Stalin. Now the war is well under way. Put that together with the place—Halifax, Canada. Also interesting. Why not the US?"

"Convenience. Dimitrov would have had an easier time getting in up there than down here."

Leonard shook his head. "Maybe it had something to do with the fact that the Canadians were already in the war. That early on, they didn't have much of a military, but they did have industrial production. I know they built an awful lot of guns and ships. And you can see how that might tie up with Dimitrov and the Communists. In the thirties and forties, the CP still had clout in the trade unions, which meant they could have had a real effect on the industrial war effort. Strikes, slowdowns, even sabotage. . . . Sensible people in the Soviet Union understood that they'd end up fighting Hitler eventually, so the real interests of the Russians required CP unions over here to *back* the war effort. Maybe Dimitrov was sent here to tell them so." He took a sip of brandy. "You can even tie in this other man, the businessman—"

"His name was Brightman."

"Was he a Red?"

"I wouldn't think so."

"No, he sounds like a capitalist who did enough business with the Russians to develop a certain rapport with them. Which would have made him perfect. . . . Say the Canadian government was worried about the effect the CP unions might have, and wanted someone from 'above' to give them a good talking to? Dimitrov, with all his prestige in the West, was a perfect man to deliver such a lecture, and this Brightman was the perfect man to arrange all the details."

This sounded like an exceedingly reasonable theory—it just didn't do me much good. If Dimitrov was connected with the child, if he was May's biological father—why had he needed Brightman at all? If he'd come to Halifax on legitimate political business, why the complicated scenario with Dr. Charlie, the passport and so forth? I said, "You can't see Dimitrov having any personal reasons for being there? Could he have been defecting?"

Leonard made a face. "He *didn't*, we know that. Almost none of them tried to escape that way, even when they had the chance."

"What about his family?" I asked. "Do you know if they were in danger?"

"If *he* was, they were. But I don't think they were."

I considered this. "He had a wife . . . children?"

"He was married twice. His first wife died before the Reichstag fire. I'm not sure whether they had children or not, but he adopted a couple with the second woman, after the war. Fanya . . . Boyko . . . there may have been another. The Bulgarians always made a fuss about it—kindly Uncle Georgi and so forth."

Somehow, I managed not to give myself away. But there it was, surely. Dimitrov, in mortal danger, had been unable or unwilling to save himself, but had wanted to rescue his child. Later, having survived, he redeemed himself with Fate by rescuing two others. Of course, that still left plenty of questions. But Leonard looked tired, and he'd given me so many answers it seemed ungrateful to ask him for more.

I drove him home, then headed back into Georgetown, coasting sedately down Q Street just before midnight. These blocks, making a village, are where Washington's rulers live in tastefully restored terrace houses. My parents had always kept a house here, giving them a place to call home as the State Department shunted them all

294

over the world. I couldn't bear to sell it but I didn't want to live in it, and so I used it now as a pied-à-terre on my trips into Washington.

There was no garage, not even a lane, and the kerb was so jammed with cars that I had to park around the corner, halfway up the next block. The street was quiet; the wind rustled gently through the trees: old oaks whose shade was so thick that you were cool even in summer, and as I walked along in their shadow, memories swelled in the darkness. My whole childhood had been spent coming back to this house, returns rendered all the more poignant by the certainty that I'd soon be leaving again. I could never walk down this street without getting the same old feelings: anxious expectancy, then glad recognition.

But now I'd reached the door: three stone steps, then you're inside. Flipping on the light in the hall, I hung up my coat and went straight upstairs, but instead of going into my room, I ascended the narrow stairs to the attic. I must have been thinking of my father, still caught up in the train of memories I'd brought into the house, for the attic had been my father's study, and after his death, my mother had kept those possessions she couldn't bear to part with up there. I opened the door. Nothing here had been changed for years. There were the neat rows of *Foreign Relations* lined up in the bookcase, the framed Foreign Service map and beneath this my father's desk, with its serried ranks of framed photographs.

Then I realized what was actually in front of my eyes.

It would be wrong to call the room a shambles—that would imply a degree of violence that just wasn't there. But someone had taken it apart, just the same. The spine of every book had been neatly sliced open with a razor. The old map had been pulled completely apart, but then neatly propped against the side of the desk. And although every photograph had been removed from its frame, all the pictures were arranged in separate, neat piles.

I was almost too tired for shock, and the question—*What were they looking for?*—barely registered. But then I felt very afraid. Quickly, I crossed the room to the window. Peering cautiously into the street, I could see two men get out of a parked car, about thirty yards down the block, and silently close the doors behind them.

Later, I was to realize how lucky I'd been. Since I'd parked so far from the house, my car had given them no warning; only my turning on the light in the hall had alerted them. I ran down the stairs to the next floor, then raced down the hall to the back stairs. These took me to the kitchen. I felt my way through the darkness to the back door; as I reached it, I could hear scratchings round at the front. I stepped into the night. The backyard was small—six feet of patchy lawn with a chest-high fence. I vaulted this, landing among my neighbour's shrubs. I scrambled ahead, then, groping along the wall of the house, I came to a gate and stepped onto the pavement. I decided against my own car. Walking quickly, but normally, I turned down 31st Street, reached Q Street, then ran all the way across to Wisconsin Street, where I flagged down a cab. I slumped down on the seat and told the cabbie to take me to the Hay-Adams. It's expensive, but that night it seemed far safer than home.

It was three days before I got back to New Hampshire. Once agai it was a question of taking the long way round to Berlin—and eve before I left I had to make several detours.

The most important, of course, involved May.

Both of us now were in danger. The search of my mother's house had changed everything. I was a target, even if I didn't understand why. But this meant that May was in danger as well—she had to be, since she was the only reason I was involved in the first place. As soon as I'd thought everything through that night in the Hay-Adams, I called her number in Toronto . . . and there was no answer. I called every ten minutes till three in the morning, and she still wasn't there. Falling asleep in a fever of guilt, I awoke at seven and called again. Still no response. Then it occurred to me that I had one other name in Toronto—Stewart Cadogan, Brightman's lawyer. So I dialled his number instead, and at seven thirty-one the old man picked up the phone himself.

There was a moment's pause as he took in my name. Then he grunted, "I'm surprised you'd start doing business this early, Mr. Thorne. But gratified. I've—"

I was in no mood for his crustiness and cut him off. "This is urgent. I'm very worried about May. I want you to send—"

"You almost make it sound as if she was in danger, Mr. Thorne."
"She is."

That made him pause for a second. "Why do you say so?"

"Because I've been calling her home since yesterday evening. There's nobody there."

"That would hardly indicate—"

"Listen, I don't want to argue. Just send somebody around there and make sure she's all right."

The anger in my voice finally got through to him. "I apologize, Mr. Thorne. I'd not understood that you were so upset. But she's not at home—she left for France yesterday afternoon."

"You're sure?"

"Yesterday afternoon she came to my office and said she was on the way to the airport. She had her bags with her."

I thought for a moment, digesting this. She did have a house in France, so it was possible.

"You weren't surprised by her leaving at such a time?"

"She said she was exhausted, that she wished to get away. She left me various instructions concerning her property, the will, her father's remains . . . indeed, yourself, Mr. Thorne."

"What do you mean?"

"Miss Brightman gave me your number in Virginia and I tried to call you yesterday. She wished me to thank you on her behalf and since—she said—your efforts would have left you considerably out of pocket, she instructed me to give you a cheque for ten thousand dollars."

I was stunned. After a moment I said, "Of course I won't accept her money, Mr. Cadogan—money has nothing to do with this and in any case that's a ludicrous sum."

"Mr. Thorne, she asked me—on her behalf—to insist."

"All right, you insisted. But I still won't accept it."

"Very well. There was one other point. She said she would write to you later and explain, but for now she wanted me to make you promise to give up all the inquiries that you've been making into her past. They'd only hurt her, she said. So I ask you for that promise, Mr. Thorne."

"I'm not sure I can give it."

"Mr. Thorne, please consider this carefully . . ." He

297

stopped himself. When he went on, he surprised me. "I'm sorry, Mr. Thorne, but I *am* worried about her . . . despite what I've said. Perhaps it would be best for all of us to do just as she asks. There is a great deal I would like to say which I can't. So I only say this. I have known the Brightmans for a good many years, and I know that May Brightman was always her father's protector and he was hers. Now, you see, all she has left are her memories. If you were to reveal that they had a false basis, you would be doing her a harm greater than you could possibly know."

"I think I'm aware of that, Mr. Cadogan."

"Very well. If you need me I can always be reached here."

"Thank you, sir."

We hung up. I felt that May must have told Cadogan about our broken engagement, because my status with the old man had changed. There seemed, under the circumstances, only one reason why she would have confided this to him: to give him an extra call on my loyalty.

I spent much of that day, and another sleepless night, thinking about May. I did not want to put her in danger, but the more I thought about what had happened, the queasier I felt. Her flight to France didn't seem natural, and, try as I might, her forgetfulness about Brightman's Jaguar still seemed peculiar. Then there was the offered money—it looked like a bribe.

I suppose it was questions like these that ultimately decided me to disregard her wishes and go on. But I had other reasons too: I'd started out as a spectator, but now I'd seized the initiative. Because I'd broken into Travin's car, I—alone?—knew about Dimitrov. More: I had a way of tracking back over Travin's footsteps. Could I live with myself if I refused to find out where they led? And there was one final matter which I could not disregard: I was a target, that was clear, and I had been from the very beginning—that's why they'd taken May's telegram from my house that very first day in Charlottesville.

So I went on.

TAKING THE MOST ROUNDABOUT ROUTE I could think of, via New York, Boston and Portland, Maine, I headed off to New Hampshire in a hired Ford. That afternoon, as I reached the White Mountain

298

area west of Berlin, I was reasonably confident I was alone. Even so, I was careful. Berlin's a small town, and there aren't that many motels. Giving them all a miss, I went on to Lancaster, about twenty-five miles to the west.

The next morning, I put my "plan" straight into action. This was simple enough. There was no listing for Travin in the local directories, and the number he'd left with the photo store didn't answer. But I had to hope that the basic information he'd given was genuine. If it was, I should be able to cross-reference the phone number and address and discover where he was living.

My first stop was the Berlin post office. No one there remembered Travin's name, but a clerk pencilled in RFD 2—the area delivery code he'd left with the store—onto my map. Following these directions, I stuck with the highway for three miles, then turned left onto a secondary road. It climbed steeply, then twisted its way through a thick stand of spruce.

The first mailbox appeared shortly afterwards.

It was at the end of a short drive leading to an aluminium "universal" home. I slowed to read the name on the box, pressing the microphone switch on my cassette recorder. W. F. Grafton came first on my list. Round the bend, in quick succession, there were three more homes. Then came a mile of cedar and spruce, and then a large New-England-style house, all turrets and dormers. Before each mailbox, I slowed and murmured the owner's name into the mike. The miles rolled on and after a time all signs of relative civilization petered out. A big sign, in the shape of an Indian, pointed down a lane to a kids' camp. Then nothing. Miles of forest. Until, with a hollow rumble, my wheels kicked up the logs on a bridge and I flashed by a hunting camp. Then nothing again. . . . By noon, I'd looped back to the main road and turned towards Lancaster.

In my motel room, I played back my tape, a list of all the people living in RFD 2. Now, tediously, I looked up all their names in the phone book—hoping to match the number Travin had left with the photo store. In twenty-five minutes, I had it. Michael Travin had been staying at something called Gerry's White Mountain Camp.

It took almost an hour to drive there, for it was at the "wilderness" end of my run. The mailbox was at the junction of a narrow dirt road that ran back into the bush. Drawing up beside it, I got out of the Ford. The gate was padlocked. The road to the camp itself, disappearing into the trees, might have run on for miles.

I drove back to Lancaster and called the camp number a couple of times, but there was no answer. I decided to check the camp at the local deed registry. The last purchaser, a man named Evans, had bought it ten months previously. Going back to the motel, I tried the number again—but still got no answer.

That evening, watching television, I wondered about this. I hadn't hunted in a long time, but this was November and we were close to the deer season: hardly the time when a hunting camp would close down. Of course, everyone might be off in the bush, or the camp might have gone bankrupt. Still, as I went on trying the number and getting no response, I decided I wasn't going to let up on the caution.

The next morning I drove into Berlin and paid a visit to a sporting-goods store on the main street. Here, a friendly clerk sold me a bush shirt, a camouflage poncho, a rubberized groundsheet, two canteens, one hatchet, a belt knife, a compass, 10-power binoculars, and a nylon pack to put everything in. I went on to a grocery store: ham, bread, a litre of Valpolicella. Back in the car, I filled up the canteens with the wine, then drove out of town.

The day was no better than yesterday, cold and wet. Slowly I climbed through the hills of RFD 2. Out of habit, I kept one eye on the mailboxes, noting that the red flags were up, a signal to people that their mail had arrived. I recognized landmarks now: a twist in the road that revealed a long, forested valley, a hill topped with an enormous, gnarled spruce.

Getting closer to the camp, I slowed. Once again, I crossed the log bridge, passed the camp gate—still locked—and began climbing steeply again. About a mile further on, a logging road ran off to the left. It was further than I would have liked, but there was no other place to pull over, and the ground, though bumpy, was firm. I nosed the car in. Ten yards on, the track pulled a bit right and became so overgrown as to be impassable. But this was perfect for me: the bend meant the Ford wouldn't be seen from the highway.

I changed inside the car. A green and black bush shirt went over my regular shirt. Then came hiking boots and a sweater, which was loose enough to be comfortable. Next I packed up the knapsack and slung it over my shoulder. Finally, on top of everything else, came the poncho. Drawing up its hood, I stepped into misery.

Cut-over coniferous forest makes about the worst bush in the world. The trees, mainly spruce, grew so tightly together that I could barely move, and their thick, heavy boughs made it impossible for me to see where I was going. Dead branches jabbed like spikes, and after ten feet my trouser legs were soaked. Eventually, I stumbled onto a deer path and for ten minutes enjoyed quick, easy going. Then spruce and pine gave way to maple and oak, and I was even able to glimpse the miserable sky overhead.

I took a breather then and tried to fix my position. I'd been walking for forty-five minutes but probably hadn't travelled a mile from my entry point. I'd been well up the mountain to begin with, but had definitely been angling downhill, which meant I'd eventually intersect the camp road. But I didn't want to do this too soon. My idea was to reconnoitre the camp, making absolutely certain that I saw the occupants—if any—long before they spotted me. I looked across the valley where there was nothing to see but a long grey sweep of trees. But looking back up the hill I'd been coming down, I saw just what I wanted: a rocky outcrop, near the summit.

Two hours later I reached it and realized it was a ledge projecting from the hillside. Up this high, even the dark, overcast sky was dazzling, and shading my eyes, I stared over the valley. I guessed it was about two miles wide; the opposite hill was a little lower than the one I was on, but higher hills rose beyond it. I caught a glint of water through the trees on the floor of the valley. On the far side of this, a little way up the hill, Gerry's Camp was clearly visible.

At the extreme edge of the outcrop, a couple of boulders made a kind of chair, and I wedged myself in and examined the camp with my binoculars. It consisted of three separate buildings. The largest, facing me, was a two-storey New England farmhouse. At the eastern end rose a hexagonal tower, and a roofed veranda wrapped around the ground floor. Parallel to this main building stood a smaller one, about the same vintage, and off to the right, and closer to me, there was a long shed with a metal roof.

Amidst all this real estate, I detected a few signs of humanity. Smoke trickled from the chimney, and just as I lifted the binoculars,

I was fairly certain that I'd heard the faint, faraway *whap* of a door slamming shut. In addition, three vehicles were parked in front of the shed: a small brown pick-up truck, a yellow Volkswagen Scirocco, and an ancient Datsun 510. So, I thought, someone was at home—why didn't they answer their phone?

I crouched in my eyrie and tried to keep warm with my wine. Half an hour slipped by. I watched a hawk drift over the valley and studied a doe taking a drink from the stream. Ten more minutes. And then, without warning, a figure stepped off the veranda. I grabbed up the binoculars, thumbed the focusing wheel.

The figure was a man, walking briskly across to the cars.

I only had him perfectly clear for a second, just as he stepped into the pick-up. Blue jeans. Windcheater, unzipped. A hint of reddish-brown hair. . . . A glimpse, that's all it was, but in a way that made him almost easier to identify.

Surprise? Elation? Fear? A little of each. I set down the glasses and let go of my breath.

A short, red-haired, weasel-faced man. The man in Halifax, at Grainger's place. The man who'd floated in the darkness beyond Brightman's study, then disappeared down the hall like a ghost.

I WATCHED THE CAMP for days.

To begin with, I used my ledge as my base, and by the time I was through, I'd even made the place halfway comfortable. An extra groundsheet, rigged between two cedars, kept off the rain; and wrapped inside the sleeping bag, with a couple of butane camp stoves angled to reflect their heat off a big rock, I stayed reasonably warm. I left my hotel around five every morning, and was normally blundering through the bush as dawn dribbled over the horizon. On the ledge by seven, I'd watch the mist uncoil over the stream. My first sighting usually came around eight: one of them would step onto the veranda with green plastic bowls for their dogs. Sometimes hours passed before I saw them again—boredom was as much my problem as anything. I had replaced my canteens of wine with a thermos of coffee, and my first coffee break, a great event, was at ten. I munched sandwiches at noon, then there was more coffee at two. I always left by four fifteen—I didn't want to get caught in that bush after dark.

There were five men staying at the camp: the red-haired man was obviously the leader. Twice I saw him ordering the others about—gesturing, pointing—and they obeyed him without hesitation. But it was equally clear that he wasn't running a hunting camp.

By the third day, I was frustrated. With the binoculars I could see well enough; the trouble was, what I wanted to see wasn't the sort of thing you ever *do* see: plans, relationships, motive. I thought of breaking into the house and searching it, but on top of all the other risks—and I wasn't sure I had the nerve—there was the problem of the dogs. They were just a couple of sheepdogs, but they were clearly turned out of the house every night to guard it.

That third night, back in my hotel room, I decided to follow the men when they left the camp in their cars. I'd observed them departing on a number of such expeditions. Most had an obvious purpose—carting their rubbish to the dump, buying groceries—but others were less clear, and they were frequent enough to arouse my curiosity.

On the fourth morning, I found a spot in RFD 2 where I could keep the gate under observation, but because of the way the road curved, I had to be almost on top of the gate to see it. I had to stay very alert to avoid being seen. As soon as someone came down the camp road, I'd pull out, as if I was just passing by, and then watch in my mirror to see which way the car turned after it had come through the gate.

Over the next three days, I followed them on seven separate trips away from the camp. I only learned anything of significance from one of them.

On the fifth day, the pick-up truck took their rubbish to the dump and I decided to do a little garbage picking. No one saw me: the dump, up a short access road, was just an open spot in the bush. I could see where the truck had parked and three yellow bags had been tossed nearby. I began poking through them, thereby discovering that rubbish is rubbish: orange rinds, eggshells, milk cartons. But the last of the bags contained newspapers and there I found two old copies of a Russian-language paper, *Nasha Stran—Our Homeland*. I'd actually heard of it: it was published in Buenos Aires and served the large Russian émigré population there. I sat in the car and read the papers, but I couldn't see anything of particular interest. Nonetheless, it established that Travin's connection to the camp hadn't been casual.

An hour later, I made another discovery—also important, even if I couldn't say precisely what its significance was.

I was back in my regular position by the side of the road when a woman in an old Toyota pulled in by the gate and delivered the US mail—one envelope, slipped into their box. The mailbox lock had long since been broken so when the woman had left I took the fat envelope and headed straight back to the hotel.

When I opened the envelope, I discovered a wad of receipts; twenty hundred-dollar bills; and a letter from a lawyer in Springfield, Massachusetts. This was addressed to "Mr. Howard Petersen, c/o Gerry's White Mountain Camp." It noted that "your usual remittance is enclosed," and concluded: "After these transactions, your funds held in trust by this firm amount to $22,736.79." It was signed by one Robert Evans.

Robert Evans—whose name was on the camp's deed. Interesting. The receipts included everything from a county tax bill to an American Express account. The Amex account included plenty of trips: Boston—Montreal, Montreal—Toronto, Toronto—New York, Brussels—New York. . . . During the previous month, Mr. Petersen had been moving around and covering his tracks: he either hid behind his lawyer or paid up in cash—and indeed it occurred to me now that I'd never seen any of them make a trip to the bank.

Given the sum of money involved, I assumed that Mr. Petersen was expecting his letter, so I drove straight to Springfield where it had come from and put it back in the mail.

Something was going on, and Berlin was one of the centres; but Brightman, Dimitrov and Travin revolved around it like mysterious planets. I couldn't see where Travin fitted in. Presumably, he'd been living at the camp. Did the people there know what had happened to him? Or had Travin been a renegade, whom they themselves had eliminated? But if I accepted that, I had to reject my previous theory—that the people who had dealt with Travin were "official". But they *had* been—I was sure of it. Which meant that I was dealing with two sets of Russians: the KGB—the men who'd killed Travin—and the people I was watching right now. But who could they be? I had a few clues. They were Russian and they might have émigré connections. What seemed to tie these facts together, albeit tenuously, were some of the remarks Travin had made to me on the phone in Detroit. "We can talk about the *byliny*," he had said, "or the *beguny* . . ." I'd taken him to mean: we can talk about anything under the sun—but perhaps he'd revealed more than he'd intended. The *byliny* are the great medieval folk epics of Russian literature, and their most famous hero—Ilya of Murom—has long been a symbol of Russian power, Russian unity, and the greatness of Russia's common man. The *beguny* were a crazy nineteenth-century religious sect (the word means "fugitive") who refused to have anything to do with authority and took to the woods, like Robin Hood.

Was it possible that Travin had hinted that these people were some sort of wild anti-Soviet émigré sect? But what was the connection to Brightman, to Dimitrov, to May—and why did the KGB take it so seriously that they were prepared to murder its members inside the United States?

The next day, when I was in my customary position near the camp gate, and as dusk began to fall, headlights swept up to the gate. The red-haired man emerged, his shadow stretching over the road. There was someone else in the car with him, which made me curious, for I'd never known them to travel in pairs. I pulled out and headed up the road. Forty seconds passed. There were still no lights in my mirror, so I doubled back and as I came round the bend I could see their taillights ahead. They were driving the Scirocco fast, away from Berlin. This wasn't the usual pattern, but then I'd never before followed them this late in the day. We came up to the highway and turned north. As the road twisted into the hills, I fumbled for my map. North of here was a place called Colebrook, very small; then the Vermont border; then Canada.

The highway climbed higher. Hanging on to the wheel, I kept my mind on my driving; the Scirocco sprinted ahead while my Ford drifted clumsily through the curves. Still, I was content to hang back, and on a road with so many bends, it was unlikely that they'd spot me. We passed through Colebrook, and then the border came up, eight or ten miles beyond. The border post here is very small— just one hut and a single guard. I pulled over as they went through and gave them five minutes.

Once I was cleared, I took off after them. The road here was gravel, twisting along the shore of a lake, and no matter what you were driving you couldn't go very fast. I picked up their lights near a town called Coaticook. Further west along the same narrow road there were more houses and farms. I hung back and when the Scirocco turned down a still smaller road, I put out my lights. The night was like ink. Driving blind, I guessed the curves by the twitch of their taillights. A mile further on, they swung down a side road. I waited till they were gone, then passed the spot where they'd turned. I could see a lane leading up through some trees, with a glimmer of light beyond. A hundred yards or so ahead, I stopped.

I rolled down my window. The night air was cool, full of the smell of grass and wet earth. I got out of the car and silently, staying on the grass at the edge of the ditch, I walked up to the lane. There was an old mailbox, with a name crudely painted in red: *N. Berri*.

I went up the drive a few steps. There was an odd smell in the air. Presumably this place was a farm, but it wasn't manure. It was different, stronger . . . I hesitated. I wanted to go further, but the two men in the Scirocco plus this N. Berri made it three against one, and if they caught me skulking around, what explanation could I possibly give? I went back to the Ford. An hour passed.

Then, around eight thirty, a terrible howl cut through the night, ending with the most pitiful whimpering sound I'd ever heard.

It was so sudden and startling that it froze me in my seat. Then a dog barked. Except—like that smell—it was different, a quicker, sharper *yip*. And then another barking voice joined in, and then another and another, and for the next twenty-five minutes it didn't stop: the desperate baying of terrified animals. Then headlights swept down the lane. The Scirocco paused at the end of the drive, then turned and headed back towards the highway.

Half of me wanted to follow the car, but to have driven away from that pitiful howling would have left too much on my conscience. So I started the Ford and moved up the lane.

The house was a small bungalow, the roof slanting steeply over a front porch. Fans of light spread out from two windows, but everything else was in shadow. I stopped the Ford and blew the horn a couple of times. The crying and barking grew even louder, but no one came out of the house.

307

Reluctantly, I stepped out of the car, then waited a moment. Beneath the grisly howling, night sounds whispered and cool air traced my cheek. The musky odour I'd smelled before was now very strong. Closing the car door softly, I went straight up to the porch. I knocked at the metal storm door; then I saw that it was slightly ajar and I just pushed it ahead of me.

Standing on the threshold, I looked into a small, cottage room crammed with old furniture. Directly in front of me, on the other side of the room, was an arch leading into the kitchen beyond, and in the middle of this arch, lashed with a rope into a straight-backed chair, was a man—but pulled over his head, like a sack, was the head and shoulders of a fox: whose lips were pulled back, grinning in death. The other half of its body was lying beside the chair, with the axe that had been used to sever the neck driven into the floor just beside it. Blood was everywhere.

I sucked in a breath, but a breath whose stench made me choke. God knows why I didn't pass out; maybe the cruelty of the scene twisted the horror I felt into anger. In any case, my shoes skidding in gore, I crossed the room. I flung the fox's head away, and for the first time the old man must have known I was there, for he started to struggle, almost overbalancing the chair. He was shaking with fear, and as I reached around behind him to get at the ropes, he started to whimper. "They said they'd kill them all one after the other . . ."

I tugged at the ropes. "It's OK," I finally said, getting him free. "They're not going to kill anyone now, Mr. Berri. You're all right. Listen: I'm a friend. Do you understand that? I'm a friend." I took him by the shoulder. "I was a friend of Harry's," I said. "Harry Brightman's."

At last something flickered into his eyes.

"Poor Harry," he whispered. "Things never end like you think."

7

As Berri later said, it wasn't as bad as it looked—but that made it quite bad enough.

They'd slapped him around, bloodied his nose, and the business with the fox's head had put him into shock; but he was more frightened than hurt. I laid him on his bed, covered him with a blanket, brought him water. He began to pull himself together pretty quickly, and then, I sensed, felt a little embarrassed. He was a proud old man, and couldn't have relished being seen by a stranger in such a state. Once I was sure he didn't need a doctor, I left him alone and went back into the kitchen. There, looking through the arch, I gawked at the full horror of the living room.

It was like the inside of an abattoir. Blood glistened on the shiny brocade of an armchair; it was sprayed on the walls. This was, I knew, a horror I couldn't ask Berri to face, so I found a shovel and wheelbarrow outside on the porch, pushed the remains of the fox into the middle of the rug, then picked it up like a sling and dumped it into the wheelbarrow. Obscenity—there's nothing you can do except bury it. I trundled the barrow round to a long strip of garden behind the house. There, with the foxes' pitiful howling as a graveside lament, I scooped out a hole and tipped everything in.

At last I could breathe again. Wandering a little away from the garden, I let the night cool me. There was no moon, but it must have been shining somewhere, for the sky had a soft, pewter sheen. In front of me a dozen old apple trees twisted their shadows against the glow of the sky, and beyond lay wire pens. Here was the source of that thick, musky odour I'd smelled, and the crying which, even now, still prickled the hairs on the back of my neck. Foxes: perhaps two dozen of them paced back and forth, dim grey shadows. With the blood of their own kind so thick on the air, they moved with the panic that only exhaustion can still. But all at once—I suppose a breeze brought them my scent—they fell silent and the emptiness of the night, like a crystal globe, dropped around me. A dozen golden eyes glowed at me in the dark. Then one voice began crying, a second joined in, and soon they were all howling again.

I went back to the house and into the kitchen. It was old and shabby, reminding me a little of Grainger's clinic. I poked around in the cupboards, and found some tea. I filled a kettle and put it on the stove, then set cups and saucers on a table at the far end of the room. While the kettle boiled, I sat down and tried to put together a picture of the man who lived in this place. He was lonely, I guessed, a bachelor—certainly no woman had any claims in this kitchen. The homemade aspect of the house and its furnishings, and the foxes

309

themselves, made me think of one of those self-sufficient men who harbour pet obsessions and projects, but who are practical enough to bring them into quirky reality. When he stepped into the room a moment later, it was clear that Berri was a very definite character: a wiry old fellow with a bristly grey crew cut and hollow, leathery cheeks. He'd changed into a rough grey sweater and a pair of old trousers, but his feet were bare and this made him seem all the more vigorous.

He hesitated a second, then managed a brief, flickering smile. "I should thank you, I guess."

"That's OK, Mr. Berri."

"Nick," he said. "Nick Berri."

"Robert Thorne."

He nodded, tried out his smile again. "Guess it was just lucky you came passing by."

I poured out the tea, trying to look cheerful. "I thought you could use some. . . ."

He nodded, crossing the room and pulling out a chair. As he took a sip of his tea, I said, "Are you sure you're all right, Mr. Berri? If you want, I could take you to a doctor."

"No." He shook his head. "I'm all right."

The defensiveness in his voice was just this side of hostile. I tried to stay neutral. "That was quite an ordeal you went through. I guess what you really need is a good rest."

"I'm fine. I thank you again for all you did, but I'm fine now."

I smiled. "And I guess you'd like me to get the hell out."

His mouth drew back in a deep, frowning crease up his cheeks. "Sorry it sounded like that. I truly am grateful. If you want to stay, you're welcome, but don't do it on my account. Those men got what they came for; they won't be back."

I asked, "Do you know who they were?"

He shook his head. "Never saw them before in my life."

"What did they want?"

"I've no idea."

"But you said—"

"Listen, Mr. Thorne, what happened tonight . . . that would be hard to explain and I'm not sure there's much of a point. But it wasn't as bad as it looked."

310

I hesitated. The foxes were still barking out in the yard, and Berri's eyes moved to the window. Obviously he had no wish to talk about what had happened to him. As easily as I could, I said, "I'm a friend of Harry's, Mr. Berri. I think I said that."

He nodded. "I guess you did."

"Do you know he's dead?"

"They said . . . they said he was."

"The police think it's suicide, and maybe it was, but those men drove him to it. You're lucky to be alive, Mr. Berri."

He squinted at me. "How come you know all this?"

"I've been following those men for days. I'm on your side. That's what you have to remember."

"Harry had a lot of friends. But some things even his best friends didn't know."

"Listen, Mr. Berri. Nothing can hurt Harry now. But other people can be hurt. *You* can be hurt—"

"*I don't give a damn!*" His voice was suddenly vehement. "Why should I? After all these years? Those bastards deserve all they get." He smiled then, a quick, rueful grimace. "That's how come I'm alive, Mr. Thorne. I just told them what they wanted to know." For a second, his eyes went to the window.

"Poor Harry," he murmured. "He called me a month or so back. He'd do that, every once in a while, to ask after the foxes. He bought them for me, you see, when I quit working—six breeding pairs, all registered. Harry loved foxes. 'They *are* cunning,' he'd say. He loved the mutations, like I've got, but he especially loved the natural reds. The most beautiful fur. Warm. Durable. He was always saying we'd go in together in a big way. Harry always liked to have plans. That's what I noticed this last time he called. No plans. It was almost as if he was saying goodbye." He shrugged. "I guess maybe he was."

I took a moment, then leaned forward a little and said, "Those men, Mr. Berri. Can you tell me about them?"

"They were Russians. They talked to each other in Russian."

"So you speak it?"

"Sure. My real name's Berzhin, though I was born in Canada. My father was Russian and we always spoke it at home. That's how come I met Harry. Because I could speak it."

"When was this, Mr. Berri?"

He shrugged. "Twenty-eight? Twenty-nine? I'm not sure. I went to Russia twice with Harry. He wanted someone who spoke the language but also knew furs. After those trips, he'd picked up enough so he could go by himself." He coughed. "The Russians were really excited about furs back then, Canadian furs especially. We got a real nice reputation. The best hotels. Our own droshky to cart us around . . ."

"This was when you met Zinoviev?"

"So you know that too? You're right, though. Kirov, then Zinoviev." He shrugged. "The very first two the Bolshevik shot."

"Yes . . ." Then, on impulse, I added, "Did you meet Anna Kostina?"

"Bolsheviks shot her, too. Poor Harry. He never had good luck with his ladies. She was interesting, though. A real Red—they say the women were even tougher than the men."

"What about Dimitrov, Mr. Berri? Wasn't that someone Anna introduced Brightman to?"

He frowned. "Been a long time since I heard that name."

"But you know it, don't you?"

His eyes went shifty. "Do I? You know a lot—maybe more than I know myself."

"I wouldn't say that, Mr. Berri, but I think you did meet him. This would have been probably the spring of 1940. Dimitrov made a secret trip to Canada that year, for the Comintern—and I think that's when you met him."

"So what if I did?"

"But isn't that where Harry Brightman came in, Mr. Berri? Dimitrov was frightened. Stalin had already amassed a huge list of victims and Dimitrov was afraid he would be next. He knew that even if he refused to go back they would get him eventually—but he thought he could save the life of one little girl. With Brightman's help he smuggled the child out of Russia and then Brightman adopted her. It was all very slick—but not slick enough. Forty years later, someone got on to him."

Berri's face concentrated in a frown of genuine puzzlement, then he shook his head slowly. "You've got it wrong."

"You tell me then, Mr. Berri."

312

His eyes held mine for a second, then shifted to the window. The foxes were still whining and barking. He listened; and I could see the pain which their pain brought into his face. Maybe I was pressing too hard. "If you like . . ." I began. But he was already shaking his head. Slowly, he pushed himself up from the table.

"No, no," he said, "that's all right. I'll tell you. Just give me a minute to settle them down."

A SIDE DOOR LED OUT of the kitchen, and beside it, on an old newspaper, was a pair of muddy rubber boots. He put these on and we stepped outside. I followed Berri through the orchard, where the sharp, sour smell of fallen apples undercut the musk of the foxes, and then onto a stretch of packed dirt. Beyond this, the cages lifted out of the gloom.

I waited, standing a little away. As Berri moved past each pen, the fox inside would leap up and bark with excitement. I caught up with him as he reached the last of the cages. The wire was torn. He murmured, "She was the mother of most of these. That's partly why they're so frightened."

I looked away, towards the foxes. I could see why he loved them. They were beautiful, their wild, golden eyes shining forth from dark, delicate faces. They moved with a slinky, elegant grace.

As the animals began barking at the far end of the row, Berri moved along. I fell into step, until, stopping in front of a cage, he drew his hand up into the sleeve of his sweater, then pushed the loose end of the sleeve through the mesh. The little fox inside was black as midnight. He ran over and tugged at the wool and started to suck. The foxes seemed calmer now, crying less. After a moment, Berri pulled the sleeve back, then moved along to the next cage and did the same trick again. And then, with his face pressed up to the mesh—as if addressing someone at the far end of the cage—Berri started to speak. I almost had the impression he wasn't speaking to me but was setting the record straight for himself.

"To understand," he began, "you've got to know something about Russia back then—1940, let's say. In those days, the Bolshevik had all sorts of problems, but his biggest was that he was broke. His money was worthless: all the roubles in the world didn't add up to a dollar. He couldn't go near a bank, on account of how Lenin, when he took over, had refused to pay off on the old Tsarist bonds. Banks all over the world were holding them, and every time the Bolshevik tried to open up an account or sell something, they'd like as not send the sheriff around. The Bolshevik tried to sell the Crown Jewels—damn near worthless, he found—and in 1923 he took all the gold and silver out of the churches. Now, gold, of course . . . that was the one thing they did have. In fact, first thing after the Great Revolution, they got the mines open again. But even that didn't do them much good. The Americans, along with the Brits and French, passed a law making it illegal to bring Russian gold into their countries. So no one would give the Bolshevik credit, they had no money and people wouldn't even go for their gold. Just to get the most ordinary things, he had to pull all sorts of tricks. You follow me this far?"

I did. And I knew that everything he'd been saying was absolutely true.

Berri went on, "It was almost impossible for the Bolshevik to get locomotives, machine tools, even food. And what about those *other* things so dear to the Bolshevik? Scientific supplies, for instance. And what about the World Revolution that would make the Bolshevik safe? These days, of course, it's no problem. They want to support the French Communist Party, they just slap some money into a bank account. They want to finance their friends over in Africa, they use the Swiss banks. Their gold's good enough now."

"What are you trying to tell me? That Brightman smuggled gold out of Russia in the furs he was buying?"

"The furs *were* gold. Year after year, Harry brought those furs back, and year after year he sold them. *But the Russians never sent him a bill.* That was his secret. They *gave* those furs to him. And though they made Harry rich, he had to use the money just like they told him." Berri chuckled then, deep in his throat.

Overhead, the moon pressed a disc of silver light through a patch of clouds and close beside me one of the foxes shoved its snout against the mesh.

"They are *cunning,"* he'd say . . . *he especially loved the natural reds.*

Harry Brightman: a red fox with golden eyes.

"I'll be damned," I whispered.

314

NOW I KNEW IT TOO, just like Travin. Yet, for a moment longer, I still couldn't take it in.

As Berri reached through the mesh to stroke the fox, he laughed again at my incredulity. "I always wanted to tell someone that story, just to see the look on their face. . . ."

"But why did he do it? Was he a Communist? Or was it just for the money?"

"Harry was a Red, all right. He *believed*. I know that because I saw how much it hurt when he *didn't* believe any more."

"You were a Communist too, weren't you?"

"Red as a fire engine."

I leaned back against the cage. "Let me get this straight. You're saying he took these furs out of Russia, all above board, and then he sold them. Which meant he turned those furs into Canadian dollars, US dollars . . . and I suppose he then passed this back to the Soviets?"

Berri shook his head. "He kept the money, built up his business. They wanted him to become a rich, respectable man."

"But if he didn't give the Soviets the money, what did he do with it?"

"At first it was political—he just gave money to the fronts, trade unions in the States, that sort of thing. Later on, though, the Bolshevik wanted him to buy things, especially scientific equipment of various kinds. Then the war came and . . ." Berri shrugged.

"So what happened then?"

"Harry bought what the Bolshevik needed, and what they needed then was . . . information, I guess you'd say. Spies cost money, Mr. Thorne, like everything else."

I was too stunned to speak. Berri laid his hand on my arm. "We can go back to the house," he murmured.

It was his turn now to make the tea, and he did so, obviously relishing my discomfiture. He'd been right: I certainly had not understood. And as the old man refilled my cup and settled down in his chair, I wanted to make sure I understood now.

"Let's go back to the beginning," I said. "When exactly did you first go to Russia?"

"I'd guess twenty-nine."

"OK. And how many trips did Harry make altogether?"

315

"Three, maybe four. Even if he didn't go, he still brought the furs in. And he bought everything. Blues and kitts. Kolinsky—a Russian weasel, that is, something like a mink. Marmot. Seal. The big item was sable."

"And how much were all these furs worth?"

"A lot. They were always big shipments and he kept it up till the start of the war. More than a million . . . but if I said more than that, I'd only be guessing."

"You're saying that the money he made out of this arrangement was ploughed back into his business?"

"Yes. But the Bolshevik kept an account. After a while, Harry even kept their share separate and turned it all into gold."

"And so far as you know, he mainly gave it to Communist Party front groups?"

Berri made a face. "That's how it started. Later, the Bolshevik wanted patents, special castings, instruments. . . ."

"And Harry bought them all this?"

"Not directly. He worked through other people, but he set them up with his money."

"Except—according to you—this all changed with the war—he ended up as a spy."

Berri made a sour face. "That's your word."

"You said he 'believed'. You're sure about that? You're sure they weren't blackmailing him?"

Berri shook his tough little head. "Don't kid yourself. He *believed*, just like the rest of us. I told you: the proof came when he *didn't* believe any more."

"And when was that?"

Berri leaned back in his chair. "That's interesting, come to think of it. You mentioned Dimitrov and his coming here—and that's when it started. Dimitrov told him the truth—about Stalin, the trials, everything. The pact with Hitler was the worst. Sometimes you hear people say it was the fault of the French or the British, that they wouldn't do a deal with the Bolshevik so they had to fall in with Hitler, but Dimitrov knew that was all so much bunk. The British couldn't give them half of Poland, Latvia, Estonia, all the rest of it— but the Nazis could, and *that* was the key."

I waited a moment; a fierce, concentrated look had come into his eyes as he'd spoken, and two red spots had sprung up on his cheeks. Finally I said, "What was Brightman's reaction to all of this?"

He shook his head slightly. "He took his cue from Dimitrov. Dimitrov told Harry a struggle was going on among the Bolshevik, that smart people knew Stalin was a fool to trust Hitler, and saw what was coming. So Harry hung on. He gritted his teeth—we all did—and waited. Of course, that got harder and harder. 1956: Hungary. 1968: Prague. I couldn't take any more after Budapest, but Harry stuck it out longer, till Czechoslovakia. Then he told them to go to hell."

"You're saying that up till the spring of 1968 Harry was still working for them?"

"Yes."

I leaned forward. "You say he finally told them to go to hell, but I wonder if that can really be true. He was in too deep. And no one tells them to go to hell anyway."

He nodded. "He shouldn't have been able to do it—but he did. He had some kind of hold . . . they were afraid of him for some reason. They left him alone."

"Until a couple of months ago. Maybe it worked for a time, Mr. Berri, but not in the end."

He sucked in his cheeks. "Don't be so sure. Those men, tonight, weren't from the Bolshevik. I don't know who they were. They *were* Russian, though, and one of them—he was like a little weasel—was called Subotin. The other one called him that."

Subotin . . . a name for my ghost. "Did they know what you've been telling me?"

"Maybe. Most of it."

"So what did they want?"

He shrugged. "The money of course. Where to find it."

"What money?"

"I 'old you—the Bolshevik's. It wasn't all spent, you see, when Harry got free. He told me he was damned if the Bolshevik would get any back, but he didn't want to spend it himself—it would only bring him bad luck. So he hid it away."

"How much?"

A quick shrug. "He told me eight hundred thousand. But it wasn't in money, you understand. He always kept the Bolshevik's share in

317

gold certificates because that made it easy to travel, and you could always cash them, no questions asked."

Gold certificates are issued by some of the big Swiss banks and a few other institutions. Each paper certificate represents a certain amount of gold, and they're far more convenient than bars or coins. I thought back. *And that's what they'd always been looking for*: in Travin's hotel in Detroit; at Grainger's clinic; in Brightman's house, where I'd first seen Subotin. And—was it possible?—even that first day, at my place in Charlottesville. Up to now, I'd assumed that whoever had broken into my place had been after the telegram from May, but perhaps they thought she might have sent the certificates to me for safekeeping.

I looked at Berri now. "Where did he hide it?"

"I don't know. That's what I told them."

I kept my voice level. "Mr. Berri, you told me yourself that they got what they came for. They killed one of your foxes and they threatened to kill all the others. Why? Because they were trying to get you to talk, or give them something you had . . ."

He took a funny, hoarse breath. "They wanted a name. . . . They knew I sometimes took messages to the people who helped Harry. They knew that Harry must have trusted those people, so they thought maybe he gave them the money to keep. I told them one name, someone who was already dead, but they knew that, and so they killed the fox, and they said . . ." He wheezed, sucked in more air. "They said they'd kill all my foxes, and then they'd kill me. So I told them."

After a moment, I whispered, "Who was it?"

"A man called Paul Hamilton. He worked in the State Department."

"Do you know where he lives?"

"Five years ago, Harry asked me to take a message to Hamilton. He was retired then, living in Paris."

I got to my feet. Now, at one level, I *did* know everything. Brightman had taken his final secret, the location of the gold, to the grave. Subotin had been going from one of Brightman's old contacts to the other in the hope of finding it. I suddenly felt very queasy: what had happened to Dr. Charlie?

Hamilton had been a spy—why mince words?—and I owed him

nothing, but simple humanity said I had to warn him. There was a phone in the bedroom. It was midnight when I dialled, which made it six in the morning in Paris. I was forty minutes getting through— you'd be surprised how many Hamiltons there are in the Paris directory. When I got him, he grumbled French into the phone, but after I'd asked if he'd once worked for the State Department and then said the name Harry Brightman, he was fully awake.

"Maybe I knew someone like that. I'm not sure."

"If you've listened this far, Mr. Hamilton, you knew him."

"All right. I knew him. Who are you?"

"Brightman's dead, Mr. Hamilton," I said. "He killed himself— he was under great pressure."

"This has nothing to do with me. It was all a long time—" An old man's voice now, a trace of a whine.

"Maybe so, Mr. Hamilton. But it *will* have something to do with you, because the people who were applying the pressure to Brightman will soon apply it to you. They believe Brightman left something with you, something valuable. Did he?"

"No. Absolutely not. I haven't seen him or heard from him in many years."

"All right. But the people who may be visiting you at any moment won't take no for an answer. I'm a friend of Brightman's. I know he'd want me to give you this warning."

"And who are these people you keep talking about?"

"I'm not entirely sure. I don't believe they are acting in an official capacity. On the other hand, I'm certain that they come from the same country as those people . . . if you follow me."

A long pause.

Then: "You're saying I'm in danger because of all this?"

"That's right, Mr. Hamilton. *Mortal* danger."

Another pause. I thought I heard him clearing his throat.

"Mr. Hamilton," I said, "just listen. You have to leave your home, and you have to leave now. Go to some place where you can't be traced. These people could be on their way now. You understand?"

"Yes."

"All right. I'll come to Paris within the next couple of days. When I arrive, I'll leave a message for you at the American Express main office, near the Opéra. . . . Then you phone me as soon as you can."

319

He'd taken it in now; he believed me. "All right, but I'll need your name."

"Robert Thorne." And then I realized something and said, "It's possible you knew my father, Mr. Hamilton. He also worked for the State Department."

"Yes. I think I do know the name. . . ."

I said, "Just remember: leave *now*. I'll tell you everything soon."

We hung up. I walked down the hall. Berri was sitting at the kitchen table, a bottle of whisky before him. I said, "It's all right. I got to him first."

He tried to keep his voice level, but didn't quite make it. "Was he worth a fox, would you say?"

I shook my head. "Probably not, Mr. Berri. Or at least he wasn't worth your love for that fox."

I sat down beside him; and then—the one gesture of sympathy I thought might be acceptable—I took a little whisky myself. I sipped, and let it burn down my throat. Then I murmured, "Just a couple of things. According to the police, Harry killed himself. And it does look that way. But if these people had been after him would he have killed himself rather than give them the money?"

Berri shrugged. "Maybe. Or maybe they threatened his daughter like they threatened my foxes. He loved her—he'd have done anything for her. Or they made it look like he killed himself."

Which was what I was wondering about. If Brightman could simply have given them the money, why would he have put himself *and May* through the horror? And Subotin wouldn't have wanted Brightman dead—not before he told him where the gold was located. But, one way or the other, Harry Brightman was dead.

I said, "There's something else I still don't get. This hold Harry had on the Bolshevik . . . did it have anything to do with the child?"

He shrugged. "I don't know. Maybe."

"There's no doubt the child came out of Russia at the same time Dimitrov made his trip here."

"Well, I'll tell you one thing. Don't kid yourself. Once upon a time, Dimitrov might have been a hero, but he ended up like the rest of them. By 1940, his hands were covered in blood. If he snatched a baby away from the Bolshevik, it was because he thought it might help save *him*, not the child."

320

Was it really possible that a *child* had protected Dimitrov, and that this protection had then been passed on to Brightman? In 1940, everyone seemed to agree, Dimitrov had been living under a genuine threat. Yet he had survived. I leaned back in my chair and, taking another sip of the old man's whisky, moved back to firmer ground. "One last point," I said. "You said he kept the money in gold certificates. Do you know if he bought them before 1970?"

He shrugged. "Long before that. What the hell difference does the year make?"

A great deal, I knew. I went into the living room, where I found what I wanted: a Montreal *Gazette* from a week ago and the box on the stock-market page which showed the commodity prices.

I took out my pen, worked it all out in the margin.

It was simple enough. Before August 15, 1971, the US Treasury had bought and sold gold at $35 an ounce, the price at which Harry Brightman must have bought his. But after 1971, the value of gold had soared. According to the *Gazette*, the present price was around $500 an ounce—which meant that Brightman's certificates were now worth between eleven and twelve *million* dollars.

I stared at this figure for a long time. It explained a great deal. More than what I'd discovered about Dimitrov, far more than what I'd found out about May's adoption. Had she known what was happening? Had she told Cadogan to stop me from going on precisely because she knew what I'd find? But then why point me down this trail in the first place?

And what did this have to do with me? Here was the last, crucial question. I'd told Hamilton I'd go to France, and I felt I had no choice about that, even if it left me dead broke. Having come this far, there was no doubt I'd go on to the end. But was there some inner, hidden logic driving me on? Paris . . . my mother's city. Paris: where my parents had met. Each step I took into Brightman's past only seemed to carry me deeper into my own, and now Travin's words drifted back: *I'll tell you something personal, something you wouldn't want a policeman to hear. . . .*

$12,000,000. . . . For most people, that was reason enough to do anything. It was reason enough for Subotin, I thought, and it would do for me too. Whatever side he was on—or Berri, or Brightman—my side was different.

But then, erasing these thoughts from my mind, the foxes once more took up their lament. Their howls rose and fell in pitiful harmony, like a ghost's agonized call to its own lost soul—the Red Fox was dead, but perhaps his shade, disturbed by this night, was restlessly moving through the forest nearby.

In the kitchen, Berri got to his feet; I heard him open the door. And then the scent that had troubled the foxes—whatever it was— must have passed on, for soon they fell silent again.

I arrived in Paris on November 9.

If you're lucky, that can be one of the city's best months, but not this time. The rain was wind-driven and unremitting, and on the bus from Charles de Gaulle Airport to Porte Maillot, the city swam mistily by the streaming window.

At the Porte Maillot *aérogare*, I reserved a car with Hertz for later that afternoon, then made my way by metro to the Left Bank. This has always been the part of the city where I've felt the most comfortable, the Paris my mother had taught me to love. It hadn't changed much, though a hint of Eastern cooking mingled with the traditional smells of bread and tobacco. Head down, I stayed tight to the buildings and let my feet find their own way through the warren of streets around St. Séverin until they brought me to the Pension Mull. I saw that the gloomy cafe underneath hadn't changed. I'd first used this place as a student, and now it was a habit, with the added virtue, this trip, of complete anonymity. After two glasses of *rouge* at the bar, I went up to my room and stretched out. In five minutes I was asleep.

I awoke at two thirty still tired, but the frigid *douche* at the end of the hall woke me up, and a brisk walk up to the Opéra got my blood flowing again. I cashed a cheque at American Express and left the cafe's number for Hamilton. It was four by the time I was finished. I decided to go on to Hertz and pick up my car, but I was back in the cafe by five.

For the next hour, I tried not to be nervous; but I was. I didn't think Subotin could have got here before me, but it was possible.

But at twenty past six, the barman waved me round to the phone.

"Thorne?" Hamilton's voice was low and tense. "I hope I haven't kept you waiting. I put off calling Amex till the very last moment to give you as much time as possible."

"That's all right. Where are you?"

"The Café Raymond on the Quai des Grands-Augustins."

"All right. I assume you've kept away from your place."

"Don't worry, Mr. Thorne. I was out of there twenty minutes after you called, and I haven't been back."

I didn't like him; he didn't like me. Somehow, that was all clear at once.

"Stay where you are," I said. "It'll only take me ten minutes to get there."

"I'm the old man at the bar, drinking Stella."

The cafe, when I reached it, was crowded with after-work drinkers. I recognized Hamilton at once, though I would hardly have described him as an old man drinking beer. He was a tall, handsome man with shiny silver hair. I couldn't be sure of his age— in my parents' generation, but on the younger side of it, and he had that glow of prosperous health that spelled "early retirement". He was dressed in a grey fisherman's sweater and grey wool trousers, the effect casual but quietly stylish.

And I still didn't like him.

I wondered why. He was a traitor of course. Yet you could say the same of Berri and I'd felt sympathy for him. Maybe it was because Berri had paid . . . not just in the beating he'd suffered, but in the wider sense of having accepted responsibility for what he'd done. But not this man. I watched him as he lit a cigarette. Very cool; very self-satisfied; but then he glanced quickly over his shoulder and I could see the anxiety in his pale, watery eyes.

Reluctantly I now moved towards him. All at once he was aware of me, but before he could say anything, I began talking rapidly in French. He played along nicely, and after a moment, quite casually, he got up from his stool and I followed him out.

Stepping outside, he paused and ground out his cigarette. "You speak excellent French, Mr. Thorne."

"My mother was French."

"Ah, yes. I was forgetting. Then that makes it definite: I did know

323

your father." He gave me a smile. "And I can clearly remember being charmed by your mother."

I wasn't that surprised—the State Department, especially before 1950, was a very small world. I merely nodded, and watched his smile fade as I didn't pick up on our family connection. Then he darted confidently into the traffic, crossing to the Seine side of the *quai*. I caught up to him at the top of a broad stone stairway leading down to the water. We went down the steps: boats were tied up all along here and beyond them, glittering with the first lights of evening, the Seine branched around the Île de la Cité. Most of the boats were barges, moored three deep. They were all about a hundred feet long, with a wheelhouse in the stern, and a long, low cabin running up to the prow. People were living on them. I smelled a charcoal fire; a radio was playing Mozart.

Hamilton had gone on a little ahead. Now he stopped and waited for me, smiling. His tanned face was marked with heavy creases. "You'll have to be a bit acrobatic," he said, then, quite gracefully, leaped across to the first of the barges. Clumsily, I thumped after him. He stopped on the far side, where the gunwales of this barge were bumpered against the next further out. Deftly, he hopped up and over. This second barge seemed deserted, its deck a dark minefield of obstructions, but finally I reached the far side and once more stormed over the gunwales.

I straightened up and tried to catch my breath. Hamilton smiled. "Welcome to *La Trompette*, Mr. Thorne."

I was standing on the deck of an old wooden barge. Its varnished decks and polished brass fittings glowed softly in the light that filtered down from the great mansions in the Place Dauphine. It was all very impressive, and I wondered how discreet it could be. "You're absolutely sure you can't be traced here?"

"I bought her in the spring, but they've been fitting her out at Janville. They only brought her up this last week."

That sounded safe enough. I nodded, then followed him into the wheelhouse. Here, shadows leaped up from paraffin lanterns, and the sounds of the great city retreated, replaced by the gentle creak of the hull.

Edging through a doorway, Hamilton beckoned me, and I followed him down a short ladder to the main cabin, a large, low mahogany chamber. Towards the bow, one section was fitted up as the salon with built-in couches, even television and stereo. Closer to us was a galley.

"Please have a seat. I'll get you a drink, if you like."

I walked through the galley and sat down on one of the couches, while, on the other side of the room, Hamilton turned a brass catch on a neatly fitted locker, and a bar descended with various bottles and implements. With his back to me, he splashed Johnnie Walker Red into crystal tumblers and murmured, "By the way, I trust you are being polite? No wires? Body recorders?"

"Don't worry, Mr. Hamilton. This is just between us."

"Good. There wouldn't be much point talking at all if we couldn't speak frankly." He turned round and handed me a glass. "So Brightman's dead?"

I nodded.

"And bad men are chasing me because I'm supposed to have something that Brightman left with me?"

I sipped my whisky. His facetiousness only increased my dislike of him. But I tried to keep my voice even. "If you don't mind, I'd like to start with my questions."

He shrugged coolly. But when he tilted his head back to drink, I could again see the anxiety in his eyes. "All right," he finally said. "Go ahead."

The small lamps on the bulkheads spilled pools of yellowish light into the leathery, masculine gloom. I said, "I'll start at the obvious place. When did you last see Brightman?"

He took a gentlemanly sip at his whisky. "I'm not sure I want to answer. I told you I want to be frank—I'd rather you let me be honestly reticent than force me into a lie."

"Have you seen him within the last six months?"

"All right. Yes."

"What did he want?"

"Help, I think, but he was vague."

"Did he leave anything with you? Or did he want to?"

"I assume you mean a variation on the letter-to-be-opened-upon-my-decease theme?"

"Not that exactly. He had something that people wanted, wanted so much that possessing it made him a target. So I think he decided to pass it on. That not only took him out of the direct line of fire but also worked as a kind of insurance. Since he was the only person who knew where it was, people interested in this item now had a vested interest in his wellbeing."

He got up and poured himself some more whisky, his back to me. "This item . . . can you tell me what it is, more specifically?"

"If you have it, you know. If not . . . perhaps that's something you'll let me reserve."

He turned around. "All right. But what makes you think I do have it? I didn't know Brightman well, you understand. Over the years, I think I met him precisely three times." He came over to the couch again and sat down. "I guess the first time was some time in the early forties. Then fifty-six. Then this last time . . . but that's it. I scarcely knew him, and had never done anything for him in a personal way."

"So what *did* you do for him?"

I watched his face. For a moment he seemed undecided, then he shrugged. "I took some science at school," he began. "Not much, but in the US foreign service, at least in my day, science was about as rare as straight talk. So at the beginning of the war I gained a number of important assignments virtually by default. Some involved various advisory panels on the export of scientific equipment. To the combatants, during the period the US was neutral, to our allies afterwards."

"Including the Soviet Union?"

He hesitated. "So far as I was concerned, Mr. Thorne, I was helping a nation that was now fighting for its life against the same enemy we were fighting."

"You were a Communist?"

"Don't be idiotic. I was trying to do the right thing." His voice, to my surprise, suddenly trembled a little. "I was surrounded by fools who couldn't see the menace Hitler represented and who let their own ideological prejudices prevent full cooperation with Russia."

I said, "In effect, you had a fundamental disagreement with US foreign policy?"

"If you like."

"And you used Brightman to . . . circumvent it."

He gave a little smile. "What a nice way to put it. . . . But you

326

needn't be so polite. I was, undoubtedly, a spy. Most of what I did revolved around scientific equipment that the Soviets were particularly anxious to know about. As well, it was useful for them to know what other Allied centres of scientific production were needing."

"And all of this," I said, "went through Harry Brightman?"

He shook his head. "I couldn't say. I was never precisely sure who received the information I transmitted."

"Then why did you meet with Brightman at all?"

"Well, the first time was in New York in the middle of the war. It turned out that he wanted to obtain a particular piece of electronic equipment. He had money, any amount—and so we worked out a plan to get hold of it."

It was clear that Hamilton was telling at least part of the truth: according to Berri, this was precisely the sort of thing that Brightman had done.

I said, "You claim you met him a second time . . . in 1956."

"Yes. Hungary, you'll remember. By this time—not that anyone ever told me—I think I was under Brightman's control. A number of people must have been, and one of them was having pangs of conscience. Apparently he believed all that talk about the Hungarian Freedom Fighters and was threatening to do something foolish. This person worked in the State Department and Brightman wanted me to calm him down."

"Who was it?"

"I've no idea. I told Brightman to forget it—I wasn't going to expose myself to somebody who was already getting cold feet."

"Was he angry?"

"No. . . . I think he understood my position well enough."

Interesting. Brightman *had* asked him for a favour, then. But Hamilton hadn't come through. I said, "These were face-to-face meetings?"

"Yes."

"But there must have been other forms of communication with him as well. Messages. And—at least once—a messenger."

"You know about that? He was a funny little fellow. A French-Canadian. I forget his name. Brightman wanted me to set up a meeting for him here, through the Soviet embassy, of course. I told him I wouldn't take the risk for him."

"Why do you think Brightman asked you to? He was higher up in the hierarchy—closer to the embassy—than you ever were."

He shrugged. "Perhaps he'd had unsatisfactory results using his normal channels and wanted to try another."

"You have to admit it's a little strange. Brightman was never close to you, personally or professionally, yet he again picked on you for a favour. Why?"

As I thought about this, Hamilton went to the bar and poured himself another whisky. "So we're back to the present," he said. "The present, and Harry Brightman. Except Harry isn't part of it, is he?" I said nothing. I watched him drink with nervous movements of his lips. He looked back at me. "He *is* dead? You're sure of it?"

"Yes, I saw his body myself. Harry Brightman is dead."

He said slowly, "I have no wish to betray him, Mr. Thorne. But there's not much point worrying if he's dead. . . ." Now he'd drawn my attention again to one crucial point: for Hamilton, Brightman's death mattered more than anything else.

"In any case," he continued, "I might as well tell you . . . about the last time I saw him, I mean." He picked up the glass again, a nice, casual gesture not quite perfectly acted, and I knew, even before he opened his mouth, that he was going to tell me a lie. "It was in September. It was clear he was in trouble and wanted my help. I tried to get out of him what it was but he refused to say, until I committed myself. I just couldn't do that. The only reason I've survived this long is because I've been very cautious."

I shook my head. "I don't believe you, Mr. Hamilton."

He turned away. "Believe what you like."

I shook my head again. "He came to you that first time and you turned him down—but he kept coming back. How come? In fact, he kept coming back to you because you always did *exactly as you were told*. He was blackmailing you, Mr. Hamilton—that's what I believe. So you had to do just what he wanted."

"Don't be ridiculous. If he could blackmail me, think of what I had on him."

"Nothing. Certainly nothing on paper. Besides, he didn't give a damn. He was a disillusioned old man, sick with himself and sick with the world. But you? Oh no . . . you've got something to lose. You want to enjoy a cosy retirement. So you did just as he told you."

He couldn't keep it out of his eyes; I was right. He looked away.

"He left a package with you because it was too dangerous to leave with his daughter or anyone else he cared for. And if you've still got that package in forty-eight hours, believe me, you're as good as dead."

Now his anxiety was coming out like sweat. "I don't believe you," he stammered. "If you're right, why was Brightman killed *after* he gave me his package? *You're* telling the lies."

I shook my head. "You've got the package, so you probably know what's inside it. A key? A combination? A document that gets you into a vault? Whatever it is, it leads to a great deal of money—but don't be tempted. It's part of the money the Soviets originally gave Brightman to buy that equipment you were putting him on to. A lot was left over. Certain Russians are trying to get hold of it, and your former employers are trying to stop them; they want to cover the whole thing up. So whatever you do, don't go to *them* for help. I think that's the mistake Brightman made."

I'd been working much of this out as I went along, but as soon as I started to speak, I knew it was true. Subotin on one side, the KGB on the other. Brightman had probably gone to his old masters to get Subotin off his back, but they'd eliminated him instead, and then done likewise with Travin. I was suddenly convinced of this—and my conviction must have got through to Hamilton. He suddenly strode across the salon and rummaged in a desk. I had a moment's panic then, thinking of a gun. But he pulled out a bottle of pills and took a few. He started to speak and I could barely hear him. "All right," he said. "I'll admit I haven't told the whole truth. But listen, you've got to help me."

"Just give me the package, the envelope . . . whatever it is. I'll get rid of it for you and I'll make sure they understand that you don't have it any more. Then you're home free."

He shook his head. "No . . . it's not that simple. You have to believe me. I need time to think." He made a quick gesture, taking in the barge. "How safe am I here?"

I shrugged. "They'll find you eventually."

"Twenty-four hours . . . I must have that long. Come back tomorrow evening. We'll work out something then."

I knew he was going to do something stupid. He had Brightman's "package", whatever that was, and he wanted some time—he was going to do something stupid, all right.

But I got up and shrugged myself into my raincoat. Then I said, "Do you have any idea who these people are?"

"I think Brightman said they were a faction of the KGB—with connections into the military. . . . Not very nice."

"You're not thinking that you can convince them that you're on their side?"

His face suddenly twisted in anger. "I'm not on anyone's side—I don't care—"

"Don't give me that. You've been on the same side from the very beginning. Your own."

I walked past him, through the galley, and climbed the stairs into the wheelhouse. Stepping outside, I looked at my watch. It was after eight; we'd talked a long time.

I made my way over the barges and climbed up to the *quai*. I felt very uneasy. I knew he was up to something, and didn't want to let him out of my sight, so I crossed the road to a cafe where I found a table that let me keep watch on the stairway up from the river.

Sure enough, twenty minutes later, Hamilton appeared; he went into a phone booth, made a call, came out again. Half an hour went by. And then a car drew up, a huge yellow Dodge Charger. A young man got out, talked with Hamilton for a minute, then drove away. Hamilton stayed where he was, smoking a cigarette and running his fingers back through his long silver hair. A few minutes later, the young man returned on foot. Together, they went down to the river. After an hour, when they still hadn't come back, I was sure they wouldn't return that night. But I was taking no chances. Making a quick tour of the streets near the *quai*, I found the Dodge squeezed into an alley, and then fetched my own little machine from the *pension* and parked up the road.

Ten twenty-two . . . Eleven sixteen . . . Slowly, one by one, the hours passed and I dozed intermittently. The front seat of a Renault Cinq doesn't make much of a bed.

AROUND FOUR O'CLOCK the city seemed to drift off, lulled into drowsiness by the distant hum of trucks on the *périphérique*, the roadway that runs around Paris, but an hour later deliveries started to the cafes, and soon afterwards the working people of the *quartier* emerged. By six, the pavements were crowded and, exhausted and unshaven, I got out of the Renault and stretched. I walked over to the *quai* and the stairway that led down to the water. On some of the barges, life was stirring, but *La Trompette* seemed to be slumbering on. I crossed the street, found a cafe, and began drinking coffee.

By seven, I felt halfway human, and began wondering what I was going to do. But almost at once, I got a surprise: the young man appeared. He popped up from the stairway and darted briskly through the traffic. I wondered if I should follow him; but then he came straight over to the cafe where I was sitting and settled down to eat, so it was easy to watch him. He ate slowly, looking about the room as he did so . . . for an instant his glance touched mine. I put his age at nineteen or twenty. Tall. A lean, elegant face but with a rather boyish lick of hair that kept falling into his eyes. He was wearing a brown leather jacket, jeans and fancy boots, and he was very tanned: Mr. Franco-California, you might have called him.

As the boy ate, I pondered. Hamilton was up to something, I was sure of that, so I was reluctant to give up my watch on the *quai*. On the other hand, the boy might be important too. Hamilton had called him immediately after seeing me and I'd half expected him to use the boy's Dodge for a midnight flit: he might still do that.

Just after eight, the boy folded his paper, rose and headed out of the cafe. I hesitated . . . and in the end, decided to follow him. He headed up the Quai des Grands-Augustins, then continued onto the Quai St. Michel, and turned up the Rue St. Jacques. He was going to his car; I took a short cut and beat him to it. I started the Renault, so its engine was already warm as the big Dodge coughed in the damp, backed out of the alley, then sped away. I had no trouble following that large splash of yellow, and forty minutes later we pulled up in the Avenue Foch in St. Mandé, an eastern suburb just outside the city proper.

I didn't know the place, but I knew lots like it: quiet streets of solid old apartments behind black wrought-iron fences. The yellow Dodge was out of place, but as I watched the boy go into one of the buildings, I had the feeling that this was where his parents lived.

He was back inside of twenty minutes, carrying two soft suitcases.

331

Throwing them into the Dodge, he now led me onto the *périphérique*. He went east as far as Gentilly and then turned in towards the Cité Universitaire, a huge educational complex. Moving onto one of its access roads, the boy headed for a car park.

I almost didn't follow—I assumed he was going to a class or was visiting someone. But striding quickly, he crossed a lawn and headed out to the street. Getting out of my car, I followed him across. He cut through a park, finally coming out at the entrance of a small side street. When I saw the name of the street I understood. It was Hamilton's street. Despite what I'd told him, he'd let the boy come here—must have *asked* him to . . . and clearly hadn't told him there was any danger, for now, with no attempt at deception, he turned into a doorway. I had a sudden spasm of guilt, but told myself that it was unlikely that Subotin had made it to Paris. I'll give the boy five minutes, I thought. Two minutes and twenty-six seconds later, he appeared, and seemed quite unconcerned.

A light drizzle began turning to rain. Hunching his shoulders, he dashed across the road, into the park. As I took off after him, the rain began to come down hard. I could see the boy up ahead; if he'd taken something out of Hamilton's apartment, it was small enough to fit into his pocket. I caught up with him as we arrived back at the Cité Universitaire. He went into one of the buildings.

I went back to the car park where I waited until he came back to the Dodge. He started the engine, and nosed past me. Returning to the *périphérique*, he led me back the way we'd come. The rain was fairly heavy now, and in the little Renault I was constantly drowned in muddy spray from big lorries, so it was a relief when he turned off the autoroute onto a smaller road running through the towns near the Marne. We wiggled along behind the river until he drove off the main road and down a small side turning. We were now about twenty-five or thirty miles from Paris. Here, all the land sloped down towards the river, whose course was marked by a grey, fuzzy line of trees in the distance.

After a couple of miles the boy turned off, to a big, barnlike, roadside restaurant. Cautiously, I drove past the entrance, then doubled back. As I parked, I was just in time to see him disappear inside.

I thought for a moment. He hadn't seemed suspicious: but he had seen me in the cafe on the *quai*. Still, there was a possibility that he might be meeting Hamilton here. Deciding to chance it, I followed him in. In front of the main dining room was a gloomy bar. I was able to sit there, pretty well hidden, and catch a glimpse of the boy every time someone opened the swing doors and went in to eat.

I ordered a vermouth and sandwiches and ate ravenously. After an hour the boy emerged. Still bearing in mind that he'd seen me in Paris, I stayed where I was until I heard the Dodge's big engine start burbling. Then I watched from the doorway as he drove across the car park. But instead of turning towards the main road, he headed down towards the river, and even as I sprinted back to the Renault, I understood. I was within ten kilometres of the Marne, which flows into the Seine near Paris. The boy *was* meeting Hamilton—but *Hamilton would be arriving by barge*. So following the boy had been a terrific stroke of good luck . . . or so I thought until I turned the key in the Renault's ignition.

Nothing happened.

After three tries I got out and propped up the bonnet. The engine was still warm after the morning's drive, and raindrops hissed on the block . . . but no matter how warm it was, there was no way it was going to start when two of the ignition cables were missing.

I sat in the car and the rain drummed on the roof. I told myself there were two possibilities, one frightening, the other merely annoying. I was certain that Subotin hadn't been in Hamilton's apartment; if he had been, he'd never have let the boy come out again. And I was *almost* sure that no one had followed us away from the place. There was no sense in getting into a panic, however; more than likely, I'd just been too confident, too careless, and the boy hadn't been as innocent as he looked. He'd led me into this place—thereby getting me out of the car—and skilfully beached me: he'd been out of my sight just long enough to do it. Very neat, I thought; except it didn't make any difference if I was right about Hamilton coming by barge. I was too close to the river; I was fairly sure I could walk there in an hour.

I ran back to the restaurant where the barman gave me plenty of sympathy, and offered to call a garage. But I knew that would end up taking hours.

One of the girls in the kitchen had a bicycle. She thought I was crazy, because of the rain, but wouldn't take any money. Her machine was padlocked to a drainpipe behind the restaurant: it was old and squeaky, with a red plastic basket on the front handlebars. I got onto it and wobbled off.

The road was downhill towards the Marne. The wheels juddered through potholes, and my trousers were soaked so completely that they moulded to my thighs. I passed a farm and a couple of cottages, but in this weather no one was out, and I didn't see a single car. After twenty minutes or so, the road narrowed and I entered a dark lane of huge oaks. The light here was soft, dim, silvery, as if everything was reflected in a misted mirror, and a sort of hush fell. I glided round a curve, and just as the road straightened out I saw the yellow Dodge ahead.

It was in the ditch: tilted sharply over on the right, with its big snout crumpled against one of the oaks.

I braked, hard. I got my feet down and straddled the bike, staring at the car.

Nothing was moving: the Dodge just lay there. The driver's door was ajar, the passenger's wide open. I listened. All I could hear was the rain. With the doors open, there should have been a warning buzzer if the keys were still in the ignition.

So . . .

The boy had driven his car off the road. Unhurt, he'd taken the keys out and was walking for help.· . . . Yes, that was possible, but I hadn't passed him, and the restaurant was the first place he'd think of going. I felt a queasiness that was becoming all too familiar. Could Subotin be here?

Reluctantly, I got back on the bicycle and rode up to the car. There was nobody in it, and no blood, which was the next thing I looked for. I walked round to the front. The right side was jammed hard against the oak, having gouged a white, gleaming wound out of the trunk. As an accident, it was nothing spectacular, assuming it *had* been an accident. Then I saw a scraped patch above the left front wheelwell, and wondered.

A crow squawked in the woods. Its call drew my eyes there. These woods were very dense, for between the ancient oaks many smaller trees were growing. The rain had beaten the leaves from their branches and they lay in great piles around the trunks . . .

334

except for the wavy path where something had been dragged through them.

I stared at that path the way you look at a door you don't want to open, but there was no getting away from what I had to do. I stepped around the car and over the ditch. The wet leaves were spongy underfoot, and each step released a pungent smell of mould. Every few yards, I stopped and listened. Birds clucked and rustled around me, and somewhere in the sky beyond the trees, a single-engine plane was droning along.

I didn't have to go far; they'd simply wanted to get him out of sight from the road. He was sitting in a little hollow, at the base of a birch tree. His arms were tied behind him, lashed around the trunk. His head too was tied back to the tree. They'd looped his belt around his neck and the tree trunk, and then they'd jammed a stick through the loop, twisting it tight, as if they were winding up the rubber band on a kid's model aeroplane. His face was very bloody. He didn't move, and a sick, guilty feeling began to spread through the pit of my stomach. . . . It *was* partly my fault. I could have stopped him. But then—thank God—his eyes opened, glittering, and his whole body strained towards me. With a tremendous sense of relief, I skidded down to him.

The belt had dug a red furrow into his throat and was tight enough to stop him from speaking. When I got it off, he gave a hoarse gasp, and then I undid his hands. He toppled onto his side and just breathed, sucking in huge, deep breaths.

I waited, kneeling in the muddy leaves. Despite the blood, I thought he was more frightened than hurt. I handed him a Kleenex, and he used it on his face. Giving him a chance to recover, I looked away, and only then realized that the ground all around the boy's feet was littered with money—French and Swiss francs, Swedish crowns, British pounds. . . .

He got his breath back. His voice trembled as he said, "I thank you. I thought no one would come. I thank you very much."

"If you like, I can go for a doctor."

He shook his head. "I'll be all right in a minute. . . . I don't know what to say. . . . I was attacked by some men. . . ." He seemed very young and frightened.

I said, "You don't have to explain. I know Hamilton . . . I know who those men are. They must have followed you from his apartment. . . . I did as well, but I didn't see them."

His head came upright but before he could speak I added, "It's all right. I'm not with them—I'm on your side. Tell me, at the restaurant, did you touch my car?"

"No . . . I don't understand. Who are you?"

"My name is Robert Thorne. I'm an American. You can ask Paul about me. But you must tell me . . . when you went to his apartment, what did you get?"

"He said he was in trouble. He said people were watching his apartment—he couldn't go there, but I could because they didn't know who I was."

"Maybe that's what he thought, but he didn't think hard enough," I said. "They followed you from the apartment. . . . They wanted to know what you were doing for Paul. What *were* you doing?"

He looked directly at me, like a child searching for trust. "You swear you are Paul's friend?"

"I swear."

The words tumbled out. "Paul had a locker in the Cité. I had to get the key from the apartment to open it. There were three envelopes inside. I was to mail one of them—I did that right there, in the Cité—and bring him the others."

I looked around us, at the bills scattered among the leaves. "This money was in one of them?"

He nodded. "Yes."

"And the others . . . you mailed one, but you had the second with you?"

"Yes. Paul said not to mail it; he wanted to look at it first. But they took it away from me. It had an address in Canada—I don't think it was important because they opened it and then crumpled it up."

"This Canadian address—did it include a name?"

"Yes. It was supposed to go to a man named Cadogan, in Toronto."

"All right. Think of the one you did mail—who was that to?"

He swallowed. "That's what they wanted to know. They said they'd choke it out of me . . ." Now his face twisted with anguish.

"Don't blame yourself," I said. "Because that's exactly what they would have done—they'd have choked you to death."

336

His voice became very soft. "It was to Russia . . . and it was in an envelope from the Russian embassy in Paris—it had a big label in the corner, printed with their address. The address it was being sent to was written in French and also in Russian—I'm sure it said Yuri Shastov in a place called Povonets. But I told them only that it was going to Russia." He looked at me, as though for approval.

"Did you have any idea from the envelopes what might have been inside them?"

"The one they took was an ordinary envelope. The other was bigger, padded. But not heavy. Even to Russia, it was just a few francs." As he finished speaking, he braced himself against the trunk of the tree and tried to stand up. He made it, but his face went pale as the blood rushed out of his head. He bent over, resting his hands on his knees.

"Take it easy," I said. With his head down, blood began to drip from his nose, patting dark red splashes on the dead leaves. I tried to understand what he'd said. I'd been right about one thing: Brightman had been holding something over Hamilton's head. Hamilton's payoff, for hanging on to Brightman's envelope, had presumably been the return of the incriminating material, whatever it had been. The letter to Cadogan would have contained instructions about this. Brightman must also have left Hamilton with orders about the other envelope, the one to Russia, and Hamilton had obeyed them. But if the second envelope contained the key to the buried treasure Subotin was looking for, why would Brightman have instructed Hamilton to send it to the Soviet Union?

I looked up at the boy. "I don't know your name."

He tried to sniff back the blood, and coughed. "Alain," he said.

"Alain . . . it's important that what you've told me is true."

"It is true." He looked straight at me, but I could tell nothing from his eyes.

"All right. What else did these men ask you about?"

Carefully, he straightened up. "They wanted to know where Paul was."

"He's coming here, isn't he? On the barge?" Now I got to my feet as well. Without noticing, I'd been feeling through the leaves, picking up the money. It amounted to several thousand dollars: Hamilton's emergency hoard.

Alain nodded. "I told them we were going to meet tonight, in Meaux, at the end of the canal. But we really intended to meet at the end of this road. There's a place where you can tie up."

I said, "Do you think they believed you?"

"I'm not sure. I thought they'd go towards Meaux to wait . . . but by the sounds of their car it's possible they turned back to Paris."

Which made sense. They'd drive back on the main road, cutting down to the water every few kilometres on a side road. Eventually, they were bound to run into him. I wondered if he was dead already, but I said, "Where do you think he is now?"

"He must be close to here. Already he's been sailing for hours."

"And when did they leave you? The men . . . the man with red hair?"

He shrugged. "Half an hour . . . forty minutes."

Probably time enough to find him. On the other hand, they could have passed him, gone too far back towards Paris.

"We must warn him."

I nodded. "Yes, but I'm going to do that. You've got to get out of here." I shoved the money into his hands. "This is very dangerous, and you're in no shape for it now. Go back to your car. There's a bicycle there. Ride it back to the place where you had lunch, then call a garage and get them to fix the red Renault in the car park— here are the keys. Take the car back to Paris. Leave it at Hertz, and then get on a plane—just listen to me—get on a plane and go anywhere outside of France. At least for a couple of weeks."

He looked down at my hand but he didn't reach for the keys. He said, "What is Paul doing? What do these men want from him?"

"I'm sorry. That's something you'll have to ask him."

"Why can't you tell me?"

"Because there's no time and it's not my story to tell."

He reached out, plucking the keys from my hands. "You're not a friend of Paul's, are you? That was a lie."

"Maybe . . . you could say he was a friend of my father's."

His hand tightened over the keys. "I will do what you say, but you tell Paul that I will write to him in a week at my uncle's."

I nodded, and, turning away, he climbed out of the hollow. He was still wobbly and he had to stop at the top. Then, straightening his shoulders, he walked off towards the road.

I LET HIM GO, then walked down to the Marne. At this point the river was really a canal, about thirty feet wide. And I could even see the spot where Alain was due to meet up with the barge: huge, rusted iron rings had been driven into the trunks of two massive oaks, making a place to tie up at. But no one was there, and there was nothing to do but slog along the towpath beside the canal.

After a couple of kilometres, the canal entered the village of Esbly. There I waited, watching a man on a railway bridge; but it wasn't Subotin and so I kept on—exhausted now, soaked to the skin—until I'd reached the other side of Coupvray. Then I saw it: even before I could read the name *La Trompette*, the gloss of the hull gave it away. The barge was tied up at the bow to an iron picket driven into the bank.

I edged closer, ducked off the path and watched the boat from behind a thick hedge. Five minutes passed. On the barge everything seemed quiet. I was about to step forward—but then I peered intently ahead as the rope from the barge to the bank suddenly tensed and a figure stepped from the wheelhouse onto the deck.

It was a woman wearing a navy blue caped raincoat, a kerchief tied on her head.

She looked away from me, down the canal, but then turned her head so I could see her in profile. I couldn't believe it—she looked just like May.

The rain streaked down, washing the image of the canal, the barge, and May—was it May?—in the silvery, monochrome tints of an old silent film. For an instant, in fact, she seemed to hang in the air like an unreal, ghostly projection. But then, as a gust of wind parted the rain, I was sure.

At once a dizzying rush of feeling swept over me—May *couldn't* be here. But she was. Peering through the hedge, I watched her unobserved as on that first day in Toronto, but the distance I'd felt from her then was now compounded a thousand times over. What was she doing on Hamilton's barge? Had she betrayed me? Now I realized we were truly strangers. She wasn't a woman I'd loved but a woman I still hadn't met. And yet . . . it was now that I felt drawn to her more powerfully and urgently than at any time since all this had begun. Shrouded in her kerchief and cape, the hissing rain scratching the air all around her, she seemed so forlorn, so remote, that something in her called out to me so strongly that I was pulled from my hiding place onto the path.

She turned then and saw me. "Robert!"

She took a step across the deck and I could see her more clearly. My last memory of her was that day in Detroit, in the waiting room, when she'd looked so drawn and tired. But now she was completely transformed. Her face shone with life, glowed with it. And her voice was strong. "Robert, what are you doing here? You have to leave. I told you—"

"Is Hamilton there?"

"No. But I don't—listen to me—"

"In a second, but get back inside."

She hesitated an instant: but now there was an edge to my voice, for Subotin might be watching. "Hurry," I said.

May disappeared. I looked down the path, but there was no sign of anyone. Dashing to the boat, I pulled myself over the rail, then ran across the deck to the wheelhouse. May was waiting anxiously inside. "Robert, I told Stewart Cadogan—"

"I got the message."

My tone made her hesitate and her glance shifted away. "It was the money, wasn't it?"

"Partly—but it's not important now. You're in great danger."

"I don't think so. I just have to be careful."

"Subotin—do you know that name?"

"No."

"Then you don't know the danger you're in. When did you get here?"

"About twenty minutes ago."

"Where was Hamilton?"

"He wasn't here. Nobody was."

"Did you look inside?"

"No, I didn't want to. I just waited. But I called out. There's nobody there. Robert—"

"Wait." I went down into the cabin and May followed. Lights

340

glowed dimly down the length of the barge. In the galley, the butter was out, along with a crock of Dundee marmalade. . . . I looked all around, but discovered no sign of a struggle. But where was Hamilton? And when I found the bright yellow oilskins neatly stowed in their wardrobe, a chill ran up my spine. Given the rain, he wouldn't have gone out without them. Peering into the dark interior of the salon, I felt its emptiness had a cold, final quality.

May felt it too. "What is it?" she whispered.

I turned to face her. "I don't know . . ."

Fringed by her long golden lashes, her eyes seemed huge; and now, for an instant, they were touched by fear. She took a step closer, instinctively seeking protection, and reached out for my arm. "Robert," she whispered, "I wish you hadn't come. I wish I hadn't . . ."

"It's all right." I squeezed her hand. "But you have to tell me everything, and you have to tell me the truth."

Her face turned up towards me and for a moment her gaze held mine. "I've tried to, I swear. In the beginning, I called you because I knew you were the only person on earth I could tell the truth to."

"Then why did you want me to stop?"

"I was afraid for you. I was afraid that . . ."

Her voice trailed away—because this was a lie that she couldn't bring off? Had she been manipulating me from the beginning? I said, "What are you doing here? How did you learn about Hamilton?"

Her eyes looked away. "I was supposed to meet him here. The day after I got back from Detroit a letter came in the mail from my father. He'd sent it from Detroit. He said that if I got this letter it would mean he was dead and he wanted me to do certain things."

"What things?"

"He said . . . he told me to go to a post-office box—he sent the key with the letter. He said I'd find an envelope inside. It was addressed to Paul Hamilton, here—in Paris—and I was to give it to him in return for another envelope, one that would be addressed to Stewart Cadogan. I was supposed to destroy that one and something else, some sort of slip. . . . Hamilton had a second envelope, you see. He was to mail it but give me a receipt—some form from the post office—to prove that he had."

'But not the envelope itself?"

"No. . . . It was dangerous. If there was no choice, my father said, I should take it, but mail it immediately."

"And in return for this . . . ?"

Reaching beneath her cape, she pulled out a thick, oversized envelope. I took it from her and squeezed it, feeling a wad of papers inside. I was certain now that this envelope contained the material that Brightman had held over Hamilton, which ultimately would have been redeemed by the letter to Cadogan—which Subotin had taken from Alain. Now, this ring-around-the-roses scarcely made any difference . . . but something else did.

"The second envelope," I said, "the one you were supposed to get the slip for . . . ? If all you had was the slip, how would you know Hamilton had really mailed it?"

Doubt passed through her eyes. To lie or not to lie—but then she made up her mind. "My father gave me the address, the address that had to be on the receipt."

"And it was an address in the Soviet Union?"

"Yes. How did you know?"

"Please—let me see it."

She took a piece of paper from the pocket of her skirt and handed it to me. The address was printed in firm block letters: *Yuri Shastov, Povonets, Karelia, USSR.*

"Do you know who this person is?"

"No. I've never heard of him. In my father's letter, there was just that name and address."

I believed her now. And I realized something else too: Subotin must know all about this. Because Alain had lied; he'd told me he'd mailed the letter, but not that he'd obtained a receipt—and why else would he do that unless he wanted to cover up the fact that Subotin had taken it from him?

I looked back at May. "You spoke to Hamilton?"

"Yes. In the letter, my father told me how I should reach him. I flew to Paris and I spoke to him yesterday—"

"When?"

"In the morning first, then late last night. That's when he told me how to get here."

I thought it through and it worked out. Yesterday, when I'd seen

Hamilton on the barge, he'd already spoken to her: which was why he'd had so many questions for me—and why, above all, he wanted reassurance that Brightman really was dead. I'd given him that; maybe that's why he'd agreed to see her. Yes, I thought, all of this fitted together, and all my suspicions about May came to nothing . . .

Because, indeed, I so much wanted to believe her. I watched her now as she stepped across the salon, peeled off her kerchief, and shook out her hair. How extraordinary she looked. In that cape and her thick wool skirt she looked like a peasant—or a perfect aristocrat, a country lady who'd just returned from a fine muddy tramp across her estate. And how alive she was. Her father was dead, she ought to be grieving, and yet she was radiant. Did she already know the truth about Harry? Was she feeling relief that his long struggle was over?

She may have sensed these questions forming in my mind, for now she broke in: "You think Hamilton's dead, don't you?"

"I'm not sure. But you should leave. There's no reason for you to stay. The first letter—the one to Cadogan—will never be mailed, and the second one, to Russia, already has been."

An anxious look crossed her face. "You can't be sure."

"I'm sure. I can't explain how, but I am."

She took this in and considered; then decision, and relief, settled into her face. "All right, then, we should leave together. If he's dead, if there's no reason to stay . . ." She came towards me, then leaned forward and kissed me, a soft press of her lips on my cheek. My response to this—the desire I felt—was as pure and unexpected a sensation as the astonishment I'd felt on first seeing her. Something had happened that had wiped the slate clean . . . whatever had kept us apart in the past was now gone—it was as if I'd never met her before, and therefore I could be attracted to her all over again. Gently, I kissed her. "I have to stay," I said. "He may have hidden something that might connect him and your father."

She stepped back. "I don't want you to do anything more. You'll hurt yourself. You'll hurt me."

"May, you're not afraid for me, or for yourself. You're still protecting *him*. But Harry's dead—anyway, I know all his secrets."

"Robert . . . you may think you do, but you don't. Nobody does—I'm not even sure that I do."

344

"You're wrong. I know everything. Russia. The gold and the furs. Who he was, what he did. What Hamilton did . . ."

"Dear God . . ."

"There's only one secret I don't know—I don't know how much *you* know, or when you found out."

She turned away and a long moment passed. In the silence, I could hear the waves working at the hull. She turned slowly around. "Can't you guess? After you asked me to marry you, I went up to see him, and that's when he told me. That's why I couldn't . . . go through with it."

Silence. The whole world suspended. I couldn't move; I couldn't feel. I could only watch my feelings mirrored in May's face—in her anguished expectation of my pain, in the consolation she longed to offer but knew was much too late.

I felt a spasm of grief, of sympathy—as if for someone else—and then a terrible regret. I could have cried—but part of the price I'd paid was the loss of all my tears. So May wept for me, a final testament to what we'd almost had. She whispered, "What a time to tell you."

I held her against me and tried to smile. "I always was a little curious. And I never did believe that nonsense . . . whatever it was you told me."

"But I couldn't tell you the truth. My father said he couldn't let me marry you without knowing because he was afraid that the police were on to him. Our lives might be ruined, but he didn't want to ruin yours. I almost did tell you later on. But it was too late then. And everything had changed with Harry; I couldn't leave him once I knew."

I'd already seen that our lives, though separate, had been on a curious parallel, both of us living in the shadow of our fathers. But Harry was dead and she was free; that had to be the reason for the transformation she'd undergone. Now, looking at her, phrases began going through my mind. We can get together now. Start again. . . . But that's where those phrases stayed—in my mind. Something held me back.

Then she tensed against me: a dull knocking sound echoed through the hull.

I held up my hand. "Wait here," I whispered.

345

But she followed me up the steps, and as I entered the wheelhouse, I had to hold her back. "Keep your head down. If something happens, get off the barge and run."

After listening a moment, I stepped out on deck. The rain drowned every sound in the splash and hiss of falling water but there didn't seem to be anything alarming; on the bank, just beyond the barge, an old man was trudging along the path, a fishing rod over his shoulder. But then I heard another thump against the hull and edged across the deck to the rail. I leaned out and took a quick look down.

Behind me, May called softly, "What is it?"

I turned. "It's all right. But look, you have to go—staying here is dangerous."

"Come with me, Robert."

I shook my head. "I can't. I have to stay and search the boat. And I'm not sure how it's happened, but this is my story now as much as yours."

She was thinking a step ahead of me. "Robert, please don't go to Russia."

"Don't worry—I'll be all right. But you must go now. You have a car?"

"Hamilton told me to leave it on a side road."

"All right. Don't go back to Paris just yet—drive around, stay in a few hotels. Then, if you want, go back to Canada."

"You'll call?"

"Of course."

"But if I'm not there . . . you mustn't worry." She tried to smile. "Who knows? I might go travelling."

"Somehow we always find each other."

She nodded, and then, quickly, she stepped across the deck and jumped down to the bank. She gave a little wave, and turned along the path.

Then I crossed the deck and leaned over the rail. My eyes searched the muddy water. It was still there. A twist of tattered cloth . . . a lump that bobbed up, then rolled under again . . . all shrouded in a cloud of greasy red.

Paul Hamilton, wrapped in the flag of his own choosing.

I stepped back and buttoned up my coat. Subotin had a good head start, and Russia—as Brightman surely knew—is a long, long way from anywhere.

There was no time to waste. I clambered off the barge and hurried down the path.

10

After Vienna, the plane headed north, over Czechoslovakia, and then east, across Poland.

Soon it became hard to know where we were, but as the miles drifted by the landscape grew whiter, and the rust-red blotches of the winter-ploughed fields showed up like the patches on a piebald pony. With the snow, my Russian memories began: closing my eyes, I could see the sun set over Lake Baikal and flash from the bright domes of Suzdal, and when I listened hard even the roar of the Kuznetsov turbofans was drowned out by the deep-throated music of the language itself.

This was an Aeroflot flight, and our destination was Leningrad. I'd been here so often before, but what was I doing here now? Charlottesville, Halifax, Paris . . . Leningrad had to be the end of the trail, yet I kept feeling I'd been moving in a circle.

But I had more concrete problems ahead of me. Who was Yuri Shastov? Why had Brightman's package ended up in Povonets, a dot on the map four hundred miles north of Leningrad? And even more difficult than these questions was the consequent one of how I was going to answer them, for I was now proposing to enter the greatest police state in history and operate in a fashion that would be both clandestine and illegal. To make matters worse, I was an American; worse still, a journalist. This meant automatic suspicion and possibly surveillance . . . which was precisely what I had to avoid.

Leningrad's airport is south of the city. There's a perfectly good airport bus that takes you right down the Nevsky, but I've always preferred a cab—and so that's what I took after we landed. It was a cold, grey day; the first snowbanks were heaped up at the side of the road, and in the fields the frozen earth was the colour of steel.

I asked the driver to take me directly to the Astoria. The beds may sag and creak, it takes about an hour to fill up your bath, but

347

the place still manages to be comfortable. I unpacked, then left the hotel and walked across St. Isaac's Square to the main office of Intourist. After a long argument and several loudly dropped names, I got what I wanted: an approved travel itinerary and a dark blue Zhiguli—a Russian Fiat—which I picked up at the Aeroflot Terminal on the Nevsky Prospekt. From there, I returned to the Astoria.

It was around three o'clock in the afternoon; I lay down on the bed and waited for the phone to ring.

Because I knew it would.

Presumably Subotin had ways of getting into the USSR without attracting attention, but for me that was impossible. Having worked here as a journalist, I was listed in too many files. Besides, in Paris I'd pulled some strings to get a visa inside twenty-four hours. Each of those strings had had a bell at the end; inevitably, they'd start to ring here.

The first call was from a man I knew in Tass's translation section, just to say hello. Then there was someone at UPI who said he'd been tipped off by Aeroflot. Lastly, at a quarter to five, I was welcomed to Leningrad by an official greeter from the Soviet Union of Journalists. I'd met Viktor Glubin before. He was a typical bureaucrat, but just this once I was glad to see him. Before picking up Subotin's trail, I had to cover my own. The KGB would have noted my arrival and to reassure them I'd carefully prepared a soothing little explanation. Now I needed someone to deliver it. For that, Viktor Glubin was perfect and I happily accepted his invitation to dinner.

Glubin was a chubby, rumpled man, with a sour, puckered mouth. I bought him a drink in the Astoria bar. Trading gossip about various journalistic acquaintances, everything proceeded quite normally. Later, he took me to the Byka, an Azerbaijani restaurant. The otherwise gloomy atmosphere was enlivened by some bright rugs on the walls and a band. In Russia, there's always a band—Russians consider dancing a necessary part of a night out.

Azerbaijan is a Soviet Socialist Republic wedged between northern Iran and the Caspian Sea, and the cuisine something like Turkish. I started with stuffed vine leaves, then went on to *shashlik kebab*—accompanied, not very authentically, by Starka vodka, which Glubin poured out remorselessly, glass after glass. With my

348

tongue thus loosened, I blurted out all my secrets, including my *true* reasons for being in Leningrad. I was writing a book, it seemed, a personal book that would contain anecdotes and reflections based on my years in Russia. The idea behind the trip was to revisit all the places where I'd lived or travelled before.

Viktor, listening dutifully, gave me an understanding nod. "It sounds very interesting, Robert. It will be a book full of feeling."

Then, showing he'd read my file, he remarked that I would have a long trip, for I'd lived in so many places—Kiev, Moscow, even Semipalatinsk—and we drank to each of these spots in turn. He grinned happily, and somehow there was nothing objectionable, or even hypocritical, about all this. We were in Russia. He knew, and I knew, that the purpose of our dinner was to enable him to make a report to the police. My story seemed to have convinced him, and after a time I set down my glass and looked around the room. The band had started up again, some tune I didn't recognize. Opposite our table a pretty blonde adjusted the straps of her dress, then gave her hand to a soldier wearing the blue beret of a Soviet paratrooper. Everyone started to dance.

After a time, even Viktor got up, though only to announce a trip to the washroom. I took another sip of vodka, then a forkful of baklava. My eyes kept coming back to the blonde: she was a real stunner. But then, as I watched her, I began to catch the quick, wary looks she kept darting to the far corner of the room. I followed those looks . . . and that's when I saw him. Short, chunky, but wearing a well-tailored dark blue suit that slimmed him down. I should have spotted him before, I realized, because he was the only person in the place with a table to himself.

I should say that I wasn't afraid, though, right away, I had no doubt that he was there because of me. KGB officers come in all shapes and sizes. Many are thugs, but most are merely the petty bureaucrats of oppression that all totalitarian states need. Very few of them actually have much involvement with espionage or even foreigners, and those that do are relatively sophisticated. Like this man. And I took that as a good sign. If they'd intended anything nasty, they would have sent someone else.

When the music stopped, he got up from his table and crossed the room.

"Mr. Thorne?"

I nodded and said, "That's right."

"My name is Valentin Loginov, Mr. Thorne. Viktor mentioned that he'd be bringing you here tonight and asked me to drop by. He thought it might be useful if we talked."

The blonde, returning to her table, looked away; a waiter, hurrying past, averted his eyes.

"May I?" he said.

I nodded.

"It's a good band?"

"Not bad."

"For rock and roll, however, a band doesn't work. All those instruments get in the way. The musicians prefer Tommy Dorsey and Benny Goodman, but the people no longer like them."

I expect he was right. As they began "Serenade in Blue", only a few people got up and danced.

"Of course," Loginov said, "Benny Goodman began with a trio—him and Gene Krupa. And then Lionel Hampton."

"I don't know much about music . . . about swing."

He smiled. "It only shows I am much older than you."

No; it showed that he was "friendly", and that he wasn't a hick. He was about fifty, with a barrel chest and a fair belly. He wore a small pin in his lapel: a cross made by a flyer's wings and a propeller, the insignia of the Soviet airforce. KGB officers frequently hold commissions in other branches of service.

I said, "I'm afraid Viktor didn't mention you'd be joining us, Mr. Loginov."

"That is because I wasn't sure that I'd be able to. Happily, however . . ." He smiled pleasantly and turned his hands palms up. Then the waiter came hurrying up, setting down an extra glass; and naturally it was Loginov who poured out the vodka—a straightforward demonstration of who was in charge.

I said, "You have the advantage, Mr. Loginov. I think you must know more about me than I do about you."

He brought out a packet of John Player's Special, and extended one to me. "I suppose that is true. To begin with, I have read almost everything you have written." He lit our cigarettes. "You've done your best to understand our country and you are a fair man, Mr.

Thorne. That doesn't make you less critical, but intelligent criticism is as rare as . . . good advice."

He lifted his glass. "Let us drink to that—to good advice."

As he put his glass down, Loginov added, "Perhaps I can return the favour, Mr. Thorne. Not with advice, exactly, but information."

"Really? Your organization isn't famous for passing it out."

He looked very levelly at me. "Look, Mr. Thorne . . . I have mentioned no organization, and there is nothing official about this conversation. Tell me to leave, and I will. And there will be no repercussions." He paused, then added, "I would simply like to help make your stay more profitable."

I said, "As you know, Mr. Loginov, I'm a journalist. Information is one thing I never have enough of."

"Good. As it happens, I am especially well informed about the subject of your current project . . . which Mr. Glubin mentioned to me."

I said, "I see," though of course Viktor Glubin had supposedly known nothing about my current "project" till twenty minutes ago.

Loginov nodded. "Yes," he said. "The dissidents. Naturally, they are a subject of great fascination in the West. But they are much misunderstood. I'm sure it would be very worthwhile for a man of your sensitivity to tackle the subject."

I leaned forward. "Mr. Loginov, just for the record, my current project has nothing to do with the dissident movement."

"No?" He looked sceptical. "Possibly it is a confusion of terminology. It may become clearer as I go on."

He was a KGB officer and this was Leningrad; if he wanted to go on, I had no intention of trying to stop him. I leaned back in my chair. "I don't suppose you're a dissident, Mr. Loginov?"

He smiled. "Not quite. But I have personal knowledge of many of them. You see, what people in the West don't understand is that the liberal dissidents are very few in number and are almost all drawn from the elite elements of Soviet society . . . our intellectuals, scientists. Of course, any regime must pay some attention to what its top people say, but in the final analysis they don't count, for they have no popular power."

"You mean, they are separated from the masses."

"Sneer at the words, Mr. Thorne, but not the idea. You

understand, this isn't because the people love Communism. In Russia, Mr. Thorne, Communism is not even a bad joke any more, just an old one. It simply doesn't work. It's like that old story about Gorky. He was supposed to have visited a wonderful, modern factory, but when he asked them what they made, they told him, 'We make signs that say LIFT OUT OF ORDER.' That's Communism for you—and everyone knows it. But this 'everyone', you see, is Russian. And 'democracy' is not Russian, 'freedom' is not Russian, 'human rights' are not Russian. These ideas come from the West, and that is why the liberal dissidents have always been doomed."

After a moment, I said, "But what does all this have to do with me?"

"For that I return to the 'liberal' dissidents. They can't succeed—they're too identified with the West. Ordinary Russians, even if they're unhappy with the state of affairs, can find nothing there—so they look to themselves, to Russia, to their past. It began in the sixties quite innocently, with our students. Something was formed called the All-Russian Society for the Protection of Historical Monuments. By sixty-seven they had three million members. . . . Which was just the tip of the iceberg. Underground, you began seeing ultranationalists taking over. . . . You must have heard of them?"

"Yes," I said. "Vladimir Osipov. A Slavic nationalist: Russia for the Russians as opposed to the Uzbeks, the Tartars, the Jews, and all the other minorities."

Now I was making connections: I was hearing Travin's voice on the phone—*We can talk about the* byliny *or the* beguny . . . and there was that émigré paper I'd found in the camp rubbish.

Carefully, I said, "You surely don't expect me to believe you're really afraid of them?"

He shook his head. "That is not the point, Mr. Thorne. No one—from 'below'—will overthrow this regime. But do you think our good Party people do not see the grave problems that now face the Soviet Union? Naturally they do. Let me give you even a single example. Everyone knows that Soviet agriculture is a disaster. But why? The reason is the system itself. It has failed, Mr. Thorne."

"So change systems."

"Yes, but how do you do that and keep the Party in power? If you take the system apart, and put it together in a different way, you must have a new glue."

"You're saying that elements in the Party are thinking that an extreme right-wing form of nationalism—"

"—might create in the country the sort of spirit that saw us through the war with the Germans. And where does this sort of ideology traditionally flourish?"

"The military, you mean?"

He nodded. "I don't wish to exaggerate," he said. "Nothing will happen about this today or even next month . . . but five years from now? Who knows . . . ? In any event, there is one aspect that you might find especially of interest. It concerns the West, you see. A clandestine group are trying to establish themselves outside of Russia. . . . They are, if you like, putting the resources together."

I saw that such a group would need a Western base. And establishing this would require resources . . . such as some old gold certificates worth a cool twelve million dollars.

Loginov now leaned forward, resting his elbows on the table. "Mr. Thorne, the men I've been describing to you are very, very dangerous. You said that you had no interest in the dissidents: if so, nothing is lost. On the other hand, if you do have an interest in this, be warned. Above all, Mr. Thorne, understand that if you ever meet *this* man, you are meeting a killer."

And then, reaching into his jacket, he drew out a small white envelope and handed it to me. Inside, there was a crudely lit photograph, a head-and-shoulders shot of a young man in a Russian army uniform. Dark eyes, the face almost squeezed, the teeth shoved forward into the mouth . . . and though the photograph was in black and white, I knew the crew-cut hair had to be red.

I said, "Can you tell me, Mr. Loginov . . . did this man ever work for your employer?"

"Let us not be coy, Mr. Thorne. Aleksandr Subotin worked for the GRU. It is even possible that he still does." The GRU: Soviet military intelligence, once a genuine rival to the KGB, but now a sort of subsidiary. "But I can tell you no more than that," Loginov added, as he got up. "From this point, you are on your own." For a moment, he stood by the table, then I watched him leave.

As I got up to go, the band began playing again—"You Light Up My Life"—and everyone was dancing cheek to cheek. Waiting till the end, I clapped with the others, and then went into the street.

IT WAS SNOWING as I left the restaurant, large, soft flakes that floated down so lazily you could follow each one individually. The snow caught on my eyelids and turned the globes of the streetlights into stars which sparkled magically in the darkness.

I thought over what Loginov had told me. Did I believe him?

Yes, I could believe it. . . . Yet the more I thought about it, the more I felt that this wasn't the real importance of Loginov's message for me. It was the manner, rather than the substance, of what he had said that struck me as crucial. He'd been so cautious: he'd offered me "information" and "advice". But he was a KGB officer, and a KGB officer shouldn't have the least reason for caution.

I thought I knew why he'd played games. May Brightman, Dr. Charlie, Dimitrov, Nick Berri, Hamilton: all the separate elements I'd discovered circled one central point—Harry Brightman and Harry Brightman's gold. This was obviously the "resource" Subotin was seeking. But Harry Brightman had been a KGB agent, so if he had buried the treasure, who had told Subotin where he should dig? There was only one possible answer: *even if Subotin and his group were rooted in the Soviet military, they must have had good lines into the KGB*. There was no other way they could have got on to Brightman in the first place. Obviously, Subotin had allies in high places; and once they got on to me, they could come down hard. So I had to move in fast and get in and out of Povonets before anyone noticed.

Assuming I was under surveillance, I tried to appear perfectly normal. I was following a reasonable route back to the hotel—and now I stopped, lit a cigarette, and looked casually down from the People's Bridge over the Moyka River. It was already beginning to freeze, the wind slithering white snakes of snow across a skin of shiny black ice. Still, it wasn't too cold for a walk, so I crossed the street, keeping to a slow pace like a man deep in thought.

Back at the hotel, I also took my time: I bought a copy of *Pravda* and left a wake-up call at reception. Then I took the lift up to my floor.

It was now eleven twenty-five. I washed my face and spruced myself up—a fresh shirt, a different tie, a navy blazer—then laid my coat out on the bed. It was an Aquascutum raincoat with a zip-in lining that now proved handy. Opening it up, I packed away a couple of shirts, a sweater and a pair of socks, then stuffed it into a pillowcase and put my boots on top. Knotted up, this made a fancy version of a hobo's satchel. Doubling a towel around my hand, I gave the window a couple of hard raps, cracking the glass. With my penknife, I wiggled the pieces of glass away from the frame. My room was at the back of the hotel, looking down on an alley. When the hole was big enough, I pushed my bundle out. It disappeared in the darkness and I didn't even hear it land.

Midnight.

I left my room, walked along to the lifts and went down to the bar. It was old, rather gloomy; a fuzzy imitation of a British club. I sat at a table with a Danish designer and two German lawyers. They all knew Leningrad well. We traded stories, compared notes. Around one o'clock, one of them asked us all back to his room for a nightcap. I declined, saying I was too tired, but went with them as far as the lifts. Then I headed straight for the lobby, and two minutes later was out on the street. No one had noticed my departure and with luck I wouldn't be missed till the next day.

Outside, the snow was still falling in sharp, slanting streaks. It took me a good ten minutes to find the alley—somehow, the world looked different down here than it had from my window. But finally, shaking with cold, I blundered into it and found the pillowcase. I got into my boots, then put on the raincoat, pulling the belt tight to stop all the stuff I'd packed inside from slipping down to the hem.

Now I made my way to my car, parked about two blocks away. The engine coughed, then kicked over, falling into a ragged, faltering idle. Letting it warm, I looked down the street. At the far end there was a glow from St. Isaac's. A block beyond this a taxi passed by, but nothing else moved; just the snow, slicing down through the glow of the streetlights. So if I was being watched, which I doubted, it was being done very well. For the time being, I'd disappeared into thin air—but now I had to pull the same trick with the car. It was the weak link. It was too easy to trace.

I turned on the headlights. The Zhiguli finally agreed to go into gear with a grind and a clunk. Slowly, I rolled down the street.

I know Leningrad like the back of my hand, and no one watching me drive would ever have guessed that I was a foreigner. I made for the Novaya Derevnya, the old country-house district on the city's far side. Here I pulled into Service Station No. 3.

It was the standard Soviet garage, with several islands dispensing *benzin* and a breezeblock building with an old woman behind a slot in the window. Since few petrol stations in Leningrad are open all night, they were doing good business. Cars, lorries and a couple of snowploughs jockeyed for position. I got into line behind an ancient Skoda and walked up to the booth .with its driver when our turn came.

"Not a good night," he said.

"If it gets any worse, I will stop in Novgorod," I replied. "At my cousin's."

We went inside, where I paid for twenty litres, then trotted briskly back to the car: in Russian petrol stations you pay the attendant for the petrol, then he dials it up on a sort of telephone gadget, which turns on the hose.

When I was finished, I pulled over to one side. I was still in the light here, but at the very edge of its arc. As cars and lorries moved in and out of the service area they hid me from anyone inside the booth.

I got out, opened the bonnet and checked the dipstick; it was fine. I wiggled the battery connections; terrific. But then, apparently discovering something wrong, I fetched the toolkit. Taking out a screwdriver, I fussed for a couple of minutes. Then, leaving the bonnet up, I got back in the car, sitting in the front seat but leaving the door open.

Five minutes passed.

Traffic, mainly lorries, kept pulling into the station. As they came up to the pumps, their powerful headlamps shone right at my little car, stretching a long wedge of shadow behind it. When I stepped into this darkened patch, I must have been almost invisible. I worked around to the service area. Extending out from the back of the building was a metal fence with a gate; I just pushed hard to shift the snow behind it and stepped quickly through.

I was in a small asphalt area where they kept the cars that were

356

waiting for repair. I saw the one I wanted in the back row. Another Zhiguli. It was dark green, but at night it would be hard to tell from the one I was driving. The front end was a twisted mess, but the licence plate was intact and hanging by only a single bolt. I levered hard with the screwdriver—one ugly screech—until it popped free. I went around to the back and set to work. In ninety seconds I had both plates shoved under my coat as I headed back to the gate. In twenty minutes, the snow would have covered my tracks and it might be days before anyone noticed the missing plates.

I returned to my car.

With its bonnet up and the door still open, it seemed part of the landscape. I slipped inside, shoving the plates under the seat, then started the engine . . . though my door remained open and the pantomime still wasn't over. I let the engine warm. At last, getting out, I slapped the bonnet back into place; and this time, getting back in, I pulled the door shut. Both my coming and going had been so gradual that I felt sure neither would have been noticed.

I edged into the road.

A mile away, in a side street, I pulled up at the kerb, and ten minutes later, despite the cold and my clumsy fingers, one Zhiguli had vanished and the other had taken its place. For one night at least, I had no official identity.

I sped out of the city and into the blackness of the subarctic night. The wind rocked the little car, but the road was level and reasonably straight. I kept the speedometer at ninety kilometres per hour, and the miles unwound.

I travelled along the southern edge of Lake Lagoda, the largest lake in all Europe, and the void beyond the car took on a limitless sheen. There were one or two towns, then at Olonets the road swung north and east, across country. Five am. . . . Now I was into Karelia, a stubby finger of rock and bush that sticks up between the Finnish border and the arctic seas.

I was tired by now; my shoulders ached and my eyes burned. At Pryazha I fell in behind a couple of empty timber lorries. Huge black chains, used to strap the logs on, jostled and jolted on their long, flat beds, and I followed their thumping music through the wind, the night, and the snow into Petrozavodsk, the capital of the Karelian Autonomous Soviet Socialist Republic.

As a grey, bleary dawn streaked the horizon, I cut through the western edge of the city, then rejoined the main road. Around nine thirty, I met a side road that led due north. It was the single track through an almost trackless waste. To my right was the pure-white desolation of Lake Onega—the second largest lake in Europe; on my left, endless pine forest, the boughs of the trees pressed low by the fresh white snow. With only an occasional glimpse of a railway line for company, I kept on, beating the miles into submission. Medvezh'yegorsk was the last sizable spot on the line. After that, the road swung inland. Two or three kilometres went by, then the road narrowed, and finally I could see a scattering of buildings along the rocky shore of the lake. I knew this was Povonets, home of the man who'd inherited Harry Brightman's strange fortune.

I eased back on the accelerator. All at once, I felt very tired. I'd come a long way; I only hoped this was the end of the line.

11

A few streets of rutted ice and mud . . . grey log buildings and metal shacks . . . black smoke oozing out of stovepipe chimneys. . . . This was Povonets. And a million other Russian villages.

In this place, a strange car would attract immediate attention, so I took the first turning I came to. It was a cul-de-sac, and at the end of it stood the burned-out shell of a breezeblock building.

I stopped the car and got out. The sound of the door closing behind me hung in the cold air. I didn't move. The trees and the snow seemed to go on for ever, stretching out under the endless grey sky. The wind worked softly, smoothing out the fresh snow.

I walked back towards the main road. It was irrational, but inside the car I'd felt a certain sense of security. Now I was feeling nervous as hell. In front of me the road sloped sharply downhill, and I could see the lake and the village in the distance.

I had to show myself some time. There was no other choice. To find Shastov, I would have to speak with someone; in fact, I'd have to pass as a Russian. I knew I could manage this up to a point, because I speak the language flawlessly. But I had no papers—one inquisitive *militsia* and I was finished—and my clothes were all wrong. I was going to be noticed. All I could do was reach Shastov as fast as I could, then get out before people began asking serious questions.

At the foot of the hill, the road levelled out and ran for three quarters of a mile until, quite suddenly, I found myself at the end of the village's "main" street.

Low, shabby buildings pressed together: log *izbas*, frame structures, one large, boxlike hut coated with peeling stucco. There were no pavements, but narrow, slushy trails, like chicken tracks, crisscrossed the street. There was an air of total abandonment.

Up ahead, a parked bus was chugging away, its exhaust spreading a sooty fan over the snow. It was in front of a dark, squat structure, probably the village store. Almost certainly they'd know where Shastov lived, though asking would create its own risks. But I had to start somewhere.

There was a porch on the front of the store, supported by heavy logs still covered with bark. A nail had been driven into one of these to hang a hurricane lamp, and the skis, snowshoes and sacks piled up around the door made me think of old steel engravings of "Life in the North".

I pushed the door open. At once, I was swallowed up in a fog of tobacco smoke and coal-oil fumes. I was in a low room divided by a wooden counter. Behind was a window, so obstructed by various pots, pans and other goods hanging from hooks that it admitted almost no light. There was a plank floor, spread with sawdust to stop the cold from seeping up.

A middle-aged woman, at the far end of the counter, grunted, "The electricity has been turned off, so I regret that the store is now closed. Tonight, at six, we will open again. When they turn it back on." In this dark corner of the room the woman was lost in the shadow of a stovepipe, which stretched from an immense black space heater to a hole in the ceiling. She was a stout woman, her bulk being further increased by layers of sweaters and shawls.

"Perhaps you could help me anyway," I said. "And . . . would you have any cigarettes?"

"Only *papirosi*."

I said, "*Papirosi* will be all right."

She reached under the counter. *Papirosi* are cardboard tubes

359

with loose tobacco inside. Inhale too deeply and you get a mouthful; puff hard and you're likely to spray ash all over the room. The woman eyed me. "You are from Moscow," she said.

I didn't argue. "That's right."

She smiled. "If you don't mind, I'll have a good look. We don't see many from there."

I smiled back, then shrugged. "I'm from Moscow, but I was born in Pestovo . . . which you've never heard of, just as people there don't know Povonets."

"So what do you want, Moscow Pestovo?"

"I'm looking for a man named Yuri Shastov. I want to know where he lives."

Her mouth tightened. She didn't like that; friends know where their friends live—and so anyone who asks isn't a friend. I tried to seem casual. "I have a message, from an old friend. He told me where to go—the road near the burned-out factory. I walked up there, but no one had heard of him."

She hesitated, then made up her mind. "He's never lived there. Everyone knows . . . I suppose there's no harm . . . he rarely comes here any more. He lives on the second road to the canal. You'll have to walk to the end of the street. You can recognize his house by the fancy roof over the well."

"Ah, I see, then. Thank you."

She smiled. "It's no trouble . . . helping a man from Pestovo."

"But you've saved me a great deal of trouble—and in Pestovo I will tell everyone that they must help you when you come there."

She laughed then, and, indeed, the chances of her ever leaving this village were purely humorous.

I retreated through the gloom. Outside, I heaved a sigh of relief. She'd found me convincing, but this just bought time. At six, when the store opened again, she would have choice gossip to sell to her customers. Who would come all the way here from Moscow to see Yuri Shastov? There was one simple solution: get out of here before six o'clock rolled round.

I turned up the street. The sun was now trying to come out, and it had grown a bit warmer; the snow was turning sticky as cake. Following the storekeeper's directions, I kept straight on. As the houses petered out, the road swung inland, away from the lake.

After a mile or so, I paused to rest at the top of a little hill. I could see a fair distance. Behind me was the white plain of the lake; further on, the woods thinned, and I guessed that I was seeing the line of the canal. It was only when the storekeeper had mentioned this word that I'd remembered the significance of Povonets. From 1931 to 1933, more than 100,000 people had starved, frozen, or otherwise perished while constructing the Belomor Canal, linking the White Sea, between Murmansk and Archangel, to Lake Onega. This was its southern end.

Ten minutes later a road crossed the one I was on: the "first" canal road, I assumed. A lorry had turned off it, giving me fresh tracks to follow through the thick snow, and now I moved faster. By one thirty I reached the second road, and then minutes after that I arrived at Shastov's house, a cabin of squared logs, with a steep, slanting roof.

I headed up the snow-covered path which ascended a gentle slope through the birch trees. It was clear no one—Subotin, for example—had passed here in hours. I knocked. And at once, as if he'd been waiting for me, a voice softly called, "Come in, come in."

I lifted the iron latch and pushed, releasing a little avalanche of snow before me.

Stepping ahead, I found myself in a darkened, smoky room. The log walls were blackened with soot, the plank floor was strewn with straw, and a fire smouldered on an open hearth. The only other light came from two paraffin lanterns. They were on a stool drawn up beside a wing chair of enormous proportions: curved legs ended in eagle's claws gripping brass balls; a seat as large as a bed. Ancient, very worn, it was covered in a faded paisley brocade, but this still had a sheen, as if it had been lovingly polished for years. In such a place, a chair like that was an incredible sight.

The light from the lamps spread through the shadows with a silky glow, transforming everything it touched; and the chair was like a jewel box with a diamond nestled inside. Appropriate to this, the chair's contents was enclosed in layers of blankets and rugs, the whole being edged by a sheet as white as tissue paper. The diamond, however, took the form of a little old man. Very wizened, he had bright dark eyes and a flowing moustache—and those eyes were the real points of light in the room. He was reading and,

clearly expecting somebody else at my knock, had gone back to his book. When he finally noticed me, he stared for a second before letting the book settle gently into his lap. Then he said, "Who are you?"

"Are you Yuri Shastov?"

"Naturally. And I ask you again: who are *you?*"

With those eyes staring into my face, I just told the truth. "My name is Robert Thorne, Mr. Shastov. I'm an American."

A log cracked on the hearth and a spark spat onto the floor. Frowning, Shastov closed the book. "I apologize, but I must ask you to confirm what you've said. You are an American?"

"Yes. I've come a long way to see you, Mr. Shastov. I just hope you'll understand . . . this isn't going to be easy to explain."

As I looked at his face, it was clear he didn't believe me. I could hardly blame him. It was almost certain that I was the only American—perhaps the only foreigner—he had ever seen. After a moment, he glanced away—but then, as if afraid to take his eyes off me, glanced quickly back. "All right, then, if you are from the United States of America, tell me this: What is the capital of South Dakota?"

Now it was my turn to gawk—not only because of the question but because he'd asked it in passable English. I shook my head. "I have no idea."

"That surprises me, since you are an American. The answer is Pierre."

"Really? And what is the capital of *North* Dakota?"

Those eyes flashed even brighter. "Bismarck. I suppose a lot of Germans must live there. Am I right?"

I smiled. "Honestly, Mr. Shastov, I don't know that one either. But I *am* an American."

He shook his head. "Your English is very good for a Chekist, but your Russian is much too good for any foreigner, let alone an American. I don't understand, however. Why did you come here?"

"I am not a Chekist, Mr. Shastov. Believe me."

A moment passed. He looked at me without fear. I said, "Your English is excellent. May I ask where you learned how to speak it?"

"Perm," he said. "In a school."

"Are you from Perm?"

"It's all in my papers. You have the authority to look at them . . . as you well know."

"No, Mr. Shastov. I assure you—I have no authority at all."

He shrugged. "In my case, I have been a resident of Povonets for many years. By order of the state, you understand. I was deported here."

"Why . . . were you deported?"

A little smile flickered over his lips. "Perhaps you *are* a foreigner. Who knows why they are deported?"

I hesitated. I couldn't tell whether he was angry or amused. "You worked on the canal?"

He laughed softly. "No, no. If I had worked on the canal, my bones would be out there somewhere. I was deported here later. I was teaching in a little village not far from Perm. But I could read and write, so the Bolsheviks decided I must be a threat and Stalin sent me and my wife to this place. I was to help run the canal. The locks, maintenance, keeping records. I have been here ever since."

All the time he'd been talking, his eyes had never left my face, and I had the feeling that now curiosity was beginning to overcome his suspicion. . . . He made a quick little gesture to indicate that I should sit.

There was a table against the right-hand wall of the room. I pulled one of the chairs away from it and drew it near his. He nodded his satisfaction at this arrangement, and from beneath the rugs covering his lap, he extracted a smoothly polished black pipe, tamped tobacco into it, found matches and set it going.

I took a breath. "Mr. Shastov, let me tell you the reason I've come to Povonets, to see you. Someone has sent you, or will send you, something very valuable from the West. It will be bigger than a letter, but it will come to you in the mail."

He peered through the smoke curling from his pipe. "A letter from the West . . . the Chekists wouldn't like that very much."

"No. But I don't think they know about it, because the man who sent this letter was very clever. It will come from Paris, in an envelope from the Soviet embassy there."

"I have not had such a letter. And I can think of no one who would send such a letter to me."

"His name is Brightman. Harry Brightman."

364

I watched his eyes, but Brightman's name didn't register . . . so far as I could tell. He shook his head. "I don't know him. You are the only American I have ever met. . . . Once, in a newspaper, I saw Nixon's face."

"Well, Brightman wasn't American. He was Canadian."

He shrugged. "I still don't know him." He sat a bit more upright. "What is in this letter?"

"A great secret . . . and valuable, the way gold is valuable."

He smiled, gesturing around his little room with his pipe stem. "Now you have proof that this letter hasn't arrived."

"You have no idea what I'm talking about?"

"Exactly. You have said it very well."

I believed him; and in the back of my mind I'd been afraid this might happen. Day one: Alain puts the envelope into the mail at the Cité Universitaire. The next day, I'm back in Paris seeing my friend at Aeroflot. Two days later, the visa arrives. Another day, arranging the flight. Then yesterday. Six days altogether—not very long for a letter to move between Paris and here . . . especially considering a detour through the censor.

I said, "You have to understand that this is serious, Mr. Shastov. Several people have been killed because of this letter. I know someone who will kill *you* to get it."

The fire spat and hissed; then there was silence, enclosed only by the soft rush of the wind around the hut. Looking at me quite calmly, Yuri Shastov said, "Mr. Thorne, I am trying to believe you. Yet there is one thing I don't understand."

"What is that?"

"Why would anyone in the world send me this letter? Why me? Why Yuri Fedorovich Shastov?"

This time I was the one who looked him in the eye. "You know the answer to that, Mr. Shastov—it's your great secret, I think . . . a secret you've spent your whole life lying about."

He smiled. "Despite what I said, Mr. Thorne, I'm just an old man. Too old to have secrets."

"But I know you have at least three. Your first secret is the one you won't tell me because you're still afraid that I might be a Chekist. Then there's the secret of how you've survived to such a great age—"

"But that is no secret, my friend. Yuri Shastov, as everyone will tell you, has led a good and virtuous life."

"And finally there's the secret—and it must be a great secret—of the chair that you're sitting in and how it ever came to be here."

He chuckled softly. "Ah, well, that is not my secret at all. It was my wife's doing. The chair was always my father's chair at our home in Perm. When he died, it became mine. Then we were sent here, and I thought I'd lost it for ever, but somehow—and she never told me how—my wife found a way to get it. All the way from Perm! Can you imagine? Two winters in a row, it was almost turned into firewood, but it always survived."

He was lying to me, of course. In the past five minutes, he'd probably told me five hundred lies—and I couldn't blame him. Why should he trust me? When I began speaking again, my remark was purely conventional, uttered only to keep the ball rolling. I said, "Your wife sounds like a very remarkable woman."

"She was. She died the year before the Great Patriotic War—and you mustn't say you are sorry, for it was a blessing to miss so much that was horrible. Only now I regret that she's not here, just to talk." He smiled then, and his right hand dived under his blankets, bringing forth a small framed photograph, which he then held out to me. "She was very beautiful, as you can see."

The frame of the photograph was heavy, conceivably silver, and the picture showed a woman in three-quarter profile. She wore a black, high-necked dress and her dark hair formed a single thick wave on one side of her face. Her beauty was striking, and very Russian; if you needed someone to play Tolstoy's Natasha, this sharply featured woman with enormous dark eyes might be a good choice. And yet it was not her beauty in itself that now made my hand tremble. Rather it was a strange, ethereal quality, part aristocratic aloofness, part shyness, which was quite unmistakable. Placing the photograph carefully on the old man's lap, I reached into my coat and brought out my wallet. I'd carried two of Travin's photographs with me: one of Dimitrov picnicking with his North American comrades, the second of May Brightman emerging from her home in Toronto. This was the photograph I laid on his lap.

"If this is your wife," I told the old man, "then this must surely be your daughter."

SHASTOV'S FACE MOVED through a dozen expressions, and when he finally tried to speak, he couldn't; I suppose forty years of the unutterable was lodged in his throat. So, in the end, I did the talking. I told him everything: about Brightman, about May, about what had happened. At a certain point, I mentioned her name. May, virtually the same word in both English and Russian, had been the name he and his wife had given their child. Brightman had kept it. The tears began trickling down his cheeks, and, as he wept, it seemed to me that his tears were as much for his wife as for anything else—she had suddenly been brought back to life by that photograph, only to die once again; and, once again, without knowing that her daughter was safe.

After that, there didn't seem to be much more to say. So I waited. But then I reminded myself that this was a Russian house, and Russian homes always have one solution for grief. There was a door that led into a kitchen. It was a small, bare room, the floor strewn with sawdust, and an iron stove with a fire burning stood on its far side. I added a log and stoked it up, then found vodka and glasses in a small cupboard and returned to the front room. When I gave the old man the vodka he drank it straight back, then held his glass out for more. I poured, and this time he sipped.

"Dear God. You will think us so wicked."

"No, I don't think that, Mr. Shastov."

He wiped at his eyes with the edge of the sheet. "We had a baby in Perm, when we were first married," he said. "A baby boy. But he died almost at once. My wife was grief-stricken and swore never to have any more. And she didn't—she was always so careful. But then she thought that was all finished, that she couldn't have any more, and shortly after, she became pregnant. I was glad. Even as we were living here then I wanted a child. But she was very upset. When the child came, it almost killed my wife. She was too old. The child was all right, but my wife knew that she was going to die, and if she died, how could the child live? There was no milk here . . . there is almost none now . . . you see?"

I could see it. In that hut—so near the canal and its graveyard of anonymous bones—I could believe desperation without any limits. "Yes . . . so she thought—"

"She asked me to let her save the child's life. She said she knew people who would take her, look after her. She didn't tell me who these people were—she wrote a letter she wouldn't let me read. But she grew weaker and weaker. . . . So I let them come and take the baby away. Not long after, she died and the war came—and I told myself that whatever might happen to me, at least our daughter was safe."

"Who were the men?"

He looked me straight in the eye; and now, without doubt, I was getting the truth. "I don't know."

"Why did *they* want the child?"

"I don't know . . . I thought then they were only taking her to somebody else."

"What did they look like?"

"Ordinary men, but from the city. Two of them. One did all the talking. He had very curly hair, like Trotsky's. The other was a big man with a big chest, and he said nothing."

Harry Brightman, taken by May Brightman with her own Brownie . . . I could see it then, the dark interior of some smoky hovel, or their corner of a barrack. A baby cries. The woman's voice is desperate and weak. And Brightman waits calmly, off to one side, with Dr. Charlie's passport in his pocket. *But why? Why Yuri Shastov's little girl?*

I said, "The second man . . . that was Brightman."

"And now he's sent me this letter?"

I nodded. "And now you know why."

"No, Mr. Thorne, I still don't understand that."

I wondered if I did. Had Harry sent the money to Shastov to put everyone off the trail? Or had he decided that Shastov might be the only person on earth who had any moral claim to the gold? But then I decided that the answer was probably simpler.

"He loved his daughter, Mr. Shastov—*your* daughter. He felt he owed you a great deal, and he was trying to repay the debt."

Shastov picked up the photograph of May, held it up to his face. He said, "I owe him more than he owed me, Mr. Thorne—and I owe you as well. It is I who have the debts to repay." He set the photograph down. "And now I shall pay them. I have that letter. Olga brought it this morning—she is a woman who helps me—and it was just as you said, from the Soviet embassy in Paris."

I sat back, startled. "You're very good at keeping secrets, Yuri Fedorovich. What did the letter say?"

"See for yourself."

Hitching himself to one side, he now reached under his blankets and drew out a heavy, padded envelope. Taking it from him, I extracted the contents. There were two items. The first was a letter, typed on very genuine-looking embassy letterhead. It read: *Your letter should have been addressed to the appropriate ministry in Moscow, or directly to the government of the Republic of France. However, on this one occasion only, we have fulfilled your request.* The "request", apparently, had concerned horticulture, for the only other item in the envelope was a thick, soft-cover book from the French Department of Agriculture on apple orchards.

"This was all?"

"Everything. I had no idea what to make of it."

Carefully, I began cutting up the envelope with my pocketknife, scattering fluff everywhere. There was nothing inside, however, so I turned to the book—and it held the treasure. Stripping the spine away from the binding revealed a length of carefully fitted plastic wrap, which protected the following:

—one flat metal key;

—one birth certificate (Province of Ontario, Canada) for Harold Charles Brightman;

—one Ontario driver's licence in the same name;

—and a receipt to Brightman from a branch of the Dauphin Deposit Bank, Harrisburg, Pennsylvania.

The old man eyed me. "Have you found what you expected?"

I nodded. "The papers let you use the key . . . and the key is the key to a great fortune."

I passed the papers across to him. Turning them over in his lap, he picked up the bank receipt and squinted at it. "Harrisburg," he said. "That is the capital of Pennsylvania."

I smiled. "That one I know, Mr. Shastov. My father was from that part of the country and we spent our summers there."

Harrisburg. . . . And even as my mind had registered the coincidence, I realized, deep in my heart, that I'd known all along.

Shastov, leaning forward, handed back the papers. "They were sent to me, Mr. Thorne, so please accept them as my gift."

I said, "It creates something of a problem in this case. Other men have been searching for this. When they come here, you'll be in danger."

"Why should I be? I'll tell them I gave it to you. Or I could say I sold it to you. They'd believe that."

I looked at the old man; his notion was logical, and I wanted to get out of here fast, not only to avoid Subotin but also to reach Leningrad before I was missed. But I didn't like it.

I shook my head. "Listen, Yuri Fedorovich. What you suggest could work, but it frightens me. These men are going to be very angry to learn that I've beaten them to this. They could hurt you."

"No. For them, that would just make more trouble."

"Maybe. But I have another idea. Remember, you have a daughter again. I'm sure she would be happy to see you. Why not go to her . . . ? Wait now—I'm not crazy. I know certain things about these other men that the Chekists would *like* to know. In return for what I could tell them, I'm sure they'd let you out of the country."

He picked up May's photograph, stared at it a moment, and then his gaze wandered away. He looked around the room: sculpted by the flickering flames, it was like the inside of a cave, a cave where men had lived for centuries, like the catacombs of the old Russian Church Fathers. Finally, he shook his head. "I don't think so," he said. "I am glad to have this"—he held up the photograph of May—"but would she really want to see me?" He shrugged. "Besides, this is my home, Mr. Thorne. It may not seem much to you, but I don't think I could live anywhere else." He shook his head. "No, I will stay here. Do you have any American money?"

"Yes."

"A lot? One hundred dollars?"

"More."

"That is enough. Give it to me. If these men come, I'll show it to them. Have no fear, they'll believe me then. And you know what they'll do? They'll threaten me . . . for it's illegal to take foreign money. All I have to do after that is act frightened and tell them everything. You came here in a car—"

"A dark Zhiguli."

"Good. And you told me you were going from here . . . ?"

"Back to Leningrad."

"So, they'll believe it. And leave me alone."

He could bring it off if anyone could. "All right," I said. "But do one more thing for me. Go and stay with someone. What about this woman, Olga . . . ?"

His expression turned sour. "She wishes to marry me. On the day before I die, I may let her—but not one minute sooner. However, I'll tell her to come here. That is more natural." Then, to my surprise, he began to get up from the chair with somewhat more locomotive power than I'd assumed he could muster.

"We should go now," he said. "She'll go down to the village when the store opens again."

Passing through a curtained doorway, he emerged a few minutes later bundled up in sweaters and coats. We stepped outside. He took my arm, and I led him down to the road.

It was late afternoon now, the sky was darkening, and the grey shadows of the birches and pines stretched over the snow. I had to slow my pace to Shastov's, but after ten minutes we reached the first canal road; it was here that Olga lived.

"I'll fetch her," the old man said, "but don't come with me. It would be best that she not see you."

I nodded. We shook hands. And then, with a little spasm of embarrassment, he reached into the folds of his clothing and drew forth a small, black, leather-covered box. "For my daughter," he said. "It was her mother's. It's all I have for her . . . if you would?"

"Yes, of course."

It was a small icon, a traditional Russian present to honour a child's "name day"—that is, the feast day of the saint whose name forms part of the child's own. The sides and top were flaps, which could be folded open and propped up as a little altar. As was usually the case, an image of the saint was embossed on a small gold disc on the top flap—I didn't recognize which one it was—and this, in turn, was superimposed over a coat of arms. The Russian nobility usually employed their own arms here, but ordinary Russians, not entitled to such dignity, borrowed the national crest, the Imperial eagles of the Romanov Tsars; and this had been done here. Beautifully enamelled, outlined in gilt—a little worn—the eagles glared up at me in all their ancient glory.

"It's very lovely," I said. "I'll see May gets it."

He smiled, and his dark eyes, peering out from under a huge wool cap that came down to his eyebrows, brightened. "And you'll also remember Pierre—"

"South Dakota—"

"And Bismarck—"

"Yes, I'll remember."

"Very good." Then, with a wave, he turned away.

It was dark now; the road was empty. I trudged towards the village in the tracks of a lorry, but then swung off to my right and waded across a rocky field towards some trees. I knew this was safer than the road.

Twenty minutes later, I arrived at the car. Saying a prayer, I turned the key . . . the battery was strong and it kicked over. As the engine warmed, I thought about this incredible day. Each aspect of this "case" which I seemed to "solve" only opened up another mystery.

Unfolding the little icon, I set it up on the dashboard. I stroked the leather; it was soft as silk and I realized that it must have been in Shastov's wife's family for generations. May was the last of her line. But who was she? And what connection was there between her real identity and Brightman's disappearance? Shastov had given me most of her story, but I had no idea what that story meant. . . . *I assume that some of what Brightman told me was true*, Grainger had written. *He did get to know many men in the senior Communist leadership. So I suspect that Brightman's daughter is the child of one of those men—someone who believed he would soon fall victim to Stalin's Terror*. But neither Shastov nor his wife had been a prominent Communist. And Berri's notion wasn't much better: *Once upon a time, Dimitrov might have been your hero, but he ended up like the rest of them. By 1940, his hands were covered in blood. If he snatched a baby away from the Bolshevik, it was because he thought it might help save* him, *not the child*. No doubt he was right about Dimitrov—but how could Yuri Shastov's child save anyone?

These were the questions that occupied my mind as I headed back to Leningrad, but they seemed unanswerable. When I got back to the hotel, no one seemed to notice, and when I returned the car—the original licence plates once again in place—there was no comment.

That last night, as I lay exhausted in the Astoria, my conscience would have given anything for the power to make a call to Povonets. Had Subotin been there? Was the old man all right? I guessed he was—when it came to survival, I would have bet on him no matter what the odds—but there was no way of telling. So, the next morning, I crossed my fingers, filled out all the forms, and headed for my plane. As I felt the big engines thrust us up, I turned my thoughts to my destination—Harrisburg, Pennsylvania. Once again Brightman's secret trail circled back upon me.

12

Everywhere I looked, as I came into Harrisburg, there was a disturbing sense of *déjà vu:* a feeling of strangeness which utterly failed to disguise the fact that what I was seeing was all too familiar.

Paris: where my parents had met.

Leningrad: my own Russian city.

Now this place, where every turning led back to my past. . . .

I was still tired after the flight back; it was ten in the morning as I drove into town, but God only knows what time my body thought it was.

I hoped that Brightman's safe-deposit box might contain the answers to a few of my questions, and for that reason I wanted to be the first one into it—which meant that I was going to commit fraud. And impersonating Brightman might not be so easy.

The bank, when I reached it, didn't do much for my nerves. Guarded by fluted Greek columns, it had the air, inside, of a proud, prosperous Victorian railway station. My request to get into Brightman's box, accepted routinely, quickly produced Looks, then Professional Concern, and finally Profuse Apologies—delivered by a civil young man named Mr. Corey.

"I'm very sorry for the delay, Mr. Brightman, but there seems to have been some sort of mix-up. According to our records, this box was cancelled and all outstanding charges cleared as of yesterday afternoon."

I took it well, on the whole. No staggers; no fainting spells. Merely the sort of frown which anyone, having been informed that their safe-deposit box has been cancelled by someone else, surely has the right to assume.

"I don't know about your records, Mr. Corey, but most of yesterday I was thirty thousand feet over the Atlantic. I certainly wasn't in Harrisburg, and I certainly didn't cancel my box." Taking the key from my pocket, I held it up. "When you cancel a box, don't you take the key back?"

He looked unhappy. I'm not sure what I felt, though my anger was only part of an act—I'd come a long, long way to get to this point. In any case, a lady was fetched, who with a prim nod solved our little mystery.

"Yesterday afternoon a lady appeared, with legal papers giving her title to the box as executor of her father's will. She was Canadian, I think. And she had a lawyer."

"Do you remember her name?"

"If I remember correctly, the lady's name was also Brightman."

I was very smooth, the Truth dawning on my face with fair conviction. "This begins to make sense, Mr. Corey. Miss Brightman is my sister . . . in fact, she *is* the executor of my father's estate. I suppose some of my papers must have got mixed up with his. It's not impossible, you see. We're both Harold; I just never use the 'junior'."

Mr. Corey looked dubious. But his ultimate concern was the bank, so he took advantage of this opening to say, "I take it, then, that no harm's been done?"

"No. And certainly nothing that the bank's responsible for." I pushed Brightman's key over the counter and, before Corey could speak, extended my hand. We shook, said goodbye, and a moment later I was out on the street.

I thought hard and fast. Had Brightman made a terrible blunder and allowed some record of the safe-deposit box to stay in his will? It seemed incredible. Wills are too public . . . but then if May hadn't learned about it from the will, how else could she have?

In confusion, I made my way back to my car, and by the time I reached it, I was beginning to feel anxious. I'd shaken off Subotin in Russia, but there was no reason to think he'd disappeared for good.

374

Had May any idea of the danger she was now in? I had to find her. Conceivably, she'd gone back to Toronto right away; on the other hand—if she was driving—she might still be here. What I needed was a phone, so I walked along Market Street to a greasy spoon called the Olympia.

Therein, I wasted five quarters. She wasn't in the Sheraton, Marriott, Holiday Inn, or any of the other big places, but then it occurred to me that she never stayed in places like that. She liked funny little residential hotels that no one else knew about. I went back to my car, and drove straight through to Blackberry Street where, on the corner with Fourth Street, stood the Alva.

It was a big old place, three storeys high with the ground floor taken up by one of those old family restaurants the fast-food chains are killing. The hotel was over the restaurant. Stepping inside brought back a flood of memories, for it had changed very little since my childhood: the same alcoves, the same photograph of the prize steer they'd bought at the State Farm Show.

I asked a waitress about May—and it seemed that my logic had been right but my timing wrong.

"This is a lady with long hair, sort of red?"

"That's right."

"I know the one you mean, then. She was here for a couple of days. Just left this morning, around ten. She had one of those old Volkswagens, the kind you don't see so much any more."

So that was that.

As consolation, I decided to get something to eat, and slid into an alcove. I ordered coffee and the *spécialité de la maison*, peanut-butter cream pie. I looked around the room. There were alcoves along the outside walls, tables elsewhere. Coming right into the centre of the room was a staircase from the hotel.

After a time, my pie arrived. It was astonishing, but also delicious. As I ate it, I listened to a pretty waitress flirting with a man a few tables away. Then another man came down the stairs from the hotel, zipping up his windcheater. As he came down the last steps into the room, I could see it was Subotin. Short, red-haired, that hard, narrow face . . . he shouldered open the front door of the restaurant and passed into the street, while I, hand trembling slightly, set a forkful of peanut-butter cream pie back on my plate.

I had the presence of mind to get up and dash out of the door. I was in time to see him crossing the road, heading for a large concrete parking garage.

Relying on luck, I ran back to my car. Then I waited, breath held—because there might be a second exit from the garage which I couldn't see. But after a couple of minutes, Subotin emerged and pointed a Chevrolet down towards Second Street. There, he picked up speed and headed towards Interstate 81. I stayed right behind him, and my brain started working. What was Subotin doing here? What had led him to the Alva? Had he been looking for May? Had he missed her, just as I had—or was he *with* her?

We hit the interchange and I concentrated on my driving. Following the Marysville signs, Subotin got onto 81 South . . . a highway I know as well as any in the world. If you stay on it, you'll end up in Washington. But beyond Marysville, Subotin swung north—and, if anything, this was a road I knew even better. It went through the Blue Mountains into the Tuscaroras beyond.

In tandem, we wound our way across the peaceful, dun-coloured slopes. Soon we left the city behind and the woods thickened. We slid into a valley where there were farms, the swathes cut by the combines neatly marking the contours of the fields, and marshalled around the crossroads were all-American villages, with their steeples, picket fences, and shiny coats of white paint. I knew all these places; one by one, their names came back to me. And every time I lifted my eyes, patches of landscape jumped out of the past: the way the road, overhung by tall oaks, doubled back through this curve; a valley, opening up to display every shade of Thanksgiving brown and gold; a scar of rock on a hill. I did not need to summon memories, they were simply there, and as we entered the Tuscaroras themselves, I could hear my father explaining that the Tuscaroras were one of the most advanced of the Indian tribes.

For a time, I had the uncanny feeling that Subotin might actually lead me back to our old cabin. But then he turned down a side road which climbed up a ridge and then curved down into a narrow valley on the far side. I remembered that a stream flowed along the floor of this valley, and soon I could see it flashing beyond the cold dark trees. Because of the bends in the road, I could stay right on Subotin's trail yet remain out of sight.

It was clear he was unfamiliar with the road, for he had a map open, and he slowed at each sign. We kept on like this for seven or eight miles, until the road swung sharp right and passed over the stream. Subotin slowed right down as he crossed the bridge; I let him get clear, then followed. I knew it would be hard to lose him now: for another two miles the road would keep the stream on its left, then climb the ridge and continue on the far side. It would eventually reach Evansville and actually pass by the steps of Father Delaney's little frame church.

Just as the road began climbing, Subotin slowed, and turned down a narrow side road. Continuing past the intersection, I pulled over and stopped. He'd probably made a wrong turn: I was almost sure the side road was a dead end.

I waited for five minutes as rain began dripping from the oaks overhead. When there was still no sign of him, I put the car back into gear. But if the road was a dead end, that meant his destination must lie along it; a car would only give me away.

Killing the engine produced an edgy, unnatural silence, and as I walked back to the intersection, the quick squawk of a jay in the woods made me jump. At the side road, I hesitated, but there was no sign of Subotin. For a hundred yards I had an unobstructed view. Reluctantly I started ahead.

Now the woods closed in on all sides and the air took on a grey, misty gloom. I walked slowly, stopping to listen every few yards. Ten minutes passed and I began to worry that I'd made a real blunder—he might be miles away—but there was nothing to do except go on. Then, a moment later, I saw my first sign of man—a crudely hand-painted sign erected at the side of the road. NO EXIT it read. . . . So I'd been right. Finally, a quarter of a mile on, I saw the car. It had been run up a narrow track leading into the woods.

I stood stock-still; the car, masked by the trees, almost seemed like a predator waiting to pounce. But Subotin couldn't have seen me; if he had, I'd probably be dead. Cautiously, I walked up the track, then peered in the car's windows . . . and saw, on the back seat, one of those canvas rifle holders. Empty.

I didn't like this at all. Where was he? Then—without comment, as it were—I simply started forward. Every twenty yards or so I stopped and listened; it was just possible, if I had any warning at all,

that I could throw myself into the bush and get away—it was so thick and dark.

Ahead, the gloom lightened. After six paces, I could see that the track opened out into a clearing fringed with birches. Something gleamed there, in the shadows. I knelt down. Looking beneath the spreading branches of the pines, I could see the bonnet of a truck.

I stood up. I knew Subotin had to be there. Waiting. With a rifle. I hurriedly retraced my steps. When the track had curved enough to take me out of sight of the clearing, I paused to consider. It was possible that Subotin had merely come here to meet someone, but more likely he was lying in ambush, no doubt expecting someone to come into the clearing from the opposite direction. But as soon as I did so, I'd be a dead man.

Backpedalling another fifty yards, I found a gap in the trees and, at right angles to the track, began working my way into the woods. When I judged I was two or three hundred yards into them, I struck out parallel to the track, to cut in behind the clearing.

I heard the rush of a stream—a constant whispering behind the steady drip of the leaves—and a few minutes later, I came to its bank. In spring it would have been deep and swift, but now there was just a thin trickle of black water along the bottom of its bed. The streambed, exposed, was gravel and hard-packed mud: as good as a path. I scrambled down from the bank. In twenty minutes or so, I must have gone the better part of a mile. Then, on the bank above me, I saw a path.

It ran up to the bank of the stream, then veered away again, like the arms in the letter "K". The upper arm, I was sure, would lead back to the clearing; the lower would continue into the woods, probably to a cabin.

I stood a moment, catching my breath, then started down the lower arm of the path. I was hurrying now as fast as I could. My panting sucked in the pungent smells of wet leaves and my flushed face began stinging with pine resin and sweat. A pale patch appeared up ahead, and a moment later I could smell woodsmoke. I crept forward and, pressed down among some ferns, I peered into a small, rocky clearing.

The cabin was merely a frame shack, with a stovepipe chimney. It had a tottering, precarious air but was nonetheless clearly inhabited. A cosy plume of smoke curled out of the chimney; fresh wood was stacked by the door. I had assumed that Subotin had stopped in the clearing, but why shouldn't he have come here? He could be inside now. Someone was, without doubt. The cabin possessed one small window and a dark shape moved past it . . . and then I held my breath as the door began to swing open.

Who, in truth, did I expect to come through that door?

My fears said Subotin. But my *heart* told me my father.

Which was crazy, of course. But, in a funny way, I wasn't far wrong, for what I saw was just as miraculous.

He was a big man, heavyset, with a broad chest sloping into a heavy belly. His face was broad and genial, his hair thick. . . .

I rose and stepped into the open.

"Who are you?" he said, staring at me.

"My name is Robert Thorne . . . Mr. Brightman."

I WAS SHOCKED, stunned . . . but perhaps I should have known. I closed my eyes, and I could see May, standing on that barge in France. How beautiful she'd looked. And what else could have transformed her so, but the knowledge that her father was still alive?

Yet whatever I'd expected to find in that cabin, it had not been Harry Brightman. So long had he been the object of my curiosity, and the subject of a thousand speculations, that his real presence was almost an affront. Harry Brightman was alive. How dare he be?

The Red Fox had been run to earth.

I must have stared at him for a long time before I finally said, "I'm not sure how to talk to the dead."

"Perhaps you're supposed to blow a trumpet, Mr. Thorne."

Brightman was certainly the most substantial ghost I'd ever laid eyes on. He communicated the physical force of a man half his age. His hands were big and strong. . . .

I said, "You *do* know who I am?"

"Yes. May's told me what a great help you were."

My smile, inevitably, was a trifle ironic. "I'm sure."

"Please, don't feel resentful. Or not at her. I know how upset she was at deceiving you. And you should understand that when she first called you, everything she said was quite true. She didn't know then that I was alive. It was only later, after you had left Detroit, that I told her."

Inside the dark cabin I watched him silently as he drew a small black cheroot from the breast pocket of his checked lumberjacket shirt. Now that I knew he was alive, a good many things began to make sense. But I still wasn't sure to what extent May had manipulated me. Or had she too been duped by her father?

Struggling to take everything in, I stepped to the cabin's single window and parted the curtain. It was late afternoon now, growing darker each minute; crouched in the woods, Subotin would be completely invisible. If he was there. . . . I turned back to the room. Brightman lit his cheroot; behind the cloud of smoke it produced, his eyes regarded me impassively.

I said, "Where is May now?"

"In Toronto, I assume."

"Did she come here first, on her way?"

"I haven't seen her for weeks, Mr. Thorne."

A lie, and it stole a little of his dignity. "We don't have time, Mr. Brightman. There's no point trying to hide things. I saw Grainger. I know all about Florence Raines. And Dimitrov. I saw Berri, and he told me the truth. Hamilton . . . your embassy package . . . Yuri Shastov . . . I know all that. I know May was in Harrisburg, and I know what she was doing."

Brightman looked at me levelly. I'd told him that I'd unravelled all the secrets of his life, but he only gave a slight nod—an acknowledgment, but hardly of defeat. I added, "The pick-up in the clearing at the end of the track . . . I assume it's yours?"

"Yes, it's mine. I was about to walk up there. You can't drink from the stream any more, so every other day I go into the village for water."

"I wouldn't advise it," I said. "You'll find a man waiting there. His name is Subotin. He's Russian, he has a gun, and he's planning to kill you—or worse."

The effect of this was immediate. The skin tightened over his skull; for an instant, he was very much his age. Steadying himself, he drew on the cheroot.

"Mr. Thorne, if you know as much as you say you do, you know how important this is. Tell me—"

"I saw him at the place May was staying, and I followed him here. He's in the clearing with the truck. I went around him, following the stream, then picked up the path." I added, "I assume he followed May when she came here."

He shook his head. "May was never here. I met her in Harrisburg."

"Then he must have followed *you* from that meeting."

He walked over to the window and looked out. "Mr. Thorne, I've been covering my tracks longer than you've been alive. No one followed me here. But you say he found Hamilton—"

"He killed Hamilton, Mr. Brightman."

He turned to me. "Years ago, Hamilton was here. It's possible—"

"Does it make any difference?"

"Oh yes. He only wants the money—but May's got it now. If he found out about this place from Hamilton—if he *doesn't* know about her—then she's safe. *That's* the difference."

And now his eyes met mine. His cunning, his duplicity, dropped away and were replaced by a look of total frankness and vulnerability. This was all that he cared about; everything else was pretence. All at once, everything May had done seemed much more reasonable; she had understood how completely he was devoted to her. Feeling an echo of this now, I said quickly, "Don't be too sure."

I was right; even this one hint of doubt as to her safety flashed life back into his eyes.

"Yes," he said, "you can *never* be too sure with Subotin. Do you know who he represents, Mr. Thorne?"

"People in the Soviet military. With friends in high places."

"You have been thorough. He was in the GRU, military intelligence. His 'friends' are in the navy."

"And they want to make the USSR safe for the Russians?"

"They want power, Mr. Thorne—and they know that Communism merely gets in the way. They want an efficient economy, national loyalty, rational political structures . . . so they can have bigger guns and more submarines. They'll try to get this power through the military and the secret police. Once they've done that, they'll turn Russia from a Communist dictatorship into a military one."

"And you want to stop this?"

"No, Mr. Thorne. I just want to be left alone. That's why—I was in despair—I sent the safe-deposit key back to Russia. Let them deal with their own problems in their own damnable country. I only want to live out my life with no more shame than I already feel."

He was lying, or partly—but then he didn't know that I knew who Shastov really was. On the other hand, I understood that he wanted to make sure: that the gold no longer served as a prize that drew everyone on . . . towards May. I said, "From what I've seen of Subotin, that's not the kind of sentiment he'll find terribly compelling. He'll kill you, Mr. Brightman. Or he'll hold you as a way of getting the money from May. So I suggest we get the hell out of here."

"That sounds like an excellent idea—for you. But not me. Even if I got away, it wouldn't do any good. Now that he knows I'm alive, he'll only track me down somewhere else."

"Not if we call the police."

He smiled. "I can hardly do that. You forget: I'm dead. Buried. If I reappear . . ."

I'd forgotten that little detail—and I suddenly realized what a nasty little detail it was. But when I looked him in the eye, his gaze didn't flinch. "Whose body was it? Was it some drunk you found in an alley?"

His face twisted sardonically. "No, Mr. Thorne. He was a 'comrade'. I was attempting, through him, to make contact with our former employers."

"And what happened?"

"I'm not sure. He had never severed his connections, or at least not as completely as myself—which is what made him useful. It is possible he transmitted my requests and received certain orders in return. Or possibly he decided to kill me on his own because he was afraid that I might expose him. I threatened to do so—I admit that. In any case, he tried to kill me. . . . I killed him instead . . . The worst part was the next half hour, sitting in the motel room with his body . . . but that's when I got the idea. Preston was smaller than me, but more or less the right age. It seemed worth a try. If I failed, after all, I could simply stick with my original plan and kill myself. So I dressed him in my clothes, set him in my car, and blew his head off. It worked—worked too well for me to undo it now." He walked over to the stove and tossed his cheroot into the fire. Turn-

383

ing back, he added, "The point is, I'm now dead, and I'm going to stay that way. With me dead, everyone else is much better off."

I sensed the despair and resignation beneath the surface of this man, and more than that: a kind of self-contempt.

Perhaps he was reading my mind, for now he said, "Do you know how you can spot a Communist, Mr. Thorne? It's very simple: a Communist is that person who can most skilfully justify the greatest number of the murdered dead. Which makes me a *failed* Communist. I could no longer *justify* murder—I've lost the greatest skill I could once claim to possess."

I nodded my head towards the window. "Very interesting . . . but a bit theoretical. We have a practical problem."

"I'm being very practical. The solution to our problem is that I stay right here. As you say, Subotin will eventually grow impatient and come and find me—and either I'll kill him or he'll kill me. What I want you to do is to make sure that you're safe. God knows, you've done enough. For reasons you may be able to guess—but for others I'm sure you can't—your safety is important to me. May and I have asked far, far too much of you already, and when I said that everyone is better off with me dead, that includes you as well."

For a second, this remark hung in the air. And of course I knew then—and knew that I'd known all along. My father had spied for this man. My father had been the other man in the State Department, whom Hamilton had refused to reveal himself to. Here, at long last, was the "something personal" that Travin had hinted at. It struck like a blow—God knows I'd let myself come to see it so gradually, but for one instant I closed my eyes and winced in pain. Turning my head, I glanced out of the window. It was raining again, hissing down on the roof . . . and hissing down on Subotin, a professional killer. For the time being, we'd have to let the dead bury the dead—or we'd be joining them.

"Do you have a gun?" I asked.

"A couple of old shotguns, and I think there might be a rifle. I won't have much of a chance, but if he makes a mistake . . ."

"Do you really expect me to walk away, leaving you here?"

"Of course. Why not? If you truly want to do me a favour, save yourself and continue being a friend to my daughter."

"Just listen to me for a moment. Subotin doesn't know I'm here—

384

and he doesn't know that *you* know *he's* here. That gives us the advantage. In that clearing, he's out in the open. If I go back by the stream and you go straight down the path, we could take him from either side."

He began to protest, but then stopped himself. Because he knew it might work.

I said, "And when I say take him, I mean take him alive. If possible. Then give me a couple of hours on a telephone. I have certain contacts—CIA contacts. I can guarantee that they'd happily take Subotin off our hands. Then I don't think you'd have to worry about him ever again."

Brightman gave a little smile. "If this fails, I'd be no worse off anyway."

"Exactly. Nor would I."

He crossed the room. Pushed into a corner was a hardboard cupboard. The guns and shells were in there. Outside it was growing much darker. Not good; Subotin would be growing restive, waiting for Brightman to show. For a moment, I wondered if this whole scheme wasn't crazy, but it was the best I could think of.

Brightman brought me the gun, a venerable double-barrelled Stevens, the sort of gun I'd learned to shoot with. I loaded both barrels, then put two more shells into my pocket and looked at my watch.

"It's almost four o'clock. Give me till half past to get into position, then wait for my signal. "I'll shout *Stoy!*—Stay where you are— when I'm ready. Wait and see what happens then before you reveal yourself."

He nodded. "All right." And then he stuck out his hand—though whether this was a sign of alliance or a farewell, I couldn't be sure.

I went to the door and stepped out. The air was cold and raw; the darkening sky held all the shades of a bruise. With the drizzle, the trees in the little clearing had lost definition while the surrounding forest blurred to a dark, indefinite smudge. Slipping the gun into the crook of my arm, I stepped down from the cabin.

Then it happened.

Three hard *cracks*—a flurry of splinters flying into my hair.

Throwing myself to the ground, I scrambled desperately under the cabin, dragging the shotgun with me.

13

My breath was knocked out of me as I hit the ground, and as I twisted under the cabin a stone slashed my knee. Yet I felt nothing—not even terror: I just kept going until I banged up against one of the pilings that held up the cabin. Wedged against this, I sprawled flat on my belly. I was in a low, dark crawl-space. Six inches above my head were the floorboards of the cabin; on either side were assorted bits of junk. All I could see in front of me was a maze of pilings and the narrow strip of light where the foundation ended. And then another shot rang out and smashed through the cabin over my head, the sound feeding back with a nasty whine.

Subotin called something, but I couldn't hear what it was. Now came two more shots, one on top of the other, and I wormed back further. Sensing light behind me, I began slewing around. A cobweb stickily matted over my mouth, but I scrambled into the open, elbows working madly. As I pulled myself up a voice hissed, "Thorne? Is it you?"

I spun around—almost more startled by this than by the shots. But then I realized it was Brightman, on the other side of the cabin wall; he was whispering, his lips pressed to a crack.

"Listen! He thinks you are me. *Run!* Get into the trees. There's a path that takes you down to the stream—*stay in the stream!* Hurry!"

I could scarcely understand this—I was too confused—but even as my brain fought to get control of my tongue, I sensed Subotin, on the far side of the cabin, making his dash up to it. Here, behind the cabin, the clearing continued for perhaps fifty yards, the black massed shadows of the trees beckoning beyond. There was no time to think; I just started to run for my life, head down, lungs gasping. Leaping over rocks, blundering through bushes, encumbered with the gun, in the dying light I barely knew where I was going. Before me, the safe shadow of the forest seemed to retreat for ever, but suddenly the dark trees reached out and grabbed me.

Only then did I allow myself a look back—the clearing was empty. At once, I began running again until I stumbled onto a path. *The path to the stream.* When it joined up with the streambed I jumped down over the edge of the bank—which gave me the protection of a parapet.

Struggling to catch my breath, my face pressed to the scurf of dead grass along the top of the bank, I looked back into the dark whorls of shadow that spread into the forest. But there was nothing to see; I was safe—for the moment. But where was Subotin? What had happened to Brightman?

He thinks you're me. . . . Run. . . . Stay in the stream. . . .

Brightman was probably right. Subotin could have had no idea that I was in the cabin at all. *Subotin thought I was Brightman.* It was probably the only reason why I was still alive. Knowing Subotin's background, it was hard to believe that he could have missed me as I came out of the cabin door. But he'd not been meaning to kill, only to frighten: *because his main interest remained the money, and for that he needed Brightman alive.*

But why the stream, why stay here? Curving through the trees, the streambed was dark as a tunnel except for the faint glitter from the trickle of water that still flowed along it. Yet the darkness made very thin cover; if he knew I was there, any man up on the bank would have had a clear shot. . . .

My mind leaped back and forth—and then the detonating sound of a shot boomed through the darkness. Instinctively, I pressed myself flat. Yet, even as the shot faded, I realized it was nowhere near here . . . and I found myself staring down the streambed; *back*, towards the road if you went far enough. I skidded down the bank and headed along the stream.

I was going in the direction of danger, towards the spot where the shot had come from, but at least, in that direction, I had the chance of reaching the road and my car, while going the other way would only carry me deeper into the bush. Then the deep boom of a second shot rolled towards me—and I knew this was the sound of a shotgun, not of Subotin's rifle. Brightman was trying to draw Subotin away from my trail.

I rushed on, and soon I had no idea where I was: the dark, hulking mass of the woods up on the bank made a featureless backdrop. Then the stream narrowed sharply, compressing the water and creating a deep enough flow to force me up on the bank. Now I had to fight through bush, in the pitch darkness, until the stream broadened, its flow fell back to the same meagre trickle, and I was able to walk along the bed once again.

Five minutes later I stopped, knowing I must be close to the spot where the shots had come from. If Brightman had been giving me a chance to escape, I'd defeated his intention—but if that *had* been his intention, why had he told me to stay in the stream? Probably I should have been able to figure out the old man's plan at this point, but a moment later I didn't need to. Moving forward cautiously, I heard a sliding, scrabbling sound up ahead.

I stopped dead in my tracks.

Someone had skidded down the bank of the stream.

I held my breath; then stone knocked against stone . . . rattled away . . .

"Brightman? I know you are there. And your old blunderbuss doesn't frighten me at all."

It was Subotin. Standing just where I was, I slowly looked around. I was virtually in the middle of the streambed, which was at its widest point here. I couldn't reach either bank before he—

"Don't try to hide. Come here. I won't hurt you, Brightman."

More silence . . . crunch of a footstep . . . then the glare of a torch.

The beam probed along the top edge of the opposite bank. Shadows leaped up and danced, then the beam started moving. Wet stones and mud glistened and gleamed . . . the arc swept closer . . . I lifted the shotgun . . .

A shot boomed through the darkness. At once the light died.

But my finger hadn't touched the trigger. The shot had been fired from high up on the far bank. Brightman . . . it had to be . . . And then he fired again, a red flashing strobe that etched my shadow into the darkness. But he'd missed, for a quick burst of rifle fire exploded in front of me and sent me scrambling for cover behind a small pile of rocks.

More shots whined up the streambed. I could hear them slash through the bush, thump into the bank . . . but all on the far side of the stream from myself. And now I understood . . . *stay with the stream* . . . and a feeling passed through me that I'd never felt before in my life. I had to kill a man—there was no other choice. Brightman and I were both foxes now, and he was deliberately

388

drawing the hound close to my teeth. What I needed was cover. The rocks weren't enough; if I missed with my first shot, he'd have me.

Then, as I listened to the stream, the simplest idea of all slipped into my mind.

Quietly, running in a low crouch, I retraced my steps down the streambed—hearing two more shots crackling behind me—until I'd reached the spot where the banks constricted. Here, the water was about two feet deep, flowing swiftly.

Silently, I stepped into it.

The first touch was like ice. With the next, a steel band gripped my ankle. My foot skidded . . . but I kept going. In the middle, where the water reached up to my knees, three big rocks formed a dam, a curve as neat as the back of a chair. Wading quietly towards them, I sat down.

The shock of the cold was a fierce grip on my chest. Yet I had what I wanted—cover: even if he'd been expecting me, he'd never look here. Scooping up mud from the bottom, I blackened my face. Now I was just another rock in the black darkness. I didn't move. And then I thought that I saw him, working along, in a crouch, on the far side . . . I waited. *Don't think. Hold your breath* . . .

And then he was there, and so close I almost jumped—a bulge in the darkness that I might have reached out and touched. Now, slowly, he came up to the water. At the edge, he stepped out, onto a stone . . . only one single step more . . . The barrel of the gun was actually under the surface, the action and butt resting on my flexed knee . . . One motion. Don't think. *Do it.* Up and point and squeeze the front trigger. . . .

Did Brightman know I was there? Had he seen me? Or did he just sense me, or perhaps Subotin himself—the old fox now turning the tables and scenting the hound? Afterwards there was no time to ask, but even as my own finger tensed on the trigger, a shot erupted high on the bank. He didn't come close to Subotin, but if he'd been trying to draw the other man out, he couldn't have done any better. Because Subotin now flashed on his light. Its beam traced a brilliant path through the darkness, glistening across the wet stones, and turning his face into a smooth, silver mask. And that's when I fired. Once. Then again. For a split second, an image was burned into my retina: the banks of the stream, the man tumbling back, his arms outflung. . . . Then there was only a vague red pulse before my eyes, and I was stumbling and splashing in horror.

"Thorne, is that you? Are you all right?"

"Yes . . . for God's sake don't shoot."

My voice, that strangled sound—it had to belong to somebody else. I was dazed and freezing and trembling all over. Brightman clattered down the bank. "I only hoped you understood what I meant. He didn't know there were two of us, I was certain . . ." But I was staring down at the bloody shape in the water. The current eddied against the curve of his shoulders; bobbed his hand on the surface. And the shot whose echo had now faded in the night air summoned another, and the sight in front of my eyes was merely a memory made real.

Brightman must have understood this, for I'm sure his words were meant only to comfort, but their kindness delivered the one blow I wasn't expecting.

"Thorne, I did all I could. That afternoon, we tried everything, your mother and I, but nothing we said, nothing we did, could have—"

I looked at him in horror. "'We'—what do you mean?"

"What I say. We . . ." But then his face turned aghast. "Dear God, I assumed you knew that. They were in it together, your mother and father. From the very beginning."

ALL I COULD SAY about the next hour was that it passed: like certain hours in the depths of an illness, it took all I had to get through it.

I was stunned, physically, spiritually—if, in fact, any spirit was left to me. Half of me was already dead; the other half wanted to die. Yet we had to move fast. This was Pennsylvania. We were into the hunting season, but it was possible that our shooting had attracted attention. We were now acting out the same scenario that Brightman and my mother had acted out long ago. A bloody corpse . . . a death that had to be turned into an accident . . . I went through Subotin's pockets for his keys and spare clips of ammunition, and checked that nothing in his wallet tied him to either of us. His gun had fallen into the stream. I found it and threw Brightman's shotgun down in its place. After that, there wasn't much we could do. This was a deserted spot and he might lie here all winter; by spring, no one would be able to say what had happened.

Though Brightman was certain that no one in the area had recognized him, we had to make the cabin look as if no one had been here for weeks. He began clearing up while I changed into a pair of his trousers and then huddled close to the fire. I made us some coffee. As its burning sweetness began washing away the bitterness that now filled my mouth, I came back to myself; rose through the fever; focused my eyes. And that's when I said, "Tell me what you know of my mother."

He hesitated. "I don't know very much."

"Maybe. But about some things, you know more than me."

There was still another instant of hesitation; then, abruptly, he said, "I didn't meet her till 1942, when she came to America. I think she had been at the Sorbonne and become involved with the French Communist Party—in those days, it was all part of being young and idealistic."

"Except with her it went further."

"Perhaps. I think that she mixed herself up with some of the expatriate leftists who were in Paris then. There were a lot of Americans. That's probably how she met your father."

"Had she been recruited by then?"

"Yes, I think so."

"So their marriage—"

"No. No, she always knew, you see, that he wasn't a Communist, not really. She once told me that. 'But I love him anyway,' she said. They each acted from slightly different motives, but both were completely sincere." He paused then, lighting one of his cheroots and throwing a tin box of them towards me. "He was a diplomat who knew what the Nazis were doing and was appalled at his own country's lack of response. He once told me that the most shameful period of his life was the years when America stayed out of the war."

I steadied myself. "At that time, though, the Russians weren't in the war, either."

"No, but he excused them. They signed the Molotov-Ribbentrop Pact to buy time, not because they wanted one quarter of Poland. And that's when he started working for them. I assumed control over him after the war."

I'd been sitting wrapped in a blanket; now I tossed it over to him and he used it to bundle up some of his food.

I said, "After the war, what did he do?"

"At first he kept on. But he became more and more uneasy. He'd supported the Russians because that seemed the best way to strike at the Germans, but as time went on, thinking like that became more and more difficult."

"He was hooked, though."

"Yes."

"By you."

"He was on the same hook I was on, Mr. Thorne. But I expect your mother was much more important. She *believed*. I was prepared to let him wriggle away, and in fact I did—he began taking himself out of the path of the more important material. But your mother would never have let him stop altogether."

"Except he did. With that gun."

"That week was terrible for him—it was the week of the Hungarian uprising. Your mother became very frightened and phoned me—she was afraid he'd turn himself in. I panicked, I admit, partly because that's just what I wanted to do myself. I called Hamilton, and asked him to do something—since they were both in the State Department—but he refused. That made me even more frightened. I knew, if he *did* turn himself in, that I was finished."

"So what happened?"

"We came here and talked. He was terribly upset. The Russians hadn't sent in the tanks yet but he knew they were going to—he had access to all the State Department estimates. I told him he couldn't be sure and calmed him down. Later, he became very despondent and your mother got a message to me, but I didn't feel safe coming here so we agreed that we would meet in the woods. I remember wondering later whether he'd brought that gun intending to shoot us all, but in fact he'd killed himself before I arrived. I remember, just as I was leaving, that there was someone—I always wondered . . ."

"That was me."

"I'm very sorry."

"What was my mother's reaction?"

"It . . . steeled her, I suppose you might say. She went on. She passed me gossip, little items . . . it made her feel she was important and let me . . . keep an eye on her."

"You mean, in case my mother ever took it into her head to betray you."

"That wasn't a worry. I just felt responsible . . . even for you, if you don't mind my saying so. One year I realized you were in New York at the same time as May, so I arranged for you to meet . . . and I suppose that's one more thing I should apologize for."

Should he have apologized for anything? I wasn't sure. But what he said after this, even if he meant it as an apology, was a hundred times better, for it seemed to explain. And though he was attempting to describe my father, his words ended by giving me a clearer picture of Brightman himself.

"I just wanted you to know something," he said, "about your father. Above all, I don't want you to think he was that much different from the person you remember—don't overestimate the importance of any of this. And don't romanticize him. Even treason can be given the golden glow of nostalgia; people were wrong—but committed; what they did was mistaken—but daring. You see? Philby, Blunt, Burgess, Maclean . . . they can all be turned into heroes. You may be tempted to think of your father that way. Don't. You'll do him a disservice.

"Closer inspection of the Communist system revealed to a good number of people enough of the truth to turn them away. Of course, a good many stayed. But each purge, murder or massacre eliminated some of them, until all that remained were the loyal, dedicated Communists who still pretended that the Gulag only existed because Stalin was mad. Your father saw the truth before many others. And where others permitted themselves to be black-mailed—literally, or through their own guilt, or simply by circumstance—he refused."

What could I say? I had neither the experience nor the wisdom to comment. Besides, there was no time. We'd done as much as we could in the hut, and Subotin's gun, disassembled, was stowed in my bag—we couldn't take a chance on the police tracing it. Staggering beneath boxes and sacks, we made our way down the path and up to the road. Last problems: inching the pick-up around Subotin's parked car. Last details: getting the gun scabbard from the back seat, remembering to shove his keys over the visor. Then, headlights off, we drove up the side road to where my car was parked. No one, we both felt certain, had seen us.

I got down from the pick-up. Now, much too late, my mind was filling with questions, questions that only Brightman could give answers to. But then, at the end, I gave him one. For just as he extended his hand, I told him to wait, went to my car, and fetched him that little travelling icon that Yuri Shastov had given me.

"For May," I said, "from all her fathers, real and imagined."

He took it from me, opened it. And then his eyes seemed to beseech me. "Do you know?" he asked. "Have you found out?"

"Whatever I've found, Mr. Brightman, you knew already."

"Then I beg you—don't look any further."

And even as I formed the words to ask what he meant, I knew I'd waited too long. He backed the truck round and finally, two headlights running over a hill—a last image of golden eyes—Harry Brightman passed out of my life.

But not quite.

14

A year passed.

I survived; I suppose you always do. There was my work, the blessed necessity of earning a living, even a lady. . . . Life went on. What I'd learned about my parents changed a great deal, but the most important things stayed just the same.

In any event, by the spring I was halfway back to myself, and with the mystery of my father's death finally resolved, all those other mysteries began to come back into my mind. There were enough of them, God knows. Would Subotin's body ever be found? Who was Travin? And what had happened to Grainger?—though, in fact, a couple of discreet phone calls to Halifax answered that one: it seemed the old man had survived and was soldiering on at his clinic.

I was able to come up with quite a few answers. Subotin—it seemed obvious—had wanted money to finance the activities of his group, and through his contacts in Soviet intelligence had learned about Brightman. Subotin had pursued him—but then, I speculated, had pushed too hard. So far as I knew, Subotin had left May alone, and indeed she would have been too obvious a person for Brightman to pass the gold to. But this wouldn't have precluded Subotin from threatening her in order to put pressure on Brightman; in fact, it was the most powerful threat he could have possibly used. *Too* powerful, however: as soon as he made it, Brightman had bolted. But this hadn't stopped Subotin at all—for, with Brightman's KGB file in his hand, he'd simply gone from one member of Brightman's old group to another: Brightman would have had to leave the gold somewhere. This suggested another explanation to the riddle of why Subotin had broken into my house. Since he knew about Brightman's group, he must also have known about my parents, and so I *might* have been one of the names on his list. And after my abortive contact with Travin, my role had become potentially dangerous.

But that brought back another question: who was Travin? It was possible that he was KGB, but, the more I thought about him, the more he seemed to be a man with his own independent agenda. After all, he'd attempted to set up a contact with me all on his own.

I put together a theory, based on what he'd said on the phone, and on that paper I'd found in the dump near Subotin's camp. Travin was an émigré: tens of thousands of former Soviet citizens have settled in the United States. The extreme Russian nationalism that Loginov had talked about had its émigré adherents, and Subotin might have used people such as Travin for assistance and cover. Travin might then have broken away. His attempt to contact me would have doomed him, though he knew far too much in any event: he'd known about Dimitrov, somehow he'd known about my father (*something personal you wouldn't want a policeman to hear*), and he'd suspected something of the truth about May: why else had he taken all those photographs of her?

But, again, there it was, the real mystery—May herself. Who was she? And why, if he so wished to protect her, hadn't Brightman just given Subotin the gold right away? I thought I knew the answer: in the end, Brightman had protected the gold only to prevent a far deeper secret from being revealed. I was back where I started, faced with the very first question of all: who was May Brightman, and why had she been so important?

Through mutual friends, I tried to find out where she'd gone, but no one knew; and a letter to Brightman's lawyer in Toronto only revealed that he didn't know either.

I knew one or two things: I was certain Shastov was her natural father; and her mother was a Russian woman who, in 1940, had tried to save her child from the desolation around her and the carnage she could see ahead. She must have been a remarkable woman (would Yuri Shastov have married anything less?), for even if many women had wished to do what she had done, few would have been able to: she possessed some sort of influence, some power which—ultimately—had enabled her to summon Harry Brightman all the way from Canada to the Soviet Union.

In September, a magazine sent me a book to review, a history of the Stalinist Comintern, and it was full of stuff on Dimitrov; so I went over that angle again. But the child wasn't Dimitrov's, and why should he have cared about Yuri Shastov's daughter? Berri must have been right: if he'd saved that baby, it was only because it might have saved him . . . which meant that May must have been a truly miraculous child.

In the end, I decided that Dimitrov must be involved in some way. In 1940 Harry Brightman had been in Povonets, in 1940 both men and the child had turned up in Halifax—the coincidence was too great to be without meaning. And Brightman would hardly have gone through the Florence Raines business without having a reason. But what was that reason? That whole story about Brightman and the woman on Zinoviev's staff—Anna Kostina—rang true, and hadn't Cadogan mentioned, right at the very beginning, that Brightman had worried aloud about someone named Anna? So one might reasonably ask: did Anna Kostina exist? Leonard Forbes hadn't heard of her, but then he doesn't know everything. I spent a day trying to find her; and, to my surprise, came across her name, *Kostina, A. P.*, in the index of one of the standard histories.

Just as Grainger had said, she'd been part of Zinoviev's entourage, and had been sentenced to a term in the Gulag during the first wave of the Purges—I could find nothing about her after 1935. Earlier, however, she'd carried out several sensitive missions on Zinoviev's behalf. Of these, the most interesting had been in 1917, for it was she who'd actually received, and transmitted, the order to murder the Tsar. Lenin and Zinoviev had dispatched her to Ekaterinburg, where the Tsar and his family were being held prisoners, with strict orders on their treatment; everything that had happened afterwards had passed through her hands . . .

The possibility which this connection raised was so improbable that I dismissed it immediately. But it kept coming back. Was it possible that Yuri Shastov's wife had a personal claim to the Imperial arms on the little icon he'd given me? Was it possible that Travin had taken all those photographs of May to compare her face to another? Was it possible to imagine a survival, an escape, a moment of pity?

If one could, then it became almost certain that Anna Kostina, alone, had known what had happened.

If any of the family had survived the original massacre, they must have done so because of her; and if any of them had ultimately been allowed to go free, that moment of pity must have come from her heart. And later, regretting her moment of weakness, she might have followed the fate of her own private hostage, realizing later, as her own pitiless fate was revealed, what a weapon she had. Except she couldn't possibly use it—*as long as the child, or the child of the child, was still inside Russia*. The child of the child. . . . But if she'd told someone, and that person had managed to get the child out— away from Stalin's long grasp—then they would have possessed a talisman, a surety, of almost magical potency.

The child of the child. . . .

Russia, as Peter the Great once said, is the land where things that don't happen, happen. And he was right about that. As the weeks passed, and Indian summer came and went, I found myself wondering if this was one of those things. Then, late in October, I received the only sign, the only help, that I ever would get: a message from May.

Except it was hardly a message.

Only a photograph: May, smiling into the sun, with a scrawl on the back: "All our love, M."

Postmarked in Schiphol, the Netherlands—the great airport for Amsterdam—it merely proved that they were alive, and might be living, or travelling, in any place in the world. The photo reminded me of that picture which had been so much in my mind, *taken by May,*

397

with her own Brownie, for it had precisely that stolid, amateur competence of a generation brought up on box cameras: Harry Brightman was positioned with the sun right over his shoulder and his shadow filled up the foreground while his daughter's eyes squinted into the glare. She was standing on a pier. Tied up to it, grand yachts jostled together, filing away in magnificent perspective, and a blue sea glittered beyond—it could have been Cannes, Rio, Palm Beach, any place where the rich spend their time. I studied May's face—she was the woman I'd loved. Was she happy? If she was who I thought she might be, did she know? It was hard to make out her expression. In fact, her face wasn't even in focus: the focus of that picture was behind her, halfway down the pier.

And about the tenth time I looked at it, that fact caught my eye. The focus was on one of the yachts behind her, one of those fine old yachts from the twenties, all bright varnish and shiny brass trim.

One afternoon, I took a glass and studied it carefully.

The yacht bore the proud lines of an era when the rich were not afraid to look rich: her deckhouse was high, the teak lovingly polished, and her name was spelled out in gilt. The name of that yacht leaped up through my glass, bright as gold and clear as life: a hint, a hope, or a last message from Brightman . . . believe what you will. In any case, I can only say what I saw, tell what I know; and I know she was called *Anastasia.*

Anthony Hyde

Anthony Hyde comes from a family of writers. His father wrote several children's novels. His brother, Christopher, has written a string of successful thrillers.

"People always ask whether our parents encouraged us to become writers," Mr. Hyde writes, "and the answer is both yes and no. In a sense, our home environment didn't give us much choice— everybody was madly scribbling away. On the other hand, my father understood what an economically precarious occupation writing can be and so he was always urging us to be more practical. 'Do something useful,' he'd say, 'take up sheet-metal work.' I actually did for a while, and though it's saved me a few dollars in car body repairs over the years, I think I'm better off in front of the typewriter."

Hyde has lived in the United Kingdom and travelled extensively, but always seems to return to Ottawa, the Canadian capital, where he was born in 1946. "It's a beautiful and very quiet city. Though we've had our share of spy scandals—beginning with the Gouzenko affair— most people would consider this place the exact opposite of Le Carré's Berlin, or Graham Greene's Vienna. Still, I rather suspect that living here has had quite an influence on the direction of my writing. Capital cities fall into two categories. London, where I've spent a lot of time, belongs to the first. Like Paris and Rome, it's the largest and most important city in the country—all sorts of things are going on. But Ottawa is more like Bonn. Here, there's nothing *but* the government. Everything happens behind closed doors, and the city is always buzzing with rumour, gossip and whispered secrets. In a small way, everyone becomes a spy."

Anthony Hyde is married to Kathleen Moses, who is partly of Canadian Indian descent, and tracing her rather complex family tree gives them one excuse for their favourite hobby, travel. In addition, Hyde enjoys gardening, his IBM computer, and an aged, cantankerous cat named Sweet Pea.

The Flame Trees
of Thika

A CONDENSATION OF THE BOOK BY

ELSPETH HUXLEY

ILLUSTRATED BY TED LEWIN

When Elspeth Huxley was a little
girl before the first World War,
her parents left England to make
a home in what was then
the Kenyan wilderness.
Slowly they learned how
to live in this new country,
how to build a grass house,
how to grow coffee and how to understand
something of the African mind.

Meanwhile, their daughter was observing
everything around her with acute but
affectionate eyes: her parents' friends and
their half-comprehended emotional
entanglements; the Masai and the Kikuyu,
their feuds and superstitions and kindnesses;
the animals which were a source
of joy to her—but also of
agony when some
mishap befell them.

This tender, warm
and enchanting
picture of a pioneer
childhood will stay long
in the memory of its readers.

Chapter I

We set off in an open cart drawn by four whip-scarred little oxen and piled high with equipment and provisions. No medieval knight could have been more closely armoured than were Tilly and I, against the rays of the sun. A mushroom-brimmed hat, built of two thicknesses of heavy felt and lined with red flannel, protected her creamy complexion, a long-sleeved white blouse clasped her by the neck, and a heavy skirt of khaki drill fell to her booted ankles.

I sat beside my mother, only a little less fortified in a pith helmet and a starched cotton dress. The oxen looked very thin and small for such a task, but moved off with resignation from the Norfolk Hotel. Everything was dusty; one's feet descended with little plops into a soft, warm, red carpet, a red plume followed every wagon down the street, and the dust had filmed over each brittle eucalyptus leaf.

We were going to Thika, a name on a map where two rivers joined. Thika in those days—the year was 1913—was a favourite camp for big-game hunters and beyond it there was only bush and plain. If you went on long enough you would come to mountains and forests no one had mapped. We were not going as far as that, only two days' journey in the oxcart to a bit of El Dorado my father had been fortunate enough to buy in the bar of the Norfolk Hotel from a man wearing an Old Etonian tie.

While everyone else strode about Nairobi's dusty cart-tracks in bush shirts and khaki shorts or riding breeches, Roger Stilbeck was always neatly dressed in a light worsted suit of perfect cut, and wore gold cufflinks and dark brogue shoes. His wife, who looked very elegant, was said to be related to the Duke of Montrose. Roger Stilbeck had met us at the station when we arrived and Mrs. Stilbeck came to see us off, a mark of grace by no means conferred on every buyer of her husband's land.

Tilly, eager as always to extract from every moment its last drop of interest or pleasure, had ridden out early on the plains to see the game, and had returned peppered with tiny red ticks. These she was picking off her clothes while she supervised the loading of the cart. Wearing a look of immense concentration, she popped them one by one with finger and thumb. Mrs. Stilbeck watched with horror. Then she put a pale, soft-skinned hand to her eyes. "Roger," she said, "I don't feel very well. You must take me home."

Tilly went on squashing ticks while a great many Africans in red blankets, with a good deal of shouting and noise, stowed our household goods in the cart. There was a mountain of boxes, bundles and packages. On top was perched a sewing machine, a crate of five Speckled Sussex pullets and a lavatory seat. The pullets had come with us in the ship from Tilbury, and Tilly had fed them every day and let them out on the deck for exercise.

Robin, my father, had gone ahead. He was locating the land and, Tilly hoped, building a house to receive us. A simple grass hut could be built in a couple of days. My father had picked out on a map five hundred acres of blank space with a wriggling line, presumed to be a river, on each side.

"Best coffee land in the country," Stilbeck had remarked.

"Has anyone planted any yet?"

"There's no need to *plant* coffee to know that. Experts have analysed the soil. Altitude and rainfall are exactly right."

Robin bought the five hundred acres for much more than he could afford. He got a map from the Land Office, from which the position of our holding could be deduced. Nothing had been properly surveyed. The boundary between the land earmarked for settlement and land reserved for the Kikuyu was about a mile away.

"Any amount of labour," Roger Stilbeck had said. "You've only got to lift your finger and in they come. Friendly enough, if a bit raw. Wonderfully healthy climate, splendid neighbours, magnificent sport. I congratulate you, my dear fellow."

Soon we were out of the town. The dusty road ran through a mixture of bush and native *shambas*, plantations, where shaven-headed women in beads and leather aprons weeded, dug, and drew water from a swampy stream in gourds or in *debes*, those four-gallon paraffin tins that had become a universal water vessel, measure and roofing material. The road had not been made, it had simply arisen from the passage of wagons. For the most part it ran across a plain whose soil was largely *murram*, a coarse red gravel that baked hard and supported only thin, wiry grass, sad-looking thorn trees, and erythrinas with flowers the colour of red sealing wax.

It became very hot on our oxcart. Tilly hoisted a parasol with black and white stripes, which helped a little, but it had not been made for tropic suns. I was fortunate; being only six or seven, I wore no stays or stockings, but Tilly was tightly laced in, her waist was wasp-like, her skirt voluminous, and the whole ensemble might have been designed to prevent the circulation of air. In a short while the dust and sweat made us look like Red Indians with strange white rings round our eyes.

Once out of the town the oxen flagged, and the driver fell into a kind of shuffle beside the beasts, who were coated now with flies. We had to keep waving flies off our own faces. When we encountered a span of sixteen oxen drawing a long, low wagon, we were immersed in a thick red fog which made us choke and smart, and settled over everything. We travelled always with its sharp, dry, peculiar smell tickling our nostrils. All day long we passed through flat country with distant ranges of hills. We saw game of many kinds. Giraffe bent their patchwork necks towards the small spreading acacias, and the plump zebra looked like highly varnished animated toys.

At last we reached Ruiru, about halfway. We were to stop there for the night. About fifteen miles a day was all the oxen could manage. Ruiru was just a few *dukas*, shops, kept by Indians, and a river crossing, not even a bridge: a causeway made by shovelling murram into the swampy stream and putting up some white posts. A small dam had been built, and a flume to carry water to a turbine which made Nairobi's electricity. Once an inquisitive hippo had got wedged in the flume, and all Nairobi's lights had failed.

Our host for the night was a flat-faced, beefy South African called Henry Oram. He had left a prosperous farm in the Transvaal, and before that in the Free State, to come to BEA (as everyone then called British East Africa) and bully into productiveness another patch of bush and veld. He had a little bougainvillaea-covered house of corrugated iron, full of sons. A number of green, shiny coffee bushes grew in rows all round it and were expected soon to make him rich, but now he could see signs of a neighbour's cultivation on the opposite ridge.

"It's getting overcrowded," he said in a South African voice, flat and strong like himself. "It's time I moved on. They're opening up a new land beyond the Plateau. No settlers yet. I'm off to have a look at it soon."

Tilly, who had the homemaking instinct, said to Mrs. Oram, "You'll be sorry to leave, now that you've made a garden."

"Oh, but the whole country is a garden; a garden God has planted. Look what He has provided—streams to drink from, trees for shade, wild fruits and honey, birds and beasts for company. How can any of His creatures improve on that?"

Tilly reacted like a clam to this sort of gushing. Yet the Orams were hard workers, their hospitality was unstinted, and their craving for the wilder places of the earth was genuine.

"They are romantics," Robin suggested later.

"They are fools," Tilly replied. She was of course a romantic herself, but she concealed it like a guilty secret.

BEFORE THE SUN was really hot next morning the little weather-beaten oxen with their humps and sagging dewlaps were inspanned, and we set off again down the wagon track.

On our right the tawny plain stretched away, a bowl of sunlight, to the Tana River and beyond; you felt that you could walk straight on across it to the rim of the world. On our left rose a long, dark-crested mountain range from which sprang rivers no larger than streams that watered a great part of Kikuyuland. Sometimes we passed Kikuyu travellers, the backs of the women always bent low under enormous burdens suspended by leather straps that bit into their sloping foreheads. They wore pointed leather aprons and trudged along looking like big brown snails.

The men were slim and upright and often had a look of fragility; their bodies were hairless, shining and light. The young warriors

406

wore their locks embellished with sheep's fat and red ochre and plaited into a large number of short pigtails to hang down all round; they walked with a loping stride quite different from the women's plod. By now the influence of missionaries and government combined had put them into blankets, which they wore like togas, knotted over one shoulder. Most of the blankets were red with black stripes and looked well against coppery skins and gay red and blue ornaments. Earlobes were pierced, and the hole enlarged to take plugs of wood, coils of wire, or bead necklaces that hung down to their shoulders; the young bloods wore a beaded belt from which depended a slim sword in a leather scabbard dyed vermilion with an extract from the root of a creeper.

We had with us a cook-cum-houseboy called Juma, lent to us by Roger Stilbeck to see us in. He was used to grander ways, and the further we travelled from Nairobi the more disapproving he became of the local inhabitants.

"They are small like pigeons," he said loftily. "They do not eat meat. Look at their legs! Thin like a bustard. And their women are like donkeys, with heads as smooth as eggs. They are not to be trusted. Why do you wish to live amongst such people?"

Juma was a Swahili from the coast, or said he was: Swahilis were fashionable, and quite a lot of people who were nothing of the sort appointed themselves as members of this race, with its Arab affinities. He was also a magician: with three stones, a few sticks and one old, black cooking pot he would produce an excellent four-course meal. He had the secret, known only to Africans, of serving food hot and promptly at any hour of the day or night. Cooks were men of substance and authority, respected and well-paid. Juma made the most of his superior position. In fact he was a bully—large, strong, and black-skinned.

"These Kikuyu are cannibals," he said facetiously, and quite untruthfully. "They will dig up corpses and eat them. Sometimes their women give birth to snakes and lizards."

"Silence, Juma," Tilly commanded. She was hot, tired, dusty, and in no mood for anatomical gossip, and her understanding of Swahili was still shaky. Although she had studied it with her usual energy on the voyage out, her phrasebook, acquired from the Society for the Propagation of the Gospel, had not always suggested sentences most helpful to intending settlers. "The idle slaves are scratching themselves", "Six drunken Europeans have killed the cook". She doubted if their recital, even in the best Swahili, would impress Juma.

After his remarks I stared at the passing Kikuyu with a new interest. They looked harmless, but that was evidently a pose. We passed a woman carrying a baby in a sling on her back, as well as a load. I could see the infant's shiny head, like a polished skittle ball, bobbing about between the mother's bent shoulders, and looked hopefully for a glimpse of a snake or a lizard.

"These oxen," Juma grumbled, "they are as old as great-grandmothers; this driver lacks the brains of a frog. When the new moon has come we shall still be travelling in this worthless cart."

"No more words," Tilly said snappily. Juma had a patronizing air that she resented, and she doubted if he was showing enough respect. Those were the days when to lack respect was a more serious crime than to neglect a child, bewitch a man or steal a cow. Indeed respect was the only protection available to unarmed Europeans who lived singly, or in scattered families, among thousands of Africans accustomed to constant warfare and armed with spears and poisoned arrows. This respect preserved them like an invisible coat of mail, and seldom failed; but it had to be carefully guarded. Kept intact, it was stronger than all the guns and locks and metal in the world; challenged, it could be brushed aside like a spider's web. So Tilly was a little sensitive about respect, and Juma was silenced.

We came at last to a stone bridge over the Chania River. Just below it, the river plunged over a waterfall into a pool with slimy rocks and thick-trunked trees all round it, and a little further on it joined the Thika. A hotel had been started just below the falls, consisting of a low-roofed, thatched grass hut whose veranda posts were painted blue and gave the place its name; of three or four whitewashed *rondavels*, circular huts, to sleep in; and a row of stables. The manager was a lean, military-looking, sprucely dressed man with a bald head and a long moustache, who was very deaf. One day a safari visitor, admiring his host's neat attire, rashly asked, "Who made your breeches?" After he had bawled this question several times, the deaf man seized his hand and shook it warmly, saying, "Ah, yes, Major Breeches, delighted to see you." After that the innkeeper was always called Major Breeches, and I never knew his real name.

Robin rode down on a mule to meet us at the Blue Posts. "I've picked out a splendid site," he said.

"Is the house built?" Tilly asked hopefully.

"Not exactly. There doesn't seem to be any labour."

"Well, we've got tents," Tilly said. I think she was glad, really; already she had fallen in love with camp life.

"There are said to be some chiefs in the reserve," Robin added. "I shall go and see them. The bush is much heavier than Stilbeck led me to believe. I shall have to do a lot of clearing before I can plough any land. And I can only find one river. The other seems to be just a sort of gully with no water in it."

"Mr. Stilbeck doesn't seem to have been very truthful."

"Perhaps he didn't know himself," suggested Robin, who always found excuses for his fellow man, and indeed for himself where necessary. "There's a lot of red oat grass, which everyone says means high fertility. The stream that is there has a nice fall and we shall be able to put in a ram. Later on perhaps a little turbine ... there's building stone by the river bank. And lots of duiker and guinea fowl; we oughtn't to go hungry."

It all sounded wonderful, except the ticks. I had already found a lot crawling up my legs and had learned to pluck them off and squash them in my fingers. They were red and active, and itched like mad when they dug into the skin. They left an itchy little bump, and if you scratched it you soon developed a sore.

There were also jiggas. These burrowed under your toenails, laid their eggs, and created a swollen, red, tormenting place. I soon learned never to go barefoot, or, if I mislaid my slippers, to walk with my toes curled up off the ground, a habit that persisted for years after jiggas had passed out of my life.

We had reached, now, the end of the road: or rather, the road continued to Fort Hall, where perhaps a quarter of a million Kikuyus were ruled by a solitary district commissioner, and we had to make our way through roadless country to our piece of land. This lay uphill, towards the Kikuyu reserve.

"I don't know how the cart will get there," Robin mused. "For one thing, there are no bridges."

"Then we must get some built," Tilly replied. She never dwelt for long on difficulties.

Robin borrowed a mule for each of us from Major Breeches and we set out early next morning. Dry, wiry-stalked brown grass reached up to the mules' shoulders and wrapped itself round my legs and knees. There were trees, but this was not forest; each tree grew on its own. Most were erythrinas, about the size of apple trees, with rough bark and twisted boughs; they bore their brilliant red flowers on bare branches. Tapering anthills, the craft of termites, thrust themselves like spires above the grass and bush; they were hard as sandstone, and the same colour.

It soon grew very hot. The erythrinas were in bloom, and glowed like torches. Small doves cooed from the branches. We followed a native path that corkscrewed about like a demented snake. Cicadas kept up a shrill, continuous chorus. It seemed that everything was quivering—air, heat, grass, even the mules twitching their hides to dislodge flies.

Once or twice, on rounding a hairpin bend, we found ourselves face to face with a Kikuyu, who stood transfixed and then stepped aside to let us pass. But the women uttered highpitched squeals and scattered into the grass, their loads and babies swaying on their backs. We could see their heads turned towards us in startled alarm, while the men shouted at them not to be fools.

The ride through sun and heat, jolted by the sluggish mules, seemed to go on for ever. We crossed a treeless *vlei* whose grass was short and wiry and where a duiker leaped away from under the mules' feet. Robin pulled up and said, "Here we are." We did not seem to be anywhere.

"You mean this is the farm?" Tilly asked. Even Robin did not sound very confident when he replied that it was.

None of us quite knew what to say, so Robin began to praise our surroundings in the rather hearty voice he always used when bolstering-up was needed: "This grass and stuff will burn off easily, we ought to be able to start our ploughing before the rains. Roger said all the land was ploughable. Except of course the river bank, which is just over there."

"I can't see a river," Tilly said.

"Of course you can't, if you don't look." Robin's testiness was a sign of disappointment; he had hoped for Tilly's enthusiasm.

"This is where I thought we'd put the house," he added, leading

410

the way up a slight rise to command a prospect of more brown grass, dark-green spiky bush and scattered trees. "There's a good view towards Mount Kenya, and we can ram the water to a reservoir on top of the hill and feed it down by gravity to the house and factory. The pulping place will be down there, and the first plantation over to the left; we might irrigate a vegetable garden, too, and start a small dairy. Lots of people will be settling here soon, and we can sell them milk and butter."

"And in the meantime," Tilly said, "it would be nice to have a grass hut to sleep in, or even a few square yards cleared to pitch the tent."

"Oh, that won't take long. But just for the next night or two, perhaps we'd better put up at the Blue Posts."

So we all rode back again, rather silently, though Robin rallied once or twice to tell us of the neighbours who would soon hem us in. All the land had been sold, he added, though the only settler actually to have arrived was a South African who was living in a tent somewhere by the river and spent all his time shooting animals.

Robin had never ploughed anything in his life. He had been in other parts of Africa, but had spent his time prospecting, and going into partnership with men who knew infallible ways to make money quickly. Something invariably went wrong, and it was always Robin's little bit of cash that vanished, together with the partner. Unfortunately his father, dying young, had left him some money, so instead of learning how to make it in an ordinary manner, he had indulged a passion for inventing things that never quite worked and starting companies to exploit them. There came a gloomy day when preparations were made to evacuate our house and sell most of our possessions. On the first occasion my nanny—to start with we had enjoyed such luxuries—replied sepulchrally to my inquiries, "Daddy has a hole in his pocket." I demanded why it could not be mended, and received no answer. So Robin had vanished to seek a new fortune in the colonies, and I had attached myself to Tilly, instead of to a nanny.

In some remote obscure region, Robin acquired a goldmine. All its previous owners had died very quickly of drink or malaria. Robin managed to get the mine into production, as he put it, though I think that consisted only of persuading some of the cannibals to hack at a hillside with picks and wash the resulting rock in a stream. In a

411

romantic moment he sent Tilly a ring made of gold from his own mine; looking at it sadly some years later, he remarked that it represented the total output of his mining career.

Still, he managed to sell the mine at a small profit, and the cash payment was enough to take him to British East Africa. All the good reports he had heard about the country seemed to him more than justified. Enthusiastic letters fired Tilly, also, with a longing for this land of splendour; and here we now were, again united, and the owners of a ninety-nine-year lease of five hundred acres of land.

If it was not quite all that Tilly had expected, it was nevertheless there, under all that coat of grass and bush. With hard work and patience, the vision could become real: a house could arise, coffee bushes put down their roots and bloom and fruit, shady trees grow up around a tidy lawn; there was order waiting to be created out of wilderness.

Chapter 2

Robin had ridden off on a mule, a few days before Tilly and myself, at the head of a peculiar cavalcade. Tents, furniture and stores made conventional if uncomfortable loads for porters to carry on their heads; as well as these, we seemed to have a lot of oddments, like a grindstone, an accordion, a light plough, rolls of barbed wire and a dressmaker's dummy.

"I wonder what the porters think about it all," Tilly speculated, watching one of them stagger off underneath a tin bath containing a sewing machine and a second-hand gramophone.

"They don't think," said Major Breeches, dismissing the notion as absurd. They sang, however, and marched off in fine style, though they did not get far before various loads fell off, or got tangled in trees, and several of the carriers grew disheartened, dumped their burdens, and fled. But the distance was only five miles, so the safari did not have to be highly organized.

The gramophone had been suggested to Robin as a convenient way of breaking the ice with the natives. It enticed them, as a light attracts insects; once, as it were, captured, the advantages of signing on for work could be explained. So when we were installed in tents,

Robin played "The Bluebells of Scotland" and "The Lost Chord" over and over again. As the records were scratched and the gramophone an old one, extraordinary sounds emerged from its trumpet. Its only effect was to deflect Juma from his labours; he listened entranced, and one of the mules was found gazing pensively down the trumpet. The local inhabitants, however, remained aloof.

Before we left the Blue Posts, a young Irishman arrived one day on a bicycle, with a broken flywheel strapped to his back. He came, he said, from Punda Milia, a stretch of country about fifteen miles further on, and he was taking the flywheel to Nairobi to be repaired. He was not much larger than a well-grown jockey, but as tough as hippo hide, and he had the quick, gay smile and bright eyes of many Irishmen, with a trace of the brogue.

His name was Randall Swift, and he found life so entertaining that he was seldom without a laugh and a smile, so that he endeared himself to everyone, and became one of my parents' closest friends. "All the same, he's been here eight years and his only form of transport is a bicycle," Tilly mused, when he had gone. "He hasn't made his fortune very quickly."

"He's a splendid fellow, but he hasn't stuck to one thing," Robin explained. "But now he's settled on sisal, he'll do well."

Randall Swift had told us how he and his partner had secured the last consignment of bulbils (the young sisal plants) to leave German East Africa, the day before the Germans put an embargo on their export. Now they would be able to supply other aspiring sisal planters with bulbils at a profit, and they had built a factory to extract fibre from the tough, prickly-tipped leaves. He gave us some good advice about labour. "Get hold of the local chief," he said. "Meanwhile, put a safari lamp up on a pole outside your tent at night. These people have never seen lamps before. Once they get over thinking it's a spirit, they can't resist a closer look at it."

When the gramophone failed him, Robin remembered this. At first nothing happened, except that insects scorched themselves to death against the glass. It was always dark by half past six or seven and, after I was sent to bed, I lay awake and watched people moving about by lantern-light and the flickering of the campfire, a small speck of comfort in a great encircling continent where cities, friends and civilized ways were not to be found for thousands of miles.

At such times, when all the furtive noises of the night beyond that speck of firelight crept into your ears, you could feel very isolated and lonely. At such times, I think, Robin and Tilly wondered whether they had set their hands to a hopeless task. For until you actually saw it and travelled across it on foot or on horseback or in a wagon, you could not possibly grasp the vastness of Africa.

On the third night, a new sound came from beyond the golden circle. I lay in bed and listened with a thumping heart. Often I used to imagine our camp to be beleaguered by creeping unseen beasts with red fiery eyes and ripping fangs, or by savage spearmen with naked limbs. The first sound was a cough which did not sound at all savage, but human; then something moved.

"They've come!" Robin exclaimed; he had not really believed in the lamp trick, as he called it. "I wonder what we do next?"

They waited. Tilly was struggling with some tapestry-work under the indifferent light. She was talented at embroidery, and never liked to sit still with nothing to do.

"Juma will deal with them," she said.

Juma had faithfully maintained his contempt and indifference towards the local inhabitants. It appeared that he, whose forebears had no doubt been slaves of the Arabs, felt that the sooner these people were enslaved the better. He was now dressed up not only in his white *kanzu*, which he always wore on duty with a red fez, but also in his scarlet sash kept normally for best occasions. Robin wore pyjamas and a dressing gown and high mosquito boots.

"Tell them we are friends, and that if they come to work in the morning I will give them all a rupee to start off with," Robin suggested.

"They are too stupid to understand rupees," Juma said.

"For heaven's sake think of *something*, Juma!"

The invisible spectators kept just beyond the firelight. They knew no language but their own, and of this Juma was ignorant. He had, however, attached to himself at some point a child, known simply as the *toto*, a fetcher and carrier. The toto was now summoned and appeared, large-headed, skinny-limbed, velvet-eyed, and rather pathetic. He stood by Juma and addressed a few quavering sentences to the unseen crowd.

The toto's voice brought forth one of them almost into the open.

414

He was young and oiled and red, with twists of ochred hair dangling all over his head and down to his eyes. He carried a spear and wore a short cloak of leather, and a belt with a throwing-club tucked into it and the usual red scabbard. His speech was soft, liquid, musical, like water over rocks.

"He asks, what is this light?" said Juma, in his mixture of English and Swahili. "He says, has it fallen from a star?"

"Show it to him," Robin instructed.

But the young man retreated as Juma advanced with the lantern in his hand. The darkness gave way before Juma and he moved in a golden glow. The light slid down a limb, caught the flash of a spearhead, flickered across a startled eye, and then all trace of the young man and his companions evaporated. Juma called. No answer. Robin swore with disappointment.

"No matter," Juma said. "They will come back."

The next night the young men were bolder, and edged more closely into the circle of light. They were like bronze statues endowed with life, and moved tautly. One felt that, just as they vanished into the void like antelopes when alarmed, they might spring forward when angered and thrust with spears. The toto spoke to them again, and the lantern was displayed at close quarters. They touched it, and one burned his hand against the glass.

Although we were astonished at their ignorance even of lamps, devices known to the Romans and indeed to others long before that, the sight of a tongue of flame imprisoned in a bubble must have appeared altogether miraculous to those confronted with it for the first time. It was those very inventions that to us appeared so simple, like lamps and matches and wheels, and putting water into pipes, that struck these people with the force of wonder and amazement. Later, when Europeans displayed the inventions in which they themselves took so much pride, like aeroplanes and radios, they were often disappointed at the Africans' indifference. But if you had lived for many centuries without control over the elements, it would be the realization that fire and water, your daily companions, could be mastered, that would come as a revelation to you, not the ingenuity of some device for enabling you to do something you had never thought of doing, like travelling through the air.

Robin had a bright idea. "Tell them," he instructed Juma, "that to

every man who comes to work for me for one month, I will give a lamp like this."

Juma, the toto and the Kikuyu conversed in their curious mixture of tongues for some time. "They say," Juma reported, "that this lamp contains a spirit which obeys Europeans. They do not believe it would stay inside and serve them."

"Explain about paraffin," Robin said briskly.

"Is there a word for paraffin?" Tilly inquired.

"It is called fat," Juma replied.

His exposition caused a stir among the young men. They uttered startled exclamations and drew back, poised for flight.

"I have told them," Juma reported with disgust. "They think it is human fat and we are cannibals."

"I could cheerfully become one," Robin said, "if this goes on. Tell them they can take this lamp away and examine it. But explain that it

will die when its food is finished and if they bring it back tomorrow, they shall have some more."

No one was brave enough to grasp the lantern. The young men backed away, and Juma left it, its flame turned low, in the grass a short distance from our tents. It stayed there till everyone had gone to sleep, but in the morning it had gone.

Two days later the natives came back, and they brought with them several older men who wore black curls, and bright bead ornaments in their ears, and snuff-horns hanging by thin chains from their necks, and a good many amulets and coils of copper wire. One or two wore red blankets and the others cloaks of monkey skin, beautifully sewn together.

These men carried no weapons, but one had a polished staff in his hand. His skin was light, his eyes keen, his voice quiet, and he was clearly accustomed to authority. This man was called Chief

417

Kupanya. It was only much later that we discovered that the Kikuyu did not have chiefs in their hierarchy. They had elders of various grades, and he was a spokesman for his particular set of elders. But the policy of the government was to appoint local chiefs where they did not exist already, and his polished staff indicated that he had been selected as ruler of the district closest to our land. He and his companions sat down under a tree near our camp and took snuff.

"I suppose I ought to give them something," Robin remarked.

"We've got some soda water siphons," Tilly suggested. In those days no camp, house or safari was complete without these useful devices, and a box of Sparklets to recharge them.

Juma fetched all our tin mugs and handed them to the Kikuyu, who examined them with interest. For themselves they used calabashes, made from the gourds we saw growing everywhere. Robin produced a siphon and squirted the frothing water into one of the mugs. This created a sensation; here was water obviously possessed of an irrepressible spirit who might well be displaying anger. Or perhaps they thought a spirit lived inside the bottle and was blowing out a kind of steam. At any rate, it said much for their courage that they did not run away. As elders, they had their dignity to preserve. Juma drank some of the soda water as a demonstration, but this was too much even for Chief Kupanya. They held the mugs gingerly, and after a while poured the soda water respectfully onto the ground.

"I want some strong young men to clear the bush," Robin explained. "I will pay them in rupees." Kupanya spoke a little Swahili, so Juma was able to act as interpreter.

Kupanya asked a great many questions: Why had Robin come, where was the shamba to be, what was he going to grow in it? Was he a relation of the district commissioner? Had he a shamba in his own country? Had he seen King George?

"We shall go on for ever at this rate," Robin said impatiently. "He doesn't seem to realize that I'm offering his young men a chance to work." No doubt the chief would have considered two or three days' conversation under the tree well spent, but in Robin's opinion this meeting was not intended as a leisurely exchange of views.

"You might get on quicker," Tilly suggested, "if you offered the chief baksheesh of some kind."

So Kupanya was told he would receive a goat for every ten young

418

men who came to work and stayed a month. There would be no payment for those who left in less than thirty days. Thereafter negotiations proceeded more swiftly. When the elders left, they took the tin mugs, which they clearly looked on as a present. After that we had nothing to drink out of but half a dozen very precious Irish cut-glass tumblers, salvaged from what was always referred to as the Crash, until Robin rode down to Thika and borrowed some more mugs from the Blue Posts.

THE YOUNG MEN ARRIVED about a week later. They were painted as for war, or perhaps a dance, with chalk and red ochre and feathers tucked into their freshly decorated hair, and they arrived in a column, stamping and chanting and waving spears. At the first sight of them Tilly and Robin were somewhat alarmed, but it soon became apparent that this was all in fun, so to speak, and to show that they were ready for anything. With them were some of the elders and, at a safe distance, a party of shy and giggling young women heavily greased and ochred and covered with beads.

When they had calmed down and communication had been established, each man who wished to work was given a small square of cardboard ruled into thirty squares and called his ticket. One square was crossed off for each day he worked. When he completed the ticket, which might take several months, he was paid.

The young men's first task was to build themselves sleeping quarters, which they did merely by felling trees, driving branches into the ground, and tying together bundles of long, dry grass to make walls. But they would not thatch the huts themselves, as this was against their custom.

Everything except the thatch was prepared on the first day. On the second, the huts were assembled. The young men had erected the walls and the skeleton of the roofs by midday. Then a file of young ladies arrived, each one bearing on her back a bundle of reeds cut from a riverbed and previously dried in the sun. These maidens clambered up onto the skeleton roofs and tied the thatch in place with twine made from forest creepers. It was very well organized and in two days the huts were done. The Kikuyu had a strict rule that every building must be completed between sunrise and sunset, lest evil spirits move in during the night.

419

After they had completed their own houses, Robin put them onto building one for us. It was to have a single living room flanked by two bedrooms, all in a straight row. This was to be a temporary arrangement, until a proper stone residence went up. He stuck some pegs in the ground to indicate the corners and cut a little trench between, to make the shape quite clear.

A young man called Njombo had emerged as the spokesman of the labourers, who were always called boys. Njombo, with several friends, looked incredulously at the trench and the pegs. "We cannot build a house like that," he said. "It will fall down."

"Not if you build it properly."

Njombo clearly thought Robin's insistence not merely peculiar, but sinister. Goodness knows how many evil spirits would find shelter in a house with corners.

"Are rectangular buildings a sign of civilization?" Robin wondered. "I can't think why they should be."

"Perhaps it's the furniture," Tilly said. "It doesn't fit very well into round houses. Natives have scarcely any furniture." This was indeed true: all they had were three-legged stools, round also, and beds made of sticks lashed together on posts high enough for goats to sleep underneath. They kept a fire burning in the middle of the hut and had no windows; you could not call it hygienic, but it was warm.

To build a rectangular house naturally took longer. Its roof was a major difficulty: the structure of rafters, purlins and a ridge-beam was a total novelty, and Robin's explanation got nowhere, although when he clambered up—we had no ladder—and, with the aid of many willing but unpractised hands, secured the main poles in position, much interest was shown. We started off with nails, but after the first day all the long ones vanished; we had no safe or store to lock things in and these handy little lengths of iron proved irresistible to the Kikuyu. Robin cursed and made up his mind to ride to Nairobi on a mule to get a fresh supply, but Njombo considered this quite unnecessary.

"It is wrong to put iron in houses," he said. "Iron is for weapons and for ornament. Let us build the house according to our custom and keep the iron for bigger things."

Robin agreed to let them try, and they bound the poles together with twine in their customary fashion. The house was standing when we left fifteen years later, and the roof withstood many storms.

After the grass walls had been tied in position, the house was lined with reed matting. The floor was made of earth rammed into a hard red clay which could be swept, and it was soon covered with skins of leopards, reedbuck, Grant's gazelle and brown-haired sheep.

The house was airy, comfortable, cool, and most companionable, for a great many creatures soon joined us in the roof and walls. The nicest were the lizards, who would stay for hours spread-eagled on a wall quite motionless, clinging to the surface with small scaly hands. They would cock their heads a little on one side and then scuttle off, or vanish into the thatch.

This thatch was always full of little rustling, secretive noises from unseen fellow-residents meaning no harm—except for white ants, those termites who will destroy anything with their tiny but ferocious jaws, and betray themselves by little tunnels, like long blisters, marking their passage across walls and beams. A constant, largely successful war was waged against termites, and our house did not get eaten away. Our light came first from safari lanterns, but later we acquired a pressure lamp that had to be pumped up at frequent intervals, emitted a faintly sinister hissing like a snake, made the room too hot, and leaked paraffin.

"On the whole, modern improvements seem to be expensive, temperamental and smelly," Robin remarked pensively.

"The bits that reach us here are rather part-worn," Tilly said. But she liked to have reminders of civilization round her, so far as she could. The evening meal always ended with black coffee drunk from tiny lustre cups of very thin china. They dwindled rapidly in number, but I remember loving their lightness and graceful shape, and their fascinating blend of tones, like mother-of-pearl. Also we had the cut glass I have mentioned, the few bits of jewellery Tilly had salvaged from the Crash, and one or two pieces of furniture which came out from England and must have looked incongruous in our earthen-floored grass hut.

Most of our furniture was made out of the packing cases that had sheltered these few salvaged possessions, such as a French bureau with ornate, curly legs, used by Tilly as a writing desk and adorned always by two tall, embossed silver flower vases. She also had a delicate little work-table where she kept her embroidery, and a fat-bellied commode which she used as a medicine chest. It was full of queer brews of turpentine, ether, linseed oil, camphor, and other strong-smelling liquids, together with calomel, castor oil, iodine, and that sovereign remedy for almost everything, Epsom salts. No more unsuitable tenants could possibly have been found for the commode. Robin noticed this one day and grew rather angry, for the commode had come from his side of the family.

"It's a shame to treat good things in that way," he said.

"How else can we treat it?" Tilly asked. "This isn't the Victoria and Albert Museum." She looked deeply hurt, and also riled by the injustice; for Robin would have been the first to have stuffed anything that came to hand into the commode.

"I wish I'd never come to this rotten country," she exclaimed when he had gone, with tears in her eyes. Sometimes she spoke aloud in my presence without exactly speaking to me; I was a kind of safety valve, helpful to her feelings even in a passive role. "The place is full of diseases and crawling with insects. No one knows how to do anything properly, and there's nobody to talk to for hundreds of miles!"

Tilly had already been upset that morning by some of those gruesome little tragedies in which Africa abounds. The first concerned the Speckled Sussex pullets she had brought from England, with a fine young cockerel, to start a new line of poultry. One of the pullets, now a hen, had been sitting, and the chicks had just emerged: fluffy yellow balls that darted about, cheeping, full of life and charm. They had hatched the day before; in the night a column of *siafu*, those black, purposeful and horribly sinister warrior ants, had marched through the nest. In the morning the yellow chicks were bedraggled little corpses with their insides eaten out. The hen was alive, and that was the worst of it, for the ants had swarmed over her and eaten half her flesh away, and her eyes, and she lay there twitching now and then. The hen was released from her pain and Tilly stood, white with misery, appalled by thoughts of the helpless chicks' last moments of agony, and by her own failure to prevent the tragedy. "They were just hatched," she said. "Why did this have to happen? What *good* do siafu do?"

"When they march, rain will come," Juma said, removing the corpses. He was unmoved; siafu were a natural hazard.

Later that morning, a woman brought along a baby that, several

422

days before, had fallen into the fire. The burns had suppurated, and the baby, like the hen, still persisted in living in spite of pain that only death could relieve. The contents of the commode were quite inadequate to deal with this situation, as was Tilly's knowledge of first aid. It was remarkable how soon the news had spread that white folk possessed healing medicines, and how women who had refused even to approach us a few weeks ago were already anxious to hand over their children for treatment. Tilly did what she could, which was very little, to treat the baby, and the operation nearly made her sick, the stinking sores were so rotten and the baby so silent, as if it accepted disaster, pain and death as its natural lot.

So that was why she was upset by Robin's rebuke about the commode. He did not know the reasons, and went off thinking her careless and touchy. He was having his troubles too. He had bought some native oxen, and was trying to train them to the plough. They were quite unfamiliar with this implement. Not only did they refuse to draw the plough but they broke chains and yokes, and cavorted all over the place like a herd of buffaloes.

It was fortunate that after tea, when both Tilly and Robin were exhausted and on edge, Randall Swift arrived. He had to push his bicycle most of the way from Thika, and he was always anxious to get back quickly to Punda Milia, but I think the inexperience and general unpreparedness of Robin and Tilly worried him, and he made it his business to see if he could help.

"You need a headman here who knows a bit about these Kikuyu fellows," Randall said cheerfully. "I think I can find one for you, and I'll send him along."

Robin accepted the offer gratefully, and resolved to build a house for him next morning. Everyone got on better at building houses than at yoking oxen to the plough.

Chapter 3

The prospect of a party, even if it consisted only of one guest with nothing but a clean pair of socks in his saddlebag, always gave Tilly's eye a sparkle and her laugh a new gaiety. Life could stab her to the heart, but her resilience was great.

423

Having lost her cherished hen in such distressing circumstances, Tilly instructed Juma to wring the neck of one of its valuable companions to provide a meal worthy of the occasion. I was allowed to stay up for the party, the first we had enjoyed in the grass hut. I picked some wild flowers and Tilly arranged them in one of the cut-glass tumblers, but we were still eating off a packing case, over which a damask tablecloth was spread.

Tilly was by nature a participator, and had a dozen enterprises under way. While Juma took care of the domestic chores, she was laying out a garden, supervising the planting of coffee seedlings, marking out a citrus plantation, paying labour in a corner of the store that served as an office, rendering first aid, and in many other ways filling her day with occupations that made her hot, dirty and tired. Now she had a chance to dress up like a lady, and she took it. She wore grey, a gentle background for her corn-gold hair and milky skin and wild-rose complexion.

"My hands are like a navvy's, the dirt won't come out of the cracks, and as for my nails..." She had been attacking them with a file, a buffer, and some polish from a tiny jar, but the result was discouraging. Tilly was downcast; I doubt if she was ever fully satisfied with anything she did. But she breasted each failure as a dinghy rides a choppy sea, and faced the next with confidence. So she frowned at her nails, remarked, "Well, they're clean anyway," and arranged her hair in a new fashion she had noticed in an illustrated magazine.

Randall was entranced, for she was a handsome woman in the fullness of youth, and had that flame of animation without which all beauty is petrified. I think he fell in love with her a little that night and never lost his admiration afterwards. He was himself a romantic, drawn to Africa less by a dream of fortune than by a wish for freedom and the danger to be found in sport. "When we make our fortune out of sisal," he said, "I shall go home every winter to hunt fox in County Meath, and in the summer I shall come back here to hunt the elephant. Ah, what a grand life that will be! And when the coffee's made a fortune for you, what will you do with it?"

"I should like a safari across the Northern Frontier into Abyssinia and home by the Nile," Tilly answered. "And I'd like to breed New Forest ponies and go to China on the trans-Siberian railway."

When the same question was put to Robin, he replied genially that he meant to buy the most expensive luxury in the world: "Doing absolutely nothing," he said. "A very expensive affair."

Then Randall asked me the same question. It baffled me. I answered at random that what I wanted most of all was a chameleon. I was fascinated by the way these creatures swivelled their deep and watchful eyes in big, baggy purple sockets that enabled them to see in any direction, and loved to feel the dry, cold, burr-like pluck of their agile little fingers on my flesh, and to observe them sway backwards and forwards, like a man about to take a tremendous leap, when they contemplated a darting, forward waddle.

My reply caused the sort of laughter any child dislikes, because it has a ring of patronage; but Juma had made a meringue-crusted pudding with which I was able to console myself, while my elders returned to their own conversation.

Randall kept his word about finding a headman, and in due course Sammy arrived. He was a tall, beak-nosed individual with fine, almost Asiatic, features and thin bones; instead of a blanket he wore a shirt and shorts and a pair of leather sandals. He brought a chit from Randall which said, "You will find this boy reliable and clever. He is half a Masai, so despises the Kikuyu, but the other half is Kikuyu so he understands them. If you give him grazing for his cattle, he will think you a king."

I became friends with Sammy. To the Kikuyu he was stern and often arrogant, but to us he was always polite and dignified. The Kikuyu, as a rule, were not much interested in their surroundings. They walked about their country without aspiring to possess it, or change or tame it. If water flowed down a valley they fetched what they wanted in a large hollow gourd; they did not push it into pipes or harass it with pumps. Consequently, when they left a piece of land and abandoned their huts (as eventually they always did, since they practised shifting cultivation), the bush and vegetation grew up again and obliterated every trace of them.

Sammy took more note of things. He showed me the nests of the small golden weavers that built in swamps: neatly woven purses, lined with seedheads, depending from bent-topped reeds; he followed the yellow-throated francolin whose clutch of speckled eggs was hidden under a grass-tuft. Also, he introduced about half a dozen of his little native cattle to graze on our land.

"This is a bad place for cows," he said, "so I shall bring only a few, enough to keep me from hunger."

"Where are the rest?"

"My father herds them for me with his own." His father was the Masai. "My father's cattle are as many as the gazelle on the plain. They are fat as lice. Kikuyu cattle are thin as grasshoppers."

Unlike the Kikuyu, he always made the most of his wealth and importance. If you asked a Kikuyu how many goats he had, he would shake his head and answer, "How should I own any goats? I am a poor man." The Kikuyu looked in others for the cunning they possessed themselves. If you believed a man to be well-off in goats and cattle, it was ten to one you were thinking of taxes, or levies of some kind. The poor, thought the Kikuyu, were like lizards who could take refuge under stones and exist even if they lost their tails. To the Masai, this attitude was contemptible. A man's glory resided in his herds and flocks, and any Masai felt himself able to defend his own against all comers, even against the government.

Work on the farm proceeded much more smoothly after Sammy came. He and Robin organized a system of piecework and gave each man a daily task. Most people finished by noon and had the afternoon free for rest and talk and the evening for eating and, if occasion offered, for dancing and making merry. But none of the young men drank beer. That was for the elders, who made up for what they had missed in their youth, when warriors had to keep themselves fit and ready to spring to arms.

Sammy was proud, but his pride was so instinctive, so unselfconscious, that it imposed upon others the obligation to respect it, and no European spoke to him in the bullying tones often adopted towards the Kikuyu. Robin and Tilly spoke to Sammy as to a fellow European. In return, he gave them his complete loyalty.

Our ploughing got on better under Sammy's care, but the oxen were still wild. They broke away quite often and had to be chased through the long grass until they were rounded up and yoked again. The ploughing looked very odd by English standards: there seemed to be no furrows, just a sea of lumps and clods, and a tangle of roots. "I don't see how anything can grow," Robin said gloomily.

Tilly pointed out that things grew without much encouragement. "The veranda posts are beginning to sprout," she added.

426

WITHIN A FEW MONTHS of our arrival, several neighbours had settled nearby. The first was a shy but determined young man called Alec Wilson, who had started life as an office boy in some drab Midland city and risen to become a solicitor's clerk. Then his health broke down and he was told to seek a dry and sunny climate if he was to survive. He came out with, I think, two hundred pounds of scraped-together capital, and was lucky enough to meet on the ship a man with somewhat larger resources, and the two between them bought a block of bush next to ours.

Alec Wilson knew even less than Robin did about the business in hand. He thought that he could learn from books, but in this he was mistaken. At that time little, if anything, that was useful or correct had been recorded. Nevertheless, the grass hut he built for himself was soon filled with government reports and textbooks on plantation industries. Robin helped him in a great many ways: lent him oxen to start his ploughing, chains to pull out tree stumps, tools, and even lent him Sammy for a week to organize his labour.

I thought him very old, as he was over thirty. At first he was pasty-faced, with a stupid toothbrush moustache. But he had good, dog-like brown eyes and wavy chestnut hair, and when the sun had cooked him he lost his underdone appearance, his shoulders grew wider and his moustache became more impressive.

On our other side was the South African hunter, Mr. Roos. The land immediately across the river was taken up by a Scot called Jock Nimmo who was always away shooting elephants. After a while he dumped a wife there to make a show of development. The regulations required every settler to spend a certain sum on his land within, I think, the first five years, and to do a certain amount in the way of clearing bush, fencing, cultivating and putting up buildings. Anyone who failed to do this lost his land. Mr. Nimmo left all this to his wife. Tilly thought that was why he had married her. She was a nursing sister from Edinburgh who had come out to the Nairobi hospital, and that was where Jock Nimmo had met her. Soon after their marriage he left her in the bush, and went off to poach ivory in the Belgian Congo.

Mrs. Nimmo had hoped to put nursing behind her, and disliked references to her former profession. She asked Tilly and myself to tea and produced a silver-plated teapot, fluted teacups decorated with

427

rosebud-chains, and many sweet cakes which I enjoyed. Conversation was difficult. Mrs. Nimmo wanted to talk about the new governor's pretty daughters, and a controversy then splitting the world of fashion as to whether sleeves should be open, or gathered in at the wrist; whereas Tilly's mind was running on such topics as pleuro-pneumonia among oxen and twisted taproots in coffee seedlings.

"I'm afraid I was a great disappointment," Tilly admitted afterwards. "The only other white woman for twenty miles and absolutely ignorant about the latest fashion in sleeves."

Early one morning a panting messenger arrived with a chit which said, "Please come at once. I have a loose murderer."

Robin collected a mule and crossed the river by a new bridge he had made. When he came back several hours later he remarked, "She's an extraordinary woman. There she was, gaily strapping up a sliced buttock and a gashed tummy. It was a ghastly sight—and when I remarked about it she said, 'Ah, weel, I've seen worse at the Infirmary on a Saturday night.'"

The Nimmos' drunken headman, it seemed, had attacked a Kikuyu, whose friends and relatives had promptly rounded on him. This was during the night. By dawn everyone had vanished, leaving the headman alone in the hut to bleed to death. But when Mrs. Nimmo had discovered him in the morning he was still alive.

"He has no chance, poor fellow," she said, drawing on a good deal of experience; but she had not reckoned with African toughness. The headman wished very much to live, and so he did. On the other hand, men who appeared to be quite healthy would sometimes die because they wanted to.

After that, Mrs. Nimmo found herself reverting more and more to her profession. People came to her at all hours and from miles away and it was very hard to refuse them, yet she lacked the medicines to treat them with, or money to buy the necessary drugs. Robin and Tilly used to buy supplies when they visited Nairobi, and a doctor Mrs. Nimmo had served under sometimes sent her things. For the rest, she worked by faith and Epsom salts.

About twice a week we sent a syce down to the post at Thika on a mule. Not much, as a rule, came back, but one day Robin received a letter from Roger Stilbeck that ran: "Some people you will like have

428

just bought a block of Thika land. His name is Hereward Palmer. He was in the Ninth. She is a dear. They are new at the game and I told them you'd give them a hand. She will be a friend for Tilly."

This letter infuriated Tilly. "He thinks he can dictate whom I'm to make friends with, just because he's sold us some land for a disgusting profit. If the Palmers are friends of his I shall have nothing to do with them."

"They won't be friends after they discover how much he's stung them," Robin said soothingly. He did not like to admit it, but he looked forward eagerly to the Palmers' arrival. After prolonged struggles with reluctant oxen, unexpected weather, and Kikuyu who had very little idea of what they were expected to be doing at all, he yearned for communication with more orderly minds.

Tilly and I ran into the Palmers at the Blue Posts Hotel. We had ridden down to the dukas and looked in on our way back to leave a pair of socks Tilly had knitted for Randall, and some guava jelly she had made. We were hot, dusty and dishevelled, and saw on the veranda two tidy figures. Tilly guessed at once who they were and tried to bolt, but Major Breeches hurried out to introduce them.

Although it is so long ago, and afterwards she changed so much, I can still remember Lettice Palmer as I saw her then for the first time: friendly, eager, and above all handsome in a stylish, natural and entirely unselfconscious manner. Her skin was fresh and translucent as the petal of a columbine. Her eyes were amber-brown and her hair an unusual colour, like dark sherry; she had a trick of tilting her head back and arching her nostrils when attentive or amused.

"What a journey!" she cried. "The grass is brown, the trees have huge flowers but no leaves, it's the women who carry everything . . . and do you really live here? You've got a house? A garden? I hope you'll help me, I feel like a lost sheep on a mountain full of wolves."

"A year ago I shouldn't have called it a house or a garden," Tilly replied. "But I suppose we have both in a sense. Of course we'll help."

"I don't know where to begin. Hereward thinks I should not have brought Chang and Zena, but I couldn't leave them behind. I love them dearly and they have the hearts of lions."

Chang and Zena were Pekinese, and lay at her feet looking disdainful and hot. Certainly on this bare veranda, beside a bougainvillaea whose concentrated purple almost screamed aloud, and surrounded by tawny vegetation much the same colour as the Pekes' silky coats, they seemed strangely out of place.

Captain Palmer had jumped to his feet when Tilly appeared, bowed slightly over her hand and now stood stiffly upright, surveying the scene with an air of male superiority and a touch of pasha-like complacency. He was a good-looking man: fair, with hair brushed straight back off a high forehead, a long bony face, strong features and a vigorous moustache. He could have been nothing on earth but an English officer. "Plenty of game, I suppose?" he inquired, feeling the bristles of his moustache with the tips of his fingers. He smelled faintly, and pleasantly, of bay rum.

"The only beautiful things in the country, so far as I can see, are the wild animals, and everyone thirsts to slaughter them," Lettice Palmer said. "When they have succeeded there'll be nothing left but ticks and dust and those pathetic little oxen. And the children! Why have they all got such big tummies?"

"Eat too much," suggested the captain.

"No, no, the wrong things," Tilly amended. "But the doctors say it's partly an enlarged spleen, from malaria."

Lettice Palmer impulsively covered her face with her hands, which were fine and white with long fingers. The gesture was theatrical, but to her natural; nothing that she did struck one as false. "How dreadful! There must be *something* we can do! All those children half deformed and the women going along like toads under those enormous burdens and the babies with flies all over their eyes!"

"My wife is very sensitive," Captain Palmer said, with some pride. "These things upset her. But she'll get used to it."

"That's just the trouble! One gets used to it and then one takes it for granted and then it all goes on as before. How dreadful it is. But I'm sure it will do me good. Layers of virtue will be added to my nature until I become a pearl for Hereward and adorn his establishment, like the record blackbuck he shot in Nepal.

"The ship was full of people," Lettice went on, "who thought they would very soon make a fortune, but I cannot think why. The natives have been here for thousands of years and all they have is a few beads. Hereward wants to own a coffee plantation...."

430

Hereward said, "Look at the fortunes made in India and Ceylon. A slow business, admittedly. Nothing back for five years."

"Five years!" Lettice looked as if he had stabbed her to the heart. "In five years I shall be fat and middle-aged. In five years our son Hugh will be nine years old and perhaps he'll have forgotten that he ever had parents at all. I find it hard to bear that he has to stay at home. But what a lot I am talking about myself; now you must tell us how we are to start setting about things on our piece of land."

Tilly gave advice, most of which dismayed Captain Palmer even more than his wife. They had with them two handsome ponies, which Tilly told Captain Palmer he ought not to take to his new farm until he had a stable.

"They'll die of horse-sickness within a few months," she said, "unless you shut them in before dark and keep them in a mosquito-proof stable."

"Roger Stilbeck said there was no horse-sickness here," the captain remarked.

"He's a great talker," Tilly cautiously remarked.

"At least the altitude makes it healthy for human beings?" Lettice suggested.

"Well, in a way; of course bubonic plague and smallpox are endemic, and the natives are riddled with yaws and parasites, so you must be sure to boil the water. There's typhoid about, and you must be very careful of those dear little Pekes; it's important to de-tick them every day. There's a form of tick fever here that affects dogs. And there's rabies, so if you see a native dog behaving suspiciously you must quickly shoot it."

"Thank you," Lettice said, "you have been a great help."

"I shall come and call on your husband," the captain added. He was looking displeased. "I'm sure he will take pity on a greenhorn and put me on the right lines."

"If you can reach him through a sea of germs," Lettice remarked. She had taken up the two Pekinese in her arms and was playing with their silky ears as if to reassure herself that something in the world was still soft and desirable.

Tilly rode back a little guiltily, for she had liked Lettice, but never could resist the urge to deflate pomposity. "I wonder why they came," she speculated to Robin. "It doesn't seem their sort of life, and if they have money . . . it might have been some kind of scandal. Perhaps she ran away with him."

"A fellow like that will want a stone house," Robin meditated. "There's some stone that looks just right for building near the river bank, on our land. I wonder if he'd like to go into partnership over a small quarry?"

ROBIN RETURNED from his first visit to the Palmers' camp only temporarily discouraged. Captain Palmer intended to employ a building contractor in Nairobi to put up his house.

"He must be very rich indeed," Robin said wistfully. "But I warned him he'd waste hundreds of pounds. I think the idea sank in; he may change his mind, and decide to develop the quarry."

After the Palmers had settled into their grass huts—larger and better ones than ours—they rode over on their superior ponies to lunch, and in the afternoon Robin showed Captain Palmer his hard-won development. The clearing of the bush had been slow and difficult, but at last a level piece of ground near our camp had been ploughed and worked down to a seedbed that would have appalled any English farmer, but that was adequate for coffee, which was planted as seedlings ten or twelve inches high. In the dry weather before the long rains, the Kikuyu dug holes for the seedlings. This task was supposed to be finished before the rains, but of course was not, and then came a crisis when the seedlings Robin had bought arrived before the ground was ready for them.

By now the first rains, which were torrential and cold and stopped the progress of all wagons and carts, had come and gone, and our seedlings had been planted in the freshly broken land. Already they had vanished beneath a carpet of weeds; the warriors had been set to work with *pangas* to demolish this and give the precious seedlings a chance to find light and air.

After the first day, Sammy came to Robin to report that the warriors refused to demolish weeds any longer. "Their pride would be injured if they were seen cutting weeds. It is women's work."

"If it's women's work," Robin said, "perhaps we had better get some women."

So Sammy went to see Chief Kupanya, and in due course a number of young women came swinging gaily down the path from the

432

reserve chanting a song which, to judge from the laughter it aroused
among the warriors, was ribald and obscene. Their heads were
clean-shaven except for a patch on top, about the circumference of
an eggcup, which showed them to be unmarried. They were bare to
the waist and had shapely breasts, and wore a triangular leather
apron in front and behind. They also wore beads and brass or copper
anklets, and objects dangling from their ears. They sang all the time
they worked, and did three times as much as the men.

When Captain Palmer rode over he saw these young women at
work with mingled disapproval and envy. "Hardly seems quite the
thing, does it?" he suggested. "With all those idle young bloods
eating their heads off and not lifting a finger."

"You know what tribal customs are," Robin answered knowingly.

Tilly took Lettice to see her hens and turkeys, a young orchard,
an embryonic garden, and rows of pegs where everyone hoped a
house would one day rise. Lettice was impressed.

"How do you find the *energy* to do so much?" she asked. "This
country's full of sloth, and the air distils it. It's become too strong for
me to resist. Or do you think I am making excuses?"

Tilly did think so, but she merely smiled. She could not help being

433

entertained by Lettice, who exuded charm as a rose its scent, and just as unwittingly. That afternoon she sat on our narrow lean-to veranda playing with the silky ears of her Pekinese and smiling a little forlornly.

"This country frightens me," she said. "Doesn't it strike you as strange that nothing people have created here has survived? No ruins of cities or temples—no tombs or burial mounds? Do you realize that quite soon *we* shall be the past? And what will there be to show that we have ever existed?"

"You're being morbid," Tilly said. "It's true the natives have done nothing yet with the country, but we shall. It all comes as a bit of a shock at first, but you'll get used to it. One sort of grows into the life."

"How confident you are! When I start some simple task, a hundred distractions spring up to prevent me from completing it. Since I've been here I find I cannot concentrate on French novels, and the other day I couldn't for the life of me remember the words of one of my songs. We've got a small grand piano on the way out. And then I shall practise, practise, practise every day!"

Lettice removed her hat, which involved the extraction of several long pins with heads of mother-of-pearl; her silky hair, wound over a frame called a sausage (I knew because Tilly used one), sat on her shapely head like a kind of plate, and threw a faint shadow over the top part of her face. The rolls of hair shone like polished mahogany, and the scent she used reminded me of heliotrope.

Hereward and Robin came back from their tour almost as brothers. Although Robin had served only for a short while in the Yeomanry, he had managed to recall one or two slight acquaintances in the Ninth; and once that had been established, Hereward had fallen into line very satisfactorily about the quarry. He would engage a mason to cut and dress enough stone for Robin's house as well as for his own. Robin would contribute the raw materials, which luckily did not need any wages.

"Now we can build some stables," Tilly said delightedly.

"And a house for my piano," Lettice suggested.

Captain Palmer stroked his moustache and smiled at Tilly. "My wife is musical," he said, as if enlisting sympathy for some distressing ailment. "I foresee difficulties in getting it here."

434

"It is with your trophies, Hereward," Lettice reminded him. "They will need a house too."

Hereward laughed. "They will share ours. Though I shouldn't say it, I have some fine specimens."

"I suppose you will add to them here," Tilly said.

"Well, of course, when we've settled in. They tell me the ladies are as keen on safari as the men. Perhaps we could persuade you to join up with us and show us the ropes?"

And so the Palmers, by and large, were a success. Lettice even paid some attention to me. I had at this time a hospital for sick animals, which included a lame hen, a baby duiker and a pigeon with a broken leg. This I had bandaged with tape and set in splints made of two matches. Lettice helped me to rearrange the pigeon's splints and to feed the duiker from a bottle.

"Which is your favourite animal," Lettice asked, "among all that you have seen here?"

Even Lettice, I thought sadly—even Lettice who fascinated me like some brilliantly plumaged bird—even she did not avoid that distressing adult habit of asking enormous questions to which there could be no sensible reply. Cornered, however—I did not want to disappoint her—I fell back on my chameleons. She looked surprised, and stroked the ruffled pigeon with slender fingers on which there sparkled several rings.

"You should keep one as a pet," she said. "No, two; you must always have animals in pairs. Most people keep only one, and try to suck all the love out of it like a vampire, but that's cruel. Look at this bird's eye, it's like a ruby in a certain light; why are pigeons' eyes red, I wonder? Yours are blue. So are Hugh's; he is much younger than you, and I've no idea whether he's fond of animals and birds, or whether he's musical. . . . We must be going, Hereward; if we are away too long we shall find the headman drunk and trying to murder someone."

"A fine woman," Robin said appreciatively, looking after their departing ponies.

"Emotional," concluded Tilly. This was a word of condemnation, because Tilly was a devotee of reason. In fact, no one was a greater victim of emotions, at least of the more generous kind, but she felt that to give way to them was rather disgraceful.

Chapter 4

One day a syce arrived with a note scrawled on sky-blue writing paper in Lettice's large and sloping hand. "Please come at once," it said. "There has been a terrible disaster." Robin climbed onto his mule and trotted off to the Palmers'.

A note came back about an hour later. "You had better come, there has been a fight. And bring iodine, bandages and scissors."

Tilly collected the equipment and set out, taking me with her. Outwardly, all seemed unruffled at the Palmers': a man in a red blanket swung a sickle-ended stick very slowly to and fro, decapitating grass-heads on what would one day be a lawn, others drooped about in various attitudes of indolence among the foundations of the future house. We asked for Lettice, and a houseboy led us to the Kikuyu huts a little way off. Lettice emerged from one of them looking white and shaky, with blood on her hands.

"Thank God you've come," she cried. "Our headman has been cut to ribbons. I've done what I can but I'm not good at it; it's dark and everything is filthy and the others have all run away." Tilly took her arm and told her to go and lie down. "First aid is not my strong point either," Tilly said, "but I'm getting used to it; where has Robin gone?"

"He and Hereward have ridden off to catch the man who did it."

Tilly vanished into the dark little hut with its horrors, while I returned to the house with Lettice, who helped herself to brandy and then lay on a sofa with her eyes closed, white and limp. "Perhaps I could have saved him," she said, opening her eyes, "but this happened in the night and they never told us till the morning; and all that time the wretched man..."

"Is he dead?" I inquired.

"Not quite, although I can't imagine why."

Lettice looked lovely and incongruous on the sofa in the rough hut. Or rather, the sofa was incongruous in the mud-floored rondavel. It was covered in green velvet, and its ends were looped together by golden cords; beside it was a low stool, on whose cushions, worked in petit point, Chang and Zena lay. The rondavel smelt of lavender.

"That man had a gash right through his skull," Lettice murmured.

"Part of his scalp was hanging down over his cheek. What a conversation for a child! Get that box from the table in the corner and I will teach you how to play chess."

The carved pieces with their pennants and prancing horses fascinated me so much that the rules of the game hardly seemed to matter, but Lettice was patient and showed me what to do. After a while Tilly came in. She was flushed, and her hands trembled. "He's still alive," she said, "but I don't think he will be much longer. They have all deserted him, which means they think it's hopeless; they won't sit with a dying person. Usually, they drag the sick person out to die; that saves the hut. If someone dies inside it, they have to burn it down."

"Let's have a game of chess," Lettice suggested. Tilly started to speak, but then changed her mind, for she saw that Lettice was very pale and her hands were shaking.

"If you are a good player, you had better give me a castle," Tilly remarked. "I haven't played since I was at school."

But Lettice only had half her mind on the game. "I am glad that Robin is with Hereward," she said. "He will have a calming influence. When Hereward is angry he doesn't bluster and shout, which gets it out of the system, he goes hard and cold as an icicle, and I'm always afraid that he will kill someone."

"He may find life here difficult, it consists so much of petty irritations."

"Life has been difficult for Hereward everywhere in the last few years. . . . I'm sorry, I'm afraid I must take your queen."

Alec Wilson, a rifle slung over his shoulder, arrived while they were still playing. "I heard there'd been trouble," he said, striding into the room in a purposeful manner. "If there's anything I can do, here I am. Where's Captain Palmer?"

Lettice explained, and Alec looked relieved. "In that case it's just as well I came; I can hold the fort while you two ladies are left on your own. One never knows what a spark may do; I sometimes wonder if we're sitting on a powder magazine."

Presently he escorted Tilly to the injured man's hut, and they returned, subdued and shaken, to say that he was dead.

Shortly thereafter Hereward and Robin returned. They had not caught the murderer, but had seen the chief, and Kupanya had promised to produce the culprit. "Meanwhile," Captain Palmer said, "half my labour force has run away and I must get the fellow buried. I'm told these Kikuyu won't touch a corpse."

This was true; but the contractor who was going to build the Palmers' house had sent out half a dozen men of another tribe. They were large and very black and liked to work stark naked, and were called Kavirondo. They did not object to handling corpses—in fact, rather the reverse. When at length we reached home on our mules, Sammy observed, "Why does the *bwana* want to bury the dead man? The Kavirondo will only dig him up again."

"But why?"

"To eat, of course. The Kavirondo much enjoy corpses."

"Then they are *shenzis*," Tilly said. *Shenzi* was a useful word, meaning anything from savage to down-at-heel or untidy.

"Yes, indeed," Sammy agreed complacently.

We had a mule called Margaret, very tame and good-natured; she would come to the veranda and eat sugar out of Tilly's hand. I was allowed to ride her, and sometimes Sammy would escort me on his bicycle along the twisting paths. That afternoon, I went to find Njombo, to ask him to saddle Margaret. But Njombo had vanished. When I found Sammy, he said, "Njombo will come back in a few days. Kupanya has sent for him."

I felt an uneasy foreboding. "Is it because of the dead man?"

Sammy smiled. "These affairs are not for children."

"If Kupanya catches him, will Njombo be sent to the district commissioner?"

"Njombo will not go to the DC," Sammy said firmly.

"Bwana Palmer will send him."

"It has nothing to do with Bwana Palmer. Njombo's father, who is dead, was Kupanya's brother. Kimani—that is the dead man—was drunk, and insulted Njombo. There was trouble between them about a woman, and Njombo hit him with a *panga*. No doubt some enemy of Njombo's used medicine to make Kimani die. As it is, there will be heavy fines to pay; Njombo is poor, and so Kupanya will have to help him to find many goats."

"But Kupanya has promised to send the murderer to the DC," I said, feeling rather at sea.

"Kupanya will find someone to send," Sammy said.

It all seemed very involved, and I was sorry Njombo had gone; I liked him, he was always cheerful, and he wore with a rakish air a little bead-edged leather cap, made from a sheep's stomach.

"Njombo is buying a wife," Sammy added. "Now all his goats will have to go to Kimani's father, so he will not be able to buy her."

"I hope he will come back," I said.

"He will come back, for he will need rupees to buy goats to pay Kimani's father. Kimani was a worthless man, but now he has died he will bring wealth to his father."

I could not mourn Kimani, as I had not known him; but next morning the pigeon with the broken leg lay in its moss-lined box stiff and cold, its eyes half closed. Tilly found me in tears and suggested an honourable funeral, so I dug a grave and interred it underneath a young fig tree, and made a small cross.

The little duiker was a comfort, and let me stroke her warm body while she waggled a stumpy tail. She had thick, stiff hair with a faint tinge of blue about it, and a line down the middle of her back. Sometimes she twitched her ears and lifted her muzzle and I knew that she was testing the air for the least whiff of other duikers, for news from home, as it were, and that if such news came, she would perhaps disappear. We called her Twinkle. When she came, her legs had been like long, thin twigs and her eyes enormous; gradually the rest of her body grew to match their scale. She walked about freely, and came into the house and nibbled titbits from my hand.

The houseboys grew used to her; although the Kikuyu killed duikers and other buck whenever they could, because of damage done to their shambas, they did not eat the flesh of wild animals, so Twinkle was safe with them. But Juma warned me against the Kavirondos. "They will eat her if they see her," he said.

A few days later a toto arrived with a wicker basket and a chit for Tilly. Inside the basket, on a bed of leaves, sat two green chameleons, a present to me from Lettice. "I hope they are a he and a she, but no one seems able to tell," she wrote. "At any rate they appear to be friends." We called them George and Mary, because Robin thought their crests looked like crowns, and they had the dignified, deliberate movements proper to royalty.

Their repertoire of colour was not very wide, but they could change from green-all-over to a patchy greenish-brown with touches

439

of yellow (suitable for bark) in
about twenty minutes. It was fascinating to watch the lightning dart
of their long, forked tongues, which
would nick a fly off a leaf too swiftly
for the eye to follow.

We built a large cage of wire
netting around a shrub, where they
could lead a natural life. To begin
with I caught flies for them, but
they ignored my offerings. They
were independent creatures, and
waved their legs as if they were
cycling when I picked them up, wriggling desperately; yet they were
not frightened of me and never tried to run away.

TILLY WAS TRYING to educate me in such time as she could spare from
the farm and garden. Luckily I liked reading, and she left me alone a
good deal with the book of the moment, but we were not well placed
to get hold of the right kind of literature, and sometimes I had to fall
back on old copies of the *Field*, manuals of instruction on everything
from lace-making to the erection of simple stills (Robin was putting
one up to distil essential oils), and the volumes of a pocket
encyclopedia in minute type.

These I found rather beyond my capacity, and when Tilly was
safely occupied I would abandon them in favour of trying to catch
George or Mary in the act of eating a fly, or playing with Twinkle,
or talking to Sammy and Njombo who (as Sammy had predicted)
had reappeared, as jaunty as ever as far as I could see. We had an
atlas and Tilly put me on to tracing and painting maps.

I was colouring a map one day when Lettice Palmer walked in,
looking, as always, fresh and elegant, although she had ridden over in
the heat of the day. She had taken off her heavy hat and her red-
brown hair was glossy and smooth. "Come," she said, "I've a surprise
for you outside."

A syce stood on the lawn holding two ponies, her own and one I
had not seen before: a small, white, dumpy animal with short legs, a
short neck, and a suspicious expression. I gazed at the pony, which

changed before my eyes into a splendid milk-white charger. An ability to match my thanks to the gift was beyond me; I muttered a few disjointed words. The pony's nostrils were soft and springy, like woodland moss, and his breath sweet. He cocked an ear as if to say he accepted my advances, and understood that he had come to stay.

"You'll have to name him," Lettice said. "Something grand like Charlemagne or Galahad. He came from a place called Moyale."

That was the name that stuck to him, Moyale. Tilly and Robin were nearly as overcome as I was. Tilly grew pink with embarrassment. She did not like receiving presents on a scale much too lavish to reciprocate, yet of course Moyale could not be returned.

"Ian Crawfurd got him for me," Lettice said. This was a name I had not heard before, but one that was to crop up often in my elders' conversation. "It came down with a batch from the Abyssinian frontier," she added. "They drove the ponies through the desert. One night they were attacked by raiders and had a pitched battle, and another time lions broke in and stampeded the ponies, and they lost three or four."

More than ever did Moyale become an object of romance and enchantment. Njombo, who was used to mules, professed himself delighted with Moyale. "What a pony!" he cried. "He will gallop like a zebra, he is strong and healthy and yet not fierce; now you have a pony fit for King George."

We found a brush and groomed him every day. His hide had many scars and gashes, and a brand on the flank. To me, these scars were relics of sabre strokes delivered in a battle. Certainly Moyale had not led a sheltered life, but he soon grew tame and learned to enjoy sugar and carrots.

For a prince's charger, full of battle scars, he was surprisingly placid. He would amble peacefully along with one ear cocked forward and the other off duty, in a resting position; but life had imposed a wary sense upon him, and sometimes I could feel a current of alertness running through his body. Once, he shied violently and threw me off into a prickly bush, but waited politely for me to remount. His main fault was a hard mouth, a result of the long, brutal bits used by Somali and Boran horsemen.

Soon after this Ian Crawfurd arrived to stay with the Palmers, who asked Tilly and Robin over for the evening. I had to go, too, as I could not be left, and they arranged for me to sleep there, rather than ride back late at night. I was given a tent, much to my satisfaction, for there was nothing I liked better than tents. By day their hot, jungly smell was delightful. At night they had the charm of a warm, protecting, secret cave, a refuge and a private kingdom. Lying on the camp bed, you could make shadows on the canvas by holding your hand near the lantern.

Tilly wanted to tie the flap back to admit plenty of air, but I implored her to shut it. "There's nothing to be afraid of," she said.

"There are cannibals."

"Cannibals! You must control your imagination."

I reminded her about the Kavirondo who had perhaps—though no one seemed to know—eaten the man Njombo had killed.

"Nonsense," Tilly said. "That was just an invention of Sammy's. In any case, they only eat people who are dead."

All the same, she did close the flap and leave the lantern burning. The tent was close enough to the living room for me to hear bursts of laughter. Ian Crawfurd was a young man who left a wake of laughter as he skimmed along. Hereward Palmer was the best-looking man I knew, but Ian Crawfurd was much more attractive. He was even fairer—his hair looked almost silver in the lamplight—and his face drew your eyes, because its expression was always changing, like cloud shadows on mountains, and because the bones were so beautifully formed. Ian was strong and lean, but he did not walk heavily like Hereward, he walked with precision and spring, like a tracker. His eyes, blue-grey in colour, were candid and clear.

Ian Crawfurd was a friendly person who found life entertaining and agreeable. He had arrived on horseback attended by a tall, thin, proud Somali who wore a shawl of bright tomato-red wound loosely round his head, and who appeared to disdain all that he saw. To him, no doubt, we were effete, heathen southerners; only loyalty, the virtue next to courage, obliged him to come amongst us, like an eagle in a parrot's cage.

When I awoke, a blade of sunlight had thrust under the flap of my tent, and outside the doves gurgled like water tumbling from a narrow-necked jar. I got up to pay my morning visit to Moyale and found Ian Crawfurd at the stable preparing for an early ride. His hair shone like kingcups in the morning light. "I'm glad you liked the pony," he said. "I picked him out from a batch of twenty or so; I thought he was the nicest."

"Did he belong to a prince?"

Ian Crawfurd replied that, in a sense, he had. "He belonged to a Ras, and a Ras is a kind of prince, if frequently a villain also. The Ras didn't want him to leave Abyssinia, even though he accepted a red cloak and a Winchester rifle and gave me his word; so he had to be smuggled out, with his nineteen companions."

I had heard of watches being smuggled, and scent; but ponies?

"That's a long story," Ian Crawfurd said. "Too long to tell before breakfast; let's ride up the ridge and you shall tell me who lives where, and what sort of animals you'd turn them into if you had been apprenticed to a witch who knew how."

Everyone (he went on to explain) had some affinity with a bird or reptile.

I thought Mrs. Nimmo might become an ostrich because she had a large behind which waggled when she hurried, and he assigned to Captain Palmer the giraffe because he was long and thin and had large feet and a thick hide; to Alec Wilson a bat-eared fox, for his large ears and big brown eyes.

When I mentioned Lettice Palmer, he laughed and shook his head. "We must leave her out of it," he said.

"But why?"

He pointed with his whip at the sun, which was climbing quickly above the tawny ridge, towards some fluffy clouds. "Suppose the sun entered the sign of Virgo, the tide turned, and an eagle perched upon the Sphinx, all at the same moment, it might really happen; and we should look fools if we got back for breakfast and found our hostess had become a wallaby."

I felt disappointed in Ian; like nearly all grown-ups, he had started something sensible and let it tail off into stupidity. But when I looked at him it was impossible to be annoyed, he was so gay and spirited, and smiled with such goodwill.

"Perhaps she'd be a sort of bird," I persisted. "With lovely feathers. A kind sort, of course."

"I'm not sure there are any," said Ian, who did not seem to have a high opinion of birds. "Rather, I think, 'the milk-white hind, immortal and unchanged', if that isn't blasphemous."

We turned our ponies for home, and took a short cut through the bush. Ian, leading the way, suddenly pulled up and signalled to me with his riding crop. It was part of the excitement of any ride that you never knew what you might encounter; apart from duiker and other small game there were plenty of leopards about, and lions came now and then on visits from the plains. The grass reached above the ponies' knees. We halted on a low hump and saw below us nothing more ferocious than a circle of beaten-down grass, like a miniature racecourse, about two feet across; and round the ring a single black and shiny-feathered bird, with a ruff like a Tudor courtier's, only black too, was prancing and hopping like a demented ballet dancer, and springing into the air. In the middle of the circle, a small, drab bird sat and brooded, thrusting its neck forwards and backwards as if something had stuck in its throat.

"Wydah birds," Ian said softly. "Watch them."

We watched in silence while the birds performed their antics ten or twelve paces away. After a while the central hen evidently grew bored and started to peck at some grass seeds. Whether because of her indifference, or for some other reason, the cock's attention also wandered, his ruff subsided, his wings drooped, his tail sagged, and suddenly he flew away. Presently a second black and shiny cock landed in the ring, ruffed up his neck feathers, arched the long plumes of his tail, and began to prance. I do not know how long we should have watched them if Moyale, growing bored, had not snorted and sneezed. There was a chattering of alarm, a flapping of wings, and both birds took off and vanished over the crest of the ridge.

It was their mating dance, Ian Crawfurd explained. One after the other, cocks came to parade in their finery before the female, who squatted in the centre with a bright appraising eye; after a while, she would choose one for her mate.

"What happens to the others?" I inquired.

"They fly away and look for another hen to fascinate."

"There must be some who never get a mate."

"Yes, they are the doomed, perpetual bachelors; no nest to go home to, no little chicks to find insects for, no one to puff out chests and sing about when other cocks go by."

"It sounds very sad."

444

"Yes, it is. There was once a cock who loved the fairest of all the wydah birds, but another cock had made her his own. So she shared the nest of another, and sat by his side, and when her chosen mate danced before her, she nodded her head at him to say bravo, bravo. The first cock knew that she could not be his, because he came too late. So he flew far away into the mountains and looked for worms and beetles and things like that."

Ian Crawfurd paused, I thought to collect words for the ending; but that seemed to be all. "What happened then?"

"Nothing happened—and that's the way to tell a true story from a made-up one. A made-up story always has a neat and tidy end. But true stories don't end, at least until their heroes and heroines die."

Ian was right, I supposed, but it was unsatisfactory, for everything ought to have a beginning, a middle and an end.

Chapter 5

Ahmed the Somali was waiting to welcome Ian back, clad in a white silk robe, a green sash, and his tomato-red turban. He bowed and brought a cupped hand to the centre of his forehead with a wide sweep of the arm. Ian threw his binoculars to this haughty noble, and expressed the hope that, in the absence of camels' milk, he had found suitable nourishment. Ahmed inclined his head and replied, "I have eaten, bwana."

At breakfast, Lettice Palmer remarked, "Ahmed makes me uneasy; I can never quite get over the feeling that I ought to be on my knees like a Circassian slave offering him a bowl of rosewater. He's the only *regal* character I've ever encountered."

"I felt the same at first," Ian admitted, "but his manners are so perfect he's managed to make me feel like a caliph born to command the service of princes; so we are both satisfied."

"I had a splendid fellow very like him once, on the Frontier," Hereward announced. "He once killed four Pathans single-handed."

"And ate them all for breakfast," Lettice said sharply. She immediately looked contrite, and asked Hereward how the farm work was getting on. Hereward replied meekly; he was her slave. He had the farm labour organized in gangs called after colours: the blue

445

squad, the red squad, and so on. In his office, a cubicle divided off from the store, he kept on the wall a large map of his farm studded with pins bearing little coloured flags, so that he could see at once where each squad was, or ought to be.

He was, however, plagued by a distressing tendency on the part of his men to wander from one squad to another as the spirit moved them. If he put the blue squad onto clearing tree stumps, a hot, strenuous activity, and the red squad onto thatching shelters for coffee seedlings, which took place by the river in the shade, by ten o'clock he would find the red squad twice its proper size and the blue squad sadly diminished.

"Not one of these fellows has an inkling of the meaning of discipline!" he would cry. "I suppose I must just go on trying to knock it into them, that's all."

He did try, very hard, and it was unjust that Lettice found his efforts ludicrous. As a rule she concealed her feelings, but Ian's presence made this more difficult. That day at breakfast, while Hereward was holding forth, I saw their eyes meet across the table and then drop to their plates. Their mouths twitched just a little, and simultaneously they both picked up their knives and forks and resumed their eating.

I was always sorry when the time came for me to leave the Palmers'. Their living room was quite different from ours, although the shape was much the same, and the reed lining, and the lizards in the roof. Their furniture had many curves and curlicues and decorations, there were quantities of books in fresh, exciting jackets, and the room always smelled delicious. Dried roseleaves and lavender mixed with patchouli in Chinese bowls were no doubt responsible.

Our own house was less exciting, and rather cramped. We lived and ate in a single, square room full of furniture, ranging from the commode and a good mahogany writing table (always piled high with account books, letters, bills and catalogues) to a roughly carpentered wooden table, homemade chairs with seats of cowhide thongs, and a couple of old armchairs upholstered in leather. One side was occupied mainly by an open stone fireplace.

There was no ceiling, only a forest of poles above us, lashed together with creeper-twine, and insect-rustling thatch; the floor undulated so much that all the furniture wobbled, and bits of wood or wads of paper were constantly being stuffed under legs to achieve an equilibrium that never lasted. We always had a lot of flowers, jostling for position among books and paintboxes, magazines and veterinary medicines, Tilly's embroidery, Robin's sketches of machinery, and my birds' eggs.

The living room was flanked on one side by Tilly's and Robin's bedroom, which they shared with several dogs, and on the other side by mine, which was divided into two, half for me and half for the tin bath. My half held little beyond a chest of drawers and a camp bed, with a colobus monkey's skin on the floor beside it. A collection of wooden or china animals stood on the chest of drawers, but no looking glass; indeed for some time no such thing existed in the house, except for a little pocket glass from Tilly's handbag which was propped up in the bathroom for Robin's use when he shaved.

ALTHOUGH NJOMBO HAD RETURNED, Hereward still did not know that he had killed the headman, and kept on pressing Chief Kupanya to produce the guilty man. Kupanya put him off with long, vague messages, so Hereward resolved to go and see the chief, and to combine his visit with a guinea fowl shoot. The guinea fowl were regarded as a pest by the Kikuyu because they came into the shambas and scratched up seed, and boys hunted them with sticks and hit them down from trees at night when they had gone to roost. The Kikuyu therefore welcomed the idea of a shoot, and so did we, because we grew tired of eating small skinny fowls, and looked forward to a meal of plump, succulent birds. So off we set one morning on mules and ponies with a picnic luncheon packed in saddlebags: the Palmers with Ian Crawfurd, Alec Wilson and our three selves.

At first we rode through landscape we were used to, but quite soon we entered the reserve and, although no boundary was marked, the nature of the country changed. Circles of round huts appeared, each fenced with split poles, and the hillsides were patchworked with small, irregular plots of cultivation. The women in the shambas straightened up to watch us, and some ran for shelter, their babies bobbing on their backs, for they had never seen mules or ponies before and thought that they were evil spirits or monstrous objects like centaurs; the whole concept of a man sitting on a beast was wild and strange.

After a steep climb up a slippery hillside we paused to rest our mounts and gaze about us at the chequered ridges, the forest darkening the scene ahead, the thatch of huts poking like mushrooms through bush and floppy-leaved banana trees. The Kikuyu liked privacy; each homestead was brush- or forest-sheltered, each had its own twisting path. The country was greener here than on our farms, and more fertile; the rainfall, you could see, was higher, the air more crisp, and the bush full of bright flowering creepers and shrubs.

Kupanya was waiting for us under a large fig tree outside his fenced enclosure, which had almost the dimensions of a village, because he had so many wives and children. He had dressed up in a cloak of grey monkey skin and wore a kind of shako made of some other fur, together with a great many ornaments and charms. This was a compliment to us; normally he wore a blanket like everyone else, and merely carried a staff with a brass knob on it to indicate his chiefly status. Round him sat a circle of dignified old men with wise, lined, authoritative faces.

"Those are the real rulers of the tribe," Ian said. "Kupanya is more or less a figurehead."

Njombo had told me that Kupanya had been a noted warrior in his time. His prowess with the spear had won him a generous share of booty. "His wealth has grown like a gourd," Njombo commented; and now indeed he looked a little like one, large and full and ripe. He gave us native beer, which Hereward spat out with a grimace and Ian sipped with interest, remarking that it tasted of sour yeast. Alec said that it would give you a bad headache if you drank more than a mouthful. Remarks about crops and weather would have continued for the rest of the day if Hereward had not grown impatient.

"I have been waiting for you to send in the man who killed my headman," he said. "Now I am tired of waiting. If you do not send him immediately to Fort Hall I shall summon the *askaris* and they will come and find him. There will be a case, with a judge, and if he is guilty he will go to prison."

"And if he is not?"

"He will be set free, but then the askaris will come and look for the real culprit. So don't think you can satisfy us with an innocent man."

448

"Why should I do such a thing?" Kupanya asked. "Am I not a chief, and is my first wish not to help the government?"

"In that case you must find the murderer."

"Have I the eyes of a spirit, not of a man? Can I see into the hearts of people and tell their business?"

"Very well," Hereward replied in his no-nonsense tone, "I will send for the askaris."

No one liked having in the askaris, the native police, they were as bad as locusts, and in some ways worse, for locusts did not eat rupees or menace daughters. Kupanya looked thoughtful and sulky. After a conversation in Kikuyu among his fellow elders he rose with dignity from his three-legged council stool. "If God will help me," he said, "I will find the man." Then he stalked off. The others remained squatting in a circle and passed round a horn filled with beer.

After a time Kupanya returned, bringing in tow a slim, drooping lad who looked as if he might evaporate at any minute. His lips were large and loose and he wore a glazed, helpless expression.

"This is the man!" Kupanya announced in tones of doom.

"He doesn't *look* like a murderer," Lettice remarked.

"Nor do I expect he is one," said Ian.

"Ask him," Kupanya said, gesturing grandly towards the boy.

"Did you kill my headman in the fight?" demanded Hereward.

"Yes, bwana."

"Why?" The boy look startled, as if this were a new idea.

"Why?"

"Yes, why, idiot. One doesn't kill people for no reason."

There was a rapid exchange of Kikuyu remarks.

"I killed him because he hit me first. I hit back, and he fell down and died."

"Well, that'll be for the DC to decide. This man must come back with us today," Hereward ordered.

The young man, as he turned to go, smiled and said in halting English, "Goodnight, sir. Save all sinners."

"Good heavens! Where did you learn that?"

"Good morning, sir. God save the King."

"A mission boy!" cried Hereward.

"Yes, bwana," the young man said, relapsing now into Swahili. "I can read a book, I can write a letter."

"Just shows you what these missions teach them," said Hereward. "You'd better send two strong men with him, Kupanya, to see he doesn't escape."

"He will not escape," Kupanya replied.

THE GUINEA FOWL could not be shot until the sun was more than halfway down the sky, and so we found a shady tree some way from Kupanya's village for the picnic. In our circle of cool shade we inhabited a different world from the sun-soaked Kikuyu ridges that stretched to meet a far, enormous sky, blue as a wild delphinium.

"If one followed those little rivers to their birthplace," Lettice inquired, "where would one be?"

"On top of the Aberdare mountains, where it's bleak and cold and marshy and the lions are said to have spots," Ian replied.

"And down there?" Lettice gestured with a sandwich towards the far distance where a brown smudge on the horizon showed us the beginning of the great plains.

"The valley of the Tana, where there's perhaps the finest concentration of game in all the world."

"I must go there one day," Lettice said.

Alec Wilson, with an air of plucking up his courage, observed, "That's not the sort of thing you're cut out for, Mrs. Palmer. Marching and camping and that sort of thing."

"If you mean that Mrs. Palmer is too good for Africa," Ian suggested, "you are probably right."

"That is rather a large claim," Lettice said.

"Surely it isn't a question of which is superior, Lettice or the continent of Africa," Tilly suggested. "It's a question of raising the level of the native conditions. That's the whole point of our being here. When we've knocked a bit of civilization into the natives, all this dirt and disease and superstition will go and they'll live like decent people." She looked quite flushed and excited when she said this, as if it was something dear to her heart.

"Captain Palmer hasn't told us yet why he came," Ian Crawfurd put in.

"I came to play a small part in building a new colony under the crown. As for the natives, they are very fortunate to come under British rule."

450

This declaration put a full stop to the conversation. We lay under the tree in silence, watching the sky through gently moving leaves and hearing the rustle of grasses, the far tinkle of goat-bells, the chirruping of crickets.

Ian lay on his back creating for himself, it almost seemed, with his bright hair, a little tarn of sunlight. He was reclining on one of the light, fine woollen shawls affected by the Somalis, and it matched the sky. Lettice was propped on one elbow, scratching patterns in the soil with a twig. An ant carrying a speck of food hurried across the dusty plain under her eye. With the twig, she gently pushed it aside to change its direction, but each time it turned back to resume the course on which it was set. Ian was watching her with a look of concentration. She raised her eyes and they gazed at one another. "Such a little thing," she remarked. "Yet its resolution is stronger than mine."

Ian spoke very quietly, so that I could hardly hear. "Lettice, you have me at your mercy like that wretched insect. You have paralysed my will."

"I have done nothing," Lettice said gently.

"You have existed. You exist now. And that is enough."

"Hush," Lettice murmured, "you are indiscreet."

"So is a volcano, so is a typhoon, so are the flames of a blast furnace. It is too late for discretion."

"Too late . . ." Lettice echoed. She was breathing quickly, as if she had walked uphill.

"What are you two talking about?" Hereward inquired.

"Ian is describing the habits of ants."

"Surely we've filled in enough time talking nonsense," Hereward said, springing to his feet. "Where have the beaters got to?"

The shooting got under way. The men were to beat homeward down the valleys, and Tilly, who was learning the sport, went with them. She was frightened of the gun at first but soon learned to control it, and Hereward remarked admiringly that she would make a splendid little shot.

I rode with Lettice along the winding paths while shadows began to advance up the red and green hillsides, turning the intervening valleys into pools of darkness. The beaters made a great deal of noise, waving sticks, and we heard a number of bangs and a good deal of

451

shouting. Small buck were about, and this worried me, for any duiker in the district might well be a relation of Twinkle's, or might leave an orphan behind if it were killed. Just then we heard cries, and saw one disappear into a patch of bush which the beaters quickly surrounded. Hereward and Tilly advanced side by side into the duiker's refuge. The little buck broke out and tried to escape up the hill, but a Kikuyu threw a stick and turned it back between Hereward and Tilly. I do not know which of them shot it, but it went down with a dreadful squeal which made Lettice put her hands to her ears.

I ran down to where it lay. It was a female, with soft grey-brown fur. Its feet were clean and sharp and delicate as those of a dancer. "I want to go home," I said, suddenly terrified lest Twinkle had escaped and been chased and killed.

"We will go home together," said Lettice, who had now arrived, "and leave the rest to slay more guinea fowl."

Several of the beaters came with us, among them the young man Kupanya had picked out as the murderer. He seemed to have forgotten all about his troubles, and had been beating with enthusiasm and energy. To mark his status as a mission boy he wore a pair of khaki shorts, whereas everyone else had a blanket. After a while our escort broke into snatches of song. These songs, always in a minor key, were, to my ears, melancholy, but they were not songs of sorrow. As a rule they celebrated some triumph of battle or of love. Perhaps this song celebrated the death of the duiker, and was its sole brief memorial.

At the last stream to be crossed before reaching home, Ian was waiting for us, sitting on a boulder with his blue Somali shawl flung over his shoulder. "I have shot enough guinea fowl," he said.

We had to ride in single file in order to keep to the narrow paths, but when we reached a stretch of open grazing, Ian drew up beside Lettice. "You will be going away soon," she said, looking ahead of her, and not at him.

"Yes: we have planned another Abyssinian safari. But I hope it will be my last."

"Have you made a fortune, and mean to retire?"

"Neither; but after a while I think the pursuit of freedom only turns one into a slave."

I followed behind them, not at all interested in the conversation

452

and anxious to get back to Twinkle. Yet I could feel a tension in the air that made their words memorable.

"There was a scandal when I ran away with Hereward," Lettice said. "You know that I was married before?"

"I am afraid all that makes no difference," Ian said. "But of course it is very interesting."

"Well, it is the plot of many hackneyed novels. I was married at eighteen to a much older man. It's true he was pushed down my throat by my parents, but I imagined myself in love."

"There's an Eastern flavour to this story," Ian commented. He had tied the blue shawl round his waist, and rode close to her side. "Ahmed would think it all a great fuss about nothing."

"Perhaps his is a better point of view, but I was not acquainted with it at eighteen. And I was most unhappy. Hereward was sympathetic, handsome and kind. He was also impulsive, and we eloped. Of course he had to resign from the army, and it was some time before I realized quite what that meant to him. So now here we are. He gave up a lot for me. So now you understand, Ian, why you must keep your freedom, or find someone else to surrender it to."

Ian was silent for so long I thought he had forgotten where he was, and when he did remember he spoke quietly. "You have warned me off, but I am not the type to go in search of tigers in Bengal. Nor to feel my heart bleed for Hereward. We are both young, and time is on my side."

"It is when one is young that time is too precious to waste."

Ian pulled up his pony and laid a hand on the reins of hers. "Look at that sunset: time can never be wasted when there are such sights to look at, and such things to enjoy."

The sunset was, indeed, spectacular. The whole western sky was aflame with the crimson of the heart of a rose. Deep-violet clouds were stained and streaked with red, and arcs of lime-green and saffron-yellow swept across the heavens.

The crimson sky, the golden light streaming down the valley, and then its obliteration by the dusk, filled me with the terrible melancholy that sometimes wrings the hearts of children, and can never be communicated or explained. It was as if the day, which was unique, and could never come again, had been struck down like the duiker and lay there bleeding, and then was swallowed into oblivion;

as if something in each of us had died with it, and could never be recalled. Then the sunset vanished, the night came swiftly and it grew cold. We made our ponies trot, and soon a light came into view that had been put on the Palmers' veranda to guide us in.

Chapter 6

One day Sammy said he was going to get married, and would like a few days' leave.

"You have two wives already," Robin said. "You are becoming very rich." He spoke resentfully, as Sammy's pay could not have brought this about and things upon the farm often disappeared, especially maize-meal locked in the store. Robin kept the key, but Sammy was always borrowing it, and in any case a Kikuyu blacksmith who could make fine chains for snuff-horns and keen-bladed swords would think nothing of copying a key.

"My father has great wealth in Masailand," Sammy said, as if guessing Robin's thoughts. "He has many daughters, and their bride-price makes him rich."

"Very well," Robin agreed, and he inquired what Sammy would like for a present. There was no hesitation about the reply: a fat ram or, better still, a bullock.

A small and skinny bullock was marked for the feast and tethered near the house to be fattened on maize and sweet-potato tops. No special ceremony seemed to be involved in Sammy's marriage, merely the making, transport and consumption of large quantities of beer. The liquor, made from sugarcane, fermented in large gourds. Once it was ready, various women attached to Sammy's household stoppered the big pots with leaves, strapped them on their backs, and set off for the homestead of the bride's father, who was one of Kupanya's fellow elders and friends.

About this time, Njombo became listless and almost sulky, in spite of the stone stables, now completed, and two new ponies, a handsome bay called Lucifer and Dorcas, a chestnut mare. Whenever Sammy appeared near the stables, Njombo walked off, his face blank and stony. His gay little cap had been abandoned, his blanket was of the plainest, and he had given up joking with his friends.

I cannot remember how I discovered that Sammy was marrying Njombo's intended wife. Poor Njombo could not pay the bride-price, everything he owned or could borrow had to go to the family of the Palmers' murdered headman. So Sammy had stepped smartly into the breach and carried off the girl.

Meanwhile, the mission boy produced for Hereward, whose name was Kamau, had gone to Fort Hall and been arrested, and would soon be tried for something he knew nothing about.

"That is unfair," I suggested.

But Njombo was unsympathetic. "That creature," he said, "his father owes a debt to Kupanya, so he must help to pay it."

It was about this time that the district commissioner rode over on a mule to make inquiries about the murder. He wore a khaki uniform with shining buttons and a topee with a badge in front, and was attended by a large retinue. He stayed the night, and next morning he held an inquiry. He sat on a camp chair under a tree while everyone squatted round him. One after the other, witnesses recalled the fight which had led to the death of the Palmers' headman. The accused youth, they said, had seized a *rungu*, one of the heavy-headed clubs that warriors carried, and bashed the headman in self-defence.

"If it was in self-defence," the DC asked, "why did the accused receive no injuries?"

The headman, they said, had gone for him with a knife, and Kamau's agility had saved him from injury.

"Who is paying blood-money to the dead man's family?"

The question provoked such a mesh of explanations involving relationships and goats, that the DC was soon wrapped round in argument. He selected three or four witnesses, instructed them to report at Fort Hall, and came in to breakfast.

"I hope that boy will not get a long sentence," Lettice said. "He looks so undersized to be a murderer, and not at all fierce."

"Mission boys," Hereward exclaimed with distaste. "The ruin of perfectly good natives. Just what you'd expect."

"I always suspect mission boys," the DC agreed. "Not of the crime, but of being picked out to be accused of it; no one likes them very much. But if all the witnesses agree on oath, and the accused says he's guilty, then it's difficult not to convict. However, in this case there's the plea of self-defence."

"Let us hope it succeeds," Lettice remarked. "Even so, it's sad to. think of him languishing in prison."

"They very seldom languish," the DC said. "There are nearly always too many prisoners. When food is short in the reserve, the warders find places for many of their relatives."

"Still," Lettice persisted, as he prepared to mount his mule, "I hope you won't be too hard on that poor creature."

The district commissioner adjusted his topee with its glittering badge, said distinctly, "I think you may trust in British justice," and rode off.

For a month or two we heard no more of the case, and then one day Kamau the mission boy reappeared, looking much fatter, and pleased with himself, and wearing a new shirt.

"I am not guilty," he said, using the English words.

"Well, it is no affair of mine," Robin replied. The foundations of our stone house were being laid slowly, and his mind was full of the complications of building. Kamau said he would like to work for us, that he was a clerk who could look after stores and tickets. So Robin signed him on for a small wage.

"Why did the DC return him?" Sammy demanded crossly. "He said he killed the headman. And all the witnesses agreed."

"Perhaps the DC thought they were all lying," Robin suggested. "As indeed they probably were."

"It is not a good thing," Sammy said firmly, without explaining why. He had, of course, become an ally of Kupanya's, which was a great help to us, as we never went short of labour. I sometimes saw his young wife, Kupanya's daughter, about her tasks near Sammy's homestead. She was called Wanjui, and was jaunty and attractive, and scarcely more than fifteen years old. Now that she was married her head was shaven and she wore a beaded leather apron and a great many coils of wire, for Sammy was a rich man. She went with his second wife (the senior was in Masailand) to plant maize, or harvest millet, according to the season. If she regretted Njombo, she showed no sign.

Some months later, after the rains, Sammy reported to Tilly in a gloomy manner that Wanjui was sick. After Tilly had visited Wanjui in the cavern of her hut, she sent for Maggy Nimmo.

"It's the usual story," Mrs. Nimmo said to Tilly when she had

456

looked at Wanjui. "A miss, and all sorts of dirty messes applied, to make matters worse. What can one do for the girl in that filthy dark hut with every sort of infection? There's only one chance, to get her into the hospital."

By now a branch line had reached Thika, and a train ran each way three times a week. The train was not well equipped for sick people, and the five miles to Thika in an oxcart or mule buggy were still an obstacle, especially in the rains, when the two streams we had to cross engulfed their homemade bridges. Still, for eight or nine months a sick person could be got to Nairobi in six or seven hours with luck, provided that he fell ill on a Monday, Wednesday or Friday.

Tilly fixed up some blankets in the mule buggy to make a bed. When everything was ready, Sammy appeared in the doorway looking sheepish and said that Wanjui had refused to go. "Some relatives have come," he said. "There are two old women ... they have their own medicines."

Tilly was furious, but it was no good. The matter had been taken over by Kupanya's family. Mrs. Nimmo reported that two old crones were in possession of the hut and that a witchdoctor with a gourd full of spells was squatting outside, and a goat tethered near him ready for sacrifice. They had managed things in this way for centuries.

My own interest was centred on the innocent goat, and I resolved to see if I could rescue the animal.

After lunch, instead of resting on my bed as I was supposed to, I slipped out to Sammy's compound. A few small children played around in the dust; there was no sign of Sammy or the old crones. And where was the doomed goat? A little corkscrew path took off from the compound and vanished into a plantation of tall maize. I followed this through a green, rustling forest, and came to an uncultivated patch round a tree where several men were squatting.

I was too late to save the goat. Its insides had been slit open, some of its organs lay on the ground and it had been partially flayed— all sights to which I was well used. The point was that the goat was still alive. I turned and ran all the way back.

Tilly found me on the lawn scratching Twinkle's back. She started to scold me for neglecting my rest, but noticed something wrong, and inquired whether I had been out without a hat, an error thought by everyone to result in instant death.

457

"Nothing must ever happen to Twinkle," I said.

"That would be a dull life," Tilly pointed out. "She's getting big enough to look for a husband."

"Then we must get one for her."

"One duiker is quite enough," Tilly said firmly. She had been obliged to have all the flowerbeds surrounded by wire netting, but Twinkle leaped over this and the beds had now become like prisons, with barbed-wire entanglements. "Sooner or later," Tilly added, "Twinkle really will have to go."

"No, no, whatever happens, nothing must hurt Twinkle."

Tilly looked at me, and also at Twinkle, and said that she wished we had never kept her in the first place, but as it was, we would look after her. I was obsessed with the fear that Twinkle would be used for a sacrifice.

Next morning Sammy, who had grown sullen and almost rude, said that Wanjui was dead. Later, I noticed smoke coming from his compound. She had died in the hut, which had therefore to be burnt down, while her body was taken out into the bush for the hyenas.

NOW THAT WE HAD three ponies, Njombo's job was an important one, for they needed more attention than mules. He had a real talent for looking after them, and was intelligent, so he was one of the few individuals, apart from Sammy and Juma, whom we looked upon as a prop and stay. It was therefore very disappointing when one day he disappeared without a word. When Robin made inquiries, he was told, "Perhaps Njombo is sick," but no one seemed to know.

So Robin rode off to see Kupanya. The chief received him with courtesy and presented him with a chicken, which ruffled Robin because he had forgotten to bring anything to give Kupanya in return.

"I will send for this man," Kupanya said, when he had heard the complaint, "but it may be that he is sick."

"If he is sick then he should have treatment," Robin replied.

"There are doctors for white men and doctors for black men. It may be that he has come to consult a black man's doctor."

"Then he is a fool," Robin retorted. "Tell him to come back at once or I will bring a case against him before the DC."

Njombo returned about a week later. He had lost weight and

looked a sick man. Quite suddenly he shrank, his bones stuck out, his cheeks grew hollow and his skin dry, as if something had literally been drained out of him. Tilly dosed him in vain with Epsom salts, cough mixture, cooking port and quinine.

Once a month, Robin drove into Nairobi in the mule buggy to fetch the wages, which came out in little sacks of rupees lying at his feet. Such a visit was now approaching, and it was decided to take Njombo to the hospital. As he would never give his consent, he was merely told to come with us in order to look after the mules. When we reached the native hospital Robin marched him in and he was virtually captured by the orderlies. His listlessness was now such that he showed little fight. Robin explained matters to a European doctor, who said that he would do his best. "But don't think we're sure to cure him," he added. "There are dozens of tropical diseases we haven't even names for, let alone treatments."

I missed Njombo, whose fondness for the ponies almost matched my own. It was noticeable that none of the Kikuyu mentioned his name. It was as if he was dead already, dead and forgotten.

And then one day Njombo reappeared, his legs like sticks, very frail and hunched. It was a wonder he had managed to walk from Thika. His skin looked grey. He carried a note which said, "I cannot do anything for this man. There is nothing wrong with him except that he has made up his mind to die."

This was a blow, not merely to the hopes Tilly and Robin had entertained of Njombo's recovery, but to their faith in European medicine. Tilly put him in her sickbay and ordered Juma to feed him on beef tea. He refused the tea, and no member of his family came to nurse him.

Then one day Alec came over. He got on well with the Kikuyu and, probably because he was a bachelor and had no one else to talk to, generally knew more than our other neighbours of what was going on. "There is only one man who can save Njombo," Alec said, "and that is Sammy; he has put a spell on him, because he thinks it was Njombo's magic that killed his wife; only he can take it off."

"But how can we make Sammy do that?" Robin protested. "He ignores everything I say."

"We must look for his Achilles' heel. That's easy, with a Masai."

"You mean his cattle?"

"Of course. If you round them up and tell him that you'll cut their throats unless Njombo recovers, I think your Sammy will very soon come to heel."

Robin summoned Sammy to his office in a corner of the store, smacked the table with his palm, and said, "Sammy, you are the headman and you have had a quarrel with Njombo, which is very wicked. You are behaving not like a man who can read, but like a savage. If Njombo dies, you will be a murderer."

"I do not understand you," Sammy stubbornly replied.

"You will understand very quickly when I seize your cattle and shoot every one of them myself. I shall do this, Sammy, if by tomorrow evening Njombo does not begin to recover."

Robin knew that, if he had the chance, Sammy would spirit his cattle away to the reserve, so he had them driven into the thorn-protected *boma* where our own oxen spent the night. "What shall I do if Sammy *doesn't* de-witch Njombo?" he wondered. "I can't really kill sixteen head of cattle."

AS THE DAY DEVELOPED, everyone realized that our bluff had failed. "I think that one of us ought to see Kupanya," Tilly remarked. "Njombo is his relation, and surely he must have some authority."

"Sammy married his daughter," Robin pointed out. "That was what started all this trouble, I suppose."

"If Njombo dies, we can make things awkward for Kupanya with the government. At any rate we can try."

Robin did not like to leave the farm with so much tension in the air, so Hereward offered to escort Tilly, and I was allowed to go with them. We set off in the heat of the afternoon, up the red path to Kupanya's, Hereward spruce and upright in a perfectly cut pair of breeches and shining boots, on a well-bred, lively polo pony, and myself jogging behind on Moyale.

Hereward took a forthright view of our troubles. "If you don't mind my saying so, Robin's too lenient with these fellows. As for Sammy, I'd put him down and give him twenty-five and that would be an end of the trouble."

"It would also be an end of Njombo," Tilly pointed out.

"That's a lot of stuff and nonsense, if you ask me. He's been poisoned, that's the long and short of it."

Tilly urged her pony into a trot, so that Hereward had to drop behind in single file. It was the time of day when heat presses down upon the earth and squeezes out the energy. Even doves can barely muster the desire to coo. Kupanya's group of huts was deserted, except for one or two naked children and an old crone, her face as crinkled as a walnut. One had a sense of watching eyes, yet Hereward's calls received no answer.

At last, after a long pause, Kupanya emerged reluctantly from a hut; he looked bleary-eyed and was clad only in a blanket. When he expected us, he dressed up in his monkey skin cloak and looked imposing. In dishabille he looked imposing in a different way: strong, well-muscled, agile, his healthy skin shining. It was easy to believe that not so long ago he had slain enemies and raided cattle.

Hereward explained our mission as if giving orders on parade. The chief listened and answered, "Njombo—I do not know this man."

"Do not give me lies! He is one of your own relations."

"If he has left my land to work for Europeans he is not mine, but theirs."

"Listen carefully," Tilly said. "Someone is trying to kill Njombo with medicine. If this does not stop by tomorrow morning, we shall tell the DC that you have allowed it. And the DC will send askaris to arrest you. He will put you in jail and fine you hundreds of goats, and he will give the staff of the chief to another. And here is our warning: if the magic has not been taken off Njombo by noon tomorrow, the DC will know about it before the sun sets."

Kupanya stood for a while in silence with his eyes on the ground. "All this has nothing to do with me," he said at last. "If the DC wishes to come, I am ready for him."

"The DC will not come," Tilly retorted. "He will send askaris to take you away with bracelets on your wrists. Have you not heard that the governor has said there must be no more bad magic? You have till noon tomorrow; and if Njombo dies first, the DC will know that you have murdered him."

With this parting shot, Tilly sprang onto her mount and we rode off without waiting for protests or denials.

"You handled that splendidly," Hereward said. "By George, I wouldn't like to come up against the rough edge of your tongue."

"I only hope he doesn't call our bluff," Tilly replied quickly, for she

461

disliked compliments, and might not have been sure whether this was one or not. "If we do send to the DC he'd probably do nothing at all, at any rate for several weeks."

"You've got the chief rattled, my dear."

"There's going to be a thunderstorm."

It was extraordinary how quickly a huge black cloud had appeared from nowhere and filled the sky. The air grew blacker and more sinister and the ridges crouched beneath a lurid, leaden light. A cold wind shook the trees, and then a fork of lightning lit the whole scene with an unreal whiteness. The crash that followed brought our ponies to a halt, quivering all over. We slid off them and held tightly to their bridles. Huge raindrops came down, as cold as ice.

"The bananas," Hereward shouted, and started to run with his pony plunging beside him. We were near a stream between two ridges, and banana trees with their arching fronds grew beside it. The storm burst fully as we reached the banana clump and the fronds were whipped about like shreds of rag. We huddled together with the quivering ponies and in a few moments were drenched to the skin. It was terrifying, yet there was something splendid and invigorating about the reverberating of the thunder, and the violence of the lightning flashes that split the sky. At last the storm rolled down the valley, leaving us cold and soaking wet.

"That was a near thing," Hereward said. "I don't want to see lightning as close as that again. Are you all right, Tilly?"

"You can see I am," Tilly replied crossly, thereby showing that she, too, had been badly frightened.

"I'd never forgive myself if anything had happened to you."

"It would hardly have been your fault, Hereward. And it would have happened to us all."

"Well, it might have been the best way out for me."

"What nonsense!" Tilly cried. "Why should you wish to get out of everything? You have everything you want."

"I am glad I have given that impression." Hereward sounded anything but glad, in fact rather offended. "I think most men would include his wife's affection among the things he wants."

"Are you trying to say that Lettice ..?"

"I may be a fool of a soldier, but I'm not blind as a bat."

It was not a pleasant ride back. Everything clung to the skin, and poor Moyale slid and slithered up and down slopes now traversed by miniature red rivers. The storm had deluged the farm, and lightning had blasted a fig tree halfway up the river slope. Hereward hurried back to Lettice, who, he said, hated thunder and hid in a cupboard with her Pekinese.

"Poor Hereward," Tilly said, "he's absurd, but one can't help feeling sorry for him."

"Pompous ass," Robin commented. "I can't think why Lettice ran off with him."

"In a way he's quite attractive, but not nearly so attractive as ..." Tilly noticed me, and added, "Go and take off your wet things at once and have a good hot bath."

I was awakened in the morning, as always, by the high, metallic ring of iron on iron (a bar struck by a rod) that was our daily summons to work. On such a soft and golden morning, night fears were silly. Yet Njombo lay as before in the dark hut—alive still, Tilly reported, but only just. She told the syce who had replaced him to saddle a mule and be ready to start at noon with a note for the DC, hoping that this would convince Kupanya's spies that we meant business.

After breakfast Robin went out as usual to the shamba, Tilly attended to business in the office, and I was employed drawing pictures of a sabre-toothed tiger being stalked by a prehistoric man.

Tilly returned to the house at noon and called on Juma to prepare beef tea. She looked angry and stern; and, glancing at my book on Early Man, remarked, "All those centuries, and nothing much has changed. When the coffee comes into bearing I think we must get a piano. Lettice would teach you; would you like to learn?"

"Very much," I said, imagining my hand sweeping up and down the keys to create rivers of splendid melody, and the plaudits of a large audience.

Juma appeared in the door without the beef tea. "It would be best to leave this thing alone a little longer, memsabu," he said. "If you wait a little perhaps something will be arranged."

"I will wait until two o'clock," Tilly agreed. She looked more cheerful, and began to think the bluff was going to work.

Robin came back from the shamba much enraged by Sammy, who had vanished in a most irresponsible way. But at lunchtime we heard that Sammy had returned, and that he would report later. "I think that's a good sign," Tilly said. "Sammy may have brought a wizard with him to work the magic."

"I think we've both gone off our heads," Robin grumbled. "We know it's all tomfoolery, the whole thing is illegal, and here we are playing their game, instead of bundling them in to the DC and letting him knock some sense into them."

The afternoon slipped by silently. I had expected something dramatic, perhaps a sound of drumming and song, or the mewing of spirits; or at least a goat's bleat, for all the time I was wondering whether some half-flayed animal was paying with its agony for the restoration of Njombo's life.

At about four o'clock Sammy came to the door. He gazed at his feet and said gruffly, "Come to see Njombo."

At any other time his almost hectoring tone would have angered Tilly, but now she was too relieved and hopeful to mind. She returned in about half an hour with news of victory. Njombo had opened his eyes and taken a little beef tea and brandy.

"When I propped him up, it was like holding up a feather," Tilly said. "There was chalk on his face and arms, and a queer smell. Heaven knows what had been going on in there, but whatever it was, I think that it has saved Njombo. And now I want my tea."

How much does one imagine, how much observe? It seemed that after tea, everything was different; songs came from the Kikuyu huts, the women laughed as they carried firewood home, the previous day's storm had vanished. It was as if a darkness had been lifted from the farm, and daylight had burst upon us all again.

Alec Wilson came over next day, full of gossip. It was Kupanya, he said, who had saved Njombo, and Kupanya had intervened only because the storm, coming immediately after our visit, had convinced him that God was angry, and did not wish Njombo to die. "Kupanya didn't give two hoots about the DC," Alec said, "but he was a bit reluctant to take on the Almighty."

"It's a good thing to have friends in high places," Tilly remarked.

The chief had sent for a wizard, who had broken the spell and so cheated Sammy of his revenge. Sammy was furious, for he believed that Njombo, out of jealousy and spite, had killed his young wife by witchcraft. If Kupanya had not changed his mind, Njombo would have run down like an unwound watch, and died.

"I should never have believed it," Tilly said, "unless I'd seen it with my own eyes."

"I suppose we believed in it ourselves until not so very long ago," Alec said.

It was remarkable how quickly Njombo recovered. He never spoke of his experience, and we never questioned him, but I always looked upon him as a man who had been raised from the dead.

Chapter 7

One day Hereward rode over to ask for Robin's help. The piano had arrived at the station in a crate, and required the united efforts of both farms to convey it to its destination.

"We shall need two span of oxen," Hereward said. "I think we shall have to cut some trees down first to widen the road."

The actual operation took on a military character, with men stationed at strategic points to direct the drivers, and others held in reserve at steep places to add manpower to oxpower. The worst danger point was a river crossing with a steep bank on either side. The stream had been roughly bridged with logs, but these were submerged in rainy periods and sometimes washed away, and the banks put a severe strain on our teams. Hereward was afraid the piano might end on its back in the stream.

We all rode down to Thika to see the crate loaded onto a wagon. A gang of lifters had been assembled and Hereward barked brisk orders that no one obeyed.

"I wonder what the boys think is inside," Tilly observed. "A house, perhaps; it's almost as big as one of theirs."

When Njombo, who accompanied us on a mule, did in fact inquire, the limitations of our Swahili forced her to reply, "It is a thing with which you make a noise. You make it with your hands."

"But who will be able to?"

"Memsabu *Mrefu.*" Hereward's official native name was *mrefu,* meaning tall.

"How can memsabu's hands use such a thing?" Njombo asked sceptically. "It would be a giant's affair."

Tilly gave up trying to explain the piano and stood in the shade of the stationmaster's tin office to watch Hereward and Robin marshalling their wagon and teams into a suitable position. The piano was eventually loaded, and lashed to the wagon. It swayed off along the rutted track, a far cry from the concert halls and drawing rooms for which its makers had intended it.

"Stupid notion, really," Hereward commented. "Lettice would have it, but what use is a piano out here?"

"I suppose Lettice will enjoy playing it."

"Oh, well, if it makes her any happier, I shall feel it's been well worth while. I'm worried about Lettice, Tilly. She gets queer notions into her head. At one moment she wants a special room built for the piano and a rose garden with a fountain in it; next day she talks of selling up and going to live in Yorkshire of all places, and pulling strings to get me back into the regiment—which is out of the question, of course. Now she's got it into her head that the natives are trying to poison Chang and Zena; she chops up their food herself and insists on sleeping in the dressing room with the little beggars, and locking the doors."

We had reached the river, and a crisis was developing upon the further bank. Egged on by a tremendous shouting and cracking of whips, the oxen had taken a run at the steep part of the bank and would have crested the rise had not the crate caught on the branches of a tree. The wagon started to slide backwards, dragging the little beasts after it, and Robin, who was riding beside the team, bellowed, "Stone, stone, stone," at the top of his voice. Everyone took up the cry; the frantic oxen scrabbled with their little hooves and several people tried to hang on to the spokes. A couple of Kikuyu at length rushed up with boulders to put under the wheels, a simple expedient which arrested the runaway in the nick of time.

The wagon reached the Palmers' without further adventures, and a week or two later we were asked over for a piano-warming. By now they had moved into their stone bungalow, which seemed to everyone the height of luxury; it had three spare rooms, teak floors, bow windows, a bathroom, and gables with curlicues. The roof was the usual corrugated iron, painted green.

"You've done your hair in a new way," Tilly remarked. Lettice wore it piled on top of her head in soft, gleaming swathes, and she had a fillet of small bronze leaves somehow woven into it.

"I thought I'd dress like a concert pianist, even if I can't play like one," she said, as she moved to the piano. "I must deputize for Orpheus, without any of his genius. Please be charitable to me."

Although Lettice might not have been a player of the first quality, the skill of her hands, darting like butterflies above the keys, summoning from the instrument a torrent of harmony, seemed to me a kind of miracle. A hissing lamp threw a circle of light over her gleaming chestnut hair, over her pale skin and her dancing hands.

When she had finished her piece there was a silence no one cared to break. Lettice herself dissolved it by arranging some music and starting to sing. Her voice was true and gentle, and she sang lively little songs in French. Ian, who had just come back from Abyssinia, jumped up and stood beside her. I suppose the music had tautened our perceptions and made me see them, together in the lamplight, as something other than they were, more handsome and accomplished, more of the spirit and less of flesh and blood.

They sang together songs as light as bubbles, and as gay. Ian's voice was clear and simple. I cannot remember any of the songs except one in which we all joined, the French-Canadian jingle "Alouette"; and afterwards, whenever I heard this little tune, it reminded me of that evening.

MOST OF THE CANNIBALS went home when the Palmers' house was finished, but two or three settled down with wives and families, a little group of aliens stuck like a splinter into the flesh of the Kikuyu. The women wore nothing but a triangle of leather, dangling from a string round their waists, but made up for it with a great deal of thick, heavy wire coiled so tightly round their arms and legs that the flesh bulged out on each side of the coil. They walked with a free, upright gait, carried things on their heads instead of on their backs, and smoked clay pipes with long stems. The Kikuyu, whose own women wore leather aprons to their knees, thought them indecent.

They soon acquired goats which, like all livestock, spent the night in thorn-fenced bomas intended to keep out marauding beasts. In this objective the Kavirondo's boma failed. They lost several goats and accused the Kikuyu of stealing them. The Kikuyu denied this hotly and blamed a leopard, whose spoor they pointed out nearby. The Kavirondo retorted that the spoor belonged to a harmless hyena and stuck to their charge, and so a *shauri* developed which came to Hereward for settlement.

This word *shauri* was one we used a great deal. It could mean a quarrel, a lawsuit, an agreement, a discussion—almost anything. Here, it meant a contest in rhetoric between Kikuyu and Kavirondo spokesmen. After several hours of this, Hereward gave a judgment of which he was proud. If the Kikuyu are so sure there *is* a leopard, he said, let them catch it, and their case will be proved. If they fail, they must restore to the Kavirondo a number of goats equal to those which disappeared.

Tilly warned Hereward to take special care of the dogs. They were a favourite food of leopards. But Hereward had taken the side of the Kavirondo and was not unduly disturbed. He paid for this—or rather, poor old Chang did. The Palmers were at dinner, the double doors giving on to their veranda were open and Chang was curled up in a wicker chair outside. He was less than six paces away, and no one imagined any danger. When it happened, Lettice heard a sort of thump, and a faint noise that might have been the chair scraping on the tiles. Hereward got up to look, and saw nothing. It was dark outside, no moon. Lettice called Chang and when he did not respond Hereward felt in the chair, which had been slewed round.

Of course there was a great hue and cry. Everyone called and walked about with lamps held high, but saw nothing. At last one of the Kikuyu shouted: he had found the spoor.

Lettice drove herself almost into a frenzy of remorse. "If I had only called him ... if only ..." Zena was seldom out of her arms, and she refused to be comforted. "She and Chang were inseparable," Lettice said. "How can she live without him? How can I?"

"The best thing is to get another quickly," Tilly suggested.

"No, I shall never get another; I ought to live in a solitary fortress somewhere. I bring disaster on everyone I love."

"You shouldn't blame yourself quite so much," Tilly said. "Leopards are one of the country's natural hazards."

"Hugh has had appendicitis, did I tell you?" Lettice seldom spoke about her son. "He very nearly died, poor little boy, and what good am I to him as a mother?"

"Perhaps you should bring him out."

"I've been hoping to; but Hereward ... I daresay he's right, in a year's time Hugh will have to go to school, and here there's nothing; but even a year would mean everything to me. Now I feel that if he came, I should let him get bitten by a snake, or eaten by a lion."

When Tilly got home she told Robin that she was going to get another Peke for Lettice, to take her mind off Chang.

"They are very expensive," Robin pointed out.

"I daresay there's something we can sell," Tilly said hopefully. She had some turkeys, reared with much care for the Christmas market. Now she decided that a pair sold for breeding ought to fetch the price of a small Pekinese.

Meanwhile, a leopard hunt was under way. Hereward went out at dawn with an enormous .450 rifle and an array of amateur trackers, gun-bearers and beaters, but the spoor was soon lost in the bush and long grass. It appeared that many different kinds of trap could be made. Someone suggested that Mr. Roos would be sure to know the best kind, so I was allowed to take a note over to him.

Although his farm was next to ours, we seldom saw Mr. Roos—he came and went unpredictably—and his life was full of mystery. He had a hut like the natives', only with a sort of veranda on one side and a fireplace made of scraps of corrugated iron on the other. Fat-tailed sheep grazed right up to the veranda, on which there stood a bare table, a camp chair and the white skull of an elephant.

My elders considered Mr. Roos a dour and uncommunicative man but he was always friendly when I saw him. Sometimes he had a black, bristly beard, sometimes a rim of stubble giving him a saturnine look. His face was creased like the bark of an olive tree, and almost as dark, but he had light-blue eyes that looked odd in such a setting, and a wide smile.

Mr. Roos was cutting bars for his ox-yokes with a bush-knife, from branches of thorn. He put the note into his pocket without even glancing at it. I suggested that he should read it. "It's about the leopard," I said.

Mr. Roos stopped dead, and asked questions. His face never showed what he was thinking, but I felt that he was pleased. The air smelled sharply of hides and alum. Skins as hard and stiff as boards were pegged out on a flat space behind his hut, and skulls with horns attached and flesh in various stages of decomposition lay about in the grass attracting flies. Pointing to a pegged-out lion skin, Mr. Roos remarked, "You see that, man? Ten feet from nose to tail, a beauty. And what a trek, for three days he led me, and he was the one tired first. He got four legs, you see, and I got two."

"You must be good at walking," I said politely.

He laughed and said that he was. Then he said that he would be over later to fix a trap for the leopard. His tone had a definite edge of contempt for us poor *rooinek* incompetents who could not fix a trap, nor shoot a large lion.

When he came over, he placed a hunk of fetid meat, which leopards really appreciate, in the fork of a tree, and concealed near the tree's foot a wicked steel gin with jagged, rusty teeth, which Hereward regarded with deep disapproval. "Not at all a sporting sort of thing."

"You want sport, or you want your cattle alive?" Hereward of course wanted both, but Lettice was in such a state of mind about her dead Chang and her threatened Zena that above all he wanted to see the dead leopard at his feet.

The trap was cleverly laid. It was in a patch of bush that invited the animal to approach the tree from one direction only, and so well concealed that, even when you knew it was there, you could not detect it.

For two nights nothing happened. Then we heard, first thing in the morning, that a leopard had been caught, but had escaped. A wounded leopard was a serious matter; knowing himself doomed, he might well try to bring a valedictory revenge down upon his enemies.

Twinkle's safety worried me. If the leopard would take Chang off a veranda, Twinkle roaming about the farm invited tragedy. She slept in a lean-to shed next to the store, but in the daytime she had taken to wandering off.

Now that the leopard was wounded, the hunt intensified. I rode with Robin, Tilly and Alec Wilson to the scene of the escape, where a lot of people had already assembled. The trap was there on the end of its chain, with fur and blood on it. There had been a terrific lashing about, until the beast had freed himself by the most desperate expedient imaginable: he had evidently bitten off his own torn, bleeding foot.

Even Mr. Roos shook his head. "Never known it happen before. Man, he's a bold one, this is."

470

Most of the Palmers' Kikuyu labour had turned back into warriors, bringing out their spears, and wearing their vermilion-sheathed swords: they stood about, as tense as coiled springs, staring into the bush with eyes brightened by anticipation. The leopard had been tracked to a patch of thick bush and boulders on the river bank a mile or two upstream, and there he was no doubt angrily lying.

"Country's too thick to beat through," Hereward said. "Wouldn't be fair on the beaters. I'll go in and walk him up with the .450; that'll settle the beggar's hash if he tries any nonsense. Alec, you see that bluff above the bit of bush he's lying up in? That's your stand. Robin, you go down by the river near that patch of reeds. And Roos, you cross the river and get up by that big tree where you'll command the bank opposite, and pick him off if he gets past the others."

The hunt was taking place on Hereward's land, so he had the right to direct it. But Mr. Roos was not a directable man. When Robin and Alec strode off obediently, Mr. Roos continued to squat on his heels like a Kikuyu. Hereward pointed out with icy displeasure that he could not proceed until Mr. Roos had taken up his forward position.

"You go ahead, man, finish him, the skin is yours."

"Good God! Is that all you're thinking of, the brute's hide?" Hereward glared at Mr. Roos's back as if at some robber of the poorbox caught in the act, and walked off.

The Kikuyu enjoyed a hunt, and their spears had been lying a long time unused. It was sad for them to stand about on the hillside, all dressed up and nowhere to go, because of Hereward's edict. Of course Hereward was only acting like a good officer who does not risk the lives of his men if it can be avoided, and puts himself in the position of greatest danger, but the young men were left baulked and silent on the hillside.

Nothing happened for a long time and I soon grew bored; even Moyale had cropped all the grass he wanted and stood half asleep. I fell into conversation with Njombo, but Tilly hushed me in case our voices should disturb the hunt. Mr. Roos had disappeared. We did not see him go. In his nondescript, untidy khaki clothing he blended into his surroundings like an antelope or lion.

Once or twice we caught a glimpse of Hereward's head and shoulders advancing at a slow pace through the green patch of bush about halfway up the bank. He was following the leopard's spoor, and it must have been a jumpy business, for he could see ahead no more than two or three yards, and might well find himself upon it before he had time to raise his rifle.

When the silence was at last broken, everything was confused. There was a very loud shot, no doubt from Hereward's enormous .450, and then another, almost at once. In the distance Robin's hat appeared above the rocks, waving in the air. Then came an outbreak of other sounds: a shout, a rifle shot but not so loud, a crashing in the bush. Tilly had a pair of binoculars and I heard her cry suddenly in a stiff voice, "Look out!" The Kikuyu poured down the slope shouting and waving their spears, musky with excitement and leaping with long strides like reedbuck from hummock to boulder and through the tufted grass. I tried to follow on Moyale, but Tilly seized the reins.

"Wait," she ordered. "Something went wrong, there was another leopard, I don't know . . ."

But she caught sight of Hereward's hat just before the warriors closed in, and we picked our way down the hill. The warriors had already started their thumping step around a circle, knees bent, buttocks out, swaying from side to side. They were chanting in short, sharp bursts which would soon coalesce into an almost endless paean. They made way for our ponies and we pushed through to the group in the centre, where Hereward glowed with pride.

There were indeed two leopards, lying perhaps fifteen yards apart, half hidden in grass of the same buff-yellow as their coats. One had a mangled stump for a leg and the flies were buzzing round it; its fur was stained and matted, its blue, rubbery lips drawn back to reveal sharp, yellow incisors and to impart to its round, cat-like face a most ferocious expression. The other leopard lay stretched out as if asleep. It was a perfect animal; the soft skin was like velvet over the stilled muscles.

Nervously, I touched it; the flesh was warm. I fingered one of its great pads, rough as sandstone and yet springy and yielding, and ran a hand down the great sweep of its flank, built for speed like the flank of a racehorse; the whole body moulded by its purpose into a yellow engine of speed, ferocity and skill. Why did it have to be dead and useless? I knew the answer that satisfied my elders— it had failed to respect their property, their goats and calves and dogs; but it was a beast so much finer than the miserable goats it preyed upon—finer

even than poor Chang—that for a moment, as I touched the leopard, that answer seemed ridiculous; rather, one would have offered goats as tribute to a creature so imperial.

Mr. Roos was bending down to stroke the pelt as I had done, but with a different purpose. He, like Hereward, looked satisfied.

Hereward had already thanked Mr. Roos, not, I expect, with the best of grace, for saving his life. For Hereward had shot the wounded leopard successfully and was bending over its corpse, when its mate, whose presence he had not suspected, came at him from the bush without a sound. Mr. Roos, who had almost miraculously been in the right position, dropped her just as she was about to leap on top of Hereward and demolish him.

"I can't think how the devil you managed to be in the right place," Hereward said. "It seems incredible luck."

Mr. Roos shook his head and chuckled. "Not luck, man. Where you find one *chui* you look for two—the mate." Mr. Roos pointed to a little rocky bluff ahead of us. "There is a likely place, those rocks. I think to myself: that is where the mate will be. She is there, she come, and so I shoot her. I keep the skin, eh?"

"Of course, my dear fellow." Hereward glanced down at it and realized, with a slight frown, that it was by far the better pelt of the two. "Worth a bit, I daresay," he added.

"A few rupees, maybe," Mr. Roos agreed cautiously, unable to suppress a tinge of complacency.

"He didn't care two hoots about my life," Hereward remarked later. "All he was after was a good skin."

"It was lucky he saved yours in the process," Tilly replied.

Chang was avenged: but Zena was lonely, and had no heart for the short walks with Lettice she had previously enjoyed so much. Tilly was already in correspondence with Roger Stilbeck, who knew someone who bred Pekinese. They were very expensive, and Tilly discovered that she would have to sell most of her turkeys, not merely a pair, to pay for a single puppy.

However, before the turkeys could be sold Tilly received a birthday present from her sister, who had come into a windfall. Anyway, she sent Tilly £25. Tilly went into Nairobi and bought Lettice a Pekinese puppy for £10, a new saddle, and a second-hand ram which Robin wanted to install, to pump out water from the river.

The puppy came out with the rupees on Robin's next monthly trip to Nairobi: a small, cream-coloured ball of fluff with a bright pink tongue, two beady eyes and a tremendous fund of energy. Lettice was delighted with it, and called it Puffball.

Chapter 8

Hereward said that we all needed a change. Fortunately, one was in sight: Ian Crawfurd suggested that he take the Palmers, Tilly and Robin on a game-shooting safari. Robin decided that he was too busy to go, but he urged Tilly to seize the chance, and Hereward implored her to keep Lettice company, so she agreed. Ian was collecting porters, equipment and stores in Nairobi, but Tilly wanted to contribute, and for some days there was a great roasting of chickens, a boiling of marmalade and a concocting of lotions according to a most valuable formula, handed down by a member of the family who had lived in India, which infallibly healed bites, alleviated sunburn and prevented the festering of sores.

Ian marched the safari out from Nairobi and camped at Thika, and Tilly and the Palmers rode down to meet him there, accompanied by

Robin and myself, who were to breakfast with them at the Blue Posts and see them leave for their long journey.

As we descended the last bit of hill above the Blue Posts, we saw the safari passing just below. The porters were marching smartly and chanting a vigorous song. Their loads were of all shapes and sizes: long tent poles, a tin bath full of lanterns, folding chairs and tables; rolls of bedding and chop-boxes of food. The porters wore all sorts of nondescript clothing—tattered shorts, vests consisting mostly of holes, football stockings, discarded greatcoats, red blankets. They were marching to far romantic places where the wild game of Africa had their wide plains and secret reeded waterholes. It was a moment to lift the heart, but also to fill the mind with anguish because the others were going and I was left behind.

"You shall come on a safari when you're older," Tilly promised, noticing my state of mind.

"I shall never be older," I said gloomily.

They were to travel first across the plains below the Kikuyu highlands, alive with game and infested with ticks, to Meru on the northern slopes of Mount Kenya, the last place where they could buy food. From Meru they were to head northwards to Archers' Post, where the shooting was excellent and water plentiful. After that, they would see. To the north lay four hundred miles of desert and then the Abyssinian mountains; to the west, more desert, great ranges of kudu-sheltering hills, and that strange, enormous lake, set in a waste of sand and lava, discovered only some twenty years before by the German von Höhnel and called after Prince Rudolph of Austria; to the east, more desert still, and then the marshes of the Lorian swamp. All around them would lie mystery and harshness, where every drop of water was hoarded by some animal or plant, and birds managed with a mist of dew that only sometimes brushed the wiry grasses. It was as well that Ian knew this country, for it had no tracks or settlements, and if you ran out of water you would die.

At the Blue Posts we ate a large breakfast, and sat on the veranda while Hereward busied himself checking girths and bridles, and once more examining the guns, helped by Ahmed, clad now in a khaki suit but with a green shawl loosely wrapped round his proud, small head. Ahmed was going to his own land, his own people, and there was a suggestion of eagerness and tension in his bearing.

476

"I would entrust my life to him a dozen times over," Ian said, "but if an unarmed, harmless youth annoyed him, he'd be as likely to stick a knife into him as to hold my stirrup when I mount." And he told us more of Ahmed's people: of the constant fights between the tribes, the deeds of bravery, the feats of endurance in this desert world so different from our own.

The time came for their departure; I cried, and so did Tilly; and we watched them mount their mules and jog away along the dusty road, and turn to wave before they disappeared round a bend.

It was tame and sad to ride back to the farm and to go on with ordinary living. Robin had desired with all his heart to go with the others, but the still he was putting up to make essential oils had reached a critical condition, and someone had to look after the farms, both ours and Hereward's. I was delivered to Mrs. Nimmo, together with instructions that I was to memorize the kings of England, learn the multiplication tables and the life cycle of the liver fluke, and draw the signs of the zodiac. I was to have an examination when they returned and if I was successful I would get another saddle for Moyale (his was almost in pieces), whereas if I failed I should have to go to bed early for a week.

Mrs. Nimmo was much stricter about hours than Tilly. At half past eight she rang a handbell and I had to keep at my lessons until ten, when I had a break for cocoa; then lessons again until twelve. Mrs. Nimmo presided over the multiplication tables and the kings of England, and she added the kings of Scotland, who were most confusing. She added Bible readings too. On the other hand, she made delicious cakes and scones.

When I next rode over to see Robin, I heard the news I had so long half dreaded. Twinkle had vanished the day before. That night her boma had been left open, but she had not returned.

"Perhaps Twinkle has gone to find a bwana of her own," Njombo said.

"Come and look at the still," Robin suggested. "It has several improvements no one has thought of before."

The still appeared to be an incoherent mass of pipes, cylinders, coils and drums, and I could not understand a word of his explanation. But I do not think he noticed this, the still was his child and, if it had faults, he would overlook them. The only one it seemed to have

477

at the moment was that it did not actually work, but this would very soon be remedied.

As I was leaving to return to Mrs. Nimmo's, Robin said, "You mustn't worry about Twinkle. She is probably quite safe somewhere, enjoying herself."

Njombo came to me a few days later. "I have news for you," he said. "There is a duiker up there"—he pointed with his chin towards the reserve—"that perhaps is Twinkle. Will you go to see?"

Mrs. Nimmo did not allow rides into the reserve with Njombo, but I pleaded with Robin, and so, with some reluctance, he agreed to come too. We followed the twisting path up the ridge towards Kupanya's, but about halfway there we diverged, and halted by a homestead whose occupants Njombo engaged for some time in conversation. At length an elderly man in a blanket led us up a hill to a large boulder and, with a monkey's agility, clambered to the top. We followed. Evening shadows had already darkened the bottom of the valley but the boulder had the warmth of day stored in it. Our elder pointed across the river and spoke in Kikuyu, and Njombo translated. "He says that two duiker come every evening to the river there. He says that one of them is Twinkle."

We waited for perhaps half an hour while shadows crept like a stain up the hillside. At last the old man pointed across the stream and said softly, "Look."

In the pool of shade, two darker shapes were moving across a flat stretch of grass. They went jerkily, stopping often to look and listen, and now and then to crop a blade of grass. One of them wore two sharp points on his brow. Was the other Twinkle? How could I tell? Yet I felt that I recognized the proud lift of her head. As I watched her, she stood still, sniffed the air and, I could have sworn, looked straight at me, as if to say, I see you, I know you, but although I shall remember you I cannot come back, for I have returned to the freedom which is my heritage.

"I must go and call her," I said.

"She will run away," Njombo warned. "She belongs now to her bwana, not to the house any more."

Nevertheless I set off down the hill and when I plunged into a plantation of bananas near the river I could see them, standing stock-still on the further bank. The bananas blotted out the view, and then

478

the stream had to be crossed by stepping-stones. At last I emerged on the other side, climbed a steep place, and stood at the foot of the slope where the duikers had browsed. The hillside lay silent and lifeless, the duikers had vanished.

I called to Twinkle, but my voice sounded alien and futile, a sound that intruded on the valley's ancient secrecy—water whispering to stones, a soft hissing of banana fronds, goat-bells from a distance, a guinea fowl's chatter, a francolin's call. I knew then it was no good trying to follow Twinkle, that the cord of trust had snapped for ever.

We rode back silently through the darkening landscape. I did not mention Twinkle again, and nor did Robin, but next time he went to Nairobi he bought me a new paintbox and a book about Buffalo Bill.

FROM THE VERANDA of our grass hut we looked over the Kikuyu ridges to Mount Kenya, which could be seen only in the early mornings and in the evenings, at certain times of the year. In colour it was a bluish-purple, save for a white cap of ice and snow from which arose cold, clear little streams bringing life to the Kikuyu uplands that formed the shoulders of this great mountain.

The snow and glaciers were also the dwelling place of God, according to Njombo, and if you wished to pray to God, you looked towards the peaks and hoped he would hear you; though this was only possible if you had offered a sacrifice. No one had ever seen God, Njombo added: he dwelt by himself without a wife, or father or mother, but he had given land and sheep and goats to the first Kikuyu, and he watched over them so long as they obeyed his laws.

Every morning the twin peaks of the mountain floated in the sky as if sketched in lightly with a pencil, and I thought of Tilly and the safari, for it was to somewhere beyond those peaks that they had travelled.

By eight o'clock the peaks of Mount Kenya had disappeared behind a cloudy muffler. The cumulus clouds that drifted all day long across a sun-filled sky reminded me of huge swirls of whipped cream, but these clouds were heavier and denser, and the colour of rosemary flowers. They meant the approach of the rains, and the planting of many more coffee seedlings.

The long rains, which in those days were expected on 25th March exactly, arrived punctually at two o'clock in the afternoon. Enormous chilly drops beat on Mrs. Nimmo's iron roof, turned our surroundings into a mess like melted chocolate, and poured in rivers down every slope. The next morning I was allowed to ride over to the farm. Rain had stirred the people. They carried on their heads boxes of bright-leaved young coffee trees, dumped them in the shamba and hurried back to the nurseries for more. The shamba boys placed each seedling carefully in a hole and packed in the chocolate mud, which they pressed down with their naked feet. Although they disliked the wet, they took an interest in this work, for they could see the plantation arising out of their labours.

There was an art in planting young coffee, because if the little taproot was not put in absolutely straight, the tree would die; so Robin hurried to and fro trying to ensure that every root was true. All the Kikuyu on the farm had been pressed into service. Njombo was there also, shouting encouragement and enjoying himself very much. "Now we will make a coffee shamba as big as a forest," he cried. "And fruit will fill many, many wagons and our bwana will be richer than King George."

I was allowed to help scoop moist earth round the seedlings and press it down with my fingers, which had all the delight of making mud pies with the added pleasure of utility.

When I got back to Mrs. Nimmo's, several Africans I had never seen before were there. None of them were Kikuyu, but blacker and fiercer, with a musky smell, large flat noses, and big sandalled feet; and two strange mules were in the stable, and safari gear was lying around. When I reached the living room, I found two men there with Mrs. Nimmo, both brown and travel-stained. One had a shirt with little slots to hold cartridges above the pockets, and both wore hunting knives, boots and puttees; a big white bull terrier with many scars lay by the fireplace.

"This is the bairn," Mrs. Nimmo cried, and she looked flustered and excited. "Come and say how do you do to Mr. Nimmo, dear. My goodness, whatever have you been doing now! Bringing all that dirt into my sitting room! Mr. Nimmo will think I've got a savage in the house! Go and clean up at once, and show Mr. Nimmo he's got a little lady to welcome him, and not a Red Indian."

I returned cleaner, and curious to see in the flesh a person who had for so long been a myth, like my bearded grandfather in Ireland or King George V. It was some time before I discovered that Mr.

Nimmo was the shorter of the two men, very solid, with broad shoulders, an unexpressive, pugnacious-looking, red, but not unkindly face, and a blue eye with a suspicion in it of a twinkle. He spoke in a dry Scots voice, and looked about him in a quiet, appraising manner, and said several times to Mrs. Nimmo, "That's changed since I was here," or, "You've treated yourself to a fine rug when there's plenty of old sacks in the store," or, to his companion, "You see, Jim, what it's like to keep a wife in luxury while you're walking after elephants with your only pair of boots worn through."

Next morning, Mr. Nimmo took charge of everything; the boy came to him for orders, and he was out early on his mule riding round the farm. Mrs. Nimmo did everything she could to please him, getting up to pour out his tea and herself making hot scones for him, and hoping that the eggs were done to his liking. In fact a great change had taken place in Mrs. Nimmo overnight and it was a surprise to me that Mr. Nimmo, who did not impress one much to look at, had been able to bring this about while he said little that was amiable, and never thanked her for her attentions.

Mrs. Nimmo was delighted when I asked permission to ride over to the farm and see if there was any news of Tilly. And there was. A telegram dispatched from Fort Hall said that she was getting a lift by car for the last stage of the safari, and would be at the Blue Posts by lunchtime. So Robin and I rode down, leading Lucifer, and there she was, sitting on the veranda in her divided riding skirt, a little thinner than when she went away, but with her bright hair shining over its wide frame, and her skin still rosy in spite of the deserts she had tramped over and the heat she had endured.

"Thank goodness you're safe," Robin said, beaming with pleasure, after they had embraced. "I have missed you . . . I'm planting out the coffee and everyone is hard at it."

"It's lovely to see you," Tilly responded. "And you look well. Do you know, I shot a lion: not a very large one, but definitely a lion; the skin is coming on with the safari."

"I've got the still in working order, except for one or two small details, and I think we shall be able to start on the geraniums in a week or two if this rain keeps on."

"It sloped off into a *donga*, and when I saw something tawny moving in the grass I let fly and hit it in the leg."

481

"We've had a bit of bad luck with the oxen, one broke its leg, and another died of colic, probably a poisonous plant."

Clearly it was more blessed, or at any rate more enjoyable, to give news than to receive it, and they continued in this independent vein for some time. Then Robin suddenly asked, "But what happened to Lettice and Hereward?"

"They've stayed behind at Nyeri—Hereward's had an accident, and must go down to Nairobi as soon as he can be moved."

When Robin asked what sort of accident, Tilly said a buffalo had charged him, and gave me her glass, telling me to get it refilled. We had lunch at the Blue Posts and rode back afterwards in the heat of the afternoon. It had been a successful safari, it seemed, except that a mysterious cloud had fallen over it towards the end. "And Ian?" Robin inquired. "I suppose he is hardly sitting at Hereward's bedside?"

"Ian is involved in a shauri about Ahmed."

"Ahmed! He's in trouble, I suppose?"

"No, it's Ian who's in trouble, up to a point. Ahmed went back to his tribe in Somaliland, or wherever he comes from. You must never breathe a word of all this."

Everyone was delighted to see Tilly. The Kikuyu were full of questions about the lands she had travelled in and the lions she had shot. "You see, we have looked after bwana very well," they said. "We have seen that he has not gone hungry and that his cattle and horses have not fallen sick, and that his shamba has thrived; and the toto also, we have looked after her."

About a week later Lettice came over to see us. Most people did not notice me when they arrived, but she always did; she kissed me and said, "I am distressed to hear that you have had a great sorrow. It is sad to lose Twinkle, but she may be happier, even if you are not."

Tilly sent me on an errand which I knew she had invented to get me out of the way, so I loitered on the veranda to listen.

"I don't know what to do, Tilly," Lettice said. "I must go back to Nairobi and there I shall meet Ian, and either we must say goodbye and he will leave the country or . . . how dreadful it is to know that whatever you do, somebody must get hurt."

"I suppose it is a question of who would get hurt the most, or recover the soonest."

"I know how you would decide that, and everyone else would think the same, but I believe you are wrong. Hereward has something to hold on to; he will always be a soldier fighting for his country, and sometimes he will suffer defeats and be betrayed, but that will not really twist the sinews of his heart, for soldiers are born to bear misfortune, and take a pride in doing so. Whereas Ian . . . if he has looked for something all his life and at last found it, and cannot keep it, that will be the end of him."

"That is all rather too deep for me," Tilly replied. "Ian is tremendously attractive, and I can understand how you feel, and wish I could help you, but I don't see how I can."

"Yes, Ian is attractive, but so are other men; it is simply that I feel as if I had come to the end of a journey, and that often there is no need for words between us at all, and yet there is never any shortage of them; even when he is not there, all my thoughts are shaped to fit his mind, and I think his fit mine also, without our intending it—a queer feeling, one I have never had before."

"There is a practical side to it," Tilly suggested. "Ian could hardly support a family by horse-trading in Abyssinia, or shooting elephants."

"Most people try to make fortunes or, if they have enough already, like Hereward, to win a name, or to add a new bit to the Empire. Ian simply wants to live. You can't live, he says, if you are trying to grow richer or greater—only by fitting into the scheme of things and not trying to alter it to fit you."

"That sounds rather Eastern," Tilly remarked with caution. "I can see he is a more interesting companion than Hereward, but not perhaps such a good provider."

"You are on Hereward's side," Lettice said sadly, "and of course you are right; and there is also Hugh."

"I know what I should do if I were in your place," Tilly observed.

"You would do your duty," Lettice said regretfully.

"No, I should not; I should do what I wanted, and enjoy it, and eventually be sorry, and never admit that I was."

"At any rate, Hereward is better; disaster was averted by a quarter of an inch. Poor Hereward, I hope that when he next loses his temper he will not speak to a Somali as he does to fellow Englishmen with their cold, phlegmatic blood."

483

"I hope Ian will be able to keep it hushed up," Tilly remarked.

"Ian says Ahmed will come back some day, when it has all blown over, because he is a faithful henchman—and because Ian owes him three months' wages. What a time we have had, Tilly!"

They continued to talk, but my attention had long since wandered, and I went out to look for birds' nests in the reeds by the river. Later, at teatime, Tilly remarked to Robin, "I expect Lettice will go off with Ian, but I can't see how it will work."

"Ian can sing and read Greek poetry, and Lettice can play and do petit point, and they are both fond of riding, and wine, and wild animals and conversation. Perhaps it will be all right."

"When you are used to luxury, you think that you despise it, but when it disappears you realize that it has grown into your life. Or so I'm told; I can't speak from experience."

Robin looked a little guilty. "Yes, my Aunt Polly was like that. She created a scandal by marrying a stockbroker—no one had ever done that before in Inverness—and then by leaving him for a sailor who hadn't a penny in the world; love in furnished rooms in Portsmouth was too much for her, she took up with a wine merchant from Bristol and ended in Jamaica with a rich old planter."

"How lucky she was to find a rich old planter," Tilly remarked. "We can only hope that you will become one, in the end."

Chapter 9

Tilly imported from England twelve more Speckled Sussex pullets and a cockerel, to make a new start. We rode down to meet them at the station, where we encountered several neighbours. They all discussed the bad news from Europe and the probability of war. Austria and Serbia were fighting, Belgrade was in flames, the Bank of England had closed its doors. All this came as a complete surprise to Tilly and Robin. People said the army was mobilizing and that if England went to war with Germany, we should at once invade German East Africa and everyone would volunteer.

Both my parents were rather silent on the ride home. There was a lot to think about. What would happen to the farm? To Tilly and me?

Robin belonged to some kind of reserve force, and began to fuss about getting back to his regiment. Next day he had a cable saying: "European war inevitable." So he packed his bag and rode off the following day to catch a train to Nairobi. Tilly felt restless, worried and out of things. She busied herself with looking after the new chickens and organizing the labour force.

Soon the district was almost deserted, with only Tilly, myself, Alec Wilson and Mrs. Nimmo left behind. Even Major Breeches had left the Blue Posts and was helping to organize rations for the volunteers who were pouring into Nairobi.

Robin returned in three or four days, full of news. People were arriving to enlist, he said, from all over the country. Some of the more forceful volunteers proceeded to form their own units, appoint their own officers and drill their followers. Thus there came spontaneously into being Wilson's Scouts, Arnoldi's Scouts (composed of Dutchmen from the plateau), and Bowker's Horse.

Robin got himself a job to do with Intelligence. He was delighted with it, and even more delighted to delve into a tin trunk in the store and extract his kilt and its accoutrements. He took it off to Nairobi, and that was the last I saw of him for some time. It was decided that Tilly was to take part in the starting of a military hospital in Nairobi. Alec Wilson offered to look after the farm, and later on he also took over the Palmers'. There remained my future to be settled. Ian Crawfurd had an elder brother, Humphrey, with a farm up-country at Molo, and a wife. Tilly had met them both and liked them; and when Mrs. Crawfurd wrote to offer me a sanctuary she accepted gratefully, and threw in the Speckled Sussex pullets for good measure. I was not allowed to take George and Mary, the chameleons, but Njombo promised to look after them faithfully. To part with Moyale was the worst of all. It was a bitter moment when he ate his last lick of sugar from my hand, nuzzling me with his soft muzzle.

We left for Nairobi in the mule buggy, with the crate of Speckled Sussex pullets, a basketful of vegetables for the hospital, and many other miscellaneous things. Nairobi was full of khaki men with rifles. Most wore breeches and puttees, bush shirts and felt hats, with gay bandanna handkerchiefs round their necks.

In the evening Tilly put me on the train, in the charge of the guard, with a good deal of luggage and some last-minute presents for Mrs.

Crawfurd, such as a box of little trees, a sack of seed potatoes, a preserving pan, an egg timer, and two new blouses that had arrived in the last boat before the war began. "They will bring nothing now but beer and bullets, I expect," Tilly remarked gloomily. The guard said he would put the Speckled Sussex in the van.

When I got off the train next morning everything smelled quite different, fresh and cold. An oxcart met me at the station with a young Dutchman, who said his name was Dirk and that he would take me to the Crawfurds' farm.

At Molo everything was much bigger than at Thika—hills, trees, distances, even sky and clouds. The trees were black and clumped, the grass tufty and bent over to one side, and you felt as if you had reached the very top of the world. We passed no round huts, no goats, no banana trees; everything was empty and cold. I was silent on the journey, and so was Dirk. At the end of the track, I told myself, would be Mr. Crawfurd, and he would be just like Ian only older. But Humphrey Crawfurd was not like Ian at all. He was much larger, dark instead of fair, with a heavy moustache and big thick hands; he was bulky, silent, he did not sparkle at all. It was only in the eyes that I could see a resemblance, proud and smoky-blue; and a little in the smile, perhaps, which made Humphrey look younger and less preoccupied.

What I remember most about him was his ability to embalm himself so deeply in thought that flies could crawl about his face, even into his ears, without his making any sign. He was a man who held to one passion at a time, and at the moment his thoughts were concentrated upon water, and ways of getting it about. He had a large farm, a ranch really, and it needed a great many pipes, channels and flumes.

Mrs. Crawfurd was as lavish with words as he was sparing. She had the knack of uncovering drama in every situation, and importance in every human being. She did not expect her husband to listen to every word of hers, for she enjoyed talking, nor did he expect an over-lively interest in his water schemes. They gave and took. They had two children, a girl called Althea who was in Scotland, and a two-year-old boy called Bay, who was with them; and a baby was expected quite soon.

After my retinue of packages had been unloaded and sorted out, and Mrs. Crawfurd had exclaimed at Tilly's generosity, I remembered the Speckled Sussex! They had not been in the oxcart. Had they been left behind?

They were not at Molo station, and Mrs. Crawfurd wrote to break the news of their disappearance to Tilly. A week or two later, we heard their fate. Tilly had received a note from the matron of the hospital, thanking her warmly for her handsome gift of a dozen young hens. "The patients have enjoyed them, such a welcome change." Poor Speckled Sussex, it was sad for them to travel five thousand miles, so much cherished, and destined to found a new colony of hens, only to end up in the roasting pan.

A few days after I arrived, Mr. Crawfurd opened a furrow that was to carry water from a spring in the forest to his house and farm. The trench was nearly two miles long and had taken over a year to dig and line with a kind of clay that had been hauled by oxcarts, with frequent adventures in the mud.

We rode up to the forest with a picnic, men with spades having gone on before. Nothing could have made Mr. Crawfurd talkative, but you could feel his excitement. The labour on the farm had decided to make this a holiday, and all the people living round about had come to join in.

Molo was not like Thika; there was no native reserve; only about fifteen years before, no humans of any sort had been living there. Too bleak for cultivators, too high even for Masai cattle, these Molo downs had lain there as God made them, empty and unchanged, with wild animals in sole possession.

After the government had built a railway from the coast to Lake Victoria, they had offered blocks of this land for nothing beyond a very small rent, but they had not found a single taker. Then a few South Africans arrived, and scratched a living by shooting the game and running transport from Londiani, the next station but one up the line, to the Uasin Gishu plateau.

It was from a South African that the Crawfurds had bought their ranch of five thousand acres. There was nothing on it, just a few huts made of split logs and some bomas for sheep and cattle. There was not even a road to link the ranch with the station. Mr. Crawfurd lacked capital, so he could only do a little bit at a time. He was building up his flocks and herds animal by animal. The Crawfurds did sell a little butter, which went once a week in an oxcart to the station, and then in small consignments to people they knew in Nairobi.

As no Africans were living on this great western wall of the Rift Valley of which Molo was a part, the earliest farmers sent to fetch some, either from the Kavirondo country or from Kikuyuland, and small native settlements arose near the European homesteads and in folds of the hills. And as everyone within ten miles or so had decided to attend the opening of the Crawfurds' furrow, we arrived to find quite a lot of people squatting round on their heels or leaning on their spears.

The head of the furrow lay a little distance inside the forest, in one of the glades. Most of the trees here were either olives, or cedars with black, bitter berries, which grew to great heights. Their foliage was hung with long, drooping beards of greenish-grey lichen. This gave them a look of ancient giants, full of wisdom and mystery.

Inside the forest's darkness the sharp cedar-smell was always in your nostrils, dry twigs cracked and whispered under your feet, the rotting fallen trunks lay deep in moss. At one moment you would be walking along a dark tunnel, scrambling over logs, pushing through creepers and listening for the squawk of a monkey. The next moment you would stand on the margin of a glade lying before you as open and inviting as a garden or park.

The Crawfurds' furrow started in one of these open glades, and the sunlight drenched us all. Large vivid butterflies, purple and gold, quivered on the bush while Mr. Crawfurd took a spade to dig away the last foot of furrow, and thus to link it with a little pool that had formed just below a spring.

"What a thrilling moment we are coming to!" Mrs. Crawfurd cried. "Humphrey, I'm sure you ought to be presented with a silver spade. We should have the date engraved on it with a motto, or quotation. Think of the sweet peas and new potatoes and the strawberries. And water from a tap! It's *too* exciting. Do you think frogs will get into the pipe, Humphrey?"

"No," Mr. Crawfurd said, digging away with his spade. When he was not listening he always said no, because it was safer. You could change to yes later, but not from yes to no.

488

"The water's going to rush through any minute! What a lot of people have come! Isn't it good that they're so interested?"

"No."

Mr. Crawfurd had now paused beside the last barrier of soil to fall before his spade. Under a cedar, a group of elders sat on their haunches taking snuff. They wore robes of stitched goat skin, and looked watchful and wise. They were fascinated by the furrow and everything about it, for the Kikuyu, although so intelligent in many ways, had never thought of irrigation.

Mr. Crawfurd straightened his back and looked round before he knocked away the last barrier. Several of the old men now came forward and made a little speech in Kikuyu; their faces were animated and they moved their skinny arms in graceful gestures. "They are saying that they are very happy to see water coming down from the mountain," the headman translated. "They ask God to see that it is good, and they hope God will help the bwana as the bwana helps the Kikuyu."

"Thank you," said Mr. Crawfurd. Then he struck away the last clod and stepped aside and down gushed the water into the clay bed. There was a murmur from the people, surprised perhaps that the water did flow along the furrow, as Mr. Crawfurd had told them it would. This they did not regard as a certain consequence of digging; it was a happy conclusion, indicating that the prayers and magic had succeeded.

There was a great deal of laughter and congratulations. I can remember still the water singing down among the cedars, and Mrs. Crawfurd standing with her hand in Bay's, her face gay with pleasure, looking from the furrow to Mr. Crawfurd as though he had indeed performed a miracle.

We ate our sandwiches beside the pool and listened to the silence of the forest, and birds moving in the foliage, and the humming of a bumblebee. The war they had talked of in Nairobi was a word without meaning.

ONE DAY I RODE with Dirk to Londiani, which was then the railhead for the Uasin Gishu plateau and all the country beyond. The Crawfurds had not wanted me to go with Dirk, whose object was to get some cartridges, but Kate Crawfurd was unwell, Mr. Crawfurd was busy and I insistent, and so they gave way. Dirk had not wanted me either, but he had little choice; I mounted the pony the Crawfurds had lent me, a white one called Snowball, and set out at his side. On the whole he was a good-natured young man, and used to children. Along the way he told me how he had come to the country as a boy, seven years earlier, with a party of Boers from the Transvaal.

As we approached Londiani, the corrugated iron roofs threw back the sunlight and we seemed to be arriving at a city of splendour and glory. Londiani shrank, however, on our arrival, and turned into a single rutted street with a few dukas, some sheds beside the railway, a *dak* bungalow, and a DC's office with a flagpole.

"Is that all there is?" I asked.

Dirk laughed. "What were you expecting?"

Whatever it had been, Londiani did not possess it. I was by then tired, sore and hungry, despite a sandwich and some roasted mealies Dirk had shared with me as we rode along.

"Now what shall I do with you?" Dirk wondered. Had I been a pony, he would have turned me out to graze.

"I'm hungry."

"We had better go to the DC."

District commissioners were accustomed to deal with any situation that might arise, and I do not remember that this one showed any great surprise at being handed over a stray child. He passed me on to his wife, who gave me a feast. On farms, the bread was made with yeast brewed from bananas or potatoes, and imported dried hops, and was nearly always sour, and hard as old boots, so that one of the luxuries farmers most enjoyed when they visited a town was baker's bread. Mrs. Pascoe's toast was pliant and delicious, and she even had apples and spicy sausages.

She was a kind-hearted woman with a well-developed sense of duty; these two attributes had made her into a dumping-ground for other people's pets, and a soft option for the locals, who caught birds and animals in the forest to bring to her for the sixpence she would generally pay to rescue them from their misery, and so the house was full of small beasts like bushbabies and mongooses.

Mr. Pascoe soon appeared, looking harassed; the war had upset everything, and this was mail-train day, so his office was full of citizens with shauris needing immediate attention. "What are we going to do with this child?" he demanded.

"I'm going back with Dirk," I said.

"That young Dutchman? What makes you think he's going back?"

"He came to get some cartridges."

"Cartridges my foot. He's probably on his way to the plateau by now, or else to Nairobi to join the party."

"But he's got Mr. Crawfurd's pony."

Mr. Pascoe only laughed. "That won't bother him."

"I can go home by myself," I said.

"You certainly can't. Perhaps there'll be someone on the train who can take you to Molo, and then the Crawfurds can collect you there."

In the end he called for Snowball, who had also breakfasted, and allowed me to ride with him to the *dak* bungalow to find out if anyone had seen Dirk.

The bungalow, a railway rest house, was full of bearded, dust-stained Dutchmen, who fell silent as Mr. Pascoe approached and addressed a man called Sandy who spoke with the accents of Scotland. When Mr. Pascoe inquired about Dirk, Sandy said, "Och, he'll have gone after his brother, up to Sixty-Four. The brother came through by the last mail, to fetch his gun before he went for a soldier."

"You mean he took the pony?" Mr. Pascoe said.

Sandy looked astonished. "You don't think a Dutchman would pay for transport when he could get his legs across a nag?"

In spite of Sandy's certainty and Mr. Pascoe's smile, I felt sure that Dirk would return the pony. Although Mr. Crawfurd would no doubt regard his action as a theft, to a Dutchman or to an African it would appear merely as a rather long borrow.

THE WAGON TRACK from Sixty-Four ended outside the *dak* bungalow, and from its veranda, where travellers waited for the mail, someone called attention to a puff of dust rolling towards us with unusual speed. A high, old-fashioned buckboard came into view. This was Whitelock's stagecoach, propelled by four oxen trained to trot (if not very swiftly) and changed every fifteen miles between Sixty-Four and Londiani.

One of the passengers who stepped stiffly down from the buckboard was a man of six feet three or four with a thick dark moustache. He seized Mr. Pascoe's hand and pumped it, and explained that he was on his way to join the war; from what he said, it was high time that someone put a little punch into it. The Germans kept on blowing up the railway line between Nairobi and Mombasa, and the arrival of troops from India had not made the difference expected. The local volunteers, who had coalesced into the East African Mounted Rifles, had been whisked up to Kisumu to man a boat on Lake Victoria, and had won a naval victory over a German vessel. But there still seemed plenty of scope for Mr. Pascoe's acquaintance, whose name was Dick Montagu.

"Oh, this is my wife," he added as an afterthought. Mrs. Montagu had been standing quite still, looking bewildered and nervous. She was as small and light as he was large and heavy; like some hesitant bird, bright-eyed and fine-limbed, she seemed to have alighted on the veranda, rather than to have climbed the steps. Dick Montagu ignored her while he got his baggage assembled, and told Mr. Pascoe that he would have to spend the night at Londiani to wait for the bulk of his kit, which was following by wagon.

"You'd better bring your wife over to our bungalow for the night," Mr. Pascoe said.

"Thanks, old man," Dick Montagu replied.

Mrs. Montagu behaved as if the Pascoes' bungalow was a palace, entered after a long sojourn in a swineherd's hut. And, indeed, that may have been her situation. Her father was one of those rich Americans who had come to shoot big game after Theodore Roosevelt had made the pastime fashionable; Dick Montagu had arranged his safari. The hunter had bagged not only a lot of large animals, but the daughter as well. She was barely eighteen, and her father forbade the match. After Dick Montagu carried her off to the Belgian Congo in a romantic elopement, her father returned to Philadelphia to cut her out of his life and his will. Dick, who was twenty years older than his bride, boasted that the old man was sure to come round, but over a year had passed, debts had gathered, and the old man was still refusing to answer letters.

Mr. Pascoe had decided that I was to stay the night too, and accompany the Montagus to Nakuru next day, where the Crawfurds would meet me as soon as they could. He had sent a syce to Molo on

Snowball with a note to this effect. I knew that Mrs. Crawfurd would be worried and Mr. Crawfurd angry, but there was nothing to be done.

We arrived in Nakuru late in the evening, and made our way to the hotel. Some time in the night, a commotion arose. The station was very close, and I awoke to hear an engine panting and grinding, bells clanging, whistles blowing, shouts and cries. Had the Germans captured Nakuru, were we all to be lined up and shot? As I did not wish to be shot in my pyjamas, I dressed and went out to investigate.

A train was in, the platform was alive with khaki men, like giant ants whose nest has been disturbed. But the Germans would be grim, orderly and helmeted; these men wore slouch hats or no hats at all, and even in the hard, shadowy light they looked young and gay. I saw Lois Montagu standing by herself, and went up to her. "It's the Mounted Rifles on their way back from a victory at Kisumu," she said. "Why, they're heroes!"

Just then I saw Dick Montagu approaching with a slighter figure at his side, on whose bare head the lamplight shone as on a new golden sovereign. Dick Montagu introduced his companion to Lois, who gazed as if bewitched at the thin and smiling face of Ian Crawfurd.

"Dick has spoken of you often," she said.

"I don't know how the devil you got yourself into uniform so quickly," Dick grumbled.

"I happened to have gone down to Nairobi, and to be there when the show started."

For a while they discussed the war, which they did not think was being well conducted. Then Ian smiled at me and said, "I saw your father in Nairobi. He had just come back from questioning some German prisoners."

"Did he shoot them?"

"Well, no; one is supposed to shoot them before they are captured, not after.... I hear you are staying with Kate and Humphrey; you must give them my love, and say that I shall write."

"All right," I said. I wanted to hold Ian's attention, not to lose him, and to find some thread to lead me on to all the questions I longed to burst out with. But the moment passed, Ian turned to speak again to the Montagus. Dick was asking him about the land he had taken up, but Ian only smiled vaguely.

"It hardly looks as though I'll need it, after all."

"Don't make any mistake, old man. That land will be worth a lot of money when we've thrashed the Hun. Don't let it slip through your hands."

"I'll remember," Ian said. "And now I must go. I'm a corporal, and have a dozen men to look after who've never heard of discipline. But two or three are good bridge players, one plays the clarinet, and another is an excellent conjurer, so we're never dull."

Ian took my hand for a moment to say goodbye.

"Did Ahmed come back?" I managed to eject one of the questions, even if it was a minor one.

"Funny you should mention that. He did, and he's joined a troop of Somali scouts and has a pony and a rifle, and glorious dreams of war and loot. So he's all right. Give my love to Tilly when you see her, and to everyone else...."

He stood for a moment looking down at me, his hat in one hand and the other resting lightly on his belt. I thought he looked thinner even than before, older perhaps. The name in both our minds lay unspoken between us like a barrier, and yet uniting us for that fleeting instant, like fish caught in the same net. So strong was this impression that I thought I heard through the chatter a clear musical voice, and sensed among the stale platform odours the scent of heliotrope.

Ian hesitated; perhaps he, too, did not want to put to flight the ghosts of happiness. Then he slipped from one wrist a little bracelet he wore—such things were then in fashion—of plaited hair pulled from a lion's tail.

"He had courage: some people eat the heart, but I doubt if that's necessary."

I took it without finding anything to say, but I knew in my own heart that it was not for me. He smiled at us, waved a hand, and vanished into the throng and bustle of the train, which was now preparing for departure. The shouts and cheers, the whistles, the hissing and chugging of the engine, filled the station as a kettle fills with steam. Men waved from windows; the guard jumped into his moving van; and we watched the rear light of the last coach vanish, and heard the chugging die away. Gradually the vast digesting dark of Africa swallowed up all traces of the hurrying train.

Chapter 10

A couple of days later I, too, found myself in the train and bound in the same direction, although not for the war. The Crawfurds, who came down from Molo together, had heard from Tilly, who had done all she could for the time being at the hospital and was returning to Thika, that she would like me back again.

Tilly was at Nairobi station, but Robin was still away somewhere on the railway, or perhaps on the German border, no one knew. The next day we took the train to Thika and rode out to the farm.

Several of the flame trees flanking the future drive, now taller than I was, had burst into flower. The young coffee trees were looking healthy and had a few green berries on them, their first. I was thankful to discover Moyale in excellent health, too plump if anything. On the farm, Sammy reported all was in order. In fact, except for Robin's absence, the war might not have existed at all. Some of the young Kikuyu were full of ardour and would shake their spears or sticks and cry, "Show me these Germani! Where are they? Have they run away? I will kill them as we used to kill the Masai!"

This bellicose atmosphere so infected me that one day Njombo came upon me chopping off the tops of old maize stalks with a hunting knife. "What are you doing?" he asked.

"Cutting off the heads of the Germans!"

The attitude of the Kikuyu was put down to a gratifying, if not surprising, loyalty to the British, who had done so much to bring civilization, law and order to the savages. No other explanation occurred to anyone but Alec Wilson, who came over soon after we were back.

"It's the prospect of law and order being removed, not their introduction, that is so much exciting them," he said. "All the men in their thirties are pulling their spears out of the thatch where they've been hidden and telling frightful whoppers about the Masai, who in fact always beat them; while the young lads are saying, 'Those old has-beens had no more fight in them than a chicken. Now you'll see something!'"

"You're a cynic, Alex, that's your trouble," Tilly said. Like most cynics, he was very kind, and frequently came over to offer Tilly help in running the farm. There was a lot to do: coffee to be weeded, citrus pruned, land ploughed, maize planted, seedlings nursed. I rode errands on Moyale, added to my collection of birds' eggs and started a scrapbook about the war.

A chit came one day from Lettice: she had returned, and she invited Tilly over for the night. I went too, because there was no one to be left with. Lettice we found pale and tired; her eyes looked huge and dark. She kept patting her hair and making other nervous gestures, and she had taken up smoking. The smell of heliotrope was still there, but almost overlaid by Turkish tobacco.

"Now I am being caught out, as I knew I would be eventually," she said, after greeting Tilly with affection. "Nothing I am good at is the least use in a war, and I cannot even help Hereward by running the farm efficiently, as you help Robin."

"How is Hereward?" Tilly inquired.

"Getting impatient. This is just a sideshow, he says, and he wants to get back to the real thing."

They fell silent, with an unspoken question lying heavily between them. Lettice had taken up her tapestry work, but she was only fiddling with it. Finally, she broke the silence. "I saw Ian in Nairobi."

"Yes. . . . May I try one of your cigarettes?" I had never seen Tilly smoke before. She puffed experimentally, blowing out the smoke in little jets.

"You know he took up some land at the back of beyond, near a mountain. He said it had caves full of bats, and wonderful butterflies. His nearest neighbour brought a house out from England in bits, and kept a cheetah chained to his veranda."

"I suppose this rotten war . . ."

"Ian is chasing Germans on the border, and Hereward's heart is set on becoming a hero. . . . Oh, Tilly, what am I to do?"

Lettice had jumped to her feet and was prowling round the room, changing the position of an arum lily in a vase, patting at a cushion. Tilly frowned at her cigarette, which had made her eyes water, as if it were the cause of all these complexities.

"You know what I think," she observed.

"Yes, and of course you were right then; everything was settled, and it only remained to face up to Hereward. But now . . . he would pay us out, I know, poor Hereward; his life comes low down on the list of things he considers important. So he would think nothing of discarding it, and for the rest of our lives, whenever we opened a cupboard we should see its skeleton. And Ian ..."

"Yes, Ian! Hereward will be in his element, he'll be a general covered with tabs, you'll see. Surely it's Ian who needs to be considered."

We rode back next morning, and a few days later Robin came home on leave, bringing me a pair of German field glasses and a lot of news about the war, which was not going well. However, the Mounted Rifles were patrolling the border and hoped to meet the Germans at any moment, and of course to win a victory.

"There's a rumour that my battalion has gone to France already. It's maddening to be stuck out here." It was a surprise to find Robin, in his new martial spirit, no longer really interested in the still. He rode off to the station again in a few days, promising to send me a button from a German uniform.

I cannot remember how long it was after Robin's leave that I was down in the coffee nursery one evening, engaged in the construction of a little furrow to irrigate some orange pips I had planted, when Alec Wilson appeared, looking for Tilly. A couple of shamba boys were repairing the banana-leaf thatch over beds of young coffee trees. The shadows had fallen already on the river, all was peaceful and serene. Alec looked dusty and smelled of pony, so I knew he had just returned from Nairobi. He asked me what I was doing.

"I'm going to have an orange shamba of my own."

"Splendid. When it's grown, you shall sit in the orange grove at dusk with hummingbirds flying round your head, playing love songs on a dulcimer, and I will come and lie at your feet."

"I haven't got a dulcimer," I objected.

"I'll buy you one the next time I go to Nairobi. And now I must find Tilly to tell her my news."

"Have the Germans run away?"

"No, they have fought a battle near a hill called Longido, and won it, I'm afraid. Now, go on with your shamba."

I took his advice for a while, but somehow I had lost interest in the oranges. So I clambered up to the house. I found Tilly on the veranda with Alec, having a cup of tea. They both looked gloomy, and Tilly's eyes were red.

497

"Run along and play with something," she said.

"With what?"

"Oh, never mind. Why don't you sit down and read a book?"

I went inside and looked at an atlas lying on the table, but I could hear them talking on the veranda.

"It would be best for you to tell her," Alec said.

"Yes, I shall have to; but it's late now to go over tonight."

"She will have the rest of her life to think about it, so you will do no harm by waiting till the morning."

"If it had been anyone else ..." Tilly's voice was hoarse and muffled.

After a pause, Alec said, "Those fools of doctors threw me out. They're idiots, I'm as sound as a bell. I shall have another shot, but meanwhile ... Goodnight, Tilly, try not to fret."

Tilly settled down on the veranda to do accounts. She was sombre and the evening sad, and I went to look for George and Mary. George was clinging to a twig, wearing his usual expression of immense self-satisfaction, but it may have been Mary; although I pretended to know them apart, I could only guess.

I knew that someone was dead. People often died, animals and people; I had seen a dead body once, lying in the grass by the side of the road. I had been hustled past it, so it did not make any great impression. It could not be connected with anyone I knew.

When I was sitting over my supper, and the lamps had been brought in, I asked Tilly if anything was wrong with Lettice.

"Nothing, so far as I know."

"Are you going to see her tomorrow?"

"Probably."

"Can I come too?"

"No, you have been neglecting your lessons; you must learn some French verbs."

"Will Ian come back soon?"

"You must eat up the white as well as the yolk, it contains albumen, which is good for you. No, Ian—well, if you must know, he has been killed. Now, don't ask any more questions and I'll read to you for twenty minutes before you go to bed."

This was a great treat—we were reading *Robbery Under Arms* at the time—and so I did not think any more then about Ian, but when I was in bed I remembered how I had seen him on the station platform, and how his hair had shone in the lamplight like a golden sovereign, and the bracelet he had given me made from a lion's tail. I had it wrapped in tissue paper and tucked safely into my scrapbook, too valuable to wear. It was hard to imagine a dead Ian, so hard in fact that I gave it up and thought of him as I had seen him when we had found the wydah birds dancing, and when he had lain under the fig tree talking to Lettice, and when they had sung together after the piano arrived. I had not seen Ian many times, but each time had been like a special treat, even though nothing unusual had happened; when he had been there it had seemed as if the sun were shining, and I thought that he would never altogether disappear from my mind.

The Kikuyu believed that when a man died, his spirit could enter an animal, and it seemed quite likely that the spirit of Ian, who was so much a part of the wild and silent places, would choose a forest creature like a bushbuck for a habitation. As for his body, I knew it would be eaten by maggots and hyenas; but if in time its remnants turned to dust, as the funeral service said, his dust, I thought, would not be quite the same as other people's, but would shine like those little specks of brightness that sometimes glitter in the sand.

THE LIFE OF THE FARM continued as usual on the surface, but underneath there was a feeling of suspense and uncertainty. Our time at Thika was running out, and everyone knew it.

Tilly was waiting for news of Robin, of the war, of our departure; and when news did come, it was never good. She hated, as she said, marking time. Hearing of a meat shortage in Nairobi, she bought a dozen native ewes and wrote up-country for a purebred ram to make a good mutton cross. The ram duly arrived in an oxcart, took one look at his scruffy little brown brides and fled into the coffee plantation, pursued by the entire labour force waving sticks and uttering cries. Before he was recaptured a number of coffee trees had been damaged.

News came at last of Hereward: he had secured his passage and would sail at once, rejoicing, to rejoin his old regiment. Lettice came over to tell us, and stayed the night. Life seemed no longer to bubble up in her. She was thinner and her arms looked brittle; her rings were loose, shadows had come into her face, and whereas before she had possessed the quality of repose, she fiddled now with things and did not pay attention, and moved in a leaden way.

I asked what was to happen to Puffball and Zena. They sat now in our only comfortable armchair, one on her lap, one tucked into her side, snuffling—a comfortable sound, like a kettle boiling—and licking their black button noses. Lettice replied that she wanted to take them with her to England. I asked, "And bring them back again?"

"If I come back."

"But you can't *not* come back!"

Lettice smiled. "Yes, I suppose it seems the centre of the world to you. But I don't belong here; it is a cruel country that will take your heart and grind it into powder."

I did not understand her meaning, and asked her what would happen to the farm and the stone house and the ponies.

"Don't ask so many questions," Tilly said. "It is bad manners."

"But if I don't ask questions, how shall I find out things?"

"You are not supposed to be a private detective."

"Shall I come and say goodnight to you when you are in bed?" Lettice offered.

This was a rare treat, so I had my supper and went off more willingly than usual. Lettice came later and sat on the edge of my camp bed, and I noticed that the Turkish tobacco prevailed over the heliotrope. She talked about Hugh: perhaps, now that she would soon be seeing him, he was more often in her mind.

"I have got something for you," I said at last.

"How nice! Is it a bird's egg, or a lizard that is indisposed?" Lettice was on the verge of making fun of me, which was unlike her. It was in such small, subtle ways that she had changed, as perhaps she was bound to; if you fall into a fire your looks are altered, and if it is a fire that burns your spirit, that must be altered too.

"It is not mine really. It is something I was given."

"If it was given to you, then it is yours."

Now that I had come to the point, I had the greatest difficulty in passing it, as if I was swimming through a pool of treacle with weights tied to my limbs. "I think it was really meant for you."

She would not help by asking who had given it to me, or what it was, and I knew that she was not really interested, so I put the little parcel on her lap without saying more. She unwrapped it and held it close to the safari lamp, and I said nervously, "It's made of lion's hair, from the tail."

I felt her stiffen and go rigid; she sat for so long without a movement that I thought she had fallen into a sort of trance. Then I felt the bed shake a little; she was trembling, and the hand that held the bracelet quivered very slightly.

"How did you. . . ? When did. . . ?"

"He gave it to me, but I think it was for you. A sort of charm."

She said nothing. Sometimes, in the garden in the early morning, I would find a snail moving forward, like a tiny ship with hunched brown sail, and would tickle it with a grass blade to watch its grey questing horns quickly curl and vanish, and the whole snail become instantly becalmed. It was like that now with Lettice. I could not help prodding with my grass blade.

"Do you want it?" Still she sat without a word. I searched for something to say that was not a question. "One of the men he was in charge of was an excellent conjurer."

Lettice got to her feet and tried to speak, but her throat had dried up. Her hand now shook so much that she could not hold the bracelet; at any rate, she dropped it on my bed, put her hand to her face and hurried away.

Now the bracelet was really mine. It was black, neatly plaited, pliable. I slipped it on and thought about the lion; perhaps he had charged from behind a rock at Ian. Although the rifle had been too much for him, he had been brave, and Ian respected him; and Ian had perhaps been killed in much the same way.

I put away the bracelet, and for a long time valued it. When I was away from Africa I would sometimes take it out and look at it, and think of the tawny lion crouching among wiry grasses and grey boulders, and the heat and aromatic smell; and dust and dryness, and the acacias with their yellow sweet-smelling flowers; and the big clouds throwing patterns on the furrowed hills, and the doves cooing, and the whistling thorns.

Hereward came over to say goodbye a few days later, and not long after that we had a telegram from Robin; he had got his passage and was coming on his final leave. He spent the time making plans for the shamba while we would be away, for how long no one knew; and going round to say goodbye to those of our neighbours who were left on the ridge. Most had gone, and the rest were going, except perhaps for Alec; even Mr. Roos had vanished, though whether in pursuit of animals or of Germans no one knew.

The time came for Tilly and me to ride down to the station to see Robin depart, as Hereward had departed a few weeks before. His belongings had gone ahead in the oxcart: his kilt and its embellishments, his sword, his surviving tweed suit that had been packed away in mothballs in a tin trunk. He had been excited, but now we were all subdued. Things were not going as they should have, either in  France or in Africa, where our troops had been routed at Tanga by the Germans and submarines had started to prey upon shipping in seas that should have been indisputably ours.

"When I get back," Robin said, "we must start at once on the coffee factory. I think it will pay us to hull our own beans, rather than to send them off in parchment. In a decent year, we ought to get a hundred and fifty tons. . . ."

Robin's calculations went on; he had been busy with scraps of paper and our fortunes were as good as made. He had bought a steam plough, a racehorse and a Mercedes before we reached Thika, and was considering a new wing for the future house. All there was of it at present was a few foundations beyond a flame tree avenue planted soon after we had arrived.

Njombo was waiting at the station to ride the extra pony back to the farm. He shook Robin's hand and said, "Goodbye, bwana, and may God help you to kill many Germans; kill one for me, since I cannot go myself. You will kill them all single-handed."

"Perhaps not quite all," said Robin.

"Here is a charm that you must wear round your neck and it will protect you from iron; it came from a very powerful *mundu mugo* near Mount Kenya and I have worn it since I was circumcised. It is a

charm for warriors, and as I cannot be a warrior any longer I give it to you."

Robin was touched, and thanked him warmly. The charm was a little leather cylinder with powder of some sort inside—it was best not to inquire too closely about its origin. Robin slipped it into his pocket and looked embarrassed; he had intended to give Njombo some money as a parting present and now this would seem like paying for the charm. He felt in his pockets but found nothing suitable.

The train snorted, the engine driver shooed everyone inside, the guard waved a flag.

In retrospect, much of one's time in that early war seems to have been spent in seeing people off on trains, or else in travelling on them. Even in peacetime there is in the departure of any train the faintest echo of the raven's croak; in times of war, trains are freighted heavily with fear and sorrow. This one, however, went off cheerfully, with many people waving from the windows, including Robin; and we mounted our ponies and rode away. About halfway home, Tilly noticed that Njombo was wearing Robin's wristwatch. "Where did you get that?" she inquired.

"Bwana gave it to me at the station. When the engine shouted, he gave it, saying, 'This is for you, so that you will know the time when memsabu calls you to help her while I am away.' This is my baksheesh, and it will bring me good fortune like a charm. Bwana is a good man, and God will help him in the war."

This sounded just like Robin, and I felt sure it was true. The watch was all that he could find to give Njombo and he gave it, and would buy another when he reached Nairobi, I supposed.

Chapter II

Berths were found for us at last in a Greek cargo vessel: no one knew when it would sail, and we were to wait for it at Mombasa.

To be torn up by the roots is a sad fate for any growing thing, and I did not want to leave Thika for the unknown. Especially I did not want to leave the animals and people of Thika, to leave Moyale and George and Mary, or Alec and Mrs. Nimmo, Njombo and Sammy and Juma, or even Kamau, and many others. Lettice had gone already. Her belongings had been packed away, her furniture sheeted, Zena and Puffball had vanished with her.

A painful moment came when Lucifer and his companion, Dorcas the chestnut mare, went away to join the war. They were to become remounts, mere units of transport in the hands of people who cared nothing for them. Moyale was spared. He was too fat and spoiled. Alec was to have him, and he could have had no better home.

I took Moyale for a farewell ride in the reserve. It was, as I remember, a cloudy day, with a sky of storms, low and threatening. Yet the sun threw long, triumphant shafts down the ridges to make huts and trees and goats look hard and solid, as if carved from wood, like objects in a toy farmyard. The green of the new grass was so

504

intense that every hillside seemed afire with an emerald flame. We made our way up to Kupanya's to say goodbye. The chief emerged to greet me in a cloak fashioned, I was distressed to see, of many duiker skins, and with elaborate bead ornaments hanging from his ears.

"Have no fear," he said. "I will look after your father's shamba until all the Germans are killed."

"When we return, will you still be here?"

"How should I not be here? The government has trusted me to look after the people, and to send them warriors."

The war had, indeed, enhanced the chief's powers and importance, not to mention his wealth, for it was understood that if a young man wished to avoid recruitment, and gave Kupanya a goat, or possibly two goats, he would not be sent to Fort Hall. And while a good fight with loot to crown it would have pleased the warriors, news had already got round that the young men, far from being given spears, much less rifles, and a prospect of booty, were expected to carry grievous loads in foreign countries and to eat poor food; as this was the work of women, not only uncongenial but insulting, no young man was going to volunteer to undertake it.

"The ponies have gone," I said, "except Moyale, who will stay with Bwana Alec."

"Good. When we see this white pony, we will think of you."

Several of Kupanya's wives, of whom he had by now at least a dozen, came up to wish me well. One, with wide cheekbones, eyes like a moth's, and an air of wisdom and sadness, spoke to me in Kikuyu and put into my hand a necklace of blue and white beads.

"These you must take and wear for us," Kupanya explained. "These beads will be like our people, the blue ones are men, the white ones are women, and the children are the spaces in between, and the thread is the river that runs past your father's shamba. If you wear it always, you will come back to greet us again."

I thanked him, and looked for something to give in return, but my pockets yielded only a crumpled handkerchief, a knife, a few beans and bits of string. I thought perhaps the knife would do and offered it to Kupanya, but he shook his head.

"The traveller does not give a present to those who stay, it is those who remain who give presents to the traveller to help him on his journey, and bring about his safe return."

The women crowded round and several of them gave me presents also—a lump of dough wrapped in a leaf, an iron bangle, a roasted maize-cob, a dried gourd, a small *kiondo* (a woven bag used for carrying grain). I stowed them away in my pockets or tied them to the saddle, and rode away rather like the White Knight, festooned with objects whose use it would have been hard to define.

The day of our departure rushed towards us. Alec came over to fetch the chameleons and Moyale. "George and Mary are planning a surprise already," he said. "There will be a row of little chameleons lined up on a branch to greet you on your return."

The Kikuyu on the farm decided to hold a dance, to celebrate our departure and bring destruction on the Germans; in Tilly's opinion it was merely an excuse to extract from her a fat ram. Grudgingly, she agreed to provide one; and then on impulse decided that the flock of mutton ewes must go, Alec would not have time to bother with them. So she gave the two biggest to the dancers and the rest to Sammy, whose delight was scarcely to be expressed in words. Sammy was getting richer and richer: he had a bicycle, a wristwatch, three wives and, in his own country, an ever-growing herd of cows; now we were going away and he was sorry, because something was ending, but glad, because the chances both to enrich himself and to exert his superiority over the Kikuyu would now become incalculable. With a charming speech about remembrance, he gave me a present of a Masai spear, the light kind used for daily herding, not the big long-bladed weapon of war, which he said would be too heavy to carry.

An immense amount of beer was brewed for the dance; big fat gourds bubbled for days in the huts by the fire that was never allowed to go out, night or day, from its lighting in the newly built home, when the timbers were white and fresh, until the home's abandonment, when the rafters were encrusted with thick, black deposits of smoke.

The young men came with white feathers in their hair, wooden rattles on their ankles, and patterns in chalk and red ochre all over their faces and their naked, glistening skins. The young women greased themselves from head to foot and put on all the ear-ornaments and wire coils they could muster, and their best leather aprons with beads sewn into the seams. They looked gay and festive, but not as decorative as the men.

Camp chairs were set for us to watch the dancing and feasting. Sammy stood beside us wearing an expression tinged with contempt for the caperings of such monkeys; had this been a Masai dance, his look implied, what nobility, what strength, what splendour we should have witnessed!

The dance would have continued, had it been allowed to, all night and all next day as well. The feet and limbs of the Kikuyu, unlike mine or Tilly's, never seemed to tire.

Next morning it was grey and drizzly and the world appeared to share our sadness. The clanger sounded promptly at half past six, but the labour force was not responsive. People drifted in with downcast eyes, walking slowly, their stomachs queasy and their heads like drums full of heavy stones. Sammy stood by the store directing them with a quiet hauteur. Already he felt the potion of authority working in his blood and brain.

Everything was packed and loaded into the mulecart. I could not believe that in a few moments the house, the garden, the farm and everything in it would be out of sight and gone, as if on another planet.

"Kiss each of the four walls of the living room," Tilly said, "and you will come back for sure." I did so and fingered Kupanya's bead necklace with the men, women and children in it, and felt better. This was only an interlude, like going to Molo, and everything would be here when we returned after the war.

WE WENT TO NAIROBI in the train, and then in a procession of three rickshaws from the station to the crowded hotel. The Norfolk was a great place for running into people: sooner or later, it was said, every up-country European climbed the steps of its veranda, or passed in front of it.

Tilly met many acquaintances, including Humphrey Crawfurd, who looked older, and tired.

"Is Kate with you?" Tilly inquired.

A strange look came over Humphrey Crawfurd's face. "You haven't heard," he said. "You see, Kate ... Kate ..."

That seemed to be all. He ducked his head and walked away, looking at the ground.

Tilly frowned. "Perhaps it is the baby," she said. "Perhaps Kate has lost it."

Later we learned that it was Kate who had been lost. "She needed a doctor," Tilly told me. "If he had got there in time, she might have been saved."

If I had been there, I would have saddled the pony and galloped so fast to Nakuru that he would have fallen dead at the doctor's feet; the doctor would have galloped through the night and reached Kate Crawfurd in the nick of time.

Kate's death had shattered Humphrey Crawfurd; he was like a tree whose taproot has been cut. Even the water-furrows had been made for Kate, as other men would bring home fine clothes or jewellery.

He came to see us off for Mombasa next day. Every corner of the train was occupied; so packed were the native coaches that you could hardly see the woodwork. We had our food with us in baskets, and bottles of soda water for drinking and for cleaning our teeth.

"Will you see Lettice," Humphrey asked, "when you get home?"

Tilly said that she would.

"Then give her this." Humphrey thrust a package into her hand. "It was Ian's. She might like something of his." It was his watch, as we saw later: a gold half-hunter, thinner than a penny-piece and engraved with his monogram. It was something she could treasure, if she felt so inclined. But it was a question whether Africans were not wiser to burn everything a dead person had owned and keep no memorial, nor try to cultivate seeds of immortality in a desert of time.

"Did Dirk send back the pony?" I asked Humphrey.

"No, he took it with him. But he sent a message to say he'd pay me back after the war."

Humphrey got our luggage on board and paid the ragged, self-appointed porters. At last the whistle blew, flags waved, and they shook hands through the window.

"My love to Robin."

"Write to us sometimes."

The engine chuffed, people shouted, smoke billowed, the carriage

508

gave a jerk. All we could do was to wave at the upright figure standing stiffly on the crowded platform. Our varied collection of packages had to be reorganized, with the aid of our fellow passengers, who eyed it with misgiving, especially a bundle done up in sacking from which a pungent odour emerged. This contained home-cured sheepskins that Tilly was taking with her to fashion into a warm waistcoat for Robin.

"I wonder if those skins were properly cured," she remarked, inspecting the bundle. "If not, they will make their presence felt in the Red Sea."

I carried the *kiondo*, the soft woven basket Kupanya's wife had given me, with a number of treasures inside: my bead necklace, a cardboard box of birds' eggs, several cocoons in matchboxes, and Njombo's gift, the little bead-edged cap made from a sheep's stomach that I had so much admired. Sammy's spear lay in the rack, together with a small native drum, a Kikuyu sword in its vermilion scabbard and my favourite hippo-hide riding whip. It was not until all our hand packages lay around us in the confined space of a railway carriage that Tilly quite realized their number and variety.

"Do you think," she inquired, "that you will really need all those weapons, as well as a drum?"

"Sammy said I was to kill Germans with the spear, and cut off their heads with the sword."

"There are no Germans at your Aunt Mildred's in Porchester Terrace, where we shall stay: only a Belgian refugee."

I was surprised to see that when she looked out of the window at the retreating wooden shacks and tin roofs of Nairobi, her eyes were red. She delved into her bag, made by an Indian from the skin of a python Robin had shot. "All this luggage," she remarked glumly, "and I seem to have left my hankies behind."

I was preoccupied with other troubles. A ripe pawpaw someone had given us had fallen from its basket on the rack into a large pith helmet resting on the seat by its owner's side. He was a red-faced gentleman with bloodshot eyes, generous moustaches and a neat, compact and well-disciplined quota of hand luggage. The pawpaw had burst, releasing a cascade of squashy yellow pulp and slimy black seeds. The helmet's owner, who had not yet noticed this accident, coughed and turned his head.

"Look at that funny animal," I cried, pointing out of the window. Everyone turned, but there was nothing to be seen except the plains, green with fresh growth, the tin sheds, a rusty siding and a knot of ragged gangers leaning on their picks.

I made a face at Tilly. She saw the pawpaw, and frowned; we were trapped, the train had no corridor. She did not hesitate; smiling with all her charm, she asked the red-faced gentleman to help her stow our soda-water bottles on the rack and in five minutes he was eating out of her hand. I looked through the open window at the undulating purple ridge-back of the Ngong hills, a haunt of lions and buffaloes, and was glad that I had kissed the four walls of the grass hut at Thika, and was bound to return.

Elspeth Huxley

Although Elspeth Huxley has lived in Wiltshire, on the edge of the Cotswolds, for the past forty years, Kenya remains very dear to her heart. She has returned there many times since the childhood she describes so vividly in *The Flame Trees of Thika* and its sequel *The Mottled Lizard*. Her most recent visit was in 1983, on the occasion of the twentieth anniversary of the country's independence.

When The Flame Trees of Thika *was filmed in Kenya for television, Elspeth Huxley visited the company on location. Here she is seen with Holly Aird, who played the part of the young Elspeth.*

At the age of eighteen, Elspeth Huxley went to Reading University to study agriculture; later she went to Cornell University in the United States. In 1931 she married Gervas Huxley, but soon the Empire Marketing Board for which they both worked was abolished, and they had to seek new jobs. Gervas found one, publicizing the benefits of Ceylon tea, which involved much travelling. Elspeth often accompanied him, paying her way with freelance journalism and photography.

In 1933 Elspeth Huxley found an occupation which took her back to her beloved Kenya. A year earlier, Lord Delamere, the pioneer of white settlement in that country, had died, so Elspeth wrote to his widow proposing she should write his biography. To her delight, her offer was accepted, and she sailed for Africa and a reunion with her parents. By this time they had moved to a new farm at Njoro, where the intrepid "Tilly" was still farming as late as 1965.

Elspeth Huxley has now written thirty-five books, and she is particularly celebrated for those about Africa. She has not only written reminiscences of Kenya—the latest of which, *Out in the Midday Sun*, has just been published—but also novels, biographies and travel books. Her wide knowledge of the African continent led to her service on the Monckton Commission which advised the government on the future of the Central African Federation, and in 1962 she was awarded the CBE.